THE LAVYRLE SPENCER COLLECTION

LaVyrle Spencer is the author of many top-selling titles, with over fifteen million copies of her books in print worldwide. She is one of today's most successful and best-loved authors of romantic fiction. She lives in Stillwater, Minnesota, with her husband, Dan.

LAVYRLE SPENCER

The LaVyrle Spencer Collection

HarperCollins_Publishers_

HarperCollins*Publishers*
77–85 Fulham Palace Road,
Hammersmith, London W6 8JB

A Paperback Original 1995
1 3 5 7 9 8 6 4 2

Published by arrangement with
The Berkley Publishing Group of
The Putnam Berkley Group, Inc.

A Promise to Cherish and *Forsaking All Others*
have previously been published together in the USA
as *A Heart Speaks*, Jove Books, 1986

The Author asserts the moral right to
be identified as the author of this work

A catalogue record for this book
is available from the British Library

ISBN 0 00 647983 9

Set in Times

Printed in Great Britain by
HarperCollinsManufacturing Glasgow

Separate Beds

*With love
to my husband, Dan,
the best thing that ever happened in my life*

Chapter 1

CIRCUMSTANCES BEING what they were, it was ironic that Catherine Anderson knew little more of Clay Forrester than his name. He must be rich, she thought, scanning the foyer, which revealed quite clearly how well-off the Forrester family was.

The deep side of the expansive entry opened into a sprawling formal living room of pale yellows and muted golds. Above was a great crystal chandelier. Behind her, a stairway climbed dramatically to the second story. She was faced by double doors, a console table whose cabriole legs touched the parquet as lightly as a ballerina's toes and a brass accent lamp reflected by a gilt-framed mirror. Beside her stood an immense brass pitcher bursting with an abundance of overpoweringly fragrant dried eucalyptus.

The pungent stuff was beginning to make her sick.

She turned her eyes to the massive carved oak entry doors. The knobs weren't shaped like any she'd ever seen. Instead, they were curved and swirled like the handles of fine cutlery. Acidly Catherine wondered how much handles like those must cost, to say nothing of the pretentious bench on which she'd been left. It was lush brown velvet, armless, tufted—the kind of absurd extravagance afforded by only the very rich.

Yes, the entire foyer was a work of art and of opulence. Everything in it fit . . . except Catherine Anderson.

The girl was attractive enough, her apricot skin and weather-streaked blond hair having a fresh, vital look. Her features bore the strikingly appealing symmetry often found in those of Scandinavian ancestry—the straight nose and fine nostrils; shapely, bowed lips and blue eyes beneath arched brows of pleasing contour.

It was her clothing that gave her away. She wore a pair of heather colored slacks and shirt that spoke of brighter days long gone. They were homemade and of poor fabric. Her trench coat was limp, frayed at hem and cuff. Her brown wedgies were made of artificial stuff, worn at the heels and curled at the toes.

Yet her clean, wind-blown appearance and fresh complexion saved Catherine from looking disreputable. That, and the proud mien with which she carried herself.

Even that was slipping now, the longer she sat here. For Catherine realized she'd been left like a naughty child about to be reprimanded, which actually wasn't far from the truth.

With a resigned sigh, she dropped her head back against the wall. Vaguely she wondered if people like the Forresters would object to a girl like her laying her head against their elegant wallpaper, supposed they would, so defiantly kept it there. Her eyes slid shut, blotting out the lush elegance, unable to blot out the angry voices from the study: her father's, harsh and accusing, followed by the constrained, angry reply of Mr. Forrester.

Why do I stay? she wondered.

But she knew the answer; her neck still hurt from the pressure of her father's fingers. And, of course, there was her mother to consider. She was in there, too, along with the luckless Forresters, and—rich or not—they had done nothing to deserve a madman like her father. It had never been Catherine's intention to let this happen. She still remembered the shocked expressions of both Mr. and Mrs. Forrester when her father had barged in upon their pastoral evening with his bald accusations. They had at first attempted civility, suggesting that they all sit down in the study and talk this over. But within moments they understood what they were up against when Herb Anderson pointed at the bench and bellowed at his daughter, "Just plant your little ass right there, girlie, and don't move it or I'll beat the livin' hell outa you!"

No, the Forresters had done nothing to deserve a madman like Herb Anderson.

Suddenly the front door opened, letting in a gust of leaf-scented autumn air and a man whose clothing looked like the interior decorator had planned it to blend with the foyer. He was a tapestry of earth tones: camel-colored trousers of soft wool, European-cut, sharply creased, falling to a stylish break upon brown cordovan loafers; sport jacket of subdued rust and camel plaid, flowing over his shoulders like soft caramel over ice cream; a softer shade of rust repeated in the lamb's wool sweater beneath; an off-white collar left casually open to foil a narrow gold chain around his neck. Even nature, it seemed, had cooperated in creating his color scheme, for his skin bore the remains of a deep summer tan, and his hair was a burnished red-gold.

He was whistling as he breezed in, unaware of Catherine who sat partially shielded by the eucalyptus. She flattened her back against the stair wall, taking advantage of her sparse camouflage, watching as he crossed to the console table and glanced through what must have been the daily mail, still whistling softly. She caught a glimpse of his classically handsome face in the mirror, its straight nose, long cheeks and sculpted eyebrows. They might have been cast in bronze, so flawless and firm were their lines. But his mouth—ah, it was too perfect, too mobile, too memorable to be anything but flesh and blood.

Unaware of her presence, he shrugged off the stylish sport coat, caught it negligently in the crook of one wrist and bounded up the stairs two at a time.

Catherine wilted against the wall.

But she stiffened again as the study door burst open and Mr. Forrester stood framed against the bookshelves within, his slate-gray eyes submerged below craggy brows with a formidable expression, his anger scarcely held in check. He wasted

7

not so much as a glance at the girl on the bench.

"Clay!" The invincible tone stopped the younger man's ascent.

"Sir?"

The voice was the same as Catherine remembered, though the formal word of address surprised her. She was not used to hearing fathers called *sir*.

"I think you had better step into the study." Then Mr. Forrester himself did so, leaving the door open as yet another command.

Had the circumstances been different, Catherine might have felt sorry for Clay Forrester. His whistling had disappeared. All she heard now was the soft shush of his footsteps coming back down the stairs.

She squeezed her ribcage with both arms, fighting the unexpected flood of panic. Don't let him see me! she thought. Let him walk right past and not turn around! Yet common sense told her she could not escape him indefinitely. Sooner or later he'd know she was here.

He reappeared around the newel post, shrugging once again into his sport coat, telling her even more about his relationship with his father.

Her heart beat in the high hollow of her throat and she held her breath, the stain of embarrassment now coloring her cheeks. He stepped to the mirror, checked his collar and his hair. To Catherine, for the briefest moment he seemed vulnerable, being watched from behind that way, unaware of her presence or of what awaited him in the study. But she reminded herself he was not only rich, he was degenerate; he deserved what was coming.

He moved then and her image became visible in the mirror. His eyes registered surprise, then he turned to face her momentarily.

"Oh, hi," he greeted her. "I didn't see you hiding back there."

She was suddenly conscious of the frightful thud of her heart, but she carefully kept her face placid, giving him no more than a silent, wide-eyed nod. Never having planned to lay eyes on him again, she was not prepared for this.

"Excuse me," he added politely, as he might have to any

8

of the clients who often waited there to do business with his father. Then he turned toward the study.

From within came his father's command. "Shut the door, Clay!"

Her eyes slid closed.

He doesn't remember me, Catherine thought. The admission made her suddenly, inexplicably want to cry, though it made no sense at all when she'd hoped he'd walk right past like a stranger, and that was precisely what he'd done.

Well, she berated herself, that *is* what you wanted, *isn't it?* She summoned up anger as an antidote to the tears which Catherine Anderson never allowed herself to shed. To feel them threatening—and here, of all places!—was unspeakable. Weaklings cried! Weaklings and fools!

But Catherine Anderson was neither weakling nor fool. The circumstances might appear otherwise just now, but in twenty-four hours everything would be far different.

From behind the study door Clay Forrester's voice exploded, "Who!" and her eyes came open.

He doesn't remember me, she thought again, resigning herself to the fact once and for all, straightening her shoulders, telling herself not to let it matter.

The study door flew open, and she affected a relaxed and unconcerned air as Clay Forrester confronted her framed in that doorway, much as his father had before. His eyes—gray, too—impaled her. His scowl immediately told her he didn't believe a word of it! But she noted with satisfaction that his hair now looked finger-combed. Pushing back both front panels of his sport coat, hands on hips, he challenged her with those angry eyes. He scanned her summarily, allowed his glance to float down to her stomach, then back up, noting her detached air.

She suffered the insolent way his gaze roved downward—like a slap in the face—and retaliated by pointedly studying his full, lower lip, which she remembered quite well, considering the brevity of their association and the time that had lapsed since. But, knowing virtually nothing about him, Catherine decided she'd best take care in dealing with him, so she carefully remained silent beneath his scrutiny.

"Catherine?" he asked at last. She expected to see his breath, the word was so cold.

9

"Hello, Clay," she replied levelly, maintaining that false air of aloofness.

Clay Forrester watched her rise, slim and seemingly assured. Almost haughty, he thought, but certainly not scared . . . and hardly supplicating!

"You belong in here too," he stated tersely, holding that implacable stance while she gave him one extended look which she hoped appeared cool. Then she walked past him into the study. Antagonism emanated from him. She could nearly smell it as she passed so close in front of him.

The room was like a storybook setting: pre-supper fire burning on the grate, stem glasses half full upon polished tables, book-lined walls, an original Terry Redlin wildlife oil on the wall behind a leather loveseat, soft carpeting underfoot. Masculine, yet warm, everything about the room spoke of an interrupted coziness, which was precisely why Herb Anderson had chosen this time of day to make his appearance, when he figured all the Forresters would be home. His exact words had been, "I'll get them rich sons-a-bitches when they're all holed up together in that fancy brick mansion, wearin' all them family jewels, and we'll see who does the paying for this!"

The contrast between Clay's parents and Catherine's was almost laughable. Mrs. Forrester was ensconced in a wing chair at one side of the fireplace. She was shaken, yet extremely proper, feet crossed at the ankles. Her clothing was impeccable and up-to-date, her hair done in a tasteful coiffure which made her features appear youthfully regal. Upon her shapely hands glittered the magnitude of gems Herb Anderson derided.

Ada Anderson, in the matching chair on the opposite side of the fireplace, picked at a slub of her bargain basement coat, keeping her eyes downcast. Her hair was mousy, her shape dumpy. Upon her hand was only a thin gold band whose apple blossom design was worn smooth from years of hard work.

Mr. Forrester, double-vested in well-tailored business gray, stood behind a morocco-topped desk that held several leather-bound books in a pair of jade bookends worth as much as the entire Anderson collection of living room furniture.

Then there was her father, decked out in a red nylon jacket boasting the words *Warpo's Bar* on its back. Catherine avoided looking at the bulging beer belly, the bloated face, the ever-present expression of cynicism that perpetually claimed the world was out to beat Herb Anderson out of something, when actually it was the other way around.

Catherine stopped beside her mother's chair, conscious that Clay had stopped behind her. She kept a shoulder turned away from him, choosing instead to face his father, easily the most formidable person in the room. Even his position behind the desk was strategically chosen to connote command. Understanding this, she chose to confront him on her feet. Her own father might swear and carry on like a drunken sailor, but this other stern adversary was by far the greater threat. Catherine sensed the man's total control, sensed, too, that should she face him with a hint of challenge on her face it would be the worst possible mistake. He was the kind of man who knew how to deal with hostility and defiance, thus she carefully kept them from her countenance.

"My son doesn't seem to remember you, does he?" His voice was like the first edge of November's ice on a Minnesota lake—cold, sharp, thin, dangerous.

"No, he doesn't," Catherine replied, looking at him squarely.

"Do you remember her?" the father snapped at his son, daring it to be true.

"No," answered Clay, raising Catherine's ire not because she wanted to be remembered, but because it was a lie. She hadn't really expected the truth out of him anyway, had she?—not once she'd suspected he had enough money to back up any lies he chose to tell. Still, his answer rankled. She turned to find him nearer than was comfortable and accosted him with blue eyes that rivaled the frost in his father's.

Liar! Her eyes seemed to shout, while he smugly perused her features, then cast a glance over her blond hair and saw the fire create sundogs on it, dancing behind her that way. And suddenly he recalled it backlit by fireworks.

Oh, he remembered her all right. . . . Now he remembered her! But he cautiously kept it from showing in his face.

"What the hell is this, a frame-up?" he accused.

"I'm afraid it isn't, and you know it," Catherine replied, wondering how long she could maintain this feigned calm.

But then Herb Anderson jumped in, yelping and pointing. "Your goddam right it isn't, lover boy, so just don't think—"

"You're in my home," Mr. Forrester interrupted explosively, "and if you want this . . . this *discussion* to continue, you will control yourself while you are here!" There was an undeniable note of sarcasm in the word *discussion;* it was obvious Herb Anderson didn't know the meaning of the word.

"Just get busy and make lover boy here own up, or, so help me, I'll squeeze the truth outa him like I done outa her."

Something slimy seemed to crawl through Clay's innards. He glanced sharply at the girl but she remained composed, her eyes now on the desk top where whitened knuckles were depressing lustrous leather.

"You will remain rational, *sir*, or you and your wife will leave at once and take your daughter with you!" Forrester ordered.

But Anderson had been waiting all his life for his ship to come in, and this . . . by God! . . . was it! He turned to confront Clay nose to nose.

"Let's hear it, lover boy," he sneered. "Let's hear you say you never laid eyes on her before, and I'll make you the sorriest lookin' mess you ever seen in your life. And when I'm done, sonny, I'll sue your old man for every goddam penny he's got. Rich bastard like you, think just because you got a few bucks your kind can go around screwing everything in skirts. Well, not this time, not this time!" He shook his fist under Clay's nose. "You're gonna pay up this time or I'll be hollering rape so fast it'll make you wish you was a fag!"

Mortified, Catherine knew it was useless to argue. Her father had been drinking all day, getting primed for this. She'd seen it coming but could do nothing about it.

"Clay, do you know this woman?" his father demanded grimly, pointedly ignoring Anderson.

Before Clay could reply, Herb Anderson pushed his face near his daughter's and sneered, "Tell him, girlie . . . tell him it was lover boy here knocked you up!" Instinctively Catherine drew away from the disgusting smell of his breath, but he reached out and grabbed her cheeks and rasped, "You tell him, sister, if you know what's good for you."

Clay stepped between the two. "Now, wait a minute! Take your hands off her! She's already pointed the finger at me or you wouldn't be here." Then, more quietly, he added, "I said I don't know her, but I remember her."

Catherine flashed him a warning look. Actually, the last thing she wanted from Clay Forrester was noble self-sacrifice.

"There! You see!" Anderson made a motion like he'd slapped a trump card on the desk top. Mrs. Forrester's face quivered. Her husband's showed the first sign of defeat as his lips fell open.

"You're admitting that this woman's child is yours?" Claiborne Forrester exclaimed disbelievingly.

"I'm not admitting any such thing. I simply said I remember her."

"From when?" Claiborne insisted.

"This summer."

"This summer, when? What month?"

"I think it was July."

"You *think* it was July! Hadn't you better do more than *think?*"

"It was."

A look of gloating turned Herb Anderson's face more detestable than ever.

"July what?" Claiborne pressed on, facing the calamity head-on, in spite of his growing dread.

"July fourth."

"And what happened on July fourth?"

Catherine held her breath again, embarrassment for Clay making her acutely uncomfortable now.

"We went on a blind date."

The room grew church-silent. Catherine sensed everyone counting off two and a half months since then.

Claiborne's chin hardened, his jaw protruded. "And?"

Only the soft hiss of the fire spoke while Clay considered, his eyes briefly lighting on Catherine. "And I absolutely refuse to answer another question until Catherine and I speak alone," he ended, surprising her.

"You, Clay Forrester, will answer my question here and

13

now!" his father exploded, rapping a fist on the desk top in frustration. "Did you or did you not have relations with this woman on July Fourth?"

"With all due respect, Father, that is none of your business," Clay said in a tightly controlled voice.

Mrs. Forrester put a trembling hand to her lips, beseeching her son with carefully made-up eyes to deny it all here and now.

"You say this is none of my business when this man threatens to bring a paternity suit against you, and to ruin your reputation along with mine in this city?"

"You've taught me well enough that a man makes his own reputation. As far as you're concerned, I don't think there's anything to worry about."

"Clay, all I want is the truth. If the answer is no, then for God's sake, quit protecting the girl and say no. If it's yes, admit it and let's get it over with."

"I refuse to answer until she and I can talk privately. Obviously we were both left out of any earlier discussion. After we've had a chance to talk, I'll give you my answer." He gestured to Catherine, motioning her to follow, but she was too stunned to move. This was one turn of events that was totally unexpected!

"Now, wait just one goddam minute there, sonny!" Herb Anderson hissed. "You ain't gonna go skipping out on me and leaving me lookin' like some jackass don't know which end is up! I know *exactly* what your game is! You take her outa here and pay her off with some measly couple o' hundred bucks and shut her up and your problem is solved, huh?"

"Let's go." Clay made a move to pass Anderson.

"I said, hold on!" Anderson stuck his pudgy fingertips in Clay's chest.

"Get out of my way." Some grim note of warning made Anderson comply. Clay strode toward the door, curtly advising Catherine, "You'd better come along with me if you know what's good for you."

She walked toward Clay like a puppet, even while her father continued his tirade at their backs. "Don't you get no ideas about givin' her the money to get rid of the kid either, you hear me! And just see to it you keep your hands offa her, lover

14

boy. She better not have no more complaints or I'll have the law down on you before the night is out!"

Face scorching, insides trembling, Catherine followed Clay into the foyer. She assumed he would lead her to another room of the house, but instead he stalked to the front door, flung it wide and ordered, "Let's take a ride." It took her off-guard and rooted her to the parquet, quite involuntarily. Realizing she hadn't followed, he turned. "We've got some talking to do, and I'll be damned if I'll do it in the same house with all of our parents."

Still she hesitated, her blue eyes wide, mistrusting. "I'd rather stay here or go for a walk or something." Not even the blazing color in her cheeks softened him. Her hesitation only made Clay more unyielding.

"I'm not giving you an alternative," he stated unequivocally, then turned on his heel. From the library came the sound of her father's voice, badgering the Forresters further. Seeing no alternative, she finally followed Clay outside.

Chapter 2

A SILVER CORVETTE was parked now in the horseshoe-shaped driveway behind her family's sedan. Without waiting, Clay yanked a door open and got in, then sat glaring straight ahead while she tried to quickly measure the risk of going for a ride with him. After all, she knew nothing about him. Did he have a temper like her father? Was he capable of violence when cornered this way? What would he do to keep her from making trouble in his life?

He glanced back to find her looking balefully over her shoulder at the front door as if help would step through it at any moment.

"Come on, let's get this over with." His choice of words did little to reassure her.

"I—I really don't care to go for a ride," she stammered.

"Don't tell me you're afraid of me!" he taunted with a dry laugh. "It's a little late for that, isn't it?" He started the engine without taking his insolent eyes off her. She moved at last, only to realize, once she was in the car, that there was one eventuality she hadn't considered. He'd kill them both before this was over! He drove like a maniac, throwing the car into gear and careening down the brick driveway while manicured shrubbery blurred past the windows. At the road, he scarcely braked, changing gears with a screech and a lurch, then tearing at breakneck speed through a maze of streets that were unfamiliar to her. He slammed his hand against a cassette that hung in the tape deck, sending throbbing rock music through the car. She couldn't do anything about his driving but she reached over and lowered the volume. He angled her a sidelong glance, then stepped a little harder on the gas. Obstinately she wedged herself into her seat and tried to ignore his childish antics, deciding to let him get it out of his system.

He steered one-handed, just to show her he could.

She sat cross-legged, just to show him she could.

They sailed around corners, up curving hills, past strange street signs until Catherine was totally lost. He took a sharp right-hand curve, gunned his way into a sharper left, flew between two stone gate markers onto gravel where they fishtailed before climbing into a pocket of wooded land. The headlights flew across a sign: PARK HOURS 10:00 A.M. to—but the lights moved too fast for Catherine to catch the rest. At the top of the last incline they broke onto a parking lot surrounded on all sides by trees. He stopped the car much as he'd driven it—too fast! She was forced to break her forward pitch with a hand on the dash or sail through the windshield!

But still she stubbornly refused to comment or to look at him.

Satisfied, anyway, that he'd managed to budge her from that damn uppity cross-kneed pose, he cut the engine and turned to her. But he remained silent, studying her dim profile, knowing it made her uncomfortable, which suited his purpose.

"All right," Clay said at last in the driest of tones, "what kind of game are you playing?"

"I wish it were a game. Unfortunately, it's very real."

He snorted. "That I don't doubt one bit. I want to know why you're trying to pin the blame on me."

"I understood your reluctance to answer with our parents present, but here, between just the two of us, there's no further need to play dumb. Not when we both know the truth."

"And just what the hell *is* the truth?"

"The truth is that I'm pregnant and you're the father."

"I'm the father!" He was in a high state of temper now, but

she found his shouting preferable to his driving.

"You sound slightly outraged," she said levelly, giving him a sideways glance.

"*Outraged* isn't the word for me right now! Did you really think I'd fall for that kangaroo court back there?" He thumbed over his shoulder.

"No," she answered. "I thought you'd flatly deny ever having laid eyes on me and that would be the end of that. We would go our separate ways and take up our lives where we'd left off."

Her unruffled detachment took some of the wind from his sails. "It's beginning to look like I should have."

"I'd survive," she said tonelessly.

Baffled, he thought, she's an odd one, so composed, almost cold, unconcerned. "If you can survive without me, tell me why you created that scene in the first place."

"I didn't; my father did."

"I suppose it was entirely his idea to storm our house tonight."

"That's right."

"You had nothing to do with it," he added sarcastically.

At last Catherine grew upset, losing her determination to remain unruffled. She whirled sideways in her seat and let him have it. "Before you say one more thing in that . . . that damnably accusing voice of yours, I want you to know that I don't want *one damn thing from you! Not one!*"

"Then why are you here, picking the flesh from my bones?"

"Your *flesh*, Mr. Forrester?" she parried. "Your flesh is the last thing I want!"

He pointedly ignored her double entendre. "Do you expect me to believe that after all the accusations that have been hurled at me tonight?"

"Believe what you will," she said, resigned again, turning away. "I don't want anything but to be left alone."

"Then why did you come?" When she only remained silent, he insisted again, "Why!"

Obstinately she remained mute. She wanted neither his sympathy nor his money nor his name. All she wanted was for tomorrow to hurry and get here.

Antagonized by her stubborn indifference, he grabbed her

18

shoulder roughly. "Listen, lady, I didn't—"

She jerked her shoulder, trying to free it from his grasp. "My name is Catherine," she hissed.

"I know what your name is!"

"It took you some time to remember it, though, didn't it?"

"And what is that supposed to mean?"

"Let go of my shoulder, Mr. Forrester, you're hurting me."

He dropped his hand, but his voice zeroed in, slightly sing-songy now. "Oh, I get it. The lady is feeling abused because I didn't recognize her right off the bat, is that it?"

She denied him an answer, but felt herself blushing in the darkness.

"Do I sense a little contradiction there? Either you want recognition from me or you don't. Now which is it?"

"I repeat, I don't want anything from you except to be taken home."

"When I take you back, it'll be when I'm satisfied about what I'm being threatened with."

"Then you can take me back now. I'm not threatening any-thing."

"Your mere presence in my home was a threat. Now let's get on with what you want for a payoff . . . that is, if you're really pregnant."

The thought had never occurred to her that he'd doubt it.

"Oh, I'm pregnant all right, make no mistake about that."

"Oh, I don't intend to," he said pointedly. "I don't intend to. I mean to make damn sure that baby is *not* mine."

"Are you saying you really do *not* remember having sexual intercourse with me last Fourth of July?" Then she added in a satirically sugary tone, "You'll notice I do not mistakenly call it making love, like so many fools are prone to do."

The dark hid the eyebrow he cocked in her direction, but it couldn't hide the cocky tone of his voice. "Of course, I remember. What does that prove? There could have been a dozen others."

She'd been expecting this sooner or later, but she wasn't expecting the anger it evoked, the way she simply had to fight back, no matter how degrading it was to have to. "How dare you say such a thing when you know perfectly well there weren't!"

19

"Now you're the one who sounds outraged. Promiscuous females have to be prepared to be doubted. After all, there's no way to prove paternity."

"No proof is necessary when it's the first time!" She smoldered, wondering why she wasted her breath on him. Without warning the overhead light came on. In its beam, Clay Forrester looked like she'd just thrown ice water on him.

"What!" he exclaimed, genuinely stunned.

"Turn that thing off," she ordered, turning her face sharply away.

"Like hell I will. Look at me." Something had changed in his voice, but it made it even more impossible to face him.

The view outside the window was totally black but she studied it as if for answers. Suddenly a hand grabbed her cheeks, the fingers sinking into them as he forced her to look at him. She glared into his surprised face as if she hated every feature of it, gritting her teeth because she didn't.

"What are you saying?" Intense gray eyes allowed her no escape. She was torn by the wish to have him know nothing of her and the equally strong wish to let him know everything. He was, after all, the father of the child she carried.

He stared into her imprisoned face, wanting to deny her words, but unable to. He tried to remember last July fourth more clearly, but they'd had too much wine that night.

"You're hurting me again," she said quietly, making him realize he still held her cheeks imprisoned in his grasp.

He dropped his hand, continuing to study her. She had a face that wasn't too easy to forget: shapely, narrow nose; long cheeks dusted with a suggestion of freckles; blue eyes trying hard not to blink, meeting him squarely now within long, sandy lashes. Her mouth was sullen, but memory flashed him a picture of it smiling. Her hair was shoulder-length, blond on blond, tabby-streaked, its bangs feathered back but falling in alluring wisps onto her forehead. It curled hither and thither around her long neck. She had a tall, thin frame. He suspected, although he could not clearly remember, she was shaped the way he liked his women shaped: long-limbed, hollow-hipped and not overly breasty.

Like Jill, he thought.

Sobered at the thought of Jill, he again fell to trying to

remember what had passed between himself and this woman.

"I . . ." Catherine began, then asked with less acid in her voice, "will you turn out that light?"

"I think I have a right to see you during this sticky conversation we're having."

She had no choice but to be studied like a printout from a lie-detector test. She tolerated it as long as she could before turning away, asking, "You don't remember, do you?"

"Parts of it, I do, but not all."

"You struck me as a man of experience, one who'd know a virgin every time."

"If you're asking me how often I do things like that, it's none of your business."

"I agree. It's none of my business . . . but I wasn't asking. I was only defending myself, which I had no intention of doing in the first place. You are the one who seemed to be asking how often *I'd* done things like that, and no girl likes to be called promiscuous. I only wanted to point out that it was undeniably my first time. I assumed you'd have known it."

"Like I said, my memory is a little fuzzy. Suppose I believe you—there could have been others after me."

That brought her anger back in full force. "I have no intention of sitting here and being insulted by you any further!" she spit out. Then she opened the door and got out. He wasn't far behind her, but she stalked off into the dark, her shoes crunching gravel, gone before he could storm around to the other side of the car.

"Get back here!" he shouted into the dark, his hands on his hips.

"Go to hell!" she yelled from somewhere down the road.

"Just where do you think you're going?"

But she just kept on walking. He broke into a run, following her shadowy form, angered more than he could say by her stony insistence that she wanted nothing from him.

She felt his hand grab her arm and swing her around in the dark. "Dammit, Catherine, get back to the car!" he warned.

"And do what!" she exclaimed, turning to face him, fists clenched at her sides, "Sit and listen to you call me the equivalent of a whore? I've taken that kind of abuse from my father, but I certainly don't have to sit still and take it from you!"

21

"All right, I'm sorry, but what do you expect a man to say when he's confronted with an accusation like yours?"

"I can't answer your question, not being a man myself. But I thought a—a worldly stud like you would know the truth, that's all!"

"I'm no worldly stud, so knock it off!"

"All right, so we're even."

They stood in the dark, unmoving combatants. She wondered if he could be as experienced as he'd seemed that night and yet not recognize the fact of her virginity. He, meanwhile, wondered if a girl of her age could possibly have remained a virgin all that time. He guessed her to be twenty or so. But in this day and age, twenty was old, sexually. Again he strove to remember anything about that night, how she'd acted, if she'd been in pain, if she'd resisted. All he knew for sure was that if she *had* resisted in any way or asked him to stop, he would have. Wine or no wine, he was no rapist!

Giving up, he said cajolingly, "You must have done all right. I never knew the difference."

His chauvinistic remark riled her so swiftly she lost good sense and swung on him, giving him a good one with her knuckles in the middle of his breastbone.

Caught off-guard, he gasped and stumbled one surprised step backward. "Ouch, that hurt, goddammit!"

"Oh, that's rich! That's so rich I could throw up! *I* must have done all right! Why, you insufferable egotistical goat! Telling me *I* must have done all right when you're the one who can't even remember clearly!"

Nursing his bruised chest, he muttered, "Christ, are you always like this?"

"I don't know. This is a first for me. How do your pregnant girl friends usually react?"

Wary now, he was careful not to touch her. "What do you say we stop trading insults, okay? Let's just forget our sexual histories and own up to the fact that we went out on a blind date and gave each other a little refreshment for the night, and take it from there. You say you were a virgin, but you can't prove it by me."

"The dates will bear it out. The baby is due on the sixth of April. That's the only other proof I have that it was you."

"Pardon me if I seem dense, but since you claim you don't want anything from me, why are you trying so hard to convince me?"

"I'm not . . . I . . . at least I wasn't until you questioned me about there being others. It was a point of self-defense and nothing more." Then, realizing she was beginning to sound more and more entreating, she muttered, "Oh, why do I waste my breath on you!" And she turned down the road again, leaving him with the diminishing sound of her footsteps.

He let her go this time and stood there with one hand on his hip in the dark, thinking to himself that she was the singularly most irritating woman he'd ever met. It was all the more frustrating to think he'd made love to a wasp like that! Then, with a rueful grin, he corrected himself, making it, had "sexual intercourse" with a wasp like that. He listened to her footsteps fading away, thinking, Good riddance, lady! But in the end he couldn't let her go.

"Catherine, don't be an ass!" he admonished, hurting her ego further as she hot-footed it down the gravel road. "You're at least three miles from my house, and God-knows-how-many miles from yours. Get back up here!"

The fragrant night resounded with her response: "Up yours, Clay Forrester!"

He cursed, returned to his car and twisted the key so violently it should have broken off in the ignition. The headlights flashed on, arced around, and the Corvette went roaring down the hill, picking out Catherine's belligerent back as she continued to stalk. He roared past her, spraying dust and gravel.

About fifty feet in front of Catherine, at the bottom of the hill, the brake lights flashed on, followed by the interior light as Clay got out again and stood leaning an elbow on top of the open door, waiting. She would have ignored him, but he wouldn't allow it. When she was abreast of him, a hand shot out and detained her. "Get in, you little spitfire," he ordered. "I'm not leaving you out here whether I want to or not. Not at this hour of the night!"

The light from the car limned her angry face as she thrust her lower lip out, beetling her brows in curled distaste. "I must have been crazy to come to your house in the first place. I should have known no good would come of it."

"Then why did you?" he insisted, holding her easily by a forearm, but well enough away so she couldn't punch him again.

"Because I didn't think your parents deserved the likes of my old man. I actually thought by going along with him I could save them from some unpleasantness they didn't deserve."

"Do you expect me to believe that?"

"I don't care what you believe, Clay Forrester! Let go of my arm, dammit!" She yanked herself free, then whirled like a bantam rooster, unable to keep explanations mute. "You've gotten a dose of my old man. It doesn't take very long to get the drift of how he operates. He's mean and vindictive and lazy, and an alcoholic to boot. He'll stop at nothing to get whatever he can out of either you or your parents. I think he's stark, raving mad to go shoving his way into your house the way he did, badgering your family."

"And what does he expect to get out of it?"

Catherine debated, decided she had nothing to lose by being frank. "A free ride."

She could tell he was surprised, for he studied her in the vague light cast from the car, then exclaimed, "You admit that?"

"Of course I admit it. It'd take a fool not to see what he's up to. He smelled money, which he's never had enough of, and it brought out his every greedy instinct. He thinks he can use this situation to make life a little easier on himself. I don't kid myself one bit that it's my reputation he's concerned about. He can harp all he wants about his little girl's loss of innocence and her ruined future. But it's really his own future he's looking out for. He wants to feather his bed till it's as soft as he thinks yours is. I don't really think he believes for one minute he can get you to marry me. I don't even think he *wants* you to. He'd rather have your guilt money, and he'll do everything in his power to get it. I warn you, he's a dangerous man. You see, he believes his ship just came in."

"And none of those thoughts entered your head?"

"I didn't know you from Adam last July. How could I possibly have smelled money?"

"Your cousin, Bobbi, lined us up. She's Stu's girl, and Stu is an old friend of mine. It follows."

She threw her hands up and paced agitatedly back and forth. "Oh, sure! First I ran a financial check on you, then got myself lined up with you on the *perfect* night to get pregnant, then I seduced you and sent my father in after the pickings." She snorted derisively. "Don't flatter yourself, Forrester! It may surprise you to learn that not every girl who finds herself pregnant wants to marry the man. I made one mistake last July, but that doesn't mean I'm going to make a second by forcing you to marry me."

"If you're innocent, tell me just how in the hell your old man knew who to come to. Somebody pointed him in my direction."

"I did not *point!*"

"Then how did he choose me to come after?"

She suddenly clammed up, turned her back on him and walked around the car, saying, "I believe I will take a ride home after all." And she got in.

He got in, too, leaving one foot out on the gravel so the light would remain on while he grilled her.

"Don't avoid the issue," he demanded. "How?"

"I did *not* give him your name. I refused to tell him anything!"

"I don't believe you. How did he find out then?" Clay saw how she worried her lower lip between her teeth, refusing to look at him.

Catherine willed her mouth to stop forming explanations for his benefit, but she was not the cunning woman he thought, and it galled her to be accused this way.

"How?" he repeated, waiting.

Her nostrils flared, she stared straight out over the dash, but finally divulged, "I keep a diary." Her tone was quieter and her eyelids flickered slightly.

"You what?"

"You heard me," she said to the window on her side.

"Yes, I heard, but I'm not sure I understand. You mean he found it?" It was beginning to dawn on Clay just what kind of unscrupulous bastard her father really was.

"Leave me alone. I've already said more than I wanted to."

"There's a lot at stake here. I deserve to know the truth if that baby is really mine. Now answer me. Did he find it?"

"Not exactly."

"What then?"

She sighed, laid her head back against the seat but continued staring out the window away from him. Then from the side he saw her eyelids slide shut wearily, almost resignedly. Her voice lost much of its agitation.

"Listen, none of this has anything to do with you. Leave it be. What he is and what he did was never supposed to enter into it. I only wanted to keep your parents from paying his demands. That's why I came along."

"Don't change the subject, Catherine. He found the diary and found my name, right?"

She swallowed. "Right," she whispered.

"How did he find it?"

"Oh, for God's sake, Clay, I've kept a diary since I was in pinafores! He knew it was there someplace. He didn't just *find* it, he ripped my room apart until he found the evidence he was always accusing me of. You wanted the truth, there it is."

Something coiled in Clay's gut. His voice softened. "Didn't anybody try to stop him?"

"I wasn't there. My mother wouldn't try to stop him if she could. She's scared of her own shadow, to say nothing of him. You don't know my old man. There's no stopping him when he gets something in his head. The man's insane."

Clay pulled his foot inside and slammed the car door. He sat brooding, putting it all together, then cradled the steering wheel in both arms, clasping a wrist behind it. At last he looked back over his shoulder at her. "I'm almost afraid to ask . . . what was in it?"

"Everything."

With a small moan he lowered his forehead to the steering wheel. "Oh, God . . ."

"Yes," she repeated quietly. "Oh, God . . ."

"I take it you remembered that night more clearly than I did?" he asked, embarrassed now himself.

"I'm no different than any other girl. It was my first time. I'm afraid I was quite explicit about my feelings and the events of that night."

The silence lengthened and Catherine's composure slipped. It was far more disconcerting having him even remotely sym-

26

pathetic than having him angry. After some time he sank back against his seat, shuddering a sigh, leaning an elbow high on the window ledge and rolling his face aside to knead the bridge of his nose. The long, strained silence became painted with provocative images that flickered through their minds until at last Clay forced his thoughts back to the present and the unpleasant aspect of her father's threats.

"So he wants reparation."

"Exactly, but whatever he says, whatever he threatens, you must not meet his demands. Don't pay him anything!" she said with sudden passion.

"Listen, it's not just up to me anymore. He's brought my father into this, and my father is...my father is the most exasperatingly honest man I've ever known. Either he'll force me to pay, or he'll pay whatever your father demands before this thing is over."

"No!" she exclaimed with an intensity that brought her near to clutching his arm. "You must not!"

"Listen, I don't understand you. You've spent the night convincing me you're carrying my baby. Now you beg me not to pay your father anything. Why?"

"Because my father is the scum of the earth!" Her words were as sharp as knives, but the knives were double-edged, for the words she was forced to utter cut her deeply. "Because I've hated him for as long as I can remember, and if it's the last thing I do, I want to make sure he doesn't cash in on any good luck due to me. He's been waiting for years for something like this to happen. Now that it has, it almost thrills me to be responsible for his coming so close, then foiling him!"

Suddenly Clay prickled with awareness. "What do you mean, if it's the last thing you do?"

She managed a sardonic laugh. "Oh, don't trouble yourself, Mr. Forrester, supposing for a minute I'd commit suicide over this. That would hardly foil him anyway."

"How then?"

"Depriving him of the payoff money will be quite enough. You don't know him or you'd realize what I mean. It'll almost be worth every time he—" But she stopped just short of being carried away by the hate she felt, by the memories she had no intention of revealing.

27

Clay again began rubbing the bridge of his nose, fighting against getting involved with her past any more than necessary. But the vindictiveness she displayed, the abusive way the man had treated her and spoken to her, the accusations she said her father undeservedly made to her—it was the classic picture of a physically violent man. But to involve himself in sympathy for this woman would be a mistake. Yet even while Clay refused to allow himself to delve any further into her past, what he knew of it was already festering in the dark silence while he grew upset over being embroiled in this fiasco in the first place. It was all so damn unnecessary, he thought. Pinching the bridge of his nose, Clay found he was now beginning to develop a headache.

He boosted himself up and outlined the wheel with his arms again. "How old are you?" he asked, out of the blue.

"What possible difference does that make?"

"How old!" he repeated, more forcefully.

"Nineteen."

He emitted a single sound, half-laugh, half-grunt. "Nineteen years old and she didn't have the sense to take some precautions," he said to the ceiling.

"Me!" she yelped. A quick, smoking anger assaulted her, making her shout louder than necessary in the close confines of the car. "Why didn't *you?* You were the one who had all the experience in these matters!"

"I wasn't planning on anything that night," he said, still disgusted.

"Well, neither was I!"

"A girl with any sense at all doesn't go around looking for sex without being prepared."

"I was not looking for sex!"

"Ha! Nineteen and a virgin and she claims she's not looking for it!"

"You conceited bastard, you think—" she began, but he cut her off.

"Conceit's got nothing to do with it," he ground out, nose to nose with her now across the narrow space, "you just don't randomly go out on the make without some kind of contraceptive!"

"Why?" she shouted. "Why me? Because I'm the woman?

28

Why not you? What was the matter with you thinking ahead a little bit, an experienced stud like you?"

"That's the second time you've called me a stud, lady, and I don't like it!"

"And that's the second time you've called me *lady*, and I don't like it either, not the way you say it!"

"We're getting off the subject, which was your neglect."

"I believe the subject was *your* neglect."

"The woman usually takes care of precautions. Naturally, I assumed—"

"Usually!" she croaked, throwing her hands in the air, then flopping back exaggeratedly, talking to the ceiling. "And *he* calls *me* promiscuous!"

"Now just a minute—"

But this time she interrupted him. "I told you, it was my first time. I wouldn't even have known how to use a contraceptive!"

"Don't hand me that! This isn't Victorian England! All you'd have had to do was open the phone book to find out how and where to learn. Or hadn't you heard—women have come of age? Only most of them prove it by showing a little common sense with their first fling. If you'd have done the same, we wouldn't be in this mess."

"What good are all these recriminations? I told you, it happened, that's all."

"It sure as hell did, and it was just my luck that it happened with an ignorant girl who doesn't know the meaning of the words *birth control*."

"Listen, *Mister* Forrester, I don't have to sit here and be preached to by you! You're equally as guilty as I am, only you're blaming me because it's easier than blaming yourself. It's bad enough I have to tolerate your inquisition without defending myself against ignorance! It took two of us, you know!"

"Okay, okay, just relax. Maybe I came down a little heavy on you, but this could have been avoided so easily."

"Well, it wasn't. That's a fact of life we have to live with."

"Clever choice of words," he muttered.

"Listen, would you mind? Just take me home. I'm tired and I don't want to sit here arguing anymore."

"Well, what about the baby—what are you going to do with it?"

"It's none of your business."

He bit the corner of his lip and asked quickly, before he lost his nerve, "Would you take money for an abortion?"

Her preliminary silence nearly made her reply redundant. "Oh, you'd like that, wouldn't you? Then your conscience would be clear. No, I wouldn't take money for any abortion!"

Long before she finished, he felt like a confirmed pervert.

"All right, all right, sorry I asked." He couldn't tell yet if he was worried or relieved by her answer. He sighed. "Well, what are we going to do about your father?"

"You're so smart, you figure it out." Catherine knew that after tomorrow, when Herb Anderson's pregnant little trump card disappeared, his ship would lose the wind from its sails. But she was damned if she'd tell Clay Forrester that. Let him stew in his own juices!

"I can't," he was saying almost contritely, "and I'm not that smart and I'm sorry I called you ignorant and I'm sorry I called you promiscuous and I shouldn't have gone flying off the handle like that, but what man wouldn't lose his temper?"

"You might be justified if I were making demands, but I'm not. I'm not holding a gun to your head or forcing you to do anything. But neither am I going to sip from your tarnished silver spoon," she ended sarcastically.

"And what is that supposed to mean?"

"It means that maybe my father was right to resent you because you're rich. It means that I resent your thinking you can sweep it all under the rug by an offer of a quick abortion. I'd have respected you more if you'd never suggested it."

"It's legal now, you know."

"And it's also murder."

"There are conflicting views on that too."

"And obviously yours and mine conflict."

"Then you plan to keep the baby?"

"That's none of your business."

"If it's my baby, it's my business."

"Wrong," she said with finality, the single word stating clearly that it was useless for him to try to get anything more from her. The silence waged war with Clay's conscience while

30

he sat disconsolately cradling the wheel. When next he spoke, the words told more truth than either of them had expected.

"Listen, I don't want that kid raised in the same house with your father."

You could have heard a leaf drop from the blackened branches that drooped above the road. Then Catherine's voice came quietly into the dark.

"Well, well, well . . ."

For answer he started the engine, threw the car into gear and tried to drive away his frustration. Brooding, he drove again one-handed, allowing the car just enough excessive speed, but not too much. She leaned back, silently watching the arch of trees spin backward above the headlights, losing all sense of direction, shutting out thoughts momentarily. The car slowed, turned, nosed along the street where he lived.

"Do you think your parents might still be here?"

"I have no idea. A madman like him just might be."

"It looks like they've gone," he said, rolling past, finding no sedan in the driveway.

"You'll just have to take me home then," she said, then added while turning her face toward her window, ". . . so sorry to put you out."

He came to a halt at a stop sign and sat waiting with feigned patience. When she only continued staring stubbornly out that window he was forced to ask, "Well, which way?"

Under the blue-white glance of the streetlight she noted the effrontery of his insolent pose: one wrist draped over the wheel, one shoulder slightly slumped toward his door.

"You really don't remember anything about that night, do you?"

"I remember what I *want* to remember. *You* remember that."

"Fair enough," she agreed, then settled her expression into one of indifference and gave him a street address and brief directions on how to reach it.

The ride from Edina to North Minneapolis took some twenty minutes—long, increasingly uncomfortable minutes during which their angers diminished at approximately the same rate as the speed of Clay's driving. With verbal combat forsaken, there was only the sound of the car purring its way through the somnolent city with an occasional streetlight intruding its

31

pale, passing glimpse into their moving world. Within the confines of that world an uninvited intimacy settled, like an unwanted guest whose presence forces politeness upon his host and hostess. The silence grew rife with unsaid things—fears, dreads, worries. Each could not be more anxious to part and be rid of this tension between them, yet for both a final separation seemed too abrupt. As Clay turned a last corner onto her street the car was nearly crawling.

"Whi . . ." His voice cracked and he cleared his throat. "Which house?"

"The third on the right."

The car rolled to a stop at the curb, and Clay shifted into neutral with deliberate slowness, then adjusted some button till only the parking lights remained on. She was free to flee now, but, curiously, remained where she was.

Clay hunched his shoulders and arms about the wheel in the way with which she was already growing familiar. He turned his eyes to the darkened house, then to her.

"You gonna be all right?" he asked.

"Yeah. What about you?"

"God, I don't know." He laid back and closed his eyes. Catherine watched the pronounced movement of his Adam's apple rising and falling.

"Well . . ." She put her hand on the door handle.

"Won't you even tell me what your plans are?"

"No. Only that I've made them."

"But what about your father?"

"Soon I'll be gone. I'll tell you that much. I'm his little ace-in-the-hole, and with me gone he'll have nothing to threaten you with."

"I wasn't thinking about me when I asked that, I was thinking about you going in there now."

"Don't say it . . . please."

"But he—"

"And don't ask any questions, okay?"

"He forced you to come to the house tonight, didn't he?" His voice was strained.

"I said, no more questions, Mr. Forrester," she said in a distractingly gentle tone.

"I feel like hell, you know, letting you go this way."

32

"Well, that makes two of us."

The vague light from the dashboard cast their eyes in shadow, but somehow the intensity conveyed itself. She looked sharply away from his face, for she would not be haunted by the conscience-stricken look she saw there. She opened her door and the overhead light came on and he reached out to stop her. Silence fell while the heat of his hold burned through the arm of her coat. She pulled, slowly, steadily, inexorably away from him, turning, straining toward the door. But her neck arched sideways, revealing under the mellow light three purple bruises strung there in a row, each a finger's width apart. Before she could prevent it, the backs of Clay's fingers glided over the spot and she cringed, lowering her jaw into her collarbone.

"Don't!" Her eyes were wide, fierce, defiant.

In a strident voice, Clay asked, "He did that, didn't he?"

Denial would have been useless, admission folly. All she could do was avoid answering.

"Don't you dare say anything sympathetic or sentimental," she warned him. "I couldn't take it right now."

"Catherine . . ." But he didn't know what to say, and he couldn't sit here restraining her any longer. He didn't want to be involved in her life, yet he was. They both knew it. How could she get out of this car and carry his child away into some hazy future without both of them realizing how fully he was already involved in her life?

"Could I give you some money anyway?" he asked, almost in a whisper.

"No . . . please . . . I want nothing of you, whether you believe it or not."

By now he believed it.

"Will you get in touch with me if you change your mind?"

"I won't." She raised her elbow, pulling it by inches out of his fingers until he no longer commanded her.

"Good luck," he said, his eyes on hers.

"Yeah, you too."

Then he leaned over to push her door open, the back of his arm faintly brushing against her stomach, sending goosebumps shimmying through her, radiating outward from the spot.

Quickly she stepped out onto the sidewalk.

"Hey, wait a minute . . ." He leaned across the seat, peered

33

up at her with a curiously sad expression about his eyes and mouth. "I—what's your last name again, Catherine?"

His question swept her with the insane urge to cry, an urge she'd felt earlier in the foyer when he'd failed to recognize her.

"Anderson. It's Anderson. So common it's easy to forget." Then she turned and ran into the house.

But when she was gone, Clay Forrester folded the arms of his expensively tailored sport coat over the wheel of his expensive sports car, laid his well-groomed head upon them, knowing he would never forget her name as long as he lived.

Chapter 3

THE ONLY LIGHT burning on the lower level was the lamp on the console table. Reaching for it, Clay caught his reflection in the mirror. A troubled frown stared back at him. *Catherine Anderson,* he thought, *Catherine Anderson.* Not liking what he saw, he quickly snapped the light off.

Upstairs the door to his parents' bedroom suite was ajar, casting a pyramid of brightness into the hall. He stopped, arms akimbo, staring at the floor in the way he was wont to do when troubled, wondering what to say.

"Clay? We heard you get home. Come in." His father moved into the open door. From the shadows Clay studied him, his heavy velour jacket shaped like a short kimono over his trousers. The older man's hair lay in soft silver waves around his healthy face. Momentarily Clay had the desire to grasp his father's neck and bury his face in the silver waves, feel that tanned cheek against his own as when he was a child and came running in for a morning hug.

"I didn't mean to keep you and Mother up."

"We'd be up in any case. Come in."

The ivory carpeting swallowed his slippered steps as Clay followed, to find his mother, wearing an ecru Eve Stillman dressing gown, her feet tucked up into the corner of a powder blue chair of watered silk.

It was like stepping back twenty years. Coming and going in their separate adult pursuits, they had little occasion to cross each other's paths except when dressed in street clothes. Gone now were the impeccable suits, high heels and jewelry from the woman curled protectively into the corner of that chair. Clay again experienced the strange sensation he'd had in the hall. He wanted to bury his head in her lap and be her little boy again.

But her face stopped him.

"We were having a glass of white wine to soothe the frayed nerves," his father said, crossing to fill his glass from a crystal decanter while Clay took the chair that matched his mother's. "Would you like one?"

"No, none for me." Sardonically he thought, wine, tricky wine.

"Clay, we assume nothing. Not yet," his father began. "We are still waiting for your answer."

Clay looked at his mother's anxious face, at that guardian-like pose which cried out that she didn't want to learn what might be true. His father stood, swirling the wine around and around in his glass, staring at it, waiting.

"It looks like Catherine is right," Clay confessed, unable to tear his eyes away from his mother's shifting expression, her widening eyes which gaped momentarily before seeking her husband's. But Claiborne studied the expression on his son's face.

"Are you sure it's yours?" Claiborne asked forthrightly.

Clay worked his hands against each other, leaning forward, studying the floor. "It seems so."

Stunned, Angela expressed what both she and her husband had been thinking for the past several hours. "Oh, Clay, you didn't even know her today. How can it possibly be true?"

"I only met her once, that's why I didn't recognize her at first."

"Once was apparently quite enough!" Claiborne interjected caustically.

"I deserve that, I know."

But suddenly Claiborne Forrester, father, became Claiborne

36

Forrester, counselor. Silently he took up pacing for a moment, then stopped directly before his son, brandishing his wineglass as he often brandished a finger at a client too quick to admit his guilt. "Clay, I want you to make damn sure you are the man responsible before we take this thing one step further, do you understand?"

Clay sighed, stood up and ran four lean fingers through his hair. "Father, I appreciate your solicitude, and . . . believe me . . . when I first found out why she was here, I was just as surprised as you. That's why I took her out for a ride. I thought maybe she was just some kind of gold digger trying to stake a claim on me, but it seems she isn't. Catherine doesn't want a thing from me, or from you, for that matter."

"Then why did she come here?"

"She claims it was all her father's idea."

"What! And you believe her?"

"Whether I believe her or not, she doesn't want one red cent from me."

His mother said hopefully, "Maybe she's had a sudden attack of conscience for blaming you unjustly."

"Mother," Clay sighed, gazing down at her. How defenseless she looked with her makeup cleansed off this way. It broke his heart to hurt her. He crossed to her chair, reached down to take both of her hands. "Mother, I won't make much of a lawyer if I can't cross-examine a witness any better than that, will I?" he asked gently. "If I could honestly say the baby's not mine, I would. But I can't say that. I'm reasonably sure it is."

Her startled eyes pleaded with her son's. "But, Clay, you don't know anything about this girl. How can you be sure? There could . . ." Her lips quivered. "Could have been others."

He squeezed the backs of her hands, looked into her despairing eyes, then spoke in the softest of tones. "Mother, she was a virgin. The dates match up."

Angela wanted to cry out, "Why, Clay, why?" But she knew it would do no good. He, too, was hurting now—she could see it in his eyes—so she only returned the pressure of his hands. But without warning, two tears slid down her cheeks, not only for herself, but for him, as well. She tugged at his hands, reaching to pull him down and kneel as she held him.

He felt a keen, sharp pain at having disappointed her, a deep welling love at her reaction.

"Oh, Clay," she said when she could speak once more, "if only you were six years old this would be so much easier. I could just punish you and send you to your room."

He smiled a little sadly. "If I were six, you wouldn't have to."

Her own wistful smile trembled and was gone. "Don't humor me, Clay. I'm deeply disappointed in you. Give me your hanky." He fished it out of his pocket. "I thought I taught you"—she dabbed her eyes, groping for a graceful phrase—"respect for women."

"You did, you both did." Abruptly Clay stood, plunged his hands in his trouser pockets and turned away. "But for God's sake, I'm twenty-five years old. Did you really think I'd never had anything to do with women at my age?"

"A mother doesn't think about it one way or the other."

"I'd be abnormal if I were pure as the driven snow. Why, you and Father were married already by the time he was twenty-five."

"Exactly," Claiborne interjected. "We were responsible enough to put things into their proper perspective. I married your mother first, no matter what my baser instincts advised me while we dated."

"I suppose you'll preach me a sermon if I say things are different now."

"You bet I will. Clay, how could you let a thing like this happen on a *blind date*, and with a girl like that! It might be understandable if you were engaged to the girl or had been seeing her for a while. If you . . . if you loved her. But don't stand there and ask me to condone your indiscriminate sex, because I will not!"

"I didn't expect you to."

"You should have had more sense!" the older man blustered, pacing feverishly.

"At the time sense didn't enter into it," Clay said dryly, and across the room Claiborne's eyes blazed.

"That goes without saying, since you obviously hadn't enough wits to see that she didn't get pregnant out of it!"

"Claiborne!"

"Well, dammit, Angela, he's an adult who *has* used the brains of a child to let a thing like this happen. I expect a man of twenty-five to display twenty-five years' worth of common sense!"

"We each assumed the other had taken precautions," Clay explained tiredly.

"Assumed! Assumed! Yes, you've assumed yourself right into the hands of that obnoxious, money-hungry father of hers with your stupidity! The man is a raving idiot, but a shrewd one. He has every intention of taking us to the cleaners!"

Clay couldn't deny it; even Catherine had said it was true.

"You're not liable for my actions."

"No, I'm not. But do you think reasoning like that is common to a man like Anderson? He wants restitution made for his little girl's seduction and he won't rest till it's made to suit the figure he has in mind."

"Did he mention how much he wants?" Clay asked, afraid to hear the answer.

"He didn't have to. I can tell his mind works best with big, round numbers. And Clay, something else has come up that bears consideration." The glance he gave his wife told their son it was something Angela, too, knew about. "I've been approached by members of a local caucus to consider running for county attorney. I hadn't mentioned it to you because I thought it best to wait until you'd passed your bar exams and become part of the firm. But frankly it's something your mother and I have been considering quite seriously. I don't have to tell you how detrimental a little muckraking can be to a potential candidate. It won't matter to the voters who the source is."

"Catherine said she has her plans made, although she won't tell me what they are. But once she leaves home, he won't have a leg to stand on as far as a paternity suit is concerned. She refuses to be a part of his scheme."

"Quit fooling yourself, Clay. You're almost a lawyer, and I am one. We both know that a paternity suit is one of the hardest nuts in the bucket to crack. It's not the outcome of a suit I'm worried about, it's the reverberations it can stir up. And there's one more issue we haven't touched on yet." He looked down into his glass, then into Clay's eyes. "Even if the man does decide to back down and cease his demands, there is a moral obligation here that you cannot deny. If you do, I will be far, far more disappointed in you than I am right now."

Clay's head came up with a jerk. "You aren't saying you expect me to marry her, are you?"

His father studied him, dissatisfaction written on every line, every plane of his face. "I don't know, Clay, I don't know. All I know is that I have attempted by both example and word to teach you the value of honesty. Is it honest for you to leave the woman high and dry?"

"Yes, if it's what she wants."

"Clay, the woman is probably scared senseless right now. She's caught between a stranger she doesn't even know and that raving lunatic of a father. Don't you think she deserves every bit of cooperation she can get from you?"

"You've said it for me. I'm a stranger to her. Do you think she would want to marry a stranger?"

"She could do worse. In spite of the thoughtlessness and insensibility you've displayed recently, I don't think you're a hopeless case."

"I would be if I married her. Jesus, I don't even like the girl."

"In the first place, don't use profanity before your mother, and in the second, let's stop calling her a girl. She's a full-grown woman, as is entirely obvious. As a woman, she should be willing to listen to reason."

"I don't understand what you're driving at. You can see what kind of a family she comes from. Her father is a lunatic; her mother is browbeaten; look at the way they dress, where they come from. That's obviously not the kind of family you'd like me to marry into, yet you stand there talking as if you want me to ask her."

"You should have considered her background before you got her pregnant, Clay."

"How could I when I didn't even know her then?"

Claiborne Forrester had the innate sense of timing peculiar to every successful lawyer, and he used the elongated moment of silence now to speak dramatically before he cinched his case. "Exactly. Which, rather than exonerate you, as you think the fact should, creates—in my estimation—an even greater responsibility toward her and the child. You acted without a thought for the repercussions. Even now you seem to have forgotten there *is* a child involved here, and that it's yours."

"It's hers!"

His father's jaw hardened and his eyes iced over. "When did you turn so callous, Clay?"

"Tonight when I walked in here and the buzzards swooped down."

"Stop this, you two," Angela demanded in her quiet way, rising from her chair. "Neither one of you is making sense, and you'll regret this later if you go on. Clay, your father is right. You do have a moral obligation to that woman. Whether or not it extends to asking her to marry you is something none of us should try to decide tonight." Crossing to her husband she laid a hand on his chest. "Darling, we all need to think about this. Clay has said the girl doesn't want to be married. He's said she's refused his offer of money. Let's let the two of them settle it between them after everyone has cooled down a little bit."

"Angela, I think our son needs—"

She placed her fingers on his lips. "Claiborne, you're running on emotions now, and you've told me countless times that a good lawyer must not do that. Let's not discuss it anymore at the moment."

He looked into her eyes, which were luminous with emotion. They were large, lovely oval eyes of warm hazel which needed none of the artifice she used daily to enhance them. Claiborne Forrester, at age fifty-nine, loved them as much now devoid of makeup as he had when he was twenty, and she'd used it to woo him. He covered the hand which lay on his chest. There was no need for him to answer. He bowed to her judgment, giving her a reaffirmation of his love with a gentle pressure of his warm palm.

Watching them thus, Clay felt again the security which emanated from them, which had emanated from them as long as he could remember. What he saw before him was what he wanted in his life with a woman. He wanted to duplicate the love and trust shining from his parents' eyes when they looked at one another. He did not want to marry a girl whose last name he'd forgotten, whose home had been fraught with the antithesis of the love he'd grown up with.

41

His mother turned, and behind her, his father's hands rested upon her shoulders. Together they looked at their son.

"Your mother is right. Let's sleep on it, Clay. Things have a way of becoming clearer with time. It lends perspective."

"I hope so." Clay's hands hung disconsolately in his pockets.

To Angela he looked like an overgrown boy in that scolded pose, his hair far from neat. Intuition told her what he was struggling with, and wisely she waited for him to get it out.

"I'm so damn sorry," Clay choked, and only then did she open her arms to him. Over her shoulder he sought his father's eyes, and in a moment the arms of the velour robe were there to rub his shoulders in brief reassurance.

"We love you, Clay, no matter what," Angela reminded him.

Claiborne added, "The proof of it may seem curious at this time, but as the saying goes, love is not always kind." Then, placing his hands once again on Angela's shoulders, he said, "Good night, son."

Leaving the two of them, Clay knew they would remain allied on whatever stand they took; they always did. He had no wish to play them one against the other, though his mother seemed the far more tractable. Their unity of purpose had created such a great part of Clay's childhood security, anything else would have been out of character now. He could not help but wonder what kind of parenting team he and the volatile Catherine Anderson would make. He shuddered to think of it.

Angela Forrester lay with her stomach nestled tightly against her husband's curled back, one hand under her pillow, the other inside his pajamas.

"Darling?" she whispered.

"Hmm?" he answered, fast enough to tell her he hadn't been asleep either.

The words seemed to stick in Angela's throat. "You don't think that girl will go and have—have an abortion, do you?"

"I've been lying here wondering the same thing, Angela. I don't know."

42

"Oh, Claiborne . . . our grandchild," she whispered, pressing her lips against his naked back, her eyelids sliding shut, her mind filling with comparisons—how it had been when she first fell in love with this man, how elated they'd been when she became pregnant with Clay. Tears sprang to Angela's eyes.

"I know, Angie, I know," Claiborne soothed, reaching behind to pull her body more securely against his. After a long, thoughtful silence he turned over, taking her in his arms. "I'd pay anyone any amount of money if it meant preventing an abortion, you know that, Angie."

"I kn . . . I know, darling, I know," she said against his chest, strengthened by his familiar caress.

"I had to make Clay face up to his responsibilities, though."

"I know that too." But the knowing didn't make it less painful.

"Good, then get some sleep."

"How can I sleep when I—I close my eyes and see that odious man pointing his finger and threatening her. Oh, God, he's ruthless, Claiborne, anyone can see that. He'll never let that girl get away while he thinks she's the key to our money."

"The money's nothing, Angie, it's nothing," he said fiercely.

"I know. It's the girl I'm thinking of and the fact that it's Clay's child. Suppose she takes it back home to the same house with that—that vile man. He's violent. He's the kind—"

In the darkness he kissed her and felt her cheeks were wet. "Angie, Angie, don't," he whispered.

"But it's our grandchild," she repeated near his ear.

"We have to have some faith in Clay."

"But the way he talked tonight . . ."

"He's reacting like any man would. In the light of day let's hope he sees his obligations more clearly."

Angela rolled onto her back, wiped her eyes with the sheet and calmed herself as best she could. After all, this was not some reprobate they were talking about. It was their son.

"He'll do the right thing, darling; he's just like you in so many ways."

Claiborne kissed his wife's cheek. "I love you, Angie." Then he rolled her onto her side and backed her up against him again, settling a hand upon her breast. Her hand crept behind to cradle the reassuring warmth inside his pajamas. And thus they drew strength from each other in the long hour before sleep eased their worries.

It took practiced skill to outwit the caginess of Herb Anderson. He had the sixth sense that inexplicably thrives in alcoholics, that uncanny intuition which can make the hazy brain suddenly work with alarming clarity. The next morning Catherine carefully maintained her customary routine, knowing any small change would trigger his suspicion. She was standing at the kitchen sink eating a fresh orange when Herb came shuffling into the room. The fruit quenched some new taste she'd developed lately, but it seemed to amuse him wickedly.

"Suckin' on your oranges again, huh?" he grated from the doorway. "Lotta good that'll do ya. If you wanna suck something, go suck up to old man Forrester and see if you can get something outa him. What the hell's the matter with you anyway? The way you stood there like some goddam lump last night—we won't get nothin' outa Forrester that way!"

"Don't start in on me again. I told you I'd go with you but I won't back your threats. I have to go to school now."

"You ain't goin' anyplace till you tell me what you got outa lover boy last night!"

"Daddy, don't! Just don't. I don't want to go through it again."

"Well, we're gonna go through it, soon as I have me a coffee roy-al, so just stand where you are, girlie. Where the hell's your mother? Does a man have to make his own damn coffee around this dump?"

"She's gone to work already. Make your own coffee."

He rubbed the side of his coarse hand across the corner of a lip. Catherine could hear the rasp of whiskers clear across the room.

"Got a little uppity since you talked to lover boy, huh?" He chuckled. She no longer tried to stop him from using the term lover boy. It pleased him immensely when she did. He came to the sink and started slamming parts of an aluminum coffeepot around, dumping the grounds out, leaving them to stain the sink, wiping his hands on his stretched-out T-shirt. She stepped

44

back as the stream of water hit the grounds and some came flying her way. He chuckled again. She leaned over the sink sideways, continuing to eat the pieces of quartered orange. But, at close range, he smelled. It made her stomach lurch.

"Well, you gonna spit it out or you gonna stand there suckin' those oranges all morning? What'd lover boy have to say for himself?"

She crossed to the garbage can beside the ancient, chipped porcelain stove, ostensibly to throw away the orange peel; actually she could not stand being so near the man.

"He doesn't want to marry me any more than I want to marry him. I told you he wouldn't."

"You *told* me! Hah! You *told* me nothin', slut! I had to search my own goddam house for any fact I wanted! If I wouldn't've had enough brains to go lookin' I still wouldn't know who your lover boy is! And if you think I'm gonna let him get off scot-free, well, sister, you better think again!" Then he fell to mumbling in the repetitive way she'd learned to despise. "Told me . . . she told me, ha! She told me goddam nothin' . . ."

"I'm going to school," she said resignedly, turning toward the doorway.

"You just keep your smart little ass where it is!"

She stopped with her back to him, sighed, waited for him to finish his tirade so she could pretend to go to classes and he'd leave the house in his usual, aimless way.

"Now I wanna know what the hell he means to do about this mess he got you in!" She heard the exaggerated slam as the coffeepot hit the stove burner.

"Daddy, I have to go to school."

Whining, mimicking, he repeated, *"Daddy, I have to go to school,"* and finished by roaring, "You wanna go to school, you answer me first! What's he intend to do about gettin' you knocked up!"

"He offered me money," she answered, truthfully enough.

"Well, that's more like it! How much?"

How much, how much, how much! she thought frantically, pulling a figure out of the air. "Five thousand dollars."

"Five thousand dollars!" he exploded. "He'll have to do better than that to see the end of me! My ship just come in and he wants to pay me off with a measly five thousand bucks? One o' them diamonds in the old lady's rings was worth ten times as much."

Slowly Catherine turned to face him. "Cash," she said, pleased with the greedy light that responded in his eyes, promising herself to remember it and laugh when she was gone. He pondered, scratching his stomach.

"What'd you tell him?" His face wore that sly weasel's expression she despised. It meant the wheels were turning; he was scheming again about the best way to get something for nothing.

"I told him you'd probably be calling his father."

"Now that's the first smart thing you said since I come in here!"

"You'll call him anyway, so why should I have lied to him? But I haven't changed my mind. You can try bleeding him all you want, but I won't have any part of it, just remember that." This too was her long-taken stand. Should she suddenly veer from it he would undoubtedly become wary.

"Sister, you ain't got the brains God gave a damn chicken!" he blasted, yanking a dirty towel off the cabinet top, then slapping the edge of the sink with it. But she'd long grown inured to his insults; she stood resignedly in the face of them, letting his spate run its course. "You not only ain't got enough brains to keep yourself from gettin' knocked up, you don't know when your ship's come in! Ain't I told you it's come in here?"

The term sickened her, she'd heard it so often, for it was part of his grand self-delusion. "Yes, Daddy, you've told me . . . a thousand times," she said sarcastically before adding firmly, "But I don't want his money. I'm making plans. I can get along without it."

"Plans," he scoffed, "what kind of plans? Don't think you're gonna sponge offa me and raise that little bastard around here 'cause I ain't raisin' his brat! I ain't made outa money, you know!"

"Don't worry, I won't ask you for a thing."

"You bet your boots you won't, sister, because you're gonna call up lover boy there and tell him to fork over!" He pointed a finger at her nose.

"To whom? You or me?"

"Just don't get smart with me, sister! I been waiting for my ship to come in one helluva long time!" She almost cringed again at the hated expression. He'd built his pipedreams upon it for so long that he was no longer aware of how often he used the term, nor the shallowness of character it only served to emphasize.

"I know," she commented dryly, but again he missed the sarcasm.

"And this here is it!" He jammed a dirty finger at the floor as if a pot of gold were there on the cracked, green linoleum.

"Your coffee is going to boil over. Turn the burner down."

He studied the pot unseeingly while the lid lifted with each perk and the man remained unaware of the hiss and smell of burnt grounds. The girl who looked on felt a sudden despair at the changelessness of the man and her situation in this household. Almost as if he'd forgotten her, he now conspired with the coffeepot, leaning the heels of his hands upon the edge of the stove, mumbling the litany Herb Anderson repeated with increasing fervor as the years crept up on him. "Yessir... a long time, and I deserve it, by God."

"I'm going. I have to catch my bus."

He came out of his reverie, looked over his shoulder with a sour expression. "Yeah, go. But just be ready to put the screws to old Forrester again tonight. Five thousand ain't a piss in a hurricane to a rich son-of-a-bitch like him."

When she was gone, Herb leaned over the sink and took up whispering to himself. He often whispered to himself. He told Herb that the world was out to get Herb, and Herb deserved better, by God, and Herb was gonna get it! And no uppity little slut was gonna ace him out of his rightful due! She had her mother's whorish blood, that one did. Didn't he always say so? And didn't she prove him right at last, getting knocked up that way? Just goes to show, things come out even in the end. Yessir. Catherine owed him—Ada owed him—hell, the whole damn country owed him, if it come down to that.

He poured himself another coffee royal to stop the shakes.

Goddam shakes, he thought, they're Ada's fault too! But after his third drink he was as still as a frog eyeing a fly. He held out his hand to verify the fact. Feeling better, he chuckled to think how clever he was, making sure old man Forrester wouldn't want any Andersons tied to his highfalutin' blood-lines! By the end of the week Forrester'd pay, and pay good to see no wedding took place between his high-class son and no knocked-up Catherine Anderson from the wrong side of the tracks.

It took Herb until nearly noon to get his fill of coffee royals and amble from the house in search of his imminent ship.

From the corner grocery store Catherine watched her father leave, hurriedly called her cousin, Bobbi Schumaker, then re-turned to the house to pack. Like Catherine, Bobbi was in her first year at the University of Minnesota, but she loved living with her family. Her home, so different from Catherine's, had been a haven for Catherine during her growing-up years, for the two girls had been best friends and allies since infancy. They kept no secrets from each other.

Bumping along an hour later in Bobbi's little yellow Beetle, Catherine felt relieved to have escaped the house at last.

"So, how'd it go?" Bobbi glanced askance through oversize tortoiseshell glasses.

"Last night or this morning?"

"Both."

"Don't ask." Catherine rested her head back tiredly and shut her eyes.

"That bad, huh?"

"I don't think the Forresters could believe it when the old man barged in there. God, you should have seen that house; it was really something."

"Did they offer to pay the bills?"

"Clay did," Catherine admitted.

"I told you he would."

"And I told you I'd refuse."

Bobbi's mouth puckered. "Why do you have to be so al-mighty stubborn? It's his baby too!"

"I told you, I don't want him to have any kind of hold on me whatsoever. If he pays, he might think he has some say in things."

"But the economics of it doesn't make sense! You can use

48

every cent you can get. How do you think you're going to pay for second semester?"

"Just like I'm paying for the first." Catherine's lips took on that determined look Bobbi knew so well. "I've still got the typewriter and sewing machine."

"And he's got his father's millions," Bobbi retorted dryly.

"Oh, come on, Bobbi, they're not quite that rich, and you know it."

"Stu says they're rolling in it. They have enough that a few measly thousands wouldn't tip the scales."

Catherine sat up straighter, her chin stubbornly thrust out. "Bobbi, I don't want to argue. I've had enough of it this morning as it is."

"Sweet old Uncle Herb on the warpath again, huh?" Bobbi questioned, with saccharine dislike. Catherine nodded. "Well, this is it; you won't have to put up with it after this." When Catherine remained despondent, Bobbi's voice brightened. "I know what you're thinking, Cath, but don't! Your mother made her choices years ago, and it's her problem to live with them or solve them."

"He's going to be in a rage when he finds out I'm gone, and she'll be there for him to take it out on." Catherine stared morosely out the window.

"Don't think about it. Consider yourself lucky you're getting out. If this hadn't happened, you'd have stayed forever to protect her. And don't forget, I'll get my mother to drop in there tonight so yours won't be alone with him. Listen, Cath . . . you're getting out, that's the important thing." She slanted a brown-eyed glance at her cousin before admitting with a grin, "You know, for that I'm not totally ungrateful to Clay Forrester."

"Bobbi!" Catherine's blue eyes held a faint gleam of humorous scolding.

"Well, I'm not." Bobbi's palms came up, then gripped the wheel again. "I mean, what the heck."

"You promised not to tell Clay, and don't forget it!" Catherine admonished.

"Don't worry—he won't find out from me, even if I think you should have your bricks counted. Half the girls on campus would give their eyeteeth to exploit the situation you've landed in and you get a case of pride instead!"

49

"Horizons is free. I'll be all right." Again Catherine resignedly looked out the window.

"But I want you to be more than just all right, Cath. Don't you see, I feel responsible?" Bobbi reached to touch her cousin's arm, and their eyes met again.

"Well, you're not. How many times do I have to repeat it?"

"But I introduced you to Clay Forrester."

"But that's all you did, Bobbi. Beyond that, the choices were my own."

They had argued the point many times. It always left Bobbi a little morose and crestfallen. Quietly, she said, "He's going to ask, you know."

"You'll just have to tell a white lie and say you don't know where I am."

"I don't like it." Bobbie's mouth showed a little stubbornness of its own.

"I don't like leaving my mother there either, but that's life, as you're so fond of saying."

"Just make sure you keep that in mind when you're tempted to give in and get in touch with her to see how she's doing."

"That's the part of it I don't like . . . making her think I'm running across the country. She'll worry herself sick."

"For a while she might, but the postcards will convince her you're doing okay and they'll keep your old man away from the university. There's no way he'll suspect you're still in town. Once the baby is born, you can see your mother again."

Catherine turned pleading eyes to her cousin. "But you'll call and check on her and let me know if . . . if she's okay, won't you?"

"I told you I would, now just relax, and remember . . . once she realizes you've had the nerve to pack up and leave him, she might just find some nerve of her own."

"I doubt it. Something holds her there . . . something I don't understand."

"Don't try to figure out the world and its problems, Cath. You've got enough of your own."

From the moment Catherine had first seen Horizons she'd felt at peace in it. It was one of those turn-of-the-century monstrosities with seemingly far too many rooms for a single family's needs. It had a vast wraparound porch, unscreened, festooned now with macrame pieces created by the various inhabitants who'd come and gone from the house. A few of the plants in the hangers looked peaked, as if they, too, had been touched by a late September frost like the maples that lined the boulevard. Inside, there was a wide entry hall, separated from the living room by a colonnade painted a yellowed ivory color. The stairway that led off the left end of the foyer took two turns, at two landings, on its way up. A rich, old, heavy handrail with spooled rails spoke of grander days. Beyond the colonnade spread the living room and dining room, like a sunny, comfortable cavern. Colored light filtered through old leaded glass, splashing across the living room like strokes of an artist's brush: amethyst, garnet, sapphire and emerald falling through the elegant old floral design as it had for eighty years and more. Wide baseboards and hip-high wainscoting had been miraculously preserved. The room was furnished with an overstuffed davenport and chairs of mismatched designs that somehow seemed more proper than the most carefully planned grouping would have been. There were tables with worn edges, but of homey design. The only incongruity present seemed to be the television set, which was off now as Catherine and Bobbi stood in the front hall watching three girls clean the room. One was on her knees sorting magazines, one was pushing a vacuum cleaner and another was dusting the tables. Beyond the far archway, a little girl bent over a dining room table that could have easily seated the entire Minnesota Viking team. Chairs of every nameable style and shape circled the table, and so did the little girl, slapping at each seat with her dishcloth. She straightened up then and placed a hand on her waist, fingers extending around to the small of her back, stretching backward. Staring, Catherine was abashed when the girl turned around to reveal a popping, full-blown stomach. The child was no more than five feet tall and hadn't even developed breasts yet. She might have been thirteen years old or so, but was at least eight months pregnant.

A glorious smile broke out on her face when she saw Catherine and Bobbi. "Hey, you guys, turn that thing off. We've got company!" she yelled toward the living room.

The vacuum cleaner sighed into silence. The magazine girl got up from her knees; the one who'd been dusting threw the cloth over her shoulder, and they all came toward the colonnade at once.

"Hi, my name's Marie. You looking for Mrs. Tollefson?" said the girl who looked like her name: very French, with tiny bones, pert, dark eyes, a wispy haircut and piquant face that Catherine immediately thought of as darling.

"Yes, I'm Catherine and this is Bobbi." -

"Welcome," Marie said, extending her hand immediately, first to one then to the other. "Which one of you is staying?"

"I am. Bobbi's my cousin; she brought me here."

"Meet the others. This is Vicky." Vicky had a plain, long face whose only redeeming feature was the bright cornflower blue of her eyes. "And Grover." Grover looked as if she should have learned better grooming habits in junior high home ec class; her hair was stringy, nails bitten, clothes unkempt. "And that's our mascot, Little Bit, playing catch with the dishcloth over there. Hey, come on over, Little Bit."

They were all in various stages of pregnancy, but what surprised Catherine was how very young they all looked. Up close, Little Bit looked even younger than before. Marie seemed to be the oldest of the four, perhaps sixteen or seventeen, but the others, Catherine was sure, were not older than fifteen. Amazingly, they all seemed cheerful, greeting Catherine with warm, genuine smiles. She had little chance to dwell on ages, for Marie took the lead, saying, "Welcome then. I'll see if I can hunt up Tolly for you. She's around here someplace. Have you seen her, Little Bit?"

"I think she's in her office."

"Great. Follow me, you guys." While they trailed after Marie, she informed them, "Like I said, Little Bit's our mascot around here. Her real name's Dulcie, but there's not much to her than a little bit, so that's what we call her. Mrs. Tollefson's a good egg. We all call her Tolly. As soon as we talk to her we'll get you settled. Hey, have you guys had your lunch yet?"

Whatever Bobbi's preconceived notions had been about this place, none of them fit. The four girls she'd met so far exuded such an air of goodwill and sorority that she felt quite Victorian at what she'd expected. They all seemed happy and industrious and helpful. Following the bouncy Marie down a hall that led to the rear of the house, Bobbi began feeling better and better about leaving Catherine here. They came to a small room tucked beneath what must have been the servants' stairway at one time. It was as comfortable as the living room, only more crowded. It housed a large desk and bookshelves, and a patchwork sofa in shades of rust and orange that gave a homespun feeling to the room. Shutters were thrown back to let the noon light flood in upon an enormous fern which hung above the desk. Behind the desk a woman was searching through the depths of an open drawer.

"Hey, d'you lose something again, Tolly?" Marie asked.

"Nothing important. It'll show up. It's just my fountain pen. Last time Francie borrowed it she hid it in this bottom drawer. I guess I'll just have to wait until she decides to tell me where it is this time."

"Hey, Tolly, we got company." The woman's gray head popped up, her face appearing for the first time from behind stacks of books. It was a flat, plain middle-aged face with smile lines at the corners of its eyes and bracketing its mouth.

"Oh, glory be, why didn't you say so?" Smiling, she said, "Well, Catherine, I wasn't expecting you quite this early or I would have told the girls to watch out for you and bring your things in. Did anyone get your suitcases yet?"

"We'll take care of it while you talk to her," Marie offered, "if Bobbi'll show us where the car is." But before they left, Marie said to Mrs. Tollefson, "I'll be her sister."

"Wonderful!" the woman exclaimed. "I take it you two have already met, so I'll dispense with introductions. Catherine, we usually have one of the established girls help each new girl, show her where things are, tell her how we arrange work schedules, what time meals are served, things like that."

"We call it being sisters," Marie added. "How'd you like to take me on?"

"I . . ." Catherine felt rather swamped by the goodwill which she had not quite expected, at least not in such immediate displays. Sensing her hesitancy, Marie reached out and took Catherine's hand for a moment. "Listen, we've all been through this first day. Everyone needs a little moral support, not only today, but on lots of days when things get you down. That's why we have sisters here. I rely on you, you rely on me. After awhile you'll find out this is really almost a terrific place to be, right, Tolly?" she chirped to Mrs. Tollefson, who seemed totally accustomed to such scenes. She wasn't in the least surprised to see Marie holding Catherine's hand that way. Catherine, who had not held the hand of another female since she'd given up jump rope and hopscotch, was far more uneasy than anyone in the room.

"Right," answered Mrs. Tollefson. "You've been lucky, Catherine, to be adopted by Marie. She's one of our friendliest residents."

Dropping Catherine's hand, flapping a palm at Mrs. Tollefson, Marie chided, "Oh, yeah, you say that about every single one of us here. Come on, Bobbi, let's get Catherine's stuff up to her room."

When they were gone, Mrs. Tollefson laughed softly and sank into her desk chair. "Oh, that Marie, she's a ball of fire, that one. You'll like her, I think. Sit down, Catherine, sit down."

"Do they all call you Tolly?"

The woman was carelessly dressed and exuded a friendly warmth that made Catherine think she ought to be wearing a cobbler's apron. Instead she wore a pair of maroon jacquard-knit slacks of definitely dated style, and a nondescript white nylon shell beneath an aged cardigan sweater that had long ago lost its shape to that of Mrs. Tollefson's rotund breasts and heavy upper arms. Altogether, Esther Tollefson was a most unstylish woman, but what she lacked in fashion, she made up in cordiality.

"No, not all of them," she answered now. "Some of them call me Tolly. Some call me 'Hey-you,' and some avoid calling me anything. Others don't stay long enough to learn my name. But they are few and far between. Some think of me as a warden, but most of them consider me a friend. I hope you will too."

Catherine nodded, unsure of what to say.

"I sense that you're self-conscious, Catherine, but there is no need to feel that way here. Here you will deal with keeping yourself and your baby as healthy as possible. You'll deal with making decisions about what to do with your life after the baby is born. You will meet young women who have all come here for the same reason as you have: to have a baby that is being born out of wedlock. We do not force you into roles here, Catherine, nor do we place labels on you or on the decisions you will make. But we do hope you'll spend time considering your future and where to pick up after you leave Horizons. We will need a little intake information for our records. Anything you answer will, of course, remain completely confidential. Your privacy will be strictly protected. Do you understand that, Catherine?"

"Yes, but I may as well tell you immediately that I don't want my parents to know where I am."

"They don't have to. That's entirely up to you."

"The rest of the information . . ." Catherine paused, looking down at the manila card, looking for a blank that said "Father's name" or "Baby's father" or something like that. She found no such thing.

"There is no coercion here of any kind. Fill out only what you want to for now. If, as time goes by, you wish to add additional information—well, the card will be here. These first few days we want you to concentrate chiefly on gaining your equilibrium, so to speak. Decisions about the future can be made in due time. You'll find that talking with all the girls will help very much. Each of them has a different outlook. There may be some fresh ideas that will help you immensely. My best advice is to remain open to the support that they may want to give. Don't shut them out, because they may be asking for your support when it appears they are giving you theirs. It won't take you long to find out what I mean."

"Are they all as friendly as the ones I've met so far?"

"Certainly not. We have those who are bitter and withdrawn. With those we try all the harder. We have—as you'll soon see—one girl whose rebellion at her situation has taken on the form of kleptomania. There is no punishment here of any kind, not even for stealing fountain pens. You'll meet Francie soon, I'm sure. If she steals something of yours please let me know. I'm sure she will, right off the bat, just to test your reaction. The best thing to do is to offer her some compliment or suggest doing something for her or ask her advice about something. It always makes her return whatever it is she's stolen."

55

"I'll remember that when I meet her."

"Good. Well, Catherine, as I said before, during the first few days we want you to relax, gain your composure again and get to know the others. I think I hear the girls coming in now. They'll find some lunch for you and show you your room."

Marie appeared in the doorway just then.

"All set?"

"All set," Mrs. Tollefson replied. "Feed this girl if she's hungry, then introduce her around."

"Aye-aye!" Marie saluted. "C'mon, Catherine. This way to the kitchen."

Some thirty minutes later Catherine walked out to the car with Bobbi. They stopped, and Bobbi turned to look back at the house.

"I don't know what I expected, but it wasn't anything like this."

"Anything's better than home," Catherine said with a definite chill in her voice. Bobbi saw the defensive veneer which always seemed to glaze Catherine's eyes when she made comments such as this. A mixture of pity and relief welled up in Bobbi—pity because her cousin's home life had been so painfully devoid of the love to which every child has a right, relief because Horizons seemed as good a haven as possible under these circumstances. Perhaps here Catherine might at last have, if not love, at least a measure of peace.

"I feel . . . well, better about leaving you here, Cath."

The introspective look faded from Catherine's face as she turned to her cousin. The brilliant autumn sun burned down through the balmy afternoon, and for a moment neither of them spoke.

"And I feel good being left here—honest," Catherine assured her. But that guilty look which Catherine had seen so often lately in Bobbi's expression was back again.

"Don't you dare think it," Catherine scolded gently.

"I can't help it," Bobbi answered, thrusting her hands into her jeans pockets and kicking at a fallen leaf. "If I hadn't lined you up with him—"

56

"Bobbi, cut it out. Just promise you won't tell anyone where I am."

Bobbi looked up, unsmiling, her shoulders hunched up, hands still strung up in those pockets. "I promise," she said quietly, then added, "Promise you'll call if you need anything at all?"

"Promise."

There hung between the two girls an intimate silence while each of them thought about that blind date last July, their many shared confidences of girlhood leading to this greatest shared secret of all. For a moment Bobbi thought maybe this time Catherine would make the move first.

But Catherine Anderson found touching a difficult thing to do. And so she hovered, waiting, until at last Bobbi plunged forward to give her the affectionate squeeze Catherine needed so badly. In a life where love was a foreign thing, Catherine's feelings for this vibrant, bubbly cousin came as close as any to that emotion. And so, the hug she returned told a wealth of things, although she herself remained dry-eyed while tears gathered in Bobbi's throat before she backed away.

"Take it easy, huh?" Bobbi managed, her hands jammed once again in her pockets while she backed away.

"Yeah, for sure . . . and thanks, huh?"

And only when Bobbi spun and headed for the car, getting in and driving off without another backward glance did Catherine admit that she felt like crying. But she didn't. She didn't. Still, she came closer than she had since, at age eleven, she'd promised herself never to allow that weakness again.

Chapter 4

IT WAS TWENTY-FOUR hours since Herb Anderson had appeared at the Forrester home with his threats and accusations, twenty-four hours during which Clay had slept little and found it quite impossible to concentrate on the evolution of the law as affected by the McGrath vs. Hardy Case he was currently analyzing in Torts II.

Angela heard the car door slam and moved toward the desk where Claiborne sat in his swivel chair. "He's home, darling. Are you quite sure about what we've decided?"

"As sure as it's possible to be, under the circumstances."

"Very well, but must you confront him seated there like some oracle behind your desk? Let's wait for him on the love-seat."

When Clay came to the study door he looked haggard. He stood in the doorway scarcely aware of the comfortable fire within the cozy room. He was too occupied with the strain upon his parents' faces.

"Come in, Clay," Angela invited, "let's talk."

"I've had a hell of a day." He came in and sank down wearily on the coffee table with his back to them, slumping

58

forward and kneading the back of his neck. "How about you two?"

"Likewise," his father said. "We spent the afternoon out at the Arboretum talking. It's quiet out there at this time of year after the picnickers have gone. Conducive to thinking."

"I might as well have stayed home for all I accomplished today. She was on my mind all day long."

"And?"

"It's no different than last night. I just want to forget she exists."

"But can you do that, Clay?"

"I can try."

"Clay," his mother's concerned voice began, "there's one possibility we did not discuss last night, although I'm sure it entered all our minds, and that is that she might possibly get an abortion. Forgive me for sounding like a grandmother, but the thought of it is utterly sickening to me."

"You might as well know, we talked about it," Clay admitted.

Angela felt a quiver begin in her stomach and travel up to her throat. "You—you did?"

"I offered her money, which she refused."

"Oh, Clay." The soft, disappointed swoon in her tone told Clay how it hurt her to hear the truth.

"Mother, I was testing her. I'm not sure what I'd have said if she had agreed." But then Clay swung around on the shiny table to face his parents. "Oh, hell, what's the use of denying it? At the time it seemed like an easy solution."

"Clay," Angela said, as near to scolding as she'd been in years, "I fail to see how your feelings for that child as its father can be any less than ours as its grandparents. How could you think of—of denying it life, or of spending the rest of your own wondering where and who the child is?"

"Mother, don't you think I've thought the same things all day long?"

"Yet you don't propose to do anything about it?" Angela asked.

"I don't know what to do, I'm just mixed up...I...oh, hell." His shoulders slumped further.

"What your mother is trying to make you see is that your

59

responsibility is to make sure the child is provided for, and that its future is made secure. She speaks for both of us. It's our grandchild. We'd like to know its life will be the best possible, under the circumstances."

"Are you saying you want me to ask that girl to marry me?"

"What we want, Clay, has been superceded by your thoughtless actions. What we want is what we've always wanted for you, an education, a career, a happy life—"

"And you think I'd have those things married to a woman I don't love?" Suddenly Clay rose and walked to a window, glanced absently at the gathering dusk outside, then turned to confront them again. "I've never said it before, not in so many words, but I want the kind of relationship you two have. I want a wife I can be proud of, someone of my own class, if it comes down to that, whose ambitions match mine, who is bright and ... and loving, and who wants what I want out of life. Someone like Jill."

"Ah ... Jill," Angela said with an arched eyebrow, then leaned forward intently, her petite elbow on her gracefully crossed knees. "Yes, I think it's time you considered Jill. Where was Jill when all of this happened?"

"We'd had a fight, that's all."

"Oh, you had a fight." Angela settled back again, her casualness belying the seriousness of the subject. "And so you took out Catherine to—to get even with Jill, or for whatever reason, and by doing so, wronged not one woman, but two. Clay, how could you!"

"Mother, you've always liked Jill far better than any of the other girls I've gone with."

"Yes, I have; both your father and I admire her immensely. But at the moment I feel your responsibility to Catherine Anderson is far greater than that to Jill. Besides, I haven't the slightest doubt that if you'd wanted to marry Jill you'd have asked her years ago."

"We've talked about it more than once, but the timing just wasn't right. I wanted to get school behind me and pass my bar exam first."

"Speaking of which, I should like to point out a few facts you may have overlooked," Claiborne said, rising from the loveseat and taking what Clay knew was his "counsel for the plaintiff" stance: both feet flat on the floor, jaw and one shoulder jutting toward the accused. "That father of hers could make more trouble for you than you might think. You are aware that your bar examinations are less than a year off, and that the State Board of Law Examiners goes to some lengths to establish that any person making application be of good moral character. Up to this point I've never given it a second thought regarding you, but I've done nothing but consider it today. Clay, something like this could be enough for them to deny you the right to take your boards! When you apply, you'll be asked for affidavits respecting your habits and general reputation, and they are fully within their rights to demand you to furnish a character investigation report to the National Bar Examiners. Do you realize that?"

The expression on Clay's face made an answer unnecessary.

"Clay, it only takes one dyed-in-the-wool conservative who still sees abortion as immoral, regardless of its legal ramifications, or who believes that siring a bastard is cause enough to doubt your moral character, and it could be the death knell to your legal career. You have less than a year left. Do you want it all to go for nothing?" Claiborne moved to his desk, touched a pen distractedly, then sought Clay's eyes. "There is a minor concern which I cannot help but inject here. As an alumnus at the university, I'm a member of the Partnership in Excellence and The Board of Visitors. I enjoy those positions and they speak well for me. They are prestigious and would undoubtedly be an asset, if I decide to run for county attorney. I should like no slur on the Forrester name, whether it be on yours or mine. And if I do run, I am counting on you to continue my established practice during my term. Of course, we all realize what is at stake here." Claiborne dropped the pen on the desk for effect. It was implicit: he was threatening to exclude Clay from the family firm, upon which Clay had always built his plans for the future. Claiborne steepled his fingertips, looked over them at his son and finished, with further innuendo, "Your decision, Clay, will affect all of us."

At that moment Herbert Anderson was stalking back and forth across Catherine's deserted bedroom like a caged cat.

61

"Goddam that girl; I'll break every bone in her body if she ain't with Forrester talking money right this minute! Talk about gratitude, that's gratitude for you!" He landed a vicious kick on a drawer that gaped at him with nothing but newspaper lining its bottom. The kick left a black scuff mark beside those he'd already put there.

From the doorway Ada stammered in a quaking voice, "Wh-where do you sup—suppose she'd of gone, Herb?"

"Well, how the hell am I supposed to know!" he yelled. "She don't tell me one damn thing about her comings and goings. If she did, she wouldn't of got herself knocked up in the first place 'cause I'd of made goddam sure she'd of known something about that lover boy of hers before she went out and got herself diddled by him!"

"Maybe—maybe he took her in after all."

"He took her in all right, and she's got a belly full of his brat to prove it!" Stalking to the telephone, he elbowed Ada rudely aside, continuing his tirade as he dialed. "Damn girl ain't got the sense God gave a cluck hen if she's not with Forrester. Wouldn't know what her ship looked like if it run her down and sliced her in half! Them Forresters was my ticket, goddammit! My ticket! Damn her hide if she run off on me and . . ."

Just then Clay picked up his ringing phone, and Anderson bawled into the mouthpiece, "Where the hell is my daughter, lover boy!" The three Forresters were still in the study discussing the situation. Claiborne and Angela didn't need to hear the far end of the conversation to know what was being said.

"She's not here." There were long pauses between Clay's responses. "I don't know . . . I haven't seen her since I dropped her off at home last night . . . Now listen to me, Anderson! I told her then that if she wanted money, I'd be happy to give it to her, but she refused. I don't know what more you expect of me . . . That's harrassment, Anderson, and it's punishable by law! . . . I'm willing to talk to your daughter but I have no intention of dealing with a small-time con artist like you. I'll say it one more time, Anderson, leave us alone! It will take no more than a call from your daughter, and financial aid will be in her hand before the day is out, but as for you, I wouldn't give you the directions to a soup line if you were dying of starvation! Do I make myself clear! . . . Fine! Bring them! She's nowhere in this house. If she were, I'd be happy to put her on the phone right now . . . Yes, your concern is very touching . . . I have no idea . . ." There followed a longer pause during which Clay pulled the receiver away from his ear while the muffled anger of Herb Anderson crackled through the wire. When Clay hung up, it was with equal portions of anger and worry.

"Well, it seems she's disappeared," he said, dropping down into his father's desk chair.

"So I gathered," Claiborne replied.

"The man is a lunatic."

"I agree. And he's not going to stop with one abusive phone call. Do you concur?"

"How should I know?" Clay jumped up again, paced across the room and stopped to sigh at the ceiling. "He threatened at least four various felonies during the course of the conversation."

"Have you any idea where the girl might have gone?" his father asked.

"None. All she would say was that she had plans. I had no idea she intended to disappear this fast."

"Do you know any of her friends?"

"Only her cousin Bobbi, the girl Stu's been dating."

"My suggestion is, you see if she knows where Catherine is, and the sooner the better. I have an idea we haven't heard the last from Anderson. I want him stopped before any word of this leaks out."

Meanwhile, in Omaha, Nebraska, the sister of a student in Bobbi Schumaker's Psych I class dropped a letter in a U.S. mail depository. It was written in Catherine Anderson's clean, distinctive hand and addressed to Ada, telling her not to worry.

The following evening the Forresters were at dinner, the table set tastefully with white damask linens, bronze-colored mums and burning tapers. Inella, the maid, had just served the chicken Kiev and returned to the kitchen when the doorbell rang. With a sigh she went to answer it. She had no more than turned the handle when the door was smacked back against the wall with a violent shove, flying out of Inella's surprised fingers.

A guttural voice rasped, "Where the hell is he!"

Too shocked to attempt forestalling him, she only gaped while the man used an elbow to thrust her aside. She landed against the side of the stairs, overturning the brass pitcher of eucalyptus. Before she could right herself, the words Warpo's Bar were disappearing into the living room, trailed by a string of filth that made Inella's ears ring worse than the thud her head had just suffered.

"I told you I'd get you, lover boy, and I'm here to do it!" Herb Anderson shouted, surprising the trio at the dining room table.

Angela's hand was poised halfway to her mouth. Claiborne dropped his napkin and Clay began getting to his feet. But halfway there he was caught in the chin by a set of crusty knuckles whistling through the candlelit room without warning. His head snapped back and the sickening sound of the fist landing on her son's face made Angela scream and grope for her husband's help. Clay reeled backward, taking his chair with him to the floor while the red nylon jacket dove after him. Before Claiborne could reach Anderson's poised arm, it cracked downward again in a second punishing blow. From the doorway Inella screamed, then covered her mouth with her hands.

"My God, call the police!" cried Angela. "Hurry!"

Inella spun from the room.

Claiborne got Anderson's arm, avoiding the swings which continued falling seemingly in every direction at once. He managed to catch the crook of Anderson's elbow, spinning the heavy man in a circle. Anderson's backside struck the edge of the table, sending crystal wine goblets, water glasses and candleholders teetering. The tablecloth caught on fire as candle wax sprayed across it, but Angela was embroiled in attempting to subdue the madman along with her husband. Clay got to his feet, bleeding, stunned, but not too stunned to throw his weight into a fist that settled satisfyingly into Anderson's paunch. The air whoofed from Anderson, and he doubled over, clutching himself, while Angela grabbed a handful of his hair and yanked as hard as she could. She was crying, even as she held the detestable hair in a painful tug. Clay stood like a crazed man himself, the look on his face pure fury as he pinned one of Anderson's arms behind his back and leaned a knee across the words on the back of the red nylon jacket. The fire on the tabletop grew, but just then a sobbing Inella ran back into the room, tipped the bouquet of chrysanthemums over to douse the flames, then stood clutching her knuckles against her lips while tears streamed down her cheeks.

"The police are coming."

"Oh, God, make them hurry," Angela prayed.

The shock of the attack was sinking in as the three Forresters looked at each other across the subdued man. Angela saw the cut on Clay's jaw, another above his right eye.

"Clay, are you all right?"

"I'm okay . . . Dad, how about you?"

"I'll get you rich sons-a-bitches!" Anderson was still vowing, his face now pressed into the yellow carpet. "Goddammit! Let go o' my hair!"

Angela only pulled harder.

Outside, sirens grew closer and Inella fled from the room to the front door, which was still yawning open. Blue uniforms sped through the house behind the maid, who was shaking uncontrollably now.

Anderson was cuffed quickly and forced to remain on the dining room floor, all the while spewing threats and oaths at the Forrester family in general. The smell of burned linens permeated the room. The officers saw the charred tablecloth, the overturned dishes and the flowers strewn across the table and onto the floor.

"Is anybody hurt?"

Everyone turned to look at Angela first, as at last she flung herself into her husband's arms, crying.

"Angie, are you hurt?" he asked concernedly, but she only shook her head, leaving it buried in his chest.

"Do you know this man?" an officer asked.

"We've only met him once, day before yesterday."

"What happened here tonight?"

"He forced his way in and accosted my son while we were having dinner."

"What's your name, Bud?" This to Anderson, who was now kneeling on the floor.

"You ask *them* what my name is, so they'll never forget it!" He jerked his head viciously in Clay's direction. "Ask lover boy there who I am. I'm the father of the girl he knocked up, that's who!"

"Do you want to press charges, sir?" an officer asked Claiborne.

"What about me?" Anderson whined. "I got some charges need pressin' here if anybody does. That son-of-a-bitch—"

"Take him to the squad car, Larry. You'll get your chance to answer later, Anderson, after we read you your rights."

He was pulled to his feet and pushed ahead of the officer to the front door. Outside the flashing scarlet light was still circling, the radio crackling a dispatcher's voice. Anderson was locked in the caged backseat to rain accusations on the entire Forrester family only to be ignored by the officer who calmly sat up front, writing on his clipboard.

Shortly before supper the following day, the hall phone at Horizons rang. Someone shouted through the house, "Phone call . . . Anderson!"

Running downstairs, Catherine knew it could only be Bobbi, and she was anxious for word about her mother.

"Hello?"

"Cath, have you read the paper today?"

"No, I had classes. I didn't have time."

"Well, you'd better."

Catherine had a sudden, horrible premonition that her fears had become reality, that Herb Anderson had taken it all out on his wife.

"Is Mom—"

"No, no . . . she's all right. It's Clay. Your old man busted into his house last night and laid one on him."

"What!"

"I'm not kidding, Cath. He pushed his way in there and popped him. The police came and hauled sweet old Uncle Herb off to jail."

"Oh, no." Catherine's fingertips covered her lips.

"Just thought you'd want to know."

There was a hesitation, then, "Is—is Clay hurt?"

"I don't know. The article didn't say. You can read it for yourself. It's on page eight-B of the morning *Trib*."

"Have you talked to my mother?"

"Yeah, she's okay. I talked to her last night, must have been while your dad was in Edina beating up Clay. She almost sounded happy that you were gone. I told her not to worry because you were safe and that she'd be hearing from you."

"Is she—"

"She's okay, Cat, I said she's okay. Just stay where you are and don't let this change your mind, huh? Clay can take care of himself, and a night in jail might even mellow out your old man."

Before she ended the conversation, Bobbi added a fact that she'd earlier decided not to tell Catherine, then had decided to tell after all.

"Clay called me and asked if I knew where you are. I lied."

The line buzzed voicelessly for a moment, then Catherine said quietly, "Thanks, kiddo."

Catherine found the article in the *Minneapolis Tribune* and read it several times, trying to picture the scene her father had created. Although she hadn't seen the dining room of the Forrester house, she could well imagine a luxurious setting there and what it must have been like when her father burst in. Clay Forrester's face welled up before her, his gray eyes, handsome jawline, and then her old man's fist ramming into it. Guilt welled up unwanted. She heard Clay's voice as he'd asked her to accept his money, and somehow knew that if she'd accepted it he would not have been assaulted by her old man. She knew, too, that her running away had thwarted Herb Anderson's plans for getting rich quick and had been further cause for him to turn his rage on Clay. At least Herb's volatile anger had been diverted away from Ada, but Catherine's conscience plagued her mercilessly until she assuaged it with the thought that, after all, the elder Mr. Forrester was an attorney and could easily prosecute his son's assailant, which would be no more than Herb deserved. The thought brought a short smile to Catherine's lips.

* * *

Bobbi wasn't surprised to answer the door the next day and find Clay Forrester there.

He said without preamble, "I've got to talk to you. Can we take a ride?"

"Sure, but it won't do any good."

"You know where she is, don't you?"

"Maybe I do, maybe I don't. Who wants to know, her old man?"

"I do."

"You're a day late and a dollar short, Clay."

"Listen, could we go somewhere and have a cup of coffee?"

She studied him a moment, shrugged, and answered, "Let me get my sweater."

The Corvette was at the curb. She eyed it appreciatively and wondered again at Catherine's foolishness in not exploiting the situation, if only financially. Watching Clay round the front fender, Bobbi couldn't help thinking that if she were in Catherine's shoes she herself might not mind exploiting Clay Forrester in more ways than one.

They drove to a small restaurant called Green's where they ordered coffee, then sat avoiding each other's eyes until it came. Clay hunched over his cup, looking totally distraught. His jawline had been altered and a bandage rode his right eyebrow.

"That's a nice little shiner you've got there, Clay." She eyed it and he scowled.

"This thing is getting out of hand, Bobbi."

"Her old man's always been out of hand. How do you like him?"

Clay sipped his coffee and looked at her over the rim of the cup. "Not exactly my idea of a model father-in-law," he said.

"So what do you want with Catherine?"

"Listen, there are things involved here which I don't care to get into. But, for starters, I want her to take some money from me so her old man will leave me alone. He's not going to stop until he's seen green, and I'll be damned if I'll lay it in his hand. All I want her to do is to accept money for the hospital bills or her keep or whatever. Do you know where she is?"

"What if I do?" There was an unmistakable note of challenge

in her attitude. He studied her a moment, then leaned back, toying with his cup handle.

"Maybe I deserved to get knocked around a little bit, is that what you're thinking?"

"Maybe I was. I love her."

"Did she tell you I offered to pay my dues, financially?"

"She also told me you offered her money for an abortion." When he remained silent Bobbi went on. "Supposing she's off having one right now?" Bobbi studied his face carefully and found the reaction she wanted: dread. She added sardonically, "Is your conscience bothering you, Clay?"

"You're damn right it is. If you think the only reason I want to see her is to get Anderson off my back, you're wrong." He closed his eyes and squeezed the bridge of his nose briefly, then muttered, "Lord, I can't get her off my mind."

Bobbi studied him as she sipped. The black eye and bruised jaw Uncle Herb had doled out could not disguise Clay Forrester's handsomeness nor the worried expression about his eyes. Something in Bobbi softened.

"I don't know why I feel compelled to tell you, but she's okay. She's got her plans all made and she's carrying through with them. Catherine's a strong person."

"I realized that the other night when I talked to her. Most girls in her position would come at a man with palms up, but not her."

"She's had it hard. She knows how to get by without any help from anybody."

"But still you won't tell me where she is?" He turned appealing eyes to her, making it extremely difficult for Bobbi to answer as she had to.

"That's right. I gave my word."

"All right. I won't try to force you to break it, but will you do just this much for me? Will you tell Catherine that if she needs anything—anything at all—to let me know? Tell her I'd like to talk to her, that it's important, and ask her if she'd call me at home tomorrow night. That way neither one of you will have to give away her whereabouts."

"I'll give her the message, but I don't think she'll call. She's stubborn . . . almost as stubborn as her old man."

Clay looked down into his cup. "Listen, she's"—He swallowed, looked up again with an expression of worry etched upon his eyebrows—"She's not having an abortion, is she?"

"No, she's not."

His shoulders seemed to wilt with relief.

That night when Catherine answered the phone, Bobbi opened by saying, "Clay came to see me."

Catherine's hand stopped where it was upon her scalp, combing her hair back from her face. Her heart seemed to stop with it. "You didn't tell him anything, did you?"

"No, I just complimented him on his shiner. Your dad really meant business!"

It took great effort for Catherine to resist asking if Clay was really all right. She affected a businesslike tone, asking, "He didn't come to show you his battle scars, I'm sure. What did he want?"

"To know where you are. He wants to talk to you."

"About what?"

"Well, what do you suppose? Cath, he's not so bad. He didn't even complain about getting beaten up. He seems genuinely worried about your welfare and wants to make some arrangements for paying for the baby, that's all."

"Bully for him!" Catherine exclaimed, casting an anxious glance down the hall to make sure no one was within earshot.

"Okay, okay! All I am is the messenger. He wants you to call him at his house tonight."

The line grew silent. The picture of his house came back all too clearly to Catherine. His house with its comfortable luxury, its fire burning at dusk, his parents in their finery, Clay walking in whistling with his hair the color of autumn. A weakness threatened Catherine, but she resisted it.

"Cath, did you hear me?"

"I heard."

"But you're not going to call him?"

"No."

"But he said he's got something he has to talk over with you." A rather persuasive tone came into Bobbi's voice then. "Listen, Cat, he kind of threw me. I thought he'd try to wheedle your whereabouts out of me, but he didn't. He said if you'd

70

call him, neither one of us would have to give away any secrets."

"Very upstanding," Catherine said tightly, haunted even further by the remembered look of concern on Clay's face as she got out of his car.

"This might sound disloyal, but I'm beginning to think he is."

"What, upstanding?"

"Well, is it so unbelievable? He really seems...well, concerned. He isn't acting at all like I thought he would. I find myself wondering what Stu would do if he found himself in Clay's situation. I think he might have left town by now. Listen, why don't you give Clay a chance?"

"I can't. I don't want his concern and I'm not going to call him. It wouldn't do any good."

"He said I should tell you if there's anything you need, just say so, and you've got the money for it."

"I know. He told me that before. I told him I don't want anything from him."

"Cath, are you sure you're doing the smart thing?"

"Bobbi...please."

"Well, heck, he's loaded. Why not take a little of it off his hands?"

"Now you sound like my old man!"

"Okay, Cath, it's your baby. I did what he asked; I gave you the message. Call him at his place tonight. From there on out it's up to you. So how's the place?"

"It's really not bad, you know?" Then, fighting off thoughts of Clay Forrester, Catherine added, "It has no men, so that's a plus right there."

The voice at the other end became pleading. "Hey, don't get that way, Cath. Not all men are like your father. Clay Forrester, for instance, is about as far from your father as a man could get."

"Bobbi, I get the distinct impression that you're changing sides."

"I'm not changing sides. But I'm getting a better view of both sides, caught in the middle like I am. I'm always on your side, but I can't help it if I think you should at least call the guy."

"Like hell I will! I don't want Clay Forrester or his money!"

"All right, all right! Enough! I'm not going to waste any more time arguing with you about it, because I know you when you get your mind made up."

Absorbed as she was in her conversation with Bobbi, Catherine was unaware that three girls had gone into the kitchen for a snack, and from there any telephone conversation could be easily heard. When she hung up, she headed back for her room, more rattled than she'd care to admit by what Bobbi had said. It would be so easy to give in, to accept money from Clay, or to solicit his moral support during the difficult months ahead, but should she rely on him in any way she feared he would have a hold on her, on the decisions about her future which must still be made. It would be better to stay here where life was better than that which she'd left. At Horizons there was no censure, for everyone here was in the same boat.

Or so they thought.

Chapter 5

THE TENSION AROUND the Forrester home grew as Catherine's whereabouts remained unknown. Angela walked around with a drawn expression about her mouth, and often Clay found her eyes upon him with such a hurt expression that he carried its memory with him to the law school building each day. His concentration was further thwarted by the fact that Herb Anderson was released after twenty-four hours without a formal charge made against him. The necessity to let him go scot-free rankled mercilessly, not only on Clay but on his father. They knew the law, knew they could pin Anderson to the wall for what he'd done. To be unable to do so only raised the pitch of their taut nerves.

Once Anderson was free, he became more self-righteous than ever. He smiled in self-satisfaction all the way home while he thought, I got them sons-a-bitches where I want them and I ain't lettin' go till they come through with the greenbacks!

When Herb got home, Ada was standing in the living room with her coat still on, reading a postcard. She looked up, startled to see him coming in the door.

"Why, Herb, you're out."

"Goddam right I'm out. Them Forresters know what's good

73

for 'em, that's why I'm out. Where's the girl?" His eyes were bloodshot, his knuckles still taped, the bandages dirty now. He already had the rank stench of gin on his breath.

"She's all right, Herb," Ada offered timorously, holding out the card. "Look, she's in Omaha with a friend who—"

"Omaha!" The word rattled the windows as Herb reeled and smacked the postcard out of his wife's hand. She cowered, watching with huge eyes as he teetered and stooped to pick up the card off the floor. He gaped at the handwriting to make sure it was Catherine's. He swiped the soiled bandage across the eyes that always wore a film of water over their ochred whites. When his vision cleared, he studied the card again, then whispered, "Them rich sons-a-bitchin' whorin' no-good bastards are gonna pay for this! Nobody makes a horse's ass outa Herb Anderson and gets away with it!" Then he shoved past Ada as if she weren't there, heading out again.

She collapsed into a chair with a shudder of relief.

At Horizons, Francie got even with a few of life's injustices by stealing a bottle of Charlie perfume from the top of Catherine Anderson's dresser.

At the University of Minnesota one of those very injustices was at that moment folding her exquisite, thoroughbred legs into Clay Forrester's Corvette.

"You're late," Jill Magnusson scolded, placing one gleaming fingernail on the door to prevent Clay from closing it, at the same time turning upon him a stunning smile that had cost her father approximately two thousand dollars in orthodontia. Jill was a beauty, and a member of the elite sorority Kappa Alpha Pheta, whose members were loosely referred to as the "Phetas," known down through the years as the rich girls' sorority at the U of M.

"Busy day," Clay answered, suddenly piqued by her method of holding them up. He was too distracted to be charmed by those supple limbs right now. He slammed the door and walked around to his side. The engine purred as they pulled away from the curb.

"I need to stop by the photo lab to check on some pictures for a research project." Jill was more than a superficial appearance; she was majoring in aviation electronics and had every intention of designing the first jet shuttle between the earth and moon. With career goals set high she wasn't the least bit interested in getting married yet. She and Clay understood each other well.

But tonight he was unusually testy. "I'm late and you're the one who's going to stop at the photo lab on our way to the party!" Clay snapped, laying a thin line of rubber as the car peeled away.

"My, aren't we touchy tonight."

"Jill, I told you I wanted to stay home and study. You're the one who insisted we go to this party. You'll forgive me if I dislike playing escort service on the way."

"Fine. Forget the lab. I can pick the photos up myself tomorrow."

Gearing down at a stop sign, he screeched to a halt, throwing Jill forcefully forward.

"What in the world is the matter with you!" she exclaimed.

"I'm not in a party mood, that's all."

"Obviously," she said dryly. "Then forget the photo lab and the party too."

"You dragged me out to this damn party, now we're going!"

"Clay Forrester, don't you speak to me in that tone of voice. If you didn't want to go with me you could have said so. You said you had a case to study this weekend. There's a vast difference between the two."

He threw the car into gear and screamed down University Avenue toward the heart of the campus, zinging in and out between other cars, intentionally laying rubber with every shift of the gears.

"You're driving like a maniac," she said coolly, her auburn hair swinging with the erratic motions of his lane changes.

"I'm feeling like one."

"Then please let me out. I'm not."

"I'll let you out at the goddam party," he said, knowing he was being despicable but unable to help it.

"Since when have you taken to insouciant cursing?"

"Since approximately six P.M. four nights ago," he said.

"Clay, for heaven's sake slow down before you get us both killed, or at the very least get yourself a walloping ticket. The campus police are thick tonight. There's a concert at Northrup."

Ahead at an intersection he could see a cop patrolling traffic, so he slowed down.

"Have you been drinking, Clay?"

"Not yet!" he snapped.

"You're going to?"

"If I'm smart, maybe."

Jill studied his profile, the firm jaw, the tight expression about his usually sensual mouth. "I don't think I know this Clay Forrester," she said softly.

"Nope, you don't." He glared straight ahead, curling his lower lip over his upper, waiting for the cop to flag the traffic through the intersection. "Neither do I."

"It sounds serious," she ventured.

Instead of replying, he hung his right wrist over the steering wheel and continued to glare at the cop, that lip still curled up with contempt at something.

"Wanna talk about it?" she asked in what she hoped was a coercive voice. She waited, dropping her head slightly forward so her hair fell like a rust curtain beyond her cheek.

He looked at her at last, thinking, God but she's beautiful. Poised, intelligent, passionate, even a little cunning. He liked that in her. Liked even more the fact that she never tried to hide it. She often teased him that she could get him to do anything she wanted, simply by using her long-limbed body. Most of the time she was right.

"What would you say if I admitted that I'm afraid to talk to you about it?"

"For starters I'd say the admission has added some common sense to your driving habits."

He had indeed begun driving more sensibly. He reached over and rubbed the back of her hand. "Do you really want to go to the party?"

"Yes. I have this gorgeous new lambswool sweater and this magnificent matching skirt and you haven't even noticed. If you won't compliment me, I'd like to find someone who will."

"All right, you got it," he said, swinging left, heading for the Alcorn Apartments, where the party was in full swing when they arrived. Inside it was a maze of voices and music, too many bodies packed into too little space. The Alcorn was a converted gingerbread house with bays, nooks and pantries, the kind of place easily gotten lost in if playing hide and seek. The furniture throughout the first-floor apartment was positively decimated, but nobody cared because nobody seemed to own it. Jill led the way through the press of people, taking Clay's hand, tugging him to the kitchen where the bar was set up on a dilapidated porcelain-topped table, the kind that went out with World War II. A guy named Eddie was tending bar.

"Hey, Jill, Clay, how's it going? What'll you have?"

"Clay wants to get smashed tonight, Eddie. Why don't you give him a little help?"

In no time Eddie extended a drink that was supposed to be mixed; it was the color of weak coffee. Clay took one sip and knew three like this would knock him smack off his feet. If he really wanted to get smashed, it wouldn't take long. Jill accepted a much weaker drink. She was too intelligent to get drunk. He'd never seen her have more than one or two cocktails in an evening.

He teased her now. "Why don't you come down one notch and show you're at least as human as me and have a couple of strong drinks tonight? Then when we go to bed you'll be as uninhibited as I intend to be."

Jill laughed and swung her waist-length hair back behind a well-turned shoulder.

"If you want to get roaring drunk go right ahead. Don't expect me to abet it by being equally as stupid."

He raised a sardonic eyebrow to Eddie. "The lady thinks I'm stupid." Then he mumbled into his drink, "If she only knew the half."

In the crush of bodies and the assault of noise Jill didn't quite hear what Clay said, but he was troubled tonight, not acting like himself. "I don't know what's gotten into you tonight, but whatever it is, I don't like it."

"You'd like it even less if you knew."

Just then somebody came by and bumped Jill from behind, spilling a splash of her drink on her new sweater at the fullest part of her left breast.

"Oh, damn!" she exclaimed, sucking in her stomach, searching in her purse for a Kleenex. "Have you got a hanky, Clay?"

He reached for his hind pocket. "That's the second time this week that a lady has needed my hanky. Here, let me help you with that, mademoiselle." He grabbed Jill by the hand, found a vacant corner beside the refrigerator and pushed her into it. With the hanky he began dabbing at the spot where the liquor had already darkened the sweater. But an odd, troubled look overtook his face. His motions stilled, and his eyes found hers. Then he grabbed hanky, sweater, breast and all and flattened himself against her long, lithe body, kissing her with a sudden fierceness that startled her. Fondling her breast, controlling her mouth, he pressed her into the corner where the refrigerator met the wall. She thought he'd lost his mind. This was not the Clay she knew, not at all. Something was more wrong than she'd guessed.

"Stop it, stop it! What's the matter with you!" she gasped, breaking away from his kiss, trying to push his hand from her breast.

"I need you tonight, Jill, that's all. Let's go someplace and leave this noisy bunch."

"I've never seen you like this, Clay. For God's sake let go of my breast!"

Abruptly he released her, backed up a step, put the guilty hand in his trouser pocket and stared at the floor. "Forget it," he said, "just forget it." He raised his drink and took an abusive swallow.

"You're going to get sick if you continue at this pace."

"Good!"

"All right, I'll go with you, but to make sense, not sex, agreed?"

He looked at her absently.

"Whatever it is that's bothering you, let's talk it out."

"Fine," he said, taking her glass almost viciously and depositing it and his back on the table which was littered with dozens of others. Without another word he grabbed Jill's wrist and started pushing his way through the mob.

When they were halfway to the door someone yelled, "Hey, Clay, hold up!" Turning, he saw Stu Glass's ruddy face making its way toward him, both hands raised above the press of elbows, trying to keep from spilling a pair of drinks. Over his shoulder Stu shouted, "Follow me close, honey; I want to talk to Clay a minute."

The two couples converged in the milling crowd. "Hey, Clay, you leaving already?".

"Hey, Stu, whaddya say?"

"Haven't seen you around all week. Dad wanted to know if you and your father decided about partridge hunting next weekend yet."

The two fell to discussing hunting plans, leaving Bobbi and Jill to exchange small talk. They knew each other only slightly, through their relation with the men, but now, for the first time, Bobbi studied Jill Magnusson more assessingly than ever before. She took in Jill's expensive wine-colored sweater and skirt, that angel's face of hers, and the negligent way Clay Forrester's arm looped around her waist while he went on talking to Stu. If ever two people were made for each other it was these two, thought Bobbi. Jill, with her burnished skin, her cover-girl's features and that glorious mane of hair, and Clay with his sun-drenched good looks, flawless taste in clothing to match the girl's, and both of them blessed with self-assurance, wealthy families and preordained success.

It struck Bobbi quite suddenly that Catherine was positively out of her class with a man like Clay. He belonged with the kind of girl he was with now. How futile it was to wish she'd used better judgment last Fourth of July, yet, observing Clay and Jill together, Bobbi felt a sting of deep regret.

All the while Clay talked with Stu he was aware of Bobbi. When at last someone from the crowd bumped through and took Jill momentarily away from his side, and Stu along with her, he got his chance.

"Hi, Bobbi."

"Hi, Clay."

The two eyed each other a little warily.

"What's new with you?"

"Same old thing."

Damn her, thought Clay, she's going to make me ask it. He threw a quick eye at Jill, who stood near enough to overhear anything being said.

"Have you heard anything from your cousin lately?"

"Yeah, just today, as a matter of fact."

"How's everything?"

"The same."

Clay's eyes shifted away and back again. "I never got that call."

"I gave her the message."

"Could you please ask her again?"

"She's not interested."

Someone from the crowd jostled his way behind Bobbi, pushing her forcibly closer to Clay. He used the opportunity to insist, "There've been some serious repercussions. I've got to talk to her!"

But just then Jill recaptured Clay, running her painted nails up his arm in a familiar way, taking his elbow in her own. There are people in this world who have things just a bit too good, thought Bobbi, and others who never get a break. Just to even the scales a little bit, some cunning gremlin inside Bobbi made her call after the couple, "I'll tell Catherine you said hello, Clay!"

He turned and burned her with a look that seemed to say he'd like to throw a hex on her. But he replied civilly, "Give her my best."

When Jill and Clay had disappeared, Stu asked, "What was that all about?"

"Oh, nothing. We lined Clay up with my cousin Catherine last summer one time, remember?"

"We did? Oh yeah, that's right, we did." Then, shrugging, he took her elbow and said, "Come on, let's go freshen our drinks."

Clay and Jill decided to drive out to the Interlachen Country Club, a place where both of their parents belonged and where they'd been coming for as long as they could remember, to play golf or eat Sunday brunch. The dining room was half empty, left now to those members who stayed to dance on the small parquet floor to the music of a trio that played old standards. They were seated at a table situated in the lee of corner windows overlooking the golf course, which was lit by single lights strewn along the fairways. The dapples of brightness created a jewelled view from this vantage point in the high, glass-walled room. The course boasted fifty different species of trees. Were it high noon, they'd be seeing every warm color of the spectrum across the expanse below, but now, night having settled over the acres of trees and manicured grass, it looked like something from a fairy tale, the trees shimmering silhouettes against the strategically placed lights.

For some minutes after they were seated, Clay continued staring out at the view below while Jill swirled her wine in its lengthy stem glass. When she'd waited as long as she intended to wait, Jill forced the issue.

"And who is Catherine?" Even a question such as this reflected Jill's breeding, for her voice grew neither accusing nor harpyish. It flowed instead like the amber liquid around the sides of her glass.

After a moment's consideration Clay answered, "Bobbi's cousin."

Raising the stem glass to her lips, Jill hummed, "Mmm..." then added, "Has she got something to do with this sour mood of yours?"

But Clay seemed far removed again, pensive.

"What's so interesting out there in the dark?"

He turned to her with a sigh, rested his elbows on the linen tabletop and kneaded his eyes with the heels of his hands. Then, leaving his eyes covered, he grunted dejectedly, so she could scarcely hear, "Damn."

"You might as well talk about it, Clay. If it's about this... *Catherine*, I think I deserve to know. It is, isn't it?"

His troubled eyes appeared once again, gazing at her, but instead of answering her question, he asked one of his own. "Do you love me, Jill?"

"I don't think that's the subject of this discussion."

"Answer me anyway."

"Why?"

"Because I've been wondering lately... a lot. Do you?"

"Could be. I don't know for sure."

"I've been asking myself the same question about you too. I don't know for sure if I love you either, but it's a very good possibility."

"That's a little too clinical to be romantic, Clay." She laughed softly, sending the lights shimmering off her sparkling lips.

81

"Yeah, I've been in a clinical mood this week—you know, dissecting things?" He gave her a brief rueful smile.

"Dissecting our relationship?"

He nodded, studied the weave of the tablecloth, then raised his eyes to study Jill's flawless face, her hair gleaming beneath the subdued lights of a massive chandelier. Her long fingers with tapered nails glistening as she absently fondled her footed glass, her grace as she relaxed back into her chair, one arm draped limply on its armrest. Jill was like a ten-karat diamond: she belonged in this setting just as surely as Catherine Anderson did not. To bring Catherine Anderson here would be like setting a rhinestone in gold filigree. But Jill...ah, Jill, he thought, how she dazzles.

"You're so damn beautiful it's absurd," Clay said, a curiously painful note in his voice.

"Thanks. Somehow it doesn't mean as much tonight as if you'd said it just that way, with just that tone of voice, with just that particular look in your eyes, say...a week ago, or, say, four days ago?"

He had no reply.

"Say before the subject of Catherine Whoever-she-is intruded?"

Clay only chewed his lower lip in a way with which she was utterly familiar.

"I can wait all night for you to spill it out, whatever it is. I'm not the one who has studying to do this weekend."

"Neither do I," Clay admitted. "I used that as an excuse because I didn't want to see you tonight."

"So that's why you pounced on me like a parolee fresh out of prison?"

He laughed softly, admiring her cool, unruffled presence. "No, that was self-flagellation."

"For?"

"For last July fourth."

A light dawned in Jill's head. She remembered quite distinctly the fight they'd had back then.

"Who was she? Catherine?" Jill asked softly.

"Exactly."

"And?"

"And she's pregnant."

Jill's poise was commendable. She drew in a deep, swift breath, her perfect nostrils flaring into slight imperfection during the length of it. The cords in her neck became momentarily taut before relaxing once more as her eyes and Clay's locked, searching. Then she gracefully braced an elbow on the tabletop and lowered her forehead onto the back of her hand.

Into the silence, a waiter intruded.

"Miss Magnusson, Mr. Forrester, can I get you anything else?"

Clay looked up, distracted. "No, thank you, Scott. We're fine."

When Scott had drifted discreetly away, Jill raised her head and asked, "Is she the reason for the shiner, which I have so graciously avoided mentioning all night?"

He nodded. "Her father." He took a drink, gazed out at the lights below again.

"I'll forgo the obvious question," Jill said, with a hint of asperity creeping into her tone, "realizing you wouldn't have told me unless the situation were clearly defined and you're certain it is yours. Are you going to marry her?"

This time it was Clay's turn to draw a ragged breath. He sat with ankle crossed over knee, one elbow slung on the edge of the table. To look at him, at the careless pose, at the classic cut of his tailored clothes, his handsome profile, one would not have guessed the slightest thing to be amiss. But inside he was a knot of nerves.

"You haven't clearly answered whether or not you love me." Slowly Clay drew his eyes back to hers, suffering now nearly as much as he could see she was.

"No, I haven't, have I?"

"Is it"—Clay searched for the correct word—"superfluous now?"

"I think so, yes, I think so."

Each of their eyes dropped down to their drinks; each of them experienced a touching sense of loss at her words.

"I don't know if I'm going to marry her or not. I'm getting a lot of pressure."

"From her parents?"

He only laughed ruefully. "Oh, Jill, that's so incredibly funny. Too bad you'll never know how incredibly funny that is."

"Sure," Jill retorted caustically, "Ha—ha—ha . . . aren't I funny, though."

He reached for her hand on the tabletop. "Jill, it was a thing that happened. You and I had had that big fight the night before. Stu and Bobbi lined me up with this cousin of Bobbi's . . . Hell, I don't know."

"And you got her pregnant because you wanted to set up housekeeping with me and I refused to leave Pheta House. How chivalrous!" She yanked her hand free.

"I expected you to be bitter. I deserve it. The whole miserable thing is a lousy mistake. The girl's father is a raving lunatic, and believe me, neither the girl nor I want anything to do with each other. But there are, shall we say, extenuating circumstances that may force me to ask her to marry me."

"Oh, she'll be overjoyed that you *have to!* What girl wouldn't be!"

He sighed, thought in exasperation, Women! "I'm being pressured in more ways than one."

"What's the matter, has your father threatened to deny you a place in the family practice?"

"You're very astute, Jill, but then I never did take you for a dumb redhead."

"Oh, don't humor me; not at a time like this."

"It's not only my father. Mother walks around looking like she's just been whipped, and to complicate matters Catherine's old man is threatening to get vocal about it. If that happens, my admission to the bar is in jeopardy. And to complicate matters even worse, Catherine has run away from home."

"Do you know where she is?"

"No, but Bobbi does."

"So you could reach her if you wanted to?"

"I think so."

"But you don't want to?"

He drew a great sighing breath and only shook his head forlornly. Then he reached for her hand again across the corner of the table. "Jill, I don't have much time to waste. All the devils of hell seem to be riding on my back right now. I'm sorry if I have to lay one of them on yours, and I'm sorry, too, if the occasion isn't what it should be at a time like this, but I want to know your feelings about me. I want to know if, at some time in our future, when all of this is straightened out, when I've completed law school and gotten my life back in working order, would you ever consider marrying me?"

Her composure slipped a notch and she cast her eyes aside as they grew too glisteny. But they were drawn back to his familiar, lovable face, of which she knew every feature so intimately. In a choked voice she answered, "Damn you, Clay Forrester. I should slap your Adonis's face."

But the softness of her words told him how very hurt she was.

"Jill, you know me. You know what I'd have planned for us if this hadn't interfered. I'd never have asked you this way, at a time like this, if I'd had the choice."

"Oh, Clay, my heart is—is . . . falling in little pieces down to the pit of my stomach. What do you expect me to say?"

"Say what you feel, Jill." He rubbed a thumb lightly across the back of her hand while she covered his face, hair and body with her eyes, letting her hand remain passively in his.

"You asked me too late, Clay."

Pained moments spun by while the piano player tinkled some old tune and a few dancers moved across the floor. At last he picked up Jill's hand, turned it over and kissed its palm. Returning his gaze to her face he whispered, "God, you're beautiful."

She swallowed. "God, you are too. That's our trouble. We're too beautiful. People see only the facade, not the pain, the faults, the human failings that don't show."

"Jill, I'm sorry I hurt you. I do love you, you know."

"I don't think you'd better bank on me, Clay."

"Do you forgive me for asking?"

"No, don't ask me to do that."

"It mattered to me, Jill. Your answer mattered a lot."

She slowly pulled her hand free of his and picked up her purse.

"Jill, I'll let you know what comes of it."

"Yeah, you do that. And I'll let you know when my space shuttle leaves for the moon."

This time it happened so fast that Clay saw nothing. He stepped out of the Corvette in the driveway and a husky shadow slinked swiftly from behind the bulk of a pyramidal arborvitae. Clay was yanked roughly around, slammed against the fender of the car just as a meaty fist smashed into his stomach, leaving no mark, breaking no bones, only cracking the wind from him viciously as he doubled over and dropped to his knees on the ground.

Through his pain he heard a grating voice informing, "That was from Anderson. The girl's run off to Omaha." Then heavy, running footsteps disappeared into the night.

When Bobbi called the following evening, she sounded breathless. "I ran into him at a party last night, Cat. He asked about you again and said to tell you it's really important. He had to talk to you."

"What good would it do? I'm not marrying him and I don't need his money!"

"Oh, jeez! You're so obstinate! What harm can it do, for heaven's sake!"

But Marie passed along the hall just then and Catherine turned her face toward the wall, couching the mouthpiece furtively. But from the knowing glance Marie had flashed her way, Catherine suspected she'd heard the last remark. Quietly she said into the phone, "I want him to think I've left town."

Bobbi's voice suddenly became critical, scolding. "If you want to know what I think, I think you owe him that much. I don't think it's enough for you to insist that *you* don't need a single thing from Clay Forrester. Maybe he needs something from you. Have you considered that?"

Dead silence at Bobbi's end of the line for a long moment.

Catherine hadn't considered that before. She clasped the receiver tightly and pressed it against her ear so hard her head began to hurt. Suddenly it tired her immensely, having to think about Clay Forrester at all. Her emotions were strung out to the limit, and her own problems were more than she wanted to handle without taking on Clay Forrester's too. She sighed and dropped her forehead against the wall.

Bobbi's voice came through again, but very calmly and quietly. "I think he's in some kind of big trouble over this, Cath. I don't know exactly what because he wouldn't say. All he said was something about serious repercussions."

"Don't!" Catherine begged, her eyelids sliding shut wearily. "J-just don't, okay? I don't want to hear it! I can't take on any of his troubles. I have all I can do to handle my own."

Again there followed a lengthy silence before Bobbi made one last observation which was to gnaw at Catherine's conscience mercilessly in the hours and days to come: "Cath... whether you want to admit it or not, I think they're one and the same."

Chapter 6

THE WIDE BLUE curve of the Mississippi River glinted beneath the autumn sky as it cut a swath through the campus of the University of Minnesota, dividing it into East Bank and West Bank. The more heavily wooded East Bank wore the school colors, maroon and gold. Homecoming was approaching, and it seemed almost as if the grounds had festooned themselves for the event. Stately old maples wore ruddy tones in startling contrast with the fiery elms. Constant activity churned along Union and Church Streets as homecoming preparations advanced. On the lawns students soaked up summer's warm leftovers. Pedestrians dawdled, waiting for buses in the shaded circle before Jones Hall. Bicycle wheels sighed through tumbled leaves. Ornamental stone parapets adorned gracious old frat houses down along University Avenue, their retaining walls, steps and balconies draped with idlers, slung there like lazing lizards. And everywhere couples kissed, heads bare to the afternoon sun.

Passing a kissing couple now, Catherine looked quickly away. Somehow the sight of them made the books ride a little more heavily upon her hip. At times lately, leaning to lift those books, twinges caught her side in newly strange places.

Clay, too, was often disarmed by the sight of a young man and woman kissing. Striding down The Mall now, he observed an embrace in progress and his thought strayed to Catherine Anderson. Pulling his eyes to the students moving along the sidewalk ahead of him, he thought the girl with the leaf-gold hair could almost be her. He studied her back while it disappeared and reappeared around others who came between them. But it was only his preoccupation with her lately that made him look twice at every blond head in a crowd.

Still, the hair was the right color and the right length. But Clay realized he could easily be mistaken, for he'd never seen her in broad daylight before.

Dammit, Forrester, get her out of your head! That's not her and you know it!

But as he watched the tall form with its straight shoulders, it swayless hips, the books riding against one of them, a queer feeling made his stomach go weightless. He wanted to call her name but knew it couldn't be Catherine. Hadn't he gotten the message loud and clear? She'd run off to Omaha.

Deliberately Clay glanced across the street to free his eyes and mind from delusions. But it was no good. Momentarily he found himself scanning the crowd more intently, seeking out the blue sweater with blond hair trailing down its back. She was gone! Absurd, but a hot flash of panic clutched Clay, making him break into a trot. He caught sight of her once more, farther ahead, and breathed easier, but continued following. Long stride, he thought. Long legs. Could it be? Suddenly the girl crooked an arm and stroked the hair away from her neck as if she were hot. Clay skipped around a group of people, studying the long legs, the erect carriage of her shoulders, remembering her air of haughtiness and defensiveness. She came to a street and hesitated for a passing car, then glanced aside to check traffic before crossing. As she stepped from the curb, her profile was clearly defined for a fraction of a second.

Clay's heart seemed to hit his throat and he broke into a run.

"Catherine?" he called, keeping his eyes riveted on her, shouldering his way, bumping people, mechanically excusing himself, running on. "Catherine?"

She evidently did not hear, only kept walking on, the sound

of traffic grown heavier as a bus pulled away from the sidewalk. He was short-winded by the time he caught up with her and swung her around by an elbow. Her books tumbled from her hip and her hair flew across her mouth and stuck to her lipstick.

"Hey, what—" she began, instinctively bending toward the books. But through the veil of hair she looked up to find Clay Forrester glowering down at her, his chest heaving, his mouth open in surprise.

Catherine's heart cracked against the walls of her chest while the sight of him made tremors dance through her stomach.

"Catherine? What are you doing here?" He reached again for her elbow and drew her up. She only stared, trying to conquer the urge to run while her heart palpitated wildly and the books lay forgotten on the sidewalk. "Do you mean you've been here all the time, right here going to school?" he asked in astonishment, still grasping her elbow as if afraid she'd vanish.

Clay could see she was stunned. Her lips parted and the look in her eyes told him she felt cornered and would surely run again. He felt the sweater slipping out of his fingers.

"Catherine, why didn't you call?" Her hair was still stuck to her lipstick. Her breath coming through billowed it out and in. Then she bent to pick up her books while he belatedly leaned to do the same. She plucked them away from his fingers and turned to escape him and the countless complications which he could mean to her.

"Catherine, wait!"

"Leave me alone," she flung over her shoulder, trying not to look as if she were running from him, running just the same.

"I've got to talk with you."

She kept half running half walking away, Clay a few steps behind her.

"Why didn't you call?"

"Dammit! How did you find me?"

"Will you stop, for God's sake!"

"I'm late! Leave me alone!"

He kept up with her, stride for stride, very easily now, while Catherine's side started aching and she pressed her free hand against it.

"Didn't you get my message from Bobbi?"

But the blond hair only swung from side to side on that proud neck as she hurried on. Irritated because she refused to stop, he grabbed her arm once again, forcing her to do his bidding. "I'm getting tired of playing Keystone Cops with you! *Will you stop!*"

The books stayed on her hip this time but she tossed her head belligerently, a yearling colt defying the bridle. She stood there glaring at him while he restrained her. When at last it seemed she wouldn't bolt, he dropped his hand.

"I gave Bobbi the message to have you call me. Did she tell you?"

Instead of answering his question, she berated herself. "This is the one thing I couldn't control, chancing running into you somewhere. I thought this campus was big enough for the two of us. I'd appreciate it if you'd keep it to yourself that I'm here."

"And I'd appreciate it if you'd give me the opportunity to explain a few things and work something out with you."

"We did all the talking we needed the last time we were together. I told you, my plans are made and you don't have to worry about me."

Curious passers-by eyed them, wondering what they were arguing about.

"Listen, we're making a spectacle here. Will you come with me someplace quiet so we can talk?"

"I said I'm in a hurry."

"And I'm in a fat lot of trouble! Will you just give me two minutes and stand still?" He'd never seen anyone so defiant in his life. It was more than just his parents' ultimatum driving him now. This had come down to a contest of wills as she strode away up The Mall with him just behind her shoulder again.

"Leave me alone," she demanded.

"There's nothing I'd like better, but my parents don't see it that way."

"Pity."

He grabbed the back of her sweater this time, and she nearly walked out of it before realizing why it wasn't coming along with her.

"Give me a time, an anonymous phone number, anything,

so I can get in touch with you and I'll leave you alone until then."

She yanked her sweater free and spun to face him defiantly. "I've already told you, I made one mistake and it was a dilly. But my life isn't ruined as long as I don't consider it ruined. I know where I'm going, what I'm going to do when I get there, and I don't want you involved in any way whatsoever."

"Are you too proud to take anything from me?"

"You can call it pride if you want. I prefer to call it good sense. I don't want you having any kind of hold over me."

"Suppose I have the solution to our problems, and it would leave neither of us indebted to the other?"

But she only eyed him acidly. "I've solved my problems. If you still have some, it's not my fault."

People were looking at them curiously again, and Clay became incensed at her stubborn refusal to listen to reason. Before she knew what was happening, he'd clamped an arm around her waist and propelled her off the sidewalk toward an old, enormous elm. She found herself thrust against it, her ears flanked by both of his palms, which leaned against the bark.

"Something else has come up," he informed her, his face no more than two inches from hers. "Seems your father's been making trouble."

She swallowed, pressing her head back, glancing first into his eyes, then aside, afraid of the determination she saw so clearly at this close range.

"I heard about that and I'm sorry," she conceded. "I really thought he'd give up when I left."

"For Omaha?" he asked sarcastically.

Her startled eyes flew to his. "How did you learn that?" She noted the remnant of a cut above his eyebrow and wondered if her father had put it there. He glowered, holding her prisoner so that all she could see was either his face or a bronze-colored sweater smack in front of her eyes. She stared at the sweater.

"Never mind. Your father is making threats, and those threats could mean the end of my law career. Something's got to be done about it. I find the idea of paying him off as distasteful as you do. Now, can we work on a reasonable alternative?"

Catherine's eyes slid shut; she was unable to think quickly enough. "Listen, I've got to go now, honest. But I'll call you tonight. We can talk about it then."

Something told him not to trust her, but he couldn't stand there restraining her indefinitely. All he could do was let her go for the time being. He knew he could find out easily where she lived, now that he knew she was a student here. As he watched her walk away he waited to see if she'd turn around to check if he was tailing her. She didn't. She entered Jones Hall and disappeared, and guessing that her patience was probably greater than his, he turned back, heading for the car.

The following day Catherine met Mrs. Tollefson in the office with its patchwork sofa and fern. Thinking Tolly would forge ahead into the subject Catherine most dreaded, Catherine was surprised when instead the matronly woman only chatted about school and asked how Catherine was getting along now that she'd settled into Horizons. When Catherine told her she was attending college on a small study grant and supplementing it by doing typing and sewing, Mrs. Tollefson noted, "You have a lot of ambition, Catherine."

"Yes, but I'll be the first to admit it's self-serving. I want something better out of life than what I've had."

Mrs. Tollefson ruminated. "College, then, is your ticket to a better life."

"Yes, it was going to be my final escape."

"Was?" Mrs. Tollefson paused. "Why do you speak in the past tense?"

Catherine's eyes opened a little wider. "I didn't do it consciously."

"But you feel you're being forced to drop out of school?"

A brief, wry laugh escaped Catherine. "Under the circumstances, who wouldn't?"

A gentle expression complemented Tolly's soft voice. "Perhaps we need to talk about that, about where you've come from, where you are, where you're going."

Catherine sighed, dropped her head back tiredly. "I don't know where I'm going anymore. I did once, but I'm not sure if I'll get there now."

"You're speaking about this baby as an obstacle."

"Yes, one I haven't wanted to make decisions about."

"Perhaps decisions will come easier once we look at all your options." Mrs. Tollefson's voice would be suited well to the reading of poetry. "I think we need to explore where your baby fits into your plans."

Oh, God, here it comes. Catherine sank deeper into the cushions of the sofa, wishing it would take her down, down, into its depth forever.

"How far along are you, Catherine?"

"Three months."

"So you've had some time to think about it already?" The kind woman watched the cords stand out in Catherine's neck as the girl swallowed, and her eyes remained closed.

"Not enough. I—I have trouble thinking about it at all. I keep pushing it to the back of my mind, thinking someone will come along and make the decision for me."

"But you know that won't happen. You knew that when you came to Horizons. From the moment you chose not to abort, you knew a further decision was in the offing."

Childlike now, Catherine sat forward, arguing, "But I want them both, college and the baby. I don't want to give up either one!"

"Then let's discuss that angle. Do you think you're strong enough to be a full-time mother and a full-time student?"

For the first time Catherine bridled. "Well, how should I know!" She flung her hands out, then subsided with a sheepish look. "I—I'm sorry."

Mrs. Tollefson only smiled. "It's okay. It's fine and healthy to be angry. Why shouldn't you be? You just started putting your life on track when along came this major complication. Who wouldn't be angry?"

"Okay, I admit it. I'm—I'm mad!"

"At whom?"

A puzzled expression curled Catherine's blond eyebrows. "At whom?" But Mrs. Tollefson only sat patiently, waiting for Catherine to come up with the answer. "At—at me?" Catherine asked skeptically in a tiny voice.

"And?"

"And . . ." Catherine swallowed. It was extremely hard to say. "And the baby's father."

"Anybody else?"

"Who else is there?"

It grew quiet for a long moment, then the older woman suggested, "The baby?"

"The baby?" Catherine looked aghast. "It's not his fault!"

"Of course it's not. But I thought you might be angry with him just the same, maybe for making you think about giving up school, or at the very least, for slowing you down."

"I'm not that kind of person."

"Maybe not now, but if your child prevents you from completing your college education, what then?"

"You're assuming I can't do both?" Catherine was growing frustrated while Mrs. Tollefson remained calm, unflappable.

"Not at all. I'm being realistic though. I'm saying it will be tough. Eighty percent of the women who become pregnant before age seventeen never complete high school. That statistic goes up with college-age women who must handle heavy tuition costs."

"There are day-care centers," Catherine noted defensively.

"Which don't accept a child until he is toilet-trained. Did you know that?"

"You're really laying it on heavy, aren't you?" Catherine accused.

"These are facts," continued the counselor. "And since you're not the kind to go man-hunting as a solution to your problem, shall we explore another option?"

"Say it," Catherine challenged tightly.

"Adoption."

To Catherine the word was as depressing as a funeral dirge, yet Mrs. Tollefson went on. "We should explore it as a very reasonable, very available answer to your dilemma. As hard as it may be for you to consider adoption—and I can see how it upsets you by the expression on your face—it may be the best route for you and the child in the long run." Mrs. Tollefson's voice droned on, relating the success of adopted children until Catherine jumped to her feet and turned her back.

"I don't want to hear it!" She clutched one hand with the other. "It's so—so cold-blooded! Childless couples! Adoptive parents! Those terms are—" She swung again to face Mrs. Tollefson. "Don't you understand? It would be like feeding my baby to the vultures!"

Even as she said it, Catherine knew her exclamation was unjust. But guilt and fear were strong within her. At last she turned away and said in a small voice, "I'm sorry."

"You're reacting naturally. I expected it all." The understanding woman allowed Catherine to regain composure, but it was her responsibility to delineate all choices clearly; thus, she went on.

Catherine again listened to the facts—adopted children tend to develop to their fullest potential; adopted children are as well- or better-adjusted as many children who live with their birthparents; child abuse is almost nonexistent in adoptive families; parents who adopt are generally in an above-average income bracket; the adopted child runs a better chance of graduating from college than if parented by an unwed mother.

A great vise seemed to tighten, thread by thread, at Catherine's temples. She dropped to the sofa, her head falling back as an overwhelming weariness pervaded her.

"You're telling me to give it up," she said to a shimmering reflection on the ceiling.

Mrs. Tollefson let the old guilt-laden term pass for the moment. "No . . . no, I'm not. I'm here to help you decide what is best for your welfare, and ultimately, for the child's. If I fail to make you aware of all eventualities, of all avenues open to you, and of all that may close, I am not doing my job thoroughly."

"How much time would I have to decide?" The question was a near whisper.

"Catherine, we try not to work with time limits here, which sounds ironic when each young woman is here for a limited time. But no decision should be made till the baby is born and you've regained your equilibrium."

Catherine considered this, then her concerns came tumbling out in an emotional potpourri. "Would that really happen? Would I resent the baby because he slowed me down? I only want to make a decent life for him so he won't have to live in the kind of home I had to live in. I set out to get a college education to make sure of that, only to find out, if I pursue it, I may defeat my purpose. I know what you said is true, and it would be hard. But a baby should have love, and I don't think anybody could love it as much as a real mother. Even if money is a problem, it seems like copping out to give the baby away because of the expense."

"Catherine." Mrs. Tollefson leaned forward, caring deeply, her face showing it. "You continue to use the term *give away*, as if you own the child and are rejecting him. Instead, think of adoption as perhaps a better alternative to parenting the child yourself."

Catherine's large blue eyes seemed to stare right through the woman before her. Finally she blinked and asked, "Have you ever seen anyone make it? With a baby, I mean?"

"All the way through college? Single parent? No, not that I can remember, but that's not to say you can't be the first."

"I could get..." She thought of Clay Forrester's offer of money. "No, I couldn't." Then she sighed. "It almost makes me look stupid for passing up an abortion, doesn't it?"

"No, not at all," the kind voice reassured.

Again Catherine sighed, blinked slowly and turned her eyes to the blue sky beyond the window. Her voice took on a rather dreamlike quality. "You know," she mused, "there's no feeling there yet. I mean the baby hasn't moved or anything. Sometimes I find it hard to believe it's in there, like maybe somebody's just pulling this big joke on me." She paused, then almost whispered, "Freshman hazing..." But when she looked at Tolly again, there was true sadness in her face, and the realization that this was no hazing at all. "If I'm already feeling so protective when there's not even any evidence of life yet, what will I feel when he moves and kicks and rolls around?"

Mrs. Tollefson had no answers.

"Do you know, they say a baby has hiccups before it's born."

The room remained still again, flooded with late sunshine and emotion while Catherine dealt with possible eventualities. At last she asked, "If I decided to give him up—" A raised index finger stopped her. "Okay, if I decide on adoption as the best route, could I see him first?"

"We encourage it, Catherine. We've found that mothers who do not see their children suffer a tremendous guilt complex which affects them the rest of their lives." Then, studying Catherine's face carefully, Mrs. Tollefson posed a question it was necessary to ask. "Catherine, since he has not been mentioned so far, and since I do not see his name on the card, I must ask if the child's father should be a consideration in all of this."

The blond young woman rose abruptly and snapped, "Absolutely not!"

And had her attitude not changed so quickly, Mrs. Tollefson might have believed Catherine.

The records office of the U of M refused to give out Catherine's home address, thus it took Clay three days to spot her again, crossing the sprawling granite plaza before Northrup Auditorium. He followed at a discreet distance as she cut between buildings, following the maze of sidewalks until finally at Fifteenth Avenue she turned northward. He kept sight of her blue sweater with the blond hair swaying upon it until she turned into an old street of homes that had been stately in their younger day, but hovered now behind massive boulevard trees in a somewhat seedy reflection of the grandeur they once knew. She entered a gargantuan yellow brick three-story with an enormous wraparound porch. The house had no marking other than a number, but while Clay stood wondering a very pregnant woman came out and stood on a chair to water a hanging fern. He might not have thought anything of it if he hadn't suddenly realized, as she turned, that she was not a woman, but was, instead, a young girl of perhaps fourteen. As she raised up on tiptoe to fetch down the plant, the sight of her swollen stomach triggered Clay's suspicion. He looked again for a sign, but there was none, nothing to indicate it was one of those homes where girls went to wait out their pregnancies. But when the girl returned inside, Clay wrote down the house number and headed back toward the campus to make some phone calls.

By the time Catherine had been at Horizons a week and a half she found herself accepted without question and knew her first taste of sorority. Because so many of the girls were in their young teens they looked up to Catherine, who, as a college student, seemed to them much more worldly. They saw her leaving each day to pursue an outside life while they themselves had forfeited theirs for the duration of the stay, and their admiration grew. Because Catherine owned a sewing machine which was often in demand, her room came to be the gathering place. Here she heard their stories: Little Bit was thirteen and wasn't sure who was the father of her baby; plain-faced Vicky was sixteen and didn't talk about the father of hers; Marie, age seventeen, spoke amiably about her Joe, and said they still planned to get married as soon as he graduated from high school; the unkempt Grover said the father of her baby was the captain of her high school football team and had taken her out on a bet with a bunch of his team members. There were some residents of Horizons who cautiously avoided getting too close to anyone, others who brazenly swore they'd get even with the boy responsible, but the majority of the girls seemed not only resigned to living here, but enjoyed it. Especially nights like this when, all together, a group was working on a pair of nightgowns for Little Bit to wear during her hospital stay, which wasn't far off.

By now Catherine was accustomed to the banter at times like these; it was a combination of teasing and gaunt truths.

"Someday I'm gonna find this guy and he's gonna have hair like . . ."

"Don't tell me. Let me guess—hair like Rex Smith."

"What's the matter with Rex Smith?"

"Nothing. We've just heard the story before and how he's just going to *know* you're the woman he was made for."

"Listen, kiddo, don't forget to tell him somebody else thought the same thing before him." Laughter followed.

"I want to be married like Ali McGraw in *Love Story* . . . you know, make up my own words and stuff."

"Fat chance."

"Fat chance? Did somebody say *fat* chance?"

"Hey, I'm not always going to be shaped like a pear."

"I want to go to school and learn to be one of those ladies who cleans teeth. The kind of job where you nestle the guy's head in your lap so you can move in close and throw your charms at him."

Laughter again.

"I'm never gonna get married. Men aren't worth it."

"Hey, they're not all bad."

"Naw, only ninety-nine percent of 'em!"

"Yeah, but it's that other one percent that's worth looking for."

"When I was little and my folks were still together, I used to look at this picture of them on their wedding day. It used to sit in their bedroom on the cedar chest. Her dress was silk and there were little pearls on top of her veil and it trailed way around the floor in front. If I ever get married, I'd like to wear that dress . . . 'cept I think she threw it away."

"Wanna know something funny?"

"What?"

"When Ma got married she was pregnant . . . with me."

"Yeah?"

"Yeah. But she didn't seem to remember it when I told her I wanted to get married."

And so the talk went. And somebody always suggested going down to the kitchen for fruit. Tonight it was Marie who won the honors. She waddled downstairs and was passing the hall phone when it rang.

"Phone call . . . Anderson!"

When Catherine came to pick it up, Marie was leaning a shoulder against the wall, a curious half-smile on her face.

"Hi, Bobbi," she answered, glancing at Marie.

"Guess again," came the deep voice over the line.

The blood dropped from Catherine's face. She sucked in a quick breath of surprise and remained motionless for a moment, gripping the phone, before the color seeped back up her neck again.

"Don't tell me. You followed me." Marie continued toward the kitchen then, but she'd heard all she needed to hear.

"That's right. It took me three days, but I did it."

"Why? What do you want from me?"

"Do you realize how ironic it sounds to have *you* asking *me* that question?"

"Why are you *hounding* me?"

"I have a business proposition for you."

"No, thank you."

"Don't you even want to hear it?"

"I've been propositioned—so to speak—by you once already. Once was enough."

"You really don't play fair, do you?"

"What do you want!"

"I don't want to talk about it on the phone. Are you free tomorrow night?"

"I already told you—"

"Spare me the repetition," he interrupted. "I didn't want to put it this way but you leave me no choice. I'm coming to get you tomorrow night at seven o'clock. If you won't come out and talk to me, I'll tell your father where to find you."

"How dare you!" Her face grew intense with rage.

"It's important, so don't put me to the test, Catherine. I don't want to do it, but I will if I have to. I have a feeling he might have ways to get you to listen to reason."

She felt cornered, lost, hopeless. Why was he doing this to her? Why, now when she'd at last found a place where she was happy, couldn't her life be peaceful? Bitterly, she replied, "You're not leaving me much choice, are you?"

The line was silent for a moment before his voice came again, slightly softer, slightly more understanding. "Catherine, I tried to get you to listen to me the other day. I said I didn't want to put it that—"

She hung up on him, frustrated beyond endurance. She stood a moment, trying to collect herself before going back upstairs. The phone rang again. She clamped her jaw so hard that her teeth hurt, put a hand on the receiver, felt it vibrate again, picked it up and snapped, "What do you want this time!"

"Seven o'clock," he ordered authoritatively. "Be ready or your father finds out!"

Then he hung up on her.

"Something wrong?" Marie asked from the kitchen doorway.

Catherine jumped, placing a hand on her throat. "I didn't know you were still there."

"I wasn't. Not for very long anyway. I just heard the last little bit. Was it anyone important?"

Distractedly, Catherine studied Marie, small, dark, her doll's face an image of perfection, wondering what Marie would do if Joe had just called wanting to talk to her tomorrow night at seven.

"No, nobody important."

"It was him, wasn't it?"

"Who?"

"The father of your baby."

Catherine's face turned red.

"No use denying it," Marie went on, "I can tell."

Catherine only glared at her and turned away.

"Well, you didn't see the color of your face or the look in your eyes when you picked up that phone and heard his voice."

Catherine spun around, exclaiming, "I have no look in my eyes for Clay Forrester!"

Marie crossed her arms, grinned and raised one eyebrow. "Is that his name, Clay Forrester?"

Infuriated with herself, Catherine spluttered, "It—it doesn't matter what his name is. I have no look in my eyes for him."

"But you can't help it." Marie shrugged as if it were a foregone conclusion.

"Oh, come on," Catherine said in exasperation.

"Once you've been in this place you realize that no girl who comes here is immune to the man who's the other half of the reason she's here. How could she be?"

Although Catherine wanted to deny it, she could not. It was true that when she'd heard Clay Forrester's voice something had gone all barmy in the pit of her stomach. She'd grown shivery and hot all at once, light-headed and flustered. How could I! she berated herself silently. How could I react so to the mere voice of a man who—two months after the fact!— forgot that he'd ever had sexual intercourse with me?

Chapter 7

THE MINUTE SHE came home from classes the following afternoon, Catherine knew something was up. The atmosphere was charged, the girls giddy, giggly. Everyone turned suddenly helpful, advising her to go upstairs and get her studying done right away, not to worry about setting the table—Vicky would do it for her. Someone suggested she do her nails and Marie suggested, "Hey, Catherine, how about if I blowdry your hair? I'm pretty good at it, you know."

"I did it this morning, thanks."

Behind her back Marie made an exasperated gesture, followed by a rash of questions about whether or not Catherine had ever worn purple eyeshadow. Apricot blush? White lipliner? By the time she went down to supper Catherine accosted the crew with a sly look on her face. "All right, you guys, I know what you're up to. Marie's been talking, hasn't she? But this is *not* a date, so don't misconstrue it as one. Yes, someone's coming for me, but I'm going exactly as I am." There stood Catherine, confronting the whole dining room full of critical faces, dressed in faded blue jeans and an outsize flannel shirt, looking like she should be slopping hogs.

"In that!" Marie fairly choked.

"There's nothing wrong with this."

"Maybe not for a game of touch football."

"Why should I primp? I told you, it's *not* a date."

"The word is out, Catherine," Grover proclaimed. "We all know it's *him!*"

Marie, without question the group leader, put a hand on her hip and sing-songed, "Not a date, huh? What'sa matter, Catherine, is he old and feeble or something? Hasn't he got any hair on his legs?"

They all started laughing, Catherine included. Someone else picked up the teasing, carrying it forward. "Maybe he's got body odor! Or halitosis. No, I know! Ringworm! Who'd want to dress up for a guy with ringworm?" By now they were circling Catherine as if she were a maypole. "I know, I bet he's married." But what had started out to be funny suddenly angered Catherine, who saw the girls as a pack of feral animals, nipping at her, closing in for the final attack.

"Nope, I know he's not married," Marie informed the group. "It's got to be something else."

"A priest then, a man of the cloth. Oh, shame, shame, Catherine."

"I thought you were my friends!" she exclaimed, confused and hurt.

"We are. All we want to do is see you dolled up for your fella."

"He's not my fella!"

"You bet he's not, and he won't be either if you don't get out of those everyday rags and paint your nails."

"I am not painting my nails for Clay Forrester. He can go to hell, and so can all of you!" Catherine broke from the circle and ran upstairs.

But she was not allowed to sulk, for momentarily Marie appeared, leaning against the door frame. "Tolly doesn't allow anybody to skip meals around here, so you'd better get back down there. The girls were just having a little fun. They're all quite a bit younger than you, you know, but you're the one who's acting childish by coming up here and sulking."

Catherine threw a derisive glance at here roommate. "I'll be back down," she said coldly, "but tell the girls to lay off!

It's nobody's business how I dress."

Supper was an uncomfortable affair for Catherine, but the rest carried on as if nothing had happened. She sat stonily, her nerves as taut as fiddlestrings.

"Pass the strawberry jam," Marie requested, eyeballing a silent message to Vicky, on Catherine's left, then to Grover, who was refilling milk glasses. When Grover reached Catherine, she made sure a cold splat of mild landed in the angry girl's lap. Catherine's chair screeched back, but she only glared silently at Grover.

Marie's voice was as smooth as melted butter. "Why, Grover, can't you be more careful?"

Grover set down the milk carton, grabbed some napkins and made a show of swabbing the wet leg of Catherine's jeans. Titters started around the table as Catherine viciously yanked the napkins away and said icily, "It's okay, forget it."

But as she leaned forward to pull her chair back up to the table, a hand shot out from her left, bearing a biscuit, oozing jam. The sticky strawberries caught Catherine on the left temple, smearing into her hair, ear and eyebrow.

"Oh, my, look what I've done," Vicky said innocently.

Catherine leaped up, anger bubbling uncontrollably. "What kind of conspiracy is this! What have I done to make you all so hateful?"

Just then Marie, their ringleader, arose, wearing her piquant smile and came to put her arms around Catherine. "We only want to help." Catherine stood in the circle of Marie's unwanted hug, holding herself stiff.

"Well, you have a strange way of showing it."

But just then Marie drew back with a false gasp, and Catherine felt something warm and cloying plastering her shirt against her back where Marie's arm had been.

"Now I've really done it. I got gravy on your shirt, Catherine." Then with a sly glance at all her coconspirators, Marie suggested, "We'll just have to see what we can do about it, won't we, girls?" And standing back, hands on hips, the shorter girl surveyed Catherine critically. "Have you ever seen such a mess in your life?"

Catherine, dumbfounded, only now began to suspect the

method behind their madness as smiles bloomed all around the table. One by one they passed her on their way upstairs, each offering something.

"You really should wash your hair. I have a bottle of strawberry shampoo."

"And I have some yummy Village Bath Oil you can borrow."

"I haven't done my laundry yet. If you'll leave your jeans and shirt in the hall, I'll throw them in with my stuff."

"Institution soap is the pits. I'll leave mine in the bathroom."

Marie swiped a finger across Catherine's temple, then sucked the jam from it. "Yuck! I guess we'll have to give you a fresh hairdo after all."

"For heaven's sake, get her upstairs and do something with that jam, Marie!"

Marie winked at Catherine, reached out a small hand, waiting. In the moment before she placed her own in it to be led upstairs, Catherine felt a lump lodge in her throat, a curious, new growing thing, a learning thing, a trusting thing. But before she quite decided how to deal with it, she was in their hands.

Many times during the next hour Catherine raised her eyes to Marie's in the mirror, understanding now, feeling warmed and grateful because they cared—they all cared so very much. "You're crazy, you know," she laughed, "you're all a little bit crazy. It's not even a date."

"By the time we get done, it will be," Marie deemed.

The pile of makeup that appeared would have put Cleopatra to shame. With gratitude but reservation, Catherine accepted pedicure, manicure, coiffure, jewelry, even lacy underwear, all offered with the best and most optimistic intentions. After holding her dress while she slipped it on, the stubby Marie stood on top of one of the beds to fasten a gold chain around Catherine's neck.

"Hey, when you gonna grow up, Marie?" someone quipped.

"Hadn't you noticed?" she rubbed her belly. "I'm growing daily, only in the wrong direction." Laughter followed, but subdued now, almost reverent, while Catherine stood in their midst, looking unbelievably lovely.

"Go on, have a look," Marie prompted, nudging Catherine's shoulder.

Catherine walked to the mirror, fully expecting to see a Kewpie doll looking back at her. But she was stunned at the surprisingly lovely woman reflected there. Her hair was glowing, flowing back from her face as if its golden streaks were blowing in the wind. The makeup had been done tastefully, giving her cheeks a delicate, hollow look, her blue eyes a new luminous size and glitter. The gloss on her lips reflected a bead of light, as if she'd just passed her tongue along them and left them provocatively wet. Small gold hoops at her ears complimented the shadowed length of her neck and emphasized her delicate jawline, while the loop of gold around her neck drew her eyes downward to the open collar of the soft, blue wool shirtwaist with its long sleeves and front closure. The collar stood up in back, flared open in front, leaving a bit of exposed skin above the highest button.

Without conscious thought, Catherine lifted a manicured fingertip and touched the hollow of her right cheek, the hollow she'd never been aware of before. Her own sober eyes stared back at her approvingly, but with a new worry in them.

My God, she thought, what will Clay Forrester think?

Behind her the girls observed the telling movement of her fingers upon her own cheek, the hand that rested briefly upon her pulsing heart as if to say, "Can it be?" And while the silent group stared, a frowsy, brown-haired fifteen-year-old with tortoiseshell glasses came forward. In the mirror, Catherine saw her coming and fought to control emotions that bubbled up and threatened. She did not want to be their hope. She did not want Clay Forrester to think she'd done all this for him. But while the hopelessly plain Francie came forward, Catherine knew that for this one evening she was doomed to play the role these girls so desperately needed her to play.

Francie, who had never spoken a word to Catherine before, came forward, bearing a bottle of Charlie perfume.

"Here," she said, "I stole this from you."

Catherine turned to take the bottle, smiling into Francie's eyes, which held no more sparkle than cold dishwater. "I have a couple of different kinds. Why don't you keep it?" But as Francie extended the bottle, Catherine could see the girl's hand tremble.

"But this one must be your favorite. It's the most used up."

Francie's eyes impaled her, wavering neither right nor left. Then Catherine smiled and took the bottle and sprayed herself lightly behind her ears and upon her wrists. When she finished she said, "You're right, Francie, it is my favorite, but why don't you put it on your dresser and when I want it, I'll just come in and take a squirt."

"Really?" Had Catherine been a movie star who suddenly stepped off the screen to materialize before Francie in flesh and blood, the girl could not have been more awed.

This is ridiculous, thought Catherine. I'm not Cinderella. I'm not what they want me to be. But something stung her eyelids as she pushed the bottle of perfume more firmly into Francie's hands, undone by the look in the younger girl's eyes.

Marie, still standing on the bed, broke the tension by quipping, "I think this is what's called a pregnant silence."

So Catherine was saved from tears, and Francie was saved from shame, and everyone laughed and began drifting from the room until Catherine was left alone with Marie. Impulsively she gave the shorter girl a hug.

"Mutt and Jeff, aren't we?" Marie joked.

"I don't know what to say. I misjudged all of you earlier. I'm sorry."

"Hey," Marie reached to fix a certain curl at the side of Catherine's cheek, "we laid it on a little heavy. We understand."

"So do I . . . now."

"You're going for all of us, Cath."

"I know, I know."

"Just hear him out, okay?"

"But he's not coming to ask me to marry him. We already—"

"Just hear him out, that's all. Give the girls a little something to hope for. Pretend for them that it's real. Promise? Just for one night?"

"Okay, Marie," Catherine agreed, "for all of you. But what happens to their hopes when it doesn't come to anything?"

"You don't seem to realize that this is a first for them. Just give them something to talk about when he comes to the door. Be nice. Make them dream a little bit tonight."

Marie wondered how any man could resist a woman as

beautiful as Catherine. Being short herself she naturally admired Catherine's height. Being dark, she admired her blondness. Being bubbly, she admired her reserve. Being round-faced, she admired the long elegance of Catherine's face. Catherine was everything that Marie was not. Perhaps that's why they felt so strangely drawn to each other.

"Hey, Cath," Marie said, "you're a knockout."

"No, I'm not. You just want me to be."

"This guy must be something to have a girl like you."

But just then someone hollered from downstairs, "Hey, what kind of car has he got?"

Knowing before she answered that her response was certain to raise a hullabaloo, Catherine mentally grimaced, then called, "A silver Corvette."

Marie looked like she'd swallowed a live crayfish. "A what!"

"You heard right."

"And you're resisting him! No wonder you look pained."

I do not look pained! thought Catherine. I *do not*.

From downstairs issued a noisy mingling of catcalls, wolf howls, whistles, and out-and-out girlish squeals, followed by violent shushing.

"Too bad you have to miss the talk after you leave," Marie giggled, smirking. "It'll be something tonight. Come on, Cleopatra, your barge has arrived."

Standing at the top of the stairs Catherine told herself this was not Cleopatra's barge nor high school prom nor Cinderella's ball. But as she clutched her knotted stomach, a little ache of expectation created a quiver there. A damning rush of blood crept up the V of exposed skin behind the blue collar. She could feel it as it rose and heated her cheeks.

This is insane, she told herself. The girls put ridiculous fancies in your head with all their giddy teenage fussing. So your nails are cinnamon and your hair is terrific and you're powdered and perfumed. But none of it is your doing, none of it is because a silver Corvette is coming to pick you up with Clay Forrester behind the wheel. So close your glistening lips, Catherine Anderson, and act like you're breathing normally and don't make more of an ass of yourself than you're already going to seem when he walks in that door and sees you!

Suddenly all the commotion stopped downstairs. Then footsteps ran in every direction and the silence that followed was ridiculous! Somebody, thankfully, got to the stereo and turned it on just as the doorbell rang.

Upstairs, Catherine felt a trembling begin somewhere down low in her groin and silently cursed every girl in this place for what they were forcing her to do. Down below she heard his voice and she closed her eyes, steadying herself.

"Is Catherine Anderson here?"

Suddenly Catherine wished she were a snail and could crawl inside her shell. Vicky's voice—utterly innocent, utterly faky—came clearly. "Just a minute, I'll see."

I'll see? thought Catherine, rolling her eyes behind closed lids. Oh, Lord!

"Catherine?" Vicky called up the stairs.

Behind her Marie whispered, "A silver Corvette, huh? Git going," and gave her a nudge.

The stairs came up to meet her high heels, and the clicks sounded like gunshots in her ears. In a last panic she thought, I should have washed off the perfume and blotted that glossy lipstick. Damn you, damn you, damn you! What am I doing?

The town idiot would not have been fooled by the obvious lack of activity downstairs. The staged poses, the casually lounging bodies, strategically placed so that each girl could see into the hall from their vantage points in the living room, the Scrabble board on the dining room table with not a wooden letter on it, and every eye in the place trained on Clay Forrester who stood by the colonnade as if framed for display and purchase.

It might not have been so bad if he hadn't dressed up, too, but he had. He was wearing a gray Continental-cut suit that made him look like an ad for some high-priced Canadian whiskey. Catherine set her eyes on the top of his wine-colored tie; it was knotted so perfectly that it stood away from his neck like a crisp, new hangman's noose. She let her gaze move up to the pale blue collar that cinched him just below the Adam's apple, where the bronze tan began.

"Hello," he said as casually as possible, considering that the change in her that made him feel like her old man's goon had only now smashed him in the stomach.

Oh, Christ! thought Clay Forrester. Oh, sweet Christ!

"Hello," she returned, trying to make the word as cool as a cucumber sandwich. But it came out wilted by the scorching heat of her face.

Her eyes were different, he thought, and her hair, and she was wearing an understated dress worthy of a travel ad in *The New Yorker*. Looking at her face again he saw that she was blushing. *Blushing.*

Catherine saw Clay's Adam's apple move like it was trying to dislodge a fishbone stuck in his throat. She bravely looked him in the face, knowing full well that her own was scarlet, silently warning him not to give away any hint of either surprise or approval. *Please!* But one glance told her it was too late. He, too, was red to the collar. To his credit, he acted as refined as his grooming, all except for one quick glance down at her stomach, followed by a quicker one at the crowd of gawking faces in the living room and dining room.

"Do you have a coat?"

Oh, God, she thought, October and I leave my coat upstairs! "I left it up—"

But of all the girls, Marie finally did the right thing. She came down at an ungainly half-gallop, bringing the coat. "Here it is." And without any sign of ill ease, thrust out a hand toward Clay. "Hi, I'm Marie. Don't keep her out too late, okay?"

"Hi. I'm Clay and I won't." He smiled for the first time, shaking her hand firmly.

Jumping Jehoshaphat! thought Marie, he looks good enough to eat! And that smile. Look at that smile!

So when Catherine reached for her coat, Marie handed it instead to Clay. Correctly trained young swain that he was, he did the proper thing, and Catherine gratefully faced the door as he slipped the coat over her shoulders.

"Have a good time," Marie said.

"Good night," Catherine wished them all.

Like a kindergarten class, they all said in unison, "Good night."

Wanting to disappear into thin air, she reached for the door-knob, but Clay's hand shot around her, forcing her to allow him to open it for her or contest his gallantry before the girls.

Catherine dropped her hand and moved out into the blessedly cool October night that touched her scorching skin in sweet relief. But still from behind them, Clay and Catherine could feel the eyes that peered out of every front window of the house.

Following her to the car, Clay caught the smell of a pleasant scent threading from her, heard the tap of high heels on the sidewalk, saw in the beam from the porch light the back of her artfully arranged hair. And although he hadn't intended to, he walked first to her side of the car and opened her door, conscious yet of all those curious eyes, his mind half on them, half on the long legs Catherine pulled into the car.

Indoors, a chorus of giddy sighs went swooning.

Within the car, the atmosphere was so tense and silent even the low rumble of the engine was welcome as Clay turned the key. Carefully, Catherine kept her eyes off him—something about a man and his car and the things he does when he gets into it, moving to start it, touching things on the dash, folding himself into the seat, the way the shoulder of a suit coat ridges high as he reaches for the mirror, disarming things that are too peculiarly masculine for comfort. She kept her eyes straight ahead.

"Where do you want to go?"

She looked at him at last. "Listen, I'm sorry about that in there. They . . . well, they . . ."

"It's all right. Where do you want to go?"

"It's not all right. I don't want you to get the wrong impression."

"I think the windows still have eyes." There was a touch of amusement in his tone as he waited, seemingly at ease now with his hands on the familiar wheel.

"Anywhere . . . I don't care. I thought we'd just go ride and sit somewhere in the car and talk like we did the other time."

The car moved away from the curb and she felt his quick assessing glance and knew he was adding up the dress, the hair, the makeup, the high heels. She wanted to die all over again. Go for a ride, indeed, she could hear him thinking.

"Do you drink?" he asked, taking his eyes back to the street. She shot him a look, remembering last summer and that wine. "I can take it or leave it. Most of the time I leave it."

He thought of her father and thought he knew why.

"I know of a quiet place where the music doesn't start up till nine. It should be uncrowded this early and we can have a drink there while we talk, okay?"

"Fine," she agreed.

He pulled out onto Washington Avenue, heading toward downtown, across the Mississippi River. The silence grew uncomfortable so he reached, found a tape, engaged it in the deck, all without taking his eyes from the road. It was the same kind of music as before, too pulsing for her taste, too lacking in subtlety and musicality. Just a bunch of noise, she thought disparagingly. Once again she reached over and turned the volume down.

"You don't like disco?"

"No."

"Then you never tried dancing it?"

"No. If I danced anything it would be ballet, but I never had the chance to take lessons. But people used to say I'd make a good ballet dancer." She realized she was rambling on to hide her nervousness.

He sensed it, too, and replied simply, "They were probably right." He recalled where the level of her hair had matched his eyebrows.

She considered telling him that her father's beer and whiskey had sopped up all the spare money that might have meant ballet lessons, but it was too personal a comment. She wanted to avoid delving into personalities at all costs.

"Are all those girls back there pregnant?" he asked.

"Yes."

They stopped for a red light and Clay's face took on an unearthly tint as he looked at her. "But they're all so young."

"I'm the oldest one there."

She could sense his amazement, and suddenly she was chattering as fast as if this were a debate she wanted to win. "Listen, they won't believe this isn't a date. They *want* it to be a date. They want it so badly *they* did all of this to me. We were at supper and..." And the whole story came tumbling out, all about how they messed her up, then fixed her up as if she were

113

a high priestess. "And I couldn't make them understand they were wrong," Catherine ended. "And it was awful . . . and wonderful . . . and pathetic."

So that's why, he thought. "Don't worry about it, okay? I understand."

"No! No! I don't think you do. I don't think you possibly can! They're making me their—their emissary!" She threw her palms up hopelessly, and related the tale about Francie and the perfume and how she was forced to put it on.

"So you smell terrific and you don't want to?"

"Don't be funny. You know what I'm trying to say. What could I do besides use the perfume, with a kleptomaniac looking at me with big eyes, begging me to make something in her life okay?"

"You did the right thing."

"I did what I had to do. But I wanted you to know it was out of my hands. When you arrived I wanted to die because I thought you'd think I—I had designs on you."

By now they'd pulled into a parking lot where a neon sign identified the place as The Mullion. Clay killed the motor, turned to her and said, "All right, I admit it was pretty uncomfortable there for a minute, but just so their efforts won't have been for nothing, you can tell them I said you looked fantastic."

"That's not what I was fishing for, don't you understand!"

"Yes, I do. But if you make anything more of it by being so insistent, I'll think you really do have designs on me." Already Clay knew the signs warning of her approaching anger. So, quickly he got out, slammed the door and came to open hers.

And though she simmered from his last comment, she couldn't help wondering, as they crossed the parking lot, why he'd worn that expensive suit.

Chapter 8

THE MULLION TOOK its name from the series of leaded bay windows facing east across the river. Clay touched Catherine's elbow, leading her to a table placed within a deepset bay which afforded semi-privacy, surrounded on three sides as it was by leaded glass and the night beyond. He reached for her coat, but she held it on like armor, sitting down before he could pull her chair out for her.

He sat down opposite, asking, "What will you have to drink?" He noticed how she now removed her coat by herself and let it fall back over the chair.

"Something soft."

"Wine?" he suggested. "White?" It was disconcerting that he remembered she preferred white to red. But then, in the early part of the evening on their one and only date, they'd been quite sober, sober enough for him to remember such a thing.

"No, softer. Orange juice—unadulterated."

He let his gaze drift to her stomach momentarily before looking back up to find her expression unreadable.

"They encourage the drinking of fruit juice there," she said, enlightening him.

Their eyes met, his rather sheepish, she thought, and she quickly looked away at the lights of automobiles threading their way across the Washington Avenue bridge, creating bleeding, golden shimmers in the water's reflection. Clay surprised Catherine by ordering two unadulterated orange juices. She braved a glance at him, but quickly shifted her eyes away. She couldn't help wondering if the baby would look like him.

"I want to know your plans," he began, then added pointedly, "first."

"First?" She met his eyes. "First before what?"

"Before I tell you why I brought you here."

"My plans should be obvious. I'm living in a home for unwed mothers."

"Don't be obtuse, Catherine. Don't make me eke every answer out of you again. You know what I'm asking. I want to know what you're planning to do with the baby after it's born."

Her face hardened. "Oh, no, not you too."

"What do you mean, not me too?"

"Just that every time I turn around lately somebody wants to know what I plan to do with the baby."

"Who else?"

She considered telling him it was none of his business, but knew it was. "Mrs. Tollefson, the director of Horizons. She says her job is not to find babies for the babyless, but any way you slice it, that's what she does."

"Are you planning to give it away, then?"

"I don't consider that anyone's business but my own."

"Meaning, you're having trouble coming to a decision?"

"Meaning, I don't want you to be part of that decision."

"Why?"

"Because you're not."

"I'm the father."

"You're the sire," she said, impaling him with a stabbing look that matched her words. "There is a big difference."

"Funny," he said in some strangely colorless voice, "but it doesn't seem to make any difference when I think of it."

"Are you saying you're suffering a fit of conscience?"

"That baby's mine. I can't just wipe it off the slate, even if I want to."

"I knew this would happen if I saw you. That's why I didn't want to. I don't want any pressure from you to either keep the baby or give it away. The responsibility is mine. Anyway, what happened to the man who offered me money for an abortion?"

"You may recall that I was under a bit of duress at the time. It was a quick reaction. Whether or not I'd have wanted you to go through with it, I don't know. Maybe I just wanted to know what kind of person you are."

"Well, I'm afraid I can't enlighten you, because I don't know what I'm going to do yet."

"Good," he said, surprising her.

The waitress arrived just then with two tall, skinny glasses of orange juice on the rocks.

Clay reached into an interior breast pocket, and Catherine automatically reached for her purse. But before she could retrieve her wallet Clay had laid a five-dollar bill on the tray.

"I want to pay for my own."

"You're too late."

The sight of his money being taken away unnerved her.

"I don't want . . ." But it was hard for her to explain what she didn't want.

"You don't want me buying orange juice for my baby?"

She stared at him, unblinking, trying to figure out her motives. "Something like that."

"The cost of a glass of orange juice doesn't constitute a lifelong debt."

"Skip it, okay? I feel you're infringing on me and I don't like it, that's all. Taking me out, buying me drinks. Just don't think it changes anything."

"All right, I won't. But I'll reiterate something that does. Your father."

"Have you told him—" she began accusingly.

"No, I haven't. He doesn't have any idea you're here. He thinks you're out in Omaha someplace. But he's been making a nuisance of himself in more ways than one, only he's sly enough to stop just short of getting pinned for anything. Now he's taken to sending his—shall we call them—emissaries around to the house occasionally to remind us that he's still waiting for a payoff."

"I thought he came himself."

"That was only the first time. There've been others."

"Oh, Cl—" She stopped herself from uttering his name, began again. "I—I'm sorry. What can we do about it?"

He was very much his lawyer-father's son as he leaned toward her, outlining the situation, his eyes intense, his expression grave. "I am a third-year law student, Catherine. I've worked very hard to get where I am, and I intend to graduate and be admitted to the bar this summer. Unfortunately, I also have to prove I'm morally upstanding. If your father continues his vendetta and it gets to the Board of Examiners that I've fathered a bastard, it could have serious repercussions. That's why we haven't pressed charges against your father so far. And while it has not been stated explicitly, it has been implied that even should I pass and be accepted to the bar, my father may deny me a place in the family practice if I've shirked my responsibility to you. Meanwhile, my mother walks around the house looking like I've just kicked her in a broken leg. Your father wants money. You want your whereabouts to remain unknown. People are pressuring you to give up the baby. A bunch of pregnant teenage girls see you as their hope for the future. What do you think we can do about it?"

The glass stopped halfway to her open, gleaming lips. "Now just a min—"

"Before you get angry, hear me out."

"Not if you say what I think you're going to say."

"It's a business proposition."

"I don't want to hear it."

Her face became highly colored and her hand shook. She turned her cheek sharply away, not quite hiding it behind a hand.

"Drink your orange juice, Catherine. Maybe it will cool you down and make you listen to reason. I propose that you marry me and we'll—"

"You're crazy!" she snapped, dumbfounded.

"Maybe," he said coolly, "maybe not."

She tried to push her chair back but he deftly hooked one foot around its leg, guessing she was preparing to bolt.

"You're really one for running out on unpleasantness, aren't you?"

"You're mad! Sitting there suggesting that we get married! Get your foot off my chair."

"Sit down," he ordered. "You're making a spectacle again."

A quick perusal told her he was right.

"Are you adult enough to sit here and discuss this level-headedly, Catherine? There are at least a dozen sensible reasons for us to get married. If you'll give me a chance, I'll delineate them, starting with your father..."

That, above all, made her ease back into her chair.

"Are you saying he's caused you to get beaten up more than once?"

"Never mind. The point is, I'm beginning to understand why you vowed never to see him benefit from this situation. He's not exactly what I'd call ideal father-in-law material, but I'd take him as a temporary one rather than give him what he wants. If you and I marry, he'll be forced to give up his harassment. And even if the Board of Examiners somehow learns that a baby is due, it won't throw a shadow on my reputation if you and I are already married. I know now that what you said is true—your father is not really interested in your welfare as much as he is in his own. But my parents are.

"I feel like a juvenile delinquent every time my mother throws those censuring looks at me. And for some ungodly reason, my father is right in there with her. They're feeling..." He glanced up briefly, then down at his glass "...they're feeling like grandparents, reacting as such. They want to keep the baby in the family. They've taken a stand they won't back down from. And as for me, I won't bore you with my emotional state. Suffice it to say that it bothers me immeasurably to think of the baby being given up for adoption."

"I didn't say I was going to."

"No, you didn't. But what will you do if you keep it? Live on welfare in some roach-infested apartment house someplace? Give up school?" Again he leaned both forearms on the table, accosting her with his too-handsome, Nordic features set in an expression of worry. "I'm not asking you to consider marrying me without getting something out of it. When I saw you crossing the campus the other day, I couldn't believe my eyes. I didn't know you were a student there. What are you using for money?"

She didn't answer; she didn't need to for him to know finances were tight for her.

"It's going to take you some time to get through, isn't it? Even without the baby?"

Again, no answer.

"Suppose . . . just suppose we marry, agreeing in advance that it will be only until I finish school and take my bar exams. Your father will leave both of us alone; you'll be able to keep the baby; I'll be able to get my *juris doctor;* I'll be taken into my father's practice. When that happens you'll have your turn, and I'll pay for your schooling and for the child's support. That's my proposition. From now until July, that's all. And six months after that we'll have our divorce. I can easily handle it, and it is far less damaging to a career than a bastard child."

"And who keeps the baby?"

"You do," he answered without hesitation. "But at least I won't lose track of him and I'll see to it that neither he nor you ever has any financial worries. You can keep the baby and finish school too. What could be more sensible?"

"And what can be more dishonest?"

A look of exasperation crossed his face, but she knew that rankled, for he sat back in his chair and studied the lights across the river in a distracted fashion. She went on.

"You told me once that your father is the most exasperatingly honest person you know. What will he and your mother think when they learn their son has deceived them?"

"Why do they have to learn? If we do it, you'll have to agree never to tell them."

"Oh," she tossed out casually, knowing her remark was barbed, "so you don't want them to know you're a liar."

"I'm not a liar, Catherine. For God's sake, be reasonable." But he ran his fingers through his perfect hair and came forward on his chair again. "I'd like to finish law school and become part of my father's business. Is that so awful? That's the way we've always planned it to be, only now he seems to have lost reason."

She mused a while, then toyed with her glass. "You never had to worry about your ship coming in, did you?"

"And you resent that?"

"Yes, I suppose in a way I do."

"Enough to reject my offer?"

"I don't think I could do it."

"Why?" He leaned forward entreatingly.

"It would require acting talent that I don't possess."

"Not for long. About a year."

"At the risk of sounding hypocritical, I have to say it: your parents seem like decent and honest people and it would not settle well with me to hoodwink them just to make things easier for myself."

"All right, I admit it. It's not honest, and that bothers me too. I'm not in the habit of lying to them, no matter what you might think. But I don't think they're being totally honest, either, by taking the stand they've taken. They're forcing me to own up to my responsibilities, and I am. But, like you, I have a certain kind of life mapped out for myself, and I don't want to give it up because of this."

"There simply is no way I would marry someone I don't love. I've had a bellyful of living in a house where two people hated each other."

"I'm not asking you to love me. All I want is for you to think sensibly about the benefits we'd both derive from the arrangement. Let's backtrack a minute and consider one question which still needs answering. Do you want to give the baby up for adoption?"

He was leaning toward her now quite beseechingly. She studied the glass within his long, lean fingers, unwilling to look into his eyes for fear he might convince her of something she did not want.

"That's not fair and you know it," she spoke in a strained voice, "not after what I told you about the girls and my conversation with Mrs. Tollefson."

He sensed her weakening and pressed on. "None of this is, is it? I'm no different than you, Catherine, no matter what you might think. I don't want that baby living with strangers, wondering for the rest of my life where he is, what he is, who he is. I'd like to at least know that he's with you, and that he's got everything he needs. Is that such a bad bargain?"

Like a recording she repeated what Mrs. Tollefson had said,

hoping to shore up her defenses. "It's a well-known fact that adopted children are exceptionally bright, happy and success-ful."

"Who told you that, your social worker?"

Her eyes flashed to his. How easily he can read me, she thought. The waitress approached, and without asking Cath-erine, Clay signaled to order two more orange juices, more to get rid of the interference than because he was thirsty. He watched the top of Catherine's hair as she toyed with her glass. "Could you really give it up?" he asked softly.

"I don't know," she admitted raggedly.

"My mother was decimated when she found out you were gone. I never saw her cry in my life, but then I did. She didn't have to mention the word abortion more than once for me to know it was on her mind night and day. I guess I learned some things about my parents and myself since this thing happened."

"It's so dishonest," she said lamely. Then after long silence, she asked, "When are the bar exams?" She could not quite believe what she was asking.

"I don't know the exact date yet, but sometime in July."

She rested her forehead against her hand, as if unutterably tired of everything.

Suddenly he felt obliged to reassure her so he reached for her arm, which lay disconsolately on the tabletop. She didn't even try to resist the small squeeze he gave it.

"Think it over," he said quietly.

"I don't want to marry you, Clay," she said, raising her sad, beautiful eyes to him, a pinched expression about their corners.

"I know. I'm not expecting it to be a regular marriage, with all the obligations. Only as a means to what we both want."

"And you'd start divorce proceedings immediately after the exams and you wouldn't use some clever tricks to get the baby away from me?"

"I would treat you fairly, Catherine. I give you my word."

"Would we live together?" Her eyelids flickered; she looked aside.

"In the same place, but not together. It would be necessary for my family to think we were married in more than name only."

"I feel utterly exhausted," she admitted.

Some musicians filed in, turned on some dim stage lights and began tuning up their guitars.

"There's not much more to be said tonight"—Clay fiddled with the table edge a moment—"only that I'd keep out of your way if you marry me. I know you don't like me, so I won't push anything like that."

"I don't dislike you, Clay. I hardly know you."

"I've given you plenty of good reason though, haven't I? I've gotten you pregnant, offered you abortion money, and now I'm suggesting a scheme to get us out of it."

"And am I so lily-white?" she asked. "I'm actually thinking it over."

"You'll consider it then?"

"You don't have to ask. Against my better judgment, I already am."

They drove back to Horizons in silence. As he pulled the car to a stop at the curb, Clay said, "I could come and pick you up at the same time tomorrow night."

"Why don't you just call?"

"There are too many inquisitive ears around here."

She knew he was right, and though it was difficult for her to be with Clay, neither did she want to give him her answer with an audience around the corner. "Okay, I'll be ready."

He let the engine run, got out and came around to open her door, but by the time he got there she was already stepping out of the car. He politely closed the door for her.

"You don't have to do all these things, you know, like opening doors and pulling out chairs. I don't expect it."

"If I didn't, would it make you feel better?" They walked toward the porch steps.

"I mean, you don't have to pretend it's *that* real."

"Force of habit," he said.

Under the garish light of the porch she at last dared to look directly into his face.

"Clay." She tested the word fully upon her tongue. "I know you've gone with a girl named Jill Magnusson for a long time." Catherine struggled to find a way to say what was on her mind, but found she couldn't say it.

He stood still as a statue, his expression void, unreadable.

Then he reached for the screen door, opened it and said, "You'd better go in now."

He turned on a heel, took the steps in one leap and ran to the car. As she watched the tail lights disappear up the street she felt, for the first time in her pregnancy, like throwing up.

Chapter 9

THE FOLLOWING DAY was one of those flawless Indian summer days in Minnesota which are like an assault on the senses. The warmth returned, dormant flies reawakened, the sky was deep azure, and the campus crimson and gold was vivid as autumn color peaked. It was October; new match-ups had been made, and to Catherine it seemed the entire population of the University moved in pairs. She found herself captivated by the sight of a male and a female hand with their fingers entwined, swinging between two pairs of hips. Without her consent her mind formed a picture of Clay Forrester's clean, lean hands on the wheel, and she wiped her damp palm on her thigh. She passed a couple kissing in the entrance to Tate Lab. The boy had his hand inside the girl's jacket just above her back waist-line. Unable to tear her eyes away, Catherine watched his hand emerge from under the garment, then pass along the girl's ribs as the two parted, went their separate ways. She remembered Clay's words, *not a regular marriage with all the obligations*, and though that's what she, too, insisted it must be, there were goosebumps on her flesh. In the late afternoon, on her way home, she spotted a couple sitting on the grass Indian style, face-to-face, studying. Without taking his eyes from his book, the boy absently ran his hand up inside the girl's pantleg to her knee. And something female prickled down low inside of Catherine.

But I'm pregnant, she thought, and Clay Forrester doesn't love me. Still, that didn't make the prickly longing disappear.

Back at Horizons Catherine carefully changed clothes, though casually enough so as not to appear seductive. But when her makeup was complete, she looked closely in the mirror. Why had she reconstructed last night's careful shadings and highlights? Subtle mauve shadow above her eyes, a faint hint of peach below them, sandy brown mascara, apricot cheeks, glistening cinnamon lips to match her nails. She told herself it had nothing to do with Clay Forrester's proposal.

Turning from the dresser, Catherine found Francie waiting hesitantly in the doorway, wearing the first suggestion of a smile Catherine had seen upon her face. In silence, Francie extended the bottle of Charlie.

Catherine forced a bright smile of her own. "Why, thank you, I was just coming to get it." The perfume followed the makeup, and a moment later Marie came in to say Clay had arrived.

When Catherine came downstairs, there was a first awkward moment while they each scanned the other's clothes and faces, that too-meaningful assessment making her heart thud heavily.

He was wearing navy blue trousers this time, stylishly pleated, and a V-neck sweater of pale blue lambswool. Beneath was an open collar, short tips clearly stating it was this season's style. He wore a simple gold chain around his neck, and it seemed to accent the golden hue of his skin. Admitting how utterly in vogue Clay always dressed, and how it pleased her, Catherine wondered for the hundredth time that day if she were doing the right thing.

There was a feeling of unreality about walking out before him, passing through the door he held open, feeling him behind her shoulder as they took the porch steps and walked toward the car. She battled to submerge the feelings of familiarity which were already cropping up: the way he leaned sideways from the hip when he opened her car door, the hug of the bucket seat as she slid in, the sound of his footsteps coming around the car, his own peculiar movements as he settled into his seat. Then once again the smell of his shaving lotion in the confined space, and all of those thrice-noticed motions of a man and his car: already she knew just in which order he would do them, wrist over wheel as he started the engine, the unnecessary touch on the rearview mirror, the single shrug and forward jut of his head as he made himself comfortable, the way he left his hand on the stick of the floor shift as the Corvette pulled away from the curb. He was driving sensibly tonight. Instead of the tape deck, the radio was on this time, softly, voices proclaiming musically that they were tuned to KS-ninety-five. Then, without warning, The Lettermen began singing, "Well, I think I'm going out of my head..." And Clay just drove. And Catherine just sat. Each of them wanting to reach over and turn the song off. Neither of them daring. Lights coming, going, flashing, waning while the car moved through the mellow Indian summer night, its engine cooing along on a note as rich as any coming from The Lettermen, whose song finally reached its medley stage and wove its way into words that were even worse: "You're just too good to be true... can't take my eyes off of you..."

Catherine thought she would do anything for some wildly pulsating disco! But she found she could not give credence to the meaningful words coming from the radio, so she braved it out until the song ended. When it had, Clay asked her a single question.

"Did the girls do all that to you tonight?"

But with the suggestive song ended, she'd regained control of her senses. There was no reason to lie. "No."

He gave her a sidelong look, then tended to his driving again.

She somehow guessed where they would go. She needn't know the exact route to be sure of the destination. He drove as if it were predetermined, out onto the Interstate, under the tunnel and west on Wayzata Boulevard to Highway 100, then south toward Edina. Again the unwanted feeling of familiarity crept over her. She had a sudden desperate hope that she might be wrong, that he'd choose to drive to some other place, thus avoiding the establishment of further familiarities. But he did not.

The wooded trail wound up into the park, taking them to

the same secluded spot as that first night. He stopped at the top of the gravel road and switched off the engine but left the radio playing softly. Outside it was full dark, but the vague light from the dash illuminated his profile as he entwined his fingers behind the steering wheel and distractedly tapped a thumb upon it in time to the music.

Panic clawed its way up her throat.

At last he turned, propping his left elbow on top of the wheel. "Have you . . . have you thought about it any more or decided anything?"

"Yes." The lone syllable sounded strained.

"Yes, you've thought about it, or yes, you'll marry me?"

"Yes, I'll marry you," she clarified, with no hint of joy in her voice. She answered instead with a throb of regret tumbling her stomach. She wished he would not study her so and wondered if he was feeling as hollow as she was at that moment. She wanted to get out of the car and run down the gravel hill again. But where would she run? To what?

"Then we might as well work out a few details as soon as possible."

His businesslike tone thrust her back to reality.

"I suppose you don't want to waste any time?"

"Considering you're three months pregnant already, no I don't. I don't suppose you do either?"

"N-no," she lied, dropping her eyes to her lap.

A short, nervous laugh escaped him. "What do you know about weddings?"

"Nothing." She gazed at him helplessly.

"Neither do I. Are you willing to go and talk to my parents?"

"Now?" She hadn't expected it so soon.

"I thought we might."

"I'd rather not." In the dim light she looked panic-stricken.

"Well, what do you want to do then, elope?"

"I hadn't given it much thought."

"I'd like to go talk to them. Do you mind?"

What else could she do? "We'll have to face them sooner or later, I guess."

"Listen, Catherine, they're not ogres. I'm sure they'll help us."

"I have no illusions about what they must think of me and

128

of my family. They can't be martyrs enough to be willing to forget all that my father has done. Can you blame me for being less than anxious to face them?"

"No."

They sat there thinking about it for a while. But neither of them knew the first thing about planning a wedding of any kind.

"My mother will know what to do."

"Yeah, like throw me out."

"You don't know her, Catherine. She's going to be happy."

"Sure," she replied sullenly.

"Well, relieved then."

But still they sat, aware of the sharp contrast between what *was* happening and what *should be* happening at a time like this.

Finally Catherine sighed. "Well, let's get it over with then."

Clay started the car abruptly. He took them back down the twisting streets, through the rolling neighborhoods of elegant lawns whose breadth spoke of estates rather than lots. She heard the unfamiliar sound of tires on cobblestone as they swept up the curve and stopped before that massive pair of front doors she had once studied so critically from inside. They cowed her now, but she made up her mind not to let it show.

Following Catherine to the house, Clay found himself thinking of Jill Magnusson, and how it should be her going with him to speak to his parents.

The foyer assaulted Catherine with memories of the last time she'd been here: the way Clay had come breezing in and the scene that had followed. She found herself before the mirror, glanced quickly away from his regarding eyes and stopped her hand from touching a wisp of hair that was out of place. Disarmingly, he read her thoughts.

"You look fine. . . . Come on." And he took her elbow.

Angela looked up as they approached the study door. The sight of them stirred her warmest blood, made it race crazily at their unexpected arrival. They were like a pair of sun-children, both of them blond, tall and strikingly beautiful. Nobody had to tell Angela Forrester how beautiful a child of theirs would be.

"Are we interrupting anything?" Clay asked. His father

glanced up from something he'd been working on at his desk. Everything in the room marked time for that interminable moment while they all allowed the surprise to run its course. Then Angela unwound her ankles in slow motion and removed a pair of reading glasses. Claiborne rose, halfway at first, as if stunned. He and Angela stared at Catherine, and she felt the blood whipping up her neck and fought the urge to duck behind Clay.

At last he spoke. "I think it's time you all met properly. Mother, Father, this is Catherine Anderson. Catherine, my parents."

And yet, for a painful moment more, the room remained a Still Life With Parents and Children.

Then Angela moved. "Hello, Catherine," she said, reaching out a flawless, jeweled hand.

Immediately Catherine sensed that Angela Forrester, like the girls at Horizons, was an ally. This woman wants me to marry her son, she thought, amazed.

But when Claiborne Forrester emerged from around his desk, it was with a less-welcoming mien, although he extended his hand and greeted Catherine, also. But where Angela's touch had been a warm peace offering, there exuded from her husband a coolness much the same as the other time Catherine had been in this room.

"So you found her, Clay," the older man noted unnecessarily.

"Yes, several days ago."

Angela and Claiborne looked at each other, then quickly away.

"Several days ago. Well..." But the word dangled there, leaving everything awkward again. "We're glad you've changed your mind and come back to talk things over a little more sensibly. Our first meeting was, well, shall we say, less than ideal."

"Father, could we forego the obvious recrim—"

"No, it's all right," Catherine interrupted.

"I think we'd all better sit down." Angela motioned toward the loveseat where she'd been sitting. "Catherine, please." Clay followed and sat down beside her. His parents took the chairs beside the fireplace.

Although her stomach was twitching, Catherine spoke calmly. "We thought it best to come and talk to you immediately."

The eagle's frown was there upon Mr. Forrester's face, just as Catherine remembered it.

"Under the circumstances, I should certainly think so," the man said.

Clay edged forward as if to respond, but Catherine hurried to speak first. "Mr. Forrester, I understand that my father has been here more than just once. I want to apologize for his behavior, both the night I was with him and any other times when I wasn't. I know how irrational he can be."

Claiborne grudgingly found himself admiring the girl's directness. "I assume Clay has told you we have refrained from pressing charges."

"Yes, he has. I'm sorry that's what you decided. I can only say I had nothing to do with his actions and hope you'll believe me."

Again Claiborne felt an unwanted twitch of admiration at the girl's straightforward manner. "We, of course, know that Clay offered you money, and that you refused his offer. Have you changed your mind?"

"I haven't come here asking for money. Clay told me you haven't paid my father anything he demanded, but I'm not here pleading his case, if that's what you think. I never intended for any of it to happen. That night I came here I had already made plans to run away from home and make it look like I was headed across the country where he couldn't catch up with me. I thought when I was gone he'd leave you alone. If any of it could have been avoided by my staying, I'm sorry."

"I make no pretense of liking your father or of excusing him, but I must admit I'm relieved Clay found you so this mess can get straightened out once and for all. I'm afraid we've all been rather anxious and have been upset with Clay's behavior."

"Yes, he told me."

Claiborne quirked an eyebrow at his son. "Seems you and Clay have been doing a lot of talking lately."

"Yes, we have."

Whatever Clay had expected, it wasn't Catherine's cool control. He was pleasantly surprised by the way she was handling his father. If there was one thing Claiborne Forrester admired it was spunk, and she was displaying an inordinate amount of it.

"Have you come to any conclusions?" Claiborne pressed on.

"I think that's for Clay to answer."

"He didn't bother to tell us that he'd found you, you know."

"I made him promise he wouldn't. I'm living in a home for unwed mothers and didn't care to have my whereabouts known."

"Because of your father?"

"Yes, among other reasons."

"Such as?"

"Such as your son's money, Mr. Forrester, and the pressure it could exert on me."

"Pressure? He offered you money, which you refused to accept. Is that what you call pressure?"

"Yes. Isn't it?"

"Are you upbraiding me, Miss Anderson?"

"Are *you* upbraiding *me*, Mr. Forrester?"

The room crackled almost electrically for a moment before Claiborne admitted in a less accusing voice, "You surprise me. I hadn't expected your . . . detachment."

"I'm not at all detached. I've been through two very hellish weeks. I've been making decisions that haven't been easy."

"So have my wife and I, and—I dare say—Clay."

"Yes, he told me about your—I dare say—ultimatum."

"Call it what you will. I don't doubt that Clay represented it to you in anything but its true light. We were grossly disappointed in the lack of good judgment he showed and took steps to see that he not only own up to his responsibilities, but that he not ruin his chances for the future."

Angela Forrester sat forward then on the edge of her chair, legs crossed, leaning a delicate elbow on one knee. "Catherine," she said, her voice the first emotional one in the room, "please understand that I—we have all been utterly distraught about your welfare and that of the child. I was so afraid you'd gone off to have an abortion anyway, in spite of what you told Clay."

Catherine could not help angling a quick glance at Clay, surprised that he'd told them he'd suggested abortion.

"They know everything that we talked about that night," he confirmed.

"You're surprised, Catherine?" Angela asked. "That Clay told us the truth or that we . . . rather . . . forced the issue?"

"At both, I guess."

"Catherine, we knew you were here against your wishes the first time. Believe me, Clay's father and I have asked ourselves countless times what is the right thing to do. We coerced Clay into bringing you back here, so are we any less guilty of force than your father?"

"My father is a man who doesn't know how to reason, or rather, who won't. Please don't think that I'm anything like him. I . . ." Catherine looked down at her lap, her first outward show of her inner turmoil. "I intensely dislike my father." Then she confronted Claiborne's eyes again, continuing. "You may as well know that part of the reason I am here now is to see that he doesn't bleed you for a single red cent, and that my reasons have little to do with altruism."

Claiborne rose, crossed back to his desk and seated himself behind it. He picked up a letter opener and began toying with it. "You're a very direct young woman."

Angela could tell this pleased her husband. While the girl's directness put her off somewhat, she was moved to sympathy by a daughter harboring such strong negative emotions for a father. The girl, it was obvious, was defensive about it, too, which meant she was hurt by it. All of this touched the mother in Angela.

"Does that bother you?" Catherine was asking.

"No, no, not at all," Claiborne blustered, ruffled that someone else controlled the conversational reins which he was accustomed to controlling.

Again Catherine dropped her eyes to her lap. "Well, anyway, I don't have to live in the same house with him anymore."

Again Angela experienced a twinge of pity; her eyes met her husband's and went to Clay, who was studying Catherine's profile.

Clay dropped his hand from the back of the loveseat onto the back of Catherine's neck, to the spot where he'd once detected the evidence of her father's abuse. Startled, she met his eyes, burned by the heat of his hand through her hair. Then the heat disappeared and Clay looked toward his father. "Catherine left home and arranged for her father to think she was running across the country so that she could continue school without being hassled by him."

Surprised, Claiborne asked, "You're a student?"

"Yes, at the university."

Again Clay spoke. "It goes without saying that she'd have a tough time of it with the baby. I managed to convince her that it was sensible to let me help with finances." He allowed a moment to pass silently before capturing Catherine's hand, pressing it onto his knee in a way she found embarrassingly familiar. "Catherine and I have talked everything over. Tonight I asked her to marry me and she accepted."

Angela carefully kept the pain from showing in her face, but her throat worked convulsively. The letter opener slipped from Claiborne's fingers and clattered onto the desktop. He then rested one elbow on each side of it and covered his face with both hands.

"We've agreed that it's best this way," Clay said quietly, and his father's eyes emerged from behind his fingertips just in time to see Catherine slip her hand cautiously off Clay's knee.

What have I done? thought Claiborne.

Angela murmured, "I'm so relieved," and wondered if she really was.

Caliborne could not help asking, "Are you sure?"

Catherine felt Clay's eyes pulling her own to his face. He gave her a secretive look which could easily be misinterpreted by his parents. Then he rested an elbow on the back of the sofa and laid a hand on her shoulder nearest his chest. "Catherine's friends and I have managed to convince her," he said, with just enough implied intimacy to give them the fully wrong impression.

Catherine felt her face redden.

Angela and Claiborne witnessed their son's eyes caressing the young woman's face, and their own startled eyes met. How could this possibly have happened so quickly? Yet they each remembered that the two had been intimate once; apparently there was some basis for attraction. Everything about Clay's attitude suggested it, and the girl's blush confirmed it. But sensing that Catherine was displeased with the way Clay allowed his appetites to show, Angela moved toward them, offering congratulations. Claiborne rose and came to clasp their hands. When he held his son's hand firmly within both of his, he said honestly, "We're proud of your decision, Clay."

But there was an undeniably painful mixture of eagerness and disappointment permeating the room. Feeling it, Catherine thought this must be how a thief felt while casing victims who were also friends.

It was some time later that the issue of the wedding came up as Angela asked, unassumingly, "Do you want your father and I in on the arrangements?"

"Of course," Clay answered without hesitation. "Catherine and I don't know the first thing about planning a wedding."

"Why not have the wedding here?" Angela asked most unexpectedly.

It was immediately apparent Catherine had not thought that far ahead. Angela placed a hand on her arm apologetically. "Oh, forgive me, have I been too assuming? From the things you've said about your father I thought perhaps..." But her words trailed away, leaving an uncomfortable void. She realized she'd put her foot in her mouth, something Angela Forrester rarely did.

Catherine attempted to ease the tension by affecting a wan laugh. "No, no, it's all right. You're probably right. My father wouldn't be inclined to lay out money when it was his intention all along to realize a profit from this situation."

"But I've embarrassed you, Catherine, and that was not my intention. I don't mean to usurp your parents' place, but I want you to understand that Clay's father and I would be more than happy to give both of you whatever you want in the way of a wedding. I simply don't want you to think we would stint you on anything. Clay is our only son—please understand, Catherine. This will happen only once. As his parents, we'd love to indulge in our dreams of a perfect wedding celebration. If you'd ... well, if you'd both agree to have the service here at the house, we'd be utterly happy, wouldn't we, darling?"

Claiborne, looking rather lost and beleaguered, could only concur. But, goddammit, he thought. It should have been Jill. *It should have been Jill!* "What Angela says is true. We cer-

135

tainly are not strapped, and we'd be happy to foot the bill."

"I don't know yet," Catherine said, floundering in this new possibility that she hadn't considered.

"Mother, we haven't had a chance to talk about it yet," Clay explained.

Angela chose her words carefully, hoping that Clay would understand there were social obligations that people of their position must fulfill.

"I see no reason for either of you to feel you must sneak off like two chastised children. A marriage should be treated as a celebration. I . . . Catherine, I can see that I *have* embarrassed you, but please take our offer in the light it is intended. We can very easily afford to pay for a small affair here. Call it selfish, if you want to. Clay is our only son, you must understand."

"Mother, Catherine and I will talk it over and let you know."

To Clay, she said, "There are so many people who would be disappointed if you eloped—not the least of whom are your father and me. I'd like the family and a few close friends anyway. You know how your grandparents would be hurt if they were eliminated. And I'm sure Catherine will want her family."

But neither Clay nor Catherine knew what the other's feelings were on the subject.

"Well"—Angela straightened her shoulders—"enough said. I've been rather premature, I realize, but whatever you decide, I know we can implement your plans."

"Thank you, Mrs. Forrester. We'll have to talk it over."

Again an awkward silence fell, and as if suddenly inspired, Claiborne clapped his hands with mock joviality, suggesting a glass of wine to honor the occasion.

Clay immediately seconded the motion, going to find an untapped bottle while Claiborne fetched four crystal goblets.

A glass of white wine of excellent vintage was placed in Catherine's hands. Momentarily the goblet blotted out Clay's face before its rim touched her lips, and above it she telegraphed Clay a message which he, thankfully, understood. The toast done, he took Catherine's glass from her hand and set it, along with his own, on the table.

136

"Catherine and I will see you... when, Catherine?" He looked to her. "Tomorrow night?"

So fast! she thought, things are moving so fast! But she found herself agreeing to tomorrow night.

Preparing to leave, Catherine tried to thank Angela, but Angela's eyes were unmistakably dewy as she said, "Things will work out." The diamonds upon her hands flashed as she made a gesture of command with the wineglass. "Go now," she finished, "and we'll see you tomorrow."

As she left the room where Claiborne and Angela stood with their arms around each other's waists, Catherine found herself comparing them to her own parents and admitted that the Forresters did not deserve to be deceived. They were the "rich sons-a-bitches" her father had despised, whom she'd nearly caught herself despising. But she saw them now only as a mother and father who wanted nothing but the best for their son. Leaving their house Catherine thought, I'm no better than my father.

Chapter 10

OUTSIDE IT HAD turned colder, and a spiritless rain had begun. The heater, not yet warmed up, breathed clammy air onto Catherine's legs as she girded her knees with both hands to keep from shivering.

Headed back to Horizons, Clay asked peremptorily, "Well, what do you think?"

"I have a feeling this thing is going to get out of hand right before our very eyes. I never thought your mother would come up with such a suggestion."

"I didn't either, but I guess I didn't have time to think. Still, it's better than the whole church thing with a thousand guests, isn't it?"

"I don't know what I expected, but it wasn't grandpas and grandmas." Somehow Clay Forrester seemed too chic to have grandparents hidden somewhere in the woodwork.

"I didn't evolve from a splitting cell, you know," he said, attempting to inject a little humor into the otherwise humorless situation.

"Right now I almost wish you had. Me too."

"Don't you have any grandparents?"

"No, they're all dead. But if I did, I think I'd burn an effigy on their front lawn to protest their having an offspring like my dad. Clay, I will not have that man at our wedding, no matter what."

"Well, it wouldn't hurt my feelings not to invite him, but how can you leave him out and still have your mother? Is that what you're suggesting?"

"I don't know what I'm suggesting. This whole idea of a— a real *ceremony* is . . . well, it's preposterous! My old man would get pickled and become obnoxious as usual and the whole scene would be worse than any so far. Either that, or he'd go around telling all the guests how his ship just came in!"

"Well, I don't see how we can avoid him."

"Clay!" she said in an I-don't-believe-this tone of voice.

"What? What does that mean—*Clay?*" He repeated her exact tone of disbelief.

"You really want to go along with this whole shindig, don't you? I mean, you think we should let your mother go through with all the preparations and the expense of a real wedding, and let them believe it's for keeps?"

"If she wants to do it, let her do it. She's in her glory when she's organizing what she calls her 'little social events,' so let her organize one. Who's it going to hurt?"

"Me! I feel like a felon already, planning what we're planning. I don't want to haze your parents any more than necessary."

"Catherine, I think you have to put things into perspective. The whole occasion will probably cost less than one of the rings on my mother's hands. So why not let her have her fun?"

"Because it's dishonest," she said stubbornly.

He grew a little irritated. "That fact is already established, so what's the difference how we go about it as long as we're going to go about it anyway?"

"Can't we just go off to some justice of the peace or something?"

"We can if that's what you really want. But I think it would only hurt my parents more. I don't know about yours—your mother anyway—but I doubt that she'd be too disappointed to see you getting married with a show of my parents' support. That's really what it boils down to, you know. My parents have chosen to accept our marriage and want it known that they do. Isn't that what weddings are all about?"

"No. Most weddings are about a lifelong commitment between a man and a woman."

But Clay sensed something more behind Catherine's refusal. "You wouldn't like any *vile ostentation* on your account, is that it? Especially if the bill was picked up by the despicable rich you've been cultured to hate so much?"

At the beginning that had been part of it, but no longer. "Okay, I'll admit it, I've been prejudiced by my father's prejudices against the rich. And, yes, I've had preformed notions about what your family would be like, but your parents are not bearing them out."

Clay worked the edges of his teeth together, noting that she did not include him in her summary of findings. "You mean you like them?"

But Catherine had decided that liking them was a pitfall she would do well to guard against.

"I respect them," she answered truthfully, "and that in itself is something new for me."

"Well, then, couldn't you respect their wishes and go along with my mother?"

Catherine sighed heavily. "Lord, I don't know. I'm not very good at any of this. I don't think I ever should have agreed to it."

"Catherine, whatever you might think, my mother is not a manipulator. She does try to do things in the accepted fashion, and I haven't mentioned it before, but I know that part of the reason for a reception of some kind is political. It may not have been mentioned, but business etiquette requires invitations to occasions such as these for certain long-established associates who have become more than just business connections down through the years. Some of them are close personal friends of my parents by now. I'm sorry if that lays an extra burden on you, but that's the way it is."

"Why didn't you tell me this when you first suggested the scheme?"

"Frankly, I didn't think of it then."

She groaned softly. "Oh, this gets worse all the time."

"If you ask Mother to scale it down, I'm sure she will. But I guarantee that whatever she has a hand in will be handled with taste and efficiency. Would that be so hard to accept?"

"I . . . it scares me, that's all. I don't know anything about . . . society weddings."

"She does. Let her guide you. I have a feeling the two of you could work well together, once you get to know each other."

Again Catherine felt cornered, this time by Clay's obvious wish to please his parents, even if it meant a wedding that was larger than prudent. And again as she remembered his light touches, the looks of implied intimacy, she decided to take up the subject now so that he clearly understood her stand on the matter.

"That was quite a performance you put on back there, and totally unnecessary. I'm sure your parents aren't that gullible."

"You may have thought it unnecessary; I didn't."

"Well, spare me in the future, please. It's bad enough as it is."

"I wanted as few questions as possible, that's all. And I think it worked."

"You have no conscience whatsoever, do you?"

"We've been over this once before, so let's not go over it again. I don't like it any more than you do, but I'm going through with it, okay? If I have to touch you now and then to make it convincing, I'm sorry."

"Well, that wasn't part of our agreement."

"Are you that insecure that a touch on the shoulder threatens you?"

She would not grace him with an answer to such nonsense. But when she sat silently stewing for some time, he added, "Just forget it. It didn't mean anything, it was only an act."

Only an act, Catherine thought. Only an act.

It was warm in the car as Catherine sighed, leaned back in the comfortable seat and let the whisper of rain beneath the tires hypnotize her. The purring syllable of the engine, the faint vibration of the road, the gentle sway now and then as they rounded a curve or changed lanes—she let it engulf her in a place halfway between sleep and wakefulness, halfway between worry and security. The swoop of the windshield wipers mesmerized her and she drifted away, playing the game of pretend, as she and Bobbi had done so often in childhood.

What happened to the girl who romanticized stories in her diary all her growing years? What happened to those dreams that had been an escape hatch then? What would it be like if this wedding were not some trumped-up scheme? What if it were real, and she and Clay both wanted it?

There was a bouquet of sweet-scented flowers in her hands as she drifted through a crowd of people with radiant smiles. She wore a stunning white gown with a skirt so voluminous it filled the width of the stairway from banister to wall. The diaphanous veil on her head tumbled around her, following like an aureole as she passed a table spread with lace and laid with silver, and another that bore an eruption of gifts which scarcely took her notice as she searched the throng for the eyes she knew so well. Bobbi was there, kissing her cheek, crying a little bit from happiness. But again the search for gray eyes and she found them and they smiled. He waited for her to reach him, and when she had she knew peace and fulfillment. Rice flew, and the bouquet flew, straight into Bobbi's upraised hands, and Bobbi tossed her a kiss that said, "See? It happened just like we pretended, you first, then me." And mother's face was in the crowd, eased of worry, because Cathy had picked the right man. Then she and the very right, very gray-eyed man were sailing through the door toward a honeymoon, a honey-life, and it was real . . . real . . . real . . .

Catherine's head leaned at a fallen angle upon the seat of the car. Clay leaned near her, shaking her elbow gently. "Hey, Catherine, wake up." The dash lights picked out a series of golden needlepoints from the tips of her eyelashes which formed a dim fan of shadows across her cheek and nose. Her hair was messed up on one side, caught against the car seat and billowed out in disarray around her ear. He noticed for the first time that the ear was pierced. She wore a tiny silver stud in it. Her lips had fallen relaxed, all of their earlier gloss now gone. The very tip of her tongue showed between her teeth. The tendons of her neck were highlighted, creating intimate shadows behind them. The faint, inviting scent of her perfume still clung there.

How defenseless she looks, thought Clay, all wilted sideways, with her usual air of aloofness erased. She was a beautiful girl this way, but when she awoke he knew her stern facade would quickly return, and with it the cold overtones that Clay already disliked so intensely. He wondered if he might not learn to love her if her personality were as warm and sweet as the look of her right now. His eyes moved down to her lap. One hand was still lightly closed around a clutch purse, the other lay against her low abdomen. Behind that hand his child thrived. He let the thought carry him. He considered what he wanted out of life and wondered what she wanted out of hers. The hand in her lap twitched and he studied it, thinking how easily she could have had an abortion. Momentarily he wished she had, then again, was relieved she hadn't. He wondered what the baby would look like. He wondered if it would be a boy or a girl. He wondered if it were a mistake, this wedding idea. He felt a momentary tenderness toward her because of the life she carried, and decided no, it was no mistake; his child deserved a better start in life than he, Clay, had given it so far. He wished, oh, how he wished, that things were different, that this girl were different, so he could love her. He realized he still held her arm, just above the elbow. He could feel her pliant flesh, her body heat through her coat sleeve.

"Catherine, wake up," he repeated softly.

Her eyelashes lifted and her tongue glanced across her lips. Her head rolled upright, and her eyelids shut once more.

"You fell asleep," he said, close to her, that hand still resting on her forearm.

"Mmmm . . ." Catherine murmured, resisting wakefulness a little longer. She stretched without stretching, using only her shoulders. She was aware of his touch, and she pretended for a minute longer, knowing now that he was very near, even though her eyes were still closed.

"You were supposed to be thinking things over instead of sleeping." But his voice was devoid of criticism, holding instead a note of warmth. She opened her eyes to find him a hovering shadow before her, his features eclipsed, for he'd slung one elbow over the wheel and half-turned her way.

"Sorry. I seem to do that so easily lately. The doctor said it was natural though."

Her words created an intimacy that lightly lifted Clay's

stomach, coming as they did upon the heels of his thoughts about the baby. He had never considered the personal changes going on inside her body before, nor the way they affected her day-to-day routine. It struck him that he was responsible for many changes she was undergoing, of which he was totally unaware.

"It's okay. I really don't mind."

It was the first time they ever had spoken unguardedly to each other. Her defenses were down, drowsy as she was.

"I was pretending," she confided.

"Pretending what?"

"Not really pretending, but remembering how Bobbi and I used to sit for hours and plan our weddings and make gowns out of dishtowels and safety pins, and veils from old curtains. Then we'd write it all in our diaries, all our glorious fantasies."

"And what did you write?"

"Oh, all the usual things. Girlish dreams."

"*Lohengrin* and trailing veils?"

She laughed softly in her throat and shrugged.

"You never said that before. If you wanted all those things, why did you argue earlier?"

"Because the traditional things will only be empty and depressing if all they do is create a front for what's missing."

"Hearts and flowers?"

She had never seen him this mellow before. Again she wondered what it would be like with him if this were real. "Don't mistake my meaning if I say yes."

He moved away slightly, squaring himself in the seat. "I won't. Do you assume that men don't want the same things?"

"I never thought about what men want."

"Would it surprise you to learn that I've recently done some wishing of my own?"

Yes, she thought, yes, it would. Have I robbed you of your dreams? She stole a glance at his profile. It was a very appealing profile, one she had looked at directly very few times. It wore an amenable expression now.

"Did you?" she asked at last, unable to stop the question.

"A little, yes. Mostly hindsight, you know."

She tried for an understanding note as she observed, "You

really don't like being a disappointment to your parents in any way, do you?"

"No."

She didn't want to seem prying, yet she had to know—it had been bothering her for so long. She took a careful breath, held it, and finally asked softly, looking down at her lap, "This other girl you've been going with . . . Jill . . . she's the one they hoped you'd marry, isn't she?"

He turned, saw the way she idled her fingers back and forth across her purse, staring down. She looked up and their eyes met.

"Maybe. I don't know." But he squared his shoulders and studied the lights on the dashboard again. A muscle in Catherine's stomach set up a light twitching. A little trail of guilt went weaseling its way upward.

"Maybe they'll get their wish when this is all over," she said.

"No, it'll never happen now."

They'd talked about it, then, Clay and Jill. Maybe this wedding would be his only chance to be feted in the recognized style. He seemed to be admitting that it bothered him. But just as Catherine came to that conclusion he spoke.

"You make the choice about the wedding, and whatever you want, it'll be okay with me. Mother will just have to accept it, that's all. But she'll be making plans in her head, so I'd like to tell her your decision as soon as possible."

"It's your wedding, too, Clay," she said quietly, undone by what she'd guessed about his feelings.

"Weddings are mostly women's doings. You make the arrangements."

"I . . . th-thank you."

"You know, it seems like every time I drop you off here, it's to give you a limited time to come to some monumental decision."

"But I've got plenty of helpers inside to help me with this one."

He chuckled. "A whole houseful of pregnant, unmarried teenagers. I can imagine how unbiased their advice will be. They're probably still pinning curtains on their heads for veils."

Catherine thought of how utterly close to the truth he was. The rain pattered on the roof, the windows had steamed up. It was warm and insular in the car, and for a minute, Catherine did not want to get out, back to reality again.

"Whatever you decide is okay, huh?" he said. "And don't let those kids talk you into anything."

He reached for his door handle, but she quickly insisted that he stay in the car. She could make it to the house just fine. When she reached to open her door, he stopped her by saying, "Catherine?"

She turned.

"It's been . . . well, I was going to say fun, but maybe I should just say better. It's been better, talking without arguing. I think we needed this."

"I think we did too."

But, getting out of his car, running to the house, Catherine knew she lied. She didn't need this at all, not at all. Oh, God, she was beginning to like Clay Forrester.

Marie was still awake, waiting, when Catherine came inside, and though she hadn't intended to, Catherine found herself admitting, "I'm going to marry Clay Forrester."

Pandemonium broke loose! Marie leaped up, hit the light switch, bounded to the center of her bed and bugled, *Wake up everybody! Catherine's getting married!"* In no time at all the place was a madhouse—everybody whooping, rejoicing, jumping and hugging.

Mrs. Tollefson called from the bottom of the stairs, "What's going on up there?" and joined the fracas to congratulate Catherine, then offered to make cocoa for everyone.

It took an hour for things to settle down, but during that time some of the girls' undaunted enthusiasm crept into Catherine. Maybe it began while they hugged her and—for the first time—she found herself unreservedly hugging back. They seemed to have given her some indefinable gift, and even now, lying in bed, wide awake, she was not sure what it was.

Marie's voice came quietly from across the way. "Hey, you asleep?"

"No."

"Give me your hand, huh?"

Catherine reached and in the dark her fingers were grasped by Marie's. There was silence then, but Catherine knew Marie, the always gay, always cheery Marie, was crying.

Chapter 11

THE FOLLOWING AFTERNOON Clay called before Catherine got home and left a message saying his mother had invited her out to the house for dinner, so would Catherine please not eat at Horizons? He'd be there to pick her up around six thirty.

Speculation ran rampant among the Horizons residents, who swarmed all over Catherine as she came in the door. When she admitted she was going there to make wedding plans, wide eyes gaped at her from every angle. "You mean they want a *real* wedding . . . *the Real McCoy!*"

The Real McCoy, it seemed, was exactly what Angela Forrester had in mind. From the moment Catherine put herself into Angela's hands, she sensed what Angela had called an "intimate affair" was destined to be an extravaganza.

Yet it was hard to resist the charming Angela, with her laugh like the song inside a Swiss music box and her constant striving to put Catherine at ease and her unaffected touches, especially for Claiborne. From the first Catherine noted how the two touched, lovingly, without conscious thought, as her parents never had, and how Angela always called him *darling* and he called her *dear*. "Isn't it wonderful, darling, we'll have a wedding here after all," Angela fairly sang.

Though the details made Catherine's head swim, she drifted along with Angela's irresistible tide of plans for caterer, florist, photographer, even engraved invitations.

There were times during the following days when Claiborne thought his wife guilty of bulldozing. But Catherine gave Angie full sway. Sometimes he met the girl's eyes and read in them a hint of helplessness. Maybe it was this, and the fact that she understood what the wedding meant to Angie, which began to make Claiborne look at the girl differently.

The subject of the guest list was the first at which Catherine assertively gainsaid Angela by refusing to have Herb Anderson included.

"But, Catherine, he's your father."

"I won't have him here," Catherine stated vehemently, and stuck to it. The Forresters were surprised when Catherine said she wanted her brother Steve to give her away. They hadn't known she had a brother stationed at Nellis Air Force Base in Las Vegas.

In her turn, Catherine was surprised at Angela's lack of compunction in inviting the residents of Horizons.

Catherine stammered, "B-but they're all pregnant."

Angela only laughed and inquired charmingly, "Are they too big to fit in my house?" That issue settled, Angela suggested Catherine call her brother immediately, using the phone in the study.

Catherine sat in the deep leather desk chair. Dialing, waiting for the phone to ring, she felt the empty longing which always overtook her at thoughts of Steve. She thought of the photographs he'd sent over the last six years, of how, during that time, he'd grown from a lean boy into a full-grown man, and she'd missed it all.

A crisp voice answered her ring. "Staff Sergeant Steven Anderson here."

"S-Steve?" she asked, a little breathlessly.

"Yes?" A brief hesitation, then, "Who's—Cathy? Babe, is that you?"

"Yes, it's me. But nobody's called me babe for a long time."

"Cathy, where are you?" he inquired with undisguised eagerness.

She glanced around the shadowed, private study, knowing

Steve wouldn't believe it if she described her whereabouts fully. "I'm in Minnesota."

"Is anything wrong?"

"No, nothing. I just wanted to call instead of writing." Phone calls were costly and rare; Catherine reminded herself to thank Mr. and Mrs. Forrester.

"It's so good to hear your voice. How are you?"

"Me?" She was close to tears. "Oh, I'm . . . why, I'm in clover."

"Hey, you sound a little shaky. Are you sure nothing's wrong?"

"No, no. I just have some news that couldn't wait."

"Yeah? Well, out with it."

"I'm getting married." As she said the words Catherine smiled.

"What! A skinny, flat-chested sack of bones like you?"

She laughed shakily. "I'm not anymore. You haven't seen me for a long time."

"I got your graduation picture so I know you're telling the truth. Hey, congratulations. And you're in college now too. Lots of changes, huh?"

"Yeah . . . lots." Her eyes dropped to the rich leather of the desk top.

"So when's the big day?"

"Soon. November fifteenth, in fact."

"But that's only a couple weeks away!"

"Three. Can you make it home?" Catherine held her breath, waiting.

The line hummed momentarily before he repeated skeptically, "Home?"

She said pleadingly, "You wouldn't have to stay at the house, Steve." When he didn't reply, she asked, "Is there any chance of you getting here?"

"What about the old man?" A coldness had crept into Steve's voice.

"He won't be there, I promise you. Only Mom and Aunt Ella and Uncle Frank and Bobbi, of course."

"Listen, I'll try like hell. How are they all? How's Mom?"

"The same. Nothing much has changed."

"She's still living with him, huh?"

"Yes, still." She rested her forehead on her knuckles a moment, then picked up the letter opener from Claiborne's desk and began toying with it. "I gave up trying to convince her to leave him, Steve. He's the same as he ever was, but she's too scared of him to make a move. You know how he is."

"Cathy, maybe if I come back there the two of us together can get her to see some sense."

"Maybe . . . I don't know. Nothing's any different, Steve. You might as well know that. I don't think she'll ever admit how she hates him."

Steve injected a false brightness into his voice. "Listen, Cathy, don't worry about it, okay? I mean, this is your time to be happy, okay? So, tell me about your husband-to-be. What's his name, what's he like?"

The question disconcerted Catherine who had never tried to put Clay into a nutshell. Her first instinct was to answer, "He's rich." But she was startled to learn there was much which mattered more. "Well . . ." She leaned back in the tilting desk chair and considered. "His name is Clay Forrester. He's twenty-five, and in his last year of law school at the U of M. Then he plans to go into practice with his father. He's . . . well . . . smart, polite, well-dressed, and not too hard on the eyes." She smiled a little at this admission. "And he has a very proper family, no brothers and sisters, but his father and mother, who want to have the wedding at their house. I'm at their house now."

"Where do they live, in the old neighborhood?"

"No." Catherine tapped the letter opener against the tip of her nose, leaning back and looking at the ceiling. "In Edina."

There was an expressive pause, then, "Well, well . . . what do y' know about that? My kid sister marrying into Old Establishment. How did you manage that, babe?"

"I-I'm afraid I managed that by becoming slightly pregnant."

"Preg—oh, well, it . . . it was none of my business. I didn't mean to—"

"No need to sound so embarrassed, Steve. You'd find out sooner or later anyway."

"I'll bet the old man had plenty to say about that, huh?"

"Don't mention it."

"Have they met him yet, the Forresters?"

Catherine recalled the small scar that still showed above Clay's eyebrow. "I'm afraid so."

"I suppose the old man thinks his ship came in this time, huh?"

"Your memory is right on target. It's been hell around here. I moved out of the house to get away from him."

"I can just imagine what he was like."

"Hey, listen, he's *not* coming to the wedding, understand? I won't have him there. I don't owe him a thing! This is one time in my life that the choice is mine, and I intend to exercise it!"

"What about Mom?"

"I haven't told her yet, but she's next. I don't know if she'll budge without him. You know how she is."

"Tell her I'll do my best to be there and take her, maybe that way she'll go."

"When will you know for sure if you can get leave?"

"In a few days. I'll put in for it right away."

"Steve?"

"Yeah?"

Catherine came forward on her chair, blinking dangerously fast, her lips compressed with emotion until at last she stammered, "I—I want you here . . . s-so bad." She dropped the letter opener, spanned her forehead with her hand, fighting tears.

"Hey, babe, are you crying? What's the matter? Cathy?"

"N-no, I'm not crying. I n-never cry. We agreed to give that up long ago, remember? It's just so damn good to hear your voice and I miss you. After six years I st-still miss you. You were the only good thing around that place."

After a long, intense silence Steve said shakily, "Listen, babe, I'll make it. One way or another, I'll make it. That's a promise."

"Hey, listen, I've got to go. I mean, I don't want to run up the phone bill here any more than I have to." She gave him the number at Horizons.

Just before they hung up, he said, "God, I'm happy for you. And tell Mom hi, and tell Clay Forrester thanks, huh?"

Catherine wilted back against the high leather chair; her eyes slipped closed and she rode the swells of memory. She and Steve, childhood allies, sharing promises of never-ending support. Steve, a freckle-nosed boy of thirteen, standing up to Herb for her, regardless of his fear of the man. Steve and Cathy, children, huddling together, waiting to see who the old man's wrath would be turned on this time; Cathy's tears when it was Steve's turn to take a licking; Steve's tears when it was Cathy's; their trembling, tearless terror when it was their mother's turn; their mute agony of helplessness. But as long as they had each other they could bear it. But then came the day Steve left, the day he was old enough. She relived again her dread sense of desertion when he was so quickly gone for good. She felt again the desolation of being the one left behind in that house where there was only hatred and fear.

"Catherine?"

Her eyes flew open at Clay's soft question. She sprang forward as if he'd caught her rifling the desk drawers. He stood in the doorway, one hand in the pocket of his trousers as if he'd been studying her for some time. He came into the dim room, and she spun to face the shuttered window as two tears scraped down to her lashes and she covertly wiped them away.

"Couldn't you reach him?"

"Y-yes, I reached him."

"Then what's wrong?"

"Nothing. He's going to put in for leave immediately."

"Then why are you upset?"

"I'm not." But she could barely get the two words out. She was uneasy knowing Clay studied her silently. His tone, when at last he spoke, was concerned and gentle.

"Do you want to talk about it, Catherine?"

"No," she answered stiffly, wanting nothing so much as to turn to him and spill out all the hurtful memories of the past, to exorcize them at last. But she found she could not, especially not to Clay Forrester, when he was only passing through her life.

Clay studied her back, recognizing the defensive stance, squared shoulders and proud set of head. How unapproachable she could make herself when she wanted to. Still, he wondered, if he crossed the short distance of the room and touched her shoulders, what would she do? For a moment he was tempted to try it, sensing her utter aloneness in whatever it was she was suffering. But before he could move, she spoke.

"Clay, I'd like to make my own dress for the wedding. I'd like to provide at least that much."

"Have I given you the impression I'll object to anything?" He couldn't help but wonder what had brought on this abrupt defensiveness again. She turned to face him.

"No, you haven't, you've been more than compromising. I only want to make sure I don't shame you before your guests in a homemade dress."

She saw questions flit through his eyes, knew he was puzzled, but how could she explain to him her need to lash out sometimes, when she didn't fully understand it herself? What was she challenging? His place in society? His safe, secure, loved upbringing? Or the fact that he'd caught her with her defenses down a moment ago?

"You don't need my permission," he said quietly, and she suddenly felt sheepish. "Do you need any money to buy things for it?"

She felt the red creep up her neck. "No. I have some saved for next quarter's tuition I won't be needing."

Now it was his turn to feel slightly uncomfortable.

Although the days before the wedding were interrupted by these emotional point counterpoints, on the whole, Clay and Catherine grew increasingly comfortable with each other. There were even times when their moods were undeniably gay, like the following night when they called Bobbi and Stu to ask them to be attendants at the wedding. Clay had settled comfortably on the loveseat in the Forrester study, to eavesdrop, he admitted. Dialing the phone, Catherine grinned, glanced up and couldn't resist revealing, "Bobbi considers you quite a catch, you know." He only smirked, stretched out comfortably with both hands locked behind his head and settled down to listen to one side of the conversation.

"Hi, this is Catherine . . . No, everything's just fine . . . No, I'm not . . . as a matter of fact, I'm out at Clay's house . . . Yes,

Clay Forrester"—The corners of Clay's mouth tipped up amusedly—"Well, he brought me out to have supper with his parents"—Catherine's eyes met his—"what do you think I'm doing? . . . Yes, a few times . . . He ran into me on campus and followed me there . . . You might call it that . . . No, he's been very polite, nothing like that"— Catherine wanted to wipe the smirk off Clay's face—"Bobbi, prepare yourself, you're in for a shock. Clay and I have decided to get married and I want you to be my maid of honor"—Catherine covered the mouthpiece, made silly eyes at Clay and let Bobbi rave on a moment—"Well, I am, I mean, I called as soon as we decided . . . Stu . . . Yes, he just talked to him . . . Steve is going to try to make it home, too . . . In three weeks, on the fifteenth . . . I know, I know, we'll have to find a dress for you . . . Listen, I'll talk to you tomorrow. I just wanted to let you know right away."

When Catherine hung up, her eyes met Clay's, and they both burst out laughing.

"That must have been quite a jolt to old Bobbi, huh?" He sat as before, amusement painted all over his face.

"Well, you heard her, didn't you?" Catherine's expression was perhaps a little bedeviling.

"And after all her efforts to keep your whereabouts a secret," he mocked.

"Did you have to sit there smirking all through my conversation?"

"Well, you sat there smirking through mine." He noted she was still doing so.

"Yes, but guys react differently than girls."

He arose lazily, sauntered toward Catherine and pressed his palms to the desk top, leaning forward as he teased, "Just getting to know my . . . bride, is all. See how she works under pressure." His gray eyes sparkled into hers.

He had never called her his bride before. It conjured up intimacy and made secret shivers tiptoe down Catherine's spine. She turned the chair aside, slid to her feet and pressed her blouse against her still-flat stomach, looking down at it. "Give me six months or so and you'll see precisely how I work under pressure."

Then she gave him one of her first genuine smiles. He thought if she'd be this way more often, the coming months could be enjoyable for both of them.

Catherine's adamant refusal to have her father at the wedding left Angela in a quandary. There was only one way she could think of to see that Herb Anderson was tidily out of the way the day of the wedding. When she tactfully brought it up to Claiborne, he reluctantly admitted the idea had been on his mind too. There was no guarantee it would work. Three weeks was a very short time; there was no assurance the case could be fitted on the docket that soon; there was no guarantee Anderson would be found guilty or be given a sentence.

But just to tip the scales, Claiborne hired the finest criminal lawyer in the twin cities. If Leon Harkness couldn't do the trick, no lawyer could.

Chapter 12

ADA ANDERSON WORKED the day shift at the Munsingwear plant on Lyndale Avenue on the north side of Minneapolis. She had worked there so long the place and its surrounding area no longer affected her. Its utilitarian setting in a dismal commercial zone, its clattery workrooms and changelessness were what she'd come to expect. But Catherine, getting off the city bus, looking up at the building, was hit by a wave of desolation at the tought of how long her mother had labored there, sewing pockets onto T-shirts and waistbands onto briefs. The factory had always depressed Catherine, but it was the only place she could talk to her mother and be sure she wouldn't run the risk of bumping into the old man.

Ada came scuffing out of the noisy, lint-strewn room with a look of fear on her simple face, put there by the fact that her supervisor had called her away from her machine to see a visitor—something highly unusual in this place. The moment Ada saw Catherine the fear disappeared, to be replaced by a smile with more seams than Ada Anderson had stitched in her sixteen years in this place.

"Why, Catherine," Ada said in that tired, surprised way.

"Hello, Mom."

"Why, I thought you was gone someplace out west."

"No, Mom, I've been in the city all the time. I just didn't want Daddy to know I was here."

"He's been awful mad about you running off."

Catherine would have welcomed a hug, but there was none, only her mother's tired acceptance of the way things were.

"Did he . . . has he taken it out on you, Mom?"

"No. Just on the bottle. Hasn't been sober a day since you left."

"Mom, is there somewhere we can sit down?"

"I don't know, honey, I don't get a break yet for another thirty minutes or so."

"How about the lunchroom?"

"Well, there's always the girls in there, and they got big ears, if y'know what I mean."

"Could we at least get away from the noise? Out on the stairway maybe?"

"Just a minute, I'll ask."

Something cracked in Catherine, some fissure of irritation at her mother's spinelessness. Not even here, after sixteen years, not even given the situation which should mean so much to her, could she simply take command and step away for a while.

"For heaven's sake, Mother. You mean you have to ask for five minutes away from your machine?"

Ada touched her chin in a feeble, troubled way, making Catherine instantly sorry for attacking her for something Ada was perhaps helpless to change in herself. Quickly Catherine touched her mother's arm. "Ask then, go ahead. I'll wait."

When they were out on the steps and the noise became a muffled clatter behind them, it somehow seemed an appropriate background for this worn woman who looked fifteen years older than she was. Catherine suddenly thought of it as a song of lament for the defeated. A surge of tenderness overtook her.

"Come on, Mom, let's just sit down here, okay? What'd you do to your finger?" There was a bandage on Ada's right index finger.

"Wasn't nothing much. I ran it under the machine last week. You'd think I'd've had more sense after all this time. They

158

said I had to have a tetanus shot, though, and that was worse than this."

Catherine wondered if her running away, then, had distracted her mother that much. "I didn't mean to make you worry, Mom. I just didn't know how to keep Daddy off my back. I thought he'd track me down at college and start making trouble for me again and for the Forresters. I thought that if he thought I was gone where he couldn't find me, he'd let it go. But he didn't."

"I tried to tell him he'd best let up, Catherine. I tried to tell him. 'Herb,' I says, 'you can't go badgerin' people like them Forresters. They ain't gonna put up with it.' But he went there and he beat up that young man and spent the night in jail. He started drinkin' worse than ever after that, and now he walks around whisperin' to himself about how he's gonna get them to pay up. It scares me. You know how he is. I says to him, 'Herb, you're gonna make yourself sick if you keep this up.'"

"Mom, he is sick. Don't you understand that by now?"

"Don't say that, honey . . . don't say things like that." The fear was back in Ada's eyes. She glanced skittishly away. "He's bound to slack off pretty soon."

"Pretty soon? Mom, you've been saying that for as long as I can remember. Why do you put up with it?"

"There's nothing else I can do."

"You could leave," Catherine said softly.

Again Ada's eyes did what Catherine expected. They grew fearful and twitchy. "Why, where would I go, honey? He wouldn't let me go nowheres."

"I'll help you any way I can. I told you I'd find out what needs to be done to get help for him. There are places, Mom, right here in the city, that could help him."

"No, no," Ada insisted in her pathetically fierce way, "that wouldn't do any good. He'd just come out and be worse than ever. I know Herb."

Catherine thought of the Johnson Institute right at their fingertips, where help could be had for a phone call. But she gave up the argument which was, by now, as shopworn as Ada herself, defeated once again by her mother's self-inflicted blindness.

159

"Listen, Mom, I have some good news."

"Some good news?" Even when her eyes registered hope they looked sad.

"I'm not exactly sure how it happened, but I'm going to marry Clay Forrester."

Catherine held both of her mother's hands, rubbing her thumbs across the shiny surfaces where the skin seemed so thin the veins looked exposed. The expression on Ada's face visibly brightened.

"You're going to marry him, honey?"

Catherine nodded her head. Her mother at last squeezed her hands.

"Marry that handsome young man who said he didn't know you? How can that be?"

"I've been seeing him, Mom, and I've been back to his house several times and have talked with his parents and they're really quite nice. They've been very understanding and helpful. Can you believe it, Mom? I'm going to have a real wedding in that beautiful house of theirs."

"A real wedding?" Ada touched Catherine's cheek while her own eyes turned glossy. "Why, honey . . ." Again she squeezed Catherine's hand. "So that's where you run off to, to that young man of yours. Well, isn't that something."

"No, Mom, I've been living out near the campus, and I've made lots of new friends, and I've seen Bobbi, and she's been letting me know how you've been all along."

"You don't have to worry about me, honey. You know I always end up on my feet. But you, look at you, ain't you something. A real wedding." Ada reached into her pocket and found a tissue and dabbed at her rheumy eyes. "Listen, honey, I got a little money saved, not much, but—"

"Shh, Mom. You don't have to worry about paying for anything. It's all taken care of."

"But you're my baby, my own little girl. It should be me that—"

"Mother, the Forresters want to take care of it, honest. I could have eloped if I'd wanted to, but Mrs. Forrester . . . well, she's really on our side, Mom. I've never met anyone like her."

"Oh, she's a fine lady all right."

"Mom, I want you there at the wedding."

Startled eyes were raised to meet Catherine's. "Oh, no, honey, why, I would never fit in that place. I couldn't."

"Listen, Mom. Steve's coming."

Surprise held Ada's tongue a moment before she repeated disbelievingly, "Steve?" Her eyes turned alight with that inextinguishable flicker of mother-love. "You talked to Steve?"

"Yes, and he's going to try to come home."

"Come home?"

Together they counted back six years.

"Yes, Mom. And he said to tell you he'll take you to the wedding with him. That's what I came to tell you."

"Steve . . . coming home?" But at the thought Ada raised those tentative fingers to her lips again. "Oh, but there'll be trouble. Herb and Steve . . ." Her eyes dropped down to her lap.

"Daddy's never going to know. Steve and you are coming to the wedding, but not Daddy." Determinedly Catherine squeezed her mother's hands.

"But I don't see how."

"Please, Mom, please listen. You can tell him you're going to play Saturday bingo like you do sometimes. I want you at my wedding, but you can see that if he came too, it would only mean trouble, can't you?"

"But he'll know, honey, he'll guess. You know how he is."

"He won't know if you don't tell him, not if you just walk out like you're meeting Mrs. Murphy for bingo like you've done a hundred Saturdays before."

"But he's got that sixth sense. He's always had it."

"Mama, Steve's not coming to the house, you know that, don't you? He swore when he left that he'd never set foot in it again, and he hasn't changed his mind. If you want to see Steve, you'll have to see him at my wedding."

"Is he all right?"

"He's just fine. He sounded really happy and asked how you are and said to give you his love."

"Steve's twenty-two now." Ada's mind seemed to drift away into the racket of the machines from the workroom. The rhythmic clack and thump accompanied her lost thoughts while she hovered on the steps with her knees almost touching her daughter's. The lines of fatigue on her face could not be smoothed, but as she reached back in time, thoughts of her son placed some new determination in the network of wrinkles about her lips. When she raised her eyes to Catherine again, she said, "Twyla's got a bolt of blue knit in the remnant room'd make me a pretty nice dress. I get it at employee's discount, you know."

"Oh, do you mean it, Mom?" Catherine smiled.

"I want to see Steve, and I want to see my little girl's wedding. Why, stitching up a dress ain't nothing to me after all the years I put in here."

"Thank you." Impulsively Catherine leaned forward to hug her mother briefly around the thin shoulders.

"I'd best get back now, or my daily quota will be low."

Catherine nodded.

"I won't say a word to Herb this time, you'll see."

"Good. And I'll let you know if Steve calls again."

Ada braced hands to knees as she creaked to her feet. "I'm glad you come, honey. I didn't like to think of you off acrosst the country someplace like Steve." She climbed two stairs, then turned around, looking down at Catherine.

"Is it gonna be the kind with flowers and cake and a white dress for you?"

"Yes, Mom, it is."

"Well, feature that," Ada said thoughtfully. Then she stopped to do so, with the expression of wonder growing grander by the minute upon her time-worn features. "Just feature that," she repeated, as if to herself.

And for the first time, Catherine was fully, totally, one hundred percent happy that she'd gone along with all of Angela Forrester's wishes.

The invitations were ice-blue, embossed with rich, ivory letters of finest English Roundhand that pirouetted across the marbled parchment like the steps of a dancer. As she lifted a card from the box, it crackled like the dancer's crinoline beneath Catherine's fingers. She touched a raised character, ran her fingertips lightly along a line, as the blind read braille. The ascenders and descenders formed graceful swirls that rose up to meet her searching touch.

You can feel these words, Catherine thought, you can feel them.

Awe-filled, she studied the invitation, not quite accustomed yet to everything that was happening so fast. The words read in that formal lexicon peculiar to occasions that mark the steppingstones of life:

Catherine Marie Anderson
and
Clay Elgin Forrester
invite you to share in their joy
as they celebrate
the solemnization of their marriage vows
at seven P.M. on November fifteenth
at the home of Claiborne and Angela Forrester
Number Seventy Nine
Highview Place
Edina, Minnesota

Again, Catherine grazed the words with her fingertips. But with a woeful sense of yearning she thought, yes, the words can be felt, but it is not enough to feel only with the fingertips.

Chapter 13

BY NOW CATHERINE and Clay could meet in the front hall of Horizons and display a friendly familiarity that lacked the edginess of those first couple of meetings. Catherine invariably found herself scanning his clothing, invariably, too, found herself pleased by what greeted her. Likewise, Clay found himself approving of her appearance. Her clothes were neat, if unostentatious, and she wore them well. He watched for a first sign of roundness on her, but so far none was showing.

"Hi," he said now, while his eyes performed that first perusal which she'd come to expect. "How are you holding up?"

She struck a pose. "How does it look like I'm holding up?"

He glanced once again over the plum wool dress, loose-belted, trimmed with top-stitched pockets at hip and chest.

"Looks like you're doing fine. Nice dress."

She dropped her pose, wondering if she'd done that on purpose to wrest a compliment from him. She found his approval pleasing. But since that night she'd fallen asleep on the way home, they had each made a conscious effort to be nicer to each other.

"Thank you."

"You're going to meet my grandparents tonight."

By now she could manage to be less alarmed at such announcements. Still, this one made her slightly apprehensive.

"Do I have to?"

"They come with the package, I'm afraid."

Her eyes moved down his length. "The package, as usual, is wrapped to perfection." And so it was, in bone colored pleated trousers and a complementary Harris Tweed sportcoat with suede elbow patches.

It was the first compliment she'd ever paid him. He smiled, suddenly warm inside.

"Thanks, glad you approve. Now let's hope my grandparents do."

"The way you put that sounds forbidding."

"No, not really. But then, I've known them all my life. My Grandmother Forrester is a crusty old gal though. You'll see what I mean."

Just then Little Bit came downstairs, stopped and hung over the banister halfway down. "Hi, Clay!"

"Hi, Little Bit. Is it okay if I take her for a while?" he asked, teasingly.

"Why don't you take me instead tonight?" Little Bit swooned farther over the railing. The girls had given up trying to hide their fascination with Clay.

But at that minute Marie came down the steps. "Who's taking you where? Oh, hi, Clay."

"Do something with that child, will you, before she drops on her head and gives birth to a dimwit?"

Marie laughed and slapped Little Bit lightly on the rump as she passed behind her. They both came the rest of the way downstairs.

"Where you off to tonight?" Marie asked, eyeing them appreciatively.

"To my house."

"Yeah? What's the occasion this time?"

"Another one of the seven tortures. Grandparents, I'm afraid."

Marie raised an eyebrow, took Little Bit's hand to tug her off toward the kitchen while giving Catherine one last conspiratorial glance over the shoulder. "Lucky thing you decided to wear your newest creation, huh, Cath?"

Clay looked the dress over a second time, with greater interest.

"We do have nimble fingers, don't we?" he asked, and without winking, gave the impression he had.

"Yes, we do. Of necessity." And Catherine laid a hand lightly upon her stomach. Smiling with Clay, she felt a little happy, a little venturesome.

Something had changed between them. The lurking sense of anger and entrapment had begun to wane. They treated each other civilly, and occasional spurts of repartee such as this were becoming more frequent.

By the time Clay turned into his parents' driveway full dark had fallen. The headlights picked out the herringbone design of red bricks while upon them the tires hummed the note that by now Catherine unconsciously listened for.

The yard was dressed for winter. Leaves were but memories, while tree trunks were swathed in white leggings. The shrubs had hunched their shoulders and pulled mulch-quilts up beneath their chins. An occasional pyramidal bush was laced into winter bindings like an Indian papoose.

The house was lit from within and without. Catherine glanced at the twin carriage lanterns on either side of the front door, then down at the tips of her high heels as she approached the house. Her pocketed hands hugged her coat close as she tried to keep her growing apprehension from getting the best of her. Without warning, from behind, Clay's fingers circled her neck, closing lightly in a warm grip.

"Hey, wait, I have to talk to you before we go in."

At his touch, she instantly turned, surprised. He left both hands on her shoulders with his thumbs pressing her coat collar against each side of her windpipe. Catherine needn't say it for him to be reminded that she'd rather not be touched this way.

"Sorry," he said, immediately raising his palms.

"What is it?"

"Just a technicality." Gingerly he inserted a single index finger into her coat sleeve, tugging until the hand came out of her coat pocket. "There's no ring on this." Her bare hand dangled out of the sleeve. While he looked at it, the fingers suddenly clenched protectively, shutting the thumb inside.

"Grandmothers tend to become suspicious when they don't

see what they expect to see," he noted wryly.

"And what do they expect to see?"

"This."

Still holding her coat sleeve, he lifted his other hand to reveal a jeweled ring riding the first knuckle of his little finger. In the meager light from the carriage lanterns it wasn't at first evident exactly what it looked like. Clay wiggled the finger a little and the gems glittered. Catherine's eyes were drawn to it as if he were a hypnotist using it to mesmerize her. Her mouth went dry.

It's so big! she thought, horrified. "Do I have to?"

He commanded her hand, sliding the ring onto the proper finger. "I'm afraid so. It's family tradition. You'll be the fourth generation to wear it."

With the ring not quite on, she gripped his fingers, stopping them, feeling the ring cut into her.

"This game is going too far," she whispered.

"The significance of a ring is in the mind of its wearer, Catherine, not in the fact that it's on a hand."

"But how can I wear this with three generations behind it?"

"Just pretend you got it in a box of Cracker Jacks," he said unconcernedly, completing the adornment of her third finger, pushing the ring all the way on. Then he dropped her cold fingers.

"Clay, this ring is worth thousands of dollars. You know it and I know it, and it is not right that I'm wearing it."

"But you'll have to anyway. If it helps to relieve your mind, remember that the Forrester side of the family made a business of gems before my father broke the tradition and went into law. Grandmother Forrester still owns a thriving business, which she refused to relinquish when Grandfather died. There are hundreds more where this came from."

"But not with this one's significance."

"So, humor an old lady." Clay smiled and shrugged.

She had no choice. Neither did she have a choice when, in the entry after he'd taken her coat, Clay returned and laced his hand half around her neck in that careless way of his. That was how they entered the living room, with him affectionately herding her along and Catherine doing her best to keep resilient under his touch.

They approached first a withered little pair of people who were dressed formally and sat side by side on a velveteen sofa. The man wore a black suit and looked like an aged orchestra conductor. The woman, in mauve lace, wore a little twinkling smile that looked as if she'd donned it seventy years ago and hadn't taken it off since. Approaching the pair, Catherine felt Clay's hand slide down her back, linger at her waist, then depart as he bent to take the woman's cheeks in both hands and plop a direct, noisy kiss on her mouth.

"Hi, sweetheart," he said irreverently. Catherine could have sworn the old girl actually blushed as she looked up at Clay. Then she twinkled as she shook a crooked, arthritic finger at him—her only greeting.

"Hello, sonny," the grandfather greeted him. "You get your grandma more excited with that word than I can anymore." Clay's hearty laugh swept the two.

"So, Granddad, are you jealous?" He put an arm around the shoulders of the bald man who might have been stepping up to a podium with his aging slump. To Catherine's surprise, the two embraced unabashedly, chuckling together.

"I want you both to meet Catherine." Clay turned back, reached out a palm and drew her forward. "Catherine, this is Grandma and Grandpa Elgin, better known around here as Sophie and Granddad."

"Hello," Catherine said, smiling easily, squeezing each parchment hand in turn. Sophie's and Granddad's smiles were so alike it was like seeing double.

Then Clay captured her elbow, turning her toward a woman who sat with a matriarchal air in a high-backed chair that need not be a throne to bespeak the woman's regal mien. The feeling was there. It permeated the very air about her. It was evident in her bearing, her facial expression, the faultless blue-white waves that crested her head, the shrewd eyes, the glitter flashing from her fingers and the glacial assessment she gave Catherine.

Before Clay could speak, the woman pierced him with an arch, amused look.

"Don't try those flirtatious tactics with me, young man. I'm not the blushing fool your Grandmother Sophie might be."

"Never, Grandmother," assured Clay, wearing a devilish

grin as he lifted one of her bejeweled hands and bent over it quite correctly. He made as if to kiss its blue-veined back, but at the last minute, turned it over and kissed the base of her thumb.

Catherine found herself amused at these cat-and-mouse goings-on. The old lady's mouth pursed to keep from smiling outright.

"I've brought Catherine to meet you," Clay said, dropping the hand, but not the half-smile. Again he urged Catherine near with a slight touch on her elbow. "Catherine, this is my Grandmother Forrester. I never call her by her first name for some reason."

"Mrs. Forrester," Catherine repeated, while her hand disappeared within all those flashing gems.

"My grandson is a precocious young upstart. You'd do well to watch your p's and q's around him, young lady."

"I intend to, Ma'am," Catherine rejoined, wondering what the old lady would think if she knew the extent to which p's and q's would need to be watched in the months ahead.

Mrs. Forrester raised an ivory-headed cane and tapped Catherine's shoulder lightly, perusing her with gray irises from beneath one straight eyebrow and one that was cocked in an aristocratic arc.

"I like that. I might have answered in just that way myself." She rested the cane on the floor again, crossed her hands upon the ivory elephant with its sapphire eyes, and angled a bemused expression again at her grandson, asking, "Where did you find this perceptive young lady?"

Clay moved a hand lingeringly up and down the inner side of Catherine's elbow while he searched her face and answered his grandmother. "I didn't. She found me." Then his hand trailed down, enclosing hers. Elizabeth Forrester's eyes followed it and registered the way the girl's fingers failed to clasp Clay's. The pair turned toward Claiborne and Angela who were pouring port and making room on a marble-topped table for the silver tray of canapés which Inella carried in at that moment.

Clay had a greeting for Inella too. He dropped a hand on her shoulder as she leaned to set down the tray. "And what kind of epicurean delights have you dreamed up tonight, Inella?

Don't you know Father's been concerned about his waistline?"

Everyone laughed.

"Epicurean delights," scoffed the pleased maid. "Where do you dream up such stuff?" She left, smiling. There followed a full-fledged hug between Clay and his mother and a clasp of hands with his father.

Catherine had never seen so much touching in her life. Nor had she seen Clay in this element before, warm, humorous, obviously loved and loving everyone in the place. The scene gripped her with something akin to envy, yet deep in some part of her, Catherine was slightly intimidated. But she could not pull away as the next warm touch fell her way and Angela's cheek pressed against her own while Claiborne—thankfully—only smiled on, and gave her a friendly verbal greeting.

"Young woman, sit here," ordered Elizabeth Forrester imperiously.

Catherine could do nothing but perch on a loveseat at a right angle to Elizabeth Forrester's chair. She was actually grateful when Clay sat down beside her. His presence somehow made her feel fortified. Elizabeth Forrester's shrewd eagle-eyes assessed Catherine, probing like a laser while she made what appeared on the surface to be inconsequential conversation.

"Catherine . . ." she mused, "what a quaint and lovely name. Not clever and will-o-the-wisp like so many of today's insubstantial titles. I dare say there are many I'd be thoroughly ashamed to be plagued with. You and I, however, have each been preceded in name by an English queen, you know. My given name is Elizabeth."

Catherine wondered if she were being given permission to use the name or being tested to see if she were so presumptuous. Assuming the latter, Catherine consciously used the more formal mode of address.

"I believe, Mrs. Forrester, that the name Elizabeth means 'consecrated to God.'"

The regal eyebrow raised a notch. The girl is astute, thought Elizabeth Forrester. "Ah, so it does, so it does. Catherine . . . is that with a *C* or a *K?*"

"With a *C.*"

"From the Greek then, meaning 'pure.'"

Catherine's stomach did somersaults. Does she *know* or does she *want* to know, Catherine wondered, making a great effort to appear unruffled.

The matriarch observed, "So, you are the one who will carry the Forrester name forward."

Catherine's stomach tightened further. But Clay, whom she didn't know whether to damn or to thank, nestled closely beside her with his thigh against the length of her own, meeting his grandmother's probe directly.

"Yes, she is. But not without some persuasion. I think Catherine was a little put off by me at first. Something to do with our having different stations in life, which I had trouble convincing her didn't matter one damn bit."

My God, thought Catherine, he's actually challenging the old girl!

Understanding that challenge very clearly, Elizabeth Forrester only chided. "In my day, your grandfather didn't pronounce vulgarities in my ear."

Clay only grinned, sparring expertly. "Oh, Grandmother, you're sterling, pure sterling. But this is not your day, and a man can get by with a little more." But then, feeling the muscle of Catherine's leg grow rigid, he dulcified his remark by adding, "*Damn* is hardly considered a vulgarity anymore, not even a crudity."

She merely cocked the eyebrow again.

"Father," Clay said, "bring your mother a glass of port. She's being testy tonight and you know how port always mellows her. Catherine, do you like port?"

"I don't know."

Elizabeth Forrester missed not a word.

"White wine then?" her grandson suggested. The girl's reaction was curious. She attempted to move her thigh away from his. Unconcerned, he arose without waiting for an answer and went to get the wine.

"How long have you known Clay?" his Grandma Sophie asked then, leaning forward with birdlike tentativeness.

"We met this summer."

"Angela says you are sewing your own dress for the wedding."

171

"Yes, but I have lots of help," Catherine answered, realizing too late that she'd left herself open for further questioning.

"Why, how nice. I never could sew a stitch, could I, Angela? Is your mother helping you?" Sophie's manner of speech was exactly the opposite of her counterpart's. Where Elizabeth Forrester was audacious and quizzing, this woman was shy and unassuming. Still, her innocent line of questioning made Catherine again feel boxed into a corner.

"No, some friends of mine are helping me with the dress. I do some sewing to help out with college expenses."

"My, Clay didn't tell us you're in college."

He came to her rescue then, returning with a stem glass of imported German liebfraumilch. As Catherine reached for it, the gems in her ring glittered like the lead crystal glass which held the wine. Before she sipped, she changed hands, resting her left, knuckles-down on her lap.

"Yes, she is. She's a clever girl too. She made the dress she's wearing tonight, Grandma. She's very good with her hands, isn't she?"

Catherine almost choked. Quickly she added, "I also type theses and manuscripts."

"You do? My, my," Grandma Sophie remarked inanely.

"You see, Grandma, now I won't have to pay to have my papers typed this year. That's really why I'm marrying her." He grinned mischievously and laid his hand along the back of the loveseat as he said it, making Sophie's eyes soften in approval.

"Mother," Angela put in, "Clay is up to his usual teasing again. Don't pay any attention to him."

The talk moved on, interspersed with the nibbling of crab-stuffed *petits choux* and marinated mushroom caps. Clay relaxed beside Catherine, his knees lolling wide so there was the ever-present intrusion of his thigh against hers. He kept up the small talk, asked once, close to Catherine's ear, if she didn't like the crab, confirmed that's what it was she was eating, murmured just loud enough that the elder Mrs. Forrester overheard him tell his fiancé there were lots of things he'd teach her to like. He bantered with Elizabeth, teased Sophie, agreed to play racquetball with his father one evening soon, and through it all, managed to act as if he doted on Catherine.

By the time they went to dinner, she was nearly undone. She wasn't used to sitting so close to him, nor being wooed in so obvious a manner for the benefit of others. At the table it went on, for Clay was seated directly beside her, and now and then during the meal he rested his elbow on the back of her chair and spoke trumped-up confidences into her ear in a highly convincing way. He could laugh just softly enough, glance at her just beguilingly enough to make his grandmothers smile at each other over their salmon steaks a la Inella. But long before the meal ended either the steaks or Clay or both had caused Catherine's stomach to begin to churn. Add to that the fact that Elizabeth Forrester brought up the ring, and Catherine wondered if she'd make it through the meal.

"I see Angela has given you the radiant. How wonderful, Angela, to see it on Catherine's hand. What does your family think of it, dear?"

Catherine forced herself to continue cutting a cheese-encrusted Irish potato.

"They haven't seen it yet," she answered truthfully, learning the game quickly, determined not to give the hawk-eyed woman an edge.

"It looks beautiful on such long, slim fingers, don't you think so, Clay?"

Clay picked up Catherine's hand, took the fork from it, kissed it, replaced the fork, and said, "Beautiful."

"Would you like to prick my grandson with that fork, Catherine, just to let a little of that self-satisfied hot air out of him? Your fondling seems to distract Catherine from her eating, Clay."

But it was as much the ring as everything else that was distracting Catherine.

Clay only laughed and delved into his food again. "Grandmother, I think I detect a note of testiness again. Nobody told you you had to pass the ring on to Mother. Would you like it back?"

"Don't be cheeky, Clay. As your bride, Catherine should and will wear the ring. Your grandfather would be thrilled to distraction if he could see it on a girl as beautiful as she."

"I give up. For once you've left me speechless because you're right."

Elizabeth Forrester was left to wonder if her suspicion was correct. The boy seemed incapable of stopping himself from fawning over the girl. Well, time would tell, soon enough.

In the car on the way home Catherine laid her head back against the seat, struggling with each passing mile to control her roiling insides. But halfway there Catherine ordered, "Stop the car!"

Clay turned to find her eyes closed, one hand convulsively gripping the console.

"What is it?"

"Stop the car...*please*."

But they were on the freeway where controlled accesses made it difficult to stop.

"Hey, are you all right?"

"I have to throw up."

An exit ramp beckoned and he pulled over, careened halfway up, drove the car completely over the curb and onto the shoulderless area of grass, then slammed on the brakes. Immediately Catherine rolled out her side of the car. He heard her retching, then she gasped and spit.

Sweat broke out under Clay's armpits. Across his chest the skin grew tight and hot, and saliva pooled beneath his own tongue as if he were the nauseated one. He got out, unsure of what to do, saw her huddled over, her hair hanging down over her cheeks.

"Catherine, are you all right?"

"Do you have a tissue?" she asked shakily.

He came up behind her, reached in his hip pocket and extracted his handkerchief. He handed it to her and took her elbow to lead her a few steps aside.

"This...is your...han...hanky. I can't use...your hanky." Her ordeal had left her fighting for breath.

"Christ, use it...anything. Are you okay now?"

"I don't know." She gulped air like a person coming up for the second time. "Don't you have any tissues?"

"Catherine, this is no time to be polite. Use the damn hanky."

In spite of her wretchedness, it suddenly dawned on Catherine that Clay Forrester swore when he was scared. She swabbed

174

the inside of her mouth with his clean-tasting handkerchief.

"Does this happen often?" His voice was shaky, concerned, and he left a solicitous hand on her arm.

She shook her head, waiting yet, unsure if there was more.

"I thought it only happened in the mornings."

"I think it was the fish and the grandmothers." She tried to laugh a little, but didn't quite succeed, so instead sucked in the starlight.

"Cat, I'm sorry. I didn't know it would be that hard on you or I wouldn't have added to it."

She heard mostly the word *Cat*. God, no, she thought, don't let him call me that. Not that!

"Do you want to go back to the car?" he asked, at a loss, feeling protective toward her, yet utterly useless.

"I think I'll stay here in the air awhile longer. I still feel funny." She refolded the hanky and wiped her forehead with it. He reached to push aside a strand of hair that had caught on her cheek.

"Are you going to keep this up when we're married?" There was a smile in his question, an attempt to make her feel better.

"If I do, I'll wash the hankies for you. I don't know, it's never happened before. I'm sorry if I embarrassed you."

"You didn't embarrass me. I just got scared, that's all. I don't know much about handling retching girls."

"Well, live and learn, huh?"

He smiled, waiting for her to gain her equilibrium again. She ran a shaky hand over her forehead and down one temple. Her stomach was calming down, but Clay's continued touch as he held her arm was unsettling. Wisely, she extricated herself from it.

"Clay, your grandmother Forrester knows." Catherine's voice shook.

"So what?"

"How can you say that when she's so . . . so . . ."

"So what? Dictatorial? She's really not, you know. She loved you, couldn't you tell that?"

"Loved me? . . . *Me?*"

"She's a shrewd old devil, and there's not much she misses. I had no notion of trying to deceive her tonight. Yes, she knows, but she's given you her stamp of approval anyway."

"She chose an odd way to show it."

"People have their ways, Catherine. Hers are . . . well, different from those of Mother's parents, but, believe me, if she hadn't approved, she would never have said what she did about the ring."

"So the ring was a test—that's why you made me wear it tonight?"

"I guess in a way it was. But it's tradition too. They all know that there's no way I'd be taking a bride without putting it on her finger. That was understood before I was ever born."

"Clay, I was . . . well, scared. It was more than just the ring and the way your grandmother quizzed me. I have to be told when I'm eating crabmeat that it's crab and I don't know port wine from a fishing port and I don't know that pink diamonds are called radiants and—"

His unconcerned laughter interrupted her. "A radiant is a cut, not a color, but what does it matter? You foiled the old girl, Catherine, don't you know that? You foiled her by letting her guess the truth and having her approve of you anyway. Why feel scared about that?"

"Because around your family I'm out of my league. I'm like a . . . like a rhinestone among diamonds, can't you see that?"

"You have a surprising lack of confidence lurking behind that composed exterior you usually display. Why do you insist on putting yourself down?"

"I know my place, that's all, and it isn't in the Forrester family."

"It is as long as I say it is, and nobody's going to contest it."

"Clay, we're making a mistake."

"The only mistake made tonight was when you ate Inella's salmon." He touched her shoulder. "Do you think you've finished with your revenge on her?"

She couldn't help smiling. "What *is* it with you that you can be so casual about all this?"

"Catherine, it's only temporary. I made up my mind to enjoy what I can of it, and not to let the rest bother me, that's all. And I'm even learning in the process, so there."

"Learning?"

"Like you said . . . how to handle a pregnant lady." He turned her toward the car. "Come on, I think you're okay now. Get in and I'll drive like a good boy."

Farther down the road, Clay began talking about Sophie and Granddad, reminiscing about them, and the stories he told made Catherine understand where Angela got all her loving ways. Riding with Clay, listening to stories about his youth, she found herself enjoying his company fully.

She laughed once, saying, "I had all I could to keep from bursting out laughing when Granddad called you 'sonny.'" She turned a skeptical grin toward Clay and repeated, *"Sonny?"*

Clay himself laughed. "Well, I guess that's how he'll always think of me. You know, I really love that old dude. When I was little, he used to take me to see the ore boats on Lake Superior. Just him and me. Once he took me up on the train, because he said trains would soon be gone, and I shouldn't miss the chance to ride on one while I could. Saturday afternoons he'd take me to see Disney movies, to museums, all kinds of places. And I'd go to the ballet with both Granddad and Sophie."

"The ballet?" She was genuinely surprised.

"Uh-huh."

"How lucky."

"You've never been to one?"

"No, only dreamed about it."

"I assumed you had, from what you said once about being a ballerina."

"No, you assumed wrong," and for the first time Catherine opened up a portion of her secret regret to him. Not much, but a little—an important little. Like wiping off a tiny peek-through from a dirt-filmed window, she gave him a first glimpse of what was inside. "My dad drank a lot, so there was never any money for the ballet."

Suddenly afraid she should not have said it, she waited for Clay's reaction. She did not want him to think she was eliciting his sympathy. She could feel his gaze on her for a moment before his words made her heart dance against her ribcage.

"There is now," was all he said.

Chapter 14

THE SHORT TRIO of weeks before the wedding, coupled with
the countless necessary arrangements, saw Catherine and Clay
together almost as much as they were apart. The thing Catherine
feared most began to happen: she grew familiar with Clay. She
began expecting things before they happened—to have her car
door opened, her coat held, her fast food paid for. Personal
things about Clay intruded too—the way he always took time
to kid the girls at Horizons before snatching Catherine away
again; the continuing sense of closeness he displayed with his
family; the endless touching about which none of them felt
inhibited; his laugh. He laughed easily, she discovered, and
seemed to accept what was happening far more readily than
Catherine herself was able to.

She grew familiar with the incidental things: the way his
eyes were drawn to the vapor trails of jets; the way he removed
the pickles from his hamburgers but added extra ketchup; the
fact that most of his clothes were brown, that he was slightly
color-blind between browns and greens and sometimes mistakenly chose socks of the wrong color. She came to know his
wardrobe and the scent of him that lingered in his car, until
one evening when it changed it came as a shock that she'd

even detected the change. She learned which of his tapes were favorites, then the particular songs on those tapes that were even more favored.

Then one day he offered her the use of his car to complete all her errands. Her wide blue eyes flew from the keys, dangling off his index finger, to his grinning eyes.

She was speechless.

"What the hell, it's only a car," he said offhandedly.

But it wasn't! Not to Clay. He took care of it the way a trainer takes care of a Kentucky Derby winner and with equally as much pride. His trusting her to drive it was another stitch in the seam of familiarity binding Clay and Catherine ever closer. She saw all this clearly as she stared at the keys. To accept them was to break down another of the barriers between them, this barrier so much more significant than any which had fallen before, for it had delineated their separate rights. Accepting the keys would only meld the two, which was something Catherine sought to avoid.

Yet she took the keys anyway, tempted by the luxury they represented, the freedom, the thrill, telling herself, "One time . . . just this once . . . because there's so much running to do, and it'll be so much easier by car than by bus."

Driving the Corvette, she felt she had usurped Clay's world, the car was so much a part of him. There was a sense of willful intrusion that made her heart race when she placed her hands on the wheel in the precise spot where his usually rested. The feel of her flesh on *his* spot was decidedly intimate, so she quickly reverted to the more cavalier pose with one wrist draped indolently over the wheel, put the machine in motion and turned on the radio, experiencing a heady jolt of freedom when the music poured from the speakers. She even used the horn once, unnecessarily, and laughed aloud at her precociousness. She adjusted the rearview mirror, amazed at how suddenly exotic Minneapolis, Minnesota, looked when viewed in reverse from a white leather bucket seat inside a sleek, silver bullet.

She watched men's heads snap around and women's faces affect expressions of disdain, and allowed herself to feel temporarily superior. She smiled at drivers of other cars while sitting at stop signs. The Corvette was superficial, ostentatious, and somebody else's. But she didn't care. She smiled anyway.

And she took first Marie, then Bobbie, out shopping in it.

And for one day—one magic day—Catherine allowed herself to pretend it was all real. And somehow, for that one day, it was. For that single day Catherine had a taste of the full flush of joy wedding preparations can bring.

The making of Catherine's wedding dress became a "family project" with almost every girl at Horizons sharing the work in some way. Then one day before the gown was finished Little Bit had her baby. It was a girl, but they all knew Little Bit had long ago made the decision for adoption, so nobody spoke much about the baby. When they visited Little Bit in the hospital they spoke of the wedding, the gown, even the Corvette ride. But on the shelf by her bed there was only an ice-blue wedding invitation where there should have been baby cards too.

After that Catherine sensed a new wistfulness when the girls touched her wedding gown. They vied for the right to zip it up the back when Catherine fit it on, touching it with a reverence she found heartbreaking. It was a lovely creation of ivory velvet, with wrist-length sleeves, an Empire waist and a miniature train. The front bodice was gathered at the shoulder and on up the high, tight neck, and draped in soft swags from shoulder to shoulder. Studying her reflection, Catherine could not help wondering what the months ahead would bring.

The plans for Catherine and Clay's immediate future came down to more personal things. They had to think about a place to live and furnishings for it. Once again the fairy-tale aura pervaded as Clay announced his father owned various properties around the twin cities and there were at least three different ones unoccupied. Would Catherine like to look at them?

He took her to a complex of town houses in the suburb of Golden Valley. Catherine stood back, watching Clay fit the key into the lock with an odd thrill of expectation. The door swung open and she stepped inside, hearing the door close behind her. She stood in the foyer of a split-level house. It was disconcertingly silent. Before her, chocolate-carpeted stairs led up one level and down one. Clay touched her arm and she jumped. They walked up the steps, unspeaking, to be greeted by a great open expanse of space which ended in sliding glass doors on the far side of the living room. To her left was a kitchen, to her right the steps leading to the sleeping level. She hadn't expected such luxury, such newness.

"Oh, Clay," was all Catherine said, sweeping the living room with her eyes.

"I know what you're thinking."

"But I'm right. It's too much."

"Don't you like it? We can look at others."

She swung to face him in the middle of the bright, vast room. "I can't live in this with you. It would be like cheating on my income tax."

"Okay, let's go. Where else do you have in mind?"

"Wait a minute." She reached out to detain him, for he'd turned impatiently toward the foyer. "I'm not the only one who has a say."

He paused, but she could tell his teeth were clenched.

"Clay, what are we going to fill all this up with?"

"Furniture, but it won't be *filled*. We'll just get what we need."

"Just . . . *get?*"

"Well, we'll go out and buy it, dammit! We have to have furniture, and that's the usual way of getting it." It was unlike him to speak in such a brittle manner. She could tell that he was disappointed and not a little angry.

"You want it, don't you?"

"I've always liked this place, but it doesn't matter. There are others."

"Yes, so you said before." She paused, met his displeased eyes and said quietly, "Show me the rest of it."

She followed him up the short flight of stairs. He switched on a light and a spacious bathroom was revealed. It had a long vanity, topped with gold-veined black marble, sporting two sinks and a mirror the size of a bedsheet. The fixtures were almond-colored, and the walls papered in a bold geometric of beige and brown with touches of silver foil adding a richness for which she was not prepared. She quickly glanced from the vanity stool to the shower stall—separate from the tub—with its opaque glass walls.

"Any of the paper can be changed," he said.

"That won't be necessary. I can see why you like it as it is—all these browns."

He switched off the light and she followed him to a small bedroom on the opposite side of the hall. Here again was a room papered in brown and tan geometric, very masculine, evidently decorated as a den or study.

Silently they moved on to the other bedroom. It was massive and could easily have been divided into two rooms. It, too, was papered in shades of brown, but this time a cool, restful dusty-blue had been added. Clay walked over and opened a door, revealing a generous walk-in closet with built-in drawers, shoe shelves and luggage racks up above.

"Clay, how much is this going to cost anyway?"

"What difference does it make?"

"I . . . we . . . it just does, that's all."

"I can afford it."

"That's not the point and you know it."

"What is the point then, Catherine?"

But for answer, her eyes slid to the spot where the bed so obviously belonged. His eyes did the same, then they quickly looked away from each other. She turned from the room and abruptly went back downstairs to check the kitchen.

It was compact, efficient, had a dishwasher, disposal, side-by-side refrigerator-freezer, glossy flooring of rich vinyl, almond-colored appliances—everything. She thought of the kitchen at home, of her father slinging coffee grounds in the sink without bothering to wash them down, of the dirty dishes that were forever piled in the sink unless she herself washed them.

Catherine thought about what it would be like working in this clean kitchen with its gleaming appliances, its wood-grained Formica countertops. She turned to eye the peninsula and imagined a pair of stools on the other side of it—a cozy, informal eating spot. She pictured Clay sitting there in the morning, drinking coffee while she fried eggs. But she'd never been with him early in the morning and didn't know if he liked coffee, or fried eggs. And furthermore, she had no business imagining such things in such a wishful way.

"Catherine?"

She jumped and whirled to find him leaning in the doorway, one elbow braced high against it. He was dressed in a rust-colored corduroy jacket with a matching vest beneath. The way he stood, the jacket flared away from his body creating inviting shadows around his torso. It struck her again how flawless his appearance was, how his trousers never seemed to wrinkle, his hair never to be out of place. She felt her mouth go dry and wondered what she was letting herself in for.

"There's only a week left," he said sensibly.

"I know." She turned toward the stove, walked over and switched on the light above it because it gave her a reason to turn her back to him and because she'd been wondering if he drank coffee in the morning and because she'd been thinking of the shadows within his corduroy jacket.

"If it's what you want, Clay, we'll take it. I know the colors suit you."

"Do you want to look at something else?" He was no longer angry, not at all. Instead his voice was mellow.

"I love this, Clay. I just don't think that we . . . that I . . ."

"Deserve it?" he finished as she faltered.

"Something like that."

"Would it make things more fair if we lived in a hovel someplace, is that what you think?"

"Yes!" She spun to face him. "No . . . oh, God, I don't know. This is more than I ever imagined I'd live in, that's all. I'm trying very hard not to be overcome."

He smiled, raised his other hand so both were now braced against the door frame above his head, then he shook his head at the vinyl floor.

"You know, sometimes I don't believe you."

"Well, sometimes I don't believe you either." She threw her hands wide, indicating the whole place in one gesture. "Now furniture too!"

"I said we'd only get the necessities."

"But I'm fast learning what you consider *necessities*."

"Well, I'll do my damnedest to hunt up some stick furniture if it'll make you happy. And I'll string some thongs from the bedroom wall and haul in a fresh load of straw for on top of them. How's that?"

His face wore the most engaging grin; it was irresistible.

He was teasing her. Standing there leaning against their future kitchen doorway looking good enough to serve for dinner, Clay Forrester was teasing. His laughter started as a soft

183

bubble of mirth deep in his throat, but when it erupted into full, uninhibited sound, all she could do was laugh back.

He chose an enormously long davenport because, he said, his mother drove him nuts with all her loveseats that a man couldn't even stretch out on. And two armchairs of tweed, and a pecan coffee table and end tables, and a lamp that cost as much as one of the chairs, although Catherine could not convince him this was utterly spendthrift and silly. He said he liked it, expensive or not, and that was that. They chose two stools for the kitchen peninsula, but Catherine adamantly refused to furnish the formal dining room. They really wouldn't need it, she said. She won on that point, but the bedroom set she said was "good enough" wasn't good enough for Clay. He picked out one that cost nearly double that of her choice, and a triple dresser *and* a chest of drawers, which she said were unnecessary because the closet had built-in drawers.

They were standing in the aisle arguing about nightstands and lamps when their salesman returned to them.

"But why do we need more lamps? There are ceiling fixtures; that's good enough."

"Because I like to read in bed!" Clay exclaimed.

The salesman began to clear his throat, thought better of it, and withdrew discreetly to let them argue it out. But Catherine knew he'd overheard Clay's last comment and was left beet-faced, feeling like a complete fool, standing there in the aisle of a furniture store arguing with a fiancé who exclaimed he liked to *read* in bed!

Things started happening so fast.

Steve called to say he'd be arriving on Thursday, the thirteenth.

Ada called to say she'd finished making her dress.

The store called to make arrangement for delivery of the furniture.

Bobbi called to say the Magnussons would definitely be at the wedding.

The doctor's office called to say Catherine's blood count was low.

Angela called and apologetically explained that Claiborne had pressed charges against Herb Anderson and successfully managed to have him convicted to ninety days in the workhouse for assault and battery.

And then one evening Catherine walked into Horizons to find a surprise bridal shower awaiting her, and not only were all the girls there, but seated side by side on the sofa were her mother and Angela. And Catherine, giving in to what is each bride's right, covered her face with both hands and burst into tears for the first time since this whole charade began.

Chapter 15

WHEN CLAY CAME to pick up Catherine and take her to meet Steve's plane, she was totally unprepared for the sight that greeted her. She stopped stupidly, dead in her tracks!

Clay was dressed in faded denims and a faded blue flannel shirt beneath a disreputable-looking old letter jacket that would have been shaped like Clay even had his body not been inside it. It was the kind of possession taken for granted. The jacket hung open haphazardly, limp from age, its pocket edges worn bare, its zipper long since grown useless. The rough clothes gave Clay a rugged look, flattering in its unexpectedness, disarming because it brought back memories of the first time Catherine had ever seen him. Oh, he was neater that night, but he'd been dressed in faded Levi's jeans and a tennis shirt.

Catherine stood transfixed while Clay, oblivious to her reaction, only greeted her with, "Hi, I brought the Bronco. I thought we'd be more comfortable in it." He'd already turned toward the door before realizing she wasn't following, so turned back to her. "What's the matter? Oh, should I have dressed up more? I was waxing the Corvette in the garage and forgot about the time . . . sorry."

"No—no, it's okay . . . You look . . ." But she didn't finish, just gaped at him.

"What?"

"I don't know—different."

"You've seen me in jeans before."

Yes, she certainly had, but she didn't think he remembered. She moved, at last, out the door with him.

At the curb was the vehicle she remembered from last July, some kind of man's toy with high bench seats and plenty of windows all around, and room for hunting equipment in the rear. She stopped walking as if she'd run up against a barbed wire fence.

"I thought we'd be a little crowded in the Corvette with your brother's gear and the three of us." Clay caught her elbow, propelling her forward. She began shivering; it was bitter for November—easy to blame her shakes on the weather. Clay moved ahead to open the door of the Bronco, but looked back again impatiently to find her eyeing him in a curious manner.

Catherine stood there, swallowing, fighting the overwhelming surge of familiarity—those jeans, and the old jacket, his hair that—for once—wasn't quite tidy. His collar was turned up, and as he stood waiting, his breath formed a white cloud. His nose was a little bit red, and he shivered, then hunched his shoulders.

"Hurry up," he said with a small smile. "Get in or you'll be scolding me for being late."

"Is this your father's?"

"Yeah."

He took his hand off the icy handle and buried it in his other pocket. Without thinking, she dropped her eyes to the zipper of his jeans, staring at the way the old, faded spots undulated between patches of deeper blue. Her eyes darted to his face, discovering that he'd been watching her. And suddenly the color of his cheeks matched his nose.

Appalled at herself, she climbed hurriedly into the seat and let him slam the door shut.

Neither of them said a word all the way out to the Air Force Reserve Base in Bloomington. Catherine stared out the side window, damning herself for letting memory play upon her this way. Clay drove, seeing over and over again the way her eyes had dropped to his zipper, recalling now the reason why. Women, he realized, placed greater importance on memories than men do. Until that happened back there he hadn't given a thought to the Bronco or his blue jeans, or the fact that he'd used them both last Fourth of July.

Clay did not touch her as they walked to the correct building. The stab of self-consciousness was again too concentrated.

A tall, strapping blond man, dressed in civvies, turned from his conversation with a uniformed desk clerk at the sound of their approach. He glanced up and hesitated. Then his mouth fell open, he smiled, and he started running toward the tall blond girl who, also, had broken into a run. They met like thwarted lovers and it came as something of a surprise to Clay, seeing for the first time a genuine display of affection from Catherine. There was a near greediness in the way her fingers dug into the back of her brother's jacket, a hungry desperation as their eyes closed while they clasped each other tightly and swallowed tears. Clay stood back uneasily, not wanting to watch them, unable not to. Steve swung Catherine off her feet, whirled her around, repeating an endearment which struck Clay as ill-suited, yet touched him all the same.

"Babe . . . oh, God, babe, is it really you?"

Her lips quivered and she clung. She could say little more than his name, backing away, spanning his tan cheeks with her palms, looking into his changed face, then at the breadth of his shoulders, then lunging into his arms again, burying herself, unable to restrain her tears now that she'd seen his.

To Clay it was a revelation. He watched Catherine's face, recalling this same expression on it that night after the long-distance call.

Finally Steve pulled back and said, "If that's Clay over there, I think we're making him uncomfortable." He tucked Catherine securely beneath his armpit, and she circled his torso with both arms while the two men shook hands.

Catherine's smile was unreserved. Her hold upon Steve was possessive. For Clay, it created an odd momentary twinge of jealousy, soon lost in the inanities of introductions, the first assessment of man to man.

"So you're the one she told me about." Steve's grip was solid, winning.

"So you're the one she told *me* about."

Clay reached for the duffel bag, and the three walked down the corridor and across the parking lot, Catherine and Steve catching up with bits of news about each other and the family. He squeezed her extra hard once and laughed. "Will you look at my baby sister. What happened to your cowlicks and pimples?" There followed another impulsive hug, then they clambered into the Bronco.

"Where to?"

"I made reservations downtown."

"But, Steve, we won't even get a chance to talk!" wailed Catherine.

"Listen, you two, why don't I drive out past the house and you can drop me off and Steve can take the Bronco?"

"Oh, Clay, really?" Catherine's blue eyes radiated appreciation.

"We've got more cars at home than we need."

Steve leaned around Catherine. "That's damn nice of you, man."

"Think nothing of it. I can't leave my future brother-in-law stranded in a downtown hotel, can I?"

Steve smiled.

"Then it's settled."

Catherine and Steve talked all the way out to the Forrester's. When they arrived, Steve took in the sprawling house, cobbled drive, extensive lawns, and said, "Well, well."

Catherine couldn't help the tiny thrill of pride, realizing how the house must appear to Steve for the first time. "This is where the wedding's going to be."

"Babe, I'm happy for you."

Clay pulled up, shifted into neutral, but he'd only dropped one leg out when Catherine laid a hand on his arm.

"Clay?"

He looked back over his shoulder at the touch on his sleeve.

"I don't know what to say."

Neither did he just then. He only looked at her, at the pleasant, warm expression she had willingly displayed toward him. She was so different today; he'd never seen her like this before. This, he thought, is how I've always wondered if she could be.

"Thank you," she said sincerely.

"It's okay. Like I said, we've got more cars around here than we know what to do with."

"Just the same—thanks." She moved impulsively toward him and brushed her cheek briefly against his, not quite kissing it, not quite missing, while he hung half in the seat, half out.

"You two have a good talk. But make sure you get some sleep, huh?"

"Promise."

"I'll see you tomorrow night then."

She nodded.

He lowered his voice and pleased her immeasurably by saying, "I think I like him."

Her only answer was the same genuine smile that he was already enjoying. Then Clay swung out, found Steve standing there waiting, and said, "Time enough for you to meet my folks tomorrow. I know you and Catherine are anxious to be alone."

"Listen, man . . ." Steve extended a hand. There followed a prolonged grip, then, "Thanks a lot." Steve then glanced up at the house and back once again at Clay. His tone changed, then he added quietly, ". . . for both of us."

There was an instantaneous sense of rapport between Clay and Steve, the inexplicable thing that happens only rarely when strangers meet. It had nothing to do with Catherine or her relationship to either of them. Neither had it anything to do with gratitude. It was simply there: some compelling invitation coursing between the clasped hands. "Here," it seemed to say, "is a man I feel good with."

Odd, thought Clay, but of all Catherine's family, this is the first person I've felt drawn to, and that includes Catherine herself.

He'd been expecting someone like Catherine's father, some harsh, forbidding younger version of Herb Anderson. Instead, he found a genuine smile, intelligent eyes, and a face much like Catherine's, only warmer. He thought perhaps the years away from home had given Steve Anderson the ability to smile at life again, which Catherine could not yet readily do. In her brother's face, Clay found the possibility of what Catherine could be, should she ever stop carrying that chip on her shoulder and that shield of armor over her emotions. Perhaps, after all, Clay liked Steve because he alone seemed able to move Catherine, to make her feel, and make it show.

When the noon break came and Ada Anderson left her machine, there was a sparkle of life in her eyes that had been missing for years. The skin about them was as corrugated as ever, but the eyes themselves were alive with expectancy. Her usual lifeless shuffle was replaced by a brisk step. Ada had even put a touch of lipstick on.

"Ada?"

She turned at the sound of her supervisor's voice, impatient to be out the door.

"I'm kind of in a hurry, Gladys. My boy is home, you know."

"Yes, I know. I checked on your output and the week's been good. The whole line had a good week, as a matter of fact. Why don't you just take the rest of the afternoon off, Ada?"

Ada stopped fussing with her coat collar. "Why, Gladys, do you mean it?"

"Of course I do. It's not every day a boy comes home from the Air Force."

Ada smiled, slid the handle of her vinyl purse onto her arm, casting one eye at the door, then back at Gladys Merkins.

"That's awful nice of you, and if you ever get in a bind when the girls get behind on their quotas, I'll put in extra."

"Get going, Ada. The quotas we'll worry about some other time."

"Thanks a lot, Gladys."

Gladys Merkins watched Ada hurry out the door, wondering how a person becomes so downtrodden, so stolid and unassuming that she doesn't even ask for a day off when she hasn't seen her son for six years. If word hadn't been passed around the shop, Gladys herself wouldn't have known. It did her heart good to see the pitiful woman with a smile on her face for once.

Outside, Ada scanned the street, clutching her coat at her throat where her heart beat in wild expectancy. The wind caught at the hem of the garment, lifting it, tugging at Ada's gray-streaked hair. She scanned the ugly street uncertainly. It sported only cold brick structures of commerce, and noisy truck traffic that never seemed to cease. Chain link fences were decorated with weathered paper scraps. There was the ever-present smell of exhaust fumes. Huddled against the wind, Ada looked like a deserted scrap of refuse herself.

But then a vehicle careened past and swerved to an abrupt halt beside the curb. A young man burst from it, forgetting to shut the door, waving, smiling, running, calling, "Mom! . . . Mom!" And the little scrap of refuse was transformed into vibrant life. Ada ran, her arms outstretched, her face tear-streaked. As her arms clung at last to her son's neck she wondered how it could possibly be him, so big, so broad, so real at last.

"Oh, Mom . . . Jesus . . . Mom."

"Steve, Steve, let me go so I can look at you."

He did, but then he saw her better too.

She appeared infinitely older, sadder. He could only hug her again, guilty because he knew some of that age, some of that sadness had been caused by his leaving. She was crying, but he saw past the tears to a much more profound sorrow, hopeful that somehow he could help erase it before he had to leave her once more.

"Come on, Mom, Cathy's in the car and we're all going out for lunch."

Chapter 16

IT WAS CATHERINE'S wedding day, the last day she would share with the girls at Horizons. So she allowed their suffocating attentions, feeling at times like she was smothering in their overcaring midst. The expressions on their faces—those doe-eyed looks—were etched on her conscience; she thought they would be her penance forever, long after she gave up her place as Mrs. Clay Forrester. The saga she had brought to Horizons would remain legend within its walls, rivaling any Hans Christian Andersen tale. But its ending, which none of them yet knew, would be her own private hair shirt.

She swallowed the knowledge of it while the girls played "wedding day" with her, dressing her up as they had their dolls as children, humming *Lohengrin* as they had for their dolls, pretending that the doll was themselves.

For Catherine it was an ordeal. Keeping the smile on her lips, the lilt in her voice, the eagerness in her pose became a task of sheer love. She realized it as the last hour neared—that she loved, genuinely loved, so many of these girls.

She sat before a mirror, her face flushed, and framed by an appealing aureole of soft blond curls, slung high and held by a winter gardenia set in baby's breath, trailing a thin white ribbon down the back. They had bought her a garter and were putting it on her calf, laughing, making silly jokes. Catherine was dressed in the sexiest undergarments she'd ever owned. Her mother had bought them from the employees' store at Munsingwear, surprising everyone at the shower. The bra was an incidental thing, plunging low in front, molding Catherine's lower breasts in lotus-shaped satin fingers that curved up to the crests of her nipples, barely covering them. Exquisite satin briefs, trimmed in peekaboo lace, left a strip of skin nearly exposed up each hip. The slip was beautiful enough to be an evening gown. It followed closely the low décolletage of the bra, flowing and clinging to her thighs and the perceptible bulge of her tummy. She placed her hands on it now, looking at the garter, at all the faces around her. Her eyes filled. She took a deep breath, fluttered a fingertip beneath her lashes, knowing the girls' eyes followed the twinkle of the diamond.

"Come on, you guys, don't!" she said, laughing shakily, quite close to breaking down completely. "Don't look so happy for me. It should be every single one of you, not me!" She widened her eyes to make room for the tears.

"Don't you dare cry, Catherine Anderson!" Marie scolded. "Not after all the work that's gone into that makeup. If you get one single tear on it, we're all going to disown you."

Another fragile, borderline laugh, and Catherine sputtered, "Oh, no, you won't. You can't disown me any more than I can disown you. Not anymore. We're all in this together."

But Catherine compressed her lips. A tear had its own way, hovered, then splashed over the edge of her lashes, and she laughed shakily, flapped her hands and demanded a tissue.

Somebody quipped, "Hey, Anderson, dry up, or else!"

It relieved the tension. The makeup passed inspection, and somebody brought the plain dress Catherine would wear in the car, her gown, carefully sheathed in plastic, her purse and the small bag she'd packed.

"Have you got your perfume in there?"

"Yes, thank you for reminding me, Francie."

"How about your Dramamine pills?"

"Dramamine pills?"

"You'll need them for flying high."

"Clay's the one that'll need them when he gets a load of that underwear!"

"Be careful of the gardenia when you get in the car now."

"Your brother is here, he just pulled up!"

They thronged downstairs. Steve was at the door. He carried Catherine's things outside, came back for a second load and for her.

Then there was nothing left to do but go. It was so hard to do, suddenly, to turn away from all the warmth and love. Mrs. Tollefson was there, hovering near the colonnade, then coming forward to be the voice of the entire group.

"Catherine, we're all so happy for you. I think you've made every girl here into something more than she used to be. Right, girls?" Catherine was hugged against Mrs. Tollefson quite roughly. She pinched her eyes shut.

"Listen . . . I—I love you all." As she said it, she experienced an explosive force of emotion. Those words, so unfamiliar to her tongue, created an expansiveness like she'd never felt before. She knew it twenty-five-fold, for at that moment it was true. She loved each woman crowded around her and suddenly wanted more than anything to stay among them, to let their hands pull her back into the security of their fold.

But that phase of her life was over. She was swept out into the November afternoon where a fine snow was falling, glittering onto her hair like stardust. The skies were pale, with smudges of gray clouds lying low, shedding their enchanting burden into Catherine's wedding day. With eyes now dry, Catherine watched their progress through the city, in a sort of enhanced state of clarity. Bare trees stood out in crisp distinction, blacker than black when wet by the snow. The snow had a pristine smell of newness, as each first snow does. It tantalized her, falling like petals strewn before the bride, touching everything with white. She stared out the window, sighed, closed her eyes, told her heart to beat right. But it beat all the more erratically as she envisioned the Forrester house, the guests who would soon be arriving, and Bobbi and Stu on their way, and somewhere, waiting . . . Clay.

Clay.

Oh, Clay, she thought, what have we done? How can all of this be happening? Me riding toward you with a velvet gown on the seat behind me and this diamond on my finger? And all those starry-eyed looks burning into my soul from the house I've just left? And your father and mother and grandparents all waiting to welcome me into your family? And guests coming, bringing gifts, and—

"Stop the car!"

"What?" Steve exclaimed, surprised.

"Stop the car. I can't go through with this."

He pulled over, watching his sister drop her face into her hands. He slid across the seat and gathered her into his arms.

"What is it, babe?"

"Oh, Steve, what should I do?"

"Shh, come on now. Don't start crying, not today. It's just the last-minute jitters. But, really, babe, I don't think you should have the slightest qualms." He lifted her chin, making her look at him. "Cathy, if I could handpick a brother-in-law, I'd probably pick Clay Forrester, from what I've seen so far. And if I could handpick a family to trust you to, it would probably be his. You're going to be loved and taken care of for the rest of your life, and I couldn't be happier with who's going to be doing it."

"That's just it. It's not for the rest of my life."

"But—"

"Clay and I are being married under duress. We've agreed to divorce as soon as the baby has a name and he's passed his bar exams and entered his father's business."

Steve sat back, absorbing this news. His brows gathered into a scowl.

"Don't look at me that way! And don't ask me how this mess got started because right now I don't think I could even explain it to myself. I only know I feel like the biggest fraud on the face of the earth, and I don't think I can go through with it. I thought I could but I can't."

Steve slid back behind the wheel and stared at the wipers that slapped disconsolately across the windshield. His eyes seemed focused on nothing. "You mean none of them know?"

"Oh, Steve, I shouldn't have told you, but I had to get it off my chest."

"Well, now that you have, you're going to listen to what I have to say. You *should* feel like a swindler. It's a damn rotten trick you're playing on some damn fine people; at least I think they are. And since you obviously do, also, you haven't got any choice but to go through with it. If you back out now, you're going to embarrass them even further than our illustrious father already has. They've been more than fair to you, Catherine. They've been supportive and decent and, in case you've forgotten, quite lavish with their money. Frankly, the things I've learned about the Forrester family have boggled my mind. I find myself wondering how I'd have accepted the situation if I were in their position and faced with the bizarre set of circumstances they've been faced with. It takes some pretty big people to be as accepting as they've been. I think you owe it to them not only to go through with this marriage, but to make a helluva stab at making it work afterward.

"Futhermore, if I were faced with the opportunity, like you are, I think I'd do my damnedest not to let a man like Clay slip out of my fingers as easily as you intend to."

"But, Steve, you don't understand. We don't love each other."

"You're carrying something that says you'd better, by God, try to!"

She'd never seen Steve so upset with her before. She, too, raised her voice. "I don't want to have to *try* to love my husband. I just *want* to!"

"Listen, you're talking to old Steve here." He tapped his chest. "I know how stubborn you can be, and if you set your mind to something you'll stick with it, come hell or high water. And what you're telling me is that you aren't going to try to make this marriage work, right?"

"You make it sound like it's all my idea. It's not. We agreed to start the divorce in July."

"Yeah, and you wait and see how far your agreement goes when he gets a load of his own kid in some hospital nursery."

Catherine's heart flew to her throat. "He promised the baby will be mine. He won't fight for it."

"Yeah, sure." His hands hung on the wheel. He stared unseeingly. "The baby goes with you, you go your way, he goes his. What the hell kind of agreement is that to make?" He looked down at his thumbs.

"You're angry with me."

"Yes, I am."

"I don't blame you, I guess."

He felt robbed, robbed of all the elation he'd held for her, angry that she'd stolen it from him. Frustrated, he slammed the butts of both hands against the steering wheel.

"I like him, goddammit!" he blustered. "I felt so damn happy for you, ending up with a guy like him." Then he stared a long time out his side window.

"Steve." She slid over and touched his shoulder. "Oh, Steve, I'm sorry. I've hurt so many people already, and hardly any of them know yet that they've been hurt. You're the only one, and look how you feel. And when Mom finds out, and his folks, well, you can see why I don't think we should go through with it."

"You back out now and you'll break Mom's heart. She thinks you're set for life, and she'll never have to worry about you living like she's done, with that—that . . ."

"I know."

"Well, Christ! She's waiting at home right now in her home-made dress, probably all nervous about it, and—Hell, you know how she gets. She's actually, honest-to-God happy, or as close to happy as I've ever seen her, with the old man gone and your future set. Don't do it to her, Cathy."

"But what about me?"

"You started it, all those people heading for your wedding, all the preparations made, and you ask 'What about me?' I think you'd better think it over and consider what happens if you back out now. Count the number of people involved."

"I have! Every day I have! Facing all those pregnant teen-agers at Horizons while they treated me like I was Snow White and they were dwarves, stitching on my wedding dress all starry-eyed. Do you think that's been easy?"

He sat stiff and silent. She slid back to her own side. The snow fell in flat plops while she stared at it unseeingly. Finally she quoted, as if to herself, "Oh, what a tangled web we weave, when first we practice to deceive."

The silence was broken only by the sweep of the windshield wipers, which were still slapping away. Catherine spoke to the snow. "I had no idea at the beginning how many lives would be touched by this wedding. It seemed like a decision that would mainly affect Clay and I and the baby. But things got out of hand somehow. Angela said he's their only son and wanted to have at least a few of the family—an intimate little affair she called it. And then all the girls at Horizons got into it, helping me make the dress. Then Mom sees me heading for what she thinks is the good life. Clay's grandparents even gave me their approval, to say nothing of the family jewels." She turned to Steve at last. "And you, my God, it even brought you home. Do you know what it means to me to have you here, and how I hated telling you the truth? I'm getting in deeper than I wanted though. Steve, please understand."

"I understand what it would do to a lot of people if you say no at the eleventh hour."

"And even after what I told you, you think I should go through with it?"

"I don't know . . . What a mess." But then he turned to her with a look of appeal on his face. "Cathy, couldn't you try to give it a chance?"

"You mean, me and Clay?"

"Yes, you and Clay. What are your feelings for him?"

That was a tough one; she thought for a minute before answering. "I honestly don't know. He's . . . well, he's able to accept all of this far more easily than I can. And the funny thing is, once he got over the first shock, he never blamed me in any way. I mean, most men would be throwing it up to a woman all the time how their plans were ruined. But he's not that way. He says he's going to make the best of it, takes me out and introduces me to his family just as if I'm his real choice, gives me this huge old ring that's been in the family forever, and treats me like a lady. Yet, at the same time, I know it's all a hoax. He does very well at keeping his family from suspecting it though. They've accepted me surprisingly well. The trouble is, Steve, I think I'm accepting them too. Oh, Steve . . . it's awful . . . I . . . don't you think I realize all those things you felt about them? They're genuinely good and loving people, and I'm drawn to them; I like them. But it's dangerous for me, don't you see? I'm to be a part of them, yet I'm not. Giving them up in a few months will be tougher than leaving Horizons was today."

"All this time you've talked about his family, but you still haven't answered my question about Clay."

"How can I? The truth is I don't know him as well as you think I do."

"Well, it's obvious you were attracted to him once."

"But it's not . . ." She paused, looked away. "I met him on a blind date. He was going with another girl at the time, and they'd had a fight or something."

"So what?"

"So it was a one-night stand, that's what."

"Are you saying he loves someone else?"

"He never mentions her."

"Hey"—Steve's voice was as gentle as his touch upon her arm—"babe, I don't know what to say, except, maybe—just maybe—Clay is worth fighting for."

"Steve, you above all people should understand that I don't want a marriage like Mom and Dad's. If there's one thing I learned in that house it's that I will not merely *survive* a marriage; I want to *live*."

"Hey, give it a chance. Had you considered that you kind of fell into the pot here and could come out smelling like a rose?"

She couldn't help smiling. "If it'll put your mind at ease, the baby will be taken care of for the rest of his life. That's part of the arrangement. After Clay graduates, he'll help me with tuition so I can go back to school."

"So the deal is made, huh? I guess we both know you can't back out of it now, don't we?"

She sighed. "You're right. I can't, and I knew it all the time, even when I told you to stop the car."

He studied her a moment before saying, "You know, little sister, I'll give you odds you won't come out of this feeling quite as platonic about him as you claim to be now. How much you wanna bet?"

"That's wishful thinking and you know it. And I'm going to be late for my own wedding if you don't get this thing into gear."

"Okay." He shifted into drive and they pulled back into traffic.

After a few minutes she touched his arm and smiled at Steve. "Thanks for letting me unload on you. I feel better now."

He winked at her. "You really are a babe, in lots of ways," he said, covering her hand with his own, hoping Clay Forrester recognized that fact.

Chapter 17

THE WINDOWS OF the Forrester home were all ablaze, throwing oblique patches of gold across the snow of early evening. Each of the front columns was festooned with an enormous arrangement of Indian corn, scarlet leaves and bearded wheat with nutmeg-colored ribbons trailing streamers that drifted in a meek breeze. Snow settled softly upon the scene and Catherine gave a soft exclamation of surprise at the liveried attendant who was sweeping the cobbled walk.

She could see that Angela's expert hand had done its work and wondered what other surprises awaited her inside. Catherine fought against the overwhelming sensation of coming home. She fought, too, against the both terrible and wonderful sense of expectation. Surely this incredible day was not happening. Yet the scent of gardenia was real. And the diamond on her hand was so large she couldn't draw her glove over it. Summoning common sense did little good. The flutter of excitement persisted, disquieting, reducing Catherine to nervous jitters.

Then the attendant was smiling, opening the door, while Catherine fought the crazy sensation that she was debarking from a coach-and-four.

The foyer door opened upon yet another dreamlike setting: bronze and yellow flowerbursts threaded with ribbons, cascading from the spooled stair rail at evenly spaced intervals. Angela appeared with Ada in tow, sweeping Catherine into a hurried hug, whispering conspiratorially, "Hurry on up. We don't want you to be seen here." \

"But, Steve—" Catherine strained to glance over her shoulder, dismayed at being whisked through the tantalizing foyer without being allowed to dote upon it. Angela's laughter tinkled into the softly glowing space as if she understood Catherine's reluctance to be swept through so hastily.

"Don't worry about Steve. He knows what to do."

The floral impressions had to be left behind momentarily. Yet a last look behind her gave Catherine the sight of two white-capped maids peeking over the banister for one forbidden glimpse of the bride.

Insanity continued as Catherine was ushered into a stunningly appropriate bedroom, trimmed in pink flounced ruffles and floor-length priscillas. It was carpeted, too, in palest pink, and furnished with a glorious brass bed and free-standing cheval mirror, ruffled pillows, and a girlish look that seemed the counterpart to Angela's giddiness.

When the door closed behind them, Angela immediately captured both of Catherine's hands. "Forgive an old-fashioned mother her whims, my dear, but I didn't want to run the risk of your meeting Clay somewhere in the hall." Angela squeezed the damp palms. "You look lovely, Catherine, so lovely. Are you excited?"

"I . . . yes . . . it . . ." She glanced at the door. "All those flowers down there . . . and a doorman!"

"Isn't it exciting? I can't think of another affair I've had more fun arranging. I believe I'm a little breathless, as well. Can I tell you a secret?" She smiled conspiratorially again, then turned to include Ada in the secret. "So is Clay."

The idea seemed preposterous, yet Catherine asked, "He is?"

"Ah! He's been driving us crazy all day, worrying if there was enough champagne and if the flowers would arrive on time and if we'd forgotten Aunt Gertie's family on the guest list. He's been the typical bridegroom, which pleases me immensely." Then Angela breezily commandeered Ada. "Now we'll leave you alone for a minute. I want to show your mother the cake and gifts. You'll find everything you need in the bath there, and if you don't find it, let one of the maids know. Come on, Ada. I think we deserve a little glass of sherry to calm our mothers' nerves."

But before they could leave, a maid opened the door and ushered in a breathless Bobbi, with a plastic clothing carrier over her arm. There followed a flurry of kisses and greetings and hanging up of gowns, and exclamations over all the subdued activity going on downstairs.

"We'll see you later, Catherine." Angela waved two fingers and took Ada away, but not before warning, "Now remember, you're not to leave this room until I come for you."

"Don't worry," Bobbi promised. "I'll see that she doesn't."

Left alone, Catherine and Bobbi had only to look at each other to burst into matching grins and hug each other again, before Bobbi exclaimed, "Have you seen what's going on down there!"

Catherine, panicked afresh, placed a hand on her hammering heart and pleaded, "Don't tell me. I'm giddy enough as it is. This is all so unbelievable!"

Whatever Catherine had expected this evening to be, she had not in her wildest dreams believed it would turn out like the make-believe weddings she and Bobbi had conjured up during childhood. Yet it seemed to be. Each of the girls realized it as they stood in the feminine bedroom, exchanging inanities, occasionally giggling. A maid knocked to ask if their dresses needed any last-minute pressing. They sent her away and went into the bathroom to check each other's hair, giving a last swish of hair spray, then laughing into each other's eyes in the huge mirror. Another knock sounded and produced a maid with two large boxes containing their bouquets.

They laid them on the bed and looked at the unopened, white containers.

"You first," Catherine said, clasping her hands beneath her chin.

"Oh, no, not this time. We're not eight-year-olds pretending anymore. You first!"

"Let's open them together then."

They did. Bobbi's held a quaint basket of bronze mums and apricot roses, with streamers of pale ribbon falling from its handle. Catherine stood back, quite unable to reach for the stunning spray of white gardenia, baby's breath, and apricot roses nestled in their transparent bag with dewy beads of moisture clinging inside. Bobbi watched her press her hands to her cheeks, then close her eyes momentarily, open them once again to remain stock-still, staring at the blossoms. So Bobbi leaned down, removed the pearl-headed pin and lifted the huge spray from its wrapper, releasing the heady fragrance of gardenia and roses into the room. She pinned one of the gardenias into Catherine's hair. Still, Catherine seemed unable to move.

"Oh, Cath, they're beautiful."

Bobbi lifted the bouquet and at last Catherine moved, wordlessly plunging her face into the nosegay. Looking up again across the flowers, she stammered, "I—I don't deserve all this."

Bobbi's voice was soft with emotion. "Of course you do. It's exactly what we dreamed about, Cath. One of us has made it, and everything turned out even better than make-believe."

"Don't say that."

"Don't dissect it, Cath, just enjoy every precious minute of it."

"But you don't know—"

"I know. Believe me, I do. I know that you have doubts about the way you and Clay got started, but don't think about them tonight. Think of the good side, okay?"

"You wanted me to marry Clay all along, didn't you, Bobbi?"

"I wanted something good for you and if it's Clay Forrester, then, yes, I wanted it."

"I think you've always been a little soft on him yourself."

"Maybe I have. Maybe not, I don't know. I only know if it were me standing there holding that bouquet, I'd be ecstatic instead of depressed."

"I'm not depressed, really I'm not. It's just more than I bargained for, and it's all so sudden."

"And so you doubt and question? Catherine, for once—just for once—in your godforsaken life, will you accept a little manna from heaven? You're so used to living in hell that a little heaven scares you. Come on, now, smile! And tell yourself that he asked you to marry him because he wanted to. It's going

205

to work. Clay is one of the nicest men I know, but if you tell Stu I said so, I'll kill you."

At last Catherine smiled, but she was affected more than she cared to admit by Bobbi's opinion of Clay.

"Now, come on, let's get your dress on."

They stripped off its protective plastic, looked at each other meaningfully once again, recalling all those childhood games, all that make-believe. But the luxurious velvet was real. Bobbi lifted it high while Catherine raised her arms. When she was halfway into it a sound—suspiciously like a harp—came from below.

"What's that?" Bobbi cocked an ear.

"I can't hear in here," came the muffled voice from inside the dress.

"Oh, here, get your ears out of there!"

When Catherine emerged, they posed like robins listening for worms. They looked at each other in disbelief.

"It sounds like a harp!"

"A harp?"

"Well, doesn't it?"

They both listened again.

"My God, it does!"

"Could there really be a harp in this house?"

"Apparently so."

"Leave it to Angela."

Then they both burst into laughter and finished drawing the dress over Catherine's arms. By now she was shaking visibly. Her palms were damp but she dared not wipe them on the velvet.

"Bobbi, I'm scared stiff."

"Why? You're the main attraction and you look it. Be proud!"

Bobbi zipped and buttoned busily, then walked around behind Catherine and extended the miniature train onto the pink carpet. Catherine caught a glimpse of herself in the mirror, pressed her hands to her tummy and asked, "Do I show a lot?"

Bobbi slapped her cousin's hands down, scolding, "Oh, for heaven's sake, will you *please!*" Then she had an inspiration; she handed over the bouquet. "If you must worry about it, hide behind this."

Catherine struck a prim pose that made them both laugh

again, but now the sounds from downstairs were definitely steadier, the hum of voices intermingling with the mellow tones of the music.

The door opened and this time it was Inella who stood there with a tiny, foil-wrapped box.

"Why, don't you look lovely, Miss Catherine," the maid said with a wide smile. "Your groom gave me the honor of delivering this." She extended the box. Catherine only gaped, then reached out a tentative hand, withdrew it, then finally took the gift.

"What is it?"

"Why, I'm sure I don't know, Miss. Why don't you open it and see?"

Catherine turned wide eyes to Bobbi.

"Inella's right, open it! I'm dying to see!"

"But what if it's something—" She stopped just short of saying "expensive." The box was too small to be anything but jewelry. It lay in her hand accusingly while she wondered with a sinking feeling why Clay had done this to her. Again her eyes sought Bobbi's, then Inella's. Quickly she stripped away the foil and found a small, velveteen ring box. Her heart was hammering, her throat went suddenly dry. She lifted the lid. Inside no jewels glittered, no rings twinkled. Instead, couched in the velvet slot was a brass key. No message, no clues. Catherine breathed again.

"What's it for?"

"Why, I'm afraid I couldn't guess, Miss Catherine."

"But— "

A knock sounded and Angela came in. As the door opened, the gentle swell of voices told that the crowd was growing below.

"It's nearly time," announced Angela.

"Look." Catherine held up the key. "It's from Clay. Do you know what it's for?"

"I'm afraid I haven't any idea. You'll have to wait until after the ceremony and ask him."

Catherine tucked the key away in her garter where it seemed to burn warmly against her leg.

"Is Mother okay?"

"Yes, dear, don't worry. She's already in her place."

Inella ventured a tidy kiss on Catherine's cheek, then said, "You do look radiant, Miss Catherine." Then she was gone to attend to her duties below.

Again Bobbi picked up Catherine's bouquet, handed it to her and gave a last caress on the cheek, and stood awaiting her signal. The door swung open and Catherine watched Angela meet Claiborne in the upstairs hall. There was a brief smile from him, a last hovering look from her before they left Catherine's range of vision. Next came Stu, in a lush tuxedo of rich spice-brown, with an abundance of starched, apricot-colored ruffles springing from his chest below a high, stiff collar and bow tie. Stu grinned in at Catherine, and she attempted a quavering smile in return before Bobbi moved out into the hall and headed for the stairs.

And then came Steve. Her beloved Steve, looking so handsome in a tuxedo of his own, holding out both hands to her as if inviting her to a minuet. He wore a smile that melted her heart, that washed away their earlier disagreement. Catherine knew she must move forward, but her feet refused. Steve, sensing her thoughts, stepped gallantly to the bedroom doorway, bowed from the waist and extended an elbow. Suddenly she realized that people below were awaiting them and were more than likely gazing up the steps.

She felt the tug of the train upon the carpet, Steve's firm arm beneath her hand and the pressure of her heart thudding high against her ribcage. From below came a collective "Oooh . . ." as she stepped to the head of the stairs. A sudden intimidation gripped her as the raised sea of faces swam into view. But Steve, sensing her hesitation, closed his free hand over hers, urging her down the first step. She was dimly aware of candles washing everything with a mellow glow. They were everywhere: in wall sconces, upon shelves and tables, gleaming and twinkling from the floral sprays attached to the railing and from within the study where an overflow of guests watched. A path emerged as she and Steve rounded the newel post and glided toward the living room. Catherine had a fleeting memory of the first time she'd been in this foyer, sitting on the velvet bench now hidden behind the multitude of guests. How apprehensive she'd been then, yet this was not really so different. Her stomach was in knots. She moved in hypnotic fashion toward the living room doorway, toward Clay. From somewhere an electronic keyboard had joined the harp in a simple Chopin prelude. And everywhere, everywhere, there was the aura of candleglow, all gold and amber and warm and serene. The smell of flowers mingled with the waxen scent of candle smoke while Catherine drifted through the throng of guests, quite unaware of their great number, of their admiring gazes, or of how, for many of them, the sight of her brought back quicksilver memories of their own breathless walk down the aisle. The living room doorway captured her every thought; the idea of Clay waiting on the other side of it sent her heart flitting and her stomach shaking.

She had a dim impression of her mother waiting in a semicircle of countenances that faced her from the bay window, of space emerging as people rustled back to clear the way. But then all others were forgotten as Catherine's eyes fell upon Clay. He stood in the classic groom's pose, hands clasped before him, feet spraddled, face unsmiling and a bit tense. She had thought to avoid his eyes, but hers had a will of their own. As if he had materialized at the whim of some talented spinner of fairy tales, both he and the setting were too perfect.

Lord help me, thought Catherine, as their eyes met. Lord help me.

He waited, his hair like ripe wheat with the sun setting over it. A tall sconce of countless candles turned his skin to amber, reflecting from the deep apricot ruffles that only added to his masculinity. He wore a vested tuxedo of rich cinnamon, a sternly tied bow tie which suddenly bobbed up, then settled back in place at his first sight of her. His eyes—in that flawless face—widened, and she caught the nearly imperceptible movement as he began locking and unlocking his left knee. Then, just before she lost his glance, his hands dropped to his sides and he wet his lips. Blessedly, he then became only an impression at her side. But she knew he turned to gaze once more at her flushed cheek while the organ and harp faded into only a murmurous background.

"Dearly beloved . . ."

The charade began. Things became surrealistic to Catherine. She was a child again, playing wedding with Bobbi, walking across a lawn dressed in dishtowels and curtains, carrying a

209

bouquet of dandelions. Pretending she was back there took away the sting of guilt at what she was doing.

"Who gives this woman?"

"I do, her brother."

Reality returned and with it Clay's arm, taking the place of Steve's. It was solid, but surprising, for minute tremors scuttled there, felt but not seen.

This time I wanna be the bride.

But, you're always the bride!

No, I ain't! You were the bride last time!

Aw, come on, don't cry. Okay, but next time I get to wear the curtain on my head!

From her left, Bobbi smiled, while sweet, naive memories came whirling back. The minister spoke; he had a mellifluous voice and could manage to sound as if what he said were being spoken solely to her and Clay. Catherine trained her eyes on the minister's lips, concentrating hard on the words as he reminded those about to be joined of the importance of patience, love and faithfulness. Some muscle tensed into a knot beneath Catherine's hand, was forcibly relaxed, then twitched again. She realized that the minister had asked all the married couples present to join their hands and renew their wedding vows silently along with the bride and groom. Silently Catherine pleaded, No! No! What you're witnessing is a sham! Don't base your reaffirmation of love on something that is meaningless!

She escaped once again into the play days of yesteryear.

When you get married, what kinda man are you gonna marry?

Rich.

Oh, Bobbi, honestly, is that all you think about?

Well, what kind you gonna marry?

One who likes to be with me so much he comes straight home instead of stopping at bars. And he's always gonna be nice to me.

The minister asked them to turn and face each other and hold hands. The profusion of gardenias and roses was given into Bobbi's hands. During the exchange their childhood fantasies were reflected within a glance the two exchanged.

Then Catherine's hands were clasped firmly in Clay's brown,

strong fingers, and she felt dampness on his palms and on her own. The minister's voice droned on, far away, and Catherine was suddenly afraid to look Clay full in the face.

I'm gonna marry a man who looks just like Rock Hudson. Not me. I like blond hair and stormy eyes.

My God, thought Catherine now, did I really say that?

She raised her eyes to blond hair, to gray, sober eyes that wore an expression of sincerity as they probed hers for the benefit of their guests. His face was limned by flickering candlelight which accented the straight nose, long cheeks and sensitive lips which were parted slightly, but somber. An errant pulsebeat showed just above his high, tight, apricot-colored collar and the stern bow tie. His manner was faultless, convincing. It created havoc within Catherine.

A man who is nice to me. Blond hair and stormy eyes. One who is rich.

Phrases from the past resounded through the chambers of Catherine's heart, filling it with remorse unlike any she'd suffered before. But those who looked on couldn't guess the turmoil within her, for she paralleled Clay's superb act, searching his eyes as he searched hers, while the pressure on her knuckles grew to sweet agony.

What are we doing? she wanted to cry. Do you know what you do to me with those eyes of yours? What do I do to myself by clenching your too-strong fingers this way, by pretending to idolize your too-perfect face? Don't you recognize the pain of a girl whose youthful dreams painted this very illusion, time and time again, who escaped into scenes just such as this when reality threatened? Don't you understand that I honestly believed those dreams would come true one day? If you do, release my hands, release my eyes, but above all keep my heart free of you. You are too flawless and this is too close to the real thing and I have suffered long enough for the lack of love. Please, Clay, turn away before it's too late. You are a temporary illusion and I must not, must not get lost in it.

But she was trapped in a farce of her own making, for Clay did not turn away, nor release her eyes, nor her hands. Her palms felt seared, her heart felt blistered. And for a moment she knew the cruel bite of wishfulness.

At last she dragged her eyes downward. Then Stu stepped

forward, drawing a ring from his pocket. She extended her trembling fingers and Clay slid a diamond-studded band halfway on and held it hovering there.

"I, Clay, take thee, Catherine..."

While his deep voice spoke the words, Catherine's cheated heart wanted suddenly for this to mean something. But this was only a fantasy. Her thoughts tumbled on while Clay completed the ring's journey to its nesting place beside the heirloom already there.

She was startled then to find a ring placed in her palm— Angela had thought of everything—and her eyes fled once more to Clay's. Another prop for the play? hers asked. But perhaps he had chosen it himself, not Angela. Obediently she dropped her gaze and adorned his finger with the wide, gold unstudded florentine band.

"I, Catherine, take thee, Clay..." Her unsteady voice was threatened by shredded nerves, lost dreams and the awful need to cry.

But still there was more to be endured as they turned once again full-face to the blurred minister's garb. Hazily Catherine heard him pronounce them man and wife. Then the cleric smiled benevolently and sealed Catherine's and Clay's joined hands with both of his own.

"May your lives together be long and happy," he wished simply, never suspecting what the words did to Catherine's already strained emotions. She stared at the wavering sight of all their hands together, quite numb now. Then the minister's hands disappeared and his voice poured out softly for the last time. "And now you may seal your vows with your first kiss as Mr. and Mrs. Clay Forrester."

Shattered already, Catherine didn't know what to do. She felt as if she aged years in the mere moment while Clay took the lead, turning toward her with every misty eye in the house upon them. She lifted her face; the breath caught in her throat. She expected no more than a faint brush of lips, but instead his face loomed near, those gray eyes were lost in closeness, and she found herself enfolded in Clay's arms, gently forced against the starched ruffles of his elegant shirtfront, besieged by soft, slightly opened lips which were far, far too compelling. Haunting memories came flooding back.

No, Clay, don't! she longed to cry. But he did. He kissed her fully. And in that moment of first contact she sensed his apology, but found herself unable to forgive him for the convincing job he was doing.

He released her then, to the accompaniment of a collective murmur, and his breath touched her nose as he stepped back and looked into her startled eyes. There followed the kind of smile she'd been waiting for since childhood, sweeping Clay's face as if the moment were genuine, and she was forced to return one equally as bright. Then Clay tucked her hand possessively within his arm and turned her to face their guests.

She wore the pasted-on smile until it held its own. She was beleaguered by hugs, kisses and congratulations, starting with Stu, who unabashedly kissed her hard on the mouth. Next came Steve, holding her a little too long, a little too protectively, rocking a little while he squeezed her and whispered "Chin up" in her ear.

"Oh, Steve," she allowed herself to say, knowing that he alone understood.

"Shh, babe, you're both doing fine. I wish you could see how you look together."

Clay's father appeared, held her by the upper arms and welcomed her to the family with a generous hug and a direct kiss—the first kiss from him ever. Over his shoulder she saw Clay with his arms wrapped around Ada. Grandma and Grandpa Elgin gave her elfin pats and smiles, and Elizabeth Forrester bestowed upon her a regal kiss for each cheek and a tap of her cane upon the right shoulder, as if she were being knighted.

"You are a beautiful young woman. I shall expect beautiful children from you," the old eagle stated sagaciously before turning away as if the matter were settled. Then Catherine was passed around like a dish of divinity, tasted by many mouths until she was actually quite grateful to be returned at last to Clay—until he pleased every guest there by voluntarily giving them what they waited for!

He swooped down, smiling boldly, and grasped Catherine firmly around her ribs, then picked her cleanly up off the floor until she hung suspended like a marionette. Indeed, she had no more choice than a marionette whose strings are controlled by the puppeteer. She could only submit to Clay's lips while the gardenias were wrapped so far around his neck that her nose was buried in them. She closed her eyes, spinning like a leaf in a whirlwind, intoxicated by the overpowering fragrance of the waxy flowers, by the awful sense that this was real, pretending momentarily that it was. The instant he touched her lips, Catherine felt the almost automatic reach of Clay's tongue toward her own, then her own surprised tongue arching in hesitation, not quite knowing what to do with itself. Then Clay's withdrawing politely again. She was faintly aware that the crowd had burst into applause but allowed herself to become mesmerized by the sensation that the world was twirling crazily. With her eyes closed and her arms around her husband's neck she endured an endless kiss while he slowly turned them both in a circle. But the kiss had grown long—difficult to find a place for a tongue in the midst of such a kiss if it does not take its natural course—until at its end, his tongue again touched hers, then, elusive as quicksilver, was gone.

But the crowd saw nothing more than a groom turning his bride in a slow circle in the middle of a candlelit room, kissing, rejoicing in the accepted fashion. They knew nothing of the elusive tongue-dance which accompanied the embrace.

Catherine came out from behind her gardenias with scarlet cheeks, which added to everyone's delight except her own. But then she was grateful to Clay for the convincing ploy, for when she turned from his arms it was to find a string of familiar faces with sparkling eyes that had just witnessed the entire scenario with awe-struck rapture. For the first time Catherine didn't need to act. Her elation was genuine as she flew to greet Marie, then Francie, and Grover and Vicky too!

Having them there made it nearly perfect. Catherine was touched by the sight of the usually unkempt Grover with her hair all shining and curled like Catherine had never seen it before. And Vicky, who had miraculously managed to let her nails grow beyond the tips of her finger and had polished them the most horrendous shade of blood-red. And Francie, smelling of Charlie perfume. Marie, tiny and petite in spite of how close she was to her due date. Marie, the sprite, the matchmaker, who had first taught Catherine to accept the contact of a caring hand. How many times had they touched hands since?

Clay arrived at Catherine's side again, encircling her waist loosely, then pulling her against his hip with a smiling expression she knew was for the girls.

"Isn't she something?" Francie demanded. And obligingly Clay tightened his grip, spread his hand upon Catherine's ribs and dropped a loving kiss on the corner of her eye.

"Yes, she's something, my bride." Catherine refused to look up at Clay. His fingers rode perilously close to her breast.

"What do you think of our dress?" Marie asked.

Again he moved the hand, caressing the velvet appreciatively, answering, "Gorgeous," then continuing to play their game by asking, "Who's going to wear it next?"

"Well, that depends on which one of us can snag a guy like you. Hey, why don'tcha let go of her and let us have our turns?"

Deftly Marie divided Clay from his bride while he gave Catherine the required Help!-what-can-I-do look, then threw his all into a tremendous kiss for the tiny Marie. Now it was Clay's turn to be passed around like a sweet. Catherine could only look on, smiling in spite of herself. He kissed them all, giving them a taste of what they wished was theirs. He returned to his bride only when they'd tasted their fill, some of them for a little too long, some with too-rapt expressions as their kiss ended.

But for his understanding, Catherine was again grateful to Clay.

They moved through the crowd again, Catherine at last realizing it was far, far larger than Angela had hinted it would be. Not only the girls from Horizons, but business associates, family friends and numerous relatives had been impetuously added to the invitation list. Angela's "intimate little affair" had blossomed into a full-blown social event of the season.

Chapter 18

SHE AND CLAY were ensconced in the study to sign the marriage certificate under the gaze of the minister. They gave away no more than shaky fingers, then the photographer was there, popping his bulbs at their hands posed upon the document, then upon Catherine's bouquet, then herding them back into the living room to pose in the bay window with the other members of the wedding party. Throughout all this Catherine succeeded in being spontaneous and gay, as brides are expected to be. Bright repartee fell from her lips and from Clay's while they touched again and again until it became automatic, this reaching for each other's waists. And somehow Catherine found herself beginning to enjoy it.

Upon the dining room table a fountain of champagne cascaded. Clay and Catherine were buffeted there to catch their glasses full and sip around each other's love-knotted arms while the cameras again recorded the moment for posterity. The gentlemen guests posed around Catherine's gartered leg. She caught Clay's eye—was it twinkling?—above the glass of champagne he sipped. Next she posed on the stairway, where she tossed her bouquet over the banister. It was caught by a young girl Catherine didn't recognize.

Small tables appeared, set up with smooth efficiency by a host of hired waiters. Angela managed to oversee the dinner arrangements with silent skill while giving the impression that she'd never left her guests' sides nor swayed her attentions away from them.

Angela's know-how brought off a masterpiece of coordination. By the time Catherine was seated beside Clay at the head table, her admiration for his mother had grown immensely. It took more than money, Catherine realized, to achieve what Angela had here tonight.

The guests were served elegant plates of chicken breast stuffed with Minnesota's rare and delectable wild rice, garnished by crisp broccoli and spiced peach halves. The plates were as delightful to look at as they were to dip into. But what was most appreciated was the almost slick transition from reception rooms to dining hall. The entire festivity was proving to be a stunning success. Gratified, Catherine leaned around Clay to tell Angela so. But she only waved a nonchalant hand and assured Catherine the joy had been hers, she'd have felt cheated to do less and every minute had been worth it. Then she squeezed Catherine's hand.

It was in the middle of the meal that Catherine remembered the key. "Clay, I got your gift. Inella brought it upstairs before the ceremony, but I don't know what it's for."

"Guess."

She was afraid to. The whole evening was already overwhelming.

"The town house?" she ventured, but there was too much noise. Clay leaned down, his ear directly in front of her lips.

"What?"

"The town house, I said."

He straightened, smiled teasingly and only shook his head. She saw his lips move, but there was such a tinkling clangor going on that she couldn't hear him either. Now she lowered her ear to his lips, but while she was thus posed, straining to hear his reply, she became aware that all voices in the room had stopped and only the demanding sound of spoons striking wineglasses filled the air.

Startled, she looked up to find every eye waiting. Then she realized Clay's hand rested on the back of her neck. It slid away and he smilingly began getting to his feet. Realization dawned, but still she hesitated, linen napkin forgotten in one hand, fork in the other, unprepared for yet another assault on her senses.

Clay stepped behind her chair, leaned near her ear. "Apparently they're not going to let us off with a couple of quick kisses that half of them didn't see."

Quick kiss, she thought, was that last what he calls a *quick kiss*?

It was an old custom, one on which Catherine hadn't reckoned. The first kiss had been part of the ceremony. The second had taken her by surprise. But this one—this one was something altogether different. This was the one where plenty of schmaltz was expected.

From behind her came the innocent invitation, "Mrs. Forrester?" But Catherine suspected that could she see his face she'd find one eyebrow cocked up saucily, along with the corners of his mouth. She had no choice, so she gave the expected nervous laugh and got to her feet. There was no evading the issue this time as Clay gave her a regular Valentino job. Oh, he laid it on with aplomb! He pinned both of her arms at her sides, bent his head sideways and her slightly backward until she thought they'd both land on the floor. Her hands spread wide, finding nothing to hold onto but the taut fabric across his back. And while his tongue plundered the inside of her mouth in no uncertain terms, everyone in the room whistled and hooted and tapped their glasses all the more noisily until Catherine thought she would die of agony or ecstasy or a combination of the two. She died of neither. Instead, she found some welcome reserve of humor. He released her, straightened, and laughed into her eyes for the benefit of their guests, holding her loosely now about the waist with his hips resting against her own.

"Ah, Valentino, I'm sure," she said with a smile.

"They love it," he rejoined above the burst of applause. If anyone cared to read lips, Catherine was sure it would appear that Clay had said, "I love it." He held her a moment longer in that relaxed and familiar slackness. From the far reaches of the room it appeared they were the typically starstruck nuptial pair. He even rocked her sideways once, then plunged forward again to whisper in her ear, "Sorry."

Catherine's stomach felt at that moment like she'd eaten too much of Inella's salmon again. But before she could dwell on it, the photographer was there, demanding that they pose, feeding each other from filled forks. It was disconcerting, watching Clay's mouth open to receive food, holding the pose like a statuette, watching the glistening tip of his tongue which had only a moment ago unabashedly invaded her own.

The meal progressed, but Catherine couldn't eat another bite. Clay poured more champagne into her glass and she dove into it like a sailor from a burning ship. It made her head light and fuzzy and she warned herself to be careful. It was confusing stuff.

But before the bubbles cleared from her eyes, the glasses were ringing out again and Clay was standing up, taking her by the upper arm. This time it was easier, better, the wine having gone to her head somewhat, and her inhibitions sagged shamelessly while Clay gave her a kiss the likes of which turned her spine to aspic.

What the heck, the bride thought, give them what they want and forget it. And so she threw a little more of her heart into it—to say nothing of her tongue, which found a readily receptive mate within Clay's mouth. She even emoted a little, plopping her hand on top of her head as if holding it on, quite tickled by her own ingenuity.

The kiss ended. Clay laughed into her eyes. "Good job, Mrs. Forrester."

"Not bad yourself, Mr. Forrester." But she was all too aware of the way his hips again nudged her own through the velvet gown and the way her slightly bubbled tummy intruded upon the spot where his crisp tuxedo jacket hung open. "But I think you'd better stop filling my glass."

"Now why would I want to do a thing like that?" He smirked cutely, raising an eyebrow suggestively. His hands skimmed lightly downward to rest upon her hips. She wondered if it were her imagination or had he pressed himself momentarily closer? But then she decided it was her imagination. After all, he was performing—just as she was—for the benefit of all the tinkling glass-tappers out there.

The cake was wheeled in on a glass cart. It was a towering creation of fluted columns and doves with ribbons threaded through their confectionary beaks, and it raised a chorus of aah's that gratified Angela. Clay's and Catherine's hands were trained upon the knife handle with its voluminous white satin bow. Flashbulbs exploded, the knife sliced through the cake, and the bride was instructed to feed her groom, this time from her fingertips. But he not only took the cake, he lipped the frosting from her knuckle while, above it, his gray eyes crinkled at the corners. Naughty sensations tingled their way down to Catherine's toes and her eyes swerved swiftly aside.

"Mmm . . . sweet stuff," he said this time.

"Bad for your teeth," she smiled up at him, ". . . and rumored to cause hyperactivity."

He reared back and laughed wholeheartedly and once again they sat down.

"Let's have one of the groom feeding the bride," the photographer suggested, zooming in on his quarry.

"How many more must we take?" Catherine asked, flustered now, but not entirely disliking the game.

"I'll be neat," Clay promised in an aside. But that same devilish crinkle tugged at the corners of his mouth and eyes. He lifted a morsel of cake and she took it, tasted sugar, swallowed, then found him still standing there with an index finger frosted and waiting.

With a smile as sweet as any confection she said, "This is getting bawdy." But all she could do was suck the end of his finger, finding it slightly salty too.

"Our guests find it amusing."

"You, Mr. Forrester, are unforgivably salty." But at that moment she caught Elizabeth Forrester's bright, knowing gaze snapping down the table at them, and she wondered what the old girl suspected.

The moment turned serious when Claiborne rose to give Catherine his official welcome. He came around the table and gave her a hug and a kiss and his approval for all to see. She sensed sobriety returning to Clay as he leaned an elbow on the table's edge and absently brushed an index finger across his lip, watching. Then he rose and shook hands with his father. Applause followed as Clay sat back down. The whole thing had been appallingly earnest on Claiborne's part, and as their eyes met, both Catherine and Clay realized it.

"On second thought, you'd better pour me another glass," she said, "and smile. Your grandmother Forrester is watching every move we make."

"Then this is for her, and for Mother and Father," Clay said, and reached a finger to tip her chin up and placed the lightest kiss upon her lips. Then he reached for the champagne bottle. But his smile and gay mood did not return.

The meal ended and dancing began. Catherine met more of Clay's relatives and spent the appropriate amount of time with each. Then she found time to move off by herself and seek out her mother, and Uncle Frank and Aunt Ella. The evening was moving inexorably toward its close, and with each passing minute Catherine's apprehension grew.

Standing with Bobbi in the living room, Catherine caught sight of Clay out in the foyer. He stood with a remarkably beautiful girl whose auburn hair trailed down to the middle of her back. She cradled a champagne glass as if she were born with it in her hand. She smiled up at Clay, gyrated her head as if to toss her hair back. But it fell alluringly across her cheek. Then the girl circled Clay's neck with the arm bearing the stem glass, raising her lips to his and kissing him differently than any of the starry-eyed girls from Horizons had. Catherine observed the somber look upon Clay's face as he spoke to the girl, dropping his eyes to the floor, then raising them to her face again with a look of apology etching his every feature. Catherine would have been lying to herself had she not admitted that the touch he gave the girl's upper arm was a caress. He spoke into her eyes, rubbed that arm, then gave it a lingering squeeze before he bent to drop an unhurried kiss upon the crest of one flawless, high-boned cheek.

Quickly Catherine turned her back. But the picture rankled until something pinched at her throat and made it hard to swallow the champagne she lifted to her lips.

"Who is that girl out there with Clay?"

Bobbi glanced toward the foyer and her smile immediately faded.

"It's her, isn't it?" Catherine questioned. "It's Jill Magnusson."

Bobbi turned her back on the couple too quickly. "Yes, it is. So what?"

"Nothing."

But try as she might, Catherine could not resist looking their way again to find Clay now relaxed, one hand in his trouser pocket while Jill threaded her arm through his and rested her breast leisurely against his biceps. She was the kind of girl who could get by with a touch like that. Her sophistication made it look chic instead of shabby. An older man had joined them now and Jill Magnusson laughed, leaned sideways without relinquishing her claim on Clay and gave the older man a swift kiss on the side of his mouth.

"And who's he?" Catherine asked, carefully keeping the ice from her tone.

"That's Jill's father."

There was a sick and empty feeling settling in the pit of Catherine's stomach. She wished she hadn't witnessed Jill leaning casually against Clay in the presence of her own father, nor her obvious lack of unease at kissing Clay with an arm looped around his neck. But Catherine was in for a further surprise, for even as she looked on, Elizabeth Forrester approached the group and it was immediately apparent that Jill Magnusson was as comfortable with the old eagle as she was with the champagne glass and Catherine's new husband. The unapproachable old woman didn't daunt Jill one bit. The brunette actually linked her remaining arm through Elizabeth's, laughing gracefully at whatever Clay's grandmother said. Then—unbelievably—the old eagle laughed too.

And Catherine finally turned away.

At that moment Clay's eyes drifted up, found Bobbi observing the quartet, and immediately he withdrew his hand from his pocket, excused himself and crossed toward her and Catherine.

"Jill and her parents were just leaving," he explained. It became apparent as soon as the words left his mouth that explanations should not have been necessary. They had not been for the other guests who'd already departed.

"Somehow it seems that Catherine was not introduced to the Magnussons."

"Oh . . . I'm sorry, Catherine. I should have seen to it." He glanced uncertainly from Catherine to the front door. But it was opening. Angela and Mrs. Magnusson were touching cheeks fondly while the two men shook hands, and Jill gave a long, last look across the expanse that separated her from Clay. Then they were gone.

"Catherine..." Clay began, but realizing Bobbi was still there, said, "Excuse us, will you, Bobbi?" He took Catherine's elbow and moved her beyond earshot. "I think it's time we left."

Certainly, now that Jill Magnusson is gone, thought Catherine. "But shouldn't we thank your parents first?"

"I've done that already. Now we're expected to simply slip away unnoticed."

"But what about the gifts?" She was grasping at straws and she knew it.

"They'll be left here. We're not expected to thank anyone for them tonight. We're only supposed to disappear while they're busy."

"Mom will be wondering..." she began lamely, looking around.

"Will she?" Clay could see how nervous Catherine had suddenly become. "Steve is with her. He'll see that she gets home okay."

Catherine saw Ada in happy conversation with Bobbi's parents and Steve. Catherine raised her glass to her lips, but found it empty. Then Clay removed it from her lifeless fingers, saying, "Slip upstairs and get your coat and I'll meet you by the side door. And don't forget the key."

Once more in the pink bedroom, Catherine at last allowed her shoulders to sag. She plopped down on the edge of the gay little bed, then leaned back and let her eyelids close wearily. She wished this were her own room, that she could snuggle in and awaken in the morning to find that no wedding had taken place after all. Absently she picked up a small pillow, toyed with the ruffled edge, staring until the design on it seemed to wriggle. She blinked, tossed the pillow aside and went to stand before the cheval mirror. She pressed her dress against her lower abdomen, visually measuring. She raised her eyes and stared at the reflected face, wondering how it could be so pink when she felt so bloodless. From the depths of the silvered glass, blue eyes watched her fingertips touch one cheek, then flutter down uncertainly to her lips. Her brows wore a troubled look as she assessed her own reflection and found countless imperfections in it.

"Jill Magnusson," she whispered. Then she turned and flung her coat loosely about her shoulders.

Outside the world wore that semi-dark glow of the first snow of the season, glittering almost as if from within. The night sky looked as though someone had spilled milk across it, obscuring the moon behind a film of white. But as if a droplet slipped off now and then, an occasional snowflake drifted down. The lights from the windows twinkled playfully upon the white frosting, and the leafless limbs of the trees looked warm now beneath their blankets. The air was brittle, though, brittle enough to freeze the tender petals of the gardenia forgotten in Catherine's hair.

Catherine clutched her coat beneath her chin, raised her face and sucked in the taste of the cold. Revitalized, she hurried through the shadows to the end of the house near the garages. It was quiet. Not even the hum of distant traffic intruded, and she savored it, trying to make it calm her.

"Sorry it took so long."

She jumped at the sound of Clay's voice and clutched her coat tighter. He materialized out of the darkness, a tall shadow with its coat collar turned up. "I got caught by a few well-wishers and couldn't get away."

"It's okay." But she drew her mouth down within the protective folds of her coat.

"Here, you're freezing." He touched her back, steered her toward a strange, dark car that waited there. Even in the blackness she could see that it had streamers trailing from it. He opened the driver's side door.

"Have you got the key?" he asked.

"The key?" she asked dumbly.

"Yes, the key." He smiled with only one side of his mouth. "I'll drive tonight, but after this, it's yours."

"M-mine?" she stammered, uncertain of which to look to for verification, the car or his face.

"Happy wedding day, Catherine," he said simply.

"The key was for this?"

"I thought you'd like a wagon, for groceries and things like that."

"But, Clay . . ." She was shivering worse now, the tremors quite pronounced in spite of the way she hugged herself into the coat.

"Have you got the key?"

"Clay, this isn't fair," she pleaded.

"All's fair in love and war."

"But this is not love or war. How can I just . . . just say 'Thank you, Mr. Forrester' and drive off in a brand new car as if I have every right to it?"

"Don't you?"

"No! It's too much and you know it."

"The Corvette isn't exactly a family car," he reasoned. "We'd have trouble getting even the wedding gifts to the town house in it."

"Well, fine, then, trade it in or—or borrow the Bronco again, but don't hand me the world on a platter that I feel guilty to eat from."

His hand dropped from the car door; his voice sounded slightly piqued. "It's a gift. Why do you have to make so much of it? I can afford it, and it will make our lives infinitely easier to have two cars. Besides, Tom Magnusson owns an auto dealership and we get great deals from him on all the cars we buy."

Common sense returned with a cold swipe. "Well, in that case, thank you."

Catherine got in and slid across to the passenger side. He got behind the wheel to find her leg angled across the transmission hump, her skirt pulled up. She produced the key from within her garter and handed it to him.

It was warm in his palm.

He seemed a little ill at ease as he started the engine, but let it idle. He adjusted the heater, cleared his throat. "Catherine, I don't know how to say this, but it seems we each got a key tonight. I got one too."

"From whom?"

"From Mother and Father."

She waited, trembling inside.

"It's for the honeymoon suite at the Regency."

She made a sound like air going out of a balloon, then moaned, "Oh, God."

"Yes, oh, God," he agreed, then laughed nervously.

"What are we going to do?" she asked.

"What do you want to do?"

"I want to go to the town house."

"And let the Regency phone tomorrow and ask why the bride and groom didn't show up?"

She sat silent, shaking.

"Catherine?"

"Well, couldn't we . . . couldn't we just"—she swallowed—"check in and leave again and go to the town house, maybe leave the key for them to find in the morning?"

"Do you want me to go back into the house and pick up a load of gifts and hope we find some sheets and blankets when we open them?"

He was right; they were trapped.

"Catherine, this is adolescent. We've just gotten married and we've agreed to spend the next several months living together. You realize that we're going to bump into each other now and then during that time, don't you?"

"Yes, but not in any honeymoon suite at the Regency." Still she knew that before the night was out they'd have put the lie to her words.

"Catherine, what the hell did you expect me to do, stuff the keys back into my father's hand and say 'Use them yourselves'?"

There was no point in arguing. They sat there thinking until finally Clay put the car in reverse, and backed away from the shadow of the garage.

"Clay, I don't have my suitcase!" she gulped.

"It's in the back with mine," he said, while the doorman grew small behind them, his arms folded and his collar turned up.

They drove along in silence, Catherine still gripping her coat although the car had long since grown warm. The smell of new, hot oil mingled with that of new vinyl. With each mile Catherine grew tighter.

Finally she said, "Why does it seem like everything important that happens between us happens in one of your cars?"

"It's one of the few places we've ever been alone."

"Well, your parents sure took care of that, didn't they?"

With an abrupt swerve he pulled to the side of the road, skidded to a halt and craned to look back over his shoulder.

She perked alert. "Now what?"

He was already turning around. "You want to go to the town house, okay, we'll go to the town house," he snapped.

She clutched his arm. "Don't," she pleaded. "Don't, not tonight."

He brooded silently, tense now too.

"I was wrong, okay?" she conceded. "Just don't drive crazy— not tonight. I know they meant well to get the room for us, and you're right. What difference does it make where we sleep?" she dropped her hand from his arm. "Please try to understand, though. It's been a nerve-wracking night. I'm not used to lavishness."

"Maybe you better get used to it, because they never do anything halfway."

He drove on more sensibly now.

"How much do you imagine it cost them to arrange all that?"

"Don't let it bother you. Mother loved it all. I've told you before, she's in her element planning things like that. Couldn't you tell how she was enjoying her success?"

"Is that supposed to ease my conscience?" she asked.

"Catherine, are we going to go through this every time we get something from them? Why do you constantly berate yourself? Had it occured to you that maybe you're not the only one benefiting from our arrangement? It may surprise you to learn that I'm actually quite happy to be moving away from home. I should have done it years ago, but it was easier to stay where I was. It's not exactly a hardship being coddled and taken care of. But I'm tired of living with them. I'm glad to be getting out. I wonder if they aren't equally relieved to have me leave at last.

"And as for my parents—don't think they didn't get something out of that production number. Did you see my father's face when he was brandishing his champagne glass? Did you see Mother when she was directing waiters around, watching while everything slipped into place like greased gears? They get high off social success, so just think of it as another autumn gala thrown by the Forresters. They throw one quite like it several times a year anyway.

"What I'm trying to say is, that it's their style. Giving us the night at the Regency is what their friends expect them to do, plus—"

"Plus what?" She shot him a look.

"Plus, giving us the right start gives them a false sense of security. It helps them believe everything will turn out right between us."

"And you don't feel guilty to accept any of it?"

"Yes, dammit!" he burst out. "But I'm not going to go out and buy a hair shirt over it, all right?"

His belligerence surprised her, for he'd been mellow for days. They arrived at the Regency in strained silence. Catherine made a move toward her door handle and Clay ordered, "Wait here until I get the suitcases out."

He walked around the car, yanking the crepe paper streamers off. His breath formed a pale pink cloud, refracting the glow from the colorful hotel sign and the lights at the entry. He opened the tailgate, and she heard the muffled swish as he tossed the streamers in.

When he opened her door and she'd stepped out, he reached for her arm. "Catherine, I'm sorry I yelled. I'm nervous too."

She studied his odd-colored visage in the neon night, but she could find nothing to reply.

Chapter 19

THE PORTER FLOURISHED his hand toward the room and Catherine followed it with her eyes. It felt as though she were couched in a Wedgwood teacup. The room was elegant and tasteful, decorated exclusively in oyster white and Wedgwood blue. The cool blue walls were trimmed with pearly moldings done in beadwork, arranged in rectangles with a carved acanthus centered in each. The design was repeated on two sets of double doors which led to closet and bath. Elegant white silk draperies were crowned by an ornate swagged valance while alabaster French Provincial furniture contrasted soothingly with the room's plush blue carpeting. Besides the enormous bed there was a pleasant grouping of furniture: a pair of chairs and coffee table of Louis XVI persuasion, with graceful cabriole legs and oval, marble tops. On the table sat a profuse bouquet of white roses whose scent was thick in the air.

When the door closed, leaving them alone, Catherine approached the flowers, found the tiny green envelope and turned questioningly to Clay.

"I don't know, open it," he said.

The card read simply, "All our love, Mother and Dad."

"It's from your parents." She extended the card, then sidled a safe distance away while he read it.

"Nice," he murmured, and stuck the card back into the roses. He pushed back his jacket and scanned the room with hands akimbo. "Nice," he repeated.

"More than nice," she seconded, "more like smashing."

Upon the triple dresser was a basket of fruit and a silver loving cup bearing a green glass bottle. Clay walked over, lifted the bottle, read the label, set it back down, then turned, tugging the knot from his bow tie and unfastening a single button of his shirt. Her eyes flew off in another direction. She walked over and gave a careful peek into the depths of the darkened bathroom.

"Can I hang up your coat for you?" he asked.

She looked surprised to find it still crumpled between her wrist and hip. "Oh—oh, sure."

He came to reach for her garment and again she retreated a step.

"Don't be skittish," he said laconically, "I'm only going to hang up your coat."

"I'm not skittish. I just don't know what to do with myself, that's all."

He opened the closet doors, spoke at the tinging hangers inside.

"I'd call that skittish. Maybe a glass of champagne would help. Do you want one?" He hung up his tux jacket too.

"I don't think so." But she wandered back to the dresser anyway and looked over the bottle and the basket. "Who is the fruit from?"

"The management. You want some? How about a last pear of the season?" A tan hand reached around her and hefted one.

"No, no pears either. I'm not hungry."

As she drifted away he tossed the fruit in the air once, twice, then forgot it in his hand, studying her.

"No champagne, no fruit, so what would you like to do to pass the time away?"

She looked up blankly, standing there in the middle of the room as if afraid to come into contact with any article in it. He sighed, dropped the pear back into the basket and moved to carry their suitcases across to the bed.

230

"Well, we're here, so we might as well make the best of it."

He stalked to the bathroom door, flicked on the light, then turned, gesturing toward it.

"Would you like to be first?"

And the next thing Catherine knew, she was laughing! It started as a silent flutter in her throat and before she could control it, it erupted and she had both hands over her mouth before she flung them wide and continued laughing to the ceiling. At last she looked across to find Clay—the corners of his eyes crinkled now—still waiting just outside the bathroom doorway.

"Come on, hey, wife, I'm trying to be gallant and it's getting tougher by the minute."

And suddenly the tension was relieved.

"Oh, Clay, if your father could see us, I think he'd demand his money back. Are we really in the honeymoon suite of the Regency?"

"I think so." Gamely, he looked around, checking.

"And did you just sign our names in the register as Mr. and Mrs. Clay Forrester?"

"I think so."

She looked up as if appealing to the heavens. "Help, I'm floundering."

"You should do that more often, you know?" He smiled her way.

"Do what, flounder?" She chuckled and made a hapless motion.

"No, laugh. Or even smile. I was beginning to think you were going to wear your stiff face all night long."

"Do I have a stiff face?" It looked mobile and amazed as she asked.

"Stiff might not be the right word. Deadpan is probably more accurate. Yes, deadpan. You put it on like armor at times."

"I do?"

"Mostly when we're alone."

"So you'd like it if I smiled more?"

He shrugged. "Yeah, I guess I would. I like smilers. I guess I'm used to being around them."

"I'll try to remember." She glanced toward the window, then back at him. "Clay, what you said down there in the car, well, I'm sorry, too." Her face had turned suddenly serious, contrite.

"No, it was me who got short with you. My timing really stunk."

"No, listen, it was partly my fault too. I don't want us to fight all the time we're married. I've been around it all my life and now I simply want . . . well, *peace* between us. I know this sounds silly, but it feels better already, just admitting that we're nervous, instead of the way we were acting on the way over here. I want you to know that I'll try to do my part to maintain some kind of status quo."

"Good. Me too. We're stuck with each other for better or for worse, so let's make the better of it instead of the worse."

She smiled a little. "Agreed. So . . . me first, huh?"

They both looked at the bathroom door.

"Yup."

What the heck, she thought, it's only a regular old bathroom, right? And I'm choking in this dress, right? And dying to get comfortable, right?

But once inside the bathroom she was too aware of his presence just outside. She turned on the faucet to cover any personal sounds. She kept glancing furtively at the doors. She confronted herself in the mirror, moving close to analyze her reflection until her breath beaded on the glass.

"Mrs. Clay Forrester, huh?" she asked her reflection. "Well, don't go getting ideas. He told you once you don't play around without paying for it, and he was right. So put on your nightie and go out there and clamber into bed with him, and if you're uncomfortable doing it, you've got nobody to blame but yourself."

Her fingers trembled as she undressed. She stared herself down with too-wide eyes as she removed her velvet wedding gown, then the slip and that ridiculously minuscule bra. Her breasts were weightier now, the nipples broad and florid. At their sudden release, dull twinges of ache flowed through them— not pain exactly, but something akin to it—and she closed her eyes and cupped one in each hand, squeezing and lifting in that way which lately could abate those unexpected throes.

Once the pangs were gone came the relief of being unbound. She watched herself scratch the red marks where her bra had bitten too tightly at the top of her ribs, then her stomach, which felt like the head of a drum and itched mercilessly now as the skin began stretching.

Unbidden the thought came that the man who waited on the other side of the door had created these changes in her body.

She shook off the thought, brushed her teeth, ran warm water and soaped a cloth. But just as she was about to scrub off her makeup, it struck her that her face had many short-comings which would be emphasized without the makeup, so she left it on.

She threw up her arms and a yellow nightgown drifted down like a parachute in the wind, followed by a matching peignoir. Her hands slowed, tying the cover-up at her throat. It was so obviously new. Would he mistake her reason for wearing such frillery? Should she march out there and announce that Ada had bought it at the company store at an employee's discount and had given it to her for a shower gift?

Through the peignoir her new girth was disguised, and she soothed the front, thoughts skittering from one to another. She was putting off opening the door and she knew it. She closed her eyes and swallowed . . . and swallowed again . . . and felt a hidden tremor deep within her stomach.

Suddenly the memory of Jill Magnusson was there in full color behind her eyelids and Catherine knew beyond a doubt that had it been Jill here getting ready to join Clay, there would be no schoolgirl shyness.

She supposed Clay was wishing right now she *were* Jill Magnusson. A hint of self-pity threatened, but she barred it. She remembered that last, long look of regret on Jill's face as she looked back across the room at Clay before walking out the door.

At last Catherine admitted, I carry his child. But it should be her, not me.

The door was soundless. Clay stood with his back to her, gazing down into her open suitcase, his tie forgotten in one hand, toothbrush in the other.

"Your turn," she said quietly, expecting him to jump guilt-ily. Instead he looked over his shoulder and smiled. His eyes

233

made one quick trip down and up the yellow peignoir.

"Feel better?"

He had pulled his shirttails out of his trousers. Her eyes went down to them like metal shavings to a magnet, to the network of wrinkles pressed into the fabric by his skin. Then farther down, to his stocking feet.

"Much."

They exchanged places and Clay moved into the bathroom, leaving the door open while he only brushed his teeth. In the suitcase, Catherine found a corner of her diary showing beneath the neatly folded clothing there. She tucked it away and closed the suitcase with a snap.

"Are you tired?" he asked, coming back from the bathroom.

"Not a bit."

"Do you mind if I break into that champagne then?"

"No, go ahead. It might help after all."

When his back was turned, she tugged at the top of her neckline; it was far from seductive, but not quite demure. His shoulders flexed and twisted as he worked away at the cork, and the wrinkles on the rear tails of his shirt did incredible things to her stomach, hanging free that way, shifting against his buttocks with each movement. The cork exploded and he swung the bottle over the loving cup.

"Here," he said, coming back with bottle in one hand, glasses in the other. She held the glasses while he poured. But his shirt was unbuttoned all the way now, exposing a thin band of skin a slightly deeper shade than the fabric itself. She dragged her eyes back to the champagne glasses, to the tan, long-fingered hand that reached out to reclaim one.

"To your happiness," he said simply, in his Clay-like, polite, usual way, while she wondered just what would make her happy right now.

"And to yours."

They drank, standing there in the middle of the room. There was a lump in her throat, she realized, as she swallowed the golden liquid. She looked down into her glass.

"Clay, I don't want either of us to pretend this is something it isn't." Rattled now, she put a palm to her forehead and swung away. "Oh, God."

"Come on, Catherine, let's sit down."

234

He led the way, set the bottle on the table beside the roses and strung himself out on a chair, lying low against its back, legs outstretched, ankles crossed, while she curled up opposite. He had a glimpse of her bare feet before she tucked them up beneath her in the corner of her chair. Together they raised their glasses, eyeing each other as they drank.

"I suppose maybe we're setting out to get drunk," she mused.

"Maybe we are."

"That doesn't make much sense, does it?"

"Not a lick."

"It won't change a thing."

"Nuh-uh."

"Then why are we doing it?"

"Because it'll make crawling into bed easier."

"Let's talk about something else."

"Whatever you say."

She fiddled with her glass, then sat back, drawing circles with it upon her turned knee. Finally she asked, "You know what was the hardest?" Across the table, he was looking very relaxed.

"Hmm-mmm." His eyes were closed.

"Your father's official welcome at the dinner table. I was very touched by it."

Clay's eyes drifted open, studied her a moment before he observed, "You know, I think my father likes you."

With a fingertip she toyed with the bubbles on the surface of her drink. "He still scares me in so many ways."

"I suppose to a stranger he seems formidable. Both he and Grandmother Forrester have an air about them that seems rather officious and puts people on their guard at first. But when you get to know them, you realize they're not that way at all."

"I don't intend to get to know them."

"Why?"

She raised expressionless eyes to his, then dropped them as she answered, "In the long run that'd be best."

"Why?"

His head lolled sideways, yet she suspected his catlike pose was not all real. She considered evading the issue, then decided against it. She leaned to take one rose from the bouquet and held it before her upper lip.

"Because I might learn to like them after all."

He seemed to be mulling that over, but he only tipped his glass again, then shut his eyes.

"Do you know what your Grandmother Forrester said to me tonight?"

"What?"

"She said, 'You are a beautiful bride. I shall expect beautiful children from you,' as if it was an official edict and she'd brook no ugly grandchildren spawned with her name."

Clay laughed appreciatively, his eyes again scrutinizing Catherine from behind half-closed lids. "Grandmother's usually right—and you were, you know."

"Was?" she asked, puzzled.

"A beautiful bride."

Immediately Catherine hid behind the rose again, became engrossed in studying the depths between its petals.

"I didn't know if I should say it or not, but—dammit, why not?—you were a knockout tonight."

"I wasn't fishing for a compliment."

"You make a habit of that, you know?"

"Of what?"

"Of withdrawing from any show of approval I make toward you. I knew before I said that that you'd turn defensive and reject it."

"I didn't reject it, did I?"

"You didn't accept it either. All I said was that you were a beautiful bride. Does that threaten you?"

"I—I don't know what you mean."

"Forget it then."

"No, you brought it up, let's finish it. Why should I feel threatened?"

"You're the one who's supposed to answer that question."

"But I'm not *threatened* in the least." She swished her rose through the air offhandedly. "You were a terrific-looking groom. There, see? Does that sound like I feel threatened by you?"

But her very tone was defensive. It reminded him of a child who, taking up a dare, says, "See? I'm not either afraid to walk up and ring Crazy Gertie's doorbell," then rings it and runs to beat hell.

"Hey, what do you think," he said in a bantering tone, "are

236

we supposed to thank each other or what?"

That at last drew a smile from her. She relaxed a little as if maybe the wine were now making her sleepy.

"Do you know what your mother said to me?" Clay asked.

"What?"

He mused silently, as if deciding whether or not to tell her. Abruptly he leaned forward and occupied himself with refilling his glass. "She said, 'Catherine used to play wedding when she and Bobbi were little girls. That's all those two would play, always arguing about who'd be the bride.'" Then he lounged back again, propped an elbow on the arm of the chair, rested his temple against two fingers and asked lazily, "Did you?"

"What does it matter?"

"I was only wondering, that's all."

"Well, don't wonder. It doesn't matter."

"Doesn't it?"

But abruptly she changed the subject. "One of your uncles mentioned that you usually go hunting at this time of year but that you haven't had much chance this year because of the wedding interruptions."

"It must've been Uncle Arnold."

"Don't change the subject."

"Did I change the subject?"

"You can go, you know, anytime you want."

"Thank you, I will."

"I mean, we're not *bound* to each other, and nothing has to change. We can still go our separate ways, keep our friends, just like before."

"Great. Agreed, Stu and I will hunt all we want."

"I wasn't really thinking about Stu."

"Oh?" He quirked an eyebrow.

"I was talking about her."

"Her? Who?"

"Jill."

Clay's eyes turned to gray iron, then he jumped up, stalked to the dresser and clapped his glass down hard. "What has Jill got to do with it?"

"I saw you standing in the foyer together. I saw the two of you kissing. I include her when I say you're not bound to me in any way."

237

He swung around, scowling. "Listen, our families have been friends for years. We've been——" He stopped himself before he could say *lovers*. "I've known her since we were kids. And furthermore, her father was right there in front of us, and so was Grandmother Forrester, for God's sake."

"Clay"—Catherine's voice was like eiderdown—"I said it's all right."

He glared at her silently, then swung toward his suitcase, shrugging his shirt off as he went, flinging it carelessly across the foot of the bed before disappearing behind the bathroom door.

When Clay returned, Catherine was sitting on the far edge of the bed with her back to him. The wilted gardenia lay discarded on the bedside table while she brushed her hair. His eyes traveled across the white satin sheets to the robe lying on the foot of the bed, to the back of her pale yellow nightgown, to the brush moving rhythmically. Without a word, he doubled his pillow over and lay down with both hands behind his head. The brush stilled. He heard her thumbnail flicking across its bristles, followed by a clack as she laid the thing down. She reached for the lamp and the room went black. The mattress shifted; the covers over his chest were pulled slightly in her direction. He had no doubt that if he reached out, he'd find her back curled against him.

Their breathing seemed amplified. Sightlessness created such intimacy. Clay lay so rigid that his shoulders began to hurt. Catherine huddled like a snail, involute, acutely aware of him behind her. She thought she could hear her eyelids scraping on her dry eyeballs with each blink. She shivered and pinioned the satin sheet tightly between her jaw and shoulder.

A rustle, barely audible, and she sensed his eyes boring into her back—invisible though it was.

"Catherine," came his voice, "you really have a low opinion of me, don't you?"

"Don't sound so wounded. There's no reason to be. Just to keep the record straight—it should have been her who was the bride today. Do you think I don't know that? Do you think I couldn't tell how she *belongs?* I felt like a square peg in a round hole. And seeing you and her together brought me back to reality. I was becoming rather swept off my feet by all the lavish trappings around me. I'll answer your question now. Yes, I did used to play wedding with Bobbi when we were kids. I'm an old pro at weddings, so this time I found myself really getting into the act. But I'm not pretending anymore. I see things for what they really are, okay?"

Goddammit, thought Clay, I should thank her for giving me permission, but instead it makes me angry. Goddammit, I shouldn't feel like I have to be faithful to a wife, but I do.

Catherine felt the bed bounce as he tossed onto his side and punched his pillow.

Somewhere outside a jet went over, its faraway whine and whistle ebbing off into oblivion. The bed was very large; neither of them had much sensation of sharing it physically, except for the sound of their breathing, far away from each other and in opposite directions. But the animosity between them was a much more palpable presence. It seemed like hours had gone by and Catherine thought Clay had gone to sleep. But then he flung himself onto his back again so abruptly she was sure he'd been wide awake all this time. She was stiff and cramped from staying in her tight curl for so long, but she refused to budge. Her shoulder got a cramp and she had to relax it. The sheet slipped off, and at last giving up, she eased onto her back.

"Are we going to get in each other's hair this way every time bedtime arrives?" he asked coldly.

"I didn't mean to get into your hair."

"Like hell you didn't. Let's at least be honest about it. You meant to bring a third party into bed with us and you succeeded very well. But just remember, if she's here it's at your request, not mine."

"Then why do you sound so angry?"

"Because it's playing havoc with my sleep. If I have to go through this for the next year, I'll be a burned-out wreck."

"So what do you think I'll be?"

Against his will, as he lay brooding, Clay had been resurrecting pictures of Catherine at the ceremony. The way she looked when she'd come around the living room doorway, when they spoke their vows, when she'd discovered all the girls from Horizons there, when he'd kissed her. He remembered the feel of her slightly rounded stomach against his. This was the damnedest thing he'd ever been through, going to bed

239

with a woman and not touching her. All the more absurd because for the first time it'd be legal, and here he lay on his own side of the bed. Dammit, he thought, I should've watched the champagne. Champagne made him horny.

He finally concluded that they were being quite childish about all this. They were husband and wife, they'd been through some decidedly sexual teasing during the course of the evening and were now trying to deny what it was that was keeping them both awake.

What the hell, he thought, things couldn't be worse. "Catherine, do you want to try it again, with no strings attached? Maybe then we can get some sleep."

The muscles in her lower abdomen cinched up tight and set to quivering. She shrank to her side of the bed, turning her back on him again.

"The wine has gone to your head" was all she said.

"Well, what the hell, you can't blame a guy for trying."

She felt like her chest bones might burst and fly into a thousand pieces. Angry with herself for wishing the night to be more than it was, angry with him for his suggestion, she wondered what exquisite torture it would be to turn to him and take him up on his invitation.

But she remained as she was, curled into herself. In the long hours before sleep she wondered over and over again if he had any pajamas on.

Chapter 20

CATHERINE WAS AWAKENED by the sound of draperies opening. She sat up as if a hundred-and-twenty-piece band had struck up a Sousa march beside her bed. Clay stood in the flood of sunlight, laughing.

"Do you always wake up like that?"

She squinted and blinked, then flopped backward like an old rag doll, covering her eyes with a forearm.

"Oh God, so you *did* have pajamas on."

He laughed again, free and easy, and turned toward the view of the awakening city washed in pink and gold below them.

"Does that mean 'good morning'?"

"That means I wasted a perfectly good night worrying about a dumb thing like whether or not you were wearing pajamas."

"Next time just ask."

Suddenly she was pulling herself off the bed, and running for the bathroom door which thwacked shut behind her.

"Don't listen!" she ordered.

Clay leaned an elbow against the window frame, chuckling to himself, thinking of the unexpected charms of married life.

She came out looking sheepish and went immediately for her cover-up.

"I'm sorry if I was a little abrupt about that, but this little feller in here has made some sudden changes and that's one of them. I'm still not used to it."

"Does this confidence mean you're not mad at me anymore?"

"Was I mad at you? I don't seem to remember." She busied herself doing up the front of the garment.

"Yeah," he said, moving away from the window, "I made some underhanded suggestion and you got huffy."

"Forget it. Let's be friends. I don't like fighting much, even with you."

He confronted her now, barechested, giving her hair the once-over so that she started combing it with her fingers.

"Listen," she explained, "I'm not at my best in the morning."

"Who is?" he returned, rubbing his jaw. Then he turned toward a suitcase and rummaged inside it, beginning to whistle softly through his teeth. Mornings she was used to her mother scuffling around the house with an air of martyrdom and tiredness as if the day were ending rather than beginning. And the old man, with his belching and scratching, drinking coffee royals and muttering imprecations under his breath.

But this was something new: a man who whistled before breakfast.

He stopped on his way to the bathroom, holding a leather case of toilet articles.

"What do you say we get dressed and find some breakfast, then go out to the house and pick up the gifts."

"I'm starved. I never did finish my dinner last night."

"And you're not the only one who's hungry?" He dropped his gaze briefly to her stomach. She was contouring it with both hands.

"No, I'm not."

"Then let me buy you both breakfast."

She colored and turned away, realizing she liked the morning Clay.

When the shower was splattering away she dropped down

242

onto the bed again, fell back supine in the sun, thinking of how different Clay seemed this morning. She even enjoyed his teasing. She heard the bar of soap drop, then a muffled exclamation, then light whistling again. She remembered him turning from that window with those coolielike pajamas hanging so tentatively low on his hips, and the thin line of red-gold hair sparkling its way down the center of his stomach. She groaned and rolled over and cradled her face in the L of an arm and the sun crept over her in warm fingers of gold and she fell asleep, waiting there that way, as pregnant women are prone to do.

He came into the bedroom wearing pajama bottoms and a towel slung around his neck. He smiled at the sight that greeted him. She lay there sprawled luxuriously and he studied the way the yellow fabric followed the contours of her shoulders, back, buttocks, the one knee drawn up, the other with its bare foot dangling over the edge of the bed.

In daylight, he decided, she was much more amiable. He'd enjoyed their little repartee upon waking.

He looked around, spied the roses, nabbed one and began tickling the sole of her foot with it. The toes curled tight, then the foot rotated on the ankle irritably. Then it kicked him in the knee and she laughed into the bedclothes.

"Cut it out," she scolded, "I told you I'm not at my best in the morning. I have an ugly disposition until almost noon."

"And here I was thinking how nice you were before."

"I'm a bear."

"What are you doing here? You're supposed to be getting ready for breakfast."

She looked at him with one cheek and an eye lost in the blankets.

"I was just catching a catnap."

"A catnap—when you just got up?"

"Well, it's your fault."

"Oh, yeah? What'd I do now?"

"Dunce. Pregnant ladies tend to sleep a lot, I told you that before." She reached backward and waggled her fingers. "Gimme."

He put the rose in her hand, and she sniffed it—one deep,

long exaggerated pull—then rolled over and said to the ceiling, "Morning has broken." And without another word went to bathe and dress.

Catherine could see that her greatest adversary was normalcy. Clay, being well-adjusted, intended to forge ahead as if their marriage were ordinary. But she, herself, was constantly on guard against the compelling gravity of the commonplace. That first day gave her glimpses of what life with Clay could be like if things were different.

They arrived at the Forresters' through the high sun of the November afternoon which had melted away all but a few hints of last night's snows. The doorman was gone now—it was just an ordinary house again. Squirrels, much the color of the lawns, chittered and chased, still on the search for winter stores. A nuthatch darted from one of the festoons beside the door where it had been dining on bearded wheat.

And as it always could, the home welcomed.

They caught Claiborne and Angela nestled together on the loveseat like a pair of mated mallards while the Minnesota Vikings radiated from the screen. There were the inevitable touches of greeting, in which Catherine was now included. They opened most of the gifts together—the four of them—with time out for instant replays, and for teasing Catherine about her ignorance of the game. Sitting on fat pillows on the floor, Catherine and Clay laughed over a grotesque cookie jar that looked like it belonged in a Swahili kitchen instead of an American town house. And she learned that Clay's favorite cookies were chocolate chip. They opened a waffle iron and she learned that he preferred pancakes. Halftime highlights came on and she learned he disliked the Chicago Bears. Angela made sandwiches and Claiborne said, "Here, open this one next," with a surprising giddiness, now that the game was over.

And amid a mound of used wrappings Catherine felt herself being sucked into the security of this family.

In the late afternoon they piled their loot into the cars and drove to the place they'd now call home. She met Clay at the door and watched as he set down his load and bent to put the

244

key in the lock. Her arms were full of gift boxes overflowing with excelsior, and she peered around, watching him pocket the key.

The door swung open and before she knew what was happening he had turned and deftly scooped up the whole works—wife, excelsior, boxes and all.

"*Clay!*"

"I know, I know. Put me down, right?"

But she only laughed while he floundered, acting like his legs had turned to rubber, and collapsed onto the steps with her in his lap.

"In the movies somehow the wife never has a paunch," he teased, leaning his elbows back on the steps behind them.

She scowled, called him a very nasty name, then felt herself being pushed from his lap. "Get off me, paunchy."

The apartment lay steeped in late afternoon dusk, silent, waiting. As they stood surveying the living room, it seemed to beckon with the intimacy of a lover about to shed her clothes: new furniture, still wearing tags and dust wrappers, waited—stacked, leaning, unassembled. Lamps with their bases encased in padding lay upon the davenport while their shades waited on the floor in plastic sleeves. Barstools and tables stood about. Pieces of bed frame lay beside the mattress and the box spring leaned against the wall. Boxes and suitcases which they'd brought earlier were stacked on the counter, strewn about the room.

The moment held a poignance that took away their laughter and made them wistful for a moment. It all seemed so ironically like the real thing. The reflection of sunset slipped its lavender fingers through the broad expanse of glass, lending an unearthly glow to the place. Catherine felt Clay's hands on her shoulders. She turned to find him startlingly close behind her, his jaw almost colliding with her temple as she swung around.

"Your coat?" he said. She thought there was a tortured expression about his mouth, wondered if he were thinking of Jill Magnusson. But—just that quick—he removed it and in its place was a grin.

They changed into blue jeans and sweatshirts and set to work—she in the kitchen, he in the living room. Again the air of normalcy returned. For Catherine it was like playing house, working away in this place that seemed too good to be true, packing away wedding gifts in the cupboards, listening to the sounds of Clay shoving furniture around. As they worked, evening spun in, and at times she allowed the line between reality and fantasy to blur.

"Come and tell me where you want the davenport," Clay called. She got up from her knees and went to ponder with him, and they arranged the room together.

And once she went laughing, asking, "What in the world do you suppose this thing is?" displaying some odd piece of steel that might have been either sculpture or a meat grinder. They laughingly agreed that it must be a sculpture of a meat grinder and relegated it to a hidden spot behind the tissue box on top of the refrigerator.

And dusk was deep when he appeared in the kitchen, asking, "Are there any lightbulbs anywhere?"
    "Shove that box over here; I think it's stuff from the shower."
    They found bulbs. A few moments later, still on her knees, she saw lamplight appear over the peninsula of cabinets from the direction of the living room, and smiled when she heard him say, "There, that's more like it."

She'd finished most of the kitchen unpacking and was lining the linen closet shelves as he passed through the hall, carrying pieces of clanging bed rail.
    "Watch the wall!" she warned . . . too late. The bed rail dug into the door frame. He shrugged and disappeared with his burden. Next he came through with the headboard, then with a toolbox from his trunk. She began unpacking linens, listening to the sounds coming from the bedroom. She was hanging up

new towels in the bathroom when he called, "Catherine, can you come here a minute?"

He was on his knees, trying to hold the headboard and bed rails at right angles while he tightened nuts and bolts—and having one hell of a time.

"Hold that up, will you?"

His hair was messed and curling across his forehead while he concentrated on his work. Holding the metal rails, she felt the vibrations wriggle their way to her palms as he plied the screwdriver.

He finished, and the thing was a square. He put the cross-slats in and stood up, saying, "I'll need a little help getting the mattress up the stairs."

"Sure," she said, uncomfortable now.

On their way up the steps with their ungainly cargo, Clay warned, "Now, just guide it, don't lift it."

She wanted to say, don't be solicitous, but bit her tongue.

And then the bed was a bed, and the room grew quiet. They looked across the short expanse—his hair all ascatter and hers slipping free of the combs with which she'd carelessly slung it behind her ears. He had sweat rings beneath his arms and she had a dust smudge on the end of her right breast. His eyes dropped down to it fleetingly.

"There," he announced, "you can take over from here, okay?"

The new, bare mattress made them both uneasy.

"Sure," she said with affected brightness, "what color sheets would you like? We've got pink with big white daisies or beige with brown stripes or—"

"It doesn't matter," he interrupted, leaning to pick up a screwdriver and drop it in the toolbox. "Make it up to suit yourself. I'll be sleeping out on the davenport."

Catherine was brushing her palms off against one another, and they suddenly fell still. Then he swung from the room. She stood a moment, staring at nothing, then she kicked their brand new box spring and left a black shoe mark on it. She stared at the mark, hands in her jeans pockets. She apologized to the box spring, then took back the apology, then spun and dropped down onto the edge of the unmade bed, suddenly feeling like crying. From the living room came the sound of

247

some bluesy music with soft piano and a husky female voice as he started up the stereo. Finally she quit her moping and made up the bed with crisp, fresh sheets, then decided to put her clothing into the new dresser drawers. She stopped with her hands full of sweaters, and called, "Clay?"

But apparently he couldn't hear her above the music.

She padded silently down the carpeted hall, down the few steps to the living room and found him standing, cowboylike, feet astraddle, thumbs hooked up in his rear pockets, staring out the sliding glass doors.

"Clay?"

He started and looked around. "What?"

"Is it okay if I take the dresser and you take the chest of drawers?"

"Sure," he said tonelessly, "whatever you want." Then he turned back to the window.

The inside of the dresser drawers smelled of new, spicy wood. Everything in the place was so spanking, so untouched, so different from what Catherine was used to. She was struck again with a sense of unreality, simply because of the inanity of what she was doing. But when Catherine considered where she was and what lay around her, she felt as if she were usurping someone else's rightful place, and again the image of Jill popped up.

The sound of a drawer opening brought her from her reverie, and she glanced over her shoulder to find Clay also putting his things away. They moved about the bedroom, doing their separate chores, silent except for an occasional *excuse me* when their proximities warranted. She snapped on the closet light to find he'd brought his hanging clothes over sometime during the week. All his sport coats hung neatly spaced, shirts squarely centered on their hangers, pantlegs meticulously flush and creased. She'd somehow imagined that Inella took care of his clothing, kept it flawless and groomed, and was surprised to find such neat precision all his doing.

The scent he wore lingered in the enclosure, much as it did in his car. She snapped out the light again and turned with her handful of hangers.

"I guess I'll take the closet in the other bedroom if it's okay with you."

248

"I can push my stuff closer together."

"No, no, it's okay. The other closet's empty anyway."

When she disappeared into the room across the hall, he stared into the drawer he'd been filling in the bureau—contemplating.

A short time later their paths crossed in the living room. Clay was occupied putting away his tapes.

"Listen, are you hungry?" Catherine asked. "We didn't have supper or anything." It was nearly ten P.M.

"Yeah, a little." He continued his sorting, never glancing up.

"Oh, well . . . gee," she stammered, "there's nothing here. We could—"

"Just forget it then. I'm really not very hungry."

"No, we could go out and get a hamburger or something."

He looked up at her stomach. "Oh, you're probably hungry."

"I'm okay."

He sighed, dropped a tape back into the cardboard box where it clacked before the room fell silent. He stared at it, kneeling there with the heels of his hands on his thighs, then shook his head in slow motion. "Aren't we even going to eat together?"

"You're the one who said first you were hungry, then you weren't."

He looked up at her squarely. "Do you want a hamburger?"

She rubbed her stomach with a timorous smile. "Yes, I'm starved."

"Then what do you say we stop playing cat and mouse and go out and get one."

"Okay."

"Let's leave the rest of this stuff for tomorrow night."

"Gladly, and tomorrow I'll get some groceries in the house."

And with that everything seemed better.

The illusion lasted till bedtime. Then, again, they walked on eggshells.

Coming in after their late supper she hurried to remove her coat before he could help her, afraid lest he should inadvertently touch her. He followed her to the living room.

"Feel better?" he asked.

"Yes, I didn't know how hungry I was. We did a lot of work today."

Then they couldn't think of anything else to say. Clay began an exaggerated stretch, twisting at the waist with his elbows in the air.

Panic hit her and made her stomach twitch. Should she simply exit or offer to make up his bed or what?

They both spoke at once.

"Well, we have to get up—"

"Should I get your—"

She flapped her hands nervously, gestured for him to speak, but he gestured for her to speak at the same time.

"I'll get your bedding," she got out.

"Just show me where it is and I'll do it myself."

She avoided his eyes, led the way up the steps to the linen closet. When she started to reach up high he hurriedly offered, "Here, I'll get them down."

He moved too quickly and bumped into her back before she could move aside. He nearly pulled the comforter down on her head. She plucked a package of sheets and another of pillowcases from the shelves and put them on top of the comforter in his arms.

"I saved the brown and beige ones for you."

Their eyes met briefly above the bedding.

"Thanks."

"I'll get your pillow." She fled to do so.

But they had only two pillows, which were both on the king-size bed, already encased in pink-flowered pillow slips. There was some sticky hesitancy as she returned with one, saying she guessed he wouldn't need that other pillowcase she'd given him. And then everything went wrong at once because he reached to take her pillow and the comforter tipped sideways and the plastic-wrapped packages slipped off the top and she lunged to try to catch them and somehow their fingers touched and the whole pile of bedding ended up on the floor at their feet.

He knelt down quickly and began gathering it up while she scuttled back to the security of the bedroom, shut the door and was about to begin changing into her nightgown when he came back for his pajamas. He knocked politely, and she let him pass before her to go in and get them, then shut the door again as he left.

By the time she donned her nightgown her stomach was in knots.

She sat down on the end of the bed, waiting for him to go in and use the bathroom first. But apparently he was sitting downstairs waiting for her to do the same thing. Naturally, they both decided to make the move at once. She was halfway down the hall and he was halfway up the steps when they spied each other headed in the same direction. Catherine's feet turned to stone, but Clay had the presence of mind to simply turn around and retreat. Afterward she closed herself into the bedroom again, climbed into the vast bed and lay there listening to the sounds that the walls couldn't quite hide, picturing Clay in those pajama bottoms as he'd been that morning. The toilet flushed, the water ran, she heard him spit after brushing his teeth.

In the bathroom, Clay studied her wet washcloth hanging on the towel rack, then opened the medicine chest to find her wet toothbrush inside. He laid his next to it, then picked up a bottle of prenatal vitamins, studied its label thoughtfully and returned it to the shelf.

She heard the bathroom light snap off, then he knocked gently on her door.

"Catherine?"

Heart clamoring, she answered, "What?"

"What time do you usually get up?"

"Six thirty."

"Did you set an alarm?"

"No, I haven't got one."

"I'll wake you at six thirty then."

"Thank you."

She stared at the hole in the dark where the door would be if she could see it.

"Good night then," he said at last.

"Good night."

He put on a tape and the sound of the music filtered through the dark, through her closed door while she tried to erase all thought from her mind and find sleep.

She was still wide awake when the tape finally stopped.

And a long time later when she heard Clay get up in the dark and get a drink of water in the kitchen.

Chapter 21

THE WAY THEY did things the first time usually set the precedent for their routine. Clay used the bathroom first in the mornings; she used it first in the evenings. He got dressed in their bedroom while she was showering, then she got dressed while he put his bedding away. He left the house first, so he opened the garage door; she left second and closed it.

Before leaving that Monday morning he asked, "What time will you get home?"

"Around two thirty."

"I'll be later by an hour or so, but if you wait I'll go grocery shopping with you."

She couldn't conceal her surprise—it was the last thing she'd expect him to want them to do together. Crisp and combed, he stood in the foyer looking up the steps at her. He put a hand on the doorknob, smiled briefly, raised his free hand and said, "Well, have a good day."

"You too."

When he was gone, she studied the door, remembering his smile, the little wave of good-bye. Juxtaposed against it came the memory of her father, scratching his belly, roaring, "Where the goddam hell is Ada? Does a man hafta make his own coffee around this dump?"

Catherine couldn't forget it all the way to school in her own car, which she kept expecting to turn back into a pumpkin.

It was an odd place to begin falling in love—in the middle of the supermarket—but that's precisely where it began for Catherine. She was still boggled by the fact that he'd come along. Again she tried to picture her father doing the same, but it was too ludicrous to ponder. She was even further dumbfounded by the silliness that sprang up between her and Clay. It had started out with the two of them learning each other's tastes, but had ended on a note of hilarity which would undoubtedly have seemed humorless to anybody else.

"Do you like fruit?" Clay asked.

"Oranges, I crave oranges lately."

"Then we shall have oranges!" he proclaimed dramatically, holding a bag aloft.

"Hey, check how much they cost first."

"It doesn't matter. These look good."

"Of course they look good," she scolded, looking at the price, "you've chosen the most expensive ones in the place."

But when she would have replaced them with cheaper ones, he waggled a finger at her and clucked, "Tut-tut!" Price was no object, he said, when he bought food. And she dropped the oranges back in the cart.

At the dairy case she reached for margarine.

"What are you going to use that for?"

"What do you think, not for a hot oil treatment for my hair."

"And not to feed to me," he said, grinning, and took the margarine from her hands. "I like real butter."

"But it's three times as much!" she exclaimed. Then she reclaimed her margarine and put his butter back in the case.

He immediately switched the two around again.

"Butter is three times as fattening too," she informed him, "and I *do* have an imminent weight problem to consider." He made an affected sideward bow, then put her margarine in the cart next to his butter as they moved on.

She spied a two-gallon jar of ketchup up ahead, and when

Clay's back was turned she picked up the ungainly thing and came waddling over with it clutched against her outthrust stomach.

"Here," she puffed, "this should hold you till next week."

He turned around and burst out laughing, then quickly relieved her of the enormous container.

"Hey, what're you trying to do, squash my kid?"

"I know how you like ketchup on your hamburgers," she said innocently. By now they were both laughing.

They wandered along behind their mountain of food, and at the frozen foods she chose orange juice and he, pineapple juice. They took turns laying them in the cart like poker players revealing their next cards.

She played a frozen pumpkin pie.

He played apple.

She drew corn.

He drew spinach.

"What's that?" she asked disgustedly.

"Spinach."

"Spinach! Yuck!"

"What's the matter with spinach? I love it!"

"I hate it. I'd as soon eat scabs!"

He perused the bags and boxes in the display case with a searching attitude. "Mmm, sorry, no scabs for sale here."

By the time they reached the meat counter they were no longer laughing, they were giggling, and people were beginning to stare.

"Do you like Swiss steak?" she asked.

"I love it. Do you like meat loaf?"

"I love it!"

"Well, I hate it. Don't you dare subject me to meat loaf!"

Warming to the game, she just had to trail her fingers threateningly over the packages of hamburger. He eyed her warningly out of the corner of his eye—a buccaneer daring her to challenge his orders.

She picked up the hamburger, weighing it on her palm a time or two, plotting the insidious deed.

"Oh, yeah, lady?" He made his voice silky. "Just try it." He grinned evilly, raking her with his pirate's eyes until she stealthily slipped it back where it had come from.

Next he turned on her, ordering autocratically, "You'd better like pork chops!" He took up a challenging stance, at a right angle to the meat counter, feet apart, one hand on a package of chops, the other on the nonexistent scabbard at his belt. The tile of the floor might very well have been the deck of his windjammer.

"Or else what?" she fairly growled, trying to keep a straight face.

He grew cocky, raised one eyebrow. "Or else"—a quick glance to the side, a hint of a smile before he snatched up a different package and brandished it at her—"we eat liver."

She hooked both thumbs up in her waist, ambled nearer, looked directly into his swashbuckler's handsome, brown face and rasped, "Suits me fine, bucko, I eats my liver rawww!"

He tilted a sardonic brow at the liver.

"More'n likely doesn't know how to cook it."

"The plague take you, I do!"

A twitch pulled at the corners of his lips. He tried to get the words out without snickering, but couldn't quite make it.

"Lucky for you, woman, be . . . cause . . . I . . . don't."

And then the two of them were dissolved in giggles again.

Where Catherine's comic instinct had come from she couldn't guess. She'd never suspected she harbored it. But she warmed to it, found herself lifted in a new, spontaneous way by their levity. Somehow Clay—who she had to admit was charming as a swashbuckler—had given her a glimpse of him that she liked. And a glimpse of herself which she liked, as well. Such bouts of good humor sprang up between them more often after that. She was surprised to find Clay not only humorous, but complaisant and even-tempered. It was the first time in her life that she lived free of the threat of erupting tempers. It was an eye-opener to Catherine to learn it was possible to live in such harmony with a male of the species.

The town house, too, wove its charm about Catherine. At times she would come up short in the middle of some mundane chore and would mentally pinch herself as a reminder not to get too used to it. She would load the dishwasher—or worse yet, watch Clay load it—and remember that in a few short months this would all be snatched away from her. He shared the housework with a singular lack of compunction which surprised Catherine. Maybe it started the night he hooked up the washer and dryer. Together they read the new manuals and figured out the machine settings and loaded the washer with their first bundle of dirty clothes and from then on a load was thrown in by whoever happened to have the time.

She returned home one time to find him vacuuming the living room—the new blankets were linty. She stopped in amazement, a smile on her face. He caught sight of her and turned off the machine.

"Hi, what's the smile for?"

"I was just trying to feature my old man doing that like you do."

"Is this supposed to threaten my masculinity or something?"

Her smile was very genuine now.

"Quite the opposite."

Then she turned and left him and the vacuum wheezed on again while he wondered what she meant.

It was inevitable that they be bound closer by inconsequential things. A telephone was installed and their number was listed under the name, Forrester, Clay. A grocery list was established on a corner of the cabinet, and on it mingled their needs and their likes. She bought herself a tape by The Lettermen and played it on his stereo, knowing full well it would not always be available for her to use. Mail began arriving, addressed to Mr. and Mrs. Clay Forrester. He ran out of shampoo and borrowed hers, and from then on they ended up buying her brand because he liked it better. Sometimes they even used the same washcloth.

But every night, out came the spare blankets, and he made up his bed on the davenport, put on a tape, and they lay in their separate darks listening to his favorite one night, hers the next.

But by now she had grown to expect that last tape of the day, and left her bedroom door open, the better to hear it.

Thanksgiving came and it was disturbingly wonderful for Catherine. Angela had included both Steve and Ada in her invitation, plus all of Clay's grandparents and a few assorted aunts, uncles and cousins. It was the first time in six years that Catherine,

Ada and Steve had celebrated a holiday together, and Catherine found herself awash in gratitude to the Forresters for this opportunity. It was a day steeped in tradition. There were warm cheeks meeting cold, cozy fires, laughter drifting up through the house from the game room below, a table veritably sagging beneath its burden of holiday foods, and of course Angela's magical touch was everywhere. There were bronze football mums laced with bittersweet in the center of the table, flanked by crystal candelabra upon imported Belgian linen. Seated at dinner, Catherine swallowed back the sickening sense of future loss and strove to enjoy the day. Her mother was truly coming out of her shell, smiling and visiting. And it was crazy the way Steve and Clay took to each other. They spent much of the meal badgering each other about a rematch at pool as soon as the meal was over, but with the best of spirits.

How the Forresters take this for granted, thought Catherine, gazing around the circle of faces, listening to the happy chatter, soothed and sated as much by their goodwill as by their food. What happened to my notions about the wicked rich? she wondered. But just then her eyes met Claiborne's. She found a disturbing gentleness there, as if he read her thoughts, and she quickly looked away lest she be drawn to him further.

In the afternoon Catherine received her first lesson in how to shoot pool. Was it accidental or intentional, the way Clay crowded his body close behind her as he leaned to show her how to extend her left hand onto the green velvet, crossing her hip with his right arm, his hard brown hand gripping hers on the cue?

"Let it slide through your hand," he instructed into her ear, sawing back and forth while his sleeve brushed across her hip. He smelled good and he was warm. There was something decidedly provocative about it all. But then he backed away and it was men against women in a round robin that pitted Clay and Steve against Catherine and a teenage cousin named Marcy. But in no time it was obvious the sides were uneven, so Catherine played with Steve as her partner, and they whipped the other two in short order. Steve, it seemed, had been dubbed

"Minnesota Skinny" during the hundreds of hours spent at pool tables during basic training and the years since. Eventually pool was preempted by football, and Catherine found herself snuggled into a comfortable cushion between Clay and Steve. During replays Catherine received her second lesson on the sport, explained succinctly by Clay, who slouched comfortably and rolled his head toward her during his comments.

At the door Claiborne and Angela bade them good-bye, and while Claiborne held her coat, Angela asked, "How are you feeling?"

She raised her eyes to twin expressions of concern, surprised to be asked in so point-blank a way about her pregnancy. This was the first time since before the wedding that anybody had brought it up.

"Pudgy," she answered with a half smile.

"Well, you're looking wonderful," Claiborne assured her.

"Yes, and don't let female vanity get you down," added Angela. "It's only temporary, you know."

On the drive home Catherine recalled their solicitous attitudes, the concern behind their simple comments, threatened by that concern more than she cared to admit.

"You're quiet tonight," Clay noted.

"I was thinking."

"About what?"

She was silent a moment, then sighed. "The whole day— what it was like. How all of your family seems to take it for granted . . . I mean, I've never had a Thanksgiving like this before."

"Like what? It was just an ordinary Thanksgiving."

"Oh, Clay, you really don't see, do you?"

"See what?"

No, he didn't see, and she doubted that he ever would, but she made a stab at comparison. "Where I came from, holidays were only excuses for the old man to get a little drunker than usual. By mealtime he'd be crocked, whether we were at home or going to Uncle Frank's. I don't ever remember a holiday that wasn't spoiled by his drinking. There was always so much tension, everybody trying to make things merry in spite of him. I used to wish . . ." But her voice trailed away. She found she could not say what it was she'd wished for, because it would seem guileful to say that she wished for a day like she'd had today.

"I'm sorry," he said softly. Then he reached over and squeezed her neck gently. "Don't let bad memories ruin your day, okay?"

"Your father was very nice to me today."

"Your mother was very nice to me."

"Clay, I . . ." But once again she stopped, uncertain of how to voice her growing trepidation. Catherine didn't think he'd understand that Thanksgiving had been just too, too nice.

"What?"

"Nothing."

But that *nothing* was a great big lump of something, something good and alive and growing which would—she was sure—be bittersweet in the end.

It was shortly after that when Clay came home one evening with a four-pound bag of popcorn.

"Four pounds!" she exclaimed.

"Well, I'm awfully fond of the stuff."

"You must be," she laughed, and flung the bag at him, nearly doubling him over.

That night they were sitting on the davenport studying with a bowl between them when Catherine suddenly dropped a handful of popcorn back into the bowl. Her eyes grew startled and the book fell from her fingers.

"Clay!" she whispered.

He sat forward, alarmed. "What's the matter?"

"Oh, God . . ." she whispered, clutching her stomach.

"What's the matter, Catherine?" He eased nearer, concern etched across his eyebrows.

She closed her eyes. "Ohhh . . ." she breathed while he wondered if she had written the doctor's number down where he could find it fast.

"For God's sake, what is it?"

"Something . . . something . . ." Her eyes remained closed while sweat suddenly broke out across his chest. Her eyes opened and a tremulous smile played at the corners of her mouth. "Something moved in there."

His eyes shot down to her stomach. Catherine held it like she was getting ready to try a two-hand set shot with it. Now he held his breath.

"There it goes again," she reported, her eyes closing as if in ecstasy. "Once more...once more...please," she whispered invocatively.

"Is it still moving?" he whispered.

"Yes...no!...wait!"

"Can I feel?"

"I don't know. Wait, there it is again—no, it's gone."

His hand advanced and retreated several times through all this.

"There it is again."

She made room for one of his hands on the gentle mound beside her own. They sat there mesmerized for a long, long time. Nothing happened. Her eyes drifted up to his. The warmth of his hand seeped through to her flesh, but the flutter within remained stilled.

"I can't feel anything." He felt cheated.

"It's all done, I think."

"There, what was that?"

"No, that wasn't it, that was probably only my own heartbeat."

"Oh." But he didn't take his hand away. It lay there warmly next to hers while he asked, "What did it feel like?"

"I don't know. Like—like when you're holding a kitten and you can feel it purr through its fur, only it lasted just a moment each time."

Clay's face felt hot. His scalp prickled. He still cupped her stomach with a hand which stubbornly wasn't going to move away without feeling *some*thing!

It's good to touch her, he thought.

"Clay, nothing's going to happen anymore, I don't think."

"Oh." Disappointed, he slid his hand from her. But where it had been, there were five buttery smudges on her green cotton blouse.

"You've marked me," she joked, stretching out the shirt by

its hem, suddenly too aware of how good his hand had felt.

He caught a glimpse of a zipper that wasn't completely zipped, a snap which wasn't snapped.

"Yes, for life," he said on a light note, but he had the sudden urge to kiss her, she looked so expectant and crestfallen at the brevity of the sensation. "Promise me you'll let me feel it next time it happens?"

But she didn't promise. Instead, she moved a safe distance away, then muttered something about getting the butter out before it set permanently and headed in the direction of the laundry.

When she returned, she was wearing a pink duster and fuzzy booties, and he had great trouble concentrating on his studying after she resumed her place on the other side of the popcorn bowl.

By now Catherine well knew how Clay enjoyed his morning coffee at the counter. He was there at his usual place, reading the morning paper a few days later when she appeared from upstairs. He blew on his coffee, took a sip, looked up over his paper, and his lips fell from the rim of the cup which hovered, forgotten, in midair.

"Well, well, well . . . lookit here," he crooned.

She pinkened, got suddenly very busy plopping a piece of bread in the toaster with her back to him.

"Turn around so I can see."

"It's just a maternity top," she said to the toaster, looking at her reflection in it.

"Then why so shy?"

"I'm not shy, for heaven's sake!" She swung around. "I just feel conspicuous, that's all."

"Why? You look cute in it."

"Cute," she muttered disparagingly, "like Dumbo the elephant."

"Well, it's got to be more comfortable than going around with your zippers open and your snaps flapping." Again she colored. "Well, I couldn't help but notice the other night when I was feeling your tummy."

"I kept thinking of facing your grandmother in maternity clothes and putting it off as long as possible."

He put down his paper and came around the peninsula to pour another cup of coffee. "Nature will have its way, and not even Elizabeth Forrester can stop it. Don't frown so, Catherine."

She turned to butter her toast. "I don't want to think about facing her for the first time wearing these."

On an impulse he moved close behind her and touched his lips to the back of her hair, his cup still in his hand. "That probably won't be until Christmas, so stop worrying."

Facing the cabinets, she was unsure of what it was she'd felt on the back of her head, and then, without warning, he slipped an arm around her middle and spread his fingers wide on her stomach.

"Is there any more activity going on in there?" he asked.

From behind, he saw her jaws stop moving. She swallowed a mouthful of toast as though it were having some difficulty going down.

"Don't touch me, Clay," she warned, low, intense, fierce, not moving a muscle. His hand stiffened, the room seemed to crackle.

"Why? You're my w—"

"I can't stand it!" she snapped, slapping the toast down on the counter. "I can't stand it!"

He felt the blood surge to his head, stung by her unexpected outburst.

"Well, I beg your goddam puritanical pardon!"

He clapped his cup down vehemently, and stormed out of the room, out of the house, without so much as a good-bye.

When the door slammed, Catherine leaned over, braced her elbows on the countertop and buried her face in both hands. She wanted to call, Come back, come back! Don't believe me, Clay. I need touching so badly. Come back and make me let you touch me, even if I argue. Smile at me and wish me your sweet-tempered good-bye like always. I need you so badly, Clay. Coddle me, comfort me, touch me, touch me, touch me. Only, make it all mean something, Clay.

* * *

She had a miserable day that day.

She made supper and waited. And waited. And waited. But he didn't come. She finally ate alone, staring at his empty stool beside her, the food like cardboard in her mouth. She ate very little.

She put on one of his favorite tapes, just for some racket in the place, but that was worse. She felt more miserable than ever, for it only brought back the memory of his slamming out the door as he had. She put on one of her favorites, but naturally, it soon rolled around to the same old song which always reminded her of him: "You're Just Too Good To Be True." That made her more miserable than ever, so she chose to wait in silence. At eleven o'clock she gave up and went to bed.

She woke up at two A.M. and crept down the dark hall and checked the living room. In the blackness it was hard to see. She felt her way to the davenport with her feet, reached out a careful hand only to find that there was no bedding there, no Clay.

Finally, at five she fell asleep only to be awakened an hour and a half later by the alarm. Catherine knew before she went downstairs that he wouldn't be there.

Chapter 22

SCHOOL WAS AN exercise in futility that day. Catherine sat through her classes like a zombie, seeing little, hearing less. All she saw was Clay's hand on her stomach the night when they'd been eating popcorn. All she heard was his voice, "Can I feel?" She remembered his eyes, those eyes she'd grown to know so well, with a brand new look, wide-gray, excited. "I can't feel anything, Catherine. What did it feel like?"

Her insides trembled at the thought of his staying away all night. She'd have to call his parents if he wasn't home when she got there. Sick at the thought that he might not come home tonight either, she delayed going there herself. She stopped at Horizons after classes for a visit with the girls. Only, she learned that Marie had gone into labor around ten o'clock that morning and they were all waiting for news from the hospital. Without a second thought, Catherine drove to Metro Medical Center and obtained permission to wait in the father's waiting room. By the time news came, it was nine o'clock. She was not allowed to see Marie, for they had taken her directly to the recovery room, so Catherine finally headed for home.

When she got there, the living room light was on. At the sight of it she felt her heartbeat go wild and racy. Catherine opened the door to silence. Slowly she hung up her coat, and even more slowly ascended the stairs. Just inside the living room Clay was standing like an outraged samurai. His shirt hung open and wrinkled, his beard was a smudge across his cheeks, his hair was unkempt and his face bore the ravages of a sleepless night.

"Where the hell were you!" he roared.

"At the hospital."

His anger swooshed away, leaving him with that gut-hollow feeling as after an elevator drops too fast. He looked at her stomach.

"Is something wrong?"

"Marie just had a six-and-a-half-pound baby girl." She turned on her heel, heading upstairs, but found herself swung around roughly by an elbow.

Madder than ever at having been duped into thinking something was wrong with Catherine, he barked, "Well, you could have called, you know!"

"Me!" she yelled back. "I could have called! What about you!"

"I'm the one that got thrown out, remember?"

"I did not throw you out!"

"Well, you sure as hell didn't make me feel anxious to come back."

"The choice was yours, Mister Forrester, and I'm sure you didn't suffer out in the cold."

"No, I sure as hell didn't."

"Did she let you paw her nice flat stomach all night long?"

"What's it to you? You gave me permission to paw anything I want of hers, didn't you?"

"That's right," she hissed, "anything you want!"

"Catherine, let's not get into it, okay? I'm beat and I—"

"Oh, you're beat! Poor baby. I didn't get two hours sleep last night worrying that you drove it out of your system until you cracked up the Corvette someplace and all the while you were with her and now you come home crying that you're tired? Spare me."

"I never said I was with her. You assumed that."

"I don't give a tinker's damn if you were with her or not. If it'll keep you off my back, fine! Spend all the time you want

266

with Jill Magnusson. Only do me the courtesy of reminding me not to cook supper for you on your nights out, all right?"

"And who do you think cooked supper for you tonight?"

Her eyes slid to the kitchen. Sure enough, there was evidence of a neglected meal all over the place. Catherine didn't know what to say.

He raged on. "Just what do you suppose I thought when you didn't show up to eat it?"

"I know what you didn't think—that I was out someplace with an old boyfriend!"

He ran a hand through his hair, as if searching for control, then turned away.

"You'd better call your mother; she's worried sick."

"My mother? How did she get into this?"

"I couldn't think of anyplace else you'd be, so I called her place."

"Oh, fine, just fine! I didn't call *your* mother to check up on you!"

"Well, maybe you should have 'cause I was there."

He stomped across the living room and plunked down on the davenport. "Lord," he said to the windows, "I don't know what got into you yesterday morning. All I did was touch you, Cat. That's all I did. Was that so bad? I mean, what do you think it makes a man feel like to be treated that way?" He got to his feet and started pacing back and forth. "I mean, I've been living like a goddam monk! Don't look! Don't touch! Watch what you say! Sleeping on this davenport like some eunuch! This setup just isn't natural!"

"Whose idea was it in the first place?"

"All right, granted, it was mine, but be reasonable, huh?"

Her voice grew taunting. "What am I to you, Clay? Another conquest? Is that what you're after? Another notch on your"—she glanced insolently at his crotch—"whatever it is you notch? I should think you could do better than one banged-up, big bellied loser like me. Listen, I plan to come out of this marriage with fewer scars than I had going in, and to do that I need to keep you away from me, do you understand? Just stay away!"

Suddenly Clay stormed across the room, grabbed one of her wrists and, in his fury, flung his other hand wide, exclaiming, "Damnit, Catherine, I'm your husband!"

Instinctively she yanked free of him, covering her head with both hands, hunkering down, waiting for the blow to fall.

At the sight of her, dropped low in that crouch, the anger fell from him to be replaced by pity, which hurt—hurt worse than the thought that she could not stand being touched by him.

He dropped to one knee beside her.

"Cat," he said hoarsely, "God, Cat, I wasn't going to hit you."

But still she cowered on her knees, sunken in some fear too big for him to fully comprehend. He reached out a hand to soothe her hair. "Hey, come on, honey, it's Clay. I'd never hit you, don't you know that?" He thought she was crying, for her body quivered terribly. She needs to cry, he thought, she needed it weeks ago. He watched her knotted fists dig into the nape of her neck. He touched her arms. "Come on, Cat." He gentled, saying, "It's only a silly fight, and it's over, huh?" He brushed back a strand of hair that fell like a golden waterfall covering her face. He leaned down to try to see around it, but she clutched her head and bounced on her haunches as if demented. Fear tore through his gut. His heart felt swollen to twice its size.

"Cat, I'm sorry. Come on, don't . . . Nobody's going to hurt you, Cat. Please, honey, I'm sorry . . ." Sobs collected in his throat. "Let me help you to bed, okay?" Something switched her back to reality. She raised her head at last, just enough to see him with one eye around that veil of gold. With infinite tenderness he promised, "I won't touch you. I just want to help you to bed; come on." The tears he expected to see were not there. She unfolded herself finally, tossed back her hair and eyed him suspiciously. Her face wore a protective mask of expressionlessness.

"I can do it." Her voice was too controlled. "I don't need your help."

With measured movements, she rose and left the room, left him kneeling there in the middle of it with a knot of emptiness inside him.

After that Catherine spent her evenings in the spare room. She either sewed maternity clothes or did typing jobs on a card table she'd set up in there. When she had studying to do, it, too, was done in the spare bedroom. Like a hermit crab, she crawled off into her shell.

After several nights of her incessant typing, Clay came to the bedroom doorway, stood there studying her back, wondering how to approach her.

"You're doing a lot of typing lately. Your professors laying on a heavy load or something?"

She didn't even turn around. "I got a couple of jobs typing term papers."

"If you needed money, why didn't you say so?" he asked impatiently.

"I want my typing to stay good."

"But you've got enough to do keeping up with your classes and things around the house without taking on more."

At last she looked over her shoulder. "I thought we agreed not to interfere with each other's private lives."

His mouth drew into a straight, hard line, then she turned back to her work.

The following evening when she was again seated at the typewriter, she heard the door slam. Her fingers fell still, hovering over the keys while she listened. Finally she got up and checked the living room and kitchen to find him gone. She sighed and returned to the spare room.

But there was undeniably a lonely feeling about the place, knowing he wasn't out there.

He got home around ten, offering no explanation of where he'd been, getting no questions from Catherine. After that, he would leave occasionally that way, preferring not to face her indifference, or the isolation of the living room with the sound of the clattering typewriter or sewing machine coming from upstairs.

One evening he surprised her by returning home earlier than usual, coming into her hideout with his jacket still on. He dropped a checkbook on the cardtable and she glanced up questioningly. He leaned from one hip a little, hands in his jacket pockets, only his eyes and hair picking up a faint reflection from the gooseneck lamp pointed down at the table.

"What's that?" she asked.

He eyed her from the shadows. "I ran out of blank checks

and had to have some new ones printed."

She looked down at the black plastic folder, opened it and found her name imprinted beside his on the top check.

"We had a deal," said Clay. "I'd support you."

She stared at the paired names on the blue rectangle, reminded of their wedding invitations, for some reason. She looked up but his features were inscrutable above her.

"But not forever," she said. "I'll need money next summer and recommendations from satisfied customers. I want to take these jobs."

He shifted feet, leaned on the opposite hip. His voice was slightly hard. "And I want you back out in that living room in the evenings."

"I've got work to do, Clay." And she turned back to her typewriter, making the keys fly. He left the checkbook where it was and strode angrily from the room.

After he was gone, she leaned her elbows on the machine and rested her face in her palms, confused by him, afraid—so afraid—of allowing her feelings for him to sway her. She thought of the coming summer, the separation that was inevitable, and sternly began typing again.

The spare bedroom soon became cluttered with her things: piles of blank paper and manuscripts lying in heaps on the floor beside patterns and fabric scraps. Textbooks, a tote bag, her schoolwork.

Christmas break arrived and she spent most of it holed up, typing, while he spent most of his time in the law library at the university, which was open seven days a week, twenty-four hours a day.

He arrived home one evening just before supper, tired of the austere law library and its dry books and rigid silence. He hung up his coat while cocking an ear toward the spare room. But everything was silent; the clack of the typewriter was disturbingly absent. He wandered upstairs, glanced into the cluttered room only to find it dark. He hurried downstairs again, to find a note.

"Bad news this time. Grover's baby born early. Going to Horizons. Back late." It was signed simply "C."

The house seemed like a tomb, silent and lifeless without her. He made himself a sandwich and wandered to the sliding glass doors to stand looking out at the snow while eating. He wished they'd have a Christmas tree, but she expressed no desire to buy one. She said they had no ornaments anyway. He thought about her cold withdrawal from him, wondered how a person could insulate herself from feeling as she did, and why. He was used to living in an environment where people conversed at the end of the day, sat and shared some talk with their dinner, sometimes watched television or read books in the same room, companionable even in silence. He missed his mother and father's house very much, picturing the enormous Christmas tree that was an annual fixture, the fires, the aunts and uncles dropping in, the gifts, the decorations which his mother lavished upon the house. For the first time ever, he wished Christmas would hurry up and get past.

He took his sandwich and wandered idly upstairs to change into a jogging suit to lounge around in. He stopped at the doorway of the dark workroom, took another bite of the sandwich, wandered in and snapped on the gooseneck lamp. He touched the keys of the typewriter, read a few words from the paper she'd left in the platen and glanced over the papers that covered the top of the crowded table.

Suddenly he stopped chewing, arrested by the dark corner of a book that was peeking from beneath a stack of papers. He licked off his fingers, slid the book out to reveal a half-filled page of Catherine's handwriting.

"Clay went out again tonight . . ." it began. He pushed the book back and hid it as it had been, took another healthy bite of tuna salad and stared at the corner of the book. It lured him, peeking out that way. Slowly he set his plate down, licked some mayonnaise from a finger again, drawn by that volume. Finally he gave in and laid the diary across the typewriter platen.

"Clay went out again tonight but didn't stay out quite as late as last time. I try not to wonder where he goes, but somehow I do. It always seems lonesome here without him but it's best not to get used to having him around. Today he mentioned buying a Christmas tree, but no matter how bad I want one, too, what's the use? It's just another tradition to break next year. He wore his brown corduroy jacket today, the one he wore the time—"

There she had stopped.

He dropped down into her chair, still staring at the words, feeling great guilt at having read them, but rereading them just the same. He pictured her sitting here, holed up in this room away from him, writing her secret feelings instead of talking about them with him. Again and again he read the words, "He wore his brown corduroy jacket today, the one he wore the time—" and wondered what she'd have written had she completed the thought. She never mentioned anything about his clothes. He'd never thought before that she even was aware of what he wore. Yet this . . .

He closed his eyes, remembering how she had said she couldn't stand to have him touch her. He opened them again and read, "He wore his brown corduroy jacket today, the one he wore the time—" Was it a pleasant memory she attached to the brown jacket? He remembered the fight they'd had over Jill. He reread, "It always seems so lonesome here without him."

Before he could do something foolish he rose, buried the book they way he'd found it, snapped off her light and went down and turned on the television. All this very abruptly. He sat through three commercials and one act of a show he didn't recognize before going back upstairs and pulling the diary out again. He told himself that this was different, that *he* was different, that he wasn't out to use anything he read against her.

She had used up so many pages last Fourth of July that he didn't waste time counting them.

"Today was a day of discovery.

"For once we were going to be all together and have a family picnic out at Lake Independence. As usual, Daddy got blind drunk and ruined everything. Mom and I had the picnic all packed when she changed her mind and called Uncle Frank to say we wouldn't be coming. One thing led to another, and Daddy accused Mom of making him the family scapegoat when all he'd had was a couple shots. Ha! He started in on her and I stepped in, so he aimed his attack at me, calling me the usual, only it was worse this time because I was wearing my bathing suit, all ready to take off for the lake. I took it as long as I could, but finally retreated to my room to contemplate Life's Injustices.

"Bobbi called in the late afternoon and said she and Stu were going to Powderhorn to watch fireworks and how would I like to come along with a friend of Stu's. If it hadn't been such a miserable day, I might not have gone. But it was, and I did, and now I'm not sure if I should have.

"His name was Clay Forrester, and when I first met him I'm afraid I made an absolute fool of myself by staring. What a face! What hair! What everything! His eyes were gray and he seemed a little brooding at first, but as the night went on, he smiled more. His eyebrows are not exactly the same. The left one quirks up a little more and gives him a teasing look at times. His chin has the suggestion of a dimple. His hair was the color of autumn leaves—not the reds, not the yellows, but the ones in between, like some maples, maybe.

"When Stu introduced us, Clay was just standing there with his thumbs hooked in his jeans pockets and all he said was Hi and smiled and just like that my heart hit my throat. I wondered if he could tell.

"What happened was insane. I'm not sure if I believe it yet. We walked around Powderhorn with this huge jug of wine, taking turns sipping, and waiting for full dark. I remember that we laughed a lot. Bobbi and Stu were ahead of us, holding hands, and sometimes Clay's shoulder bumped mine and shivers went up my arm. By the time the fireworks started, we were all nearly as high as they were!

"It turned out there were blankets in the truck and pretty soon Bobbi and Stu disappeared with one of them. I remember just the way Clay stood there with the bottle of wine in one hand and the handle of the truck door in the other. He asked if I wanted to sit in the truck and watch the fireworks or use the other blanket. I still can't believe I really answered, 'Let's use the blanket' but I did.

"We sat down under a huge tree with lacy black branches, and Clay pulled the cork out of the wine bottle with his teeth and spit it high in the air and we both laughed. I remember thinking how different it felt, getting drunk, when you were the one doing it instead of watching somebody else.

273

"He was leaning on one elbow, stretched-out-like on the blanket, resting the bottle on the ground between us when he leaned over and put an arm around my neck and pulled me over to kiss me the first time, and somehow my breast came up against his hand and the neck of that bottle. 'Fireworks,' he whispered in my ear afterward. He put his hand under my hair and held me there, moving the back of his hand and the top of the bottle against me. I guess I said 'Yeah' or something, just to see what'd happen. What happened was that he said 'Come here' and put his other arm around me, wine and all, and pulled me over there beside him and stretched out. I went willingly, remembering the names that Daddy had called me that morning, thinking to myself that maybe I'd prove him right.

"Clay took his time. He was some kind of a kisser. I've kissed boys before but this was different. And I've been pulled tight against guys before, but somehow they always were panting and clumsy and overeager and I was repelled. I waited for that to happen again, but it didn't. Instead, when I stretched out beside Clay, he gave me all the time I needed to make up my mind. I had it made up long before he pressed himself against me. I could feel the wine bottle bump against my back, cold through my shirt compared to his tongue, warm in my mouth. Lazy, it was at first, lazy and slow. I remember the feeling of his teeth against my own tongue, and the taste of wine in both of our mouths together. I remember him using his lips to urge me to open my mouth wider, then the feel of his tongue exploring me made me go all barmy and warmy. Funny thing was, while he did it, he loosened his hold on me and I found myself lying there drifting into submission more from his lack of force than the presence of it. At last he nudged himself away and collapsed onto his back with a wrist over his eyes. He was still holding onto the wine bottle with the heel of it against the ground, rocking it back and forth.

"He said something like 'Whew, you're good at that.' Did I say 'So are you' or not? I don't remember. I only know I felt all loose and woozy, and by then my heart was pounding between my legs and both of us were breathing so hard you could hear it above the boom of the fireworks.

"I think it was me who said I needed more wine, and I think

it was him who said he needed less. Anyway, we both laughed then and when the wine bottle was corked up again and not hindering him, he pulled me over half on top of him and this time the kisses were harder and hotter and wetter and both of our bodies were doing a lot of talking. He rolled me onto my back, lying half across me and I remember thinking how secure it felt to have somebody hold me that way. It seemed to take away the hurt of the awful things Daddy was always yelling at me. It was like coming home ought to feel, or like Christmas, or like all the best scenes from all the best movies all rolled into one. He flattened me with the length of his body and began moving, moving, moving against my hips, kissing me all over my face. Once he broke away and groaned, 'Oh, God,' but I wouldn't let him go. I pulled him back on top of me and made him not stop. Maybe if I hadn't done that, things would have eased up a little. But by that time I didn't want them to ease up.

" 'Hey, listen, I think we're both a little drunk,' he finally said, and rolled off of me. But I found the wine bottle and said, 'Not yet.' Then I took a mouthful of wine and leaned over and kissed him and when his mouth opened, I let the wine drizzle into it. He took the bottle and sat up and filled his mouth, pushed me onto my back again and did what I'd just done to him. The wine was warm from the inside of his mouth. When I swallowed it, he bathed my lips with his tongue, running it over them like a mother cat washes her kitten. And before I knew what was happening, he ran his tongue down my jaw and laced his fingers through my hair and forced my head back. Then I felt the neck of the bottle against my own neck and the cool trickle of the wine as he poured it in the hollow of my arched throat.

"Crazy! I thought. We're crazy! But I felt like my pores were alive for the first time ever while he lapped the wine from my neck, then he moved up to continue kissing me under my jaw, intentionally touching me nowhere else, I think.

"I remember the pulsing happening in my body in places where I wished he'd pour the wine and cool me off. But I knew pouring the wine wouldn't really cool me off, and anyway, I didn't want to be cooled. When his tongue left me again, my hand groped for the wine bottle and he played along, letting me take my turn at drinking from him. I made him lie on his side and we were both giggling terribly while I tried to pour wine into his ear and he said, 'What are you doing?' and I said, 'Deafening you' and he said, 'What?' and I said, 'Deafening you!' and he said, 'What?' again, louder and louder and we were laughing and I was taking wine from his ear with the tip of my tongue. Only most of it had gone running down behind it and into the soft hair at the back of his neck and I followed it and we laughed and laughed.

"When it was his turn again, he teased me by pretending to consider for a long, long time, and finally he rolled me onto my stomach and said, 'Pick your hips up off the blanket a little.' I did and felt him pull my shirttails out of my jeans. Next I felt the wine run into the hollow of my spine before he slipped his arm under me and held me up a little while taking the wine off my back. And always we were laughing, laughing, even when he lay down on top of me and started kissing the back of my neck, using his hips from behind to tease me, while I pleaded breathlessness with his weight on top of me that way.

"My turn next, and there was only one place I could think of—if you could call it thinking by that time, my mind was so fuzzy. We were kissing when I pushed him onto his back again. Then I sat up and boldly unbuttoned his shirt and—like he'd done to me—pulled it out of his jeans. I poured my turn into the shallow valley between his ribs, and tried to lap it up before it ran down to his stomach, but of course I couldn't and we started giggling foolishly, getting hotter all the time, avoiding the final confrontation with this silliness we'd somehow cooked up together. I've read about different kinds of foreplay before, but this one beat anything I'd ever read about.

"Next it was his turn, and suddenly the giggling stopped. He unbuttoned my blouse in the flashes from the fireworks, and without uttering a word, poured wine in my navel, and ever so slowly pushed the cork into the bottle and threw it far away onto the grass someplace. He leaned over and no sooner had I felt his tongue on my stomach than he got both arms around my hips some way, and we rolled back and forth with his face against my stomach, and one of his hands swept up and down from the small of my back to the back of my thighs, and I knew what would happen if I didn't stop him, so I reached

276

down to pull at his shoulders, but he rolled over and pinned the bottom half of me down, kissing his way around the waist of my jeans. Then he tried to open the snap with his teeth. Finally I managed to make him come up and join me, stretched out again. But my blouse was opened and he had my bra off before his lips got to mine. Again we were flattened against each other and his skin felt so good against mine. He ground himself against me and I ground right back. He raised his knee and pressed it high between my legs and I clung to him, to the very, very good and right feeling of being close that way to another human being.

"He had a way of moving his hands over my breasts that made me forget all the names Daddy had ever called me, that made me feel utterly right to lie there beneath his touch, letting his knee ride hard and high between my thighs, letting him pull one of my legs over his hip until we were as close to joined as it's possible to be when you're both still wearing jeans.

"Once he whispered, 'Hey, listen, are you sure you want to do this?' and something about him not usually doing this with strangers and I think I stopped his words with my mouth and then his hand plunged down into the back of my jeans and I gave him every permission with the movement of my body. Names Daddy had called me came teasing, but somehow they didn't apply. I wanted that closeness, needed it like nothing I had ever needed in my life. And when Clay zipped down my zipper and tucked the backs of his fingers against my bare skin, I sucked in my stomach to make it easier for him. His hand moved down and I closed my eyes and lay there pretending that at last somebody loved me. Who was I at that minute? Was I some heroine from a forgotten childhood film or was I myself, the me that had gone without affection all her life? I think maybe I was a little of each, for I knew a treasured feeling that could only happen in the movies. At least, I'd always believed it only happened in the movies, yet here it was, happening to me. I felt like all nineteen years of my life had been pointed to this moment, to this man who was showing me that there was more than hate in this world, there was love too. He called me Cat then. 'Ah, Cat,' he said, 'you feel good' and I was sure that he could feel me throbbing, touching the inside of me that way, and I wanted to say to him that I'd never felt that way before, not ever, not even close. But I didn't. I only closed my eyes and let everything in me swim toward his touch until my body thrust against his hand of its own accord, and I knew my mouth hung slack but could not seem to close it. I seemed to forget how to kiss even, but lay there beneath his kiss nearly unaware of it, for its adequacy seemed to pale compared to the sensations that wanted completion in the lower half of my body. And the wine led my hands to search his hard hips, feeling them pull away, giving me consent, freedom, space.

"The heat of him was a surprise and I felt awkward and graceful, both at once, knowing this was what I was expected to do, yet unsure of how to go about it. At my touch he grunted, pressed closer against my hand, moved sinuously. 'Go ahead, Cat,' he said in my ear and his breath on my neck was equally as hot as the beating of his blood through denim.

"I did it, in slow motion, I think, fearing with every opening tooth of his zipper that somehow my father would know what I was doing. Then I put him from my mind. No, that's not true. I didn't have to put him from it, because thoughts of him and everything else fled when I touched Clay Forrester for the first time. Whatever I had expected, I had not expected such heat. Neither had I expected the silkiness. But he was both hot and silky and I had enough sanity about me to marvel at the fluid way he could move, his thrust and ebb making me feel the experienced one holding his flesh in my hands, when I feared being naive and inexpert.

"When I used to imagine making love, I always thought it must be awkward and clumsy. First times are bound to be, I thought. But it wasn't. Instead, it was easy and as graceful as any dance. When he came into me, he called me Cat again, plunging deep while little of the discomfort I'd been led to expect happened. I learned that my body had had some hidden knowledge all along that my mind had not, for it undulated and surprised me and pleased Clay (I think) and it really was like the ballet, each movement so in tune with the other. It was effortless and natural and rhythmic, and would be beautiful to watch, I thought later. But when we were soaring everything came clear, and I suddenly knew why I was doing it. I was

278

doing it to get even with Daddy, and maybe even Mom.

"In the middle of it all, my muscles suddenly lost motion and I only clung to Clay and let him finish without me. I wanted to cry out loud, 'Why didn't you love me? Why didn't you hug me? Why did you make me do this? You see, it's not so hard to touch, to be tender. Look, a total stranger can show me all this, why couldn't you? I didn't want much, just a smile, a hug, a kiss sometime to know you approved of me.' I wanted to cry then but made myself not. And maybe I hung onto Clay too tight, but that's all. I'll show them! I'll show them all!"

The room was a circle of dark around the lightblot shining over the cluttered tabletop. The words on the page became hazy and Clay's hand shook as he replaced the diary where he'd found it. He propped his elbows on the typewriter and pressed his lips against his folded hands. His eyes closed. He tried to gulp down the lump in his throat but it stubbornly remained. He dropped his face into his palms, picturing a father reading that from his daughter. Further, he tried to conceive of a father so devoid of emotion as to fail to respond to such a cry for love. His mind wandered back to the evening he'd first learned that Catherine expected his child. Vividly he recalled her stubborn refusal to ask anything of him, and for the first time he thought he understood. He thought he understood, too, why she had done such a convincing job during the wedding and reception. *I'll show them! I'll show them all!* He felt a new and oppressive weight of responsibility that he'd not known until now. He recalled her aversion to being touched, her defensiveness, and realized why it was so necessary for her to build such a barrier around herself. He pictured her face the few times he'd seen it genuinely happy, knowing now the reasons for her quicksilver changes and why she had been striving so hard to remain independent of him.

His elbows hurt. He realized he'd been sitting for a long time with them digging into the sharp edges of the typewriter. He opened his eyes and the light hurt them. Listlessly he rose and turned off the lamp, wandered into the bedroom and fell on the bed. He lay there with his mind reeling and groping, waiting for her return.

Clay heard her come in, sat up, wondering how to treat her, an odd sensation, for now his concern was with her, not with himself. When he came downstairs, she was sitting with her coat still on, her head laid back against the davenport, eyelids closed but quivering.

"Hi," he said, stopping way across the room from her.

"Hi," she said, without opening her eyes.

"Something wrong?" The lamplight shone on her wind-strewn hair. She hugged her coat very tightly around herself and turned the collar up around her jaw.

"The baby died."

Without another word he crossed the room, sat down on the arm of the davenport and put a hand on top of her hair. She allowed it but said nothing, showed no signs of the heartbreak and fear that bubbled inside her. He moved his hand, rubbing in warm circles upon her hair, then smoothing it down in wordless communion with her. She swallowed convulsively. He wanted desperately to kneel down before her and bury his head in her lap and press his face to her stomach. Instead, he only whispered, "I'm sorry."

"They said its l-lungs were underdeveloped, that wh-when a baby comes early there's always a ch-chance of . . ." But her sentence went unfinished. Her eyes opened wider than normal, focused on the ceiling and he waited for only a single sob, but it never came. He tightened his fingers gently on the back of her neck—an invitation to avail herself of him in whatever way she needed. He could tell how she needed to be held and comforted but she overcame it and sprang up, away from his touch, jerking her coat off almost angrily.

He stopped the coat while it drooped yet over her shoulder blades, grasping her upper arms from behind, expecting her to yank free of his touch. But she didn't. Her head sagged forward as if her neck had suddenly gone limp.

"It doesn't mean ours is in danger," he assured her. "Don't let it upset you, Catherine."

Now she yanked free and spun. "Don't let it upset me! What do you think I am? How can I not let it upset me when I've just seen Grover crying for a baby she never wanted! Do you know how she got pregnant? Well, let me tell you. She was suckered into a date with a high school jock who did it on a dare because she was such a troll! That's how! And she thought she hated the thing growing inside her and now it's dead and she cried like she wished she had died too. And you say 'don't let it upset you?' I don't understand h-how this w-world got s-so . . . screwed up . . ."

He moved suddenly before he could change his mind, before she could run from him again or hide her need behind more of her anger. He wrapped both arms around her and gripped her fiercely. He cradled the back of her head and forced it into the hollow of his neck and made her stay that way, their muscles quivering, straining until at last she gave in and he felt her arms cling to his back. More like combatants than lovers, they clung. Her nails dug into his sweater as she gripped it. Then he felt her fists thumping against the small of his back in desperation, although she wasn't trying to escape him anymore. Just those pitiful thumps, growing weaker and weaker while he waited.

"Catherine," he whispered, "you don't have to be so strong all the time."

"Oh, God, Clay, it was a boy. I saw him in the incubator. He was so beautiful and fragile."

"I know, I know."

"Her mom and dad wouldn't come. Clay, they wouldn't come!" A fist hit his back again.

Let her cry, he thought. If only she'd cry at last. "But your mom's going to come and so is mine."

"What are you trying to do to me?" She suddenly started pushing, palms against his chest, almost thrashing.

"Catherine, trust me."

"No, no! Let me go! This is hard enough without you mixing me all up even worse."

Then she ran up the stairs, taking with her all her years of bottled-up hurt. But now he knew that gentleness would work. It would take time, but eventually, it would work.

Chapter 23

IT BEGAN SNOWING shortly after noon on Christmas Eve day. It came down like diamond dust, in light, puffy featherflakes. By evening the earth looked clean-white. The sky bore a soft luminescence, lit from below by the lights of the city reflecting off the snow.

Catherine wore a new homemade jumper of mellow rust wool, with a tie that cinched it loosely beneath her breasts. She had decided to meet Elizabeth Forrester head-on this time. Yet, approaching the front door, some of Catherine's aplomb quavered at the thought of the grand dame eyeing her popping stomach for the first time.

"Do you think she's here yet?" she asked Clay timorously, while he paused with his hand on the door latch.

"I'm sure she is. Just do like I said, face her squarely. She admires that."

The smile she managed nearly faded as they entered, for Elizabeth Forrester was advancing upon them from the height of the open stairway. Her cane led the way, but it had a surprising tuft of Christmas greenery tied about its handle with a red ribbon.

"Well, it's about time, children!" she scolded imperiously.

"Merry Christmas, Grandmother," Clay greeted, taking her arm as she approached the lowest step.

"Yes, I'm given to understand that it certainly is. I can help myself down the steps, if you please. If you want to pamper someone, I understand that your wife is in the way of a woman who needs pampering. Is that so, my dear?" She turned her hawk-eyes on Catherine.

"Hardly. I'm as healthy as a horse," replied the girl, removing her coat into Clay's hands, revealing the maternity dress.

About Elizabeth Forrester's lips a thin smile threatened, and the eyes that pointedly refrained from dropping to Catherine's abdomen glittered like the jewels upon her fingers. Then she cocked a brow at her grandson.

"You know, I like this young woman's style. Not unlike my own, I might add." The ivory-headed cane pecked twice at Catherine's stomach while the matriarch passed on her decree. "As I've said once before, I shall most assuredly expect him to be beautiful, not to mention bright. Merry Christmas, my dear." She bestowed a cheek to Catherine's, miming a kiss which did not quite land, then exited to the living room in her usual grand style to leave Catherine gaping at Clay.

"That's all?" she whispered, wide-eyed.

"All?" he smiled. "Beautiful *and* bright? That's a pretty big order."

A smile began about the corners of Catherine's eyes. "But what if *she* is only *cute* and of *average intelligence?*"

Clay looked shocked. "You wouldn't dare!"

"No, I don't suppose I would, would I?"

Their smiles lingered for a long moment, the encounter with Elizabeth Forrester somehow already forgotten. Gazing up at Clay, at the smile upon his firm cheeks, his charmingly handsome mouth, and that brow that curled provocatively over his left eye, Catherine found her self-restraint slipping. She realized she'd been standing there with her eyes in his for some time, and thought, It's this house. What is it that happens to me when I'm in this house with him? Breaking the spell, Catherine swept her glance around the magnificent foyer, searching for something to say.

"I think this place deserves to have its gentlemen arrive in capes tonight, and its ladies with fur muffs, with sleighs outside and nickering horses."

"Yes, Mother's been having fun, as usual."

Then they turned to join the others.

If the house exuded cordiality at other times of the year, it had a special spell at Christmas. Pine swags looped their way up the banister, their pungent aroma a heady greeting to all, while red candles sprang from freshly cut holly branches on tables everywhere. The pine scent mingled with that of smoke from the blazing fireplaces and cooking aromas from the kitchen. Within the study, hurricane lanterns couched blazing candles on the mantel, while a childish rendition of "Deck the Halls" came from the piano in the living room. There, within the bay window, stood a tree of enormous size, a proud old balsam with traditional multicolored lights that cast their rainbows across the walls and faces there and were redoubled in gilded swags of tinsel garland that threaded the balsam's limbs. It bore so many dazzling ornaments that its green arms fairly drooped. A mountain of gifts—foiled, beribboned, sprigged with greens—cascaded around the foot of the tree. Upon the longest living room wall was an outsized wreath of nuts, garnished with a red velvet bow whose streamers were caught within the beaks of gilded partridges which hung on either side of the wreath. Everywhere there was the buzz and babble of happy voices, and above them came the laugh of Angela, who'd been ladling eggnog in the dining room, looking like some delicate little Christmas ornament herself in a pale lavender lounging outfit of soft velour, her tiny silver slippers matching the thin belt at her waist and the fine chains around her neck.

"Catherine, darling," she greeted, immediately leaving her task and crossing to them, "and Clay!" Her melodious voice carried its usual note of welcome, but Clay affected an injured expression.

"You know, it used to be 'Clay-darling' first and then 'Catherine-darling,' but I seem to have been upstaged."

Angela gave him a scolding pout, but nevertheless kissed Catherine first, then him, flush on the mouth.

"There. Is that what you were waiting for, standing there so innocently?"

She quirked an eyebrow at the archway above his head,

which held a kissing ball of mistletoe. "As if you didn't know," teased Angela, "it's there every year."

Clay quickly ducked aside, playing the beleaguered male while Angela only laughed and bore Catherine away toward the eggnog where Claiborne now turned with a warm greeting.

The doorbell kept ringing until the laughter and voices were doubled. Left momentarily alone, Catherine scanned the ceiling to find the place peppered with mistletoe. Someone approached to congratulate her on her pregnancy, and she tried to forget about mistletoe. But everybody else was using it to great advantage, and it made for a gay mood. Catherine assiduously avoided it.

The food was served buffet style, crowned by real English plum pudding that arrived steaming from the kitchen. That was when Granddad Elgin caught Inella under the mistletoe in the kitchen doorway as she fussily gave orders not to touch the pudding until she returned with the warmed dessert plates. Catherine laughed to herself, standing nearby with a cup of coffee in her hand. It was delightful and so unexpected to see little birdlike Granddad Elgin kissing the maid in the kitchen doorway. Catherine felt someone behind her and glanced over her shoulder to find Clay there. He raised his eyebrows, then his eyes, to a spot over her head.

"Better watch out. Granddad Elgin will get you next," he said.

She quickly scuttled from beneath the mistletoe. "I wouldn't have suspected it of your Granddad," she said smilingly.

"Things get a little crazy around here at Christmastime. It's always this way."

"They certainly do," Clay's father said, approaching just then. "Do you mind, Young Mister Forrester, if Old Mister Forrester kisses your wife while she's standing in that advantageous spot?"

Catherine wasn't under the greens anymore; still, she looked up and backed up a step. "I wasn't—"

"Not at all, Mr. Forrester."

Claiborne captured her for a hearty kiss, then stepped back, squeezing her biceps, looking into her face.

"You're lovelier than usual tonight, my dear." He put one arm around her shoulders, his other around Clay's. He looked first into one face, then into the other. "I don't think I remember a happier Christmas."

"I think a little of the glow might be from you spiking the eggnog," Clay teased his father.

"A little, not all though."

Catherine and Clay found a corner to sit in and eat their plum pudding, but she only dabbled at hers. It seemed they had little to say to each other, although time and again she felt Clay's eyes on her.

Soon Angela rounded everyone up and took her place at the piano to accompany the younger children who piped carols off-key until the entire group ended with "Silent Night." Claiborne stood behind Angela as she played, with his hands on her shoulders, singing robustly. When the last note finished, she kissed one of his hands.

"You weren't singing," Clay said behind Catherine.

"I'm a little inhibited, I guess."

He was close enough to smell her hair. He thought of what he'd read in her diary. He'd been wanting her ever since. "People will be leaving now. I'll help them find their coats."

"And I'll start picking up glasses. I'm sure Inella is tired."

It was after midnight. Clay and Catherine had ushered the last straggler out the door, for somehow Angela and Claiborne had disappeared. The entry was dim, pine-scented and private. With slow steps, Catherine radiated toward the living room and the soft glow of tree lights. Clay was just behind her, where it seemed he'd hovered more and more as the night moved on. His hands were in his pockets. She ran her fingers through her hair, brushing it behind an ear as they ambled thoughtlessly toward the archway.

But there Catherine stopped, warned by a movement in the shadows at the far end of the dining room. Claiborne and Angela stood there, wrapped in each other's arms, kissing in an impassioned way in which Catherine did not think people of their age kissed. Claiborne had a dishtowel slung over his shoulder and Angela was shoeless. His hand moved over Angela's back, then stroked her side and moved to her breast. Quickly Catherine turned away, feeling like an intruder, for the two were certainly unaware of her presence across the wide, dimly lit rooms. But as she turned discreetly to withdraw, she bumped into Clay, who, instead of retreating, only placed a single finger over his lips, then raised it to point at the mistletoe above their heads. His hair and face and shirt were illuminated in the muted hues of Christmas, all red, blue, green and yellow, and he looked as inviting as the gifts beneath the tree. His eyes, too, reflected the glow of the tree lights as with a single finger he traced the line of Catherine's jaw, burning its path to the hollow beneath her lower lip. Her startled eyes widened and the breath clawed its way into her throat. She laid a hand against his light-dappled shirt, meaning to hold him off, but he captured it, along with her other, and carried them around his neck.

"My turn," he whispered.

Then he lowered his lips to hers, caught them opened in surprise, expecting the struggle to begin. But it didn't. He knew he did not play fair, catching her while his parents were right there doing the same thing. But it had been on his mind all night, and playing fair was the farthest thing from his mind as he delved into the silken depths of her mouth. Their warm tongues touched. He plied her with singular lack of insistence, remembering what she had written about such things, inviting rather than plundering, with a luxuriant slowness. He felt fingers curve around the back of his collar and stilled his tongue— waiting, waiting, with his hold still merely a suggestion upon her body. Then a single fingertip found the skin of his neck and gently he tightened the arm about her waist.

Her body had grown since their wedding. It had blossomed into a captivating fullness that now held their hips apart. But he ran a hand possessively up and down her back, wishing that now the baby would kick—just once—so he could know the feel of it against his loins.

Reluctantly he ended the kiss.

"Merry Christmas," he whispered, near her face.

"Merry Christmas," she whispered back, her lips so close he felt the whisper of breath from her words. The room was utterly still. A needle dropped from the Christmas tree, making an audible ping as they gazed into each other's eyes. Then their lips were willing and warm and seeking again and her

287

stomach was pressed lightly against him. She wished this could go on forever, but the very wish reminded her that it couldn't, wouldn't, and she withdrew. But when she would have been turned loose he instead entwined his fingers loosely behind her back, leaning away, swiveling lazily back and forth with her, smiling down at her hair, her lips and her breasts, which were undeniably growing.

She knew she should insist on being turned loose, but he was tempting, tender this way, handsome with his face limned by the low lights, his hair colored like fire. They turned their faces to look at the Christmas tree. Contented for the moment, she let him pull her lightly near him until her temple rested on his jaw. And from the shadows, the pale faces of Angela and Claiborne—in a like embrace—watched the younger couple, and Claiborne wordlessly tightened his embrace.

"I have a marvelous idea," Angela said softly.

Catherine started slightly, but when she would have pulled away, Clay prevented it.

"Why don't the two of you spend the night and that way we'll be able to creep down in the wee hours in our nighties and robes just like we've always done."

Clay felt Catherine stiffen.

"Fine by me," he said, rocking her as before, the picture of a satisfied spouse.

"But I don't have my nightie," she said, alarmed.

"I'm sure I can find one for you, and we must have a spare toothbrush around here someplace. You could stay in the pink room."

Catherine groped for excuses, came up with one. "But we have to pick up Mother on our way over tomorrow morning anyway."

"Oh, that's right."

Clay's heart fell.

"Well," Angela mused, "it was a good idea anyway. But you two make sure you get here bright and early."

At home, Clay took his sweet old time about dragging out his own bedding and using the bathroom. He hovered around the upstairs hall, leaning against her doorway, watching while she slipped off her earrings and shoes, "Want a glass of soda or something?" he asked.

"No, I'm stuffed."

"I'm not very tired, are you?"

"I'm beat."

He unbuttoned his shirt. "I guess that's to be expected, huh?"

"Yes, the heavier I get the less zip I have."

"How much longer are you planning to stay in school? Shouldn't you be quitting pretty soon?" He finally decided to come into the bedroom, passing close behind her to stand beside the chest of drawers and empty his pockets.

"I can go as long as I want."

"How long is that?"

"A while yet, maybe till the end of second semester."

He watched her moving around the room, knew she was making motions at inconsequential things to look like she was busy. He wandered to the closet door, idle himself, leaning against the door frame and watching while she opened a dresser drawer. Her fair hair swayed forward over her shoulder as she leaned to retrieve something from inside. The skin across his chest felt as tight as a piano string. His heart beat upon it like a velvet hammer. His voice, when he spoke, was a deep, resonant note, softly struck.

"How long can a pregnant woman safely have intercourse?"

Catherine's hands fell still. Her head jerked up and she met his eyes in the mirror. The muscles of her groin involuntarily tightened, as did her hands upon the garments she'd been needlessly straightening in that drawer. Clay didn't move a muscle, just lounged there against that door frame with a hand strung negligently in his trouser pocket and a thin strip of golden-haired skin showing behind his open shirt. His expression was unreadable as she struggled to think of a reply.

"I want to, you know," he said, in that same hushed tone that raised every hair along the base of her spine. "And since you're already pregnant, what else could happen? I mean, if it's safe for you, of course." But she only stared at him. "I've been wanting to for weeks, and I've told you in every possible way except in words. Tonight when we were kissing under that mistletoe I decided I'd tell you. You're a very desirable wife, did you know that, Catherine?"

At last she found her voice, trembling though it was. "I'm a very pregnant wife."

"Ah, but that doesn't detract from your desirability in the least. Particularly since it's my baby you're carrying."

"Don't say any more, Clay," she warned.

"Don't be afraid of me, Catherine. I'm not going to force the issue. It's entirely up to you."

"I'm not afraid of you, and the answer is no." Suddenly she found what she was looking for in that drawer and slammed it shut.

"Why?"

She kept her back to him, looking down at something on the dresser top, but in the mirror he could see how she pressed herself against the edge of it, clutching some blue filmy thing in her hand.

"Why are you doing this tonight when it's been such a perfect day?"

"I told you, I'd like to go to bed with you. Would it be dangerous?"

"The subject never came up at the doctor's."

"Well, why don't you bring it up next time you're there?"

"There's no point in it."

"Isn't there?"

The silence that followed was as pregnant as the woman leaning against the dresser. Then Clay's voice became convincing.

"I'm tired of sleeping out there on that davenport when there's a luxurious king-size bed in here and a perfectly good, warm woman to snuggle up to. And I think she'd enjoy it, too, if she'd let herself. What do you say, Catherine, it's Christmas."

"Don't, Clay. You promised."

"I'm breaking my promise," he said, bringing his shoulder away from that door frame in slow-motion.

"Clay," she said warningly, turning to face him.

"How can you kiss that way and not get turned on, will you tell me that?"

"Stay away from me."

"I've been staying away. All it does is make me need it all the more." He advanced halfway across the room.

"I am not going to bed with you, so you can just forget it!"

"Convince me," he said low, still advancing.

"Do you know what your problem is? It's your ego. You simply can't believe I can live with you and not give in to your deadly charms, can you?"

In a voice like velvet he accused, "Cat, you're a goddam liar. You're forgetting I'm the one that was kissing you earlier. What's the harm in it? After all, it's legal, if it comes down to that—all signed, sealed and documented by the preacher. What are you afraid of?"

He was no more than an arm's length in front of her now, his gray eyes warmer than she'd ever seen them. Unconsciously she covered her widening girth with both hands.

"Why do you do that? Why do you try to hide from me? Always keeping me at a distance, avoiding even being in the same room with me. Why can't you be like you were earlier tonight more often? Why don't you talk to me, tell me how you're feeling, even complain about something? I need some human contact, Cat. I'm not used to living this insular life."

"Don't call me Cat!"

"Why? Tell me why."

"No." She would have turned away, but his arm stopped her.

"Don't turn away from me. Talk to me."

"Oh, Clay, please. It's been the most wonderful night. Please don't ruin it now. I'm tired, and happier than I've been for the longest time; at least I was until you started this. Can't we pretend the kiss never happened and be friends?"

He wanted to put voice to the root of her problem, to say to her that making love with him would not make her the slut her father told her she was. But she wasn't ready for it yet, and furthermore, it was a truth she must discover for herself. He knew if he forced her before she recognized that truth, the damage would be irreparable.

"If you mean it, and you're genuinely going to be friendly toward me from now on, that's a start. But don't expect me to forget that kiss ever happened, and don't expect me to believe that you'll forget it either."

"It's that house. Something about that house. I feel different when I go there, and somehow I do crazy things."

"Like letting your husband kiss you under the mistletoe?"

She was struggling with emotions she could not control,

wanting him, afraid of the heartbreak he could cause her in the end. He reached out one brown hand, capturing the back of her neck, pulling her a little nearer, though she stiffly resisted.

"You are afraid of me, Catherine. But you don't have to be. When and if . . . the decision will be yours."

Then he kissed her lightly on the mouth, still holding her with that single hand on her tight neck muscles.

"Good night, Cat," he whispered, and was gone.

Her determination to resist Clay was further weakened when on Christmas morning she opened up a small package from him and found two tickets to *Swan Lake*, coming up at Northrup Auditorium in late January. She read the words on the tickets and raised her eyes, but he was tearing into a gift from his mother, so Catherine leaned over and touched his arm softly. He looked up.

"You remembered," she said, with the warmth expanding in her chest. "I . . . well, thank you, Clay. I'm sorry I have no gift for you."

"I haven't been to a ballet in a long time," he said.

The moment grew complicated by the looks in their eyes, then she broke the tension by teasing, "Who says you're invited?"

But next Catherine bestowed one of her rare smiles.

Chapter 24

DURING THE FOLLOWING week, Clay invited Catherine to go shopping with him. He needed something to wear on New Year's Eve, which they'd agreed to spend with Claiborne and Angela at the country club. But Catherine declined, believing it best to avoid such little domestic sallies.

Clay came home one night with a pair of plastic-sheathed garment bags, and tossed one casually across the back of a living room chair. "Here, I thought we both ought to have something new."

"You bought something for *me?*" she asked from the kitchen.

"Sure. You were stubborn so I had to. It's quite formal at the club—kind of a tradition."

Then he bounded up the stairs with his hanger. She wiped her hands on a dishcloth and walked around the peninsula with her eyes riveted on the dress bag.

When Clay came back, she was standing with the dress aloft, holding the black crepe skirt like an opened fan.

"Clay, you shouldn't have."

"Do you like it?"

"Well, yes, but it's so impractical. I'll probably only wear it once."

"I want you looking just as classy as every other woman there."

"But I'm not. I've never owned a dress like this in my life. I'll feel funny." She looked momentarily crestfallen, but he could tell how much she liked it.

"Listen, Catherine, you're my wife, and you have as much right to be at the club as anyone else. Understand?"

"Yes, but—"

"*Yes, but* nothing. All I'm worried about is if the thing will fit. It's a first for me, you know—buying a maternity dress."

She couldn't help chuckling. "What did you do, go in the store and say 'Gimme a dress that's, say, four ax-handles around?"

He rubbed his chin, measuring her visually. "No, I figured more like five."

She scarcely looked at him as she laughed; she had eyes for nothing but the dress.

"I'll look like a circus tent, but I love it . . . really."

"You're awfully touchy about losing your shape. Isn't it time you accept it? I have."

"It's easy for a man to say when he doesn't have to face getting blown up like some dirigible and having to lose the extra pounds afterward. If I'm not careful, no man will look twice at me next summer."

As soon as Catherine said it she felt him bristle. His good humor fled as Clay remarked, "Oh, so you plan to go husband-hunting then?"

"I didn't mean it that way. But I certainly don't intend this marriage to mean the end of my love life."

For Clay the pleasure of giving her the dress suddenly dissolved, leaving him feeling angry, his ego stung. It irritated him that she could make a comment like that while she wouldn't even let him lay a hand on her. He'd given her the best home she'd ever had, all the things he could think of to make her life easy. He'd taken on his share of the housework, given her the freedom to come and go and to do her abominable typing— which irked him no end and made him want to drop the damn typewriter off the balcony. And he'd been more than patient with her, even when he wanted more attention than she gave.

And how did she repay him? By being cold and standoffish, then bemoaning the fact that no man would look twice at her if she didn't preserve her shape? What the hell was she trying to do to him anyway?

While they were getting ready to go out on New Year's Eve, Clay was as stony as he'd been during the three days since he brought the dress home. Catherine had learned how lonely it felt to be the one on the receiving end of such treatment.

She put the finishing touches on her hair. Just then Clay came in the bedroom to rummage through his jewelry box for a tie pin. From behind, he was tantalizingly thin and tapered in the new smoky-blue suit with its trim cut and double vents at the rear.

Clay swung around to find her studying him.

"I'm almost ready. Excuse me," he said, edging around her briskly.

"I see that. Is that your new suit?"

He didn't answer, just moved to the mirror to insert the needle of the pin through a new striped tie.

"You always manage to look like an ad in *The New Yorker*," she tried.

"Thank you," he replied icily.

"And the dress fits, see?"

"Good."

She was stung by his indifference. "Clay, you've hardly talked to me at all this week. What's wrong now?"

"If you don't understand it, I'm not going to waste my breath explaining."

She knew very well what was wrong, but it was hard for her to apologize.

He dropped the back clasp of the tie pin and muttered, "Damn."

"Clay, I know I act ungrateful sometimes, but I'm not. And you and I had an agreement before we got married."

"Oh, sure! So why are you in here offering me compliments? Why do I suddenly merit applause for how I dress?"

"Because it's true, that's all."

"Catherine, don't, okay? I don't know how to handle you anymore. You've walked around me like I was some cigar-store Indian for weeks now. And when you finally decide to start talking to me, it's to tell me you're worried you might gain too much weight so it'll be tough when you go on the make again. How do you think that makes me feel when you practically start shopping for chastity belts every time I try anything with you?"

"Oh, for heaven's sake, what's the matter with you, any-way!"

"You want to know what's the matter with me?" he barked, whirling on her, accosting her face-to-face. "What's the matter with me is the same damn thing that was the matter with me last week and the week before that and the week before that. I'm horny! That's what's the matter with me! You want the truth, lady? There it is in a nutshell! So don't come sashaying in here after all this time and suddenly start fawning over my looks, which are the same as when you married me! You know what you are?"

She had never seen Clay this angry. His face was suffused with color; the veins above his collar stood out boldly.

"You, Mrs. Forrester are a——" But even as angry as he was he couldn't say it.

"What!" she yelled. "Finish it! Say it!"

But he got control of himself and turned away, tugging at his lapels and adjusting the knot of his tie.

"My mother raised me to speak with respect around fe-males, so I'll refrain from using the four-letter prefix to the word ——teaser."

"How dare you, you bastard!"

He gave her an insolent look in the mirror. "Take a look at what happens to you after a few days of being ignored. You come in here with your cute little compliments, just enough to keep me swimming after the bait, huh? Do you know how many times you've warmed up to me just enough to keep me interested? I won't bother to recount them because you'd deny it anyway. But it's the truth. You've accused me of being the one exploiting you to boost my ego, but I believe the shoe's on the other foot."

"That's not true! I've never led you on!"

"Catherine, at least I've been honest about it, starting with our wedding night. I've come right out and said that I wanted to make love to you. But do you know what you do? You skirt the issue, you skitter away, then allow me close enough only when it suits you. Your problem is you want to forget you're a woman but you can't. You like being pursued, but on the other hand, you're afraid if you break down and allow yourself to be made love to, you'll be what your father always accused you of being. What you don't realize is, that makes you as sick as your old man!"

"You bastard," she growled, low in her throat.

"Go ahead, call me names so you don't have to face yourself."

"You said, 'no sex,' when you asked me to marry you."

"You got it. I've decided not to harass you anymore. You want to sleep in your big bed alone, fine. But let's end this sweet little charade we play in between bedtimes, okay? I won't press you for attention, and you won't give me cute little compliments you don't mean, huh? Let's just keep out of each other's way until July, like we agreed."

There was nothing in the world she wanted to do less than go to the club that night. Things became even less tolerable when, shortly after they arrived, so did Jill Magnusson, along with her date and her family.

Clay put on a devoted-husband act, timing his repeated returns to Catherine's side very assiduously all night long, making sure she had whatever drink she wanted, making sure introductions were made where necessary, making sure she was never left at the table alone when every other woman was dancing. Around his parents Clay was the epitome of husbandly courtesies, but Catherine lost track of how many times he danced with Jill. At two minutes before midnight Clay was dancing with his wife, but when the band broke into "Auld Lang Syne" and he kissed her, it was the most impersonal, tongueless kiss she'd ever had. Furthermore, he had artfully maneuvered them near enough to Jill and her partner that it appeared quite natural when they were the first couple to exchange partners. Catherine found herself pressed into the arms of a stocky, black-haired man who solicitously refrained from embracing the pregnant lady too tightly. But while she and the dark man kissed, her eyes were open, watching Clay and Jill sending a silent message into each other's eyes—long and tenuous—before enfolding each other in a painfully familiar fashion. Clay's hands caressed Jill's bare back, his fingers spread seductively so that his little finger hooked beneath a red spaghetti strap, traveled up Jill's shoulder blade and disappeared beneath her cascading hair. Catherine dropped her eyes only to see Clay's hips pressed provocatively against Jill's. The couple broke apart momentarily, then Jill laughed and half-turned to Clay as she captured him again. Now Catherine could see Jill's long fingernails glittering through Clay's hair. Unable to drag her eyes away, Catherine watched as their mouths opened wide upon each other and could see a movement at Clay's cheek as his tongue danced into Jill's mouth.

Then, thankfully, Stu was there to claim a kiss from Catherine. But he could see the way she fought the intimidating rush of tears and whispered, "Don't think anything of it, kiddo, okay? We've all been kissing each other Happy New Year since we were too young to know what it meant."

Then Stu smoothly parted Clay and Jill and moved in for a kiss. But Catherine noticed when Stu kissed Jill there was none of that open-mouthed business, nor did she run her glistening nails through *his* hair.

Before one o'clock arrived, Jill and Clay were both mysteriously missing. Nobody seemed to notice except Catherine, who checked the clock at least twenty times during the twenty minutes they were gone. When they returned, they entered carefully from opposite doors. But Clay's tie had been loosened and she could tell he'd freshly run a comb through his hair.

Dreary January settled in, bringing snow and cold and little to cheer anyone. Clay began leaving the house in the evenings again, although he never stayed out overnight. He and Catherine withdrew into their polite roles of roommates, and nothing

298

more. The spirited teasing they'd once shared seemed gone forever, and the consideration Clay had once shown Catherine disappeared with New Year's Eve. When they were at home at the same time, they rarely ate together, avoided even passing each other in the hall. With Herb still in the workhouse, Catherine visited her mother more often, raising no objection in Clay when she'd return home later than he. The night before the ballet she reminded him of it, but without looking up from his book he suggested she take Bobbi or her mother because he wouldn't be free to go with her. Catherine took Bobbi, but somehow the ballet had lost its appeal.

Clay spent the night of the ballet at home. Occasionally his thoughts meandered to Catherine, remembering her pleasure at receiving the tickets. He'd thought back then that it would be fun to take her to see her first performance. Most of the time when he was alone he tried not to think of her at all, but tonight it was hard, knowing where she was. There had been times during the past month when, if she would have offered even the slightest warming toward him, he might have reneged and dropped the uncaring front behind which he'd been posing. But he'd been hurt by her rebuffs too many times to approach her again. A man could stand being turned away only to a point before withdrawing a safe distance, or—better yet—going where he knew he'd find a positive response.

When Catherine came home, Clay was drowsing in the living room with a book on his lap. He yawned, sat up and ran a hand through his hair. It had been a long time since they'd said anything civil to each other. He thought, maybe . . .

"How was it?" he inquired.

She glanced over his tousled hair, wondering why he bothered to make it appear as if he'd been home all night when she hadn't the slightest doubt whom he'd been with. She kept her voice intentionally expressionless as she replied, "I didn't like the way you could hear the dancers' feet echoing on the floor every time they landed."

Clay withdrew further into his protective shield.

February came, bringing gray days that thwarted even the most blithe spirits. Catherine decided to stay in school until the semester ended in mid-March, but the chore became harder and harder as she grew heavier and more listless.

And in the town house in Golden Valley not even the briefest word was spoken between husband and wife.

Chapter 25

THE DAY THEY released Herb Anderson from the Hennepin County Workhouse, the Chenook winds were blowing elsewhere in the country, but in Minnesota the cold leaden skies matched Anderson's temperament. Gusty winds lapped at his ankles, whipping their icy tongues along the frozen slush beside the road as he walked. It was hard going without overshoes. Time and again his slick soles skittered on the uneven wayside and he swore under his breath. He hitchhiked his way into Minneapolis, finding the city as dismal as the highway had been, malcontent under the dirty blanket of late-winter ice that bore the remnants of the road crews' seasonal efforts at sanding and salting.

It was late afternoon, everybody scurrying with their chins pulled low into coat collars, scarcely looking up. Herb was forced to take a city bus to the old neighborhood, and even on it, the cold seeped in. He rode with arms crossed tight, staring out the window with unsmiling eyes.

Jesus, a drink sounds good. Kept me dry all these months, thinking they finally got old Herb. Hah, just who in the hell do they think they are, taking away a man's free will? I can dry out any damn time I want to. Didn't I always say I could!

Well, I did it, by God, just like I said I could. But what gave them sons-a-bitches the right to force it on me? When I get to Haley's I'll show them sons-a-bitches that Herb Anderson quits drinkin' when Herb Anderson's good and ready, and not one day sooner!

At Haley's Bar the usual old crowd was there, picking up glasses instead of their kids.

"Well, look who's here! Been keepin' a stool warm for ya, Herb."

All of his cronies moved aside to make room, slapping him on the shoulder, settin' 'em up.

"First one's on me, huh? Hey, Georgie, bring Herb here a taste of what he's been missin'!"

Ah, this is what a man needs, thought Herb. Friends who talk your language.

The feel of the varnished bar was like balm beneath his elbows. The smoky, neon haze around the jukebox burned his unaccustomed eyes wonderfully. The blaring medley of good ole country songs about wronged loves and foiled hearts made the wounds bleed like ulcers, self-opened. Herb raised another shot and downed it, then squeezed the shot glass and reveled in being the center of attention.

And all the while the alcohol did its dirty work; all the outrage that life had handed Herb Anderson came doubling back.

Ada tensed, placed trembling fingers to her lips at the sound of someone fumbling at the door. It was locked, but there came the click of a key. Then the door was flung wide and Herb wavered before her.

"Well, well, well, if it isn't Ada, keeping the home fires burning," he observed thickly.

"Why, Herb," she exclaimed in her timid way, "you're out."

"Goddam right I am, no thanks to you."

"Why, Herb, you should've told me you were coming home."

"So you coulda had lover boy here to keep me out?"

"Shut the door, Herb, it's cold."

He eyed the door sullenly. "You think it's cold in here, you oughta try prison a while." He swung wide and slapped hard at the door, which cracked against the frame and bounced back open. Ada edged around him and shut it again. He watched her suspiciously, weaving slightly, hanging onto the front edges of his jacket with both hands.

"H-how are you, Herb?"

He continued to glower at her with sallow eyes. "What the hell do you care, Ada? Where was your concern in November? Man expects his wife to stand behind him at a time like that."

"They told me I didn't need to come, Herb, and Steve was home."

"So I heard. Bet the bunch of you got together and saw to it I wouldn't even see my own kid, didn't you!"

"He was just here for a little while."

"Ada, he's my only goddam kid, and I got rights!"

She dropped her eyes and fidgeted with a button on her duster.

"You know what a man thinks about in prison, Ada?"

"It wasn't prison, it was just the workh—"

"It was the same as a prison and you know it!" he roared.

Ada began to turn away, but he caught one thin arm and swung her around to face him. "Why the hell'd you do it to me? Why!" The blast of his breath made Ada turn her face sharply away but he caught a fistful of her duster and lifted her to her toes, an inch from his mouth. "Who was he? I deserve to know after all these years."

"Please, Herb." She plucked at his knotted fist but he only clenched the cotton all the tighter.

"Who! I sat in that stinkin' hole and made up my mind I'd get it out of you once and for all."

"It don't matter. I stayed with you, didn't I?"

"You stayed because I'd've found you and your lover boy and killed you both, and you knew it!" He suddenly thrust her away and she fell sprawling upon the sofa behind her. "Just like I'd like to kill that slut of a daughter you spawned while I was off fighting the goddam Vietcong! How could you do a thing like that? How! Everybody looks at you and me together and I can read their minds. Poor little Ada, living with that no-'count bum, Herb! You had 'em all fooled, all these years with your little mouse-in-the-corner act. But not me, not me! I never forgot, not for one minute, what you done to me while

303

I was good enough to go out and fight your war for you. Every time I look at that blond hair and that bastard face of hers I remember, and I swore long ago I'd get even with the pair of you one day. And finally I get my chance when the little slut gets herself knocked up by that rich son-of-a-bitch, and I figger for once in his life Old Herb is gonna get paid back for what he put up with all those years. And do you know how sweet it was to think it was comin' straight from the hand of one who owed it to me—that whorin' no-good who's just like her mother?" Herb was weaving, his eyes bright with rage. "You owed it to me, Ada! You both owed it to me! But what did you do? You saw to it that I ended up empty-handed again, didn't you!"

"I never—"

"Shut up!" he barked, pointing a finger straight at her nose, "Shut up!" He towered over her, leaning dangerously near. "You had this comin' for nineteen years, Ada. Nineteen years I looked at your bastard and seen my own flesh and blood turned against me by the two of you till he finally run away from home. Then when he comes back the first time, you side with them and let them railroad me into prison. And just to twist the knife in the wound, you marry her off to my meal ticket. Goddamit, Ada, I had to read about the wedding in a *newspaper*. You kept me away on purpose, and I never even got to see Steve!"

"I didn't have nothing to do with—"

But Ada's cowering body was jerked to its feet.

"Don't lie to me, slut! I took nineteen years of your lies, and what does it get me but prison!"

He reeled back and swung the first blow to the side of Ada's head, sending it twirling while she fought to cover her face.

"You was on their side all the time, always siding against me!"

The next blow fell on her jaw and dropped Ada to the floor.

"That was my ship comin' in and you knew it!"

A savage kick raised Ada and dropped her back onto the floor.

Incensed now beyond reason, Herb Anderson's injustices fed upon themselves. The hate that had been too shallowly submerged for so long erupted in a wild red rage that found

304

vent upon the hapless Ada. The alcohol lent its beastly hand in raising the man's temper and fists until the deed he'd begun lay senseless and broken on the floor before him. He stared at the huddled heap, wiped a trickle of sputum from the side of his mouth, then tasted her blood on his knuckles and ran from the house, then from the neighborhood, and the next day from the town, then the state.

Catherine was typing when the phone rang downstairs. A moment later she heard Clay's footsteps pelting up the stairs, then his voice behind her.

"Catherine?"

He watched as she raised an elbow and kneaded the back of her neck.

"Cat?" he said gently.

The word—that above all others—made her suddenly swing around to find apprehension written on Clay's face.

"What is it?"

"That was Mrs. Sullivan, your mother's neighbor."

"Mother?" She half-rose from her chair. "What's wrong?"

Clay saw the lines of fright that suddenly pinched up her face. Instinctively he moved to her and laid a hand on her shoulder. "Your mother is in the hospital. They want us to come right away."

"But what's wrong?"

"Come on, we'll talk about it on the way."

"Clay, tell me!"

"Catherine, don't panic, okay?" He took her hand and led her hurriedly through the house. "It's not good for you in your condition. Here, put your coat on and I'll back the car out."

She nearly tore his jacket sleeve off stopping him. "Don't coddle me, Clay. Tell me what's wrong."

He covered her hand, squeezed it so hard that he curled it up. "Cat, your father is out of the workhouse. He got drunk and went home that way."

"Oh, no," she wailed from behind her fingertips.

Fear trickled through Clay, but not for her mother, for her.

"Come on, we'd better hurry, Cat," he said gently.

For the first time ever Catherine was grateful for Clay's

305

penchant for speed. He drove the Corvette with the grim determination of an Indy-500 racer, taking curves and lane-changes in robotlike fashion, taking his sight from the road only long enough to assure himself Catherine was still all right. She sat huddled and shivering, reaching out to clasp the dashboard occasionally, eyes riveted straight ahead. Once they arrived at the hospital, she was out of the car like a shot, and Clay had to jog to catch up with her. When they reached the emergency ward, Catherine broke away from Clay, surging toward the broad-beamed woman who immediately rose from a chair and came forward with outstretched hands.

"Cathy, I'm so sorry."

"How is she, Mrs. Sullivan?"

The woman's eyes immediately sought Clay's. He nodded.

"The doctors are still with her. I don't know yet. Oh, girl, what that man done to her..." And Mrs. Sullivan dissolved into tears. Clay's first thought was for Catherine, and he urged her into a chair while Mrs. Sullivan whimpered into a limp handkerchief. He stood before the pair, clutching Catherine's icy hand in his.

"She—she made it to the phone to call me," choked Mrs. Sullivan. "I don't know how, though."

Clay felt utterly helpless. He could do nothing but take the chair next to Catherine's and hold her hand while she stared with glazed eyes at the other pieces of cold, uncomfortable furniture across the room. Finally a nurse approached, saying the doctor would talk to them now. Clay restrained Catherine, pulling on her hand.

"Maybe I should go."

"No!" she insisted, yanking her hand out of his. "She's my mother. I'll go."

"Not alone then."

The doctor introduced himself, shook their hands and glanced at Catherine's roundness.

"Mrs. Forrester, your mother is in no danger of dying, do you understand?"

"Yes." But Catherine's eyes were locked on the door behind which her mother lay.

"She has been badly beaten and has a very bruised face.

She's been sedated so there's really no point in your seeing her. Perhaps tomorrow would be just as well."

"She insists," Clay said.

The doctor took a deep breath and sighed.

"Very well, but before you go in I must warn you that she is not a pretty sight. I want you to be prepared for that. In your condition, shock won't help you at all. Don't be frightened by the amount of equipment—it looks far more complicated than it is. Your mother has suffered a fractured nasal septum, which is why her nose appears to be pushed to one side. She also has two fractured ribs. They compromised the breathing so a tracheotomy had to be performed, and she has a tube projecting from her throat. The respirator machine looks alarming, but is only helping her breath temporarily. She'll soon be doing it on her own again. She has a nasal-gastric tube, a prophylaxis, to empty the stomach and prevent vomiting, and of course we are giving her some IV's, a little plasma.

"Now, do you still think you want to go inside?" He found himself wishing the girl would spare herself the sight. But she nodded, so the doctor was given one of the unpalatable tasks that sometimes made him ask himself why he'd chosen this profession.

The woman on the bed did not even remotely resemble Ada. Her nose was flattened. Her forehead was grotesque with bulging, strawberrylike welts. The cracked lips were puffed beyond recognition and showed telltale marks of blood. Tubes seemed to be stitched into her everywhere, leading to inverted bottles above the bed, a plastic sack hanging beside the mattress, and the respirator which created the only sound in the room with its bellowslike mechanism breathing steadily. A blood-pressure cuff circled her arm, its cords connected to a computer which gave a constant digital printout of vital signs. In contrast to her puffed face, the rest of Ada looked shrunken and dissipated. Her hands lay limp and blue; the little finger of the left was in a splint.

Clay found himself swallowing repeatedly at the pitiful sight before him. He clutched Catherine's hand and felt the tremor there. She gave no other sign of the struggle within, but he was smitten with pity for her, knowing how she held her emotions in check. He thought of his own feelings, should this be Angela, and rubbed the inside of Catherine's elbow and pulled her arm hard against him. After only a brief moment, the doctor ushered them silently out. Catherine walked like a zombie all the way to the car.

When Clay opened the car door, he had to gently urge Catherine to bend, to sit, to turn her legs inside. He wished the doctor could have prescribed a tranquilizer for her, but it would be dangerous in so advanced a pregnancy. Starting the car, Clay felt a double fear now, for both Catherine and the baby. She sat woodenly while he fastened the top button of her coat, tugged at the collar and urged, "You've got to keep warm, Cat." But she only stared straight ahead, dry-eyed, unmoving. There were no trite phrases Clay could bring himself to utter. *Don't worry* or *She'll be all right* were more . . . or less . . . than he wanted to say to the tormented woman beside him. All he could do was find her hand in the dark and lace his fingers through hers as he drove, hoping that the meager offering might help somehow. But her lifeless fingers lay inert within his hold all the way home.

He suffered an agony of helplessness, driving through the night with his thumb brushing against the back of her hand in silent communication to which she did not respond. Their hands lay upon her narrow lap, the back of Clay's resting lightly against her now fully round stomach. He thought of the pain children bear at their parents' expense and hoped his child need never suffer what Catherine now suffered.

At home he helped her with her coat, then watched as she listlessly mounted the steps.

"Catherine, what can I do? Can I fix you something?"

She had stopped, as if she didn't know where she was. He came behind her, his hands in his pockets, wishing she would say, "Make me some cocoa, rub my back, put on some music, hold me . . ." But she shut him out instead, insulated within her carefully guarded solitariness.

"No, there's nothing. I'm very tired, Clay. I just want to go to bed." She walked upstairs with rigid back, directly to the bedroom, and closed the door upon the comfort he sought to offer.

He stood in the middle of the living room looking at nothing for a long time. He shut his eyes. His Adam's apple bobbed up and down convulsively. He pictured Ada, then Catherine's face as she'd looked at her mother's still figure. He sat down on the edge of the davenport with his face in his hands. He did not know how much time had passed before he sighed, rose, and made a phone call to his father. He made up his bed on the davenport and wearily took off his trousers and shirt, but when the light was out he went instead to stand before the sliding glass door, staring out at the ebony night.

He needed the woman upstairs as badly right now as she needed him.

A faint, muffled sound intruded itself into the bruised night, bringing him to turn from the window. He strained to listen and it came again, high, distant, like the wind behind walls— hurt wind, wailing wind—and he knew what it was before he felt his way up the stairs in the dark. He paused at her bedroom door and listened. He laid his palm against the wood, then his forehead too. When he could stand it no longer, he found the doorknob and soundlessly turned it. In the dimness, he made out the blur of the pale blue bedspread, padded silently across to lean and explore it with his hands. He felt her curled beneath the covers, clutching them over her head. He ran his hands along the snail-shaped form, the pity in his heart a choking thing while her high keening came muffled from the womb she had crawled back into. He pulled gently at the covers but she only clung to them the tighter.

"Catherine," he began, but found his throat clotted with emotion.

She gripped the guardian covers fiercely until at last he ebbed them from her fingers to reveal her curled with her head covered with both arms, her elbows tucked between her knees. Gently he lifted the blankets and lay down behind her, then covered them both up again. He tried to pull her into his arms but she only huddled tighter, wailing in that solitary, high syllable that made Clay's eyes sting.

His voice quavered as he whispered, "Cat, oh, Cat, let me help you."

He found her fists clenched in her hair and eased them away, running a palm along her arm, then pressing his chest upon her curved back until he could bear it no longer. Bracing himself on an elbow, he leaned over the curled ball of her, brushing back her hair, assuring her throatily, "I'm here, Cat, I'm here. Don't go through this all alone."

"Mamaaaaaa..." she wailed pitifully into the dark, "Ma-maaaaa..."

"Please, Cat, please," Clay begged, running his hand down her arm to find her hands fiercely knotted between her knees.

"Mama," she wailed again.

He felt her body quaking and sought to calm her by cradling her as best he could with one arm along her thigh, cupping a knee and pulling her back against him.

"Darling, it's Clay. Please don't do this. Let me help you... let me hold you, please. Turn around, Cat, just turn around. I'm here."

"Mama, I didn't mean to," she quailed in that same childlike voice that frightened Clay so terribly. He stroked her hair, her shoulder, braced up and rested his cheek on the back of her head, waiting for some sign that she understood.

"Please, Catherine... I... don't shut me out."

He felt the first soundless spasm, the first sob that was not yet a sob, and gently, gently, pulled at her shoulder, turning her toward him until, like a broken spring, she unwound all at once and burrowed into his arms, while painful sobs wrenched from her throat.

"Hold me, Clay, hold me, hold me," she begged, clinging like a drowning person while her hot tears scalded his neck. Her grip was like iron while she quaked wretchedly and cried into him.

"Catherine, oh, God, I'm so sorry," he said throatily into her hair.

"Mama, mama, it's all my fault."

"No, Cat, no," he murmured, clasping her to him all the more closely, as if to pull her within his very body that he might absorb her pain. "It's not your fault," he soothed, kissing the top of her head while she babbled and cried and blamed herself. All the pent-up tears that Catherine had so long refused to shed for herself came rushing out for her mother while she clung to Clay with arms and hands that could not hold tightly enough. He cradled the back of her head, pulling her cheek against the silken hair of his chest, rocking at times, lost in pity, aching with the feeling of her heaving stomach pressed at last to his, but for the wrong reason. She muttered unintelligible sounds, broken by sobs which Clay welcomed, knowing they were the cure of her.

"It's all my f-fault, all my faul . . ."

He forced her mouth hard against his chest to stop the words. He swallowed convulsively before he could speak.

"No, Cat, you can't blame yourself. I won't let you."

"B-but it's t-true. It's because I'm pre-pregnant. I should've kn-known he wa-wanted the money . . . ba-bad enough. I hate him, I h-hate him. Why did he do it . . . Hold me, Clay . . . I had to get away fr-from him. I had to, but to get a-away I had to b-be those things he c-called me, but I d-didn't care, I didn't care. You're so warm . . . They never hugged m-me, never k-kissed me. I was good, I was al-w-ways good, just that one t-time with you, but he sh-shouldn't take it out on her."

Clay's heart thundered at her pitiful outpouring. She babbled on, almost mindlessly.

"I shouldn't have le-left her. I should have stayed, b-but it was s-so awful there when St-Steve left. He was the only one who ever—"

A deep sob broke from Catherine and she clung more desperately to Clay. Now he softly encouraged her, knowing she must say these things.

"Who ever what?"

"Who ever l-loved me. Not even M-Mama could, but I n-never understood wh-why. They never took me pl-places or bought me th-things like other kids got, or played with m-me. Uncle Fr-Frank used to kiss me and I'd pretend he w-was Daddy. Steve loved me, but af-after he was gone there was nobody and I used to pr-pretend I had a baby who'd love me. I thought if only I had a b-baby I'd never be lonely."

She stopped then, having discovered this truth at last.

Clay squeezed his eyes shut hard. Her heart was hammering against his, her arms clinging tenaciously to his neck. Pity and compassion and the overwhelming need to heal her welled high in Clay. He was deluged by the desire to protect, fulfill, calm her, and to provide the missing years of love that could never be made up for. He fought against tears, holding her long and hard against his body, unable to hold her long enough, hard enough, pressing her so fiercely that at last he opened his legs to let one of hers in, high against him. And hers opened and his knee found shelter against her too. They clung that way, sharing a new bond of warmth and comfort until, pressed between them, the baby objected to all that crowding and moved restlessly within Catherine. A wild exhilaration lifted Clay's stomach, as if he'd just reached the downhill slope of a roller coaster. And everything—the horror Catherine had suffered this day, the first feel of his child's movement in her belly, her own desperate cry for love—made his motions somehow right as his hands skimmed over her body, up her back, down her side, down her warm buttock and leg that lay over his hip. And even as Catherine cried against his chest, Clay found the hollow behind her knee and pulled her more securely into her nestling place. He ran his hand again up her hip, up her side, finding her breast and cradling it, and the side of her stomach with his forearm. She was warm and reaching and unresisting against him, and he whispered raspily against her ear, "Cat, oh, Cat, why did you wait so long? Why did it take all this?"

With a hand, he commanded the back of her head and lowered his mouth into her salt-kiss. Her mouth opened wide and took him in, and it ceased to matter that it was only in desperation she turned to him. It ceased to matter that she might later feel he took advantage of her in her weakness. His hand, warm and soft and seeking, trailed, unchecked, from her full breast to the hard, taut stomach that protruded because of him. He fondled it searchingly, awed by its solidness, by the thought of the life it carried. And as if the baby heard its father's pleas, it moved within. Clay lay stock-still then, stunned, with his palm conforming to the shape of Catherine's flesh, willing the child to move once more. And when it had, and he'd again known the feel of it, Clay reached unhesitatingly to pull Catherine's wide gown up and run his hands over the bare, firm skin beneath. He skimmed his palm again and again over the warm curve of her belly, discovering things that his body had caused in hers: the protruding navel, the engorged breasts, the widened, enlarged nipples, and—yet again—the fluttery motion of life beneath his hand. How often he had wondered. How often he had thought it his right to explore these changes of his making. How often she, too, had longed to share them but had steeled herself against him, shielded in an armor of assumed remoteness.

But what had started out as a journey of pity and compassion became one of sensuality as Clay's caressing hand moved lower, touching the crisp hair that couched the spot where Catherine's burden thrust itself sharply outward from her body. Wordlessly he slipped his hand between her thighs, covering her, swollen there, with the length of his long, closed fingers, pressing gently upward, feeling her pulse throbbing there, learning her. Thoughts of her sexuality, her pregnancy, what he knew he could not do, made him curiously callow in his exploration of her. He moved his hand once more to her stomach.

"Oh, Cat," he whispered, "your stomach's so hard. Does it hurt?"

She moved her head to answer no, amazed by his naïveté.

"I felt the baby move," he whispered almost reverently, yet his breath was warm and labored on her skin. "It moved right there under my hand." He spread his fingers over her stomach again, as if in invitation, but when nothing happened his hand again sought the intimate world between her legs.

And Catherine closed her eyes and let him . . . let him . . . let him, drifting in a myriad of emotions she'd held at bay so long, thinking to her child, It's your father.

And the father's hand filled itself with the mother's body that readied itself for their baby's birth.

"It's too late, Clay," she murmured once.

"I know." But he kissed the hard, warm orb of her stomach anyway, then lay his face in the juncture of her legs as if he must, unable to solace himself and her any other way. The child kicked against his ear.

Catherine was drawn painfully back to reality from the secure place in which she'd allowed herself to drift. The thrum of her heart in odd spots in her body told her she had let Clay go too far to pull away from him unhurt when the time came.

"Stop, Clay," she said in a loving whisper.

"I'm only touching, that's all."

"Stop, it's not right."

"I won't go any further. Just let me touch you," he murmured.

"No, stop," she insisted, stiffening.

"Don't pull away . . . come here."

But now she resisted even more, having come fully to her senses.

He moved and tried to take her in his arms, then asked, "Why do you pull away all of a sudden?"

"Because it doesn't seem right with my mother lying in that hospital."

"I don't believe you. A minute ago you had forgotten all about your mother, hadn't you? Why did you really turn away?"

She didn't know.

Very gently he said, "Catherine, I'm not your father. I won't call you names and make you feel guilty afterward. It's not because of your mother that you turn away, it's because of your father, isn't it?"

She only shivered.

"If you keep pulling away now, he'll have beaten you just as surely as he beat her, only the marks he leaves on you won't go away like hers will, don't you see that?"

"It's my fault he beat her up, because once before I gave in to you. And now here I am again . . . I . . . you . . ." But she stopped, confused, afraid.

"He's making an emotional cripple out of you. Can't you see it, Catherine?"

"I'm not! I'm not! I feel things, I want things, I need things, just like everybody else!"

"Then why don't you let yourself show it?"

"I j-just did."

"But look what it took," he said in a pained whisper.

"Get your hands off me," she quavered. She was crying again but he would not allow her to roll away from him. "Why? What are you afraid of, Catherine?"

"I'm not afraid!" But her voice caught in her throat even as she said it.

He held her flat on her back, silently willing her to admit what it was that had held her emotionally sterile for too long, afraid that what he was doing might backfire and hurt her more.

"Of those names?"

He held her prisoner while her mind raced backward to ugly, unwanted memories which would not set her free. Clay's

314

breath on her face brought her careening back to the present, to this man whom she loved and was so afraid of loving, of losing.

"I-I'm not," she choked, while Clay felt her pulse pounding against him in places where he held her down. The muscles in her forearms tensed beneath his hands as she repeated, "I'm not, I'm not—"

He eased his hold, prompting softly, "What aren't you? Say it, say it, and be free of it. What?" She ceased struggling against him, and when he had freed her arms she flung one across her eyes and sobbed behind it. With infinite tenderness he touched her breasts, her stomach, the swollen world between her legs again, whispering urgently, "What aren't you, Catherine? Say it, say it."

"I'm not—" she tried again, but choked to a halt.

"No, you're not, you're not. Believe me. Say it, Catherine. You're not what?"

It came out in a rush, tumblewords finding voice at last as she covered her face with both hands.

"I'm not bad I'm not a slut I'm not a whore I'm not I'm not I'm not!"

He enfolded her protectively against him, pinching his eyes shut while she flung her arms around his neck and clung. He felt a shudder possess her body and spoke into her hair.

"No, you never were, no matter how many times he said it. You never were any of those things."

"Then why did he say them, Clay, why?"

"I don't know ... Shh ... The important thing is that you don't believe him, that you don't let him hurt you anymore."

They rested at last against each other, exhausted, silent. Before she slept, Catherine again pictured her mother and realized she herself had just escaped becoming the same kind of self-contained, undemonstrative being.

And for the first time ever, she felt she had beaten Herb Anderson instead of the other way around.

Chapter 26

ADA OPENED HER eye. It looked like a soft-poached egg. Her mouth tried to wince but couldn't.

"Mom?" Cathy whispered.

"Caffy?" Ada's lips were still grotesquely swollen.

"You've been asleep a long time."

"Have I?"

"Shh, don't move. Try to rest. You have a cracked rib and if you move it'll hurt."

"I'm so tired," the old woman breathed, succumbing, letting her eye slide shut again. But even in her bleary state she'd observed something that startled her eye open again.

"You've veen crying." She couldn't pronounce her *b*'s.

"A little. Don't worry about me, just worry about—" But tears stung her eyes again, burning the swollen lids. Ada saw and fluttered a hand. Catherine took it, feeling the small sparrow-bones and how little strength her mother had. The same helplessness which Clay had felt the night before, now assaulted Catherine.

"I ain't seen you cry since you was a little girl," Ada whispered, trying her hardest to squeeze her daughter's hand.

316

"I gave it up long ago, Mom, or I would've been doing it all the time."

"It ain't a good fing to give up."

"No—no it isn't." Catherine swallowed. "Mom, you don't have to talk."

"Funny fing, you sayin' I don't hafta talk, me sayin' you don't hafta cry—least not for each other. Vut I guess we gotta do it for ourselves."

"Why don't you wait till you're feeling stronger."

"Veen waiting nineteen years to get stronger."

"Mom, please . . ."

A gentle pressure on Catherine's hand silenced her. Ada spoke with an effort.

"Time it was said. Just listen. I'm a weak woman, always have veen, vut mayve now I faid my dues. Got to tell you. Herv, he was good to me once, when I was first married to him. When Steve was a vavy you shoulda seen Herv with Steve, why you wouldn'ta known him." She closed her eyes, rested momentarily before continuing. "And then all that vusiness started in the Gulf of Tonkin and Herv, he was in the reserves. When his unit got called to active duty, I figured he'd ve vack in no time. Vut it was worse'n we thought, and he was gone two years. He saw a mighty lot in them two years. He saw so much that he come home liking the liquor too much. The drinking he mighta got over, but what he never got over was findin' me expectin' a vavy when he got home."

Catherine wondered if she had understood Ada's distorted words correctly.

"A—a baby?"

The room was still. Ada's single, open eye stared at the ceiling.

"Yes, a vavy. That was you, o' course."

"Me?"

"I told you I was a weak woman." Ada's eye teared.

"I'm not his?"

The bruised head moved back and forth weakly on the pillow while a rippling sense of freedom seeped into Catherine.

"So you see, it wasn't all his fault, Caffy. I done that to him, and he could never forgive me, nor you either."

317

"I never understood till now."

"I was always so scared to tell you."

"But, why didn't you?" Catherine leaned nearer so her mother could see her face better. "Mom, please, I'm not blaming you, I just need to know, that's all. Why didn't you ever stand up for me? I thought you didn't—" Catherine stopped, her eyes flickered away from her mother's.

"Love you? I know that's what you was gonna say. It's no excuse at all, vut Herv, he was just waiting for me to show you some favoritism. Why, he'd use any excuse to vlow up. I was scared of him, Caffy, I was always scared after that."

"Then why didn't you leave him?"

"I figured I owed him to stay. Vesides, where would I go?"

"Where are you going to go now? Surely you aren't going to go back to him?"

"No, I don't need to now that you know. Vesides, it's different now. You and Steve all grown up, all I have to worry avout is myself. Steve, he's made a good life for himself in the service and you got Clay. I don't need to worry avout you no more."

A prickle of guilt traced through Catherine's veins. She rubbed the back of her mother's hand absently, then sat forward to study Ada's face.

"Who was he, Mom?" she asked wistfully.

A contorted smile tried to find its way through the swollen lips.

"It don't matter who, just what. He was a fine man. He was the vest thing that ever happened to me. I'd go through all the years of hell with Herv again if I could live those days once more with your father."

"Then you loved him?"

"I did . . . oh, how I did."

"Then why didn't you leave Da—Herb, and marry him?"

"He was already married."

Hearing all this, Catherine realized that within her mother dwelled an Ada she would never know, except for the glint of remembrance in the bloodshot eye.

"Is he still alive?" Catherine asked, suddenly wanting to know everything about him.

"Lives right here in the city. That's why it's best if I don't tell you who he is."

"Will you tell me someday?"

"I can't make that fromise. See, he went flaces. He's *something* now. You'd never have to ve ashamed of having a father like him. My—my mouth is a little dry. Do you think I could have some water?"

Catherine helped her mother drink, listened to her weary sigh as she sank back again.

"Mom, I have a confession to make too."

"You, Caffy?" The surprised way her mother said it made Catherine wonder if Ada might not have always thought her above wrong, only she herself had been too busy looking for outward shows of affection to see the deeper, intrinsic feeling.

"Mom, I did it on purpose—got pregnant, I mean. At least, I think I did. I wanted to get even with Herb for all the times he'd called me names, and I wanted to get away from both of you, from that house where there was never anything but fighting and his drunkenness. I guess subconsciously I believed a baby would get me out and provide me with love. I didn't think he'd take it out on you, but I feel somehow it is part of the reason he beat you, wasn't it?"

"No, no, don't vlame yourself, Caffy. It was a long time coming. He said I shoulda been at his trial, and that it was my fault he never got no money outa Clay. Vut the real reason was because you wasn't his. I don't kid myself that's the real reason, and I don't want you to go vlaming yourself."

"But I've made such a mess of things."

"No, honey. Now you just get that out of your head. You got Clay, and the vavy coming, and with a father like Clay, why, that vavy's vound to ve somevody too."

"Mom, Clay and I—" But Catherine could not tell her mother the truth about her future with Clay.

"What?"

"We were wondering if when the baby is born, if you're strong enough then, you'd come and stay with us and help out for a couple days."

The pathetic excuse for a smile tore at Catherine's heartstrings as her mother sighed contentedly and closed her eye.

It was the day after Clay and Catherine had shared the same bed, but he'd left her asleep that morning. Returning home in the late afternoon, he was eager to see her.

She heard the door slam and her hands grew idle, the water splattering unheeded over the paring knife and the rib of celery she'd been washing. He came up the stairs, across the kitchen behind her, and laid a hand lightly on her shoulder.

"How was she today?"

A warmth seeped through her blouse at his touch, going beyond skin, beyond muscle, to the core of her. She wanted to turn, take his palm, kiss it and place it on her breast and say, How were you today? How was I? Were we happier for what passed between us last night?

"She hurt a lot, but they gave her painkillers whenever she asked for them. It was very hard for her to talk with her mouth that way."

Clay squeezed her shoulder, waiting for her to turn around, to need him again as she had last night. He could smell her hair, fresh, flower-scented. He watched her hands as water splashed over them and she peeled green, stringy fibers from the celery.

Why doesn't she turn around, he wondered. Can't she read my touch? She must know that I, too, am afraid.

Catherine began to clean another rib of celery she didn't need. She longed to look into his eyes and ask, "What do I mean to you, Clay?" But if he loved her, surely he would have said so by now.

Last night they had been bound together by her vast need for comfort, and by the accident of her pregnancy. At the time that had been justification for the swift siege of intimacy. But he had not said he loved her. Never, during all their months together had he even hinted that he loved her.

Their senses pounded with awareness of each other. Clay saw Catherine's hands fall still. He moved his fingers to the bare skin of her neck, slipping them behind her collar, his thumb brushing her earlobe. The water ran uselessly now, but Catherine's eyes were closed, her wrists dangling against the edge of the sink.

"Catherine . . ." His voice was thick.

"Clay, last night never should have happened," she got out.

Disappointments assaulted him. "Why?" He took the paring knife from her fingers, dropped it into the sink and turned off the water. When he'd forced her to face him he asked again, quietly, "Why?"

"Because we did it for the wrong reasons. It wasn't enough—just my mother's problems and the fact that this baby is yours. Don't you see?"

"But we need each other, Catherine. We're married, I want—"

Suddenly she put her wet hands on his cheeks, interrupting. "Cool off, Clay. It's the easiest way, because we are not going to have a repeat performance of last night."

"Dammit, I don't understand you!" he said angrily, pulling her hands from his face, holding her by the forearms.

"You don't love me, Clay," she said with quiet dignity. "Now do you understand me?"

His eyes pierced hers, steely gray into dusky blue, and he wished he could deny her words. He could easily drown in her tempting eyes, in her smooth skin and beautiful features with which he'd grown so familiar. He could look at her across a room and want to fill his hands with her breasts, lower his mouth to hers, to know the taste and touch of her. But could he say he loved her?

Deliberately now he reached to cup both of her breasts, as if to prove this was all that was necessary. Through the smock and her bra he could tell her nipples were drawn tight. Her breath was heavy and fast.

"You want it too," he said, knowing it was true, for he felt the truth beneath the thumbs that stroked the crests of her breasts.

"You're confusing lust and love."

"I thought last night you finally agreed with me that it's a healthy thing to be touched, to touch back."

"Is this healthy now?"

"You're damn right. Can't you feel what's happening to you?"

Stoically she allowed his hands their freedom, and though she could not prevent her body from responding, she would

321

not give him the satisfaction of moving willfully in any way suggesting acquiescence. "I can feel it. Oh, I can feel it, all right. Does it make you feel macho, knowing what it does to me?"

He dropped his hands suddenly. "Catherine, I can't exist with this coldness of yours. I need more than you put into this relationship."

"And I cannot put more into this relationship without love. And so it's a vicious circle, isn't it, Clay?" She looked straight at his face still glistening with water. She respected him if for nothing more than not lying. "Clay, I'm only being realistic to protect myself. It would have been so easy all these months with you to delude myself every time you turned your eyes on me with that certain look that makes me go all liquid, that you loved me. But I know it's not true."

"To be loved you have to be lovable, Catherine. Don't you understand that? You never try in the least. You carry yourself like you're wearing armor. You don't know how to return a smile or a touch or—"

"Clay, I never learned!" She defended herself. "Do you think things like that come naturally? Do you think it's something you're born with, like you were born with your father's gray eyes and your mother's blond hair? Well, it's not. Love is a learned thing. It's been taught to you since you were in knee pants whether you know it or not. You were one of the lucky ones who had it happening around him all the time. You never questioned it but you always expected it, didn't you? If you fell and got hurt, you were kissed and coddled. If you were gone, then came back, you were hugged and welcomed. If you tried and failed, you were told it didn't matter, they were proud anyway, right? If you misbehaved and were punished, they made you understand it hurt them as badly as it hurt you. None of those lessons were taught to me. Instead, I had the other kind, and I learned to exist without your kind. You take all signs of affection too lightly; you set too little store by them. It's different for me. I can't . . . I can't be—oh, I don't know how to make you understand. When something's in short supply its value goes up. And it's like that with me, Clay. I've never had anyone treat me nice before, so every gesture, every touch, every overture you make toward me is

322

of far greater value to me than it is to you. And I know perfectly well that if I learn to accept them, learn to accept you, I'll be hurt far more than you will when it's time for us to separate. And so I've promised myself I will not grow dependent on you—not emotionally anyway."

"What you're really saying is that we're back where we started, before last night."

"Not exactly." Catherine looked down at her hands; they were fidgeting.

"What's different?"

She looked up, met his gaze directly, then squared her shoulders almost imperceptibly. "My mother told me today that Herb is not my real father. That frees me from him—really frees me—at last. It also gives me even better insight into what happens when people stay in a loveless marriage for all the wrong reasons. I'm never going to end up like her. Never."

During the weeks that followed, Clay mulled over what Catherine had said about love being taught. He had never before dissected the many ways in which his parents had shown him affection. But Catherine was right about one thing: he'd always taken it for granted. He had been so secure in their approval, so certain of their love, he'd never questioned their tactics. He admitted she was right, also, about his placing less value than she upon physical contact. He began to evaluate outward signs of affection by looking at them from Catherine's viewpoint and admitted that he'd taken them too lightly. He began to understand her awful need to remain free of him emotionally, to understand that the idea of loving him loomed like a threat, in light of their agreement to divorce soon after the baby arrived. He analyzed his feelings for her only to find that he honestly did not believe he loved her. He found her physically desirable, but because she had never been demonstrative toward him, it was difficult to imagine he ever would love her. What he wanted was a woman who was capable of impulsively lifting her arms and seeking his kiss. One who could close her eyes against his cheek and make him feel utterly wanted and wanting. He doubted that he could ever achieve with Catherine the kind of free-wheeling spontaneity he needed in a wife.

They bought a spooled crib and matching chest of drawers. He set it up in the second bedroom where the walls still wore that masculine paper of brown designs, totally inappropriate for a nursery.

But when the baby was born, who would stay and who would go?

Her suitcase appeared on the bedroom floor, packed, ready to go at a moment's notice. The first time he came in and saw it, he sank down heavily on the edge of the bed and buried his face in both hands, utterly miserable. He thought about Jill— willing Jill who understood his needs so well, and wished that it were she who was expecting his child. But Jill didn't want babies.

April Fool's Day came, bringing bursting buds and the redolent scent of moist earth that marks spring's arrival. Catherine was given a lavish baby shower by Angela, whose pleasure over the upcoming arrival of her first grandchild was a burning wound to Catherine.

Claiborne surprised Catherine by stopping by one afternoon with "a little something" he'd picked up for the baby: a windup swing Catherine knew the baby wouldn't be big enough to sit in until long after she and Clay were apart.

Ada was back home and called every day to ask how Catherine was. Catherine, grown now to enormous proportions and slothlike slowness, answered, "fine, fine, fine," until finally after hanging up one day, she burst into a torrent of tears, not understanding at all any more what it was she wanted.

She awakened Clay in the middle of the night, hesitant to touch his sleeping form.

"What?" He braced up on an elbow, hazy yet from sleep.

"The pains have started. They're ten minutes apart."

He flung back the covers and sat up on the davenport, finding her hand in the dark and tugging at it. "Here, sit down."

She got back up immediately, if clumsily. "The doctor said to keep on the move."

"The doctor? You mean you've called him already?"

"Yes, a couple of hours ago."

"But why didn't you wake me?"

"I..." But she didn't know why.

"You mean you've been walking around here for two hours in the dark?"

"Clay, I think you should drive me to the hospital, but I don't expect you to stay with me or anything. I'd drive myself, but the doctor said that I shouldn't."

Her words caused a sudden stab of hurt, followed by another of anger.

"You can't keep me out, Catherine; I'm the baby's father."

Surprised, she only answered, "I don't think we'd better waste time arguing now. Do whatever you want when we get there."

They were greeted in the maternity ward by a young nurse whose name tag identified her as Christine Flemming. It did not occur to Ms. Flemming to question Clay's presence. She assumed he would want to stay with Catherine. And so, he was asked to have a seat in a well-lit room with an empty bed in it. When Catherine returned after being blood-typed, she was having a contraction and Ms. Flemming spoke in soothing instructions to her patient, telling her how to breathe properly and how to relax as much as possible. When the contraction ended she turned to Clay and said, "Your job will be to remind her to relax and breathe properly. You can be a big help." So rather than try to explain, Clay listened to her instructions, then stayed in the labor room when the nurse left, holding Catherine's hand, reminding her to keep her breathing quick and shallow, timing the length of contractions and the minutes between.

Soon the gentle-voiced nurse returned and spoke soothingly to Catherine. "Let's see how far along you are now. Try to relax, and tell me if a contraction should start while I'm checking you." It happened so fast that Clay had no time to gracefully withdraw nor to be embarrassed. Neither was he asked to leave, as he thought he'd be at this time. Instead, he stood on the other side of the bed, holding Catherine's hand while her dilation was checked, amazed to find how appropriate it felt to be included in such a natural way. When the nurse finished her examination she pulled Catherine's gown back down, sat on the edge of the bed and lightly stroked the wide base of Catherine's abdomen.

"Here comes another one, Catherine. Now just relax with it and count—one, two, three..." Catherine's hand gripped Clay's like the jaws of a trap. Sweat broke out under his arms while beads of perspiration gathered into runnels on Catherine's temples and trailed into her hair. Her eyes were closed and her mouth was tightly shut.

He remembered what he was there for. "Open your mouth, Catherine," he reminded softly. "Pant, pant, little breaths."

And through her pain Catherine knew she was happy Clay was there. His voice seemed to calm her when she was most afraid.

After the pain was over, she opened her eyes and asked Ms. Flemming, "How could you tell it was coming?"

Christine Flemming had a pretty face with a madonnalike smile and a very patient way about her that made both Catherine and Clay feel comfortable in her presence. Her voice was silken, soothing. She was a woman well-suited to her profession.

"Why, I could feel it. Here, give me your hand, Catherine." She took Catherine's hand and curved it low around her stomach. "Mr. Forrester," she instructed, "put your hand here on the other side. Now wait—you'll feel it when it starts. The muscles begin to tighten, starting at the sides, and the stomach arches and changes shape during the height of the contraction. When it ends, the muscles relax and settle down again. Here it comes; it will take half a minute or so until it's at its peak."

Catherine's and Clay's fingertips touched, their hands forming a light cradle around the base of her stomach. Together they shared the exhilaration of discovery as the muscles tensed and changed the contours of Catherine's abdomen. For Clay, it made her pain a palpable thing. He stared, big-eyed, at what was happening beneath his hand. But in the middle of the contraction, Catherine's hand flew above her head and Clay tore his eyes away to her face to find her lips pursed, jaw clenched against the pain. He leaned to soothe her hair back from her forehead, and at the touch of his hand, her lips relaxed and fell open. He spoke his litany again in quiet tones, reminding her, and felt a curious sense of fulfillment that he had the power to ease her, even in the height of her labor.

"That one was longer than the last," Christine Flemming said when it was over. "As they get closer, it's more important for you to relax between them. Sometimes it helps to have your tummy rubbed lightly, like this. I like to think that the baby can feel it, too, and knows you're out here waiting to welcome him." With a gentle palm the nurse stroked the outer perimeter of Catherine's stomach. Catherine's eyes remained closed, one wrist over her forehead, her other hand in Clay's. He felt her grip slacken as the nurse continued those feather-light strokes over her distended abdomen. With a smile, Christine Flemming looked up at Clay and said softly, "You're doing very well, so I'll let you take over for a while. I'll be back in a few minutes." Then on silent white shoes she was gone and Clay was left to stroke Catherine's stomach.

He understood things in that time of closeness with Catherine, things as deep and eternal as the force of life trying to repeat itself in her body. He understood that nature had planned this time of travail to draw man and woman closer than at any other time. Thus the pain had purpose beyond bringing a child into the world.

When they took Catherine to the delivery room, Clay felt suddenly bereft, as if his role was being usurped by strangers. But when they'd asked if he'd taken the classes required for fathers to be in the delivery room, he'd had to answer honestly, "No."

The University of Minnesota Hospital did not use delivery tables any more. Instead, Catherine found herself placed in a birthing chair, which allowed gravity to pull while she pushed. Christine Flemming was there through the delivery, supportive and smiling, and once Catherine even joked with her, saying, "We're not so smart. The Indians knew this secret long ago when they squatted in the woods to have their babies."

The daughter of Catherine and Clay Forrester was born with the fifth contraction in the birthing chair, and Catherine knew before she faded off into blessed sleep—lying flat now—that it was a girl.

Catherine swam upward through a lake of cotton fuzziness. When she surfaced and opened heavy-lidded eyes, she found Clay dozing in a chair, his cheek propped on one hand. His hair was disheveled and he needed a shave. He looks terrific, she thought through a crazy, disoriented fog. Her mind was still moony and wandering as she studied him. The rhythm of his breathing was lengthened by her drug-induced lethargy. Between pains, hazily she thought, I still love him.

"Clay?" The word was a little mumbled.

His eyes flew open and he jumped to his feet. "Cat," he said softly, "you're awake."

Her eyes drifted closed. "Barely. I did the wrong thing again, didn't I, Clay?" She felt him take her hand, felt the back of it pressed against his lips.

"You mean having a girl?"

She nodded her head which felt like it weighed hundreds of pounds.

"You won't think so when you see her."

Catherine smiled a little bit. Her lips were very dry and he wished he had something to put on them for her.

"Clay?"

"I'm here."

"Thanks for helping."

She drifted into oblivion again, her breathing heavy and rhythmic. He sat on the chair beside her bed with his elbows on his knees, holding her hand long after he knew she was asleep again. Then with a heavy sigh he lowered his forehead against her knuckles and closed his eyes as well.

Grandmother Forrester's cane announced her imminent arrival. When she rounded the doorway, the first thing she said was, "Young lady, I am seventy-eight years old. The next one had better be a boy." But she limped to the bed and bestowed an honest-to-goodness kiss upon the consummate perfection of her firstborn great-granddaughter.

Marie came, laughing as ever, with the announcement that

she and Joe are going to get married at last, as soon as he graduated from high school in a couple of months. She added that she'd been inspired to "give it a whirl" by Catherine and Clay's success.

Claiborne and Angela came daily, never empty-handed. They brought dresses so absurdly frilly the baby would surely get lost in all those ruffles, stuffed toys so big they would dwarf an infant, a music box that played "Eidelweiss." Although they both fawned over Melissa, Claiborne's reaction to her was heart-touching. He would stand at the nursery window with his fingertips against the glass as if transfixed. Walking away, his head was the last to be turned forward. He even stopped on his way home from work one day, although it was decidedly inconvenient for him to do so. He said things like, "When she's old enough to ride a trike, Grampa will see that she gets the best one in town." Or, "Wait until she walks—won't that be something?" Or, "You and Clay will have to take a weekend away by yourselves soon and leave the baby with us."

Bobbi came. She stood in front of the window with her thumbs strung up on her rear jeans pockets, her feet rolled over until she was almost standing on the sides of her shoes. "Well, wouldja look at that!" she exclaimed softly. "And to think I had a hand in it."

Ada came with the news that she'd signed up for a course in driver's education so she could come to Catherine and Clay's house to see the baby now and then. Herb had disappeared.

Steve wired an enormous bouquet of pink carnations and baby's breath and followed it with a long-distance phone call in which his main message was that he'd be getting leave again in August, and when he got to Minnesota, he wanted to see Cathy and Clay and Melissa all living under one roof.

And, of course, there was Clay.

Clay, who was just across the river at the law school and popped in at any time of day. Clay, who stood at the end of Catherine's bed when they were alone together and couldn't seem to think of anything to say. Clay, who played the father's role well when other visitors were there, laughing at their jokes about waiting until Melissa was bringing boyfriends home, turning his smile on Catherine, exclaiming over the never-ending stream of gifts, but spending long minutes at the nursery window alone, swallowing at the lump that never disappeared from his throat.

Ada came and helped out for three days after Catherine and Melissa went home. During that time Ada slept on the davenport. It became particularly hellish for Clay, sleeping with Catherine. Each night he would awaken to the tiny sounds of suckling from the other side of the bed and he wanted more than anything to turn the light on and watch them. But he knew Catherine would be bothered by both the light and his watching, so he lay silent, pretending to be asleep. How surprised he'd been at the news that she intended to breast-feed the baby. At first he supposed she made the choice out of a sense of duty, for there was a lot of propaganda on the subject. But as the days wore on, he realized that everything Catherine did for and with Melissa was done instead from a deep sense of mother-love.

Catherine began to change.

There were times when he came upon her with her face buried in Melissa's little tummy, cooing to her, talking in soft expressions of love. Once he saw her lightly suck on Melissa's toes. When she gave the baby a bath, there was a steady stream of talking and light laughter. When the baby slept too long, Catherine actually hounded her bedroom doorway, as if she couldn't wait for Melissa to wake up again and want to be fed. Catherine began singing a lot, at first only to Melissa, but then seeming to forget herself and singing absently when she worked around the house. It seemed she had found her source of smiles, too, and there was always a ready one waiting for Clay when he got home.

But while Catherine's contentment increased, Clay's virtually disappeared. He astutely refrained from getting involved with the baby, though it was beginning to have a growing, adverse effect on him. His temper flared at the slightest provocation while Catherine's seemed as unassailable as Melissa's— for Melissa was truly a satisfied baby with a flowery disposition. As graduation neared, Clay blamed his crossness on the pressure of finals, and the bar exams coming up shortly.

330

Angela called and asked his permission to plan a little Sunday brunch on the weekend following his graduation. When she said she'd already received Catherine's approval, Clay snapped into the phone, "Since the two of you already have the whole thing planned, why are you bothering to ask me!"

Then he had to do some fancy skirting to get around his mother's demand to know what on earth was eating him.

Clay graduated from the University of Minnesota law school with honors when Melissa was two months old. Now he held a degree, but he had never held his daughter.

Chapter 27

THE DAY OF the brunch would have been well-suited to a June wedding. The sprawling backyard of the Forresters was at its finest. The view over the flaming chafing dishes on the semi-circular terrace was lush with color. The terrace itself was delineated by carefully pruned global arborvitae, which in turn were edged with alternating clumps of marigold and ageratum, the purple and gold contrast creating a stunning effect. The yard stretched in falling terraces to the far reaches of the property where a file of blue spruce marked its boundaries. The rose gardens of phalanx symmetry were in full bloom, in full scent. Shapely maples and lindens dotted the grass with vast splashes of shade. It was like a pastoral scene from an impressionist's brush: ladies in filmy dresses drifting from the terrace across the lawn, men sitting on the parapet of the terrace, everyone nibbling on melon and berries.

Catherine was sitting on the grass when a shadow fell over her and she glanced sunward, blinded at first and unable to make out who stood above her.

"All by yourself?" It was Jill Magnusson's rich, lazy voice. "May I join you?"

Catherine held up a forearm to shade her eyes. "Of course, have a chair."

Dropping to the grass, Jill doubled up her Thoroughbred legs and folded them elegantly to the side—like a ballerina in a swan scene, thought Catherine. Jill tossed back her thick mane and smiled directly at Catherine.

"I guess I should apologize for not sending a gift when the baby was born, but you know how it is."

"Do I?" Catherine replied sweetly—a little too sweetly.

Jill's gaze drifted over Catherine before she smiled archly. "Well . . . don't you?"

"I don't know what you're getting at."

"You know precisely what I'm getting at, and I won't be a hypocrite about it. I'm completely jealous of that baby of yours and Clay's. Not that I'd want one, you understand, but it should have been mine."

Catherine controlled the urge to slap her. "Should have been yours? Why, how gauche of you to say so."

"Gauche maybe, but we both know it's true. I've been damning myself ever since last October, but I've finally decided to lay my cards on the table. I want Clay; it's as simple as that."

Some stirring of pride made Catherine answer, "I'm afraid he's already taken."

"Taken for a fool maybe. He's told me what kind of relationship you two have. Why do you want to hold a man you don't love and who doesn't love you?"

"Maybe to give our daughter a father."

"Not the healthiest reason, you'll have to admit."

"I don't have to admit anything to you, Jill."

"Very well—don't. But ask yourself why Clay asked me to wait for him until he could get this mess straightened out." Then Jill's voice became quite purring. "Oh, I see this is news to you, isn't it? You didn't know that Clay asked me to marry him right after he found out you were pregnant? Well, he did. But my silly pride was shattered and I was totally wrong in turning him down. But now I've changed my mind."

"And what does he have to say about it?"

"Actions speak louder than words. Surely you know that

while you turned a cold shoulder on him all last winter he knew where to find a warm one."

Catherine's stomach was aquiver. "What do you want from me?" she demanded coldly.

"I want you to do the right thing, turn Clay free before he falls in love with his daughter and stays for the wrong reason."

"He chose me over you. That's hard for you to swallow, isn't it?"

Jill tossed her hair behind a shoulder. "Kiddo, you didn't fool me with that trumped-up wedding of yours. This is Jill you're talking to. I was *there* that night and it's no hallucination that Clay kissed me far more intimately than grooms are supposed to kiss other women." Jill paused for dramatic effect, then finished, "And he told me he still loved me. Strange for a man on his wedding night, huh?"

The memory of that night came back to Catherine, but she hid her chagrin behind a mask of indifference. She turned now to see Clay sitting on the terrace, deep in conversation with Jill's father.

Jill went on. "There's no doubt in my mind that if this . . . . mistake"—Jill's pause seemed to denigrate the word further— "hadn't happened between you, Clay and I would be planning our wedding right now. It was always implicitly understood that Clay and I would eventually marry. Why, we've been intimate since the days when our mothers plunked us naked together into our little plastic backyard pools. In October when he asked me to marry him, he admitted you were nothing more than a tragic mistake to him. Why not do him a favor and bow out of the picture?"

It was clear that Jill Magnusson was used to getting what she wanted, by fair means or foul. The woman's manner was insolent and rude. There was no note of appeal in her attitude, only brazen self-assurance.

Oh, she was as cool as Inella's tomato aspic up there on its bed of crushed ice, thought Catherine. But Catherine disliked tomato aspic too.

"You assume a lot, Jill," Catherine said now with a little ice of her own.

"I assume nothing. I know. I know because Clay has confided in me. I know that you've thrown him out of his own bed, that you've encouraged him to live a life of his own, to keep his old friends, his old pursuits. The baby's born now, she has a name, and Clay is financially responsible for her for life. You got what you wanted out of him, so why don't you free him?"

Catherine rose, brushed off her skirt and pointedly raised an arm to wave at Clay, who waved back. Without looking again at Jill, she said, "He's a big boy. If he wants to be free, don't you think he'd ask?"

Catherine headed in the direction of the terrace, but before she could get away, Jill threw one last parting shot, and this one hit its mark: "Where do you think he was while you were in the hospital having his baby?"

Insane thoughts came to Catherine, childlike in their vindictiveness. She wished that Inella's superb tomato aspic was made with Jill's blood. She wanted to shave Jill's head, roll her naked in poison ivy, feed her chocolate laced with laxative. These thoughts didn't strike Catherine as immature. She felt hurt and degraded; she wanted revenge and could think of no way to get it.

And Clay! She felt like taking a handful of melon balls and firing them at him like artillery. Like overturning the chafing dishes, getting everyone's attention, telling everyone here what a liar and a libertine he was! How could he! How could he! It wasn't bad enough that he'd continued his sexual relationship with Jill, but the thought of him confiding the intimate truths about their marriage cut deeper than Catherine ever thought possible. Painful memories came back, bolder than ever: New Year's Eve and Clay kissing Jill with his little finger under her spaghetti strap; the night he hadn't come home at all while she'd fixed supper and waited; and worst of all—four nights while she lay in a maternity ward...

It was several days after the brunch.

Catherine had submerged her anger until it lay at the base of her tongue like bile, waiting to be spewed. He'd known for days that she was seething and would soon erupt. What he didn't know was what would trigger it.

All he was doing was standing beside the crib watching

Melissa sleep. Suddenly, behind him, Catherine hissed, "What are you doing! Get away from her!"

His hands came halfway out of his pockets and he turned, surprised by her vehemence. "I didn't wake her up," he whispered.

"I know what you're thinking, standing there staring at her all the time, and you can just get it off your mind, Clay Forrester, because it won't work! I'll fight you till my dying day before I let you take her from me!"

With a quick glance to make sure the baby hadn't been disturbed, he moved toward the hall.

"Catherine, you're imagining things. I told you I—"

"You told me a lot of things you wouldn't do, like keep your affair going with Jill Magnusson, but she certainly set me straight about that! Well, if you want her, what's holding you up?"

"What did Jill say to you Sunday anyway?"

"Enough that I know I want to see you gone from this house, and the sooner the better."

"What did she say?"

"Do I need to repeat it? Do you want to rub my nose in it? All right!" Catherine marched into the master bedroom, slammed a hand against the light switch and paraded to his chest of drawers, flinging clothes out to punctuate her words. "You've been sleeping with her all the time you lied to me and said you weren't, so why not move in with her permanently? Do you think everybody doesn't know what's been going on between you when you stood at your own wedding reception and French-kissed her in front of everybody there? Did you tell your mother you'd stepped out for air when you disappeared with Jill on New Year's Eve? How dumb do you think I am, Clay? And why are you hanging around here like a stray dog? I'm not going to take you in and feed you and ask you if you'd like to live with me, because I want this farce to be over. I don't want your phony condescension or your two-bit psychoanalysis about my being emotionally crippled! I don't want you coming in here fawning over *my* daughter—the one I had while you were staying nights at Jill's house. All I want is what you agreed to give me. Child support for Melissa and my college education paid for. And I want you out of here—out!—so I can get on with my life!"

The pile of clothes lay in disarray between them. The air seemed thick, as if her shouting had actually raised dust.

"She told you a pack of lies, Catherine."

Catherine closed her eyes, but the lids quivered. She raised both palms up to Clay.

"Don't . . . just don't. Don't make it worse than it already is." Her voice shook.

"If she said I've been sleeping with her, it's a goddam lie. I've seen her, yes, but I told you I wouldn't sleep with her and I haven't."

"Why are we arguing? This is only what we knew was coming all along. Do you want me to go so you can stay? Okay—"she grew obstinate—"okay, fine." She started dumping armfuls of his things back in the drawers. "Fine, I'll go. I can easily go back home now that Herb is gone." She headed for her own dresser and yanked the drawers open.

"Catherine, you're acting childish. Will you stop it! I don't want you to go! Do you think I'd toss you and Melissa out?"

"Oh, then you want to go."

She marched back to the bureau and stubbornly began to empty it again. He caught her by an arm and swung her around none too gently.

"You're an adult now. Will you start acting like one?"

"I . . . want . . . this . . . over!" she said with emphatic pauses. "I want your parents to know the turth so I don't have to listen to your dad babbling about us leaving Melissa at their house. I'm sick of your mother giving her Polly Flinders dresses that cost forty dollars apiece and making me feel guilty as Judas! I'm sick of you standing over her crib plotting how you can get her away from me! Jill doesn't want her. Don't you understand that, Clay? All she wants is you! And since you want her, too, why don't we cut through all the crap and give little Jill what she wants?"

Something inside Catherine cringed at her rudeness, her gutter language so like her father's, but she couldn't stop it. The need to hurt Clay like he'd hurt her was too strong.

"I can see Jill really did a number on you. She's very good

337

with words, but did she ever actually say I slept with her, or did she *imply* it? I have no doubt she made me sound totally conniving and guilty."

"You told her!" Catherine raged. "You told her I threw you out of your bed when it was you who chose to sleep on that davenport. You picked out that . . . that damn long davenport, I didn't! And you had no right to tell her such private things about us!"

"I told her we were having problems; she must have guessed the rest."

"It doesn't take much guessing, does it? Not when a man sleeps with one woman while another is in the hospital having his baby!"

Clay's eyebrows lowered ominously. He ran a hand through his hair. "Goddam that Jill." Then he swung around with a palm up entreatingly. "Catherine, it's not true. I saw her the second night you were in the hospital. She was waiting outside in her car when I came home, and she followed me in."

"You had her *here?*" Catherine's voice cracked into a high falsetto. "Here in *my* house?"

"I didn't *have her here,* not the way you put it. I said she followed me in. She said she had to talk to me. We didn't do anything."

But Catherine was done arguing. "If you're leaving, leave. If not, I'm going to start my own packing. Which will it be?"

In the moments during which she stood confronting Clay, waiting for him to make the move, some bereft voice seemed to be calling from within her, beating on the inside of her stomach with tiny fists, "Why are you doing this? Why are you treating him this way when you love him? Why can't you be forgiving? Why can't you reach out and beg him to start over with you? Is that pain in his face? If you don't risk finding out, he'll be gone, and you'll be left to wonder. But then it will be too late." She stood before him, aching for him to love her, knowing she was making herself unlovable again because she loved him so much that the idea of having him—truly having him—as a husband, then losing him, would annihilate her in the end.

"I'll need to know where you'll be so my lawyer can serve

the divorce papers" was all he said. Then he went to the closet to get his luggage.

Catherine hid in the kitchen while Clay packed, listening to him making trips out to the car. Her stomach felt queasy. It lifted nauseatingly until she pressed it firmly against the edge of the kitchen counter. She sensed when Clay went in to look at Melissa for the last time. In the silence she pictured him, his blond head bent over the crib, gazing down at the baby's head—blond, too—and she felt heartless and sick with herself. She swallowed back tears, pressing against the counter until her hipbones hurt. The awful need to cry made her throat ache unbearably. It felt like she'd swallowed a tennis ball.

He came quietly to the kitchen doorway, found her standing in the lightless room.

"All of my things wouldn't fit in the car. I'll have to come back for them."

She nodded her head at the wall.

"Good-bye, Catherine," he said softly.

She raised a hand, hoping that from behind, he couldn't tell what a struggle she was having to keep from crying.

A moment later she heard the door shut.

It took him two days to clear out all his belongings for good. It took another two days before a deputy sheriff appeared at her door and served her with divorce papers. It took another week before Angela called, her voice very shaken, obviously grieved by the news. It took a week and a half before Catherine worked up the courage to visit Ada and tell her.

But it took less than an hour for Catherine to begin to miss him.

The days that followed were the most hollow of Catherine's life. She found herself staring listlessly at Clay's favorite things in the house; there were so many earth-tone items he loved so much. The place was more his than hers. She remembered how awed she'd been by its luxury the first day he'd brought her here. Guilt was her constant companion. She ate with it, slept with it, paced the rooms with it, knowing full well that it was she who should have gone, he who should have stayed. And though she had once feared leaving, she now feared staying, for the house seemed to echo Clay's voice, reflect his tastes, and always, always, remind her of his absence. She remembered how much fun it had been to fill the cabinets with wedding gifts, to go grocery shopping together, to work in the bright, well-equipped kitchen. She hated it now. Cooking for one was decidedly the most desolate chore in the world. Even making coffee in the mornings became a miserable task, for it reminded her sharply of all the mornings Clay had sat at the counter with a cup and the early paper, often attempting to tease her out of her morning grouchiness. She admitted now how hard she'd been to get along with, and marveled at how amiable Clay had always remained, no matter how bearish her morning temper. She had the bathroom all to herself whenever she wanted it, but found she missed the occasional trace of whiskers she used to find in the sink, his toothbrush lying wet beside hers, the smell of his after-shave that lingered in the room after he was gone. One day she made popcorn, but after it was buttered, she burst into tears and threw it all down the garbage disposal.

Telling Ada proved to be a terrible ordeal. Ada, whose life was being painfully rebuilt, a day at a time, looked much like she used to when Herb raised his fist at her. She seemed to cower, her shoulders curling, shriveling before Catherine's eyes.

"Mom, please don't act that way. It's not the end of the world."

"But, Cathy, why would you want to go and do a thing like that, divorce a man like Clay? Why he's—he's . . ." But for lack of a better word, Ada finished lamely, "perfect."

"No, Mother, he's not perfect and neither am I."

"But that wedding they give you, and the way Clay give you that beautiful place and everything you wanted—"

"Mother, please understand. It was a mistake for us to get married in the first place."

"But if Melissa is his—" But Ada placed trembling fingertips over her thin lips and whispered, "Oh, she is, isn't she?"

"Yes, Mother, she's his."

"Why, of course, she is," Ada reasoned. "She's got his nose and chin. But if Melissa is his, then why did he leave?"

"We tried it for Melissa's sake, but it just didn't work. You, above all people, should understand that I didn't want to stay with him when he didn't love me."

"No—no, I guess you wouldn't want to do that. But, honey, it breaks my heart to see you give up that good life you had. I was so happy to see you settled that way. Why, you had everything that I never had. Everything I always hoped my little girl would get. And I figured I'd buy myself a little used car soon and come—come over." Then, without changing the hopeless expression on her face, Ada began to cry. She did it silently, sitting in her beaten-up living room chair that she had recently covered with a new slipcover. The tears rolled down her sad cheeks, and she acted too empty and weary to lift a hand and swipe at them.

"Mom, you can still get a little car, and you can still come to see Melissa. And I'm not coming out of this a total loser. I've got Melissa, haven't I? And Clay is going to pay for me to go back to school in the fall."

"And you'd rather have that than be married to him?" Ada asked sadly.

"Mother, that's not the point. The point is, Clay and I are getting divorced, and we have to accept that. If you're honest with yourself, you'll admit that I never really fit into his class of people anyway."

"Why, I thought you did. The way Angela seemed to love you and—"

"Mother, please." Catherine put a hand to her forehead and turned away. The thought of Angela hurt almost as much as the thought of her son.

"Why, okay, honey, I'm sorry. Only it's so sudden and it takes some getting used to when I've been feeling so good about you being fixed for life."

From then on, whenever Catherine visited her mother, Ada rambled on about all that Catherine would give up in divorcing Clay. It didn't matter how many times Catherine pointed out the ways in which she'd benefited, Ada refused to see it that way.

In late July there came an unannounced visit from Clay's father. Opening the door and finding Claiborne there, Catherine immediately felt her throat swell. He was so strikingly handsome; she knew that Clay would look much like him some day. Missing Clay as she did, there was a swift surge of bittersweet joy at seeing his father at the door.

"Hello, Catherine, may I come in?"

"H-hello. Well, certainly."

There was a moment of hesitation during which each assessed the other. And each saw pain. Then Claiborne moved to pull Catherine briefly into his arms and kiss the crest of her cheek. She closed her eyes, fighting the overwhelming sense of déjà vu, fending off the love she felt for this man because he was Clay's father, Melissa's grandfather. She felt suddenly secure and protected in his hold.

When they were seated in the living room, Claiborne stated simply, "Angela and I were decimated by the news."

"I'm sorry."

It was easier for Catherine if she didn't look at her father-in-law, but she couldn't keep her eyes from his, they were so like Clay's.

"I waited, thinking Clay would come to his senses and come back here, but when we realized he wasn't going to, Angela and I had to know how you are."

"I'm fine, just fine. As you can see, I have everything I need. Clay . . . and you . . . have seen to that."

He leaned forward on the edge of his chair, cupped his palms and seemed to study them.

"Catherine, I'm afraid I must ask your forgiveness. I made such a mistake."

"Please, Mr. Forrester, if you're going to tell me about the ultimatum you issued to Clay, I know all about it. Believe me, we're no less guilty than you. We should have known better than to think marriage would automatically solve our problems. And we weren't truthful with you either."

"He told us about the agreement you two made."

"Oh." Catherine's eyebrows shot up.

"Don't look so guilty about it. None of us is too lily-white, are we?"

"I wanted to tell you long ago, but I just couldn't."

"Angela and I guessed that everything wasn't as calm as it appeared on the surface." He stood up and walked to the sliding door, gazing out much as Clay had often done. "You know,

I've only seen this place once since you and Clay moved." He glanced over his shoulder at her. "That was one of the things that made Angela and I wonder. It hurt, the fact that you never invited us here, but I guess we had it coming."

"No . . . oh, no." Catherine followed him to the window, reaching out to touch his elbow. "Oh, God, what good are recriminations? I thought it would be best not to—not to grow to love you, too, under the circumstances, I mean, knowing that Clay and I would be separating soon."

"Too?" he repeated hopefully. She should have remembered, he was a lawyer; he picked up on slips like that.

"You know what I mean. You and Angela were so good to us, you didn't deserve to be hurt."

He sighed, turned his eyes to the summer lawn where sprinklers threw cascades of droplets out across the greens between buildings. It was a warm, lazy afternoon.

"I'm a rich man," he ruminated, "I own all this. But there's very little pleasure in the thought right now."

"Please," she pleaded, "don't blame yourself."

"I thought I could buy Clay and you and my grandchild, but I was wrong."

"I'm not going to deny you the right to see Melissa. I couldn't do that."

"How is she?" The first trace of joy crossed his face at the thought of Melissa.

"She's getting a double chin, but she's healthy and very happy. I never thought a baby could be so good. She's napping now, but due to wake up soon. I could wake her if you like."

Claiborne's smile was answer enough, and she went to get Melissa up, then brought her out to see her grandpa. From his pocket he produced a small teething toy, and his smile was far wider than Melissa's when he gave it to her.

"Listen, Catherine, if there's anything she needs, or anything you need—ever—you must promise to let us know. Is that understood?"

"You've done more for me than you should already. Besides, Clay sends us money regularly." Then she studied Melissa's head, reached to lightly ruffle the feather-fine curls there as she asked, "How is he?"

Claiborne watched Catherine's hand on Melissa's fair head.

343

"I don't know. We don't see much of him these days." Their eyes met above the baby. There was deep pain in Claiborne's.

"You don't?"

"No. He went to work in the legal department of General Mills as soon as he passed his bar exam."

"But isn't he living with you?"

Claiborne became occupied with the toy, trying to get the baby to hold it in her pudgy hand.

"No, he's not. He's—"

"No need to feel uncomfortable. I think I know where he's living. With Jill, right? But that's really where he belonged all along."

"I thought you knew, Catherine. I didn't mean to spring it on you."

She laughed lightly, got up and spoke over her shoulder while she moved to the kitchen. "Oh, for heaven's sake, don't be silly. He can do whatever he pleases now."

But when Claiborne was gone, it was Catherine who stood staring out the window across the lawns, hollow-eyed, seeing Clay and Jill in the prismatic colors that jetted from the sprayers outside. Without thinking, she clutched Melissa a little too tightly, then kissed her a little too forcefully, and the baby started to cry.

Chapter 28

DURING THAT SUMMER Melissa was Catherine's greatest joy. The love Catherine found so difficult to display toward others she could lavish readily upon her child. Simply touching Melissa seemed to heal Catherine's wounded spirit and bring it back to life. Sometimes she'd flop on her side on the bed, taking Melissa with her, and with five tiny toes against her lips, would tell the child all the hidden feelings she had. In a voice as soft as cotton candy she poured out her feelings.

"Do you know how much I loved your daddy? I loved him so much that I didn't think I'd survive when he left. But there you were and I loved you, too, and you helped me through. It wasn't as bad after a while. Your daddy is handsome, know that? You have his nostrils and pretty hair like his. I'm glad you didn't get my straight hair. It's hard to tell about your mouth yet, whose it is. Why, Melissa, did you smile at me? When did you learn how to do that? Do it again, come on. That's the way. When you smile you look like your Grandma Angela. She's a wonderful lady, and your Grandpa Claiborne is wonderful too. You're a very lucky girl, you know, to come from people like them. They all love you, Grandma Ada too. But I'm the lucky one. I got you, and I love you best. Always remember that, and remember, too, how much I wanted you."

Her soliloquies to Melissa were punctuated by kisses and touches while the baby lay unblinking, her eyes, of yet-undefined color, wide and trusting.

There came a day when Melissa learned to reach. When she first reached for Catherine's face the mother knew a joy of love such as she'd never experienced before. It was pure, unconfounded by conflicts such as other loves she'd experienced. The tremendous outpouring of emotion left Catherine's eyes awash and her heart full. As the baby grew and responded to Catherine's love, there grew within Catherine the realization that she possessed qualities she hadn't known she possessed: patience, kindness, gentleness, an ease of laughter, a modicum of mother-sense and the innate knowledge of how to make a baby feel secure.

They did everything together. Sunbathed on the deck, swam in the pool, took showers—it was during a shower that Melissa first laughed aloud, ate bottled baby food—one spoon for Melissa, one spoon for Mommy—visited Ada, went grocery shopping, and registered Catherine for the next quarter. But Catherine had enough sense not to fall into the habit of taking Melissa to bed with her at night, no matter how comforting it would have been to have the baby there for company. At bedtime, she resolutely tucked Melissa into the crib in her own room, facing the king-size bed alone. She never lay down on it without thinking of Clay and the few nights they'd shared it. She couldn't help wondering if he'd still be here, had she invited him into it from the beginning. Catherine now found recriminations helpful, for she was learning much from them about herself and her shortcomings. And through Melissa she was learning it was far more satisfying to be a warm, loving person than a cold, remote one.

She learned what an abundant harvest love can reap, that the old saying is true: the more love you give away, the more you have.

* * *

In late August Steve came home. He was so dismayed to find Catherine and Clay separated that he blew up at his sister, blaming her for not trying harder to hold a man who'd done his damnedest to do right by her.

"I know you, Cathy. I know how godawful stubborn you can be, and how once your mind is made up it sets harder than a plaster cast. You don't have to tell me you didn't love him because I know different. What I want to know is why the hell you wouldn't swallow a little of your pride and fight for him!"

He was the only one who understood all the forces behind Catherine's belligerence and stubbornness, those old millstones which had ultimately alienated Clay. Steve was the first one to come right out and blame her, and Catherine surprised him by admitting he was right. By the time Steve left he realized Catherine had done a vast amount of growing up since her wedding.

In September she went back to school, leaving Melissa with a babysitter. Catherine had to contact Clay to let him know there would be another bill for him to pay. He asked if he could drop by and bring her a check and see Melissa at the same time.

From the moment the door opened, he could tell that Catherine was different. There was an openness about her, starting with the smile on her face. His attention was torn between it and the wide gaze of curiosity upon the face of his daughter.

"Hi, Clay, come on in."

He couldn't control the size of his smile. "Holy cow! Has she grown!"

Catherine laughed, plopped a loud kiss on the baby's neck and turned to lead the way inside. "She's got lots of chins to nuzzle, haven'tcha, Lissy?" And Catherine did so. "She's kind of getting to that shy stage, so it might take a while for her to warm up to you. But don't feel bad, she's that way with everybody lately."

Following Catherine upstairs, Clay glanced quickly up and down her jean-clad figure. Her old shape was back, and when she turned to face him again he noticed how tan she was. Her hair seemed lighter, bleached into streaks like honey and peanut-butter.

"Sit down, you two, and say hello while I bring us a glass of Cola or something."

She put Melissa into the crank-up swing that occupied the center of the living room, then ducked into the kitchen. Melissa immediately realized she'd been left alone with a stranger and stuck out her lip.

"Didn't you warn her I was coming and tell her to put on her best manners?" Clay called.

"I did. I told her you were the fella paying the bills, so she'd better watch her *p*'s and *q*'s."

Melissa began to squall, but quieted as soon as Catherine reappeared. She handed a glass to Clay, cranked up the swing, then sat cross-legged on the floor beside it.

"Oh, before I forget—here." Clay dug a check out of his pocket and handed it to her.

"Oh, thank you. I hated to ask for more."

"You earned it," he said without thinking. But Catherine seemed to take no offense. Instead, she began to describe the babysitter who cared for Melissa, as if to put him at ease about the woman's coming well-recommended.

"You don't have to reassure me about that, Catherine. If there's one thing I don't worry about, it's the kind of care Melissa will get."

"She's a good baby, Clay, really good. She's got your temperament." Then Catherine smiled, shook her head in gay self-deprecation. "Boy, I'm sure glad she didn't get mine or she'd be driving her mother nuts!"

"You had to put up with plenty of temper from me."

"Usually after I started it, though. Oh, well, water over the dam, huh? So, how's everything with you and Jill? Are you happy?"

Clay seemed startled. The last thing he'd expected Catherine to ask about was Jill, especially in that free and easy way.

"Yes, we are. We don't—" But he stopped self-consciously.

"Hey, it's okay. I mean, I didn't mean to pry."

"No, you weren't prying. I was just going to say that Jill and I don't fight like you and I used to, or give each other the silent treatment. We coexist rather peacefully."

348

"Good for you. So do Melissa and I. Peace is nice, isn't it, Clay?"

He sipped his drink, assessing this changed Catherine who seemed utterly satisfied with herself and her life. She reached over and tucked the baby's collar down, keeping up with the swing while she did it, smiling and saying, "Melissa, this is your daddy. You remember him, don't you? Shame on you for sticking your lip out and crying at him." Again she glanced up at Clay. "Your father came to visit us once. He brought Melissa a toy and asked how we were and said to let him know if we needed anything. But he's been so good to us already I'd feel guilty to take anything from him."

"What is it you need?"

"Nothing. Clay, you've been great about the money part. I really appreciate it. School is going to be great this year, I know. I mean, it's so much easier going to school when you're not pregnant." She flung her arms up and let them flop back down. "I feel like I could conquer the world every day, you know?"

Clay used to feel that way; he didn't anymore. "Are you still sewing and typing?"

"Yes, now that school is in session again it's easy to find jobs. Don't worry, I'll help with the money any way I can. Mostly it goes for groceries. Baby food is kind of expensive." She chuckled and fluffed Melissa's hair as the swing went past. " 'Course, I could save a lot on it if I didn't eat so much of it myself. We kind of share stuff, Melissa and I. I share my shower with her and she shares her food with me, huh, Lissy?"

"You take her in the shower!" exclaimed Clay. "At her age?"

"Oh, she loves it. And the pool too. You should have seen her in the pool this summer, just like a baby otter." While she rambled on, she took Melissa out of the swing and sat the baby in her lap facing Clay. He noticed a new contentment in Catherine as she touched Melissa's hair or ear or gently clapped the bottoms of the tiny feet together. There was a naturalness about it that made Clay feel left out. The longer he observed Catherine with the baby the more he sensed how much she'd changed. She was freer than he'd ever seen her, talkative and happy, trying to withhold nothing about Melissa from him. It almost seemed as if she must share everything she could remember. But she did it guilelessly, shifting her attention from the baby to Clay all the while. Finally she said, "I think she's used to you now if you want to hold her."

But when he took Melissa, she immediately complained, so, disappointed, he handed the baby back to her mother.

Catherine shrugged. "Sorry."

He stood up to leave.

"Clay, is there anything you want from the house? I feel awful about taking everything from you. It seems like everything here is yours and I've ended up with it all. If there's anything you want, just say so, it's yours."

He glanced around the neat living room where the only thing out of place was the swing. He thought of the disarray Jill always left in her wake.

"Jill had everything already, thanks."

"Aren't there even any of the wedding gifts you want?"

"No, you keep 'em."

"Not even the popcorn popper?" She looked like a sprite while asking it.

"That wasn't a wedding gift. We bought that together."

"Oh, that's right. Well, I don't make much popcorn, so just say if you want it."

She seemed to have thoroughly adjusted to her life without him. She led the way to the door, opened it and sauntered out to the car with him.

"Thanks for bringing the check over, Clay; we really appreciate it."

"Anytime."

"Clay, one more thing before you go."

He stood beside the open car door, grateful for something that kept him here a little longer. Catherine stared at the ground, kicking a pebble, then looked directly into his eyes.

"Your father mentioned that they don't see much of you anymore. It's none of my business, but he seemed terribly hurt by that. Clay, there's no reason for you to feel like you've failed them or—or whatever." This was the first time she'd acted flustered. Her cheeks were pink. "Oh, you know what I mean. Your parents are really great. Don't sell them short, okay?"

350

"They don't exactly approve of my living with Jill."

"Give them a chance," she said, her voice gone quite low and musical, persuasive somehow. "How can they approve if they never see you to do it?" Then, quite suddenly, she flashed him a smile. "Oh, forget it. It's none of my business. Say good-bye to your daddy, Melissa." She backed away, manipulating the baby's arm in a wave.

Why was it that Clay, too, felt she was manipulating his heart in some obscure way?

Six weeks after school started a history professor named Frank Barrett asked Catherine to a show at the Orpheum. They returned to her house after an exhilarating live performance of *A Chorus Line*, and Frank Barrett tried to exact payment for the evening. He was handsome enough, in a rugged, dark-whiskered way, and Catherine thought of it as therapy when she let herself be pulled into his arms and kissed. But his beard, which she'd liked earlier, was less likable when his tongue came through it. His body, which had nothing to speak against it, was less appealing when it flattened Catherine's against the entry wall. His hands, which were square-nailed and clean, were too abruptly intimate, and when she pushed them away, it was with a healthy, negative feeling against him that had nothing to do with hang-ups. She simply was not attracted to him, and found it glorious to turn him away for such a reason.

When he apologized, she actually smiled, saying, "Oh, no need to apologize. It was wonderful."

Misreading her reply, he moved in again only to be staved off a second time.

"No, Frank. I meant *saying* no was wonderful!"

The poor, puzzled Frank Barrett left Catherine believing that she was somewhat wacky, not at all like she'd seemed when he'd first noticed her in his classroom.

In late November the law caught up with Herb Anderson and he was returned to Minnesota for trial. When Catherine saw him in the courtroom, she could scarcely believe it was he. His beer belly was gone, his face sallow, his hands shaky; life on the lam had obviously been unkind to him. But the same cynical expression still marred his face, the same droop of lips said Old Herb still thought he deserved a square deal from life and wasn't getting it.

To Catherine's surprise, Clay was in the courtroom, and so were his parents. With an effort, she forced her thoughts back to the proceedings, noting the satisfied smirk that crossed Herb's face when he saw that the Forresters did not seat themselves in the same row with Catherine and Ada.

The trial did not last long, for there was no one to come to Herb Anderson's defense, save two of his booze-buddies from the old days, who looked even more desreputable than Herb, who'd at least been cleaned up and offered fresh clothing, courtesy of the county. Herb Anderson's history of violence was clearly presented in the testimony of Ada, Catherine and even Herb's own sister and brother-in-law, Aunt Ella and Uncle Frank. The past assault on Clay was brought up as evidence and dismissed, yet its impact remained. The doctor who had treated Ada testified, as did the ambulance drivers and Mrs. Sullivan. As the trial proceeded, Herb's usually florid face grew pastier and pastier. There were no verbal outbursts from him this time, only a quivering of his flaccid jowls and a persecuted expression when the judge sentenced Herbert Anderson to two years in the Stillwater State Penitentiary.

Leaving her seat, holding Ada's arm, Catherine saw Clay and his parents moving, also, toward the center aisle. He wore a stylish cashmere coat of spice brown, its collar flipped up. His eyes sought and held hers as she moved toward him, and wings seemed to flutter within Catherine's chest as she realized he was waiting for her. There was a welcome feeling of security about anticipating his touch upon her arm. Without a word— for the bench had called the next case—it was somehow understood: Angela and Claiborne separated to make room for Ada between them as they left the courtroom, followed by Catherine, with Clay's hand guiding her elbow. Walking beside him, she caught a hint of his familiar cologne. She gave in to the urge to look up at him again, tightening her arm and pulling his hand against her ribs.

"Thank you, Clay," she smiled appreciatively. "We really needed your support today."

He squeezed her elbow. The impact of his smile sent flurries deep into her stomach, and she looked away.

Once again Clay sensed the changes in her. She had gained a new self-assurance that was totally attractive on her, while at the same time, she'd become dulcified. She was no longer skittish nor defensive. He noticed that she'd changed her hairstyle and that the summer's streaks were now blending into its natural gold color. He studied it as she walked a step ahead of him, mentally approving of the appealing way in which it was caught up with combs behind her ears, falling in blithe curls down past her shoulder blades now.

They reached the corridor and found Angela waiting there, gazing at Catherine, fighting tears.

"Oh, Catherine, it's so wonderful to see you."

"I've missed you too," Catherine got out. Then the two were in each other's arms and tears were hovering in the corners of both pairs of eyes.

Observing them, Clay remembered how Catherine had vowed not to let herself grow fond of his parents, but he saw that it hadn't worked, for from Angela's embrace she went to Claiborne's. It was the first time Clay ever remembered Catherine moving unguardedly into a hug, except that time with Steve.

Claiborne's bear hug made Catherine gasp and laugh, breaking the tension, but over his shoulder Catherine's eyes were again drawn to Clay, who was studying her with a faraway expression.

They all seemed to remember Ada then, and the reason for their being there. After they spoke of the case she had just won, the talk moved on to other things, growing a little fast and clipped, as if too much needed crowding into too little time. At last Angela suggested, "Why don't we all go somewhere and have a sandwich or a drink, somewhere we can talk for a while. There's so much I want to hear about Melissa and you, Catherine."

"How about The Mullion?" Claiborne suggested. "It's a favorite place of mine and not far from here."

Catherine glanced sharply at Clay, then at her mother.

Ada's hand fluttered to draw her coat closed. "Why, I don't know. I rode in with Margaret." They now took note of Mrs. Sullivan standing by, waiting with Ella and Frank.

"If you'd like, we'll take you home," Claiborne offered.

"Well, it's up to Cathy."

Catherine heard Clay say, "Catherine can ride with me." She slid him a look then, but he was buttoning up his coat as if it were already decided.

"I have my own car," she said.

"Whatever you'd like. You can ride with me if you like, and I'll bring you back uptown afterward to pick up your car."

The old Catherine intruded, with her impulse to fend off her feelings of attraction for Clay. But the newer Catherine was secure now and decided to go ahead and enjoy him while she could.

"All right," she agreed. "There's no sense in burning up extra gas."

Smiling at the others, Clay said, "We'll see you there then." And Catherine felt her elbow firmly clasped and snuggled against Clay's warm side.

Outside the wind was howling, eddying in miniature twisters in the valleys between tall buildings. Catherine savored the icy sting upon her cheeks, for they were warm, almost burning. She and Clay got to a corner and stood waiting for a light to change. Catherine kept her eyes on the luminous red circle across the street, but she could feel Clay's eyes on her. She reached to turn up her collar but it caught on the long angora scarf twined around her neck, and Clay reached a gloved hand to help. Through all those layers of wool, his touch could still raise goosebumps up and down Catherine's spine. The light changed then.

"My car's in the parking ramp," Clay said, taking her arm again as they crossed the windy street, then crossing behind her as they turned the corner. Taking the outside, he brushed her shoulder. The touch made her tingle. She searched for something to say, but the only sound came from their heels on the sidewalk. He turned her into the echoing dungeon of a concrete parking ramp, its floor slick with motor oil. The heel of her shoe skittered, dumping her sideways, but she felt herself hoisted upright by that hand so secure on her elbow.

"You okay?"

"Yes, winter is no time for high heels."

354

He watched her trim ankles, mentally disagreeing with her.

At the elevator he dropped her arm, leaned to push the button, and the silence seemed insurmountable while they waited, shivering, their shoulders hunched against the cold that seemed so much more intense in the concrete dimness. The elevator arrived; Clay stood aside while Catherine boarded. He pushed an orange button. Still they said nothing, and Catherine frantically wished she'd kept up a steady stream of chatter all the way because the privacy of the elevator was unbearable, yet she couldn't think of how to start.

Clay watched the light indicate the floors as they went up. "How's Melissa?" he asked the lights.

"Melissa's fine. She just loves the babysitter's; at least I'm told she's very content and happy there."

The hum of the elevator sounded like a buzz saw.

"How's Jill?"

Clay looked sharply at Catherine, hesitating only a moment before answering, "Jill's fine, at least she tells me she's very content and happy."

"And how about you?" Catherine's heart slammed around inside her. "What do you tell her?"

They had arrived at the correct level. The doors opened. Neither of them moved. The frigid air invaded their cell, but they stood as if unaware of it, gazing into each other's faces.

"My car is off to the right," he said, confused by the confusion in his chest, afraid of making the wrong move with her.

"I'm sorry, Clay, I shouldn't have asked that," she said in a rush, hurrying along beside him. "You have every right to ask about Melissa, but I have none to ask about Jill. I do wonder about you, though, and hope you're happy. I want you to be."

They stopped beside the Corvette. He leaned to unlock the door. He straightened, looked at her. "I'm working on it."

Riding to The Mullion they were both remembering the other time he'd taken her there. Suddenly it seemed childish to Catherine, the way they had grown so ill at ease with each other.

"Are you thinking about it, too, about the last time we went here?" she asked.

"I wasn't going to mention it."

"We're big kids now. We should be able to handle it."

355

"You know, you've changed, Catherine. Half a year ago you'd have bristled and acted threatened at the idea of going there."

"I felt threatened then."

"And now you don't?"

"I'm not sure of your question. Do you mean threatened by you?"

"It wasn't always against me that you put up your defenses. It was other things, places, circumstances, your own fears. I think you've outgrown a lot of that."

"I think I have too."

"Since you asked me, I'll ask you—are you happy?"

"Yes. And do you know what made the difference?"

"What?" He angled a glance at her and found her watching him in the failing light of late afternoon.

"Melissa," she answered softly. "There have been countless times when I've looked at her and fought the urge to call you and say thank you for giving her to me."

"Why didn't you?"

He'd had his eyes on her for so long she wondered how the car stayed on the road. Catherine moved her head and shoulders in a vague way that said she did not have the answer. He turned back to watch the lane, and the familiarity struck her with a breath-taking blow: his profile there behind the wheel, the wrist draped negligently as he drove with the ease she remembered so well. She let her impulses have their way and suddenly leaned over, putting a hand on his jaw and pulling his cheek briefly against her lips.

"That's for both of us, for Melissa and me. Because I think she's just as grateful to have me as I am to have her." Quickly Catherine centered herself in her own seat and went on. "And you know what, Clay? I'm a fabulous mother. Don't ask me how it happened, but I know I am."

He couldn't help grinning. "And humble too."

She snuggled into her seat contentedly. "There aren't a lot of things I'm good at, but being Melissa's mother is . . . well, it's great. It's a little harder since school started, but I cut a few corners of housework time here and there, let a few things stay dusty, and I still find time for her. But I have to admit,

I'll be glad when school is over and I don't have to divide my time so many ways."

The kiss then had been purely a kiss of thanks. It was clearer than ever that Catherine's life was full and happy. She had it all together. Clay listened to her relating stories about it and suffered pangs of regret that she'd been unable to feel this fulfilled when she was living with him. He came from his reverie to realize she'd just said she was dating again. He submerged the twinge of possessiveness to which he no longer had a right, and asked, "How does it feel?"

"Terrific!" She flung up her palms. "Just terrific! I can kiss back without the slightest bit of guilt. Sometimes I can even enjoy it."

She looked at him with an impish grin and they both laughed. But a hundred queries bubbled up in his mind about those kisses, the ones she shared them with, queries which, again, he had no right to ask.

They stayed at The Mullion for over two hours, until Angela had learned about each of Melissa's toys and teeth and vaccinations. Catherine was her new, free, easy self all the while. Clay spoke little, sitting back and studying her, comparing her to the way she used to be. And subconsciously comparing her to Jill. He wondered if she was dating only one man or several. He planned to ask her when he drove her back to her car.

But when the time came to leave, Catherine pointed out that it was actually closer to Claiborne and Angela's route to drop her back uptown, and she rode with them.

Chapter 29

CLAY STOOD IN the window of the high-rise apartment he shared with Jill, staring down at the icy expanse of Lake Minnetonka in the cold, purple dusk below. The lake was a sprawling network of bays, channels and inlets in a western suburb bearing its name. Clay wished it were summer. In summer the lake was a water-lover's paradise, dappled by sails, dotted with skiers, peopled with fishermen, rimmed by intermittent beach and woodland. Its islands emerged like emeralds from sapphire waters. In spots where its shoreline was left to nature's whims, watery fingers erupted in lavender explosions of loosestrife, come August.

But now, in early December, Clay studied the frozen surface in distaste. Winds had whipped it into a froth as it froze, leaving it the pitted texture and color of lava. Rowboats and schooners alike looked bereft, overturned on the shore. Hoisted above the waterline their soiled canvas covers held dirty snow. On a spar below, a trio of dissolute sparrows fluffed their feathers against an arctic wind until they were blown off, trundled sideways as they flew. A small flock of mallards fought a headwind, then disappeared in their search of open water.

Watching the ducks, Clay wondered where the autumn had

gone. He had drifted through it listlessly, free this year to enjoy the hunting he so dearly loved, yet somehow never even getting his gun out of its case. In the past he'd hunted with his father more than anyone else. He missed his father. But as winter thickened and intensified, so had his parents' disapproval over his living with Jill. Although they occasionally phoned, Clay sensed their silent chastisement, thus never called them back.

He saw Jill's car curve into the parking lot below and disappear toward the garages. Minutes later he heard her key in the door. Normally he'd have hurried to open it, but today he only continued staring morosely at the chill scene outside.

"Oh, God, it's cold! I hope there's a nice hot toddy waiting for me," Jill said. She crossed to Clay, dropping gloves, scarf, purse and coat across the room like rings from a skipping stone, only—unlike ripples—the articles would not disappear. It aggravated Clay, for he'd just cleaned up the place again when he got home. Jill crooked an arm through his and rubbed her cold nose against his jaw in greeting.

"I like it when you get home first and you're here waiting."

"Jill, do you have to drop your stuff everyplace like that?"

"Oh, did I drop something?" She looked at the trail behind her, then nuzzled Clay again. "Just anxious to get to you, darling, that's all. Besides, you know I always had a maid at home."

"Yes, I know. That's always your excuse." He couldn't help recalling how Catherine used to enjoy keeping the town house clean and neat.

"Irritable tonight, darling?"

"No, I'm just tired of living in a mess."

"You're irritable. In need of some liquid refreshment. What have you been standing here brooding about, your parents again? If it bothers you so much, why don't you go over and see them tonight?"

But it only irritated him further that she simplified it so, as if his problems could be solved by a simple visit. She dropped her shoes in the middle of the room on her way to the liquor cabinet. She picked up a brandy decanter, swung around loosely to face him, and said, "Let's have a drink, then go out and get some supper."

It was Friday night, bleak and cold, and he was tired of

running. He wished just for once she'd suggest making dinner at home, doing something cozy and relaxing. The memory of sharing popcorn and studying with Catherine came back, so inviting now. He pictured the town house, Melissa in her swing with Catherine cross-legged beside it in her jeans. Looking out at the cold, icy lake which was receding into dusk's hold, he wondered what Catherine's reaction would be if he showed up at her door. Abruptly, he walked over and closed the draperies. Before he could reach for the lamp switch, Jill moved close in the dark. She wrapped her arms around him, pressed her breasts to his chest and sighed.

"Maybe I can think of a way to coax you out of your bad mood," she whispered huskily against his lips.

He kissed her, waiting for arousal to grip him. Instead, he was gripped only by hunger pangs; he'd skipped lunch that day. It struck him that the state of his stomach overrode his bodily response to Jill. It made him feel emptier, hungrier, but for something that went beyond either food or sex.

"Later," he said, brushing her hair back, guilty now for his lack of desire. "Get your coat and let's go out and eat."

Melissa was teething and fussy and whiny these days. She resisted bedtime, so Catherine often brought her out onto the living room floor until she fell asleep there, then carried her up to her crib.

The doorbell rang and Melissa's eyes flew open again.

Oh, damn, thought Catherine. But she leaned over, kissed Melissa's forehead and whispered, "Mommy'll be right back, punkin."

Melissa started sucking on her bottle again.

Through the door Clay heard her muffled voice.

"Who is it?"

"It's Clay," he said, close to the wood.

Suddenly Catherine forgot her irritation. Her stomach seemed to suspend itself, then drift back into place in an unnervingly tentative way. It's Clay, it's Clay, it's Clay, she thought, deliriously happy.

On the other side of the door Clay wondered what he'd say

to her; she'd surely see through his flimsy excuse for coming here.

The door fairly flew open, but when it swung back she stood motionless. First impression made her momentarily mute: his wind-whipped hair in a whorl of inviting imperfection above the turned-up collar of an old letter jacket; faded jeans hugging his slim hips; his hands in his pockets like some uncertain high-school sophomore ringing a girl's bell for the first time. He hesitated as if he didn't know what to say, then his eyes traveled down to her knees, then back up, then seemed not to know where to rest. Everything in her went all loose and jellyish.

"Hi, Catherine."

"Hi, Clay."

Suddenly she realized how long it had been since either of them had moved and remembered that Melissa was on the floor with the cold wafting in.

"I brought Melissa a Christmas gift."

She stepped back, let him in, then closed the door to find herself disarmingly close to him in the rather confined area of the entry.

Clay briefly glanced down at her attire. "Were you in bed already?"

"Oh—oh, no." Self-consciously she tugged the zipper of her robe the remaining two inches up her neck, then jammed her hands into its pockets.

"I guess I should have called first." He stood there feeling graceless and intrusive. The robe was fleecy pink, with a hood, and pockets on the front like a sweatshirt. Her hair was pulled back with a plastic headband and the ends of it were still wet. Her face had that scrubbed, shiny look that he recognized so well. With a start, he realized she'd just gotten out of the shower. He knew perfectly well there was no bra beneath that fuzzy, pink fleece—he remembered that untethered look of hers.

"It doesn't matter, it's okay."

"Next time I'll make sure I call first. I just bought something on impulse, and I was driving past and decided to drop it off."

"I said it was okay. We weren't doing anything special anyway."

361

"You weren't?" he asked dumbly.

"I was studying and Melissa was teething."

He smiled then, a big, warm, wonderful smile, and she hunched up her shoulders and pushed her hands as far down in her pockets as they'd go because she didn't know how else to contain her happiness at his being here.

Suddenly there was a loud thump and the living room was plunged into darkness, followed by a second of silence before Melissa's wail of panic billowed through the blackness.

"Oh, my God!" Clay heard. He groped, touched the fleecy robe and followed it up the stairs in the direction of the living room.

"Where is she, Catherine?"

"I left her on the floor."

"You get her. I'll get the kitchen light."

Melissa was screaming and Catherine's heart threatened to explode. Fumbling for the light switch, Clay, too, felt a stab of panic. He found the switch, then in five long-legged strides was kneeling behind Catherine who had scooped up the baby and was muffling Melissa's cries against her neck. In the dim light Clay could see the table lamp on the floor, but unbroken. He touched Catherine's shoulder, then Melissa's head.

"Catherine, let's take her into the light and see if she's hurt." He put his hands on Catherine's sides, urging her up and felt through the robe that she was crying too. "Come on," he said sensibly, "let's take her to the bathroom."

They laid Melissa on a fat Turkish towel on the vanity top. They could see right away where the lamp had hit the back of the baby's head. There was a tiny gash there and already it was starting to swell into a goose egg. Catherine was so upset that her distress was conveyed to Melissa, who squalled all the louder. So Clay was the one who swabbed the bruise and calmed them both.

"It's all my fault." Catherine blamed herself. "I've never left her on the floor like that before. I should have known she'd go straight for the lamp cords—she does every chance she gets. But she was asleep when the doorbell rang and I didn't think anything of it. She started sucking on her bottle again and I was just—"

"Hey, it's nothing serious. I'm not blaming you, am I?"

Clay's eyes met hers in the mirror.

"But a lamp that size could have killed her."

"But it didn't. And it's not the last bump she'll take. Do you realize that you're more upset than Melissa?"

He was right. Melissa wasn't even crying anymore, just sitting there wet-eyed, watching them. Sheepishly Catherine smiled, sniffled, yanked out a tissue and blew her nose. Clay put his arm around her shoulder and bumped her up against his side a couple of times as if to say, silly girl. At that moment he understood why nature had created a two-parent system. Yes, you're a good mother, Catherine, he thought, but not in emergencies. At times like this, you need me.

"What do you say we show her the Christmas present I bought for her and that'll make her forget she even had an accident."

"All right. But, Clay, do you think this needs stitches? I don't know anything about cuts. She's never had one before."

They fought Melissa's tiny hands and caused her to start complaining again while they inspected the damage.

"I don't know much about it, either, but I don't think so. It's awfully tiny. And anyway, it's in her hair, so if there's a scar it won't show."

Finally, Melissa left the bathroom on her mother's arm, looking back at Clay with a wide-eyed look of inquiry. He set up the lamp and plugged it in again, and they all sat down on the living room floor, the baby in her yellow footed pajamas staring so silently at Clay that he finally laughed at her. Her bottom lip started quivering again, so Clay suggested, "Hurry and open that before I get a complex."

The sight and sound of the bright red, crackly paper captured the baby's attention as Catherine tore it off the white koala bear with its flat nose and lifelike eyes. At the sight of it, Melissa's mouth made a tiny "ooo," then she gurgled. The koala had a music box inside, and it wasn't long before it accompanied Melissa to bed.

Coming back down from Melissa's room, Catherine found Clay waiting at the bottom of the stairs, his green and gold letter jacket slung over one shoulder as if he were going to leave. A throb of disappointment thudded through her. She stopped on the bottom step, curling her toes over the edge, hanging on by her heels only. Her fingertips unconsciously toyed upon the handrails. He stood before her, their eyes nearly on the same level, trying to think of something to say to each other.

"She'll sleep now," Catherine said—not quite an invitation, not quite not.

"Good . . . well . . ." He looked at the carpet while he slowly threaded his arms into his jacket sleeves. Still studying the floor, he straightened the old shapeless collar while Catherine gripped the handrails tightly. He buried his hands in the jacket pockets and cleared his throat.

"I guess I'd better get going." His voice sounded a little raspy, trying to talk soft that way so he wouldn't wake Melissa.

"Yes, I guess so." It took great effort for Catherine to breathe. The banister felt suddenly slippery.

Clay's head came up slowly, his inscrutable eyes meeting hers. He gestured with one of his hidden hands as if waving good-bye—jacket and all.

"So long."

She could barely hear it, he said it so softly.

"So long."

But instead of moving, he stood there studying her, the way she perched on that bottom step like a sparrow on a limb. Her eyes were wide and unsmiling, and he could see the way she forced herself to take shallow, fluttering breaths. His own breath wasn't any too calm. He wished she wouldn't look so stricken, but knew she had good reason to be scared, just as scared as he was at that moment. Her hair was dry now, the ends curling wispily upon her shoulders, upon the folds of the hood that hilled up around her jaw. She stood there all still, arms straight out from her sides, looking almost breastless in her robe. Face shiny, devoid of makeup, hair unstyled, feet bare. He tried not to analyze, not to think either "I should" or "I shouldn't," because he only knew he had to. He took three agonizingly slow footsteps toward her, his eyes roving her face. Then he leaned silently and put his face in the spot where her hair lay, lifted by that hood. He breathed of her remembered fragrance— soft, powdery, feminine scent that he'd always loved. Catherine's lips fell open and she moved her jaw against his temple while deep in her body things went liquid, deep in his things went hard. Her heart scrambled to make sense of this while it seemed to take light-years of time before he straightened and their eyes met. They asked tacit questions, remembered old hurts they'd caused each other. Then, still with his hands in his pockets, Clay leaned and touched her lips softly with his own, seeing her lashes drop just before his own eyes slid shut. He kissed her with a light lingering of flesh upon flesh, letting the past slip into obscurity, yet unable to prevent it from being part of the kiss. He told himself he must go, but when he drew away her lips followed, telling him not to. Their eyelids flickered open to breach that moment of uncertainty before he moved more surely against her lips. There was a timorous, first opening of mouths, warm touch of tongue upon tongue, then Clay wrapped his hands, jacket and all, around her, pulling her inside of it with him. Handlessly they embraced, for she still clutched the rails, and his hands were lost in his pockets behind her, quite afraid to pull them out and start something they certainly should not finish. But it was impossible, unbearable, this handlessness. Then Catherine seemed to lean off the steps, drifting into the warm place he opened up to her, losing her arms deep inside his jacket. He enclosed her in the cocoon of soft, old wool and leather, and hard, young flesh and blood, lifting her off that step, turning, holding her suspended against him while the kiss became reckless and she went sliding down his body. Her bare toes touched canvas and she was standing on his tennis shoes. One hand came out of his pocket and found her hair, cradling the back of her head, pulling her against his mouth. His other hand left the safe confines of its pocket and flattened itself upon the center of her back, then drifted lower, lower, to the shallows of her spine, to bring the length of her body against his. Through her robe she could feel his belt buckle and the hard zipper of his jeans, and she remembered drinking wine from his skin. Ironically, the thought sobered her and she tried to push away. But he pulled her almost violently against the thunder of his heart, crushing her.

"Oh, God, Cat," he whispered in a strangled voice, "this is where we started."

"Not at all," came her shaky reply. "We've come a long way since then."

"You have, Cat, you have. You're so different now."

"I've grown up a little, that's all."

"Then what the hell's the matter with me?"

"Don't you know?"

"Nothing's right in my life anymore. Everything's gone wrong since you and I made that damn agreement. The last year has been miserable. I don't know who I am or where I'm going anymore."

"Is this going to tell you?"

"I don't know. I only know it feels right here with you."

"The first time we met it felt right, and look where it landed us."

"I want you," he half-groaned against her hair, wrapping his arms around her so far she heard old stitches pop up the back of his jacket. She closed her eyes and swam in a warm, wet place of his making, secure enough now to take the plunge, to say that which she'd refused to say during the agonizing months she'd lived with him.

"But I love you, Clay, and there's a difference."

He pulled back to search her face, and she willed him to say it, but he didn't. He read her thoughts and knew what it was she waited for, but found he could not say it unless he was certain. Things had happened so fast he didn't know if he was running on impulse or emotion. He only knew she looked beguiling, and that she was the mother of his child and that they were still husband and wife.

He came back against her hard, and the momentum swept them to the carpeted stairs. All in one motion he pressed her down and lifted his knee, riding it across her stomach, hip and thigh, caressing her with it while he searched the neck of her robe for the zipper, slid it down and plunged his hand inside to slake it with her breast, then run it down her stomach.

"Stop it, Clay, stop it," she implored, dying because she wanted nothing more than to turn her body inside-out for him.

Against her warm neck he said throatily, "You don't want this to stop, not any more than you did the first time."

"Our divorce will be final in less than a month, and you're living with another woman."

"And lately all I do is compare her to you."

"Is that why you're here, Clay, to make comparisons?"

"No, no, I didn't mean it that way." His hand swept down

her ribs, down her stomach, heading again for the spot that wept for him. "Oh, Cat, you're under my skin."

"Like an itch you can't reach, Clay?" She grabbed his wrist and stopped it again.

"Don't play games with me."

"I'm not the one playing games, Clay, you are."

He felt her nails now, digging into his wrist. He pushed himself back, leaning on one elbow to see her better.

"I'm not playing games. I want you."

"Why? Because I'm the first thing in your life that you can't have?"

His face changed, grew stormy, then abruptly he sat up on the step beside her and buried his fingers in his hair. God, is she right, he wondered. Is that all it is with me—ego? Am I that kind of a bastard? He heard her zipper go back up but remained as he was, touching his scalp, which tingled at the thought of all that naked skin beneath her robe. He sat that way a long time, then pulled his palms down over his face. But in them he could smell the fragrance of her perfume, gathered from her skin like spring flowers.

She sat beside him, watching him do battle with himself. After a long time, he stretched his frame back against the edges of the steps, lying there at an angle. With his eyes closed he lifted up his hips and tugged at the crotch of his jeans. She could see the telltale bulge there. He rested the back of a wrist over his eyes, let his other hand lie limply down along his groin. He sighed.

Finally she spoke, but her voice was unangry, reasonable. "I think you'd better decide what it is you want, me or her. You can't have us both."

"I know that, I goddam know that," he said tiredly. "I'm sorry, Catherine."

"Yes, you should be, doing this to me again. I'm not as resilient as you are, Clay. When I get hurt it hurts for a long time. And I have no alternate lover to fall back on for support."

"I feel like I'm spinning in circles; nothing's in focus."

"I don't doubt it, living with her, coming here, your parents right in the middle. What about them, Clay? What are you trying to prove by rejecting them the way you have and going to work for someone else?"

She saw his Adam's apple slide up and down, but he didn't answer.

"If you want to punish yourself, Clay, keep me out of it. If you want to go on putting yourself into situations that rub you raw, fine. I don't. I've made a new life with Melissa, and I've proven to myself that I can live without you. When we met, you were the one with direction, the secure one. Now it seems we've changed places. What happened to that direction, that purpose you used to have?"

Maybe it left me when I left you, he thought.

At last he sat up, then pulled himself to his feet and stood with his back to her, staring at the floor.

She said, "I think you'd better go someplace and get sorted out, get your priorities straight. If and when you manage that and think you want to see me again . . ." But instead of finishing the thought, she ended, "Just don't ever come back here asking for me unless it's for keeps."

She heard the snaps of his jacket, like whipcracks in the silence. Clay's shoulders squared, then slumped, then he waved wordlessly, without looking back at her, and left the house, closing the door softly behind him.

Chapter 30

EMOTIONALLY, CATHERINE FOUND herself in that painful, bittersweet state she'd faced and gotten through once before when Clay left her. Again, she suffered reveries from which she emerged to find her hands idle, her thoughts and eyes meandering out the window, across the snowy city to Clay. Clay, whom she'd have on one condition only, thus would probably never have at all. The contentment she'd known from loving Melissa ceased to sustain her. Emptiness crept into her unexpectedly, in the middle of the most everyday activities: studying, folding laundry, walking across campus, giving Melissa a bath, driving in the car. Clay's visage appeared before her constantly, his absence again robbing her of joy, making life seem wan and empty, at times bringing tears to her eyes. And like all lorn loves, she found reminders of him in countless places that were only illusory: in the reddish-gold hair of some stranger on the street; in the cut of a sport coat on a muscular shoulder; in the inflection of someone's laughter; in the way certain men crossed their ankles over their knees, dropped their hands into their pockets or straightened their ties. One of Catherine's professors, when he lectured intensely, had Clay's habit of standing with arms akimbo, holding his sport coat back with his wrists, studying the floor between his outspread feet. His body language was so like Clay's that Catherine became obsessed with the man. It did no good to tell herself she was transferring her feelings for Clay to a veritable stranger. Each time Professor Neuman stood before class that way, Catherine's heart would react.

She counted off the days until Christmas break when she would no longer have to be subjected to Professor Neuman and his similarities to Clay. But Christmas brought its own bittersweet memories of last year. In an effort to stave them off, she called Aunt Ella and wangled an invitation for herself and Ada for Christmas Day. But even having plans didn't help much, for she never turned on the lights of her tiny tree without having to quell the soft, seductive memories of last year at Angela and Claiborne's house. She would walk to the sliding glass door and look out at the snow-laden world and jam her hands into the pockets of her jeans and remember, remember, remember. That magical house with all its love, lights, music and family.

Family. Ah, family. It was so much the root of Catherine's unhappiness, had been all her life. She would look at Melissa and tears would gather, for that family security the child would never know, no matter how much she herself lavished her daughter with love. She fantasized about Clay coming to the door again, only this time it would be different. This time he'd say he loved her, and only her, and they'd bundle Melissa into her little blue snowsuit and when the three of them arrived at the big house it would be just like last year, only better. Catherine closed her eyes, hugging herself, smelling again the tang of newly blown-out candles, remembering soft mistletoe kisses...

But that was fantasy. Reality was making it through Christmas alone, as a single parent, with no one to place gifts beneath her lonely tree but herself.

"Let's get a tree and put it up," Clay said.

"What for?" asked Jill.

"Because it's Christmas, that's what for."

"I don't have time. If you want one, put it up yourself."

"You never seem to have time for anything around the house."

"Clay, I work eight hours a day! Besides, why cultivate interests you never intend to use?"

"Never?"

"Oh, Clay, don't start in on me now. I lost my blue cashmere sweater and I wanted to wear it tomorrow. Dammit, where could it be?"

"If you'd muck the place out once a month or so, maybe you wouldn't lose track of your things." The bedroom looked like an explosion in a Chinese laundry.

"Oh, I know!" Jill suddenly brightened. "I'll bet I took it to the cleaners last week. Clay, be a darling and run over and pick it up for me, will you?"

"I'm not your laundry boy. If you want it, go get it yourself."

She picked her way across the littered floor and cooed close to his face, "Don't be cross, darling. I just didn't think you were busy right now." When she would have teasingly inserted her glittering nail into the smile line on his cheek, he jerked his head aside.

"Jill, you never think I'm busy. You always think you're the only one who's busy."

"But, darling, I am. I'm meeting the project engineer for the first time tomorrow and I want to look my best." She tried to put him into good humor with a quick caress. But that was the third time she'd called him *darling,* and lately it had started to bother him. She used the term so loosely it sometimes stung. It reminded him of what Catherine said about the value of affection going up when it was in short supply.

"Jill, why did you want me back?" he asked abruptly.

"Darling, what a question. I was lost without you, you know that."

"Besides being *lost* without me, what else?"

"What is this, the Spanish Inquisition? How do you like this dress?" She held up a pink crepe de chine and swirled in a little side-step, eyeing him provocatively.

"Jill, I'm trying to talk to you; will you forget the damn dress?"

"Sure. It's forgotten." She dropped it negligently on the foot of the bed and turned to grab a brush and begin stroking her hair. "So talk."

"Listen, I—" He hardly knew where to begin. "I thought our life-styles, our backgrounds, our futures were so alike that we were practically made for each other. But, this—this isn't working out for me."

"Isn't working out? Clarify that for me, will you, Clay?" she asked crisply, stroking her hair all the harder.

He gestured at the room. "Jill, we're different, that's all. I have trouble living with the clutter, the meals in the restaurants, and the laundry that's never clean and the kitchen cabinets that are full of magazines!"

"I didn't think you wanted me for my domestic abilities."

"Jill, I'm willing to do my share, but I need some sense of home, do you understand that?"

"No, I'm not sure I do. It sounds to me like you're asking me to give up my career to push dust around."

"I'm not asking you to give up anything, just to give me some straight answers."

"I would if I knew exactly what it is you're asking."

Clay picked up a lace-trimmed violet petticoat from a chair and sat down wearily. He studied the expensive garment, rubbing it between his fingers. Quietly he asked, "What about kids, Jill?"

"Kids?"

Her brush stopped stroking. Clay looked up.

"A family. Do you ever want to have a family?"

She whirled on him angrily. "And you said you're not asking me to give anything up!"

"I'm not, and I'm not even talking about right away, but someday. Do you want a baby someday?"

"I've just put in all these years getting a degree; I have a future ahead of me in one of the fastest-growing fields there is, and you're talking babies?"

Without warning, Clay pictured Catherine crying because Grover's baby had died, then in the labor room with their hands together on her stomach as the contractions built; he thought of her cross-legged on the living room floor clapping Melissa's feet together, and the way she'd cried because Melissa had bumped her head.

Suddenly Jill threw the brush down. It cracked upon the dresser top, went skittering off the mirror and landed on the floor inside an abandoned high-heel pump.

"You've seen her, haven't you?"

"Who?"

"Your . . . wife." The word galled Jill.

Clay didn't even consider lying. "Yes."

"I knew it! As soon as you came in here complaining about the mess, I knew it! Did you take her to bed?"

"For God's sake." Clay stood up, turning away from her.

"Well, did you?"

"That's got nothing to do with this."

"Oh, doesn't it? Well, think again, buster, because I'm not playing second fiddle to any woman, wife or not!" Jill turned back to the mirror, picked up a fat brush and savagely began applying blush to her cheeks.

"That's part of this arrangement we have here, isn't it, Jill?"

She glared at him in the looking glass. "What is?"

"Egos, yours and mine. Part of the reason you wanted me was because you've never had to do without anything you wanted. Part of the reason I left Catherine is because I've never had to do without anything I wanted."

Her eyes glittered dangerously as she swung around to face him. "Well, we're two of a kind then, aren't we, Clay?"

"No, we're not. I thought we were, but we're not. Not anymore."

They stood with eyes locked, hers angry, his sorry, in the meadow of strewn garments, coffee cups, newspapers and makeup.

At last Jill said, "I can compete with Catherine, but I can't compete with Melissa. That's it, isn't it?"

"She's there, Jill. She exists, and I'm her father and I can't forget it. And Catherine has changed so much."

Without warning she flung the makeup brush at him and it hit him on the cheek as she yelled, "Oh, damn you! Damn you! Damn you! How dare you stand there mooning over her! If you want her so bad, what are you doing here? But once

373

you leave, don't think your half of the bed will be cold for long!"

"Jill, please, I never meant to hurt you."

"Hurt? How could you hurt me? You only hurt the one you love, isn't that how the song goes?"

When Clay left Lake Minnetonka, he drove aimlessly for hours. He headed for Minneapolis proper, circled Lake Calhoun, headed east on Lake Street past the quaint little artsy shops at the Lake Hennepin area, farther east where seedy theaters gave way to seedier used-furniture stores. He turned south, caught the strip that cut Bloomington in half and circled west again. The lights of the Radisson South split the night sky with its twenty-two stories of windows as Clay turned onto the Belt Line, unconsciously heading for Golden Valley.

He took the exit of Golden Valley Road without deciding to, and threaded through the streets that once had been his route home, passing Byerly's Supermarket where he and Catherine had first gone grocery shopping. He pulled into the lot beside the town house but let the engine idle, leaving only the parking lights on. He looked up at the sliding glass door and there, shining out onto the snowy balcony were the multi-colored lights from a Christmas tree. As he sat staring at them, they blinked out and the window grew dark. Then he put the car in gear and headed for a motel.

When Clay appeared in the doorway of the study, Claiborne looked up, tried to mask his surprise, but couldn't quite bring it off. He half rose from his chair, then settled down again behind the desk with a bald look of hope.

"Hi, Dad."

"Hello, Clay. We haven't seen you for a long time."

"Yeah, well, don't tell Mother I'm here just yet. I'd like to talk to you alone first."

"Of course, come in, come in." Claiborne removed a pair of silver-rimmed reading glasses from his nose and dropped them on the desk.

"The glasses are new."

"I've had them for a couple of months, can't get used to the damn things, though."

They both looked at the glasses. The room was still. Suddenly, as if inspired, the older man rose.

"How about a brandy?"

"No, thanks, I—"

"A Scotch?" Claiborne asked too anxiously. "Or maybe some white wine. I seem to remember that you liked white."

"Dad, please. We both know white wine isn't going to fix a damn thing."

Claiborne dropped back into his chair. A log hissed in the fire and shot a tongue of blue flame sideways. Clay sighed, wondering as he had so often recently, where to begin. He sat on the edge of the leather loveseat and pressed his thumb knuckles deep into his eyes.

"What the hell went wrong?" he finally asked. His voice was quiet and searching and pained.

"Absolutely nothing that can't be fixed," his father answered. And even before their eyes met again, their hearts seemed to drop burdens which each had borne for too long.

The telephone rang for the fifth time and Clay's hopes waned. He angled the receiver away from his ear, leaning his head back against the headboard and shut his eyes. Traffic roared past on the highway outside. He studied his stocking feet stretched out before him, his suitcases lying open, sighed, and was just about to give up when Catherine said hello.

She stood in the dark bedroom dripping bath water onto the carpet, trying to get a towel wrapped around her without dropping the receiver.

"Hello, Catherine?"

Her heart seemed to flip up into her windpipe and her hands stopped messing with the towel. It slid down off her back and she clutched it to her breast, feeling her battering heart through the terry cloth.

At last she said, "H-hello."

He heard the catch in her voice and swallowed. "It's Clay."

"Yes, I know."

"I didn't think you were home."

"I was in the tub."

The line buzzed for an interminable moment while he wondered which phone she'd picked up and what she was wearing.

"I'm sorry, I can call back."

"No!" Then she calmed herself a little. "No, but . . . can you wait a minute, Clay, while I get a robe on? I'm freezing."

"Sure, I'll hang on." And hang on he did, clutching the receiver in his damp palm while hours seemed to drag past and visions of a pink hooded robe filled his mind.

Catherine flew to the closet, dropping the towel, scrambling for her robe, frantic, impatient, fumbling, thinking, oh, my God, it's Clay, it's Clay! Oh, Lord, oh, damn, where's my robe? He'll hang up . . . Where is it? Wait, Clay, wait! I'm coming!

She tried running back to the phone and stepping into the robe at the same time, but the zipper went only halfway down the front of the thing, and she stumbled, arriving at the phone breathless.

"Clay?" he heard, and the sound of her anxiousness made him smile and feel warm inside.

"I'm here."

She released a pent-up breath, got the zipper up and perched on the edge of the bed in the semidarkness, with only the light from the closet easing around the corner into the room.

"Sorry it took so long."

He figured it had probably taken seven seconds. Still, he was afraid now to ask what he'd called to ask, afraid she'd turn him down, sick at the thought that she might.

"How are you?" he asked instead.

She pictured his face, the face she'd been searching crowds for ever since she'd last seen it, pictured his hair which she'd imagined she'd seen on hundreds of strangers, his eyes, his mouth. Long moments passed before she admitted, "Not so happy since you were here last."

He swallowed, surprised at her answer when he'd expected the usual trite, "Fine."

"Me either."

It was incredible how two such simple words managed to slam the breath out of her. Frantically she searched for something to say, but her mind remained filled only with his face, and she wondered where he was and what he was wearing.

"How's Melissa's head?" he asked.

"Oh, fine. It's all healed up, no worse for the wear."

They both laughed nervously, but the strained sound ended abruptly at both ends of the wire, followed by silence again. Clay raised one knee, propped an elbow on it and kneaded the bridge of his nose, his heart thundering so loud it seemed she must hear it at her end.

"Catherine, I was wondering what you're doing tomorrow night."

She clutched the phone in both hands. "To-tomorrow night? But that's Christmas Eve."

"Yes, I know."

Clay quit kneading his eyes, took up pressing the crease of one trouser leg between his fingers instead. "I was wondering if you and Melissa have plans."

Catherine's eyes slid shut. She raised the mouthpiece up to her forehead so he couldn't hear her jerky breathing. She got control.

"No, not for tomorrow night. We're going to Uncle Frank and Aunt Ella's on Christmas Day, but nothing for tomorrow." Up went the receiver to her forehead again.

"Would you like to come out to the house with me?"

She put her hand on the top of her head to keep it from leaving her body, struggled to sound calm.

"Out to your parents' house?"

"Yes."

He felt physically sick during the interminable moments while she thought, What about Jill? Where is Jill? I told you not to call me unless it was forever.

"Where are you, Clay?" she asked, so quietly he had to strain to hear the words.

"I'm in a motel."

"A motel?"

"Alone."

Joy sluiced through every vein of her body. Her throat and eyes felt flooded while she sat there gripping the phone like some babbling idiot.

377

"Catherine?" His voice cracked as he said it.

"Yes, I'm here," she got out.

In a stranger's voice he managed, "For Chrissake, answer me, will you?" And she remembered how Clay swore when he was scared.

"Yes," she whispered, and slid down with a thump onto the floor.

"What?"

"Yes," she said, louder, smiling great-big.

The line grew silent for a long, long time, with only the sound of some distant electronic bleeps making music in their ears, then disappearing.

"Where are you?" he asked then, wishing he were with her now.

"I'm in the bedroom, sitting on the floor beside the bed."

"Is Melissa asleep?"

"Yes, for a long time."

"Has she got the koala bear with her?"

"Yes," Catherine whispered, "it's in the crib by her head."

The line went quiet once more. After a long time Clay said, "I'm going back to work with Dad, as soon as possible."

"Oh, Clay . . ."

She heard him laugh, but it was a deeply emotional laugh, as if it were very hard to bring from his throat.

"Oh, Cat, you were right, you were so right."

"I was only guessing."

This time when he laughed it was less strained, then she heard him sigh.

"Listen, I've got to get some sleep. I didn't get much last night or the night before that or the night before that."

"Me either."

"I'll pick you up at five or so?"

"We'll be ready."

Silence roared between them again, a long, quivering silence that said as much as the soft words which followed:

"Good night, Catherine."

"Good night, Clay."

And again, silence, while each waited for the other to hang up first.

"Good night, I said," he said.

"So did I."

"Then let's do it together."

"Do what together?"

She never knew before that you could hear a smile.

"That too. But later. For now, just hang up so I can get some sleep."

"Okay, on three, then?"

"One . . . two . . . three."

This time they hung up together.

But they were both sadly mistaken if they thought they'd get much sleep.

Chapter 31

THE NEXT DAY crawled. Catherine felt light-headed, at times giddy, almost removed from herself. Passing a mirror, she found herself staring at her reflection long and assessingly before covering her cheeks with both hands, closing her eyes and reveling in the heartbeat that seemed to extend into every nerve ending of her body, its cadence fast-tripping. She opened her eyes and warned herself this might be a false alarm. Maybe just Clay's way of seeing Melissa, giving his parents a chance to see her, too, during the holiday. But then Catherine would remember his voice on the phone, and she knew somehow this was what she'd been dreaming of. Her thoughts flew to the oncoming evening. Hurry, hurry!

Finally, to kill time, she bundled Melissa into the car and went out shopping for something new to wear. She moved through the crowds of last-minuters in a thoroughly changed state from the previous day. She smiled at strangers. She hummed along with piped-in carols. She was eminently patient when forced to wait behind slow-moving lines at cash registers. Once she even spoke to an older man whose temper was on edge, whose face was red and quivery and impatient. A new feeling of ebullience lifted Catherine as she saw his impatience dissolve beneath her own good spirits. And she thought, see what love can do?

Back at home she put Melissa down for a nap and took a leisurely bath in an explosion of bubbles. Emerging from the tub, she stood before the wide vanity mirror blotting her skin. She felt giddily gay, childish and womanly all at once. She made a moue at her reflection, then struck a seductive pose with the towel partially shielding her nudity, then tried a different pose, a different facial expression. She leaned nearer the mirror, tugging tendrils of hair out of the hastily secured topknot, giving herself a kittenish look with loose wisps at her temples and the back of her neck. She wet her lips, allowed them to fall slightly open, lowered her lids to a smoky expression, and breathed, "Hello, Clay." Then she tried standing with her back to the mirror, looking over one shoulder, saying impishly, "Hi, Clay." Next she turned, slung the towel around her neck, its ends covering the rosy peaks of her breasts, put her hands on her bare hips and said sexily, "Whaddya say, Clay-boy?"

But suddenly she dropped the charade; she was none of these characters. She was not a little girl anymore, she was a woman. What was happening in her life was real, and she must present only the genuine Catherine to Clay. The real Catherine dropped the towel at her feet. She stood straight and tall, studying her body, her face, her hair. She took up the bottle of lightly scented lotion she'd splurged on that morning, her eyes never leaving her reflection as she poured some within her palm and began applying it to her long, supple arms, her shoulders, her neck, circling it and reaching as far onto her back as she could. She cupped her hand for another cool, sleek helping, its smell—the scent she knew Clay loved—all around her now in the warm, steamy bathroom. She rubbed it into her stomach, up the cove between her ribs, her eyes sliding closed as her palms slipped over her breasts, feeling the vaguely welcome discomfort at touching the nipples puckered into gem-hard points. Standing there touching herself, she thought of Clay, of the night ahead. I want you, Clay, she thought, I've wanted you for so long. She imagined it was Clay's hands rubbing her breasts. Her eyelids fluttered open and she took more lotion, watched her palms rub slowly together before she raised one foot, resting it on the vanity, pointing her toes as she spread the scented coolness from the arched top of the foot up the calf, behind the knee, thigh, over the buttock, the sheltered spot between her legs. I'm wanton, she thought. Then, No, I'm a woman, with a woman's needs. The scent Clay loved was all over her now.

Slowly she took the combs from her hair and began brushing it, remembering that night of their blind date, then the night the girls at Horizons had played handmaiden. That was the night of her second date with Clay. She took as much care now with her toilette as the girls had taken that night. She dressed in the minuscule bra and panties that Clay had never seen on their wedding night. She worked over her makeup until it was a subtle work of art. But she kept her hair loose, simple, lightly curled back from her face much as she wore it when she first met Clay.

The new dress was of pale plum crepe de Chine, a wrap-around that dropped from lightly gathered shoulders to the hem in an easy looseness. It was collarless, leaving a V of skin exposed at the neck. When she tied the string-belt, the dress gained shape, accenting her hollow-hipped thinness. She buttoned the cuffs at her wrists, then stood back to study herself. She pressed her palms to her dancing stomach, then brushed back a wayward wisp of hair. The movement stirred the scent of Charlie which was trapped now in the fabric of the new dress. Gold loops for her ears, a simple, short chain that fell only to the hollow of her throat, and sling-back shoes of black patent. She chose them because they were the highest she had, knowing how heartily Clay approved of a woman's foot in high heels.

It struck Catherine that she was, without a doubt, trying to be alluring to Clay, and for a moment she felt guilty. But then Melissa called, in her after-nap gibberish, and Catherine hurried to get the baby ready.

Clay had gone out and bought a whole new outfit as well. But now, on his way to Catherine's, he wondered for the tenth time whether the silk tie looked too formal. He wondered if he'd appear to be a spit-combed, nervous schoolboy, all trussed up and tightly knotted this way. What the hell was the matter with him anyway? He'd never had the vaguest doubt about choosing his clothing before. But as he sat at a red light, Clay twisted the rearview mirror so he could study the tie once more. He yanked the Windsor knot halfway down, then changed his mind and slipped it back into place. He glanced at his hair, smoothed a palm over it, although not a filament was out of place. Someone behind him honked the horn and he muttered a curse and proceeded through the green light. Suddenly, as if just remembering, he withdrew a tape from the deck, found another and put it in the track, filling the car with the music of The Lettermen. Too obvious! he reprimanded himself, and tucked The Lettermen out of sight again.

With more than a half hour to spare, Catherine was all ready. She pictured Clay, somewhere out there getting prepared to come for her, wondered what he was feeling, what he was thinking. Melissa seemed to pick up her mother's distraction and capitalized on it, getting into things she knew she wasn't supposed to touch: the tree decorations, the knobs of the television, the philodendron on the coffee table. Finally, unnerved further by constantly pulling Melissa away from trouble, Catherine deposited her in the playpen, and continued her pacing without interference.

The bell rang.

Twice, let him ring twice, she scolded her impatient feet, while outside, Clay crammed his hand into his coat pocket to keep from ringing again too soon.

What should I say, she wondered wildly.

What should I say, he wondered frantically.

The door opened and she stood there in a loosely belted thing that made her look willowy and wonderful.

Snow fell upon the shoulders of Clay's rich, brown leather topcoat.

"Merry Christmas," he said, his eyes on her face while he took in details of her slender feet arched into high-heeled shoes, and the way the dress draped over her hips.

"Merry Christmas," she answered, smiling a small, nervous smile, stepping aside with a hand still on the doorknob to let him pass into the house. He turned around to watch her close the door, letting his eyes travel down to the backs of her calves, then up to the hair on her shoulders. When she met his eyes he said, "Nice dress."

"Thank you. It's new. I . . . well, I spent a little of your money on it."

Why did you say that! she scolded herself, but then he was smiling, saying, "I heartily approve, especially since I did the same thing."

"You did?"

"Christmas present for myself." He opened his topcoat to give her a brief glimpse of herringbone tweed the color of coffee with cream in it.

"In browns, of course."

"Of course."

"But then you always did look your best in browns." The entry suddenly seemed to grow too small, hemming them in, and Catherine moved to lead the way up to the living room, chattering, "Melissa's wearing a new dress, too, one your mother gave her that she just grew into. Come and see her."

"Hey, she'll outshine us both," Clay said right behind her. "Hi, Melissa." And for once Melissa didn't cry at the sight of him.

Catherine stooped and lifted the child, turning with her on her arm, carefully avoiding Clay's eyes as she said, "Can you say hi to Daddy, Melissa?" Their baby only gazed at Clay with bright, unblinking eyes. Catherine whispered something Clay couldn't make out and nudged Melissa's little hand. Still staring, the baby opened and closed her chubby fingers once.

"That's hi," Catherine interpreted, and briefly met Clay's pleased smile. Then she sat down on the davenport and began stuffing Melissa's hands and feet into a blue snowsuit. "Clay, would it be all right if we took my car, then we could take the playpen along."

"We won't need a playpen. Mother had one of the bedrooms redone into a nursery."

Startled, Catherine looked up. "She did?"

Clay nodded.

"When?"

"Last summer."

"She never told me."

"She never had a chance."

"Does she . . . I mean, do they know we're coming tonight, Melissa and I?"

"No. I didn't want to disappoint them if it didn't turn out."

Like a scene from a long-remembered favorite movie, the car moved through the streets while along the way streetlights eased on, signaling the arrival of dark. Catherine was filled with such an odd combination of emotions. The peaceful feeling of being again where she belonged was combined with the breath-halting sense of anticipation leading ever closer to a place where she belonged even more. She counted the hours until the end of the evening.

Clay cast careful glances her way. Christmas did things to a person, he thought, smiling appreciatively at the sight of Melissa reaching for knobs on the dash while Catherine pulled the tiny hands away time and again, and gently scolded. He glanced at Catherine's profile once more, his nostrils almost flaring in the light, powdery fragrance emanating from her, and he wondered how he'd make it till the end of the night when he could get her alone again.

The driveway curved to meet them, and Catherine couldn't control the small gasp. "I've missed it," she said, almost to herself. An expression of pleasure tipped up the corners of her mouth beguilingly.

They swept up in front of the door and Clay was around the car, reaching for Melissa, taking her up and into the crook of his arm, then taking Catherine's elbow as she stepped from the car. They stood for a moment in the mellow glow, splashing their faces from the carriage lanterns. The streamers of a red ribbon made a light tapping sound as they flicked against the bricks in a light, crisp wind. That wind lifted Clay's hair from his forehead, then set it gently back down as Catherine gazed at him. It toyed with the gold hoops at her ears, sending them swinging against her jawline where he wanted to bury his lips. But that would have to wait.

"Let's ring the bell," he said puckishly.

"Let's," she seconded.

When Angela opened the door she was already saying, "I wondered when—" But the words faded and she placed delicate fingers over her lips.

"Do you have room for three more?" Clay asked.

Angela didn't move for the longest time. Her eyes grew too sparkly, going from the smiling face of Catherine, in the shelter of Clay's arm, to that of Melissa, in his other arm.

"Angela," Catherine said softly. And suddenly the older woman in the pale yellow dress moved to encompass all three as best she could, unable to quite contend with everything at once, with the tears threatening to spill over her lids, with getting them all inside, beckoning Claiborne, taking Melissa— blue snowsuit and all—getting kissed by Clay and by Catherine.

When Claiborne saw who it was, he was as excited as Angela. There were more hugs, interrupted by a surprised Inella who stopped short and broke into a pleased smile at the sight of the newest arrivals and was immediately drawn to Melissa who was sitting on her grandmother's lap on the steps, having her snowsuit removed.

The tap of Elizabeth Forrester's cane announced her arrival from the living room. She cast a haughty eye over the assemblage in the foyer, stated to nobody in particular, "High time somebody came to their senses around here," and tapped her way back to the dining room, where she ladled herself a cup of eggnog, added a tot of rum, then mumbled, "Oh, why the bloody heck not," and tipped up the brandy bottle again with a satisfied smile.

The mistletoe was there again, everywhere. Catherine tried neither to avoid it nor seek it, but to ignore it, which was virtually impossible, for each time she looked up she found Clay's eyes seeking her across the room. Those eyes need not stray up to remind her of mistletoe. All evening she felt as if she wore a sprig of it in her hair, so suggestive were the glances they exchanged. It was odd, Clay staying away from her, always eyeing her across the room that way. Time and again she turned from conversation on which she had difficulty concentrating to the tug of his eyes on her back. And always, she would be the first to look away. The food was laid out upon the buffet and they found themselves elbow to elbow moving down the serving line.

"Are you having a good time?" he asked.

"Wonderful. Are you?"

He thought about answering truthfully, No, I'm miserable, but lied instead. "Wonderful, yes."

"Aren't you going to eat anything?"

He glanced at his plate, realized he was halfway past the food and his plate was still empty. She stabbed a Swedish meatball out of the wine sauce and dropped it on his plate.

"A little sustenance," she said, matter-of-factly, never raising her eyes as she moved on to the next chafing dish. He looked at the forlorn piece of meat all alone on the plate and smiled. She knew as well as he did what kind of sustenance he needed tonight.

Melissa let it be known immediately that she resented being left in this strange room, in this strange crib, all alone. Catherine sighed and went back into the room, and immediately her daughter stopped crying.

"Melissa, Mommy's going to be right here all the time. You're so tired, sweetheart, won't you lie down?"

She laid Melissa down, covered her, and hadn't even made it as far as the door before Melissa was standing, clutching the rail and crying pitifully.

"Shame on you, punkin," Catherine said, relenting and picking the baby up again, "you're going to hurt Grandma's feelings after she made this beautiful room all for you." It was beautiful. It had all the charm Angela could so easily bestow on everything she touched: bright patches of gingham checks in pastel pink, blue and yellow, blended skillfully into tiered curtains, patchwork comforter and an adorable padded rocker. Turning around to study the room in the glow of the small night-light, Catherine stopped short at the sight of Clay standing in the doorway.

"Is she giving you trouble?"

"It's a strange room, you know."

"Yes, I know," he said, crossing toward them to stand behind Catherine, talking to Melissa over her shoulder. "How about some music then, Melissa? Would you like that better?" And then, to Catherine, "Mother is starting the carols now. Why not bring her back downstairs? Maybe the music would make her sleepy."

Catherine turned to glance past Melissa's blond head at Clay. The look on his face made her pulse race. She realized they were alone, the sounds of the piano and voices drifted up to them from below. Clay moved, extending a hand to touch her . . .

But it was Melissa he reached for, and in the next instant the weight was gone from Catherine's arm.

"Come on," he said, taking Melissa, but never pulling his eyes away from Catherine's, "I'll take her. You've had her all night."

Melissa fell asleep in Clay's arms during the singing, but when she was returned to the crib, her eyes flew open instantly and she began to whimper.

"It's no use, Clay," Catherine whispered. "She's exhausted, but she won't give up."

"Should we take her home then?"

Something in the way he said the word *home*, something in the beckoning, wistful tone of his voice made the blood clamor in Catherine's head.

"Yes, I think we'd better."

"You get her dressed and I'll make our excuses."

All the way to the town house they didn't utter a word to each other. He switched on the radio and found that every station was playing Christmas carols. To the lull of them, Melissa at last fell soundly asleep in her mother's lap.

It was as if Catherine had played this scene before, putting Melissa to bed, then coming down to find Clay waiting for her. He was sitting on a swivel stool this time, with his coat still on. He had one foot propped on a rung of the opposite stool, an elbow leaning nonchalantly on the edge of the counter. Something caught Catherine's eye, something he twirled between thumb and forefinger, something green. Silently he twirled

388

it—back and forth, back and forth—and it held her gaze like the watch of a hypnotist. Then the thing stopped and she realized it was a sprig of mistletoe he held by its stem.

Staring at it, she stammered, "Th-the baby's . . ."

"Forget the baby," he ordered softly.

"Would you like a drink or something?" she asked stupidly.

"Would you?"

Her eyes were drawn to his, to the level, unsmiling study in gray. The silence hummed, enveloping her momentarily. Then without moving a muscle, he said, "You know what I want, Catherine."

She looked at her feet. "Yes." She felt as if she'd turned into a pillar of salt. Why didn't he move? Why didn't he come and get her then?

"Do you know how many times you've turned me away, though?"

"Yes, eight," she gulped.

The blood leaped wildly to her face as she admitted it. She raised her eyes to him, and he read in them the cost of each of those times. And in the silence the mistletoe again began twirling.

"I wouldn't care to make it nine," he said at last.

"Neither would I."

"Then meet me halfway, Catherine," he invited, stretching out a hand, palm-up, waiting.

"You know what my conditions are."

"Yes, I know." He held the hand as before, in invitation.

"Then—then . . ." She felt like she was choking. Didn't he understand yet?

"Then say it?"

"Yes, say it first," she begged, staring at his long, beautiful fingers, the palm that waited.

"Come here so I can say it up close." It was almost whispered.

Slowly, slowly, she reached to touch the tips of his fingers with her own. But he did not move them until she herself had traveled a share of the distance, telling him what she, too, wanted, as her cold palm slid over his warm one. His fingers closed over hers in slow motion and he pulled her toward him more slowly yet. Her heart slammed against the walls of her chest and her eyes drifted to his as he reeled her close, settling her there against his open legs, his one foot still propped wide onto the rung of that other stool. There was no question then about what it was he wanted. His heat and hardness spoke for itself. He pressed her firmly, securely against his loins, then closed his eyes as his lips opened over hers. The mistletoe grew lost in the long sweep of her hair. She felt his hand, warm and forceful against her buttocks, holding her tight while his warmth and hardness branded her stomach. His kiss became all seeking and fevered, a wild crushing of tongue and lips, and she felt their teeth meet, then tasted blood, but had no thought for whose it was. His hands came one to each side of her face, and he jerked her fiercely away from his lips, looked into her eyes with a tortured expression.

"I love you, Cat, I love you. Why did it take me so long to realize it?"

"Oh, Clay, promise me you won't ever leave me again, so I know what I'm getting into."

"I promise, I promise, I promi—"

She stopped his words by flattening herself against him with such force that he grunted. He pulled the whole long, supple, welcome length of her against him. She felt his raised knee rubbing possessively against her hip and wound her arms around his neck, holding him tenaciously. Then she felt herself hoisted off the floor as he swiveled the stool around and in a single motion half leaned, half fell, pressing her back against the edge of the counter. But it cut into her shoulders, so she pushed him back, turning him, taking him with her on a brief journey together on that swiveling stool until she stood again on the floor between his open knees. They kissed, warm against each other, and somehow while they did it, the stool began twisting back and forth, back and forth, almost like the mistletoe had done twirling earlier in his fingers. And each time the stool moved, Clay's erect body brushed provocatively against hers while she rose up on tiptoe to meet it, brushing harder each time. She felt his hand leave her hair and seek the knot of her belt. Dimly she thought about helping him, but leaned against his loose hold instead, pleasured at the feel of his hand there between them, then at the touch of the belt as it glided down

390

the backs of her legs to the floor. One-handed, he opened the dress, touching the skin of her throat first with his fingers, then with his lips, then moving lower, lower, lower, until his hand lay warm on the lowest part of her stomach. He backed away to look at her while he wrested the dress from her shoulders, and when he saw the brief garments beneath, he groaned and buried his face in the band of bareness between bra and panties, wetting the skin there with his tongue.

"Did you know I wore these on my wedding night?" she asked in a husky voice that sounded strangely unlike her own.

"Did you?" His eyes burned into hers, his hands traced the lotus petals along the top of the bra. "But tonight will be our wedding night." Then both of his arms went around her, and she felt her bra go tight, then loose, then fall away in his hands. His head swooped forward while hers dropped back. His kiss fell upon her bare breast, and a faint growl sounded in her arched throat as his tongue circled the nipple, then the edges of his teeth rode lightly against the cockled point. Strangling in delight, she threaded her fingers in his soft hair, directing him to her other hungering breast. Carried away, his teeth tugged too hard and she flinched, her nostrils distended. With a sound of apology deep in his throat, he suckled more lightly. Deep in her body, sensations sluiced and impatiently she tugged at the shoulders of the leather topcoat he still wore. Without taking his mouth from her flesh, he freed his arms, let her take the coat from his shoulders and drop it, unheeded, behind him, followed by his sport coat. Nuzzling each other, dropping kisses wherever they chose to fall, he worked the knot from his tie while she unbuttoned his shirt. Then it joined the rest on the floor. One-armed, he brought her back where she belonged, with her naked breasts against his bare chest. He eased away from her then, to watch the sight of his hands cupping her breasts. He flattened one hand against her stomach and ran it down inside the front of her bikini until he touched her intimately.

"Do you want me to take the rest off?" he asked, nuzzling her neck, tonguing her skin there, even tasting her perfume now.

"We're in the middle of the kitchen, Clay."

"I don't give a damn. Should I take it off or will you?"

"This was your idea," she whispered coquettishly, smiling against his hair.

"Like hell." But in one swift motion he had her panty hose and bikini down to her knees, then he picked her up effortlessly and set her on the edge of the counter, hooking a stool and sending it out of the way with a foot. He knelt down, raised his eyes to hers as he removed first one high heel, then the other, then with a sweep of both hands had her last two garments lying in a soft heap on the floor. He moved up next to the counter and she raised her arms, looped them around his neck, opened her knees and looped them around his waist and said, "Take me upstairs to our bedroom." He pulled her off the counter until she was astraddle his waist, her ankles locked behind him. Her naked flesh was pressed against his navel and the smell of her perfume was like a cloud about them as they walked that way, kissing, upstairs to the bedroom. He stood by the lamp and said, "Turn it on." She let go of his neck with one hand and reached.

Standing beside the bed he whispered "Let go" into her mouth.

"Never," she whispered back.

"Then how can I get my pants off?"

Without another word she unhooked her ankles and fell backward with a bounce onto the mattress, lying there watching him while he unbuckled his belt, unzipped his trousers, never taking his eyes off her. When he was naked, he knelt above her on one knee, his hands on either side of her head.

"Catherine, I know I'm a year and a half late asking this, but are you going to get pregnant out of this?"

"But if you'd asked that Fourth of July, we wouldn't be here now, would we?"

"Cat, I just don't want you pregnant for a while. I want to enjoy you flat and thirsty for a while first."

"Flat and thirsty?"

He realized he'd given himself away, so he leaned his head down to kiss her and stop her questions. She turned her mouth aside.

"What does that mean, flat and thirsty?"

"Nothing." He nudged around at her lips, trying to get her to stop talking and touch him.

"You answer me and I'll answer you," she said, avoiding another pass of his lips against hers.

If she got mad at him now, he thought, he'd never forgive himself for opening up his big mouth. But he had to answer.

"Okay. I read your diary. All that stuff we did with the wine—that's what I meant by flat and thirsty."

She burned now, but not with anger, with embarrassment and sensuality. "Clay, I feel like I'm dying of thirst right now, and believe me, I won't get pregnant."

She could feel his muscles quivering on each side of her head. His voice was racked as he asked. "Then how long do I have to hang here before you touch me?"

No longer, she thought, no longer, Clay, and reached to touch him lightly with the backs of her fingers, measuring his ardor with feather-strokes that robbed him of breath. The months of want drifted into oblivion at her first caress. The days of searching had their answer. Her hand explored, enclosed, stroked, cupped and thrilled, until Clay's elbows turned to water. He collapsed beside her, reaching, seeking her warm skin. Her stomach was a little softer now, but the old hollows were back below her hipbones. Her thigh was smooth and firm, lifting at his touch to free the spot his hand sought. As he moved toward it, her hand fell still upon his tumescence. Sensing her urgency, her expectancy, he lay his head upon her breast and listened to the thunder of her heart beneath his ear as he touched her depths for the first time. It thundered there in double time, and he could feel it lifting the weight of his head with each beat. Outwardly she lay limp and passive, but her heartbeat told the truth. He moved his fingers once, and she lurched and gulped for air. He rolled half over her, kissing her eyes, her temple, the corner of her mouth, her lips which lay slack, as if what was happening to the inside of her body robbed her of the will to do anything but drift in the grip of pleasure. He aroused her with butterfly touches, bent again to cover her breasts with kisses, sliding his lips over her stomach, feeling it rise with each lift of her hips. Low animal sounds scraped from her throat, then his name, repeated as an accent

393

to each thrust she could no longer control.

He spoke her name—Cat—over and over, letting her soar, experiencing a new high, a sharing of purpose with her as he brought her near climax and sent her shivering. This, he knew, was what he had not given her the first time, and he meant to make it up to her all the other times of their lives.

"Let it happen, Cat," he whispered hoarsely.

But suddenly he knew he had to share the sensation to its fullest. Easing onto her, he sought and found, entered and plunged, murmuring soft sounds; lovesounds that took on their own meaning.

She shuddered and arched first, and he was close behind her, so close that the film of dampness dried from their skins at the same time.

Into her hair he spoke weakly, "Ah, Cat, it was good for me."

"For me too."

He lay his palm on her stomach, then ran it lower, let it rest peacefully upon her body, then just barely inside it. She could feel his jaw move in the hollow of her shoulder as he spoke.

"Cat, remember in the hospital when the nurse showed us the way the contractions build up?"

"Mmm-hmm," she murmured, toying sleepily with his hair.

"It felt the same way inside you a minute ago."

"It did?"

"It made me think of how close pleasure and pain are. It even seems as if the same things happen in your body during the moments of your greatest pleasure and your greatest pain. Isn't that odd?"

"I never thought about it before, but then I never—"

He raised up, leaned on an elbow and looked down into her face. He touched a lock of hair, easing it back from her forehead.

"Was that your first time, Cat?"

Suddenly timid, she surrounded him, hugged him too close for him to see her face.

"Yes," she admitted.

"Hey." Gently he removed her tight grip so he could look at her again. "After all that we've been through, are you getting modest on me?"

"How could I possibly claim modesty now?"

"Just don't ever be afraid to talk to me about anything, okay? If you don't trust me with the things that bother you, how can I help you? All that business about the past and your feelings for Herb, do you see that we seem to have conquered that already, together?"

"Ah, Clay." She sighed and leaned against him, promising herself she'd never withhold her feelings from him again. A short time later she said, "Did you know that I started falling in love with you while you were courting me at Horizons?"

"That long ago?"

"Oh, Clay, how could I help it? All those girls panting after you and telling me how perfect you were, and you coming by in your sexy little Corvette, with your sexy clothes and that sexy smile and all those sterling good manners of yours to offset all that sexiness. God, you drove me crazy."

"Idiot girl," he laughed. "Do you know how much time you could have saved if you'd just once let on what you were feeling?"

"But I was so scared. What if you didn't feel the same way about me? I'd have been shattered."

"Yet every time I made advances I felt like you couldn't stand me."

"Clay, I told you that first night that my dad made me come to your house—marriage had to be for love only. Please, let's always be this way, like we are tonight. Let's be good to each other and promise all those things that we never really promised in that trumped-up marriage ceremony."

Lying naked, with their limbs entwined, secure in each other's love, they sealed those vows at last.

"I promise them, Cat."

"I do, too, Clay."

On Christmas morning Melissa woke them up, babbling and thumping her heels on the crib. Clay came awake groggily, stretched and felt bare skin on the other side of the bed. He turned to study the woman who lay on her stomach, sleeping beneath a swirl of blond hair.

He started to creep from bed noiselessly.

"Where you going?" came a voice from under the hair.

"To get Melissa and bring her in with us, okay?"

"Okay, but don't be gone long, huh?"

They came back together, the one in aqua-blue footed pajamas, the other one in nothing. When Catherine rolled over, Clay plopped Melissa down beside her, then got in too.

"Hi, Lissy-girl. Got a kiss for Mommy?"

Melissa leaned over and sucked her mother's chin, her version of a kiss.

Clay watched with a glad expression on his face.

Catherine looked at his tousled blond hair, his smiling gray eyes and asked, "Hi, Clay-boy, got a kiss for Mommy?"

"More than one," he said, smiling. "This is one child who's going to learn early the value of touching."

He leaned across the baby then, to give his wife what she wanted.

Forsaking All Others

With love
to my friend
Dorothy Garlock

Chapter 1

"NORTH STAR AGENCY," answered the voice on the phone.

Allison Scott crossed her ankles, rested a heel on her desk, and leaned back in her ancient, creaking swivel chair. "I need the sexiest man you've ever seen and I need him right now," she said, smiling.

"Hey, who doesn't?" came the glib reply. "Allison, is that you?"

"Yes, Mattie, it's me, and I mean it. I need the man to end all men. He's got to be handsome, honed, with hair the color of waving wheat, blue eyes—but I could get by with brown—a jaw like Dick Tracy's and a nose like the hand of a sundial, a body like—"

"Hey, hey, hey! Hold on there, girl. What are you using him for anyway, a screen test?"

"Not quite. A book cover."

"*A what!*"

"A book cover." Allison's voice became exhilarated. "I got the offer about a month ago, and I said I'd see what I thought after reading the book. It came in yesterday's mail, and I took it home last night, read it from cover to cover, and decided to give it a try. I just called New York and—oh, Mattie, this could be the break I've been waiting for. They'll be sending a contract within the week. Now all I need from you is Mister Right for the cover."

"Let me get his vital stats on paper and look through the

files and see what I can come up with. Okay, shoot."

Allison's feet hit the floor as she reached for the manuscript, flipped to the right page, and followed the words with her finger. "Blond, blue eyed, virile, handsome, about twenty-five years old, six feet, sinewy...God, Mattie, can you believe they really believe men who look like that are worth anything?" Allison slapped the manuscript closed in disgust.

Mattie's voice came back critically. "Were you hired as a book critic or cover artist?"

"All right, I deserved that. It's really none of my business what these star-struck authors put between the covers. This is a chance I've been waiting for, and if they want me to give them a picture that'll convince the readers people fall in love at first sight and live happily ever after, that's what I'll give 'em. You just send me the raw material and watch me!"

"Okay. So describe the woman."

"Ah, let's see..." Again a slender finger scanned a page. "Oh, here it is. Early twenties, ginger-colored hair, blue eyes, tall, willowy. And listen, Mattie, hair color is important, seems the readers tend to notice if it's wrong, so shoulder length and ginger, right?"

"Ginger it is. Let me see what I can dig up, and I'll get the photos over to you in tomorrow's mail."

"Okay, Mattie, I appreciate it."

"Hey, Allison?"

"Yeah?"

A brief silence hummed before Mattie asked guardedly, "Is he back yet?"

Allison Scott's back wilted. Her elbow dropped to the desk, and she rubbed her forehead as if to ease a sudden shooting pain. "No, he's not. I'm really not expecting him anymore, Mattie."

"Have you heard from him?"

"Not a word."

Allison thought she could hear Mattie sigh. "I'm sorry I asked. Forgive me, huh?"

Allison sighed herself. "Mattie, it's not your fault Jason Ederlie turned out to be a first-class bastard."

"I know it, but I shouldn't have asked."

"My skin's gotten a lot tougher since he disappeared."

"I know that, too. That's what worries me."

"What do you mean by that!"

Mattie backed off at Allison's sharp tone. "Nothing. Forget I said it, okay? The glossies will be in tomorrow's mail."

The click at the other end of the line ended any further questions Allison might have posed, but her ebullient mood was gone, snuffed away at the mention of Jason Ederlie's name. Pushing his memory aside, she swiveled abruptly, rocked to her feet, and thrust belligerent hands deep into the pockets of her khaki-colored jeans. Standing with feet spread, she stared out the ceiling-to-floor windows that overlooked downtown Minneapolis. The building was old and drafty but spacious and bright, thus well suited for a photography studio. At one time it had housed the offices of a flour-milling company that had long ago turned to carpets, subdued lighting, well-insulated walls, and piped-in music.

But as Allison stared out unseeingly, the only music she heard was that of aged water pipes overhead, the clang of the expanding metal in ancient radiators that heated the place— but never quite adequately, it seemed.

The January cold had condensed moisture on the north-facing panes. Now and then a rivulet streamed down and joined the drift of ice that had formed at the corners of the small panes. With the edge of a clenched fist Allison cleared the center of a square, but the view beyond remained foggy.

Her fist slid down the cold glass, then rapped hard against an icy frame.

"Damn you, Jason, damn you!" she exclaimed aloud. Her forehead fell to her arm and tears trickled down her cheek as she indulged in the memory of his face, his voice, his body, all those things she had learned to trust.

Abruptly her head jerked up and she tossed it defiantly, sending her hair flying back in a rusty swirl of obstinance. She dragged the back of one wrist across her nose, sniffed, dashed the errant tears from her eyes, and swallowed the lump of memory in her throat. "I'll get over you, Jason Ederlie, if it's the last thing I do!" she promised the empty studio, the sky-line, herself. Then Allison Scott turned back to the balm of work.

* * *

It was a simple book, an uncomplicated story of a man and woman who meet on vacation on Sanibel Island, look at each other while sparks fly, make their way into each other's arms within fifty pages, out of them by a hundred, right their misconceptions some fifty pages later, and regain bliss together as the book ends. Perhaps because the hero's description matched that of Jason Ederlie, Allison had found herself lost in the pages. Maybe that, too, was the reason she'd at first been reluctant to accept the contract to do the cover art, for without Jason to pose, something would be missing. But realizing what a boon it would mean to her career and her finances, she'd accepted, even though it galled Allison that women readers sopped up such Cinderellaism as if it really happened.

Allison Scott knew better. Cinderella endings were found only in paperback romances on the shelves of the grocery store.

At the end of the day, reaching for a can of spaghetti and meatballs at the PDQ Market, she felt the bluntness of that fact all too fully, for she hated the thought of walking into the emptiness awaiting her at home, now that Jason was gone.

Home. She thought about the word as she drove from downtown Minneapolis around "the lakes," as they were loosely called. There were five of them—Calhoun, Harriet, Nokomis, Lake of the Isles, and Cedar—forming the heart of the beautiful "City of the Lakes." Allison lived on the west side of Lake of the Isles, in a second-story apartment in a regal old house that had been well preserved since the turn of the century.

She could barely see the first-floor windows as she turned in the driveway and threaded her Chevy van to the detached garage at the rear, for the snow had been inordinately heavy this year, and the banks beside the drive were shoulder high. She closed the garage door and glanced at the frozen surface of the lake. Shivering, she tucked her chin deep into the collar of her warm jacket as she headed for the private stairway running up the outside of the house.

Home. She turned the key but dreaded going in, a feeling she'd been unable to overcome during the last six weeks. As

404

she moved inside and shut the door on the subzero temperature, her eyes scanned the living room that she'd carefully decorated to bring a little bit of summer into the Minnesota winters—gleaming hardwood floors, the old kind they don't lay any more; the Scandinavian import rug she'd searched so long to find, with its clever blending of greens, yellow, and white in an unimposing oblique swirl of design; airy rattan and wicker furniture with fat cushions of a green-and-yellow print that brought to mind warm, tropical rain forests; a multitude of potted palms, scheffleras, philodendrons, and more, flourishing on windowsills, tables, and on a small white stepladder in front of four long, narrow windows; lime-and-white Roman shades of woven wood that added to the tropical air; a pair of French doors leading to the summer sun porch overlooking the lake; a hanging lamp with white wicker shade that matched the floor lamp behind her favorite renovated wicker rocker with its rolled arms and thick pillows. And everywhere an impression of light and space.

Yes, it was like a breath of summer. Oh, how she'd loved this place . . . until Jason.

But now whenever she returned it was only to remember him here, slouched in the enfolding basket chair that hung from the ceiling, in one corner, his heel resting on the floor as he made the thing go wiggly-waggly, all the while teasing her with those gorgeous grinning eyes or that sensuous pair of lips that photographed like no others she'd ever caught in her viewfinder.

Jason . . . Jason . . . he was everywhere. Leaning over his morning coffee at the glass-topped dining table with its chrome-and-wicker chairs, often as not with one leg thrown over a chair arm, foot bare, swinging in time to the music he always seemed to hear in his head, whether it was playing on the stereo or not. Jason . . . sprawled diagonally across the squeaky old bed, studying the ceiling with fingers entwined behind his neck, talking about making it big. Jason . . . digging through the clothing that had hung beside hers in the closet, searching for just the right look that'd finally catch some producer's eye. Jason . . . blow-drying his razor-cut hair in the bathroom, nothing but a towel twisted around his hips, whistling absently as she leaned against the doorway watching him . . . just watching. Jason . . . spread-eagled on the living room floor, teasing, tempting, while The Five Senses sang, "When I'm stretched on the floor after loving once more, with your skin pressing mine, and we're tired and fine. . . ."

Jason, with the face and body of Adonis. It had never ceased to amaze Allison that he should have chosen such an ordinary looking girl as herself. He was beauty personified, a spellbinding combination of muscle, grace, and facial symmetry that spoke as poignantly to the artist in Allison Scott as to the woman in her. With Jason before the camera there could be no poor shots—his face wasn't capable of being captured at an unflattering angle. So while she'd had him, business had soared. Sport coats, leather goods, candy bars, road machinery—it seemed there was no product Jason's face could not sell, or so thought Twin Cities ad agencies.

Meanwhile, the portfolio of photos grew, and they made plans for a fashion layout in *Gentlemen's Review* magazine. It had been Allison's dream. But to sell to *GR,* to even approach them, Allison needed between three and four thousand photos. So she shot him everywhere, in every light, in every pose, against every background, learning with each clicking of the shutter to love him more.

And then six weeks ago she'd returned home to find half the closet empty, the razor gone from the bathroom, a damp towel over the sink, and the entire collection of negatives gone, too, and along with them, her dreams. He had left one thing—their favorite photo of him, blown up to poster size, on the four-foot easel in the living room. Across the bottom of it he had scrawled, "Sorry, babe . . . Love, Jason."

The easel stood now at the far end of the room, in the opposite corner from the hanging basket chair. Its pegs were empty, for when Allison had finally admitted that Jason wasn't coming back, she'd taken that overblown ego symbol, with all its memories, and stuffed it behind a bunch of unsold works stacked against the bedroom wall. She could hide the photo, but it seemed she could not hide the hurt. For it was back as keen as ever, resurrected by a simple thing like a two-dollar romance for which she'd agreed to do the cover.

Only she needed Jason to do it.

She turned away, toward the small kitchen alcove where she heated the spaghetti and ate it standing up, leaning against the kitchen cabinet, for she dreaded sitting at the table alone with Jason's image shimmering again as if he were still there, opposite her, as he'd been for the better part of a year.

Damn that story! Damn that hero who had to bring Jason's memory back all fresh and vibrant! Damn Mattie and her innocent questions!

The spaghetti tasted like wallpaper paste, but it filled the hole, and that's all Allison cared about anymore. Mealtimes were to be endured now, not savored as when there'd been the two of them together.

The way the apartment was arranged there was little to distinguish where the kitchen stopped and the dining area began. They ran together, then on to become the living room. Leaning now against the cabinets with a kettle in one hand and a fork in the other, Allison studied the empty easel, wondering where he was, who he was with, if he was modeling again. As tears filled her eyes, she thought: Damn you, Jason Ederlie, if you ever come back expecting to find your gorgeous face and body still haunting me from the corner of the living room, you'll be sadly disappointed!

But the fork dropped into the kettle, the kettle into the sink, and her head onto her arms as despair and regret welled up in her throat.

The following day was one of those grim efforts to make a living. Working with a pre-set camera, Allison spent six hours taking elementary-school pictures of gap-toothed second-graders, measuring the distance from camera to nose with the string that dangled from the tripod. It wasn't art, but it paid the rent on the studio.

By three o'clock in the afternoon, when the school session finished, the temperature was already dropping outside. Allison pulled a fat, fuzzy bobcap low over her forehead, wound a matching scarf twice around her neck, and headed for the van and downtown.

The ice on the studio windows was thick, the floor drafty. But the promised portfolio of glossies was in the mail. A quick check with the answering service turned up nothing needing immediate attention, so Allison headed home, her spirits a little higher than they'd been yesterday when she'd faced the empty apartment.

She made a cup of hot cocoa, slammed a tape into the tapedeck, and curled up against the puffy pillows of the sofa to see what Mattie had come up with.

Inside the mustard-colored envelope was a note in Mattie's writing: "Sorry they're not all in color, but I pulled some that looked as if coloring would be right. Love, M."

The girls came first, a bevy of fifteen faces, some in color, some in black and white, all with shoulder-length hair, as requested. One by one she laid them on the end table and against the cushions of the sofa. Some of the faces were passable, but none bowled Allison over. Semi-perturbed, she started looking through the men.

A smiling face with one tooth slightly crooked, giving an appealing little-boy look. Another with a sober aspect that somehow lacked character. Next, a glamour boy whose face was handsome enough but who somehow made Allison sure he wouldn't have any hair on his chest—for the poses she had planned, that was important. Next came a rugged type who'd adapt well to a Stetson and cigar.

But when the rugged type fell face down with the others, the cup of cocoa stopped halfway to Allison's lips, her eyes became riveted, and her back came away from the pillows. For a long moment she only stared, then her hand brought the cup toward her lips, and the next thing she knew, she'd burned her tongue.

"Ouch, dammit!" Depositing the cup and saucer on the glass-topped coffee table, she rose to her feet, scattering male faces from lap to floor as she held the single, striking face at arm's length.

"Holy cow," she breathed, stricken. "Holy . . . holy . . . cow." The face seemed too perfect to be flesh, the hair too disorderly to be accidental, the eyes so warm they seemed to reflect the change beneath the light from the table lamp. The nose was straight, with gorgeous nostrils. He had long cheeks and a strong jaw. And the mouth—ah, what a mouth. She studied it as an artist, but reacted as a woman.

408

The upper lip was utter perfection, its outline crisp, bowed with two peaks into perfect symmetry—a rare thing, no matter what the untutored layman might think. The lower lip was fuller than the upper, and the half smile seemed to hint at amusing things on his mind. Flat ears, strong neck—but not too thick—good shoulders, one leaning at an angle into the picture. He wore what appeared to be a wrinkled dress shirt with its collar askew, not the customary satin showman's costume, nor what Allison had come to think of as the "Tom Jones Look"—open-necked shirt plunging low underneath a body-hugging, open suit jacket. Still, she smiled.

I'll bet any money there'll be hair on his chest, she thought.

Allison flipped the picture over.

Richard Lang . . . 4-11-57 . . . blond . . . blue.

She read the words again, and somehow they didn't seem enough. Richard Lang . . . 4-11-57 . . . blond . . . blue. God, was that all they had to say about a face like this? Who was he? Why hadn't she ever seen his photo in the North Star files before? He had the kind of features photographers dream of. Bone structure that created angles and hollows, beautiful for shadowing. The jaw and chin seemed to be living, the mouth made for mobility. She imagined it scowling, smiling, scolding. She wondered if it were as mobile in real life as it seemed on paper. Something said "dimples" when there actually were none, only attractive smile lines on either side of his mouth, as if smiling came easily.

Richard Lang.

Twenty-five years old, blond hair, blue eyes, face as captivating as . . . but Allison stopped herself just short of finishing, "Jason's."

Richard Lang, you're the one!

She leaned the eight-by-ten glossy against the base of a table lamp and backed off, studying it while she unbuttoned her cuffs, then the buttons up the front of her shirt. She reached for her cup, took it a reasonable distance away while blowing and sipping, and studied the face, already posing him, figuring the camera angles, the lighting, the background, which could not be too involved lest it detract from that face.

There wasn't a girl in the lot pretty enough for him. The

girl, she could see, was going to give her trouble. It had been made clear to Allison that in the photograph the hero must appear to be overcome by the heroine, yet that was going to be hard to do with a face like his! It would overshadow any other within a country mile!

Allison, you're getting carried away.

To bring Richard Lang back into perspective, Allison deposited her empty cup in the sink, clumped into the bedroom, flung off her shirt, squirmed out of her jeans, and snuggled into a blue, fleecy robe, thinking all the while that when she returned to the living room she'd find the flaw she must have overlooked.

But he leaned there against the base of the lamp, more handsome than she'd remembered, making her hand move in slow motion as she zipped up the front of her robe.

She wished the photo was in color. Maybe his skin wasn't as clear as the black and white made it appear. Maybe he had freckles, ruddiness, sallow coloring. But she somehow knew his skin would be as smooth and healthy as a lifeguard's. Still searching for flaws, she thought maybe he has a horrible temper. Catching herself, she scolded, well, what does that matter, Allison Scott! You're taking his photo, not his name. If he has the temperament of a weasel, it's no affair of yours!

Nevertheless, it was hard to sleep that night. She hadn't been this exhilarated about her work since Jason had left.

The following morning she called Mattie to request more glossies of girls, and the two agreed to meet for lunch. Over steaming bowls of chicken-and-dumpling soup at Peter's Grill, Allison found herself hungry—actually hungry!—for the first time in weeks.

When Mattie asked which male model she'd chosen, Allison produced the photo of Richard Lang and laid it on the table between them.

"Him!" Mattie pointed a stubby finger. "I knew it! I knew he was the one you'd pick. All I had to hear was blond and blue, and I had him pegged in a second. He's just the type you can do wonders with on film."

"I'm sure as hell going to try, Mattie," Allison said thoughtfully. Then, studying the photo, struck again by his perfection, she asked, "What do you know about him?"

"Not much. He doesn't seem to give a fig leaf for what he wears. The times I've seen him he's been in battered-up tennies, washed out blue jeans, and wrinkled shirts that look like no woman ever touched an iron to them. Kind of strange, since most of our clients tend to overdo it when they dress for a booking."

"Mmm . . . so I noticed. His shirt looks like it's been through the Hundred Years War, and his hair . . . lord, Mattie, would you look at that hair! It's . . . it's . . ."

"Natural," Mattie finished.

"Yeah." Allison cocked her head and eyed the photo. "Natural, just like the rest of him. I wonder what the giant flaw is going to be when I get a look at him in person."

"Probably ego, like most of the pretty boys we handle."

The thought was depressing. "Probably," Allison agreed, stuffing the picture away again. "You don't have to teach me about ego in male models. Not after Jason Ederlie."

"I'm sorry I brought him up yes—"

"No, Mattie, it's okay." Allison held up her palms. "If I can't be adult enough to accept his being gone, I shouldn't have invited him to move in in the first place without any commitments on either side. It was . . . it was an idyll, a dream. But it's over, and I'm done licking my wounds. I'm going to throw myself into my work and make a name for myself, and when it's made I'll choose the man I want to live with, he won't choose me."

"Well, when you do, honey, why don't you make him a nice, stable plumber or grocer or accountant? Somebody who smiles at more than just himself in the mirror."

"Don't worry, Mattie. I've learned my lesson. When I find him, he'll be generous, humble, and honorable, and he'll dote upon my every desire."

Mattie laughed. "Hey, wherever you find him, could you pick up two—one for me?"

They laughed together, Mattie in her size sixteen slacks and Allison with her shattered illusions. But in the end Allison wondered if such men existed.

Chapter 2

THE OLD GENESIS Building had two elevators, one for passengers and one for freight. Naturally the old relics were both out of order when Allison got there, so she was totally out of breath as she unlocked the studio door after climbing six flights of stairs.

The phone was shrilling, and she tore across the room to grab it, puffing breathlessly as she answered, "Ph...photo Images."

"Hello, this is Rick Lang. I was told to call this number, that you may possibly have a booking for me over there."

"Rick...L...." Suddenly the light dawned. "Oh! *Richard* Lang! The one in the photo from North Star's files."

"Right, but I go by Rick."

Allison was caught off guard by the pleasant, unaffected voice on the other end. It was deep, masculine, and easy. If she was looking for shortcomings in the man, his voice wasn't offering any clues.

"Rick...all right. Listen, I never make decisions from photos alone. I'd like to see you before we sign any contracts, okay?"

"Sure, that's understandable."

The image of his face came back to Allison, suddenly making her feel like a damn fool for insisting. What could she possibly find wrong with a face like that?

"Please understand, I'll be relying heavily on this job to

bring in other similar work. If there's anything about you that—"

"Hey, sure, I understand. Sometimes black-and-whites can be misleading."

Of all things, Allison felt herself blushing. Blushing! Talking on the phone clear across a city where he couldn't even see her, she was stammering and blushing while he maintained perfect poise.

"When are you free?"

"I'm my own man. When would you like to see me?"

"How about tomorrow at one o'clock?"

"Fine."

"Can you come up to my studio?"

"Sure, if you tell me how to get there." She gave him instructions on where to park and what to do if the creaking old elevator was still balking, and more careful instructions on what to do if it wasn't. She heard his laughter then for the first time, a light, mirthful enjoyment in deep tones, before he ended, "I'll see you at one o'clock, then."

When she'd wished him good-bye, she fell back into her swivel chair, linked her fingers and hung her palms on the top of her head. This was ridiculous. She was becoming paranoid, looking for faults in him even before she met him, hoping to hear an effeminate tone in his voice, poor grammar, a lisp . . . something!

Scott, get your ass going! she chided, and jumped to her feet. He's not Jason, and he's not going to move in with you, so call a sand-and-gravel company and get a promise of free sand in exchange for free publicity shots of their operation or free photos of the owner's grandchildren or whatever it takes to get that sand up here. But get your mind off Rick Lang!

The following afternoon, Rick Lang entered the door of Photo Images to find a woman with her back to him, talking on the phone. She was tilted far back in an ancient oak swivel chair, the high heel of one brown leather boot propped high onto a frame of a huge wall of windows, the other ankle crossed over her knee. Spicy brown hair hung to her shoulder blades, held behind her ears by a pair of oversized sunglasses pushed onto the top of her head. His eyes followed the taut blue jeans on the outstretched leg, took in a bulky gray sweater and a coordinated woolen scarf wrapped twice around her neck. Suddenly she gestured at the ceiling like an Italian fruit vendor haggling over the price of an apple.

"But what if I sign up and get the bends or something, can I get my money back?" She gestured again, more exasperatedly, and the foot that rested on the knee started tapping the air sideways. Rick stood there, smiling, listening. The foot stopped tapping, the chin came down. "Oh, you can't?" she asked. "Not in a swimming pool?" She lowered the sunglasses to their proper place, and her voice turned innocent. "Well, to tell the truth, I really don't want to learn to scuba." She scratched the blue denim on her knee, nervously. "I just needed to use the gear for a couple of days for a photo project I'm planning and—"

She yanked the phone away from her ear, while across the room Rick heard snatches of a man's angry reply. "Lady . . . every curious . . . try diving . . . out of business . . . no time . . . want lessons."

The chair rocked forward, and her boots hit the floor with a slap. "Well, you don't have to get so—" She stopped, cut off, listened a moment longer, then spit, "Mister, I'm not after free—" Again she listened, then abruptly slammed the receiver onto the cradle in her lap, made a most obscene gesture at it, crossed her arms belligerently, and hissed, "That's for you, sweetheart!"

Rick Lang smiled widely, carefully wiped the expression from his face, and quietly said, "Excuse me."

The chair whirled around so fast, her sunglasses slipped down her nose, and the receiver flew off its cradle. She caught it by the cord, set the whole thing on her desk, and came to her feet, blushing a deep crimson.

"How long have you been standing there?" she snapped.

"A while." He watched the color flood her face, her lips compress, and studied the oversized lenses that hid her eyes. "Sorry, I got here a little early." He smiled as he came forward, hand extended. "Rick Lang," he greeted simply.

"Allison Scott," she returned as his warm palm enfolded hers, pumped once, then disappeared into the pocket of a misshapen garment that had once been a letter jacket.

"You wanted to look me over." He stood back, absolutely at ease, weight on one foot, not so much as a hint of nervousness while that easy smile turned his mouth to magic and Allison had the distinct impression that if anyone was being looked over, it was she.

"Yes . . . I . . ." Her cheeks were positively hot. "Listen, I . . . I'm not a dishonest person." She gestured toward the phone, certain he'd seen her rude, unladylike gesture at the end of the conversation. "You heard me tell him I didn't really want to take scuba lessons, didn't you? I don't con people out of things, it's just that it's kind of tough to come up with props for pictures sometimes, and I need scuba gear for a project I'm planning, so I . . . I thought I just might give scuba diving a try if it'd get me the gear and they'd let me have my money back after lesson number one, but the guy got nasty and I . . . I . . ." She suddenly realized she was blubbering to hide her embarrassment, so fell silent. Being at a disadvantage was something new to Allison Scott, and letting it show was even rarer.

Rick laughed engagingly, managing at the same time to admire her upbeat look, the sleek jeans and body sweater ending nearly at her knees, and her face, now pink and flushed with embarrassment.

"I'm not here to judge you, you're here to judge me, so forget I even heard it."

She told herself to cool down, that he was just another handsome face, another ego, another Jason. Yet even at first glance she sensed a difference. The cocky self-assurance was absent. Even his clothes were unsensational. He was dressed as Mattie had warned he might be—that seen-better-days jacket with the collar worn absolutely threadbare, faded jeans; a pair of scuffed, well-traveled almost-cowboy boots. The jacket was partly unsnapped. Beneath it she saw a purple sweatshirt bearing a white number 12. Her eyes moved from it to his face, which again affected her like a 110-volt shock.

Ruddy skin, bitten to a becoming pink by the wind outside, but smooth and unblemished; nose straight and shining from the cold. His hair had been styled by the feckless whims and guileless artistry of the January winds. That hair was, indeed, blond, a rich color that seemed a gift in the middle of this snowbound January, when most people bundled beneath warm caps. The lightly curled strands of hair were blown about his ears, temples, and forehead in engaging disarray. To comb it would be folly, she thought.

She suddenly realized she'd been staring, and looked away. He was, beyond a doubt, even better than his pictures.

"Did the agency tell you what this assignment is?" she asked.

"No, just that I should contact you to find out." He glanced across the studio—full gunny sacks resting against the front of an old, beaten desk; an ancient refrigerator; rolls of back-drop paper hanging from between the pipes on the ceiling; an assortment of chairs, stools, artificial plants, pillows, and cream cans in one corner; cameras on tripods, umbrella reflectors, strobes, a variety of photographic equipment. But mostly space—lots of space—and bright afternoon light flooding the place through the frost-laced windows. The corner where her desk stood was her "office," separated by two metal file cabinets against the wall, to one side. A nearby door led to a windowless room, but it was dark inside, and he couldn't tell what it was used for.

While he studied the studio, she studied him, wishing he were wearing a deep-necked shirt so she could see if there was hair on his chest. She wasn't quite sure how to ask him if there was. His eyes wandered back to hers, and she felt the color rise along her neck again.

"It's a book cover, and they need two poses, one for the front, one for the back."

"What kind of book?"

"A romance."

His eyebrows rose briefly, speculatively, then he shrugged and nodded.

"Have you ever posed with another model?"

"A few times."

"A woman?"

"Once."

"What was the ad for?"

"His and hers jogging suits or something like that."

She'd guessed right when studying the black-and-white glossy. He had the most utterly mobile mouth she'd ever seen and brows that expressed his mood almost before the words were out of his mouth.

"Will you do something for me?" Allison asked.

"If you'll do something for me." His eyes stopped roving and stared at his own reflection in her sunglasses. "Take off the glasses so I can see you."

"Oh!" She pushed the glasses up to rest on her hair. "I didn't realize."

"Better. Now where were we?"

"You were going to do something for me."

His hands came out of those drooping pockets, palms up. "Name it."

She moved from behind the desk to stand several feet before him, her hands slipped into the tight front pockets of her jeans, her shoulders hunched while she assessed him.

"Look angry," she ordered.

Again came the magic. In a split second his brows lowered, curling just enough to gain a viewer's sympathy yet not enough to make him look mean.

"Wily," she shot at him.

"What?"

"Look wily," she demanded, pointing a finger at his nose.

Immediately his gaze shifted until he peered from the corner of his eye at the refrigerator, as if it were there to thwart him but he had the goods on it.

Allison smiled, clapped her hands once in delight, then ordered, "Tired!"

His lips fell open slightly, a droop tugged the corners of his mouth down, and the sparkle disappeared from his spiky-lashed eyes, which he cast disconsolately at the floor between them. . . . Perfect, she thought.

Her heart went tripping over itself in delight. He was a natural! She went into a semi-crouch, hands grasping knees as if she were a lineman on a football team.

"Give me belligerent!" she threw at him.

The beautiful lips puckered up like a drawstring bag. The eyes scowled. The skin seemed to stretch tight over the sculptured cheekbones. She forgot his name, age, coloring, handsomeness, and saw only magic happening before her eyes. And while she was intensely captivated, caught up in discovering him, she didn't realize how her own eyes danced, how her face took on life, mirroring the responses he effortlessly brought forth with each new order she issued. No matter what it was, his face changed with each brusque command. "Threatened . . . amused . . . puzzled . . . pleased. . . ." As fast as she snapped out the words, he expressed them.

"Ardent!" she threw out.

For the first time his eyes settled on hers, remained on them, in full, while he leaned toward her as if only the merest thread of restraint compelled him not to touch. His eyes spoke poems, his lips hinted kisses, and his stance was so questing that she actually straightened and took a quick step backward.

Immediately he dropped the pose and took up his own lazy, loose-boned stance again, his eyes asking how he'd done.

The breath she expelled lifted wispy Pekingese bangs away from her forehead and temples, then she laughed, a bit nervously, but enormously pleased.

"Hey, do you do this all the time?" she asked.

"What?"

"This . . . this immediacy!"

He looked surprised. "Am I immediate?" He laughed a little.

"Immediate!" She became animated, pacing back and forth before him, boot heels clicking on the floor. "You're as immediate as electricity! Do you know what it sometimes takes to pull those kinds of responses out of models?"

"I never thought about it much. I haven't been in this racket very long. I just did what I was told."

"Yeah, you sure did." She came right up to him, smiling now, shaking her head in disbelief. Involuntarily, she took two steps backward.

Holy Moses! He didn't even know what he had. It was more than looks, more than bone structure and vibrant skin and come-hither eyes. It was . . . charisma! The kind photographers search for and rarely find. He quickly grasped each mood she sought to create and portrayed them not only with facial expression but with body language so poignant and natural that she hardly sensed him changing from one pose to the other until his mood caught her in the gut and telegraphed itself.

Suddenly realizing she was standing there clasping the top of her head as if trying to hold it on, she let her hands slide down and moved toward her desk, crossed her arms, and stared at the windows while stammering, "The . . . there's one other thing I have to ask you to do, and it may be rather unorthodox, but . . . I . . . I . . ."

He noted the defensive way she turned her back and crossed her arms. "You haven't seen me running yet, have you? So what's next?" He smiled.

She glanced back over her shoulder. "Take off your jacket."

"It's off," he claimed, snaps flying open even as he spoke. He dropped the jacket nonchalantly across one corner of her desk.

His arms and chest filled out the jersey beautifully. She took a gulp and reminded herself he was just a model.

"Now the jersey."

That one slowed him down for a fraction of a minute.

"The jersey . . . sure." It came off, but a little slower than the jacket.

He was now in a white V-neck T-shirt, the jersey bunched up in one uncertain hand as if he were getting ready to pitch it at the first thing that threatened.

"The T-shirt, too," she ordered.

He illustrated "suspicious" without being ordered to. His magnificent eyes skittered to her, to the desk top, to the wall where a few totally unobjectionable samples of her work were displayed. Finally, frowning, his eyes came to rest on her. "Hey, lady—"

She spun to face him fully. "The name is Scott, Allison Scott."

"Okay, Ms. Scott, I don't do any of that kinky stuff that I've heard—"

"Neither do I, Mr. Lang!"

"Well, just what kind of book is this, anyway?"

"It's not pornography, if that's what you're thinking. But if you're scared to take off the shirt, I've got a file full of faces that'll suffice just as nicely as yours!"

"I guess I'd like to know why first."

"I told you, it's a romance. It takes place on Sanibel

Island." Why was she being so defensive, she wondered. Because suddenly, when confronted with such an impressive physical specimen, she found she was wondering what he looked like bare-chested—and wondering out of mere female curiosity, not just artistic professionalism. Immediately she realized her mistake—it was amateurish and childish to be hedging the issue. She should have asked him immediately and avoided all mystery. Allison decided to be honest.

"All I need to know is if you have hair on your chest, but I felt a little silly asking."

Without another word the T-shirt came off. He stood before her in those tight, washed-out blue jeans, the nipples of his chest puckered up in the old icebox of a building, while zephyrs of too-fresh air sneaked along the floors. His was the first naked chest she'd seen since Jason departed, and Allison found she had to force her thoughts into structured paths while viewing it. But it was difficult to disassociate herself from the fact that he was—masculinely speaking—superb. Allison felt her body radiating enough heat to melt every shred of ice off those windows while he stood before her, shivering, letting her study him.

He looked down his chest, then back up at her. "Enough?" he asked.

For a moment she felt like a curious teenager peeping at the boys through a knothole in the changing-room wall, while he stood before her thoroughly at ease.

"Yes," she answered, and immediately the shirts started coming back over his head. From inside the first he asked, "So what am I going to wear for this picture?"

"Bathing trunks. Have you got any?"

"Sure." His head popped out, hair tousled in gamin boyishness that belied the mature, well-proportioned body she'd just assessed.

"What color are they?" she asked, moving back around the desk.

"White."

"Perfect, since we'll be shooting at night and they'll show up more."

His eyebrows curled and again he watched her warily as she moved, businesslike, to pick up pencil and clipboard, making a note while asking, "Do you have any scars on your legs or back?"

"No." He tossed the jersey on, shivering visibly now.

"Do you have any objections to kissing a stranger?"

With one arm half drawn into his jacket sleeve, he stopped, as if struck dumb.

"Kissing a stranger?"

"Yes." She raised serious eyes to his, making a desperate effort to appear calm.

"Who?"

Allison plucked the photo of the chosen female model from the pile on her desk and handed it to him. "Her."

He gave it a cursory glance. "The other subject in the photo, I take it?"

"Yes, if her coloring turns out to be right when I see her."

He turned it over and read the name on the back. "Vivien Zuchinski." He laughed and shook his head, lifting some of the tension from the room. "With a name like that she'd better know how to kiss!"

It broke the ice. Their eyes met and he chuckled first, followed by her mellow sounds of mirth.

"I feel like an ass," she admitted, relaxing even further, at last able to look him in the eye again.

"Well, I was a little uncomfortable there for a minute myself."

She ambled past the windows, toward the back of the studio, away from him. "I've never hired anybody for this kind of assignment before. I went about it all wrong. I apologize for making you feel ill at ease." She turned a brief glance back over her shoulder. He was still beside the desk.

"It's okay . . . as long as I get to kiss . . ." He checked the back of the photo again, "Vivien Zuchinski," he finished with a grin. He tossed the photo back onto the desk and followed Allison along the length of the studio.

"Do you mind my asking *you* a few things?" Rick Lang queried.

"No, ask away."

"Well, for starters, why are we shooting at night?"

She couldn't help smiling. "I can see you're still suspicious, Mr. Lang."

"Well, you have to admit it sounds a little fishy."

"Not when you want a nighttime effect. It's going to be a beach scene with a fire. I'll need total darkness outside so I can control the lighting. As you can see, the place is solid windows." She waved a hand at the glass wall and scanned the length of the studio before her eyes came to rest on him.

"A fire?" he repeated dubiously.

"Yup." With her hands in her pockets, one eyebrow raised slightly higher than the other, she looked a trifle smug.

"In here?" he asked skeptically.

"In here. You don't believe I can do it?"

He shrugged. "It'll be a good trick if you do. How many shots are you planning to take?"

"Oh, sixty-five maybe . . . of each cover, front and back."

He whistled softly. If she took that many shots, she was serious, dedicated, and thorough. He glanced around, obviously searching for a beach.

"Trust me," she said. "When you come for the session there'll be a beach. And all you have to do is wear a bathing suit and kiss a pretty girl. Is that so tough?"

"Not at all."

"Then do you want the job or not, Mr. Lang?"

"This is really on the level? Nothing kinky?"

"Honestly, you *are* a skeptic, aren't you? I admit the poses will be sensual. There'll be body contact—after all, it is a romance. But the final result will be tasteful."

A teasing light came into Rick's eyes. "Hmm . . . it's beginning to sound like more fun all the time."

"Then you'll do it?"

"When do we shoot?"

"Thursday night, if things go right. I've got to create the set first, and this one might give me a little trouble."

"The scuba gear?"

"No, not that. That's for the next series I'm doing. I was just planning ahead. It's the beach that's going to give me trouble on this one. I'll face the scuba gear later."

"Would it help you out if I borrowed some from a friend of mine?"

Her face registered pleased surprise. "Could you really?"

He glanced at the snowy city below. "I really don't think

he's putting it to very hard use right now, do you?"

"And I wouldn't have to take scuba lessons and get the bends?" She feigned great relief, then added seriously, "Taking the pictures is often the easiest part. It's setting them up that makes my hair turn gray sometimes."

"I hadn't noticed." He raised his eyes to the top of her head, then let them drift back to her face, an easy smile on his lips.

Immediately she was on her guard. It was the kind of remark Jason might have made, that sly, flattering brand of innuendo that had broken down her barriers and made her break her one basic rule of thumb: never get personal with the male models.

Though it was meant as banter, not flattery, the moment the words were out of Rick Lang's mouth he noticed how she crossed her arms tightly across her ribs. She was a classy-looking woman, particularly when she let her guard down. But often she set up unconscious barriers—the crossed arms, the lowered sunglasses, jumping behind the desk. He couldn't help but wonder what made her so defensive.

"I'll drop the gear by some afternoon."

"Oh, you don't have to do that. I can pick it up, wherever he lives."

"It's no trouble."

"I appreciate it, really. And thanks."

"Think nothing of it." He opened the door, turned with a grin, and finished, "As long as I get to kiss Vivien Zucchini."

"Zuchinski," she corrected, unable to stop the smile from spreading across her lips.

"Zuchinski."

Then he was gone.

Allison's arms slowly came uncrossed. She stared at the door, picturing his face, his form, his too-good-to-be-true physique. Unconsciously she slipped one hand through her long hair, kneading the back of her neck where pleasant tingles displaced common sense.

Haven't you learned your lesson yet, Scott? He's just another pretty boy out to make a score, and don't forget it!

Chapter 3

VIVIEN ZUCHINSKI TURNED out to have exactly the right color and length of hair. Her face wasn't quite as long as her publicity photo made it appear, but she had flawless skin, still clinging to most of last summer's tan, and a mouth that could be called nothing but voluptuous. Her eyes were a stunning blue, as big as fifty-cent pieces, eyes, Allison knew, that would photograph beautifully, for they were fringed with sooty lashes so thick it seemed they'd weigh her down. Her breasts, it seemed, threatened to do the same. Oh, Vivien Zuchinski had all the qualifications, all right. Her main shortcoming, Allison could tell immediately, was that the girl was stupid, which—thankfully—would not show in a photograph. She chewed gum like an earth-breaking machine, had a fixation with lip gloss, which she constantly pulled out of her shoulder bag and painted on her pouting lips, whether in the midst of conversation or not. Her favorite word, which made Allison grimace, was "nice."

"Hey, *nice* studio," Vivien said immediately upon entering. "Hey, *nice* boots! Wheredja get them? I got a pair's kinda like them but not as nice. Those're really nice."

Allison cringed. Most of the models she worked with were intelligent, upbeat, many of them students on their way to professional careers in another field, helping themselves through college with the money they earned modeling. Vivien Zuchinski was definitely the exception to the rule.

"Hey, ah, what's the guy look like? Is he a fox, I mean, you know, ah, has he got a nice bod?"

"Very nice," Allison answered dryly. "Almost as nice as yours, Vivien."

"Hey, really? I like a guy with a nice bod."

It was all Allison could do to keep from rolling her eyes. "Have you got a bathing suit?"

"Oh, yeah, sure, got a bunch of 'em, nice ones, too."

"Would you mind bringing them along when you come?"

"Sure, you bet."

"The girl in the book wears a blue bikini."

"Hey, no sweat! I got this really nice blue bikini, bought it last summer when this lifeguard up at Madden's kinda started givin' me the eye, you know? And I figure I'd just put on a little show for him and come out on the beach with a different bikini every day, but I only had five and I was gonna be there for six days, so, gol, what was I s'posed to do?" She flipped her palms up at shoulder height, hopelessly. "So I find this nice blue bik—"

"Vivien, bring them all, would you?"

Vivien was too much of a stereotype to be believable. She hung a hand on one hip, threw Allison a wide-eyed look of innocence, and answered, "Oh, sure . . . yeah, sure thing."

"Then I'll see you Thursday."

"Yeah, sure. Where'd you say you got them boots again?"

By the time Allison had gotten rid of Vivien she wondered if she'd made a mistake hiring her. Allison stood with hands on hips, shaking her head at the door through which Vivien had left, then glanced down at her own high-heeled boots and said to herself, "Nice boots, hey."

The following afternoon Allison was standing disgruntledly with a broom and dustpan in her hand, spilled sand around her feet, when Rick Lang showed up with air tanks, flippers, hoses, and pipes.

"Hi."

She looked up, surprised, realizing in a flash how glad she was to see him again. "Oh, hi . . . oh, you brought them!" She dropped the dustpan, wiped her hands on her thighs, and came eagerly toward the door.

"Where do you want this stuff? It's kind of heavy."

She motioned toward the wall, sighed, and ran a hand through her hair. "Thanks. At least that's one thing that's gone right today."

"Have you got troubles?" He noted the sand, then her disgusted face. She noted his same old jeans and letter jacket, not at all the kind of clothing a guy wears to turn a girl's head.

"Have I ever." She glared at the mess. "I'm thinking about flying us down to Florida to do these shots! Except I think Vivien Zuchinski would drive me crazy before we got there."

"Vivien didn't turn out to be what you wanted?"

"Vivien's . . ." Allison searched for the proper word and turned a sardonic smirk his way. "Vivien's . . . *nice*."

He eyed the upward tilt of Allison's lips as she enjoyed some private joke. When she smiled, her eyes smiled with her mouth. She was dressed in off-white corduroy trousers with some kind of stylish, little army-green rubber shoes with bumpy white soles and long tongues and laces. They looked like something a socialite might wear duck hunting. Cute, he thought, taking in her modish hooded jacket and turtleneck sweater. Again she wore the sunglasses, pushed high up on her head.

"What's wrong with Vivien?"

"Nothing!" But there was a smirk of sarcasm in the quick word as she flipped her palms up innocently, then repeated, "Nothing. She has a terrific face and a very nice body."

"Good for me," he teased. "When can I kiss her?"

"Anytime you want . . . I'm sure she'll make that abundantly clear. You see, Miss Zuchinski has already pointed out the fact that she likes a guy with a, quote, 'nice bod,' unquote. Also, she likes her men foxy."

He laughed, leaning back, but it had a nice, easy sound, uncluttered by ego. "Need a hand?" he asked.

"I thought you'd never ask. The damn gunny sacks weigh a ton, and the first one came open halfway across the floor, which is not where I wanted to build my beach."

Already he was shucking off his frowsy letter jacket, laying it across the top of the refrigerator. "Just show me where."

She pointed to the area where the backdrop paper hung in huge rolls from the ceiling, then led the way, rolling aside some tall strobe lights on stands while he grabbed the ears of the closest gunny sack and dragged it over. She went to work cleaning up the loose sand while he moved the rest of the sacks. Covertly she watched the play of his back muscles as he lugged the bags.

"Do you go through this with every job you do?" He grunted, letting the first sack roll to its resting spot.

"Sometimes. I do what has to be done, get whatever props are necessary. You'd be surprised where trying to find them sometimes leads me."

"So I guessed when I walked in here the other day."

"A gentleman would tactfully refrain from mentioning the other day," she stated, her eyes on the broom while she swept. "Now the sand . . . I got it from a sand-and-gravel company, even got them to haul it up here free. In return I'll do a series of free shots of their operation when it's in full swing next summer. The kind of thing they can use on their Christmas calendar or whatever."

He glanced around the studio. "I never realized how much went into your kind of photography. In my kind the settings are already made for me."

"You're a photographer, too?" she asked, surprised.

"No, I'm a wildlife artist, but I paint from original photos."

She couldn't have been more surprised had he said he moonlighted as a fat man at the fair.

"An artist?" Yet the clothes fit, the lack of guile, of style.

"It's not a very lucrative business until you make a name for yourself. I only do the modeling to pay the bills."

"Like my school pictures."

"Your what?"

"I take school pictures . . . you know—little kids, stool, string-to-nose, smile and say *gravee-e-e!*" She made a clown face, tipping her head to one side, hands spread wide beside her ears, while the broom handle rested against her chest. "It pays the bills here, too."

"I thought that, working with publishers from New York, your career was going full swing."

"Not yet it isn't, but it will be," she stated, then set to work sweeping determinedly. "I had a good start once, but . . ."

Suddenly her face closed over, and she bit off the remark abruptly. He waited, studying her as she again attacked her sweeping, this time too intensely.

"But what?" he couldn't resist asking.

"Nothing." Suddenly she dropped the broom and turned toward her files. "Hey, wanna see some of the things I've done for local ad agencies?"

"Sure, I'd love to," he answered agreeably, following her.

It took no more than thirty seconds of viewing her work for Rick Lang to see she had enormous talent. "You're good," he complimented, scarcely glancing up as he studied her work. "Your concepts are fresh and vital." It was true. Still objects seemed to have motion, moving objects to have speed, scented objects smell, and flavored objects taste. He noted that she had two favorite models—one male, one female— whom she'd used predominantly, as was the case with most commercial photographers.

"Thanks. I love the work, absolutely do."

"It shows." He glanced up, but she was staring at the top photo, one of the favorite male model. The man wore a textured shirt and was posed against a background of bleached barn boards and a rich, rough stone foundation. The ancient building created the perfect foil for the man's handsome face and classic clothing. This was no manufactured set. She'd taken the shot when the sun was low in the sky, either early morning or sunset, for the shadows, even on the rocks and boards, were dark, rich, and intense. Shot after shot showed an artist's soul, an enviable talent behind the viewfinder.

While Rick Lang leafed through the matted enlargements, Allison saw Jason's face flash past time and again. She felt a sense of loss as keenly as ever, this time a professional loss, for the works featuring him were the best of the lot. Oh yes, she'd lost much more than a lover when she'd lost Jason Ederlie.

Rick looked up and caught an expression of unconcealed pain on her features. Realizing he was studying her, a tinge of color stained Allison's cheeks before she quickly reached to flip through the pictures to one she particularly liked. "I sold this one to *Bon Appetit* magazine." It was a photo of freshly sliced apples and cheese viewed through a bottle of pale amber wine.

"Mmm . . . you make my mouth water," Rick said.

She shot him a censorious look, but he was only studying the photo. How often Jason had said things like that—glib, quick, thoughtless compliments, laced with his irresistible teasing grin that were meant to do a snow job on her emotions while together they worked up an impressive portfolio of fashion shots on him alone. And, like a fool, she'd believed it all when he strung her along.

She swallowed now, trying to forget. Abruptly she lowered the sunglasses to cover her eyes, squared her shoulders, slipped her palms into her hip pockets, and walked away.

"Listen, thanks a lot for helping me haul the sand to where it belongs," she said. "I really appreciate it." The cool dismissal was unmistakable. It chilled the studio like air currents blowing across an icy tundra. Taken aback at her swift change, Rick's eyes narrowed, but he moved immediately toward his jacket.

"Sure. Anything else I can do before I leave?"

"No, I'm just about to close up here for the day."

"How about a cup of coffee? It's colder in here than it is outside."

"It always is, even though I crank up the radiators till they clank like a rhythm section. I'm used to it by now."

He waited, realizing she'd artfully glossed past his invitation without either accepting or rejecting it. "Maybe I'd better find one of those old-fashioned bathing suits, the ones shaped like long underwear, if it's always this cold in here."

"Oh, don't worry. Vivien will warm you up."

"You know, you've really got me wondering about this Vivien."

He managed to make Allison smile again, but her gaity seemed to have seeped away. Her lips turned up, but this time the smile seemed forced.

"Oh, I never should have made any comment about Vivien. She's just a little . . . inane, that's all," Allison noted apologetically.

"Which is a polite way for saying she's not too bright."

"Who am I to say?" She hadn't been too bright herself, falling for Jason's line all those months. Maybe it was better to be like Vivien Zuchinski and look for a man with a nice body, have a good time with it for as long as you both were willing, and forget in-depth relationships.

Rick Lang had snapped up his old jacket, and stood now with his hands lost in its pockets.

"How come you hide behind those glasses like that all the time?"

"What? Oh . . . these!" She flipped them up with a false laugh. "I didn't even realize I had them on."

"I know."

Their eyes met, serious now, his gaze steady, blue, and determined. He stood between Allison and the door.

"A minute ago I asked you if you wanted to have a cup of coffee. I thought maybe you were hiding so you wouldn't have to answer."

She experienced a brief thrill before quelling it to wonder why he asked. Goodness, he was nice enough—Vivien's word, but apropos at the moment—and handsome enough to land any woman in the city. But no matter how inviting it sounded, Allison had learned her lesson.

"Thanks, but my work's not done for the day. I still have to find a log."

He shook his head slightly, as if to clear it. "A what? You lost me somewhere."

"A log. I need a log for the beach, and I've kept putting it off and putting it off because it's been so cold, and I have to go out in the woods somewhere—if I can find a woods—and haul a log in here."

He gestured across the room. "You couldn't haul those bags of sand across the floor, yet you're going to haul a log out of the woods, into your car—"

"It's a van."

"Into your van, up the freight elevator that works whenever it feels like it, down the hall, and in here, all by yourself?"

She shrugged. "I'm going to try."

"No, you're not. You'll slip a disc, and I'll never get to kiss Vivien Zucchini."

Without warning she spurted into laughter. "Zuchinski,"

she corrected, "and I'm not too sure it would be such a great loss if you missed the chance."

"Oh yeah? Let me be the judge of that. I'm helping you do the logging because Miss Zucchini sounds like something mighty delicious. Maybe I like women with nice bods, too, and foxy faces." But his eyes were filled with mischief. He stood there in those raunchy old boots and that shapeless old jacket, with his hair all messed, for all the world as ordinary as any plumber or grocer or accountant. And dammit! she liked him. Not just because he had a face fit for the silver screen, but because he managed to be persuasive without being pushy, had a swift sense of humor, and was the first man who'd invited Allison out for coffee in over a year—and that included Jason Ederlie, who'd only drunk hers and never even washed his cup!

"Maybe we could pick up a cup of coffee and take it with us in the van," she suggested, then admitted, "I *am* freezing, and we're running out of daylight if we expect to come up with a log."

He smiled—not big, not phony, not even at her—and gestured with a shoulder. "Let's go." From the coat tree behind the door she grabbed her jacket, but he plucked it from her hands and helped her put it on. It was something Jason had never done. Thinking back on it, in that passing instant, Allison realized there were actually times when *she'd* held *his* sport coat while he slipped flawless shirtsleeves into it. Often, afterward, she hugged him from behind, using the jacket for an excuse to touch, to caress.

She'd forgotten how it felt to have a man help her into a coat. It made her more conscious than ever of Rick Lang as they rode down in the clanking old freight elevator together. She stared at the brass expansion gate, then at the ancient floor indicator, ill at ease as she sensed him studying her.

When they reached her van, he surprised her by following her to the driver's side, taking the keys from her gloved hand, removing his own gloves and unlocking the door. She found herself staring in disbelief. Did men actually do these things anymore?

He smiled, handed her the keys, waited for her to climb in so he could slam the door, then jogged around to the other side. He climbed in, hunched up, and chafed his arms.

"Not many guys do that anymore," she noted.

"Do what?"

"Help with coats and car doors and things."

"My mother used to cuff me on the side of the head if I forgot. After about the twenty-ninth cuff, I managed to remember. After that it kind of stuck with me. Guess I still think she'll manage to get me if I forget."

She couldn't help laughing. The story made him seem infinitely more human.

"God, but it's cold." He shivered, then pointed out the windshield and peered through the frosty glass as the engine chugged to life. "Go south and take Highway 12. I'll show you a place right in the middle of the city limits where we can get you your log."

"In the middle of the city?"

"Well, almost. Theodore Wirth Park."

"Theodore Wirth! But it's public land! It's against the law. If they catch us, we'll get fined."

He grinned, all lopsided and little-boyish. "Guess my mother didn't cuff me quite enough. Sounds like fun, trying to put one over on the law. Course, it's up to you . . . I mean, I don't want to be the one responsible for getting your name on the FBI's Ten Most Wanted List."

She laughed again. "You do that, and I'll personally see to it you never kiss Vivien Zucchini."

"Zuchinski," he returned with a smile coming from deep inside his turned-up collar and hunched-up shoulders. "And you'll have a tough time of it from behind the walls of the state pen."

They were thoroughly enjoying each other as the van headed toward Theodore Wirth Park. Allison stopped at a sandwich shop and Rick jumped out, returning a few minutes later with cups of hot coffee. The late-afternoon sun lit the clouds around it into crazy zigzags of aqua blue and vibrant pink. But suddenly Allison didn't mind the frigid temperatures.

Rick handed her a cup of coffee, watching appreciatively while she caught the fingers of her gloves between her teeth and yanked them off. He grinned broadly at the sight of her in the worst-looking bobcap he'd ever seen, pulled so low that her eyebrows scarcely showed.

"Forgot to ask if you like cream or sugar," he said.

"Sugar, usually, but I'd drink it any way today."

"Sorry. I'll remember next time." He sipped, looking around. "Nice van."

"Yup, it is, isn't it? Only another year and a half and it'll be paid for. I need it. I'm always hauling junk back and forth from the studio. Buying a van was the smartest move I ever made."

"I'm not big on vehicles," he offered. "Don't really care if I have a tin lizzy or an XKE—as long as it'll get me there, that's all that matters."

It had always been Jason's dream to have a sleek, silver Porsche, one that would set off his looks with a touch of panache. How refreshing to find a man whose values were so different.

"Would you look at that sky," Rick Lang said admiringly, almost as if reading her mind.

"Beautiful, huh?" They fell into comfortable silence, driving westward, squinting into the lowering sun against which every object became bold, black, and striking. Even the telephone lines, power poles, and road signs became artistic creations when viewed against the brilliant sky.

How long had it been since she had enjoyed a ride through an icy, stinging wintry afternoon and not complained about the cold? Allison wondered. Now she found herself noting the silhouettes of oaks standing blackly against their backdrop as she turned the van onto Wirth Parkway and entered the sprawling, woodsy park.

Children were sliding down the enormous hills between sections of wooded land. Skiers were out on the runs in gaily colored clothing. Even a sweatsuited jogger could be seen, his breath labored and hanging frozen in the air.

The road wove into the heart of the public land, past frozen Wirth Lake, the ski chalet, the ski jump, and acres of untouched woodland, which surprised and delighted Allison, situated as it was in the center of the teeming city. The van moved in and out of shadows as the late sun rested lower and lower in the west, behind the trees, making long, skinny shadow fingers across the road.

Rick directed Allison up a steep incline at a sign that read Eloise Butler Wildflower Garden and Bird Sanctuary.

"Anybody who's looking for wildflowers today is going to be disappointed," he commented. "I think we can steal our log up there without getting caught."

At the top was a paved parking lot the plows hadn't bothered to clear. Tracks left by cross-country skiers showed that only they had disturbed the snow here.

"You gonna be warm enough?" Allison asked as Rick opened his door.

"Yup!" He produced warm leather gloves from his pocket, yanked his collar higher for good measure, and got out.

It was getting dark quickly as they entered the woods, following the foot trails whose wooden identification signs now wore caps of snow. The trails were easy to follow, and when Allison and Rick were scarcely twenty-five feet from the van, they spotted a long, oblique lump beneath a thick coat of snow. Rick brushed it off, revealing a four-foot section of tree trunk.

"How's this?" he asked, squatting beside it and looking up.

She glanced measuringly from the log to the van. "Close, but too heavy, I think."

He walked to the end, kicked around in the snow, knelt, and boosted it up from the ground. "Must be half-rotten, just the kind we need so we can run fast when the posse comes."

"Think I can lift it?" she asked.

"I don't know. Give it a try."

She shuffled through the snow to the other end of the log, rummaged around to find a handhold, grunted exaggeratedly, and hoisted up her end. "I did it! I did it!" She staggered a little for good measure.

Rick trained his eyes on a spot behind her shoulder and said with grave seriousness, "Oh, officer, it wasn't me! I was just coming to turn in this lady for stealing this rotten log. Ninety-nine years should certainly be fair, yes, whatever you say."

Allison gave a giant shove, and the log rammed Rick Lang

in his beautifully muscled belly like a battering ram, then thudded to the earth at his feet as he dramatically clutched his gut. He staggered around as if he'd just had his lights punched out, hugged himself, and grunted, "I . . . I take that back . . . off . . . officer, let her go. I'll pay for the damn log!"

She affected a wholly superior air and joined his farce. "Officer, all this man's done all day long is talk about kissing girls. Can you blame a woman for grabbing the first thing in sight to protect herself with?"

Rick raised both gloved hands as if a gun were pointed at his chest. "Oh no . . . oh no, no, no, I'm innocent. Furthermore, after this display, you can put your damn log in your van by yourself! I'm going for a walk!"

He turned and continued along the trail, leaving her standing up to her knees in snow, laughing.

"Hey, no fair, you've got high boots and my shoes only go up to my ankles. . . ." She paused to check for sure, lifting one foot. She raised her voice and called after him, "Not even that high!"

"Come on. I'll make tracks," he said without pausing, dragging his feet to plow a way for her. It was somewhat better, but certainly left plenty of snow for her to trudge through. With high, running steps she hurried to catch up with him.

"Hey, wait up, you crazy man!" she hollered.

He paused, only half-turned to watch her over his shoulder. When she was close behind, he headed again along the footpath, with her at his heels.

It had been years and years since Allison had been in the woods at this time of day. The sky turned lavender as the sun sank. Snow blanketed everything, muffling sound, softening edges, warming—in its own way—all that lay around them.

Suddenly Rick stopped short and stood with his back to her, stalk still. Automatically she stopped, too. Sparrows tittered from branches above their heads, the notes crisp in the clear air. Wordlessly, Rick pointed. Allison's eyes followed. There on the snow beneath a giant tree sat a brilliant red cardinal.

"That's the kind of stuff I photograph and paint," he whispered.

435

The cardinal flitted away at the sound of his voice. Allison watched it flash through the trees. Suddenly she felt curiously refreshed and renewed. She turned in a circle, gazing at the white-rimmed branches overhead. "It's hard to believe we're in the heart of the city."

"Haven't you ever been here before?" He still faced away from her, and she looked up at blond hair curling over his upturned collar, then scanned the peaceful woods again.

"No. Not up here. I've been through the park, but I never bothered to come up here and see what was at the end of the trail."

He stood in silence, studying the sky, his head tipped sharply back. After a long time he said, "It's peaceful, isn't it?"

"Mmm-hmm." Even the birds had stopped twittering. She realized she could actually hear Rick Lang's breathing. They fell silent again, two people whose busy lives afforded too little of such elemental joys as this. There came a faint popping, as if bark were stretching in its sleep, growing restless for spring.

"This is what I miss about not living where I was born and raised."

"Are you a country boy?"

"Yup." Suddenly he seemed to grow aware of how long they'd been standing motionless, knee-deep in snow. "Your feet must be frozen."

"It's worth it," she replied, and found it true.

"Better get you back though, and steal that log if we're going to."

"I guess." Still, she was reluctant to return to the highway, to the sound of cars that was totally absent here, to the road signs instead of boles and branches.

"Can you even feel your feet anymore?"

Grinning, she looked down, then back up at him. His face was almost obscured by oncoming dark. "What feet?"

He laughed. "Just a minute, stay where you are," he ordered, then jogged off the path, circled around her, hunched over, and said, "Climb on."

"What!"

"Climb on." His butt pointed her way. "I got you into this mess, I'll get you out."

"Won't do you a bit of good. They're gone. The feet are gone. Can't feel a thing down there," she said woefully, staring at her hidden calves.

"Get the hell on, you're making me feel guiltier by the minute."

"Oh, lord, if I do, you'll be the one with the slipped disc."

"From a willow whip like you? Don't make me laugh."

So she clambered aboard Rick Lang's back, and he clamped a strong arm around each leg. She found herself with her cheek pressed against the back of his jacket, gloved hands clasped around his neck as she rode piggyback to the parking lot. Childish, foolish . . . fun, she thought.

He smelled of cold air and slightly of something scented, like soap or shaving lotion. Bumping along, she tried to think back to how she had managed to end up in such a spot. She could scarcely remember. Only that it had been painless, fun, and that somehow he'd managed to make her laugh again.

At the van she slipped off him and they loaded the log without mishap, but by that time Allison was shivering like a wet pup.

"Do you want me to drive back?" Rick asked. "You could stick your feet up underneath the heater and start thawing out."

"No, they're too cold. If I thaw them out that fast I'll lose 'em for sure."

"Minnesota girls!" he exclaimed in disgust. "Never know how to dress for the weather, even though they're born and raised in it."

"How do you know I was born and raised in it?"

"Were you?"

"Nope, South Dakota."

"Hey, you wanna talk all night or get back to town so you can thaw out?"

When they were halfway back to the city, the headlights picking the way through the dark, she asked, "Are you always this way?"

"What way?"

She shrugged. "I don't know . . . amusing."

She felt his eyes scan her for a moment before he turned away and answered, "When I'm happy."

Memories of Jason came flooding back, warning her again of how sweet words such as these had hurt her once before, led her into a trap that had been sprung with such suddenness that she hadn't yet healed. This man was too new, too irresistible, too perfect. She was reacting to the loss of Jason, spinning Rick into a fanciful hero of her liking.

They parked the van on the nearly deserted downtown street and unloaded the log. Carrying it down the hall of the Genesis Building, they met the night watchman. As congenially and off the cuff as if the enormous log were only a toothpick he'd been picking his teeth with, Rick nodded to the curious old man, asked, "Hey, how's it going?" and marched on past without so much as a snicker.

After they'd gotten into the ancient elevator and propped the ungainly log in the corner, between them, they turned around to see the gates closing on the night watchman's suspicious face.

Allison and Rick looked at each other and crumpled against the sides of the elevator in laughter.

"He's probably still standing there with his tonsils showing," she managed at last.

"This is probably the most intrigue he's had since he got the job. We'll keep him wondering for months what we did with a log this size on the sixth floor of a downtown office building."

They were still in stitches as they lugged the clunky log down the hall and into the studio, stumbling under its weight, which was far more appreciable the farther they went. When they'd deposited it inside, near the sandbags, Rick dropped down heavily on it, puffing.

"When I took this modeling job, I had no idea what else it would entail."

"Listen . . . thanks. I realize now I'd never have been able to do it alone."

"Any time."

The room grew quiet. Somewhere in the hall the elevator reverberated as it moved in the silent building.

"Probably the night watchman coming up to see what those two crazy people are up to," suggested Rick.

"I'll explain to him someday."

Rick clamped his hands to his knees and lunged to his feet.

"Well, I've got an appointment on a log with Vivien Zucchini Thursday night. I'd better get home and get my beauty rest."

Allison led the way to the door, switched out the lights, locked up, and walked with Rick to the elevator. The night watchman was standing there again, studying them with a curious look on his face.

As the cage was cutting him off from view, Rick waved two fingers at him. "G'night."

Unable to resist, Allison did the same.

"He has the master key. How much you wanna bet he goes into the studio and figures it all out?"

There seemed little more to say. Allison felt a strange reluctance to leave Rick. He walked her to the van and opened her door again.

"Well, thanks for the ride," he said.

"Same to you." She smiled.

He grinned, slammed the door, gave a good-bye salute, and sent Allison on her way wondering again where his hidden flaw was. Surely it would show up soon. The man was too good to be true.

Chapter 4

THE FOLLOWING DAY Allison had an argument with a stubborn fool at the Anderson Lumberyard who refused to deliver a partial pallet of bricks because its value was under fifty dollars. When she explained her situation, he became even more belligerent, his raspy voice taking on an insolent tone. "Lady, we don't deliver bricks to no sixth floor of no office building. If we can't unload 'em with a forklift, we don't unload 'em at all. You want your bricks up there, you carry 'em up yourself!"

"But—"

The dead wire told her she was talking to nobody. She slammed the receiver down and kicked the corner of her desk, angered as she so often was by things beyond her control.

The phone rang and without thinking she jerked it to her ear and bawled into the mouthpiece, "Yaa, hullo!"

A few seconds of surprised silence passed, then a man's voice said, "Oh, I must have the wrong number."

Realizing how rudely she'd answered, she clutched the phone and put on a far more congenial voice. "No . . . wait, sorry, this is Photo Images. What can I do for you?"

"Ms. Scott?"

"Yes, who . . . oh God, is this Rick Lang?"

"You guessed it. Caught you being nasty on the phone again."

She sank into her swivel chair and hooked her boot heels

on the edge of the desk. "Listen, I'm sorry. You must think I'm a real asp, but sometimes I get so mad at . . . at . . . well, at men!"

"Hey, what'd I do?"

"Oh, it's not you, but do you mind if I blow off a little steam? I mean, all I asked for was a little partial load of bricks, and you'd think that damn fool could tell his truck driver to pull his truck up in front of the building and deposit them on the sidewalk or something! I mean, I wasn't asking to have them hand carried up six flights! But no, the load isn't worth enough for them to waste the gas. If they can't take it off with a forklift, they won't take it off at all!"

From his end Lang heard an ending sound like the growl of an angry bear while she worked off her frustration.

At her end, Allison felt slightly sheepish when his understanding laugh came over the wire and he asked good-naturedly, "There, do you feel better now?"

"No, dammit, I'll have to carry those bricks by myself . . . yes, kind of . . . oh hell, I don't know!" she blurted out in exasperation. But a minute later, Allison found her anger losing steam and finally disintegrating into self-effacing laughter. "Hey, I'm really sorry I took it out on you. It's not your fault. And what if you'd been a paying customer wanting to hire me? I'd have alienated you with the first word."

"How do you know you didn't? You still don't know what I called for."

Allison dropped her feet to the floor, crossed her legs, leaned an elbow on the desk, and affected a sultry, ingratiating feminine drawl. "Good mawnin' dahlin', this's Photo Images —hot coffee, hugs of greetin', and free makeup with every sittin', honey, so y'all come back, heah?"

She was twisting a strand of hair coyly around an index finger as Lang's full-throated laughter came over the wire, and she pictured him as he'd been last night in the woods, goofing around with the log, giving her a piggyback ride.

But now he reminded Allison, "Hey, I didn't get any hugs of greeting, and if I remember right, I'm the one who bought the coffee."

"But you'll get free makeup when I take the shots, and I'll buy you a cup of coffee then, so we'll be even."

"What about the hug?"

Something fluttery and warm lifted Allison's heart. She knew she was engaging in mild flirtation and shouldn't be. She searched for a glib answer, leaning back and gazing at the ceiling. "Mmm, what about when you gave me that piggyback ride? What would you call that?"

"You're too quick, Ms. Allison Scott. I'll let you off this time. What I called for was to check on your health today after last night's frostbite in those flimsy little duck shoes of yours."

"No worse for wear."

"Not even a head cold?"

"Not even."

"Well, good, at least I didn't add another item to your list of grievances against . . . men."

Allison smiled, toying now with the dial on the phone, warmed by his thoughtfulness, though she didn't want to be. But it had been a long time since anyone other than Mattie had been concerned about her welfare. Certainly Jason had never been. With Jason it was always her catering to him.

"Listen, what's all this about the bricks anyway? Can I help?" he offered.

"No, it's not your problem, it's mine. I need them to weigh down the plastic so I can build a lake."

"You're kidding!"

"No, I'm not! Have you ever heard of a beach without a lake?"

"Wouldn't it have been easier to take the pictures in the summer and use a real lake?"

"No challenge in that."

"Oh, you like a challenge, do you, Ms. Scott?"

"Rather. Besides, contracts like this don't always accommodate the seasons. I knew when I accepted that it would present problems, but it was just too good a chance to pass up. This cover will be for a new line of books coming out next year, and if I give them what they want, chances are I'll have my foot in the door. It'd be wonderful to know where my next month's grocery money was coming from . . . and the next, and the next."

"I know the feeling well and I admire your guts, but I'll

still have to see it to believe it—a lake, a beach, and a bon-fire?"

"Do you doubt me, Mr. Lang?"

"I have the feeling I shouldn't, but I do. It sounds impossible."

"Nothing is impossible if you want it badly enough, and I want this to be the best damn cover Hathaway Romances sees between now and June, so they beat my door down to get me to do a hundred more."

Rick Lang was beginning to admire the lady more and more. He couldn't wait to see how in the world she would build that lake. "So what about the bricks? Could I help? I haven't got a forklift, but I've got two good hands."

"Listen, you've done enough already, helping me get that log up here. I can handle the rest myself. The only thing is, if it takes me longer than I thought, we might have to delay the shooting for a day. But I'll call you and let you know when the set is ready. If we can't shoot Thursday, could you make it Friday instead?"

"Sure . . . whenever."

There was a pause in the conversation, and Allison suddenly felt reluctant to end it. Rick Lang was turning out to be one of the most congenial and warm men she'd ever met.

"Well . . . thank you again for checking on me, but as I said, there's no need to start cooking chicken soup."

"My pet hen will be glad to hear that."

They laughed together for a moment, and the line seemed to hum with expectancy.

"I'll call," Allison promised. "See you either Thursday or Friday night, six o'clock."

"Right. Bye."

But after the word was spoken Allison waited for a click, telling her Rick Lang had hung up. A full ten seconds passed, and she heard nothing. A curious throat-filling exhilaration tightened her skin, like back in high school when the boy you had a crush on stared at you across the classroom for the first time. Five more seconds of silence hummed past, and at last Allison heard the click. As if the phone had turned hot, she dropped the receiver onto the cradle, jumped back, and jammed her hands hard into her pants pockets, staring at the instrument with her heart hammering in her temples.

Scott, you're a giddy fool! she harped silently. Go get your load of bricks!

She drove the van to the lumber yard, where she bought a roll of strong, black plastic and the partial pallet of bricks. When she started loading them single-handedly, the men at the loading dock felt sheepish enough to lend a hand.

Back at the Genesis Building it took almost two hours to round up the head janitor and locate a freight dolly, and by that time Allison's temper was flaring again. At this rate she might as well wait and shoot the scenes at Lake Calhoun, come summer!

By four o'clock in the afternoon it was cold and windy in the canyons between the tall buildings as she backed the van up to the dock platform. The alley was dismal, foreboding, and the cold was no palliative for her temper. Allison shivered, then pulled on leather gloves and began the arduous task of transferring the bricks two at a time from the van to the wide, flat dolly. According to the radio, the windchill had sent the temperature down to minus forty. Allison tugged the thick knit cap lower over her ears and forehead. The icy air caused a pain smack between her eyes. As she bent and stooped, the wind seemed to swirl and chill and find every hidden path into the breaks between her layers of clothing.

Damn that stingy lumberyard! she cursed silently, thunking down two bricks and turning back for two more. Allison's nose was drippy, and her fingers had turned to icicles. She looked like a disgruntled kodiak bear, bundled up in an ugly old army-green parka with her hat covering her eyebrows.

"Ms. Scott, you're going to give yourself a hernia if you don't slow down."

Allison spun around, a brick in each hand, and peered from the depths of the van to find Rick Lang lounging against the doorway beside the freight dolly, smiling in amusement. The ugly, utilitarian bobcap had slipped so far down it now almost covered her eyes. She had to tip her head way back to peer at him from under it. At that moment, to Allison's horror, she felt a trickle of mucous run warmly from her nose down to her lip. Sniffing frantically, she thought, Oh no! Oh dear! I look

444

like the abominable snowman! And damn, why did my nose have to run right now?

"Oh God, how did you find me here?" she wailed.

"The studio was unlocked and the lights were on, so I figured you must be unloading bricks—I thought you'd be at the loading dock."

Before she could hide or run, he was pulling on thick leather gloves and bounding onto the back of the van. Automatically she bent over and covered her head with both hands. From the muffled depths came the wail, "Ohhhhhhh, hell! I look like the wrath of God."

He answered with a wide-mouthed laugh, then she felt a hand rough up her bobcap teasingly and push her face momentarily farther toward her knees.

"Hey, you look like an honest working woman, so let's get to work."

When spring comes, she promised herself, I'm gonna bury this ugly cap in the garden!

She stood up, knowing her face was beet red, thankful he couldn't see much of it in the dim light of the dock area. She peered up into his smiling blue eyes, sliding the bobcap farther back on her head. Immediately it slid back where it wanted to be, and any lingering delusions Allison might have had about her appearance vanished. She must be about as appealing as a seven-year-old boy after an afternoon of sledding. Horrified, she felt her nose dripping again. Rick Lang just stood there and boldly laughed at her, a pair of bricks in his hands.

"Hey, your nose is dripping," he informed her merrily.

She sniffed loudly, leaned farther back, purposely exaggerating her snot-nosed, childish appearance, swiped at her nose with the back of her gloved hand and pouted, "Well, I don't have a tissue, smarty! And if you were any kind of a gentleman whatsoever, you would politely refrain from mentioning it!"

He chuckled and dropped one brick. "It's rather hard to pretend when it's running right down." Leaning sideways, he fished in a hind pocket and came up with a crumpled white hanky. "It looks like it's been used, but it hasn't," he informed

Allison. "I do my own laundry and ironing isn't really one of my favorite pastimes."

"Beggars can't be choosers," she returned, yanking off a glove and turning her back while she buried her nose in his hanky and honked. To the best of her knowledge it was the first time she'd ever used a man's hanky.

"How come in the movies when this happens to girls they are somehow always daintily indisposed, with clinging tendrils of hair coming seductively loose from their topknot?" she grumbled.

"I think I see one now." Behind her she felt a tug as he lightly pulled a frowsy chunk of hair that must have been hanging from beneath her cap.

Never in her life had Allison felt more like an unfeminine klutz!

Rick Lang didn't mind one bit. He thought she looked delightful, bundled up in that ugly war-surplus parka, red nose running, scarcely an eyelash visible underneath that unflattering bobcap. She finished blowing her nose, turned, offered him the hanky, realized her mistake, and withdrew it with a snap. "Oh, I'll wash it first."

He unceremoniously yanked it out of her hand and buried it in his pocket. "Don't be silly. Let's load bricks."

He set to work with a refreshing vigor, unlike what she might have expected from a man with a cushy job like modeling. Somehow, when she'd first laid eyes on his snapshot, she'd visualized a self-pampering hedonist, but she was learning he was no such thing.

They had little breath for talking while they transferred the bricks from van to dolly. Their breath formed white puffs in the air as they worked. When they were finished, he ordered, "Toss me the keys. I'll pull the van in the lot, but wait for me. We'll take that dolly up together. Don't try to push it yourself."

He disappeared around the front of the van, and Allison lowered the big overhead door, evaluating Rick Lang anew. It was wonderful to have a man offering to help with the heavy work. She had done it alone for so many years, she never thought much about it anymore. But a warm glow spread through her at his admonition to wait for him.

He came back in, handed her the keys, and took up his place at the far end of the dolly, gesturing toward the other end. "You steer, I'll push."

"Aye, aye, sir," she replied with a grin.

The dolly filled almost the entire area of the freight elevator. When they'd eased it on, Rick sat down on top of the bricks and indicated a place beside him. "Your chariot awaits," he quipped.

Allison laughed and plopped herself down beside him, Indian fashion, for the ride up to the sixth floor. From the corner of her eye she saw him turn his gaze from the floor indicator to her. Self-consciously she realized she was wearing the most ridiculously ugly pac boots ever manufactured. Resolutely she kept her head tilted back, eyes trained on the numbers above the door.

"That's a damn nice cap," he teased.

Without taking her eyes off the numbers, she pulled the disreputable hat even farther down over her forehead, until only a slit of eyes remained visible beneath the turned-back brim.

"For a stupid South Dakota girl who doesn't know how to dress for the weather, it ain't too bad." She flashed him a smart smirk and a brief glimpse of the corner of one eye as it angled his way.

"I'll take that back when I see a beach, a lake, and a bonfire on the sixth floor."

"Doubting Thomas," she scoffed, and grinned.

They arrived at the sixth floor, and she leaped off the dolly and opened the clanking brass gate, then together they worked the ungainly vehicle into the hall. Wouldn't you know, the night watchman had just come on duty. He rounded a corner of the hall and saw the two of them maneuvering a load of bricks off the elevator.

Rick raised a hand in greeting and informed the wide-eyed fellow, "Just takin' my girl for a ride is all." He swept a theatrical bow toward the bricks, and Allison played along, clambering on board to again sit Indian fashion in snow boots, parka and bobcap, while Rick pushed her down the hall to the studio door.

When they got inside they closed the door, looked at each

other, and burst into laughter, as it seemed they were doing with increasing regularity. Rick dropped down onto the dolly. Allison leaned against the door, holding her sides, filled with rich amusement such as she hadn't shared with anyone in years.

"Oh, you were so glib, I think he believed you!" she managed to get out, quite weak now, reaching a tired hand to doff the cap from her head, leaving behind a mop of hair as disheveled as a serving of spaghetti.

"So were you—climbing on, sitting there like some Indian princess on her way to a fertility rite. You were superb!"

"I was, wasn't I?" she preened.

Immediately he reconsidered, scanning her from head to foot. He shook his head in mock despair. "I think I take that back. You're the biggest mess I've ever seen in my life."

"How would you like a brick implanted in the middle of your forehead?" She picked one up and threatened him with it.

"Hey, come on." He raised his arms protectively above his head. "Take a look in the mirror."

"*You* take a look in the mirror! Your hair looks like somebody styled it with a cattle prod, so don't point fingers at me." She deposited the brick and turned toward the doorway, across the room. Rick saw a light come on as she moved inside, and the next minute he heard a blood-curdling shriek.

He got up off the dolly and ambled over to the doorway, where he stood smiling. The well-lit room was apparently a dressing room, and Allison stood in front of a mirror, sticking her tongue out at herself.

"See? I told you," he nettled.

"Yep," she agreed dryly. She found a comb in a nearby drawer and dragged it unceremoniously through her hair.

He stood watching, noting the way the winter air had tinted her nose a becoming pink, the way her feminine shape was lost inside the enormous parka, which now hung unzipped, dwarfing her shoulders.

At that moment a furious pounding sounded on the studio door, followed by the concerned voice of the night watchman. "Hey, you all right in there, miss?"

Allison's and Rick's eyes met in the mirror, and they giggled.

"The night watchman. Thinks you're being assaulted in here."

"You'd better stop making fun of my appearance or I'll tell him it's true." She gave him a warning glance.

"Hello in there!" came another shout from the hall.

Allison hot-footed it around Rick Lang, opened the hall door, and confronted the frowning, grandfatherly man who peered past her to the pallet of bricks, the log at the far end of the room, and Rick lounging against the doorway of the dressing room. "Everything all right in here?" he asked. "Thought I heard somebody screamin'."

"Oh, that was me." She pointed over her shoulder. "He tried to get fresh, but I've got a black belt in karate. Thanks for inquiring, but I can take care of myself."

The watchman turned away, shaking his head and muttering to himself.

In the studio, Rick threatened, "If he sics the law on me, I'll tell 'em about the log you stole from a public park."

"I didn't steal that log, *you* did!"

"Oh yeah? Then what's it doing in your studio?"

She shrugged innocently. "Don't know. It just showed up here uninvited, like you."

Rick lazily pulled his shoulder away from the door frame, pulling on his gloves while he sauntered to the dolly and ordered, "Get your butt over here and help me unload these bricks, lady, before I take offense and leave you to do it yourself."

They worked companionably for the next two hours, placing the bricks in two roughly concentric circles on the floor at the far end of the studio. While Rick returned the dolly to the loading area, Allison unrolled the black plastic and sliced off an enormous piece to act as their lake bottom. When Rick came back, the two of them arranged the plastic, draping it over the inner circle of bricks, then weighing it with the outer circle. They crawled back and forth on their hands and knees in their stocking feet so they would not puncture the plastic, taking up slack, gauging how big the makeshift puddle of water had to be to produce an adequate reflection from the fill light that would simulate the moon shimmering upon the lake.

Next they worked with the sand. Allison was grateful to

have Rick there to lug the clumsy sacks around the edge of the "lake." As they emptied them one by one, covering the brick-work, the setting slowly took shape, appearing less and less artificial. The last item to be positioned was the log. Together they hefted it, placed it in the foreground where Allison indi-cated, then stood back while she formed a square with her palms to confine the view the camera would see and to judge the results of their labor. She hadn't yet set up a camera on the tripod, but she asked Rick, "Will you sit on the log for a minute so I can get a general idea of how we did?"

"That's what I'm being paid for." Obligingly he sat on the log, his arms draped loosely over his knees while she studied the composition as best she could without everything in it.

He watched her kneel, her face serious now as she peered at him from about hip level, where the camera would be come Thursday night. Again she was all brisk self-assurance, a stu-dious expression on her face as she did what she loved doing best. She had removed the army parka a while ago and now wore a white sweatshirt and blue jeans. As she bent forward, her hair fell across her cheek, but she seemed totally unaware of it, of anything but her work.

Suddenly she stood up, biting her upper lip while deep in thought. She glanced at the darkened strobes standing around the edges of the room, thought for a moment longer, abruptly smiled, clapped her hands, and declared, "Yup! It'll work just fine."

"Good," he returned, then sighed. He looked at his watch and reminded her, "Do you know what time it is? It's eight-thirty, and I haven't had any supper. Neither have you." He heaved himself to his feet, gestured with a sideward quirk of the head as he passed her, and led the way to the front door. "Come on, let me buy you a hamburger."

Walking toward their jackets, piled on her desk, she scolded, "Oh no, not after all the help you've given me. It's me who'll do the buying."

He automatically picked up her parka first and held it, waiting for her arms to slip in. "I asked first."

"I buy or I'm not going," she declared stubbornly. "It's the least I can do."

"Are you always this obstinate?"

"Nope. Only when guys come along and save my discs."

"All right, you win." He shook the jacket slightly. "Come on, get in, I'm starved."

At last she complied, buttoning up, retrieving her bobcap, and pulling it clownishly low over her forehead again while he slid his arms into his jacket and snapped it up.

"My car or yours?" he asked as they walked toward the elevator.

"How 'bout both of ours, then we can just hit for home after we eat."

"Right."

On the first floor he turned toward the front of the building, she toward the rear, having agreed upon where to meet. But when Allison got to her van she realized, chagrined, that she was almost flat out of cash. She counted the money in her billfold and her loose change. She had a single one-dollar bill and hardly enough change to make up the price of two hamburgers, much less drinks to go with them.

God, how embarrassing, she thought, and frantically started the van, thinking of her checkbook at home on the kitchen cabinet. The city streets were almost deserted. She had no idea what Rick's car looked like, so she had no recourse but to drive to the appointed restaurant and wait in the parking lot for him to arrive.

When she saw his face behind the window of a Ford sedan, she jumped from the van, left it idling, and was waiting when he came to a stop. She tapped on the window, and he rolled it down. She plunged her hands into her jacket pockets and looked up sheepishly.

"I feel like a real dope, but I haven't got enough money with me after all, so would you settle for an omelette at my place?"

"Sounds good."

"It's not far. I live on Lake of the Isles."

"I'll follow you."

She shivered, ran back to her van, and twenty minutes later the headlights of his car followed hers into the driveway between the high snowbanks.

When she emerged from the depths of the dark garage, he was waiting to lower the door for her, and once again Allison was struck by his unfailing good manners. He performed each

451

courtesy with a naturalness that most men seemed to have long forgotten in this day of women's independence. Allison felt special when he treated her in this gentlemanly way. Inwardly she chuckled as she led the way up the stairway to her apartment, realizing she was dressed more like a combat soldier than a lady. Yet he still afforded her chivalry at every opportunity. And he did it in so offhand a manner as to make her feel foolish for giving it a second thought.

They stamped the snow off their boots and walked into her gaily decorated apartment. He was already pulling off his boots before she could turn around to protest, "Oh, you don't have to."

But he tugged them off anyway, then stood looking around the room while she removed her jacket and waited for his.

"Hey, this is like a touch of summer. You do all this your-self?" he asked.

"Yes. I like green, as you can see."

"Me too." His eyes scanned the room, moving from item to item while he shrugged from his jacket and absently handed it to her. "You have a nice touch. Looks to me like if you ever wanted to give up photography, you could take up interior decorating."

"Thank you, but you're making me blush. Please, just . . . just sit down and make yourself at home."

One brow raised, he glanced back over his shoulder with a grin to see if she was really blushing, but she was busy hanging up their jackets in a small closet behind the door.

She turned, caught him grinning at her, and gave him a little shove toward the living room. "Go . . . sit down or something. I'll be right back."

While she was gone, he walked around the room, noticing the tape player, the healthy plants, the daybed out on the closed-off sun porch. The main room was marvelous, full of light and color, its rich wood floor gleaming, tasteful art prints in chrome frames hanging on the walls. A decorator easel stood in one corner, and he wondered why it was empty. Hands in pockets, he ambled over to the opposite corner and was gazing at the ceiling hook that held up the suspended chair when she returned to the room.

"Doubting Thomas?" she inquired archly.

He glanced over his shoulder. She had put on some lip gloss and combed her hair. On her feet were huge, blue fuzzy slippers. "You read my mind so easily, do you?"

"Everybody who comes in here goes over to that chair, looks up, and asks 'Will this thing really hold me?'"

"Not me. I didn't ask."

"No, but you were about to."

"No, I wasn't."

She went to the kitchen end of the room and opened the refrigerator, in search of eggs. Funny, she had an inkling he'd ask it, even before he asked it.

"Hey, will this thing hold me?"

But he was already inserting himself into the almost circular basket, but very, very gingerly, as if it were going to drop him the moment he settled his full weight in it.

"Nope!" she answered.

He laughed, crossed his hands over his belly, pushed gently with his heel, and called across the room, "Hey, I want an under-duck."

"A what?" she asked, popping her head up from the depths of the cabinet where she was searching for a bowl.

"An under-duck. You know . . . when you were a little kid and you got pushed on a swing, didn't you call it an under-duck when they'd go running right under you?"

"Oh, *that!*" She laughed, cracked the eggs into the bowl, and remembered back. "No, I think we used to call it . . ." She screwed up her face, trying to remember. "Would you believe I can't think of what we used to call it."

"Shame on you. How will you teach your kids those all-important things if you forget them yourself?"

"Haven't got any kids."

From the depths of the basket chair Rick studied her while she beat the eggs with a wire whisk. The movement made her shining hair bounce at the ends, and inside her baggy sweatshirt he could make out the outline of her breasts bouncing, too. He let his glance rove down to her derrière—tiny, shapely buns . . . trim hips . . . long, supple legs.

You will have kids, he decided, admiring what he saw. "Do you plan to have kids?" he asked.

"Not for a while. I've got a career to establish first. I'm

453

just getting up a good head of steam."

He liked the way she moved, brisk and sure, taking a moment to wipe her palms on her thighs before reaching into the cabinet for a salt shaker.

Allison was conscious of his eyes following her, though she wasn't even facing him. It was disconcerting, yet welcome in a way, too. She was standing uncertainly, gazing into an open cabinet as she admitted, "This is awful, but all I have to put in an omelette is tuna fish."

She turned apologetically to find him six inches behind her. Startled, she drew back a step.

"Tuna-fish omelette?" he repeated, grimacing. "You lured me up here for a tuna-fish omelette?"

"I didn't lure you up here, and besides, experimentation is the mother of invention."

"I thought that was necessity."

"Well . . . whatever." She gestured haplessly. "Right now it's necessary for me to experiment, all right?"

"Okay, tuna-fish omelette. I'll grin and bear it, but we could have had a perfectly good hamburger and french fries if you hadn't been so stubborn."

"I get that way sometimes . . . female pride or something like that." She turned her back on him and rummaged for a can opener, her heart fluttering giddily at his nearness. When the tuna can was open, he reached around her, took a pinch, and popped it into his mouth. "Sorry," he offered, without the least note of contrition in his voice, "but I'm starving, and I thought I'd get at least one good taste before you ruin it."

"Would you rather have a tuna sandwich?" But immediately she waggled her palms. "No, forget I asked that. I just remembered I'm out of bread."

"There's one thing a person can't accuse you of, and that's trying to finagle your way to a man's heart through his stomach." He turned away and wandered to the tape deck, squatting down on his haunches to scan the titles on the shelf below. "You like The Five Senses, huh?" he noted.

At his question something tight and constricting seemed to settle across Allison's chest. A lump formed in her throat as she stared, unseeing, at Rick's back.

He swung around on the balls of his feet to look at her, and immediately she whirled to face the cabinet. "Yeah," she said, so crisply the word held an edge of ice.

Immediately he sensed he'd touched a nerve. She exuded defensiveness that chilled him clear across the room. "Do you mind if I put something on?"

She stared at the frying pan, seeing Jason Ederlie instead, wondering how she'd react if Rick happened by accident to put on the wrong song. Yet she'd just said she liked The Five Senses, so how could she possibly say what she was thinking: *anything* but The Five Senses.

"Go ahead," she answered lifelessly, leaving him to wonder what motivated her quicksilver change of mood.

She busied herself with the omelette, and a few minutes later the music of Melissa Manchester drifted through the apartment. Relieved, she cast him a quick glance to find he was standing by the stereo, studying her across the room.

Don't ask, she begged silently. *Don't ask, please.* Thankfully, he didn't, but went to sit on the davenport and wait to be called to the table. He stretched out, crossed his feet at the ankles, threaded his fingers together, and hung them over his belly, watching her covertly as she put the food on the table and wondering what had caused her sudden defensiveness.

A guy, he supposed. When it involved music it was usually a guy and some song the two of them had considered special. He made a mental note never to play any of The Five Senses tapes if he ever got up here again.

"It's ready," she announced soberly, standing beside the table with a long face.

He eased slowly to his feet, walked across the room, and stood by a chair next to hers. "Listen, I'm sorry for whatever I said that upset you. Whatever it was, I'm sorry."

Her lips parted slightly, and for a moment she looked as if she might cry. Then she slipped her hands into her jeans pockets, her throat working convulsively. "It's not your fault, okay?" she offered softly. "It's just something I have to get over, that's all."

His sober eyes rested on her questioningly, but he asked nothing further. Wordlessly he leaned across the corner of the table to pull out her chair. "Agreed. Now sit down so I can, too."

She gave him a shaky smile and sat, but the gaity had evaporated from the evening. They shared their meal in strained silence, as if another presence were in the room separating them.

Allison avoided Rick's eyes as he intermittently studied her, the downcast mouth, the forlorn droop of shoulder. His eyes moved to her left hand—no ring. Covertly they moved around the room in search of evidence of a man sharing the place or having shared it. There were no pictures, magazines, articles of any kind intimating a male presence in her life. His gaze moved to her again, to her shapely mouth, breasts, fine-boned jaw, shell-like ears, downcast eyes, and slender hand picking disinterestedly at the omelette. He leaned toward her slightly, resting his forearms on the edge of the table.

"Stop me if I'm stepping on hallowed ground," he began, "but are you committed to someone?"

Her head snapped up, and a shield seemed to drop over her eyes.

"Yes." She dropped her fork, giving up all pretense of eating. "To myself."

A brief flare of anger shone in his eyes. "That's not what I meant, and you know it. Is there some man in your life right now?"

Her heart began to beat furiously, but immediately memories of Jason came to quell it. "No," she answered truthfully, "and I don't want one."

He scrutinized her silently for a moment, his lips compressed. "Fair enough, but I had to ask. I enjoyed myself tremendously the last two evenings." He watched her carefully while relaxing back in his chair, leaning his elbows on the chrome armrests.

She propped her elbows beside her plate, entwined her fingers, and rested her forehead against white thumb knuckles. A shaky sigh escaped her lips. "I did too, but that's as far as it goes."

"Is it?"

"Yes!" she snapped, but her eyes remained hidden while her lips trembled.

"Somebody hurt you, and you're going to make damn sure nobody does again."

"It's none of your business!" Her shoulders stiffened, and her head came up.

"We'll see," he said with disarming certainty, not a flicker of doubt in his unsmiling countenance.

"I make it a practice never to get personally involved with my models. I'm sorry if you thought . . ." Her eyelids fluttered self-consciously before her gaze fell to her plate. "I mean, I never meant to lead you on."

"You didn't. You've been a lady every inch of the way, all right?"

Her eyes met his again—unsteady brown to steady blue. Against her will Allison was struck again by his flawless handsomeness, even as it filled her with mistrust. She wanted to believe he was sincere, perhaps for a moment. His face wore a look of quiet determination, warning her that he wouldn't back off without a fight.

She swallowed. "It's been a long day—"

"Say no more, I'm gone." Immediately he was on his feet, plate in hand, heading for the sink.

She felt small and guilty for giving him such an obvious brushoff when he'd been a perfect gentleman. But since Jason her instinct for self-preservation was finely honed. The faster she got Rick Lang out of here, the better.

He padded over to the entry, picked up a boot, and leaned his backside against the door while pulling it on. From the closet she retrieved his coat, and before she realized what she was doing, held it out as she'd often done for Jason. A surprised expression flitted across Rick's face before he turned, slipped his arms in, and faced her once more, slowly closing the snaps while she waited uncomfortably for him to finish and leave.

She trained her eyes on the frayed collar, afraid to raise them further, for she knew he was studying her while the sound of the snaps seemed to tick away the strained seconds.

His hands reached the last one, and he leisurely tugged his gloves from the jacket pocket, slowly pulled them on while she stared at them, knowing no other place to safely rest her eyes. He jammed his spread fingers into the gloves, all the while studying her averted face.

He was dressed for outside, ready to go, yet he stood there

without making a motion toward the door.

"I heard what you said before. I know what you were telling me," he said in a low voice. "But I just have to do this . . ."

She had a vague impression of the scent of leather while his glove tipped her chin up. Soft, warm, slightly opened lips touched hers. A tongue tip briefly flicked. Two strong gloved hands squeezed her upper arms, pulling her upward, forcing her to her toes momentarily, catching her totally off guard. Almost as if it were a harbinger of things to come, the kiss ended with a slow separation of their mouths. He lifted his head, studying her eyes for a brief moment, then dropped his gaze to her surprised, open lips.

"Nice," he said softly. Then he was gone, leaving behind only a rush of cold air and a trembling in her stomach.

Chapter 5

ALLISON HALF EXPECTED Rick to call the following day, Wednesday, but he didn't. She wondered what he'd say when he walked into the studio Thursday night. She wondered how to act, then decided she would act no differently than she had all along. Maintaining the same light, teasing banter would be the best way to remain at ease and keep their relationship on a nonpersonal level.

One of Allison's Wednesday chores was to talk her landlord out of a garden hose and lug it up to the studio in preparation for filling the "lake." Then she made a trip to get firewood and a piece of asbestos for under it, so the heat wouldn't raise the linoleum off the studio floor. If that night watchman found out she was going to start a fire in the middle of the building, she'd be out on her ear. Thankfully the building was such a relic it had no smoke alarm or sprinkler system.

Thursday she filled the pool, checking to make sure there were no leaks, then set up her lights, deciding how many she'd need, the general positioning of both key light and fill lights, and what color filters to use on each. She cut out a circle in the backdrop paper, inserted an orange filter on one of the strobes, and positioned it to simulate the moon, which would appear only as a hazy, out-of-focus orb in the finished photograph, its reflection on the water being the chief reason she needed it at all.

By five o'clock she was loading her camera with nervous fingers, telling herself this was stupid, this was business, and Rick Lang was only a model.

Then why was she shaking?

She secured the camera on its tripod, coiled up the hose, disconnected it from the bathroom faucet, then cursed softly to find it had left a trail of water across the floor. Mopping up the spill, she suddenly remembered she hadn't asked the janitor for a wet vac to have on hand in case of an emergency, and ran to do so.

Returning to the studio, pushing the clumsy machine, Allison found Rick standing in front of the set, studying it.

He looked up as she entered and smiled.

"Hi," he said simply.

Something joyfully warm and appreciative crept along her veins at the sight of him. It was impossible to forget his brief parting kiss.

"Hi."

"You did it." He grinned, glancing at the lake, the sand, the bonfire ready for lighting.

"I told you I would." She sauntered over to the edge of the set.

"Clever lighting, with the moon—I presume—reflecting across the water." He turned to indicate the strobe showing through the backdrop, the low positioning of the camera on the tripod.

"Let's hope so. We haven't taken the shots or seen the results yet."

"How did you get that lake filled up?"

"With a garden hose."

"And you're going to suck it up with that when you're done?" He indicated the wet vac.

"Yup." She flipped her palms up and gave him a plucky smile. "Simple."

"Don't underrate yourself. It's more than simple, it's ingenious." Glancing at the set again he commented, "I see you made another trip for firewood."

"Yup."

"Who carried you out this time?" he teased.

"I wore my boots like a good girl. How 'bout you? Did you bring your bathing trunks?"

"Yup!" He pulled them out of a pocket, rolled up tight. "Got 'em right here, but I'm not anxious to put 'em on. It's like a meat locker in here, as usual."

"Don't worry, the fire will warm you up."

"Oh, I thought Vivien Zucchini was supposed to do that." He grinned down at Allison, hooked his thumbs in the pockets of his letter jacket, and watched her swing away.

"Zuchinski," she corrected without turning around.

Rick grinned in amusement, watching her trim hips and thighs take no-nonsense steps. Her hair swayed. Her backside was firm and athletic as she strode toward the dressing-room doorway, reached inside, and flipped the lights on. Slipping her hands into the pockets of her slacks, she turned and leaned one shoulder against the dressing-room doorway like a model in a chic shampoo ad. He scanned her long-sleeved khaki safari jacket, which was belted and had epaulets at the shoulders, his eyes lingering only a fraction of a second on the breast pockets with their button-down flaps. Matching trousers were tucked into thigh-high boots. Her hair was again held behind her ears by the upraised sunglasses, though night had fallen outside and inside the lights were dim.

"I've had the door to the dressing room closed so it would warm up in there," she said. "I don't want you to freeze and break in half before we get you posed and the fire started."

"Where's Miss Zucchini?"

She laughed, hands still in pockets, bending forward at the waist, then peering at him with mock admonishment. "If you say that one more time, she's going to walk in here and I'm going to pour tomato sauce over her instead of oil!"

Rick leaned back and laughed appreciatively while Allison checked her wristwatch. "She's due any minute. If you want to use the dressing room first, we can get started oiling you."

The oiling was news to him, though it was common practice to oil skin to simulate wetness and bring out highlights on the skin.

But at that moment the door opened and in came a stunning blue-eyed brunette bundled up to her ears in fake fur. In an affronted tone she said, "I hope it's warmer in here than it was the other day, or my unmentionables will shrivel up like raisins."

Both Rick and Allison burst out laughing. The woman gazed at them with wide, innocent eyes, as if she had no idea she'd made a graceless, tasteless opening remark.

"Rick Lang, I'd like you to meet Vivien Zuchinski." It was all Allison could do to hold a straight face and get the name right. "Vivien, this is Rick Lang, the man you'll be posing with."

Rick extended his hand.

In slow, sultry motion, Vivien's came out to meet it. She wrapped it tightly in long, shapely fingers with long, shapely nails of a ghastly vermilion that looked surprisingly right on her. Sweeping her spaghetti-length lashes up and down Rick's body, Vivien cooed, "Ooooo, *nice*."

Rick laughed good-naturedly, playing along when Vivien refused to relinquish his hand. "Likewise, I'm sure, Vivien," he said congenially. "I'm happy to share a book cover with a pretty face like yours."

She teased the hairs on the back of his hand with a tapered nail and widened her devastating eyes on him. "Heyyyy, no . . . lisssen, I'm the one that's really knocked out. I mean, you're really somethin', Rick. I'm already forgetting how cold it is in here."

Allison cleared her throat, and Vivien turned to find her leaning against the doorway to the dressing room, one foot crossed in front of the other, with a toe to the floor.

"Mr. Lang has been complaining about how cold it is in here, too, so maybe the two of you can warm each other up, huh?" Bringing her shoulder away from the door frame, Allison gestured Vivien into the brightly lit dressing room. "Would you like to be first, Miss Zook—" She caught herself just in time and finished, "Miss Zuchinski?"

Vivien swooped into the dressing room, shedding her coat and looking around. "Heyyyy, *nice*. Lots of good light for putting on makeup."

"Yours looks great already, so don't change a thing. Just put on your suit, and I'll give you a bottle of baby oil. Is your hair naturally curly?"

"What?" Vivien momentarily gave up studying her pouting lips in the mirror.

"Your hair—is it naturally curly? I'd like to put baby oil on it, too, to create the illusion of wetness."

Vivien patted her tresses with deep concern. "Oil! On my hair? I'd rather not."

"How about just on the ends then, to make it look like you've been in the water?"

"Well, you're the boss . . . but, gee!" She looked crest-fallen, her face much more expressive than her vocabulary.

"Why don't you change first, then we'll experiment a lit-tle," Allison advised.

Vivien closed the door all but a crack, through which she waggled two fingers at Rick before closing it the rest of the way. Allison bit her lip to keep from laughing, but she couldn't resist glancing Rick's way to check his reaction. When their eyes met, he feigned a wolfish grin and rubbed his palms together in anticipation. "Hey, I can't wait," he teased in a whisper.

"I'll just bet you can't."

The door opened a short time later, and Vivien appeared, clad in a minuscule two-piece bathing suit that showed off every voluptuous hill and valley to great advantage. Out she came, hands thrown wide. "How's this?"

"Wow!" Rick exclaimed exuberantly.

"Nice," Allison commented dryly.

"I'm ready for oiling," Vivien declared.

"Let me get the tomato sauce, and I'll get you started," Allison quipped.

"The wha-a-a-t?" Vivien questioned, a puzzled frown on her face, dropping her hands to her hips.

"Rick, go ahead and change," Allison suggested. "It's just an old inside term, Vivien. Come on."

Allison felt rather small, having resorted to such catty tac-tics with Vivien. It wasn't like her at all. What in the world had she been thinking to say such a thing? Vivien was here as a professional, and if anyone was acting unprofessional, it was Allison herself. The truth was, Vivien Zuchinski was a beauti-ful woman with impressive proportions. Allison was abashed to find herself slightly jealous.

463

In two minutes the changing-room door opened again. "Hey, come on in, ladies, it's warmer in here."

Standing behind her desk, Allison lifted her eyes, and her mouth went dry. Rick stood in the doorway, barefooted, bare chested, bare legged, only that tight white suit striping his midsection, dividing his dark skin. Unlike Vivien, he didn't flaunt his assets, but just appeared at the door, invited them in, then stepped inside himself.

"Heyyyy, sugar, I'm comin'!" Vivien giggled.

There was an awkward moment when Allison stepped to the door and handed Rick a full bottle of baby oil. Her eyes had lost all hint of teasing. He was magnificent! Sparkling golden hair covered not only his chest, but also dove in a thin line down his belly, covering his legs and arms lightly. He turned to face the mirror and poured a modicum of oil into his palm, then began applying it to his shoulders while Allison saw his back for the first time. Her eyes drifted from wide shoulders to narrow hips, taking in firm skin and fine-toned muscle. His derrière was flat, his legs well shaped without the bulging muscles that ruined the male form when it came to photographing it. Truly, his body was an artist's concept of beauty.

In the mirror Allison caught his eye and knew he'd been watching her assess him, but he only looked away and continued applying oil briskly. Unlike Jason, who used every such opportunity to smirk and flaunt and tease with his eyes, Rick accepted his physical assets with dignity, but not ego. He radiated no sexy innuendo, but merely turned to the mirror and vigorously continued what he was doing.

Vivien sat on a chair and hooked her shapely toes—vermilion, too, Allison noted—on the edge of the vanity, squirting a line of oil up a perfect leg. Spreading it, she kept her eyes on Rick.

"I'll put some on your back," Allison offered, moving behind Vivien, who swiveled sideways a little on the chair.

It seemed Vivien had dreams of becoming a Playboy bunny, and she prattled on about a trip she had taken to the Playboy Club in Chicago, all the while scouring Rick with admiring gazes.

"I think we'll need some oil on the ends of your hair any-

464

way, Vivien. Do you want me to put it on?" Allison asked.

"Do we have to?" Again Vivien appeared devastated.

"Unless you have some other suggestion as to how we can make it appear wet."

Vivien stood before the giant mirror beside Rick, leaning forward while she concentrated on the monumental decision, then began applying carefully controlled amounts of oil to selected strands of hair.

"Will you help me with my back?" Rick asked Allison, offhandedly passing the bottle of oil over his shoulder and catching her eyes in the mirror.

She was suddenly reluctant to lay a hand on him. She had little choice, however, and accepted the bottle from his slippery fingers. Thank God he didn't grin or tease, just handed the bottle over and waited. Allison poured oil into her palm, thinking: This is how it all started with Jason.

She went at it energetically to hide the fact that her hand shook when she touched Rick's bare skin for the first time. She was unaware of how she glowered or that behind closed lips she held the tip of her tongue tightly between her teeth. Sensations of touch came flooding back to her, filling her memory and her body at this first touch of a man's flesh since Jason's. How many times had she done this for him? How many times had he done this to her? How many times had their oiled skins delighted each other?

Don't think about Jason. Don't think about the fragrance of the oil. Don't think about all the times he was sleek and slippery and seductive.

But Rick's flesh beneath Allison's hand was warm and firm, and her palm slipped over it, conforming to its strong, sleek lines. The shoulder was tough, the shoulder blade hard, the neck unyielding with a tensile strength. Her fingertips inadvertently touched Rick's hair and learned its fine softness, so different from the hardness of his muscles. The contrast jolted her, and she raised her eyes to the mirror to find Rick studying her solemnly.

She was suddenly swept with the awkward feeling that he'd read her mind. Immediately she dropped her eyes to his back again. Taking more oil, she worked it down the warm center of his back to the waistband of his trunks. The memory of his light, undemanding kiss came back to her, and his words, "I just have to do this." With her hands on his skin he somehow became all mixed up in her mind with Jason. Love, hurt, sensuality, and bitterness welled up within Allison, leaving her confused. Then her fingertips slipped over Rick's ribs, and he flinched and tipped guardedly sideways.

Allison came back to the present, realizing it was Rick, not Jason. Their eyes met in the mirror.

"I'm ticklish," he informed her, and the spell was—thankfully—broken.

"I'll remember next time." She handed him the bottle, said, "Excuse me," and reached around him for a roll of paper towels on the vanity.

"Your hair, too," she instructed, brushing alarmingly close to his chest as she reached.

"What?"

Wiping her hands gave her an excuse not to look up at his reflection in the mirror. "Oil your hair, too. How're you doing, Vivien?"

"Can't say I like getting all greasy like this, but I hear oil makes the hair healthy, huh?"

"As soon as you two are done, come on out to the set. I'll get the lighting started."

Outside the wide wall of windows it was totally black. Inside, the only light came from the dressing room. Allison shook off thoughts of Rick Lang and set to work, adjusting the direction of the strobes, firing them time after time to see the effect they created on log, water, sand. Working with a light meter, she took readings from various points, adjusting the rheostats on individual strobes, which were all connected to a single triggering device that would fire them simultaneously with the shutter release when connected to the camera.

Rick and Vivien padded out, barefoot and shivering, to find Allison's shadowy form darting back and forth amid the equipment.

"Oh, good, you're ready. Listen, this sounds like a joke, but I have to crack a window a little bit to let the smoke out once I start the fire. But the room should warm up as soon as the fire gets going. I'm really sorry about the chill in here, but bear with me, okay? I didn't want to strike the match until you

466

two were out here, because I don't want that fire going any longer than necessary.

"Okay, Rick, I want you on the log, Vivien laying on the sand below him, facing him and rather leaning up onto his outstretched leg, gazing up into his face. For now, take the general positions, but don't strain yourselves to hold them. Just relax and I'll light the fire and do a final metering on all the strobes once the flame is going."

A shivering Vivien moved toward the set, rubbing her goose-pimpled arms.

"Step lightly on that sand," Allison warned, "and move slowly across it so it doesn't get spread out any more than necessary." Vivien's teeth were chattering. "Rick, why don't you sit down on the log first?" Allison continued. "Maybe Vivien can lean against your legs for a minute and keep warm." There was no joking now in Allison's voice. As Vivien picked her way gingerly across the sand, Allison touched a match to the hidden chunk of Dura-Flame log that gave a clean, smokeless *pouff* before the small twigs caught. Immediately Allison was moving about, taking readings, firing the strobes time and time again, resetting the angle of the camera now that she had bodies to compose in the viewfinder. Crouching, she peered into the camera to assess the angle of the moon's reflection on the water, firing the strobes repeatedly, making minute adjustments.

The oil caught the gleam of the strobes and sent it shimmering to the eye of the camera, creating precisely the illusion of wetness Allison was aiming for. She decided it would not be necessary to further discomfort Rick and Vivien by sprinkling water on their already shivering skin. In the night light the oil was all that was necessary.

The key light had a blue filter to simulate moonlight. When Allison fired it, Rick's hair took on a life of its own, haloed to perfection in all its glorious disarray. Vivien's, too, became a moonlit nimbus about her head, the oiled ends perfect.

By using fill lights with orange filters, Allison had eliminated shadows that were too stark, tempering them with simulated firelight at each flash.

"Okay, all set," she declared, moving toward the set now, standing just beyond the sand, leaning over with hands on thighs, giving orders. She positioned Rick with his far knee raised slightly, the near leg stretched out with only its heel resting on the sand. Touching his shoulders, she ordered, "Turn . . . no, not so much . . . good. Now tip that head down, and Vivien, I want you to look like you want to crawl right up his body. Roll onto your far hip just a little . . . a little more, let me see just a hint of tummy. Good, now brace on your left hand any way you can to keep from falling over, and put your right hand on his chest." There followed a single reflex drawing apart as Vivien's biceps inadvertently came up against Rick's vitals, for she lay in the lee of his legs now. But the two of them reverted to faultless professionalism in an instant, settling into the pose again.

Allison produced a small jar of petroleum jelly, touched a spot of it to the corner of Vivien's mouth, produced a comb from her pocket, and tugged free a strand of Vivien's beautiful hair to fasten to the corner of her lips. Perfect!

"There . . . don't move," Allison breathed, backing away. Immediately she returned, touched the comb to a few wayward strands of hair at the back of Rick's neck, flicked it through a lock above his ear to partially cover the top of it, then stepped to the camera to evaluate the composition in the viewfinder. Immediately she saw sand where it wasn't supposed to be, produced a small, soft barber's brush and whisked it off the top of Vivien's leg. Another check in the viewfinder, a flash of strobes, and she found the stunning fire glow had created exactly the skin effect she wanted. But the sand that she'd found distracting on Vivien seemed lacking on Rick. Quickly she stepped around the tripod, picked up a handful and threw it at his near shoulder.

This time the scene in the viewfinder was flawless. Another quick check of all the strobes, firing them six times in quick succession before connecting them to synchronize with the camera.

Allison's voice became silk as she stepped behind the camera, crouching low, ready to shoot.

"All right, I want you to think about that skin you're touching . . . sleek, desirable . . . wet those lips, come on." Their tongues came out, leaving lips glossy in the firelight. The strobes flashed as the shutter opened for the first time, capturing the image on film. Allison's heart hammered with excitement. They were perfect together!

"Ease up a little higher, Vivien, and droop those eyelids just a li-i-i-i-tle more . . . more . . . no, too far, lift your chin now, think of how much you love him."

Flash!

"Great!" Exhilaration filled Allison as she moved deftly around the camera, giving sharp orders at times, soft compelling orders at others.

"Rick, I want a long, caressing thumb touching the hair that's caught in her mouth, but don't cover those beautiful lips of hers . . . let my camera see them . . . good with the thumb, now closer with your lips . . . think about tongues . . ."

Flash!

"Let's see the tip of your tongue, Vivien, and ease up with that hand on his chest. You're caressing it, not hanging suspended from it."

The perfection broke and both Rick and Vivien laughed, falling out of their poses momentarily.

Allison waited only briefly before saying, "Okay, back at it, lovers. Let's get messages going between those eyes, and Vivien, I want that tongue peeking out . . . open the teeth only slightly . . . good, good."

Flash!

"All right, Rick, spread those fingers and bury them in her hair . . . you love that magnificent hair, you're lost in it . . . not so deep, we're losing those beautiful fingers of yours, gently . . . gently."

Flash!

"You have wonderful hands, Rick. Let's use them some more, give me sensuality with your hands . . . wing it, fly with it, Vivien, respond to his every touch . . ."

· Rick relaxed, curled his fingers, and lay the knuckles gently against the crest of Vivien's cheek. At his touch she turned her head slightly as if to take more, lips falling open, eyelids drooping with sensuality.

Flash!

"Now you, Vivien, what can you do with those delicate fingers . . . touch him where he wants to be touched, turn him on, tell him with your fingertips what's on your mind. . . ."

469

Vivien's hands slid down to Rick's bare thigh, and immediately his face reacted. His shoulders and arms spoke to the camera of wanting to express more than the photograph would allow.

They continued for a series of twenty-four shots, and during that time Allison all but forgot who Vivien Zuchinski and Rick Lang were. She moved with an unconscious purity of purpose and saw her subjects with uncanny acuity, missing not one hair that needed straightening or messing. Halfway through the first roll of film she repositioned Vivien, raising her farther up until her head rested against Rick's chest. Ordering Rick to place his hand almost on the side of Vivien's breast, hers on his hip, she received immediate, professional response, then hustled back to the camera.

Rick and Vivien were subjects, integral parts of the art she created, nothing less. Allison's vitality and enthusiasm brought out the best in them, and her businesslike attitude put both Rick and Vivien at ease in a situation that otherwise might have been embarrassing.

When it was time to change film, Allison straightened. "Okay, stretch for a minute, but watch that sand—don't get it anyplace I don't want it."

She fetched fresh film from the old refrigerator and in a matter of minutes had reloaded. A quick check of the fire, another stick on it, and it was back to work.

They resumed shooting, with Allison issuing rapid-fire orders that immediately brought changes of pose, expression, and body language. With the next change of film came a change of camera angle. This time Allison posed Rick and Vivien hip to hip, facing each other, creating sensuality not only with near kisses, but with hands on each other's ankles and calves. Another pose had Rick leaning across Vivien's lap, his lips just above the fullest part of her breast while her head hung back in abandon.

As the session moved on, the models' muscles grew stiff, and, quite naturally, their facial expression and body language did, too. Allison worked quickly, efficiently, noting the first times Rick and Vivien sighed wearily, understanding that cramps and outright pain were very real afflictions for models. But when Vivien suddenly jumped and raised her backside sharply off the sand, ruining a shot, Allison's head popped out from behind the camera.

"Tired, Vivien?"

"No, something bit me." She scratched the underside of a thigh, then settled back into the pose again.

But just as Allison pushed the shutter release again, Rick twitched, ruining a second shot.

"You two need a break?"

"No," they answered in unison.

"Let's keep going and get finished," Rick advised. "All right, Vivien?" He gave her a considerate glance.

"Sure, this sand is . . . ouch!" This time Vivien leapt to her feet.

Now Allison became concerned. What was troubling Vivien?

"You too?" Rick questioned, suddenly getting to his feet and straining around, twisting at the waist in an attempt to see the backs of his thighs. "I could swear something's been having me for dinner, but I didn't want to say anything."

"Honey, you and me both!" Vivien seconded, scratching her legs now, lifting one foot to rake her nails on the back of an ankle.

Allison stepped to the light switch. A moment later the room was flooded with light while she knelt at the edge of the fake beach, studying the sand. She could see nothing. She fetched a large white sheet of paper and laid it on the sand, stooping again to watch carefully. A moment later she saw a tiny black dot hit the paper and disappear so fast her eyes couldn't follow.

Horrified, she stood up, biting her lip. "I hope you two have a good sense of humor, because it looks like sand fleas."

"Sand fleas!" Vivien yelped. "Eating *me?*"

"I'm afraid so. They must have come to life when the heat from the fire thawed them out." Immediately Vivien began scratching harder. "I'm . . . I'm really sorry about this," Allison apologized, more than a little embarrassed. Lord, what next! she thought. How was she going to control the insects and finish the rest of the shots? There was no bug spray in the studio. Crestfallen, Allison added, "I don't have anything to get rid of the pesky things. I guess we'll have to stop shooting and go with what we have. Hey, I'm really sorry."

"How many shots do you have left on that roll?" Rick inquired.

Allison checked. "Thirteen."

Rick turned to Vivien. "Well, I can stand it for thirteen more if you can. What do you say, Vivien?"

Suddenly Vivien grinned, and with a rueful gesture said, "Ah, what the heck. Fleas have to eat, too."

To Allison's surprise, they resumed their places and suffered through the rest of the shots with the best of humor.

"Ah, that one likes his steak rare," Rick joked.

"I would too if I could take a bite out of the back of your leg," Vivien countered.

"Do you suppose we should demand to see a certificate from the local exterminator before setting foot in this place again?"

"To say nothing of the fire marshal."

"I think maybe an extra life-insurance policy is in order before taking a job at Photo Images. How about you, Vivien?"

"Why, whatever makes you ask? I have a bad case of pneumonia, slivers in my back from this log, flea bites, and my feet are scorching!"

"All right, you two . . . that's it!" Allison announced, ending the session.

By this time it was almost ten o'clock, and they were all grateful to stretch and bend. As the overhead fluorescent lights came on, Allison rejoiced, "A hundred and fifty-four shots, and you two were fabulous!"

"I think she's soothing our egos in hopes we won't sue for damages," Rick kidded as he and Vivien hurried off the sand.

"Damn pesky things!" Vivien exclaimed, dancing, scratching again.

"I really am sorry, and I mean that. You were both . . ." Allison searched for the proper word. "Intrepid!"

Vivien, looking puzzled, turned to Rick and asked, "Is she sayin' I didn't do so hot?"

They all laughed. "You were great, and I mean that sincerely," Allison clarified. She had gained a new, healthy respect for the girl who—true—might not be exceptionally bright. But she had a glow that looked wonderful through the viewfinder and, more important, a willingness and tenacity, even under less than ideal conditions. Allison had worked with lots of models who grew increasingly irritable as their muscles tightened and the hours passed. Who knew what would happen if they were asked to pose in a nest of sand fleas! But throughout it all Vivien had remained adamantly good humored and uncomplaining. "I know a lot of models who *would* sue!" Allison commented.

"Only thing that'll make me sue is if you don't let me get this oil off. I feel like a regular grease ball!" Vivien complained volubly, now that the session was over.

"Go ahead, you deserve it," Allison said. "Straight through the dressing room to the shower. There are clean washcloths and towels back there and plenty of soap."

Vivien disappeared through the dressing room, and Rick watched Allison remove the camera from the tripod, rewind the final roll of film, then begin disconnecting cables, pushing lights aside, seeing to the equipment.

"Can I help?"

"Absolutely not. You've done enough already." She placed a lens cap on the camera. Looking up, she found him carefully scrutinizing her. Immediately she dropped her eyes to her work. Now that the camera was no longer before her eye, it was too easy to view Rick Lang as a man instead of a model.

Just as Allison had gained a healthy respect for Vivien, Rick had gained the same for Allison. She was a true professional, with an attitude and ability that made working with her a rewarding experience.

"Hey, you're shivering," she said, and Rick snapped out of his reverie. She was wrapping an electrical cord around her arm with brisk, efficient movements.

"Am I?"

"Yeah. Why don't you see if you can find a robe in the dressing room until the shower's free?"

Instead he moved across the space between them, taking the cord from her arm while she protested, "Hey, I can—"

"So can I. Don't be so bullheaded and independent."

"But you must be tired." Somehow she acquiesced without realizing it.

"Yup, I am tired. How about you?"

473

"In a way, but whenever I finish a session that's gone particularly well, like this one has, I'm so high I can't come down for hours. I'll go home and feel like I'm falling off my feet, but when my head hits the pillow it'll take forever to fall asleep."

"You do love it, don't you?"

Suddenly their eyes met, and they forgot what they'd been doing. Allison's hands fell still.

"Yes, I do," she said, almost reverently. "There's no feeling like it in the world . . . not for me. Tonight was . . ." She glanced at the set, the shrouded equipment, the cable release in her hands. Finally her eyes came back to his. "It was unadulterated joy for me," she finished solemnly.

"You're damned good, Allison, do you know that?" He spoke quietly, admiring the strong sense of purpose she emanated. Her love of work seemed to radiate from her glittering, eager eyes.

The softly spoken compliment went straight to her heart. She smiled, and her eyes fluttered away. He had never called her Allison before. It warmed her almost as much as his opinion and the ungushing way he'd voiced it. In all the months she'd worked with Jason, he'd never once come right out and said as much. He'd glanced at the finished products with an eyebrow cocked. But if he admired them, it was always with a hint of egoism that left Allison feeling slightly empty.

She studied Rick now, comparing him to Jason, finding him totally opposite—warm, sensitive, considerate.

"Thank you," she replied quietly, giving him the rare gift that to some comes so hard—accepting a compliment at face value, thereby lending it a value of its own. "So are you," she added softly.

Their eyes lingered on each other, and at last, unsmiling, he replied, "Thank you."

Just then Vivien came bouncing out of the dressing room, swaddled in her fake fur and looking considerably revived. "Shower's all yours, honey!" she announced, perkily strutting over to Rick. "But before I lose you, I want one real honest-to-goodness kiss out of that hundred-dollar-an-hour mouth of yours. I deserve it after all the suffering I've been through

474

resisting it while it was half an inch away from me for four hours."

Boldly, Vivien slipped her fingers around Rick's neck and pulled his head down for an unabashedly lingering kiss.

He was taken off guard, and though Allison had a brief impression of his surprise, he acquiesced gracefully while Vivien audaciously demanded a full-fledged French kiss, holding his head until she'd received what she was after.

Looking on, Allison felt a little red around the collar, and again was bothered by a faint twinge of jealousy at the impudent woman who had no compunctions whatsoever about being so outlandishly forward.

Backing away, finally, Vivien gave Rick a sultry once-over. "You are *reeeeeally* something. You ever want to get together where there's no camera lookin' on, you just give li'l Vivien a call, okay?"

Rick laughed into her upraised face, his hands resting on her waist. "Vivien, I just might take you up on that. Maybe we can compare fleabites," he managed, ending the touchy moment gracefully, with exactly the proper touch of humor.

Vivien socked him playfully on the shoulder. "Hey, I like that. I like a man with a nice bod and a good sense of humor. You're a real fox, fella." She flitted out of his arms with no more compunction than she'd flitted in. "Well . . . gotta run."

Allison, discomfited by watching Vivien's dauntless, straightforward display, turned her back on Rick as she gave the woman a one-armed hug and walked her toward the door.

"Vivien, you're marvelous to work with, and I'd like to do it again." She meant it. In spite of the past sixty seconds, which had been embarrassing, Allison meant it.

Chapter 6

WHEN RICK EMERGED from the dressing room, Vivien was gone. Allison had wet down the coals and was scooping the sodden lumps into a metal garbage can. She heard the door open and watched him cross the long, open length of the room. She attended to her chore, conscious of his eyes on her while he stood nearby with his hands in his pockets, conscious, too, of the flustering memory of Vivien's mouth demanding his to open. Throughout the shooting Allison had managed to keep her thoughts separate from her personal feelings, but with Rick standing beside her in street clothes, and after Vivien forcing that impromptu, final pose on him, Allison was suddenly at a loss, searching frantically for something to say. Her hand trembled as she dumped the last dustpan of coals and clapped the cover over the garbage can. As the tiny clang drifted away into silence, she looked up at last.

"Vivien's gone," she said inanely. Rick's hair was damp, clinging to his temples, coiling about his ears. The overhead lights reflected off his fresh-scrubbed forehead and nose, highlighting his skin.

"I know. And I'm sorry about what happened. I didn't mean to embarrass you."

Her cheeks flushed. "Oh, that's okay, it's none of my business." She frantically tried to appear busy, to disguise her discomposure. She wiped her hands on her thighs and looked around. Everything was done. "I'll clean up the rest tomorrow." She checked her watch. "Goodness, it's late! I'll get your check so you can go."

She escaped to her desk, picked up the check she'd made out while he was in the shower, and handed it to him, extending, too, her other hand in a gesture of good will.

Without taking his eyes from hers, he accepted the check with one hand, her cold palm with the other. But instead of shaking it, he held her hand firmly, refusing to relinquish it when she tugged away. She flashed him what she hoped was a dismissing smile and reiterated, "I really meant it when I said you were wonderful to work with. As soon as the transparencies come in, I'll give you a call so you can see them."

"Fine," he replied, obviously not giving a damn about transparencies as he still refused to release her hand.

His touch sent paths of fire up her arm, and she frantically raked her mind for something more to say. "M . . . maybe I'll get some extra color stats of the cover when it has the title and copy on, so you can see what the finished product looks like, too."

"Fine," he agreed disinterestedly, brushing a thumb against the back of her hand. His eyes remained fixed on hers. She knew instinctively it would not bother him in the least if he never saw the finished photos. It was becoming increasingly difficult to dream up things to say. Finally she stammered, "I . . . I'll call when the stats come in."

"And how long will that be?"

She forcibly pulled her palm from his. "Oh, maybe three months."

"Too long." He folded the check in half and creased it with his thumbnail without removing his eyes from her face.

"I'm afraid that's entirely up to New York. After the transparencies leave here, my part is done."

"That's not what I meant." With unnerving slowness he pulled a billfold from his hip pocket, inserted the payment, then tucked the billfold away again. "Thank you, though it doesn't seem right taking money for a job I've enjoyed as much as tonight's."

Common sense told her this was no time to make jokes about Vivien or fleas or pneumonia. "You earned it, Rick," she said simply, gesturing nervously, then twisting her fingers together.

He shrugged, dropped his eyes to her desk, and still didn't move. He stood there, his weight on one foot, considering the clutter of photos, bills, lenses, filters. The old building emitted faraway nighttime sounds—the soft clang of a radiator pipe, the hum of a clock, a janitor's pail way off in the distance.

Finally Rick looked up. "I didn't have any supper, did you?" he asked.

"No." Her eyes met his, then flitted away. "But I'm all out of tuna and eggs."

A long silence followed while Allison commanded her eyes to stay off Rick, who seemed to be considering deeply as he stood before her.

"I don't want any of your damn tuna and eggs. I want to go somewhere and talk to you and get to know you."

Her startled eyes flew up. "I told you—"

"Hey, wait." He pressed open palms against the air. "A sandwich and a cup of coffee and some talk, okay? No commitments, I promise. You said yourself you're so keyed up you won't sleep if you do go home, so let me do the buying and you can bubble off your enthusiasm on me, okay?"

"Thank you, Rick, but the answer is no."

A slow grin climbed one cheek. "Would you reconsider if I threatened to sue for the fleabites?"

A quavering smile tipped her lips up, but a warning fluttered through her heart. Afraid of eventualities, afraid of letting anyone close again, afraid of being hurt as before, she drew in a sharp breath, stifling the sweet enjoyment she felt being with him.

"I think I'll have to call your bluff, and just hope you won't."

"Then just come because I ask, and because I can't sleep if I go straight home, either."

Uncertainly she stood before him, pressing her thighs hard against the edge of the desk, as if its solidity might anchor her to earth when she was so tempted to drift above it at his invitation.

His eyes fell to her tight-clenched hands, then rose to her

478

face again. He moved around the side of the desk, captured one of her wrists, turned and towed her toward the door, affecting an injured tone. "Hey, you owe me. After I helped you lug six tons of bricks up here for that set, not to mention one illegal log, which put me in jeopardy with the law, and after almost getting pneumonia from the cold in here, as well as a bad case of fleabites. You can't put a man through all that, then refuse to have a cup of coffee with him."

"Rick, listen—"

"Listen, my ass, I'm done listening. You're coming with me." He moved decisively, retrieving her jacket from the hat tree and turning again to face her with the garment held wide, waiting.

With a sigh of resignation, she turned to slip her arms in. As she buttoned up, he hit the light switch, plunging the room into darkness, except for the vague light from the hallway, which fell through the old-fashioned glass window of the door.

He stood close behind her—too close for comfort—so, rather than turn again to face him, she reached for the doorknob. His hand moved quickly to cover hers and prevent her from turning it. Immediately she yanked free of his touch, burying her hand in a pocket. But his palms fell lightly on her shoulders, turning her to face him once more.

His fingers circled her neck, under the jacket hood, pressing on her collarbone, the thumbs pushing the wool fabric lightly against her throat. A spill of brightness from the hallway washed one side of his face, leaving the other in shadow, and Allison experienced an unruly wish to photograph him this way, for his profile was pure, sharp, perfect, the sober expression in his eyes accentuated by the fact that one eye was thrown totally into shadow.

She was conscious of the scent of soap lingering on his skin and of the warmth from his hands seeping through her coat to circle her neck.

"For some reason you don't trust me," he said softly. "I can tell it. Yet I think you enjoy being with me, and I know I enjoy being with you. I won't push—that's a promise—but neither will I give up on a relationship with definite possibilities."

479

"I . . . I'm not looking for a relationship. I already told you that."

"Hey." He shook her gently, cajolingly. "People don't look for relationships. They just happen, Allison, like heaven-sent gifts, don't you know that? Afterward, the two people can work on them. But meeting is the accident."

"No, I don't know any such thing." She herself had spent years, it seemed, always *looking* for a relationship, only to be wounded when she found it, and it ended just like the one before, against her wishes.

His gaze was intense as he studied her face, half-lit from the hall. She found it impossible to pull her eyes away. "What are you afraid of?" he asked, his voice gone slightly gruff.

"I'm not afraid. I just view things . . . people . . . more cynically than you do. Besides, heaven has never sent me a gift that turned out to be worth two cents, so you'll pardon me if I don't take a very optimistic view of heaven."

"Maybe I can change your mind," he ventured.

"I doubt it."

"Do you mind if I try?"

"That depends."

"On what?"

"On what you want from me."

"Why do you think I want something?"

"Everybody wants something." She swallowed. "Only they usually want it for nothing."

"Who was the last person who wanted something from you for nothing?"

"Nobody!" she retorted too sharply. Then quieter, "Nobody."

His eyes assessed her, carefully tracking the defensive expressions across her face with its downturned mouth. "You're lying," he said softly. "Somebody hurt you and left you distrusting the rest of mankind, and left me with the job of proving to you that not everyone in this world is a rat."

"You'll have a tough time doing that during the course of a quick cup of coffee."

"I believe I will," he agreed amiably, leaning around Allison to open the door. "It may take more than just tonight, but you'll find that I'm a very patient fellow." Waiting for the elevator, he asked, "Would you like to ride in my car?"

Again she watched the changing numbers above the door, knowing he was studying her. "No, I'll take the van and meet you."

"Where?"

She eyed him sideways. "Wherever we're going for coffee."

"Where would you like to go?"

She shrugged, caring only that it wasn't too dimly lit or intimate.

"Do you like big, fat, juicy hamburgers dripping with cheese and crisscrossed with bacon srips and sour pickles and fries?" He sounded like an ad for a fast-food hamburger place.

She couldn't help grinning. "I think I'm being prompted. Do *you* like big, fat, juicy hamburgers dripping with cheese and crisscrossed with bacon and dill pickles and fries?"

His eyes lit up merrily. "How'd you guess?"

"Go ahead, name it."

"The Embers—my favorite."

"And what if I said no, I don't like big, fat, juicy hamburgers, that I want a . . . a bowl of chili and a corn dog?" She pursed up her mouth in mock petulance.

"I'd say, tough! I said first, and I said hamburger. So whaddya make of it, huh, lady?" The elevator arrived and he punched her arm playfully, dancing through the open doors on the balls of his feet.

She fell back convincingly against the elevator wall. "I give!" Her hands reached for the sky. "I love hamburgers, I swear I love 'em!"

He shadowboxed his way to her, stopping close, playfully raising her chin with one gloved fist. "Yeah?" He grinned into her eyes. "Well, youse is one smart broad if youse already learned not to cross me when I want hamburgers."

By now she was laughing out loud, her shoulders shaking as she leaned against the elevator wall. He was incorrigible. If he couldn't get her one way, he got her another. It was becoming harder and harder to resist him. She found herself smiling all the way to the restaurant. Entering and scanning the booths, she found she'd arrived first.

When Rick came in minutes later, he sauntered up to her

booth, leaning negligently against the backrest across from her, looked around shiftily, and asked, "Hey, ah . . . lady, ah, you're a pretty good-looker. You got anybody in particular hidin' in the men's room or somethin'?"

"That'd be tellin'," she replied in her best gun moll's accent. "With me you take your chances, bud."

Smiling, he slipped into the booth, across from her. They talked for two hours. During that time he learned she was from a small farming town in South Dakota, where her family still lived, that she'd come to Minneapolis to attend school at Communication Arts, and had stayed because the city offered opportunities for an aspiring young photographer that couldn't be found in Watertown, South Dakota. Her ambitions were to own a Hasselblad camera and to sell a fashion layout to *Gentlemen's Review* magazine.

"Why *Gentlemen's Review?*" he asked.

"Why not? It's the epitome of prestige to be published in *GR,* so why not set my goal as high as possible?"

"But why a man's magazine?"

Without thinking, she answered, "Because I'm good with men."

"Are you now?" he purred. His eyelids drooped to half-mast, and he picked up his cup, smirking as his lips touched its rim.

She colored and stammered, "I . . . I mean with a camera, of course."

"Of course," he agreed, clearing his throat, again hiding behind his cup.

"Quit smirking and get your mind out of the gutter," she scolded, sitting up straighter. "I can see you leering behind that cup. It's the truth, I *am* good with men. I have a good eye for men's clothing and for backgrounds that flatter masculine features and for bringing out ruggedness, suaveness—whatever. I have to work much harder to achieve those things with women." She toyed with her cup. "I suppose that sounds egotistical, but it's imperative in my line of work to recognize where my strengths lie and pursue that direction."

"You're forgetting, I'm an artist, too. The same is true with my work."

She leaned forward eagerly, caught up in the subject she

482

loved best. "It's disconcerting sometimes, isn't it, having your work so . . . so *visual!*" She gestured at the table top. "I mean, whatever we produce is right there for the world to judge us by."

They talked on about the common interest they shared. Her cheeks grew pink, her eyes excited, body language intent, and he absorbed it all with growing enjoyment.

"Do you know you become vibrant when you talk about your work?" he asked.

"I do?"

"Your cheeks get pink, and your eyes dance around, and you get all animated and turned-on looking."

She leaned back, retreating into the booth. "I guess I do. It exhilarates me."

"Like nothing else can?" The implication was clear in his voice. The memory of his kiss came back vividly, and she dropped her eyes from his carefully expressionless face. She thought it best to lighten the atmosphere. "There's one other thing that does as much for me."

"And what's that?"

"The mere thought of working with a Hasselblad." She shivered, pressing folded hands between her knees as if even the word itself were sensual.

He lifted his cup, took a sip, mentioned casually, "I own a Hasselblad."

Her eyes grew wide. Her back came away from the booth. "You do?" She gulped.

"Is that covetousness I see gleaming in your eye?"

"Is it ever!" She rolled her eyes toward the ceiling. "Oh, those enormous two-and-a-quarter-inch negatives!" she swooned. "Oh, those lenses! Oh, the dream of owning the camera the astronauts took to the moon!" She sank back as if overcome, then pressed a hand to her heart. "I'd sell my soul for one of those things."

"Sold!" he put in quickly.

"Figuratively speaking, of course. You actually own one? You're not kidding?"

"I worked one whole summer on a road-construction crew and saved every cent I possibly could, and by fall I had enough to pay for the camera."

Her face became clownishly sad. "Somehow I don't think a road-construction crew would hire me on to drive a cat."

"Don't bother applying. You can try my camera any time."

Again she sat up, surprised, a new look of fire in her eyes. "You mean that? You'd actually let me?"

He gestured nonchalantly. "I mostly use the thing when I make trips up north to Emily, where my folks live. They have a cabin on Roosevelt Lake, too, and I do most of my photography around the lake and in the woods up there. I stay in the city because the modeling pays for the wildlife art, which doesn't pay for itself yet. But, like I said, the camera's yours whenever you'd like to try it."

"You mean it, don't you?" she said, flabbergasted.

"Of course I mean it." He leaned back, crossed his arms over his chest, and hooked a boot on the seat beside her. "But I didn't offer to give it to you, just to let you try it."

She smiled, overjoyed. Her nostrils flared slightly as her eyes drifted shut for a moment. She opened them to meet his, a hint of naughtiness about her lips while she made circles around the lip of her coffee cup with an index finger.

"I might abscond with it."

They leaned back lazily, playing teasing games with half-shut eyes.

"Then I'll have to make sure I stay very close to it . . . and to you, won't I?"

Allison was suddenly very aware of his foot propped on the seat, almost touching her hip. And of how incredibly handsome he was, lazy that way, almost as if he were half asleep. And of the dancing eyes that told her he was far from asleep. And of the fact that, when the waitress asked, he had remembered she liked sugar in her coffee. And of the fact that she had laughed with him more in the last couple days than she'd laughed with Jason during all the months they'd lived together. And of the dawning realization that she and Rick Lang had an incredibly lot in common.

It was well past midnight when Rick paid their bill. Allison stood behind him, watching him shrug as he dug in his tight jeans pocket for change. His hair was flattened where he'd leaned his head against the booth. The collar of his old jacket was turned up, crinkled leather touching the back of his head. Without warning she itched to touch it, too.

Allison shook off the thought, buttoning her jacket up high and twisting her scarf twice about her neck.

"All set?" Rick asked, turning.

She nodded and moved toward the door. He reached around her, almost brushing her arm as he pushed the heavy plate glass open for her to pass through. Outside, crossing the parking lot, she was too keenly aware of the fact that he walked very near, just behind her shoulder, pulling leather gloves on while she buried her chin in her scarf, hands in pockets.

She stopped in the middle of the snow-packed parking lot and turned toward him. "Well, my car's over here."

He gestured in the opposite direction with a sideward bob of the head. "Mine's over there."

An uncertain pause followed, then, "Well, thanks for the hamburger. It was good, after all."

"Anytime."

It was quiet, late. All that could be heard were the exhaust fans on top of the restaurant humming into the neon-lit night. Allison looked up at Rick. His breath came in intermittent white clouds on the chill air. He stood before her, not a hint of smile on his face, pushing his gloves on tighter, tighter, while perusing her in the night light that turned her face pink.

"Well . . . good night," she said, hunching her shoulders against the cold.

"G'night." Still he didn't move away, but stood there studying her until she became giddily aware of how fast he was breathing. There was no hiding it, for each breath was broadcast by its spreading vapor cloud. Reactions spread through her in a warm drift of awareness. Her heart seemed to be beating everywhere at once. Then common sense took over, and she turned quickly toward the van, only to find him still following behind her shoulder. He slipped a gloved hand on her elbow, squeezing tight as they picked their precarious way along the icy footing. Though his touch was far from intimate through layers and layers of winter clothing, it sent shivers up her spine.

At the van she reached to open the door, but he beat her to

it, reaching easily around her, then standing back, waiting, with his glove on the handle.

She turned to give him a last brief glance over her shoulder.

"Well, good night and thanks again."

"Yeah," he tried, but it came out cracky, so he cleared his voice and tried again. "Yeah." Clearer this time, but low, soft, disconcerting.

Just as she was about to raise a foot and climb into the van, his hand captured her elbow once more, tugging her around.

"Allison?"

Her startled eyes met his as he circled both of her elbows with gloved hands. They stood in the narrow space between the open door and the vehicle as Rick's hands compelled her closer. The freezing night air seemed suddenly hot against her skin. He pulled her closer by degrees, his head tipping to one side, blotting out the lights behind him as his lips neared.

"Don't," she demanded at the last moment, turning aside and raising her palms to press him away, though her heartbeats were driving hard against the hollow of her throat.

The pressure on her elbows increased. "What are you afraid of?"

"You promised you wouldn't push."

"Do you call one kiss pushing?" His breath was so close it brushed her cheek, sending a cloud of warm air over her skin.

"I . . . yes," she managed, refusing to look up at him.

"Why don't you try it and see if I push any farther?" The hands commanded her again until their bodies were so close that their jackets touched. Again Allison's eyes met Rick's, which were shadows only, though his hair, forehead, and nose were rimmed with a pinkish glow from the lights of the parking lot. "One kiss, all right? I've been thinking about it ever since the shooting session, watching you all fired up behind your camera. We were sharing something together then, I thought. Something that caught both of us up and exhilarated us, excited us. Don't tell me you didn't feel it. I thought maybe that common ground was reason enough to end the night with a simple kiss."

"I told you, I'm not looking for a relationship."

"Neither am I. I'm looking for a kiss—nothing more.

486

Because I like you, and I've enjoyed being with you and working with you, and kissing is a helluva nifty way of telling a person things like that."

There was little she could do—and in another moment, little she wanted to do—to combat him. He lowered his lips the remaining fraction of an inch, touching her mouth lightly with warm, warm lips, made all the more warm by the contrast of his cold, cold nose against the side of her face while he held her by her upper arms. Her eyes slid closed, and her guard grew shaky while the gentle pressure of his mouth lingered, growing more welcome as the seconds passed. Without removing his lips from hers, he pulled her lightly against him, guiding her resisting arms around his sides, then clamping them securely with his elbows. When he felt her stiff resistance melt, he slowly, cautiously moved his hands to her back, wrapping her up, tightening inexorably while he started things with the sensuous movement of his head—nudging, now harder, now softer, back and forth, while she felt the warm proddings of his tongue. The warning voices, reminding Allison of Jason and the hurtful past, echoed away into silence. Only the thrumming of her own heart filled her ears as her hands rested on the back of his jacket, holding him lightly. Her lips parted, and his tongue came seeking. She met the warm, wet tip with her own and felt the heart-tripping thrill of wet flesh meeting wet flesh in a first seeking dance.

Behind her she felt his hands moving brusquely and wondered what he was doing as the motion jerked his mouth sideways on hers momentarily. The next moment she knew he'd removed a glove, for she felt his bare hand seek her warm neck, under the cascade of hair, nestling in under the twist of scarves, massaging the back of her neck and head, commanding it to tip as he willed it, holding her captive though she no longer sought escape.

Her heart hammered everywhere, everywhere as she drifted beneath his warm, wet tongue while it slid along the soft, velvet skin of her inner lips, drew circular patterns around her own before he softened the pressure of his entire mouth, nibbling at the rim of her lips, making the complete circle before widening again, the kiss now grown wholly demanding.

Their jackets were waist length. He held her around her hips with a strong arm, and she felt his body spring to life with hardness as he pressed the zipper of his blue jeans firmly against her stomach, and before she knew what she was doing, she was moving in afterbeats, making circles with her hips that chased those he made with his.

As if realizing he'd taken the kiss farther than he'd intended, Rick closed his fingers around a fistful of Allison's hair, tugging gently, gently as he dropped his head back and swallowed convulsively.

Their breaths came strident and rushed, falling in blending clouds of white as she leaned her forehead against his chin.

Rick's eyes slid closed while he bid his body to slow down.

"Wow," he got out, the word a guttural half gulp.

She chuckled, a high, tight sound of unexpectedness before two strained, little words squeezed from her throat. "Yeah... wow."

Her hips rested lightly against him. She waited for her body to cool down and be sensible, but against her she could feel the difficulty he, too, was having talking sense into his body.

"One kiss," he managed in a gruff voice. "That's what I promised, and I keep my promises."

Seeking to control emotions that seemed to be running away like horses with the bits between their teeth, she teased, "Would you believe I did that so convincingly just so I could get my hands on your Hasselblad?"

He laughed, raised his head, and answered, "No."

She disengaged herself from his arms, and Rick complied without further resistance.

"Well, I did," she teased, jamming her hands deep into her pockets and backing a step away. "I told you I'd sell my soul for one of them."

He smiled, his eyes on her upturned face as he drew his glove back on. "You keep that up and you might end up doing exactly that."

For a moment she had the urge to step into his embrace and try that one more time. But if she did, it might be more than his Hasselblad she wanted to get her hands on.

While she pondered, he indicated the van with an upward

nudge of chin, ordering, "Get the hell in, do you hear?"

Obediently she turned and climbed aboard.

"I'll call you," he said tersely, as if trusting himself to say no more at the moment.

Then the door slammed shut, and he stepped back, feet spread wide, moving not a muscle as he watched the van back up and drive away. In the rear-view mirror she saw him as she rounded the corner. He hadn't moved from the spot.

Chapter 7

THE PHONE RANG exactly six times the following day. Each time Allison expected to hear Rick's voice but was disappointed. Neither did he call all weekend. During the following week Allison grew more and more impatient for the sound of his voice on the other end of the line. But he didn't call.

The transparencies for the book cover came back from processing and she tried calling him but got no answer. Vivien came to see them one afternoon, gushing in her own inimitable way that the shots were *"re-e-eally* nice." Then she asked for Rick Lang's phone number.

After giving it to her, Allison wondered if Vivien called men and asked them for dates. Probably. Remembering the freewheeling kiss Vivien had laid on Rick, and the kiss she herself had shared with him, Allison couldn't say she blamed Vivien one bit.

Friday night and Saturday seemed to crawl by, and still he didn't call. Sunday morning Allison was up early and in the shower when the phone rang.

She burst from the spray stark naked and dripping, flying around the corner of the hall into the living room, skittering on the slick floor in her bare feet.

"Hello!" she exclaimed breathlessly.

"Hi." One deep-voiced syllable turned her heart into a jackhammer. "Did I wake you?"

"No. I was in the shower."

"Oh! Why don't I call you back in a few minutes?" he returned apologetically.

"No!" she almost yelped, then consciously calmed her voice. "No, it's all right." There was a puddle on the floorboards at her feet. Her breasts were covered with goose pimples, which also blossomed up and down her belly like the curried nap of a carpet. Wet hair was dripping into her eyes and streaming into her mouth. She pushed a straggly strand away from one eye as she lied, "I wasn't really in the shower. I was all done."

"Are you sure?"

"Sure I'm sure. You should see me—all bright eyed and bushy tailed." She glanced at her naked, shivering body and controlled an urge to laugh out loud.

"It's been over a week," he reminded her unnecessarily.

"Oh, has it?" Allison was shivering so badly she covered her breasts with one arm and hand, trying to keep warm.

"Very funny—*has it*," he repeated dryly, "as if I haven't been counting off every damned day."

"Then why didn't you call?"

"I was up north taking winter shots while there's still some snow left, getting last dibbs in on my Hasselblad before somebody else gets her hands on it. I just got back."

"Just? You mean just now?" She checked the kitchen clock. It wasn't quite nine yet. Emily was a three-hour ride from here.

"Yes. I wanted to leave yesterday, but my mother insisted on cooking my favorites for supper last night—a convenient ruse to keep me another day, so I just pulled in."

"And?" she prompted innocently.

"And can I see you?" Beneath the hand that cupped her naked, wet breast a rush of sensuality tingled the nerve endings of her flesh. She closed her eyes and pretended it was Rick's hand.

"I have the transparencies here to sho—"

"Screw the transparencies! When can I come?"

"I have to do my—"

"When?" he demanded, then decided for her. "Never mind answering that. I'll be there in fifteen minutes."

"Fif—hey, wait!"

But it was too late. The line had gone dead. She flew back to the bathroom, stubbed her toe on the corner of the vanity, cursed volubly, and flung a towel over her hair. Frantically rubbing, she wondered which to do, hair or makeup? There wasn't time for both. Oh God, he was going to walk in here and she would look like she had just had a Baptist baptism! She flung the towel aside just as the phone rang again.

"Yes, what is it?" she demanded impatiently.

It was him again. "Have you had breakfast?"

"No."

"Well, don't!" The line went dead in her hand again, and she stared at it a moment, smiled then flew back to the bathroom. When the doorbell rang less than twelve minutes later, she was sure it was him.

"Oh, *no-o-o!*" she wailed at her reflection in the mirror, her face sans lip gloss, blush, mascara, or even dry hair. Only one eye had pale mauve shadow above it. Like a half made-up clown she opened the door to find Rick standing on her landing hugging a grocery sack in both arms.

"Hi," he said quietly, a slow smile spreading over his face.

"Hi." A beguiling fluttering began just beneath her left breast as they stood in the cold morning air, measuring each other while the draft swirled into the apartment.

"Can I buy you breakfast?"

She couldn't seem to take in enough of him at once as her eyes wandered over his face, freshly shaved and shining, while he let his gaze roam over her half made-up face.

She nodded mutely, forgetting to step back and let him in. Still holding the brown paper bag, he reached one gloved hand out and captured her neck, pulling her half outside while he leaned down to kiss her, the zigzagged edge of the crackly bag cutting into her chin. His lips were warm and impatient as his tongue slipped out to touch her surprised lips. Then he straightened, released her, and smiled sheepishly.

"Oops, I'm sorry. Here I am letting all the warm air out while your hair turns to icicles." He moved inside and glanced down her legs. She had whipped on a pair of faded jeans and a plaid cotton shirt but hadn't had a chance to put her shoes on.

492

Self-consciously she tried to cover the bare toes of her left foot with those of her right.

His eyes moved to her wet, straight hair, and from her left eye to her right. Next he caught sight of the puddle of water on the living room floor, by the telephone.

One eyebrow lifted skeptically. "All bright eyed and bushy tailed, huh?"

"Well, sort of." She flipped her hands out only to realize she still held the brush from her eyeshadow.

The room was flooded with bright morning sunlight, cascading across the yellows and greens, dappling the gleaming hardwood floors where the plants cast leaf shadows. Rick's glance moved around, lingering longest on the puddle before returning to her face.

"Should I have waited until later to call?" he asked.

Her heart threatened to explode in her chest as she admitted, "No, I'd have gone mad waiting another hour."

The brown paper bag slid down his leg and landed on the floor with a thump. Rick's eyes devoured Allison's face while he reached out and brought her up hard against his chest, lifting her completely off the floor while he kissed her thoroughly. His tongue sought her mouth, and hers eagerly waited to meet it, moving in wild, eager greeting as if these last eight days had been agony for each of them. His teeth trapped her bottom lip, but she neither knew nor cared when she tasted the faint saltiness of blood. He fell back against the door, taking her with him, letting her body slide back down until her toes touched the floor. And in passing she realized he was hard, aroused, and marveled that she could make him so even while her hair was wet, her makeup still in its plastic cases. His hands disappeared from her back, and she began to pull away, only to be stopped.

"No, wait, don't go," he said, close to her ear, "I just want to get my gloves off so I can touch you." Behind her she heard the gloves hit the floor, then his hands pulled her close again, and she clambered right up on top of his boots with her bare feet, leaning willingly, feeling the welcome length of his body against hers. His palms slid to her buttocks to draw her harder, harder against him. She circled his neck with both arms, straining toward his lips, tongue, chest, and hips while desire flared in her. His cold palm slid beneath her shirt. When it brushed the skin just above her waistband, she flinched and shivered.

He pulled back, looking down into her eyes. "What's the matter?" His voice was deep and ragged.

"Your hands are like ice."

"Do you mind?" he asked with gruff tenderness, one cold hand already warming on her soft, willing skin.

She searched his eyes, her own gone somber, her lips fallen open, slightly swollen and glistening with moisture from his tongue.

"No." It was difficult to speak, her heartbeats were so erratic. She had missed him incredibly, found herself undeniably eager for more of his lips and hands on her. Those hands now spread wide over her ribs, which rose and fell in sharp gusts while the driving thrum of her heart seemed to lift her from his chest and drop her back against it heavily.

And then his face was lost in closeness as he kissed the side of her nose, her colored eyelid, her uncolored eyelid, her temple, and after that impossibly long wait—her mouth. He took it with tender, demanding ease, playing with her tongue, nuzzling even as he tasted, tempted, tried. His hand rode up her ribs until one thumb rested in the hollow beneath her left breast, where it gently stroked. Surprised when he found no bra, he lifted his head, smiled, and murmured, "Mmmm?"

Her arms still looped about his neck, she replied, "Well, you only gave me ten minutes." Then she reached to catch his upper lip between her teeth and tugged him back where he belonged. His kiss grew ardent and searching while his hand at last filled itself with her naked breast, its nipple puckered tight with desire.

Into his open mouth she whispered throatily, "Rick, what did you do to me in these last eight days?"

"Exactly what you did to me, I hope—drove me crazy."

"But I don't want you to think I just . . . just fall against every man who walks through that door with a grocery bag in his arms."

"How many have walked through it that way?"

"One."

494

"Hell, one's not too many. Your reputation's safe." But he backed away, grinned into her eyes, and added, "For the time being."

And she knew her days—maybe hours—of celibacy were numbered. She was falling for him more swiftly than she'd fallen for Jason, and more surely, for while she had learned to love Jason, she'd never really liked him. But she had liked Rick Lang even before falling in love with him.

Restraining his desires, he smiled down into her eyes. "Hey, lady, did you know you have purple stuff above one eye and not the other?"

"It's mauve, not purple, and it's eyeshadow, not stuff, and I was hoping you'd be so overcome by me you wouldn't notice."

"And what about that mop of hair? You intend to leave it that way or do you want to dry it while I cook us a *real* omelette?"

"Inferring that the one I fixed us was not a real omelette?" she returned in an injured tone.

"Exactly. Mine will have ham and green pepper and onion and tomato in it, and it'll be topped with cheddar cheese."

"I can't stand green peckers," she stated tartly.

"Green *whats!*"

Immediately she colored. "Oh, Rick, I'm sorry. I . . . I . . ." She turned her back, horrified to have let the familiarity pop out unrestrained. It was an old joke between her and Jason.

"Go dry your hair. I'll holler if I can't find everything I need."

In the bathroom she glowered at her reflection in the mirror.

"Stupid twit!" she scolded her reflection.

To turn the odds in her favor, she made her bed, put on a bra, and took extra pains with her hair, styling it with the curling iron until it fluffed about her collar in wispy tendrils that bounced on her shoulders.

The sound of the stereo came to her. Smiling, Allison glanced toward the doorway, then began humming as she turned toward the mirror again.

Her makeup was subtle and iridescent, applied with a light but knowledgeable hand, for she'd made up many models in

495

her day. As an afterthought she placed light touches of perfume behind each ear, on each wrist, then on impulse snaked a hand beneath her shirt and touched the valley between her breasts before bending to touch each ankle, too.

Straightening up, she turned to find Rick leaning indolently against the bathroom doorframe, grinning as he watched her. He let his head tip speculatively to one side while teasing, "So that's where you women put perfume, huh? I counted—there were seven places." He pulled his shoulder from the door and turned away. "Your breakfast is ready, Cleopatra."

Allison could have died on the spot.

She might have felt self-conscious meeting his eyes when she took her place at the table, but he put her at ease with his teasing. Swinging around, bearing two plates with enormous, fluffy Spanish omelettes, he unceremoniously plopped them on the table, advising, "Eat up, skinny, you look like you can use it."

"Oh, do I now? I didn't hear any complaints a few minutes ago when you came in."

"You may not have heard them, but you may recall I had a hand on your ribs, and you're about as fat as a sparrow's kneecap."

She smiled. "You sound just like my mother. Every time I go home it's, 'Allison, eat up. Allison, you just don't look healthy. Allison, have a second helping.' It drives me crazy. Why is it that mothers and grandmothers think a woman isn't healthy unless she's at least twenty pounds overweight?"

"Probably because they love you and mean the best for you. If they didn't they wouldn't bother to notice. I get the same thing from my dad when I go home, only about being single. 'Rick, you know that Benson girl moved back home and got a job in Doc Wassall's office. Didn't you used to date her when you were in high school?'" Rich grinned sardonically. "That Benson girl probably weighs a hundred and eighty now and wears support hose and orthopedic shoes. Besides, I don't think Dad would believe it if I told him I can actually cook an omelette. He's never cooked one in his life. Mom's always there to do it for him . . . *and* his laundry, his housecleaning, and reminding him when it's time to pay the electric bill. That's their way of life. If they try to force it on me, I understand it's because they want me to be happy. So I just grin and tell Dad maybe I'll give old Ellen Marie Benson a call before I leave."

"And do you?" Allison peered up at him, suddenly curious about the women he'd dated.

"Occasionally . . . oh, not Ellen Marie, but a couple of others my folks don't know about."

"Anyone in particular?" she inquired, watching his expression carefully.

It remained noncommittal. "Nope," he answered shortly and took another mouthful of eggs.

"Speaking of calling girls, you're going to get a call from one."

"Who?" He looked up over the rim of his coffee cup.

"Vivien. She asked me for your phone number."

He chuckled. "Oh, *Vivien*." He drew out the name and followed it with a salacious grin.

Allison leaned an elbow on the table, smirking. "Do girls actually do that, I mean, call guys and . . . and boldly . . ." She stammered to a halt.

"And boldly what?"

"And boldly . . ." Allison gestured vacantly. "I don't know. What do girls boldly ask when they call guys? I've always wondered."

"Meaning you've never done it yourself?"

"Hardly. It's not my style."

His eyes danced over her pink cheeks, and he leaned his elbows on either side of his plate, a coffee cup in one hand. "I'm glad."

"You are?" Her eyes were wide and innocent now, meeting his over the cup.

"Yes, I am. Because I'm one of those guys who still wants to do the pursuing as if women's lib never came along and gave women the idea of doing it themselves."

"Judging from the kiss Vivien treated you to, I'd say you're in for some mighty diligent pursuing from that quarter."

He lifted his chin and laughed lightly, leaning back in his chair. "Oh, that Vivien, she's incorrigible." Yet he didn't fawn over the fact. Instead he made light of it, suffering no bloated ego, which pleased Allison. All of a sudden the corners of his mouth drifted down into a placid expression as he studied her. His eyes moved over her hair, ears, mouth, cheeks, and came at last to her wide brown eyes. "Your hair is very pretty," he said quietly.

A stab of warmth flooded her cheeks, and her eyelids fluttered down momentarily. He crossed his hands over his stomach and continued studying her pink, flustered cheeks and the self-conscious way her eyes cast about for something to settle on. They came to rest on his knuckles. "And so is the rest of you," he added.

A warning signal went off in her head. Was this his line? It was different from Jason's, which never included compliments quite this simple, but rather effusive hosannas on how she "turned him on." Remembering them now, Allison told herself to slow down, beware, things were going too fast.

But she experienced a heady feeling of pleasure in being the object of his admiring scrutiny as he leaned back in his chair with casual ease, his voice coming softly again. "You have butter on your top lip." Her hand reacted self-consciously, grabbing the paper napkin from her lap and lifting it toward her mouth. Halfway there, his came out to stop it. He leaned across the corner of the table while her eyes flew up in alarm.

"Would you mind very much if I kissed it off?"

His eyes remained steady on Allison while her throat muscles shifted as she swallowed. Her brown gaze held a startled expression. Her lips fell open in surprise while she sat as still as a bird in deep camouflage, staring back at Rick.

"Would you?" he repeated so softly it was nearly a murmur.

Her wariness fled, chased away by his soft, persuasive question. The negative movement of her head was almost imperceptible. Eyes locked with hers, Rick removed the napkin from her numb fingers, crossed her palm with his, in the fashion of an Indian handshake, only gently, as if he held a crushable flower. As he leaned by degrees across the corner of the table, the pressure of his fingers increased, and he brought the back of her hand firmly against his chest. She felt the heavy thud of his heart as his eyes slid closed, and his lips

498

touched her buttery upper lip, lightly sucking, licking, moving across its width from corner to corner before he did the same to her bottom lip. Allison felt as if melting butter were rippling down the center of her stomach, ending in a fluttering delight between her legs.

He backed away a fraction of an inch so that only the tip of his tongue circled her mouth, which eased more fully open until her own tongue did his bidding, just its tip caressing the tip of his while beneath her hand the hammering of his heart grew almost violent.

He took his long, sweet time at it, tempting her with unhurried leisure, backing away an inch that made her eyes drift open to find his had done the same. He rested his forehead against hers, nudging softly, then backing away again so they could gaze into each other's eyes. His calculated slowness caused an insistent throbbing within the deep reaches of Allison's body. His eyes stayed on hers while he gradually brought her hand between their two mouths, opening his lips in slow motion, taking her thumb gently between his teeth, making miniature, caressing motions of gnawing, while his chin moved left and right, left and right, and his eyes burned into hers. He moved on to her index finger, biting its knuckle before straightening it with a flick of his thumb. She watched, fascinated and sensualized as it disappeared into the warm, wet confines of his mouth.

The gushing responses in her body were like nothing Jason had ever elicited from her, short of climaxes, which he had carefully regulated and often delighted in denying until she begged. Now, as Allison's finger was caressed by Rick's tongue, her body felt ready to explode. Gradually he slipped the finger from his mouth, then turned her hand over and gently bit its outer edge, his eyelashes drifting down to create a fan of shadow on his cheek while his labored breathing told her what this foreplay was doing to him, too.

He fell utterly still for a long, long moment, resting the backs of her fingertips against his lips, eyes closed as if in deep meditation. When he lifted his lids to study her, he spoke hoarsely, with her knuckles still touching his lips, muffling the words. "I didn't think I'd make it through these last eight days. You don't know how many times I went to the phone

499

and stood there staring at it, wanting to call. But I remembered what you said about not wanting a relationship, and I was sure you'd say you didn't want to see me again."

His words sent a wild reverberation of joy through Allison.

"Are you for real?" she managed at last, letting her eyes travel over what she could see of his face behind their hands. "I mean, look at yourself. Look at your face and your . . . your form, and tell me why you should be worried about whether or not one girl wanted to see you again."

"Is that all you see when you look at me? A face and a . . . a form?" he queried.

"No." She swallowed, retrieved her hand, and picked up her coffee cup to have a reason for withdrawing from him. "But why me?"

"If you don't know, if you can't feel it, I can't explain. I thought what was just happening here a moment ago was explanation enough—that, along with some enjoyable hours we've spent together."

"Rick . . . I . . ." She quickly rose to her feet, taking their plates to the sink so she could turn her back on him. She heard his chair scrape back and knew he was standing directly behind her.

"You don't trust me, do you? You think I'm handing you a practiced line of bull."

"Something like that," she admitted. In her entire life no man had ever so effectively seduced her as he'd just done across the corner of a breakfast table, touching no more than her hand. He had to know his appeal—all he had to do was look in the mirror to see he was no Hunchback of Notre Dame. And he had a wooing, winning way that could easily turn a woman's head.

"You want me to act like an admiring monk, is that it?"

She rested the palms of her hands against the edge of the sink, staring straight ahead, not knowing what she wanted, afraid of things her body was compelling her to do.

"I don't know," she choked, near tears, so confused by her impulses to trust him, those impulses juxtaposed against past experiences that had always turned out disastrously when she too eagerly placed her trust in another person.

A heavy hand fell on the side of her neck, kneading lightly. "I'm sorry, Allison. I promised, didn't I?" Even the touch he bestowed so casually made her heart race. Silence ticked by for several seconds, then Rick said quietly, "But after what happened at the door when I came in, I thought—"

"My mistake, letting it happen, okay?" she quickly interjected, afraid to turn around and face him. "I *was* glad to see you, and you just caught me a little off guard, that's all."

"You feel you have to erect a guard against me, is that want you're saying?"

"I . . . yes," she admitted.

"Why?"

She refused to answer. His warm hand lowered to the center of her back and began stroking up and down. "I'm not him, Allison," he said in the gentlest tone imaginable.

The hair at the back of her neck bristled. Her shoulder blades tensed. "Who?" she snapped.

"I don't know. You tell me." His hands circled her upper arms and forced her to turn around.

"I don't know what you're talking about," she lied, staring at the floor.

"Neither do I. What was his name?"

Her lips compressed into a thin line. He watched her face for every nuance of truth while dropping his hands from her. He stepped back, crossing his arms, then his calves, leaning his hips against the edge of the kitchen stove behind him.

"Do you want to tell me about him?"

"Him! Him!" she spouted belligerently. "You don't know what you're talking about."

"The man who made you so defensive and jumpy and wary of me, that's who I'm talking about. What was his name?"

"There is no such man!"

"Bull!" he returned tightly.

Her eyes met his determinedly. *"There is no man in my life,"* she stated unequivocably.

"No, but there was, wasn't there?"

"It's none of your business."

"Like hell it isn't. If he's what's keeping you from me, it's my business."

501

"I'm what's keeping me from you! I'm cautious, all right? Is there any crime in that?" she shouted in a sudden display of hot temper.

Rick scowled, studying her with a hard expression about his mouth. "Boy, he soured you on men but good, didn't he? Made up your mind you'll never trust one of us again, is that it?"

"Trust is another thing that never profited me one damn bit in the end," she stated bitterly.

"And so you're done with it, no matter what your gut feeling tells you?"

She suddenly bristled, gesturing angrily with her hands in the air, storming away. "I don't have to stand here for this . . . this third degree! This is my house, and just because I let you come in and cook breakfast for me doesn't give you the right to assess my motives. I thought of you, too, during the last week." She swung around to face him. "Is that what you want to hear? All right, I did! And I knew before the second day was gone that I wanted to see you again. But don't probe into my past if you want to share any of my future, be it a day, a week, or a month, because I won't stand for it!" She was back before him, practically nose to nose, bristling with defensiveness, striking out at him because she was afraid of the overwhelming urges she felt to like him, to trust him, maybe even to fall in love with him.

He stared at her angrily for a moment, and she saw his eyebrows finally relax from their tightly knit curl, his mouth take on a less pinched expression as he made a conscious effort to quell the urge to argue.

"You're right. It's none of my business," he agreed, backing off, shelving the issue for the time being. "Peace offering, all right?"

He pulled away from the stove and dipped a hand into the brown paper bag that was still on top of the counter. The next moment he lifted a camera in a black leather case. He held it aloft in invitation, its wide, woven strap swinging in the sudden silence between them.

Her animosity fell away with amusing speed, to be replaced by excited surprise. "The . . . the Hasselblad?" she asked breathlessly.

"The Hasselblad."

She reached for it, but he pulled it back just beyond her fingertips. "Wait a minute. Aren't you the woman who said you'd sell your soul for a chance to use it?"

Here it comes, Allison thought, the proposition.

But he only grinned one-sidedly, leaning over from the hip to place his mouth within easy kissing distance. "I won't ask for your soul, just one little kiss to bring peace back between us."

She gave him the price he asked, a quick, fleeting smack, but he still refused to give her the camera. "Friends?" he inquired, grinning into her face.

"Friends," she agreed, and snatched the camera from his hand.

Behind her she heard a throaty chuckle as she whirled toward the sunny living room to sit cross-legged on the shag rug. He ambled over and joined her, sitting almost knee to knee with her. He produced a roll of film and smiled, watching as she loaded the camera, exhilarated now, all attention given over to the coveted piece of equipment.

"Here's the film advance." He pointed to a silver crank. "And here's the shutter release." Her face was a picture of radiance as she looked down into the magnified square to study the light falling through the long, narrow windows. She spun around on her derrière, then rolled to her knees, walking on them across the hardwood floor while scanning the room through the viewfinder, looking for a setting that caught her eye.

The camera fell against her tummy. "Over there!" she ordered, pointing.

"Where? What?" He played dumb.

She wagged a finger at the floor to an oblique square of morning sun. "Over there, quick! Just sit the way you are, only do it over there, and face the kitchen so your face is sidelit."

He complied, smiling, sitting on the floor in the warm wash of sunlight, drawing his knees up, crossing his arms loosely over them. Allison lay on the floor before him, flat on her belly with her elbows braced on the floor, directing the tilt of his head in this direction and that. The natural window light illuminated the side of his face, put highlights on one side of his thick hair, lit the top of an ear, and left a solid line of shadow beyond the ridge of his forehead, nose, lips, and chin. She took two shots, then popped up, dragged a schefflera plant across two feet of floor, and ordered, "Now, with the shadows of the leaves on your face . . . but no smiles, okay? Turn a little more toward the window and give me that hand-some seriousness and let the mouth speak of thoughtfulness." The shutter clicked two more times, and her exuberant face appeared above the Hasselblad, a puckish smile on her mouth. "You're stunning, Rick Lang, do you know that?"

The camera freed her and let her natural impulses bubble out. With it around her neck, she felt totally uninhibited, released to speak what she felt. Only without the camera was she thwarted by the idea of getting involved with personal emotions.

"How about the basket chair?" he suggested next.

"Ahhh, perfect. Get in."

He pushed himself up off the floor and plopped onto the cushioned seat while she directed the chair opening toward the light source with an acute instinct for shadow effect and camera angle. She peered down into the viewfinder, checked the composition, lowered the camera, and looked around. She bounced across the room to drag a potted palm over, knelt down, and framed the shot with a spiky frond, making sounds of delight deep in her throat when she found the composition to her liking.

When she'd satisfied her artist's eye at that setting, she scanned the room, pointed to the French doors leading to the porch, and asked if he'd mind going out there where it was cold.

"What'll you give me?" he teased. "I work by the hour, you know."

She plopped a passing kiss on his mouth, hardly conscious of what she was doing, so caught up was she with the joy of photographing with the prized piece of equipment.

She framed him through the panes of the French door, adjusting the angle of the camera time and again in an attempt to create a well-composed photo without hiding his features behind the crossbars of the window frames.

"Hey, hurry up!" he complained, his voice coming muffled through the closed door. "My nipples are puckering up."

She laughed, snapped two quick ones, told him he could come back in, then admitted, "Mine, too," adding impudently, "they always do when I get turned on, and your camera really turns me on."

"Only my camera, huh?"

"I didn't say that, did I?"

"Well, let me know when you want to indulge in a little puckering. Maybe we can work together on it, without the help of porch or camera."

When she'd exhausted all the best possibilities the apartment offered for settings, she was still rarin' to go. "How about doing some outside shots?" he suggested. "There's a Winterfest going on at Lake Calhoun this afternoon, and I was planning to ask if you wanted to go over and fool around anyway."

"Fool around?" she repeated archly.

"With the camera, of course," he returned. "There's all kinds of stuff going on over there. What do you say we bundle up warm and check it out?"

He was irresistible, and she *did* want a chance to get to know him better. And she *did* want to work with the camera a little longer. And she *did* so enjoy being with him.

"Why not?" Allison replied, jubilant at the thought of spending a whole afternoon with him without having to talk her emotions into a state of equilibrium because privacy offered him a chance to kiss or touch her.

Chapter 8

SHE DONNED HER disreputable bobcap and scarf, and thigh-high boots lined with fur and a hip-length jacket belted at the waist. From the trunk of his car Rick dug out an enormous parka. He let the hood flop down his back, but the wolf-fur lining, framing his chin and jaw, set off his masculinity to great advantage. Even before they got in the car, Allison snapped a shot of him, having adjusted the f-stop to compensate for the blinding brightness of the snow outside.

It was a dazzling day, as bright as their spirits as they drove the short distance to Lake Calhoun. The Winterfest was already in full swing when they arrived, the activities taking place right on the frozen lake, which looked like a confetti blanket, its white surface dotted with multicolored wool caps and bright ski jackets. Wandering from event to event, Allison snapped random shots—two runny-nosed eight-year-olds angling for sunfish through a hole in the ice; the laughing face of a man who'd fallen onto his back like an overturned turtle during a game of broomball; a young married couple sculpturing an ice mermaid by wetting down snow and compacting it with mittens covered with plastic bags; a string of red-nosed youngsters at the finish line of an ice-skating race, their lips set in grim determination; a boy and girl kissing, unaware that Allison was snapping them because their eyes were closed; an ice boat with its orange-and-yellow sail furled by the breeze, its rider hanging over the edge at a precarious angle; Rick lying flat on his back, making an angel in the snow; the grand, old Calhoun Beach Hotel Building—which was a hotel no longer—standing across the road from the lake in majestic watchfulness while funseekers romped and played and totally disregarded the fact that the temperature was only twelve degrees above zero.

Rick brought hot chocolate from a stand that had also been on the ice. They sat on a snowbank, squinting through the steam rising from their cups, watching a judge measuring a ridiculously short pickerel with a tape measure while a small boy looked on hopefully. Allison felt Rick's eyes on her instead of on the fishing contest, and turned to meet his gaze.

"You're the neatest girl I ever met, you know that?"

Flustered, she looked away and hid behind a sip of cocoa.

"Don't hide, it's nothing to be ashamed of. You're game for anything—bundling up and clumping out here in this cold, taking pictures of stuff that to some would seem so ridiculously bourgeois they'd scoff at the suggestion of even coming here, much less recording the homey events on film."

"It's been fun," she replied honestly, then braved a look into his eyes, adding, "and I've had a wonderful day."

"Me too."

For a moment she thought he was going to kiss her. With her heart already fluttering greedily in her throat, she suddenly didn't trust her own common sense, so she put on a pained expression and informed him, "But my derrière is so damn cold there's no feeling left in it."

Abruptly he laughed. "How 'bout your nipples?" he teased secretively. "Anything happening to them?"

"None of your business, you dirty old lech."

He licked his lips, gave her a suggestive head-to-toe scan, and grinned. "Like hell it isn't."

She hauled herself to her feet and reached out a mittened hand to give him a tug. When he was on his feet, Rick bracketed her temples with gloved hands. Her heart went a-thudding in anticipation, but he only pushed her drooping bobcap up out of her eyes and teased, "Nice cap, Scott." Then he kissed the end of her icy nose, bundled her up against his side, and hauled her with him, pressed hip to hip while they walked to the car.

Pulling up in her driveway sometime later, she moved a hand toward the door handle. His glove crossed over her arm. "Wait," he commanded.

She listened to his footsteps crunch around the rear of the car, and a moment later her door was opened. She had to giggle at his gallantry when she was dressed in her urchin's outfit, totally unflattering and unfeminine.

He followed close behind her as they climbed the stairs in slow motion. At the landing, when she aimed the key for the lock, he took it from her hand and opened the door for her, then dropped the key into her mitten. He looked into her eyes and once more pressed his palms to the sides of her head and pushed the bobcap back where it was supposed to be. But he left his hands on her cheeks this time and said into her eyes, "I want to come in."

Her lips opened to say no, it was dangerous, their feelings were rioting too fast, they needed time to assess what was happening. But before she could speak he slowly lowered his mouth to hers and her heart fluttered to life and sent quivers to her breasts. As the kiss lingered, he released her face, taking her in his arms to pull her against his bulky jacket.

She pressed her mittened hands against his back, drawing close and moving her mouth languorously beneath his, opening her lips to invite his seeking tongue. It was hot, wet, tantalizing, seductive, and it stroked away the memory of Jason. His hands roved down the back of her jacket, then underneath it. Spreading his hands wide, he gathered her close against him, spanning her icy buttocks with warm, wide palms.

His lips left her mouth. He bent his face into the warm hair at her neck, burrowing deep to find skin inside the folds of scarf. "Allison," he murmured gruffly, "let me come in. I want to warm you up."

You already have, she thought, delighting in the feel of his palms against that intimate part of her body. He drew back, deliberately lifting first the hem of his parka, then her jacket, recapturing her buttocks to pull her against the long ridge of flesh inside his jeans, to let it speak for him as he pressed its heat against her stomach. He undulated his hips, grinding against her while on her backside his hands asserted themselves and controlled her.

He kissed her with a wild thrusting of tongues, rhythmically matching the strokes of tongue and hip before jerking his mouth aside and begging in a raspy voice, "Let me come in, Allison."

She knew what he was asking and was abashed to find she wanted to do his bidding, to invite him not only into her house, but into her body as well. But she pressed her hands against his chest, begging, "Please, Rick, please stop. It's too soon, too sudden."

"What are you afraid of?" he asked.

She swallowed, reached for his hands, and brought them between them, folding his palms between her own while looking deeply into his eyes.

"Me," she admitted.

He drew in a deep, shuddering breath, put a few more inches between their bodies, and asked, "So you'd turn a man away hungry?"

"Is it supper you want?" She knew it wasn't, not any more than it was what she wanted.

"I guess I'll have to settle for it, if that's the only way I can stay."

It seemed a reprieve. She wanted him with her yet, and supper was a plausible excuse to keep him a while longer.

"I have a pizza in the freezer. How does that sound?"

"Like a hell of a poor second, but I accept."

They moved inside, but when the door was closed and the lights snapped on, there was no denying that the sexual tension remained, as vibrant as before. She hung up their jackets and turned from the pursuit in his eyes, telling her heart to calm down. But it felt deliciously good, this business of being pursued. It was beginning to dawn on her why Jason Ederlie had eaten it up so.

Allison was halfway across the living room when she was swung around abruptly by an elbow. "What's the hurry?" he teased, swinging her against him, holding her loosely around the waist, leaning back so their hips touched.

"Are you about to extract payment for the use of your Hasselblad?" she asked, resting her hands on his inner elbows, striving to keep the mood light.

"Not at all. You can keep it awhile . . . unconditionally."

"God, how can you let a camera like that lay around in its case all the time, then lend it out to some girl who . . . who . . ."

"Puckers up at the sight of it?" he finished. "Well, if you can't make the girl pucker up at the sight of you, you do the next best thing, right?" His hand wandered to her breast to brush it testingly with the backs of his fingers.

"Rick, stop it. You came in here for pizza."

"Did I?" But the humor fell from his face as he reached to take the back of her head with both hands and pull her hard against his mouth. She forgot caution and flung her arms around his neck, a hand twining into the thick hair above his collar as he made sounds of frustrated passion deep in his throat. Stars and suns and moons seemed to flash across the darkness behind Allison's closed eyelids while she let her tongue and hips and hands respond to the plea in his eyes. He tore his lips from hers. They buried their faces in each other's necks, clinging, learning the scent of each other, the texture of skin, of hair, of clothing as his hands played over her hips, and hers over the taut muscles of his shoulders and back.

"Allison, this afternoon seemed like a year," he ground out, his voice gone low. His hand cupped the back of her head, losing itself in her hair. "I swear, woman, I don't know what's happening to me."

In an effort to control the body that threatened to burst its skin, she laughed—a throaty, deep sound that came out very shaky. "I think it's called hunger pains. Let me put the pizza in."

Reluctantly he released her, his eyes darkly following the sway of her narrow hips while she crossed to the kitchen, turned on the oven, and opened the freezer door. He turned away, unable to watch her and retain control. He ambled to the component set and switched on the radio, wandered aimlessly about the living room to find himself once again drawn near the kitchen, his eyes riveted to her backside while she leaned over to slip the pizza into the oven. The back of her jeans was faded to a paler blue in twin patches just below the pockets. His eyes roved over them and he inhaled a deep, shaky breath before letting his eyelids slide closed. He ran a palm down the zipper of his jeans and pressed it hard against his tumescence.

When he opened his eyes again, she was facing him. Her cheeks lit up to a fiery red, and she bit her bottom lip, then swallowed hard.

"It's no secret," he admitted gruffly, "so why pretend? I've spent the entire afternoon thinking about one handful of warm breast in the early morning when I came here today, and somehow it just hasn't been enough."

She backed up against the oven door, reaching behind her to grab the handle in both hands to steady herself. Her face was a mask of uncertainty, and her breath fell hard and heavy from her chest.

"Rick, I'm no virgin," she admitted, abashed, yet facing him squarely.

"Neither am I. So what?"

"I'm a woman, and we're the ones who have been taught since puberty that it's up to us to control situations like this. But I feel like I'm losing control, and I don't want you to think I'm easy." She suddenly covered her face with both hands and spun around, afraid to face the hour of reckoning she knew was at hand.

How long did she think she could play with fire? How long did she think she could string along a healthy, virile, and willing twenty-five-year-old man? And what was she going to do now that she'd backed herself into this corner?

"Rick, you were right, I'm scared."

"Of what?" he asked, close behind her. "Of me?" His hand touched her hair, smoothing it gently, without the slightest hint of force. "Allison, look at me . . . please. Don't hide from it. It's nothing to be scared of."

She turned at the gentle pressure of his fingers on her neck and lifted quavering eyes to his. A moment later her voice came, shaky, unsure, doubtful. "I don't think I like being a woman in this . . . this liberated age," she admitted. "I'm not very good at being a . . . a casual lay."

His hands bracketed her jaw, lifting her face so he could look deeply into her eyes. A thumb stroked the hollow of her cheek. "Thank God," he said softly.

She lunged against him, turning her cheek upon his chest, squeezing her eyes shut, wrapping her arms tightly about his sides. "Oh, Rick, what happened to the days when a man and woman went to the altar as virgins and learned about each other in their wedding bed and stayed in it for seventy-five years, forsaking all others? That's what I'm afraid of . . . It's not there anymore!"

She could hear the steady thrum of his heart beneath her ear, then the deep rumble of his voice as he spoke reassuringly. "Allison, I don't care if there's been someone else. It doesn't change how I feel about you. What you are now you wouldn't be if you hadn't lived your life as you have so far. Does that make any sense?"

"Nothing makes any sense when I'm near you. I try to think clearly, but everything goes blurry. The only time things aren't blurry is when I'm behind the camera. Then things are clear, uncomplicated, I can understand them. If I could . . . could turn a focus ring on my life and bring it into focus as easily as I can a picture, I'd feel I had control of my life."

"And if you let your defenses down with me, your life goes out of control?"

"Yes!" She pulled back, looking up at him with haunted eyes. "Don't you see? It's like turning it all over to you. That's what scares me."

"I don't want to control your life, Allison. I want to make love to you." Gently he drew her near, raising her chin while he spoke.

She studied him, wanting to believe but afraid to. "They're both the same thing," she said shakily.

"Not with the right person."

He kissed her left eyelid closed, then her right.

"Don't," she breathed.

As if she hadn't spoken, he wrapped his arms around her, pinning her arms to her sides in the strong circle of his own. He leaned to kiss her neck. Her eyelids remained closed as she dropped her head to the side.

"Don't," she whispered raggedly.

But his lips moved to hers while he held her with one arm, peering past her cheek as he turned off the oven. Continuing to control her movements with his own, he opened the oven door while pulling her two steps away to make room for its downward swing.

"Don't."

Keeping his arm around her, he leaned to pick up a pot-holder from the top of the stove, then bent her over half backwards, half sideways, while he got the pizza out of the oven and set it on a burner.

The heat on the backs of her legs was nothing compared to that springing through her body as she repeated weakly, "Don't."

He manipulated her at will, dipping to reach the oven door and close it again before marching her slowly backwards in his arms across the kitchen, kissing her all the way. He stopped to turn off the dining room light, but didn't stop kissing, only opened his eyes and peered across her nose to find the light switch and snap it down while she mumbled with her lips pressed against his, "Don't."

He danced her backwards with slow, deliberate pushes of his thighs against hers, kissing her now open mouth as they progressed across the dining area toward the living room. He released her arms, found them with his hands, and forced them up over his shoulders, still walking her inexorably backwards while her body tingled and strained against him with each step.

At the stereo he dipped again, punched a button, then let his eyelids drift closed, kissing her while his tongue delved deep into her mouth, all the while idly playing the radio dial across the scanner until he'd found something soft and vocal with a guitar background. Her arms were now looped around his neck without resistance, and her words were nearly unrecognizable, spoken as they were with her tongue pressed flat against his: "Don't . . . waste . . . so . . . much . . . time."

He smiled, devouring her mouth while his hands slid down to her buttocks, pressing their shifting muscles as he hauled her step by agonizingly slow step to the light switch by the entry door. After he'd fumbled for it behind her back, his hand returned to her buttocks. He held her firmly against him in the dark until neither of them seemed able to strain close enough against the other. His thighs pushed against hers again, and she took a faltering step back to feel something solid against her shoulder blades. Wedged between his warm flesh and the wall, her breath came in onslaughts as he pressed his hips against hers, moving in sensual circles until she responded, beginning to move, too. Her shirt went sliding out of her jeans as he pulled it up with both hands, easing away from her with all but his mouth, which continued plundering in welcome attack. Behind his neck she unbuttoned her cuffs. He sensed what she was doing, stopped kissing her, and leaned his forearms on the wall beside her head.

"Unbutton the rest of it for me," he begged, his voice gravelly with emotion while his breath whisked her lips. With scarcely a pause, her trembling fingers moved to the top button. He leaned his head low in the dark, feeling with his mouth to see if she was doing as he asked. When the first button was free, his lips pressed warmly against the skin inside, above the bra. She hesitated, lost in delight as the touch of his tongue fell on her flesh. Then, keeping his palms pressed flat on the wall, he bent his head even lower, nudging her fingers to the next button, which opened at his wordless command. This time when he pressed his lips inside he met the small embroidered flower at the center of her bra. He breathed outward gently, warming her skin beneath the garment, sending shivers of desire to the peaks of her breasts. When at last her blouse hung completely open, he ordered in a husky whisper, "Now mine," hovering so close his breath left warm, damp dew on her nose.

She reached out in the dark, exploring the front-button band of his shirt running down its length. When her hand reached the waistband of his jeans he sucked in a hard, quick breath and jerked slightly. With both hands she explored his hips, just above the tight cinch of waistband. He was hard, honed, not a ripple of flesh that shouldn't be there. When her hands reached the hollow of his spine, she slowly tugged his shirttails out.

"Allison." His voice was thick and throaty. "How I've wished for this."

"And how I wanted to wish, but I was afraid."

"Are you always this slow?" came his gruff question at her cheek, and in the dark she smiled.

"Mmm-hmm, I like it slow."

"Me too, but I can't wait any long..." The last word was swallowed up by her mouth as his came against it while he speedily loosened his remaining buttons.

He laid his warm hand inside the open neck of her shirt, caressing her throat before pushing the garment back from her shoulders to fall to the floor behind her. His arms slid around her ribs, fingers testing their way to the clasp of her bra. It came away in his hands, leaving her half naked, eager for the caress of his palm upon her bare flesh. He stepped back, taking the bra down her arms, and in the dark she heard a rustle as he tucked it into his hind pocket. She waited, breath caught in her throat, for the return of his touch, expecting a warm cupping of her breast.

But he, too, seemed to be hovering in wait.

She reached out a tentative hand, seeking texture, seeking warmth, remembering the look of him standing in the studio, straight, erect, with his shirt off, while she assessed his almost square chest muscles studded with lightly strewn hair as pale in color as a glass of champagne, the light refracting off them as if caught in champagne bubbles.

Her hands now found what they sought, sensitive fingertips fanning across the hard muscles, the soft hair, the firm skin that shuddered beneath her touch, surprising her.

"Richard Lang," she murmured, almost as if to remind herself she was here, that it was he whose skin had just reacted so sensuously to her touch.

An almost pained sound came raspily from his throat while he scooped her against him, coaxing her bare breasts to his half-exposed chest. His lips and tongue swooped down again, working their magic as he pulled her away from the wall and took her with him, this time stepping backwards himself, feeling her legs brush his as she followed his lead.

In front of the stereo he stopped, studying her face by the dim light radiating from the face of the dial. Scant though it was, Allison could make out the outline of his features, the points of light caught in his eyes as he wrestled his shirt off, then draped it across the top of the closed turntable. He stood away from Allison, reaching first to touch her eyebrows while her lids lowered and a shudder possessed her body. His fingertips trailed over her cheeks, touched her lips, then after what seemed an eternity, found her waiting breasts.

She opened her eyes languorously. His were cast down, watching his hands. She, too, followed his glance to witness long fingers gently adoring, caressing, exploring, while beside them a voice sang, "It was easy to love her, easier than whiling away a summer's day..."

He touched her with tentative reserve, almost a reverence, until she could stand it no longer and covered the backs of his hands with her own, pulling his palms full and hard against her, twisting repeatedly at the waist to abrade his palms with the side to side brushing of her nipples, all hard and eager and tightened into little knots of desire.

"Allison..." he uttered, and dropped to one knee, reaching his mouth up to cover the hardened peak with his lips and suckle it with his tongue. "You're beautiful."

She felt beautiful as his words washed over her and a strong forearm pulled her hips against the fullest part of his chest. Her head fell back weakly, a soft sound of abandon issuing from her throat while she undulated slowly against him, brushing, brushing, with light strokes that moved her in sensual rhythm. She ran languid fingers through his hair, lost in sensation, while he moved his mouth to her other breast and took its nipple gently between his teeth, tugging lightly before circling it with his tongue, sending shivers of desire coursing through her body.

The song on the radio changed, and as if to verify the softly uttered confidences of minutes ago, a feminine voice crooned about wanting a man with a slow hand.

And a slow hand it was, slow and sensual and arousing Allison's passions until her breathing grew labored and her limbs felt as if she were moving against swift water.

Rick was on his feet again, moving against her in the age-old language of rhythm and thrust, compelling her hips to seek a mate. He backed away, guiding Allison to the soft cushions of the wicker sofa, leading her by a wrist, then urging her down with the gentle pressure of his hands on her shoulders until she lay on her back while he knelt on the floor beside her.

A strong hand found the hollow beneath her jaw, while his

other one slipped behind her head, controlling the kiss that moved from mouth to nose to eyes, questing, testing. When Rick's mouth found hers again, his tongue slipped within, riding against hers in rhythm to the music, the song's sensual words underlining their feelings about this act they were sharing.

While his left hand remained buried in her hair, his right traveled down the center of her bare stomach, following the zipper of her jeans until he cupped the warmth between her legs, pressing, pressing, unable to press hard enough to satisfy either of them, exploring through tight, restrictive denim until she raised one knee and her hips jutted up, bringing her body hard and thrusting against his touch.

Lowering his mouth to her breast, he continued his exploration, pressing the heel of his hand against the mound of flesh hidden yet from him, delighting in her response as small sounds of passion came from her throat, and she strained upward with arousal and the need for more. He kissed the hollow between her ribs, burying his face in the wider hollow just above her waistband, feeling the driving beats of her breath as her stomach lifted his face time and again.

He raised his head. With one tug, the snap of her jeans gave, and she fell utterly still, not breathing, not moving, but waiting . . . waiting. The rasp of the zipper seemed to match the sound of Rick's strident breathing.

When his palm slipped inside, against her stomach, pent-up breath fell from Allison in a wild rush, and she flung one arm above her head while wholly giving over the control of her body to him. His hand slid lower, fingers delving inside brief, silken bikinis until they brushed flattened hair and moved beyond, contouring her flesh, seeking, finding, sliding within the warm wet confines of her femininity. Her ribs arched high off the cushions as he began a slow, rhythmic stroking to which her body answered.

She lowered the arm from above her head, seeking to know him in the dark, then rolled slightly toward him and found his hot, hard body, while he knelt with knees spread wide, ready. He made a guttural sound deep in his throat, and she caressed him more boldly, learning the shape of him through his jeans. He leaned to nuzzle her neck, and as his nipple touched hers she could feel the torturous hammering of his heart against her own.

The moments that followed were a rapturous swirl of sensation as they pleasured each other with touches. There no longer seemed a need for lips to join. Only their cheeks rested lightly against each other while they savored this bodily prelude and honed their senses to a fine edge.

He was so different from Jason, unrushed and sensitive to her every need. "You like that?" he whispered against her breast, laughing deep in his throat when she answered, "Yes, do it again." He washed the entire orb of her breast with his tongue again, wetting all of its surface until shivers radiated across the aroused skin.

He slid his lips to the corner of her mouth. "Lift up," he whispered, hands at her hips. And in the next moment, both denim and satin were down around her hips, then gone, whispered away from her ankles. His hands deserted her body, and she listened to the rustle, snap, and zip as he freed himself in like manner, found her hand, and once again led it to him.

He leaned over, burying his face in the warm hollow of her waistline as a shudder overcame him and he held her wrist, guiding her to stroke his velvet sleekness. Then they were lost in each other, in the moving, touching, and trembling. They reveled in the taking and giving of sensory delights while the darkness whispered their intimacies. Time had no limits as they explored with slow ease, thrilling to the realization that they had found each other. Somehow, in this wide world of countless souls, theirs had managed to meet and strike a chord of kindred need and compatibility.

They felt rich and blessed, at times awed that they should be this lucky. They were, in those minutes, open and unencumbered, hiding neither the passion to give nor the pleasure in taking, extending the anticipation of the final blending until their bodies writhed and burned.

But soon the heat and height grew too great for Rick. "Allison, stop . . . stop . . ." He grabbed her wrist and pinned it above her head, pulled in a deep, shuddering breath and lay his hips just beside hers. "I'm outdistancing you, darling," he whispered thickly, "but there's no hurry, we have all night." He kissed her eyelid, the side of her nose, continuing his silken arousal of her even while temporarily denying himself fulfillment. Again his mouth was at her breast, teeth, tongue, and lips sending ripples of impatience radiating everywhere. The tumult he'd started rumbled close to the surface—higher, higher, until Allison's head arched back, her body now moving to meet his velvet touches. Through clenched teeth she whispered a single word, "Please..." knowing he would stop, leaving her at the brink of that hellish heaven where her body would be exposed in its most vulnerable state.

But it was Rick, not Jason, who wielded the touch of fire in which she burned. And rather than withdraw it, he extended it as Allison had never known it could be extended, until her muscles went taut and the goodness lengthened and strengthened and took her tumbling into the world of sensation as her body became a choreographed dance of muscle and motion.

In the height of her passion, Allison's palms unknowingly pressed his mouth away from her nipples, which had suddenly gone sensitive while she shuddered and cried out in a half sob, half laugh.

When she drifted down to earth from the place of lush quickening, his hand was stroking her languid legs, his kiss etching its mark upon her damp stomach. Weakly she reached to lift his face back to hers. "I didn't mean to push you away. I'm sorry..."

His kiss cut off her apology. "For what?" came his throaty whisper. "Allison, that was beautiful. I never thought you'd be so...so free and open with me." He kissed her neck, his voice a loud rumble in her ear as a hand ran from her knees to her waist and back again. "God, Allison, that was more than beautiful. It was an accolade."

"It was selfish," she insisted, abashed at her total abandon.

"No...no," he assured her against her lips.

"But I forgot all about you in the middle of it." She lay a palm along his cheek and felt him smile as he chuckled.

"But I'm next, darling."

She rolled to her side, brushed her hand down his stomach to find him taut, silken, waiting. The next moment, she felt herself being tugged into a sitting position, insistent hands stroking her spine and urging her toward the edge of the cushions. He leaned away. Warm touches guided her to do his

519

bidding. Her knee brushed his hard stomach as he parted her knees and settled himself between them. "Come here," came his voice thickly. Then he pulled her hard and tight against him and tilted her back with a gentle pressure of his palm upon her chest. There came a rustle in the dark, and she felt a cushion fill the void between her back and the sofa. His hands found her hips, moved sleekly down the backs of her legs to the hollows behind her knees. Then he was touching and kissing her everywhere. The sated feeling of moments ago slipped away to be replaced by renewed desire as he laced his brushing caresses with random kisses, dropping them along her darkened skin wherever they happened to fall—on a breast, an inner elbow, a hip, her stomach . . .

She tensed, tightened her stomach muscles, and held a pent-up breath, sensing his destination. She reached for his shoulders to stop him, but it was too late. His tongue touched her intimately, leaving her feeling utterly vulnerable and undeniably prurient.

"Rick . . . I . . ." His hand reached blindly to cover her lips while his lambent touches sent currents of sensation firing her veins with new life. Resistance fled beneath the onslaught of sensations, and she fell back, a strangled sound issuing from her throat, until at last he knelt to her, entering the silken front of sensuality with easy grace. When he clutched her hips and pressed deep, a soft growl escaped his throat, then the dark was filled only with music and breathing and the magnificence they shared as his body blended into hers.

He murmured her name, interspersing it with endearments, and somehow the beats of their bodies matched, became rhythm and rhyme as she lay back, remembering the sheen of these muscles the first time she'd rubbed them with oil, picturing his perfect face as vividly as if the room were not cast into darkness.

Her fingers flexed into the flesh of his shoulders as he moved within her, taking her beyond the point of no return. And when her nails unconsciously dug in, he jerked her wrists down, pinning them against the cushions while together they thrust closer . . . closer . . . closer.

His breath was tortured, her voice a ragged plea as she begged, "Let . . . m . . . my . . . hands . . . g . . . go." The pressure left her wrists, but her fingers remained clenched as she clung to his strong back while beat for beat she rode with him to their devastating climaxes.

Oh, it was good. Everything about it was good.

He, too, was trembling, trying to control it by pressing her hard against him, holding the back of her head with a wide-spread palm. They had slipped down, their bodies now wilting toward the floor. Finally they gave in to the inertia that dumped their sated limbs in a loose heap onto the shaggy rug.

The radio was still playing. It intruded now where before they'd been unconscious of it in the background. Side by side they rested, neither able to conjure up the strength to move, while tomorrow's weather was followed by a time check and a tuneful commercial for soft drinks. Then from the speakers came a guitar intro to a soulful melody and a man's voice singing into their intimate world: "When I'm stretched on the floor after loving once more with your skin pressing mine and we're tired and fine . . ."

The words broke into Allison's consciousness in an unwelcome reminder of the past. But this was Rick, not Jason! Yet he was lying just as the words of the song described, flat out on the floor, and the enormity of what they'd done together struck Allison. Committed. She'd committed herself to a man again by sharing the most intimate of acts. Almost as if it possessed a clairvoyance, the radio reminded her that once before she'd done this, trusted like this, only. . .

Rick's warm hand rested on the soft skin of her inner elbow, and slowly she eased away from his touch and left his side to search for her clothing in the dark.

"Allison?" She sensed how he'd braced up on an elbow, but she didn't answer, feeling along the seat of the sofa. Through the dark the song kept playing. Then a moment later she heard his heels thud across the floor toward the radio, and an angry hand slam against it, thrusting the room into silence. He found her again, but as his hand touched her shoulder, she ducked aside and evaded it.

"Allison, what's wrong?"

"Nothing."

"Don't lie to me." He touched her again, but she retreated to the sofa, curling up with her feet beneath her. The light switch sounded, and Allison flinched.

"Don't . . . don't turn the light on, please."

The light flooded over her shoulder from the table lamp behind her, revealing her strewn hair and withdrawn pose as Rick studied her.

"You want to talk about it?" he asked.

"Just . . . let it be." The only garment at hand was her jeans. She pulled them across her lap and slumped her shoulders as if to shield her naked breasts.

He leaned forward to touch her knee. "No, it's too important."

"Don't look at me." She huddled now, shivering while he hesitated uncertainly for a moment, then retrieved his shirt from the top of the stereo and draped it over her shivering arms and shoulders. He slipped into his pants, then returned to kneel on one knee before her, searching for words, for meanings, for reasons. But she remained closed against him as he tiredly rested an elbow on a knee and kneaded the bridge of his nose, waiting—for what, he didn't know. Insight perhaps, guidance, a hint of where to start.

"Allison, tell me about it. Tell me about him."

Her head snapped up. "It's none of your business. I told you, no questions. Just . . . leave me alone, Jas . . ." Realizing her slip, she cut the word in half.

"Is that his name . . . Jason?"

"I said don't probe, dammit! Don't try to ch—"

"Don't probe!" he shouted, coming to his feet, towering over her. "Don't probe?" He flung a palm angrily at the sofa cushions. "You just came close to calling me by his name and you say don't probe?" He laughed once, ruefully. "What the hell do you think I am, stupid? I heard your precious Five Senses song come on the radio, and I felt what it did to you. All of a sudden you weren't there any more. How do you expect me to react?"

"Please, I . . . I . . . we shouldn't have done this." She turned her eyes aside. "I think you should go."

She saw how he braced one hand on his waistband and locked his knees, his feet spread wide.

"I'll need my shirt," he stated coldly.

She waited, expecting him to yank it from her, dreading

522

the moment when she'd be exposed to him again. Instead his angry footsteps moved across the hardwood floor to her bedroom. She heard the closet door open, then he came back, stood before her with her blue robe clenched in his hands, and repeated tightly, "I have to take my shirt." A hand reached out, and she thought she saw it tremble before she clamped her eyelids shut, and the cool air covered her naked skin.

He glanced at her arms, crossed now protectively over her breasts. "I want to fling this thing at you and tell you to go to hell, you know that?"

Her eyes opened and met his. He was so totally honest—why couldn't she be that honest about her feelings? He dropped the robe in her lap, then donned his shirt, tucked it in, and stood contemplatively. He sighed heavily at last, ran a hand through his hair, and squatted down beside the sofa again, studying the floor. "We can't drop it here, you know. We have to talk," he said.

"Not now, okay?" she asked tremulously.

He nodded. His knees cracked as he stood up again. "I'll call you."

Still he didn't go, but stood above her, looking down on her hair, which stood out like a dark nimbus in the light drenching her shoulder as she fought to hold back the tears.

"Hey," he asked huskily, "you gonna be all right?"

She nodded jerkily, once, and he turned away. She heard him pause at the door to pull on his boots, heard the snaps of his jacket, and knew he was watching her through the long silent pause before the door opened, then quietly closed behind him.

At its soft click Allison flung herself around and fell across the back of the sofa, burying her head in her arms. And there in her loneliness and confusion she cried. For Jason. For Rick. And for herself.

Chapter 9

RICK LANG HAD left his Hasselblad behind. Guilt stricken at how she'd treated him, Allison at first declined to use it. He didn't call on Monday or Tuesday, and by Wednesday the shots of the Winterfest came back from processing—crisp, clear and breathtaking. After viewing them, she found herself staring at the phone, wanting terribly to call him, to apologize. But she had hurt him so badly . . . so badly. She stared out the studio windows, seeing only Rick Lang, whom she'd likened to Jason when he was nothing at all like Jason. He cared so little about his looks, he hadn't even asked to see the transparencies of the book cover.

She sighed and turned back to her work—a layout for a Tiffany diamond. The engagement ring nestled within the petals of an apricot rose to which she had applied a single drop of water with an eyedropper. Against a backdrop of lush salmon satin, the composition was stunning. She glanced at the Hasselblad again, weakened, picked it up, and was loading it a moment later.

The diamond, the rose and the camera again worked on Allison's conscience, and she promised herself she'd call Rick and apologize as soon as she got home. But before she finished the series of photos the phone rang, and Mattie said, "Prepare yourself, kiddo, I've got some news you aren't going to like."

"What?"

"Remember that series of shots you took of Jason last fall —the ones in the Harris tweeds?"

"Of course I remember."

"Well, get ready for a surprise—they're in this month's *Gentlemen's Review*."

The shock set Allison in her chair with a plop. "What!"

"You heard me right. They're in this month's *GR*."

"B . . . but that's impossible! He only stole them a few weeks ago."

"Apparently not. It appears he lifted them months ago and submitted them then. When did you realize they were missing?"

A sick feeling made Allison's stomach go hollow. "When he left, of course. I wasn't running to the files daily while he was living with me to see if his intentions were honorable or not."

"Well, the creep was about as honorable as Judas Iscariot! The photo credit lists the photographer as Herbert Wells."

"Undoubtedly with a post office box in some eastern city to which *GR* was instructed to send the handsome paycheck," Allison surmised bitterly.

"You're going to tell the police, aren't you?"

Allison sighed uselessly. "Without the negatives to prove the originals were mine?"

There was silence, then Mattie's sympathetic voice. "Listen, honey, I'm really sorry I had to give you the bad news."

"Yeah, sure," said the lifeless voice in the wide, drafty, echoey studio.

Allison hung up and shot to her feet, taking a defiant, angry stance as she stared unseeingly at the glittering diamond that seemed to wink hauntingly from the velvety folds of the rose. Two diamond-hard tears glittered from Allison's eyes.

Damn you, Jason, you bastard! Even while you were taking me to bed night after night you were lying all the time, using your body to get me to do exactly what you wanted. Well, you certainly saw me coming! You must've been standing on the sidewalk watching while this stupid little South Dakota farm girl came rolling off the turnip truck!

I fell for your line like some sex-starved ninny, while you

525

stole the one thing that meant more to me than even you. All those transparencies—my God!—all of them good enough for publication, while I never suspected. But you knew, didn't you? You knew and you used me. You picked my body and my files clean and made sure I'd know exactly how, by selling them to *GR!*

Where are you now? Laughing in some other woman's arms while you tell her about the ignorant little farm wench from Watertown?

It all flooded back, redoubling Allison's sick realization of how gullible she'd been—of all the times she'd fawned over his body, adored it, both in clothing before the lens and out of it in bed. What a fool she'd been not to see how one-sided her affection was. He took her every compliment as if it were his due while giving back nothing but his body. And that he gave with a hint of smugness, as if doing her a favor.

She cringed now at the memory of how openly she'd displayed her need, her desire, her love. For she *had* loved him. That's what hurt the most. She had. And Jason had fed off her, figuratively as well as literally, for she'd paid all the bills as long as he posed, posed, posed, while she collected the portfolio of photos he was systematicaly rifling all along.

She lived again the anguish and disbelief of that afternoon she'd returned to the apartment to find his message scrawled across the bottom of the picture on the easel. How typical of him to leave his parting message in that way, as if she were some adolescent groupie.

Allison sighed, deep and long, then dropped to her desk chair forlornly. Jason Ederlie had done it all to her, everything a man could possibly do to a woman. He'd taken all a man could take, left as little as a man could leave.

Well, she'd learned her lesson but good. She'd been taken in once by a stunning face and a talented body, but no man would ever reduce her this way again. Not even Rick Lang! Whether he doled out kisses like Eros himself, nobody was going to worm his way into her heart or her bed or her files again!

The telephone rang once more that afternoon. When Allison recognized Rick's voice, she told him this was the answering service and that she would have Ms. Scott return his call.

There followed a puzzled hesitation before he thanked her and hung up.

At home that night during supper Allison's phone rang twice. Later she lay in bed listening to its jangling insistence for the fourth time since she'd gotten home. Determinedly she buried her head under the pillow.

The following morning her answering service reported that a man named Rick Lang had been calling and was becoming abusive to the woman on duty, who could not make him believe they weren't withholding his messages from Ms. Scott.

Late Thursday Allison made the sudden decision to go to Watertown for the weekend. But she was restless and irritable even there, for the farmhouse felt confining. She wished she could talk to her mother about Jason and Rick, but her mother would never understand Allison's having had a sexual relationship with a man before marriage, much less having lived with him for the better part of a year. Sexual intercourse had never, never been a discussed subject at home, and Allison knew her mother would be extremely uncomfortable to confront it with her daughter, even now.

Allison's married brother Wendell farmed nearby, but they weren't close enough for her to seek his counsel either. Then, too, every time Allison's mother looked at her it was with a shake of the head as she declared, "Land, you're nothing but skin and bones, girl." At mealtime the woman invariably added another spoonful from each dish after Allison had already filled her plate.

Finally over Sunday breakfast Allison's irritation churned out of control, and she exploded, "Dammit, Mother, I'm twenty-five years old! I don't need any help deciding how many scrambled eggs to eat for breakfast!"

The stunned silence that followed left Allison feeling guilty and far less adult than she claimed to be. She returned to the city more discontent than ever, and bearing one more niggling burden of guilt.

She was sitting in her empty, silent apartment eating a TV dinner that tasted like plastic when the phone rang. She glared at it, dumped her unfinished food into the garbage can, and went to do her washing. The damn phone rang with extreme regularity through three loads of washing and the ironing, too. She was sure it was Rick, but refused to take the phone off the hook, and let him know she was home.

But the ringing finally raised her hackles beyond soothing. She yanked the receiver up and blared, "Yes, yes, yes! What do you want!"

There was a moment of silence, then his voice. "Allison?"

"Yes?"

"Just where in the hell have you been for three days!" he exploded.

"I went home to South Dakota."

"While you let me wonder if you'd dropped off the face of the earth!"

"I didn't want to see you or talk to you," she explained expressionlessly.

"Oh, well, that's just dandy! You didn't want to see me! Just like that! Did you happen to think I might be going crazy worrying about you while you traipsed off and ignored my calls!"

He was so angry the receiver seemed to quiver in her palm. Allison's hand was shaking too as she backed up against the wall, let her eyes droop shut, sighed, and slid down until her butt hit the floor. "No," she answered wearily, "no, I didn't stop to consider that. I'm sorry."

"Well, you should be, for crissakes," he raged on. "You don't just disappear into thin air to leave a man wondering if you're alive or dead or what the hell is going through your impossible female head. You were pretty damned upset when I left you the other night, you know. Did you think I—"

"I said I was sorry!" she hissed.

"Well, dammit, I was worried sick! I've been up to your apartment no less than eight times in the last three days, and all the people downstairs could tell me was that they hadn't seen you since some time Thursday morning, and they didn't know where you'd gone. And I couldn't get one damn thing out of your answering service except some catty little snoot placating me with 'I'm sorry, Mr. Lang, but we've given her all your messages.' So just what the hell kind of game are you playing!"

"It's no game," Allison assured him. "We had some laughs

together and took a few pictures and ended up making love, that's all. That doesn't constitute a commitment of any kind. It was just a . . . a mistake."

"Just a mistake," Rick repeated, thunderstruck, his voice now holding a sharp edge of hurt. "You call what happened between us a mistake? Who the hell are you trying to kid, Allison?"

"It *was* a mistake for me. It's too . . ." She stopped, drew a deep breath, and went on. "I can't see you anymore, Rick. I'm sorry, I'm just not as resilient as I thought I was. I can't forget that fast—"

"Forget what! Something I did or something *he* did? I'm not him, damn it, yet you're judging me as if I were! If you're going to judge a man, at least do it on his own merits and shortcomings instead of someone else's."

Damn him, he was right! But the full sting of Jason's duplicity was too fresh within Allison to allow her to feel unthreatened by the thought of committing herself to a new relationship. To commit was to become vulnerable again.

"So why are you wasting your time on me?" It hurt, it hurt, having to say those words to him. And even across the telephone wire she could tell they hurt him, too.

"I don't know. I felt what we did together *does* constitute a commitment, and I thought you were the kind of woman who felt the same way, but apparently I was wrong." A pause followed, then he muttered, "Oh, hell," and his voice grew persuasive. "I don't know how to say this, but you and I spent some hours together that were far, far above the ordinary for first times. We worked and laughed and learned we had a lot in common. And after such a great day last Sunday, the way we ended it was as natural an ending as . . . as . . . you know what I'm talking about, Allison. We're good together, so I kissed you and you kissed me back and we made love . . ." His voice had gone low and gruff. "And don't lie to me. It was like fireworks." She heard him swallow. "And then you ran, and I deserve some answers, Allison. I have a right to know why."

"Because I'm afraid, okay?" she answered truthfully.

"Tell me what Jason—"

"I don't understand why you're bothering. I'm not even a

very good . . ." But abruptly she gulped to a halt.

"Lover?" he filled in. "Is that what you were going to say? Because if it is, you might be interested in knowing that not every guy thinks of that first. Some people honestly look for the person inside the body first. Some people actually base their feelings on more than just superficial appearances." He paused. "And you are a hell of a good lover."

"Stop it! Stop it! You want to know why I'm afraid to trust you, I'll tell you why. Because I trusted Jason Ederlie and all I got for it was taken. We lived together and I paid his way. Like a stupid, lovesick fool I took him in and stroked his ego and let him live scot free off me, thinking all the time we were working toward . . . toward something permanent. He posed for me. Oh, did he pose! And he knew his charms very well. I laid my whole future on the line with him, and one day I walked into this house and found him gone—lock, stock, and negatives! You want to know why I'm afraid to commit myself to a man again? Open up this month's issue of *Gentlemen's Review* and find out. You'll recognize his face—it's the one from my files. They say a picture is worth a thousand words—well, in *GR* it's also worth about a thousand dollars and a fixed career, and there's a whole layout of them. Only the photo credit, you'll note, is not quite accurate!"

By now Allison was quivering, viewing the chrome legs of the dining room chairs through a blur of angry tears.

"All that doesn't change one thing that's gone on between you and me, Allison, because it's past. It's done. What about what we shared?"

"What about it?" she retorted, wanting to draw back the words, but unable to, hurting him, hurting herself.

First came stunned, hurt silence, then carefully controlled words. "Nothing—nothing at all. I've been talking to the wrong girl all night long. And I mean *girl!* Why don't you grow up, Allison, and stop blaming the rest of the world for one man's transgressions? Then maybe you'll find somebody *worthy* of your lofty attention!"

Without saying good-bye, Rick Lang hung up.

The days and weeks that followed were filled with the deepest despair Allison had ever known, deeper than that she'd suffered when Jason deserted her, for then she'd been fortified by justifiable anger. Now she had no blame to lay on Rick Lang and thereby assuage her own shortcomings.

Rick had done nothing to earn her callous rejection—nothing. Her own insecurity had caused her to treat him so cruelly. A hundred times a day she considered calling him, apologizing, telling him it wasn't his fault, that he was innocent of everything she had accused him of. But she was utterly ashamed of how she'd acted. And now, too, she felt unworthy of him.

The vision of Rick filled her thoughts as the days stretched into weeks. In her memories she no longer searched for flaws, for he possessed none, none with which he had ever sought to hurt her, to dominate her, even to bolster his own ego. Those were crutches Jason had used—Jason, not Rick. He had entered the relationship honestly; it was she who had hidden truths from him and disguised her fears behind a façade of wariness and distrust.

Ah, what a sorry human being she was. She deserved the hurt and the sense of loss she now suffered as the dreary days of February paraded past and she heard nothing from Rick Lang.

The photographs of their day at the Winterfest brought painful memories of what she had so carelessly cast aside. Leafing through them one day, she recalled a time she now longed for, a man she now longed for, who had treated her decently, honorably. In a spate of self-disgust she threw the pictures across her desk and lowered her head to her arms to cry again.

She was so tired of crying.

When she blew her nose and dried her eyes, she felt better. Resting her chin on a fist on the desk top, she scanned again the scattered scenes with their bright colors and bittersweet memories.

Call him, call him, a lonely voice cried.

He'll have nothing to say—you've hurt him too badly.

Apologize, came the taunting, haunting voice.

After the way you treated him? You have no right to call him.

Her head came up off her fist, and she collected the photos, sniffling still, and rubbed a wrist under her eyes and laid the collection in a row. Studying them in a series, she realized they were remarkably well-done, giving an overall effect of vibrant Minnesotans hard at play in the midst of an icy winter's day.

On a sudden impulse she dashed off a cover letter and jammed them into an envelope along with it, and put them in the mail to *Mpls./St. Paul* magazine.

To Allison's amazement, she received a call three days later from a man who wanted to buy the series for their April issue.

But the joy she would otherwise have basked in was dulled by the fact that she couldn't share it with Rick, who had been so much a part of that day. When Allison hung up the phone, she stood for long minutes, hands hugging her thin hips through tight jeans pockets as she stared at the phone.

Again she had the sudden urge to call him and tell him the news. But once more she felt guilty and undeserving and decided against it.

The Hasselblad was still here. She worked with it daily, realizing she must return it, afraid to call and tell him he could either come and get it or she would take it to his place.

On the first day of March she returned home to find an envelope with strange handwriting in her mailbox. Racing up the stairs, she flung off her cap and scarf, her heart warming, warning—it's from him! It's from him!

She curled her feet beneath her on the sofa, studying the writing. The envelope was pink. She began to rip it open, then suddenly changed her mind, wanting to keep it flawless and neat if it truly were from him. She found a knife in the kitchen and slit the envelope open carefully.

Back on the sofa she slipped the greeting card slowly from its holder. There came into view a hand-painted card done in pastel watercolors of a single stalk of forget-me-nots forcing their way up between an old brick wall and a weathered gnarl of driftwood around which wild grasses waved in dappled shadow.

Even before she opened it, Allison's eyes had filled with tears. She ran her fingertips over the rough texture of the watercolor paper, realizing it was the first of his work she'd seen.

A wildlife artist, he'd said, but she'd never asked once to see his work, never displayed an interest in it at all. Yet she'd heartlessly accused *him* of egoism! She was the egotist, so wrapped up in her own career she'd never bothered to ask about his.

Considering the sensitivity that radiated from the simple drawing, she realized an enormous truth—Rick Lang didn't give a damn about his physical appearance and did not feed off it, because it was wholly secondary to what was most important in his life—his art.

She opened the folded sheet. His writing, done with black ink and calligraphy pen, slanted across the page: *I haven't forgotten. Rick.*

Allison clamped a hand over her mouth, swallowing repeatedly at the sudden surge of emotion that welled up in her throat. His face came back, beguiling, entreating.

No, Rick, I haven't forgotten either, but I'm so ashamed, how can I face you again?

She sat there for a long time with her legs drawn up tightly against her chest, thinking of him, remembering, reliving all the enjoyable hours spent with him, their teasing and laughter, the disastrous omelette, their exuberant forays into the winter days, the night they'd shared that wonderful sense of oneness after the studio session, and, of course, the night he'd made love to her.

His words came back clearly. "I'm still one of those guys who wants to do the pursuing." She now wanted so badly to call him, but the memory of those words stopped her.

She glanced at the telephone and decided that if he wanted to see her again, he'd call.

In mid-March she sent him a brief note telling him she'd leave the Hasselblad at the North Star Modeling Agency, and he could pick it up there. She debated for a long time before adding, "I loved your card. You're gifted with a paintbrush." Debating again about how to sign it, she finally decided on, "Yours, A."

The last two weeks of March dragged past. The buds on the trees along Nicollet Mall were bursting with new life, ready to sprout greenery into the heart of downtown Minneapolis, which was vibrant with expectancy now that spring was just around the corner. In downtown bank plazas noontime fashion shows offered spring garments in an array of bright colors—short sleeved and breezy in anticipation of the balmy season ahead.

Allison bought a chic suit of pale yellow linen to take home to Watertown for Easter, which fell in mid-April. But the new suit did little to lift her spirits as day after day she hoped to find another letter in her mailbox from Rick. But none came.

She broke down in early April and tried calling him for three days in a row, but got no answer.

Carefully nonchalant, she went to North Star's office one day to ask Mattie if Rick Lang had come by to pick up his camera.

"Sure did," Mattie answered. "Said he was happy to have it back because he was going home, wherever that is, to get some spring shots for his files."

Depressed at the idea of his being miles away, in a town where she'd never been, Allison submerged herself in work, trying to put him out of her mind.

Hathaway Books called, saying they loved the cover concept and photography she'd done and offering her a contract to do two more. It should have elated Allison, but while she was happy, that ebullient feeling she'd expected to experience at a time like this was curiously absent.

In mid-April another envelope bearing Rick's writing showed up in the mail—a hastily scrawled pencil sketch of a fawn standing beneath a leafless tree. Inside he'd written, "I've been out of town, reevaluating. Just got back and saw the spread in *Mpls./St. Paul*. Congratulations! You, too, are gifted . . . with my Hasselblad. Yours, Rick."

The spirits that had lain unlifted by either the new spring suit or the two-book contract offer were buoyed to the heights by his simple message.

Again she considered calling him, but studied the word "reevaluating" and decided it was best to leave the pursuing to him, if he ever decided to see her again.

Easter came and at the last minute before leaving town on

Good Friday, Allison picked up an Easter card at the drugstore and addressed it to him, writing beneath the printed message, "I, too, am reevaluating. Yours, Allison."

Spending two days at home this time, Allison remembered Rick's analysis of her parents' motives and found herself less critical of them, enjoying her weekend immensely.

The winter wheat was already sprouting in the limitless fields around the farmhouse, and she took time for a long walk through them, evaluating not only herself but also Rick, their relationship, and the far too great importance she had put on the treatment given her by Jason Ederlie.

What was she afraid of?

The answer, she found now, was nothing! She wasn't afraid; she was eager. She wanted the chance to see Rick Lang again, to apologize, to laugh with him, make love with him if he would have her, and to prove that she was willing to judge him for himself alone, not by measuring him against a man who, during the past few months, had become only a vague recollection and whose memory had almost ceased to bring the hurt and despondency it once had.

No word came again until the first of May. A long, narrow, hand-painted card bearing a basket of mayflowers with a ribbon tied to its handle, streamers flying breezily in the wind.

Inside it said, "There's an old May Day tradition that if a girl likes a boy, she leaves a May basket on his step, rings his doorbell, then runs, in the hopes that he'll catch her and kiss her. I'm not sure if boys are allowed to do the same thing, but . . . Love, Rick."

Allison's cheeks grew as pink as the May blossoms on his painting, and a glorious smile lit her face. She felt as if a bouquet of flowers had burst to profusion within her very heart. Breathing became suddenly difficult, and she turned, studying the sofa in her bright living room where late afternoon sun now streamed through the windows of the sun porch, whose French doors were opened.

She remembered Rick here in his many poses and knew beyond a doubt that he would be here again . . . soon.

She would invite him over for supper, she thought, immediately tossing the idea out as too forward. Not here, not in this place where memories of the past might come to threaten. They needed neutral territory on which to meet and assess the changes they were sure to find in each other.

Unsure of what his message meant, she was still reluctant to be the one to call him. Rick Lang, pursuer, she thought with a smile.

She waited another day, and in the mail at the studio there arrived the answer to her quandary—the announcement of a two-day symposium and workshop at University of Wisconsin-Madison, at which the keynote speaker would be Roberto Finelli, a renowned instructor of photography from Brooks Institute in Santa Barbara.

Subject: Photographing People for Profit
Requirements: 35mm camera, colored film and a model
            of your choice
Dates: May 19–20
Registration Fee: $160.00
Meals: Available at the college cafeteria at student rates
Lodging: Not arranged for, hotels and motels available
            in vicinity near the campus

Odd how insignificant her lifetime dream of meeting Finelli suddenly seemed when offered beside the opportunity of seeing Rick Lang again, of working with him and in the process rectifying the mistake she'd made with him.

The hands of the clock seemed to creep by so slowly that at one point Allison actually called for correct time, verifying that it was her own eagerness and not some electrical malfunction that made the hours move so slowly. She could have called Rick from the studio, but for some reason she wanted to be at home when she did.

But when five o'clock finally arrived and Allison got home, she dawdled unnecessarily through a tuna salad sandwich, reaching for the phone three times while the heartbeats in her throat threatened to choke her. Each time she pulled back the sweating hand, wiping it on her thigh, turning around to pace the living room and work up her courage.

He wouldn't be home, she thought frantically. Or he might be home but have somebody else with him and not be able to talk. Or maybe he would be able to talk but would refuse—then what?

Chicken, Allison?

Damn right, I'm chicken!

Then don't call—spend the rest of your life wishing you had!

Oh shut up, I'll do it when I'm good and ready!

Ha!

He would have called if he wanted to see me.

You're the one who threw him out, remember!

But he said he's old-fashioned about these things.

He's made it abundantly clear he wants to see you.

She grabbed the phone and dialed so fast she had no chance to change her mind. Waiting while it rang, she wildly wished he wouldn't be home, for she had no idea how to begin.

"Hello?"

She clutched the phone, but not a word squeaked through her throat.

"Hello? . . . Hello?"

"Rick?" Was that her voice, so cool, so low, so controlled, when her heart was thumping out of her chest?

A long pause, then his surprised voice. "Allison?"

"Yeah . . . hi."

"Hi yourself." The ensuing silence seemed to stretch across light-years of time before he added, "I pretty much gave up hope of hearing from you again."

"I gave up hope of hearing from you."

Silence roared along, carrying her thumping heart with it. He began to say something but had a frog in his throat and had to clear it to start again. "So how are you doing?"

"Better."

"Obviously, with the sale to *Mpls./St. Paul* and everything. The pictures were really great, I mean that. I couldn't believe it when I opened my copy and saw them."

"It . . . it was a surprise when they called to say they'd buy them. I . . . well, I sent them off on kind of an impulse, you know?"

"Lucky impulse."

"Yeah . . . yeah, lucky."

She shrugged as if he could see her and stared at the floor

between her feet, but neither of them seemed able to think of anything more to say now that that subject was exhausted.

"Oh, guess what!" she said, remembering. "Hathaway offered me a contract to do two more book covers!"

"Hey, congratulations! Now you'll know where next month's groceries are coming from, and the month's after that."

Old simple words from their past—did he forget nothing? —but the memories they conjured up were rife with other things she wanted them to say to one another.

Finally Allison remembered what she'd called for.

"Listen, are you still modeling?"

"Sure. It pays the bills, same as always."

"Would you like a job?"

"Sure."

"For me?"

To Rick she sounded uncertain, as if she thought he might say no when he found out who it was for. "Why not?" he asked.

"It's not the regular kind of job, you know—I mean, not the book covers again, but I figure we can both learn a little something if we do it together. I mean, it's a workshop and symposium down at University of Wisconsin called Photographing People for Profit. The guest speaker is going to be Roberto Finelli. I've . . . well, I've always wanted a chance to meet him." Her words tumbled out one after the other to hide her nervousness.

"When is it?"

"May nineteenth and twentieth."

"Two full days?"

She realized the implications of staying overnight and swallowed hard, wondering what he was thinking.

"Yeah," she finally answered, trying to sound noncommittal. He's going to say no! He's going to say no! she thought, her palms now sweating profusely, her cheeks already flushing with embarrassment.

"It sounds fun."

The sun burst forth inside her head with a blazing flash of wonder.

"It does?" Her lips dropped open, her eyes were wide with pleasant shock.

"Of course it does. Did you think I'd refuse?" She thought she detected a slight lilt of teasing in his question.

"I . . . I wasn't sure." She had clapped one hand over the top of her head to hold it on. You like to do the pursuing, she thought—you told me so!

"You'll have to tell me what kind of clothes to wear," he was saying, while she controlled her euphoria in order to settle the final details.

They made plans for her to pick him up at four A.M. on the appointed day. This settled, there came a lull in the conversation.

Allison was on her feet, pacing the length of the phone cord. She stopped and stared at the daybed on the sun porch, wondering if summer would find them on it. "Well . . ." she muttered stupidly.

Well, she thought . . . *well?* Is that all you can think of to say, *well!* Think of some bright, witty ending to this conversation, Scott!

He cleared his throat and said, "Yeah . . . well."

Silence.

Allison's palms were sweating. She wiped them on her thighs. "I'll see you on the nineteenth then."

"The nineteenth," he repeated. "Good-bye."

"Good-bye."

But Allison didn't want to be the first one to hang up. She stood in the sunset-washed living room, staring at the spot where they'd made love, hugging the receiver to her ear, listening to him breathe. After a long, long moment she lowered the receiver and pressed it firmly between her breasts, her heart racing, a feeling of imminent fullness overpowering her senses.

"Rick Lang, I love you," she whispered to the picture of him behind her closed eyelids, unsure if he could hear the muffled words or the crazy commotion of her heart, suddenly not caring if he knew the full extent of her feelings for him.

She lifted the receiver to her ear again and listened, but could not be sure if he was still there. At last she hung up.

Chapter 10

THE MORNING OF May nineteenth had not yet dawned when Allison Scott drove her Chevy van through the winding streets of the elegant old part of Minneapolis called Kenwood. Situated in the hills behind the Walker Art Center and the Guthrie Theater, it was once home to the city's oldest monied families. But in more recent years the founding families had moved to lake-shore estates, and Kenwood had been captured by young architects, lawyers, and doctors who'd brought new life, and children, to the staid, old sector.

Thick wooded hills and winding streets twisted through the area, making addresses hard to find. But Allison followed Rick's precise instructions through the sleeping hulks of old homes that in the daytime drew sightseers to admire cupolas, porches, bannisters, turrets, carriage houses, dormers, gables, and more, for no two homes in the area were alike.

Just off Kenwood Parkway Allison found the designated street and number, an elegant old three-story building of English Tudor styling buried beneath overhanging elms, its front door flanked by soldier-straight bushes trimmed to military precision. A sidewalk wound its way around to the back of the house, and Allison followed it beside a high wall of honeysuckle hedge that dripped dew, its full blossoms giving off a heady scent.

A light was on above a second-story door much like hers, and she took the steps with a queer sense of familiarity, of coming home. He'd never told her he lived in a place so much like her own.

She paused, searching for a bell. There was none, but she clutched the tiny woven Easter basket in her hands, wondering if it was wise to give it to him after all. It was large enough to hold only one Easter egg, which it had when her brother Wendell's little daughter had given it to her Aunt Allison with beaming pride, declaring she had dyed the egg herself.

The basket now held two candy kisses and a tiny cluster of lilies of the valley that Allison had stolen from her landlady's garden and tied with a small pink grosgrain ribbon.

Allison drew a deep, deep breath, held it for an interminable length of time, let it gush out, then soundly rapped on the door.

She heard footsteps approaching on the opposite side, and her heart threatened to stop up her throat.

The door opened, and she forgot the basket, forgot the words she'd rehearsed, forgot the businesslike air she'd vowed to maintain, forgot everything except Rick Lang, standing before her in a pair of crisply ironed blue jeans with an open-necked white shirt underneath a flawless lightweight sport coat of muted spring plaid that gaped away from his ribs as his hand hung on the edge of the door.

Through Allison's tumult of emotions it struck her that he'd dressed up for her. His hair, she thought—he had combed his hair! How could she ever have imagined it would be folly to touch a comb to it? She'd never seen such a tempting head of hair in her life. It was blow-combed to a neat feathered perfection, covering the tips of his ears on its backward sweep, touching his forehead as it fell faultlessly forward.

Rick Lang neither smiled nor stepped back nor spoke, but studied her with an expression that told Allison little about what he was thinking.

At last she came to her senses. "Good morning." Her voice sounded pinched and squeaky.

"Good morning." His sounded deep and even.

Again Allison struggled to find something to say. Suddenly she jumped as if she'd just touched an electric fence and thrust the silly little basket forward.

"Here . . . for you." She added a quavering smile. "But I'm not running."

He looked down, smiled, and slowly reached out for the basket, hooking its tiny handle over a single index finger.

Immediately she clasped both hands behind her back.

He looked up with a grin. "Of course not. It's not May Day."

She felt herself blushing and cast about for a quick reply, but none came. Still clutching her hands behind her, Allison leaned forward from the waist, peering around him inquisitively. "Mmm . . . nice house. It reminds me of mine."

He stepped back quickly. "Mine doesn't have a sun porch, and somebody covered up all the hardwood floors with these ugly brown carpets, but it's roomy, close to town, and has all the conveniences."

"Yes, it's nice." *Nice*, she thought . . . you *ninny!* "It's really . . ." Allison stopped her examination of the premises. Realizing it had grown silent behind her, she turned to find his eyes following her with a hint of amusement in their expression.

"You were about to say?" he prompted.

"I . . . nothing." She ordered the blood to stop rushing to her head.

"We'd better get going if we're going to make it to Madison by ten." He turned away and headed toward a door leading off the opposite side of the living room. "Be right back," he called over his shoulder.

She scanned the room again, wishing she had hours to study it so that she might learn of him, his likes, his ways. An easel stood near a north window, but it was turned to catch the window's light, and she couldn't see what he was working on. There were deep leather chairs and a matching davenport and bookcases with hundreds of items other than books. His old, worn letter jacket lay across the back of one of the chairs. She walked over and touched it lightly.

"Ready?" he asked.

She jerked her hand back as if he'd caught her stealing. "Yes."

He held a suitcase in one hand, a zippered clothing bag slung over the opposite shoulder, and in the buttonhole of his

542

jacket lapel he'd stuck the cluster of lilies of the valley.

She pulled her eyes away from the flowers with an effort and came forward. "Here, I can take something."

She reached for the garment bag, but he said, "No, I'll get that, but you can take this." There was some confusion while he attempted to shrug a wide woven strap from his shoulder, but it got tangled in the ends of the hangers.

At last it was free and in her hands. "The Hasselblad?" she asked, looking up with surprise in her face.

"What else?" He smiled.

"But—"

"When she's working under Finelli for the first time, a woman ought to be really turned on, right?"

She beamed radiantly, hung the wide strap over her shoulder, and hugged the case protectively against her belly. "Thanks, Rick, I'll treat it like spun glass."

He stepped out onto the landing, set his suitcase down, and held the door, waiting for her to pass before him. "If I remember right," Rick teased, "that's where all this started."

As she crossed in front of him, she caught the intoxicating drift of lily of the valley, and it did little to still the heart that beat at double time, because she was with him again.

They stowed his gear in the back of the van. Rick slammed the doors shut and asked, "You want me to drive?"

"I'd love it."

She dropped the keys into his palm, and a minute later they were backing down the driveway, heading through the sleeping city toward the interstate.

"I've got coffee." She twisted around in her seat and dug out a thermos and chubby earthen mugs while he glanced sideways briefly, then back to the road, checking the rearview mirror as the scent of coffee filled the van.

"One black . . . one with sugar," he remembered, reminding Allison of the first time they'd shared coffee this way. But his eyes remained on the road as he reached blindly and she placed the mug in his hand.

The horrible uncertainty of her first moments with him were gone, spinning farther into the distance as the miles rolled away beneath the wheels. She slumped back in her bucket seat, resting one high-heeled boot against the corner of the dash, balancing the coffee mug on her stomach. Occasionally she sipped, but mostly she basked in a feeling of supreme well-being at going off with him alone, attuned to his nearness, covertly watching his familiar hand on the wheel, listening to him sip his coffee now and then.

Rick, meanwhile, glanced time and again at the blue denim stretched tightly over her upraised knee and occasionally at the coffee mug resting on her stomach. At first only the lights from the dashboard illuminated the outline of her legs, but within half an hour the first strands of dawn lit the eastern sky as they headed directly into the sunrise. It was one of those explosive dawns that splash across the sky in layers of blue, pink, and orange. As the sun slipped above the horizon, they crossed the border into Wisconsin.

Rick turned to find Allison's cup slipping sideways. He smiled to himself, turning lazy eyes toward her sleeping face. He had time for a longer, more intimate look as she slept trustfully beside him. He scanned her body with its chin settled onto a shoulder, that shoulder wedged at an uncomfortable angle in the corner of the seat, while her upraised knee swung indolently back and forth with the motion of the vehicle. The way she was scrunched up made her blouse buckle away from her chest. A shadowed hollow invited his eyes, and inside he saw a wisp of white lace. His eyes moved back to the road momentarily.

Her cup slipped farther askance and he reached to slide it from her fingers, but as it slipped away she jerked awake and sat up, looking sheepish.

"It's okay, go back to sleep."

"No, I'm not tired. I slept like a log last night."

He grinned and turned back to the road, making no comment while she wondered how he could possibly believe such a fat lie!

She sat up, entwined her fingers, and stretched her palms toward her knees, writhing a little, stiff-elbowed, and catlike.

"Looks like we're in for a knockout sunrise," Rick observed.

"Mmm . . . and I nearly missed it." She scanned the eastern horizon from north to south, her artist's eye appreciating this masterpiece the more for sharing it with him. She leaned for-

544

ward, clasping her hands back to back between her knees, and savored being with him.

Wisconsin was devastatingly beautiful in its May costume. Fields of freshly tilled soil rolled along like flags waving in the wind, interspersed with blankets of budding forests where an occasional burst of wild plum blossoms could be seen in the distance. Immense promontories of sharp, gray rock loomed above the roadside, high and straight, their tops flat. They were awesome.

"It seems as if there should be an Indian on top of every one of them," Allison observed, "sitting there on a painted pony with a feathered lance in his hand."

"I've often thought the same thing myself."

Still they spoke of nothing personal. The remainder of the trip passed in companionable silence, but Allison knew they were only delaying what could inevitably not be delayed.

As they turned off the interstate at the Madison exit and followed Washington Avenue straight into the heart of the city, the dome of the state Capitol proudly guided them to its very center, seemingly built in the middle of the highway. They circled the Capitol grounds on quaint city streets arranged like a spiderweb around it.

The college town was bustling, its sidewalks swarming with students on bikes and on foot, bare armed, hurrying through the warm spring weather.

Allison and Rick found the correct building, parked the van and collected the Hasselblad, its equipment bag, and Allison's clipboard.

Finelli in the flesh inspired every photographer there with his opening speech and the narrative that accompanied a slide presentation of some of his most stunning work, many famous faces from film stars to politicians, cover girls to cardinals.

The lunch break came all too soon. Rick and Allison shared it in the campus cafeteria. Allison had difficulty coming down from the high inspired by the man who epitomized success in her chosen field.

Rick's voice repeated her name for the second time. "Allison?"

"Hmm?" She came up from her fanciful world where success was wholly achievable, pulling her eyes from her bowl of chili and grilled cheese sandwich to find Rick laughing at her.

"Hey there, dreamy, you haven't got Finelli's job yet. We have a workshop to attend and pictures to take. You gonna sit there and dream in your chili all day?"

She braced her chin on a palm and smiled dimly. "I will one day—have his job, I mean. Just you watch and see."

During the actual workshop cameras were set up in various lighting situations and personalized guidance given to the photographers, allowing them to experiment with newly marketed equipment and various techniques. Ideas were exchanged freely, live models wandered about, and the country's most noted teachers of photography gave advice and inspiration.

Allison looked up to see Rick approaching after having changed his clothes. He came striding toward her in a set of clothes the likes of which she'd never seen on him before. She was stunned. He was dressed in a thick-textured sweater of pale gray with a bulky collar; dress trousers of smooth navy gabardine, slightly pleated at the waist; a small-collared button-down dress shirt of pale smoky blue; highly polished black loafers; a gold identification bracelet with a large-linked chain; and a pendant bearing his sign of the zodiac—Aries— lying just below the hollow of his throat, nestled in the pale gold hair above his open collar.

"I'm ready," he announced quietly.

Wow, so am I! she thought, then realized her mouth was hanging open and shut it with a snap. He moved to the camera case to take out extra backs for the Hasselblad, while her eyes followed him like those of a hungry puppy. As he stepped close to show her how to load the several backs in advance, the scent of his aftershave set her quivering. "Each roll has only twelve shots, you know, so I thought I'd bring the extra backs. You can preload them," he said. But it was hard for her to concentrate on the words. She watched his long fingers showing her how to line up two double dots on the back of the camera if she wanted to double expose.

With an effort Allison forced her mind from Rick Lang to the business at hand. The renowned Finelli offered advice on back-lighting the hair with a colored filter to achieve a sunset effect. She produced the color print of the book cover, showing how she'd used the same technique with blue filters to create the effect of moon glow. He complimented her, watched as she proceeded, and offered kindly, "Young lady, it looks to me like you're wasting your time here. I'll move along to someone who needs my advice."

She looked up to see Rick stepping toward her. "Mind if I see that?"

She handed it to him silently, and they both studied Rick Lang leaning over Vivien Zuchinski with his hand near the side of her breast.

"It's damn good," he said quickly.

She looked at his temple as he studied the picture. "You're damn good." Before he could look into her eyes, she turned back to the camera.

By the end of the day's workshops it was four P.M. and both Allison and Rick were exhausted, yet curiously exhilarated. Heading back toward the van, he asked, "Is this going to be one of those nights when you're too high to sleep?"

She squeezed her eyes shut, opened them again, flung her arms wide, and bubbled joyously, "Yes! Yes! Yes!"

He watched the back of her hair swinging as she walked a step ahead of him, so energized she seemed ready to do cartwheels up the sidewalk.

"In that case I won't be keeping you from sleeping if I take you out to dinner."

"Oh, you don't have to do that." She turned to insist, but found her shoulder nearly colliding with his chest as he walked along, the sweater slung over his shoulder on two fingers.

"I know. I want to."

They studied each other for a silent moment. "Yeah?" she inquired cutely.

"Yeah," he repeated, grinning at her tilted chin and giving her a slow-motion mock punch on the jaw.

"Don't mind if I do," she decided. "I hardly touched my lunch, I was so off in another world. Sorry I get that way, but I can't help it. Lord, but I'm half starved, and I just realized it when you mentioned dinner."

"Half starved? Then how about a kiss to hold you over?"

She raised her eyes in surprise, feeling the thrill of anticipation already leaping up in the form of a blush. But he only pulled one of the paper-wrapped candy kisses from his pocket, and held it between index and middle fingers, offering it to Allison.

Their eyes met above it as they continued along the sidewalk. Her heart suddenly felt as if spring were burgeoning within it as well as in the apple, myrtle, and plum trees along the Madison streets.

"Oh, is that all?" she asked impishly. She plucked the candy from his fingers, opened it, and popped it into her mouth.

It seemed preordained that he drive again. "Where to?" he inquired, nosing the van into the busy end-of-the-day traffic near the Capitol.

"Back the way we came. There are plenty of cut-rate motels out that way." Without another word he headed out to Washington Avenue.

They entered the lobby of the Excel Motel together, each of them signing the register separately, ignoring the assessing glances cast their way by the clerk who asked, "Smoking or nonsmoking?"

Rick and Allison gaped at each other, then at the clerk.

"What?" they asked in unison.

"We got smoking rooms and nonsmoking rooms. Which one you want?"

"Nonsmoking," they answered, again in unison, and the clerk let his eyes drift from Allison to Rick as if to say, separate rooms, huh? He picked two keys from the wall, dropped them on the desk, and said, "Enjoy your stay."

On their way to the van—obviously the only vehicle parked out front, obviously the vehicle in which they had arrived together, obviously the vehicle which would take them to door C and rooms 239 and 240—Allison could feel the clerk's eyes following them.

"Do you think he believed us?" Rick asked, casting her a sidelong glance.

"Not after we both spouted out 'Nonsmoking.' Have you ever heard of such a thing before?"

"Never."

"Me neither."

They climbed into the van, and Allison couldn't resist wagging two fingers at the desk clerk as they pulled away from the sidewalk—shades of the night watchman in days past.

In the hall, standing between the two assigned doors that were exactly opposite each other, Rick asked, "Which one do you want?"

"Where's east?"

"That way." He pointed to 240.

"Then that one. I like the sun in the morning."

"Two-forty, milady," he said with a slight bow from the waist after he'd opened the door and dropped the key into her palm. She stepped uncertainly inside. It was vaguely creepy going into the motel room alone. She poked her nose around the corner to eye the double bed, the floor, the closed draperies, then glanced over her shoulder to find Rick standing in the open doorway to his room, watching her.

"How's yours?" he asked.

She shivered and shrugged. "Cold."

"There's probably a heater they leave turned off until guests are in. Just a minute." He hung up his clothing bag on the rack in his closet and crossed the hall, moving into her room without apparent self-consciousness, while she felt as if every eye in Madison, Wisconsin, was somehow watching them on closed-circuit TV. He bent to the heater on the wall and studied its dials. Abruptly he stood up. "Nope, that's just for air." He came toward her, and she stood as if rooted to the floor. "Excuse me," he said, taking her by the elbows to move her aside to adjust the thermostat behind her.

"There, it'll warm up in a minute. Everything else okay?"

"Sure, thanks." But suddenly she didn't want him to go back across the hall. The room seemed too impersonal and quiet, a queer, lonely place when she faced it alone.

Rick paused in the doorway. "Would it be all right if we didn't go to dinner right away? I thought I'd lie down awhile and catch a nap. It was a long drive. Maybe you should do the same."

"I don't mind."

"What time then?"

She shrugged again, feeling more lost and lonely than ever,

realizing he was, indeed, going to leave her and close himself away in his own room. She wondered despondently if nothing more personal would come of the two days than candy kisses.

After all, she had been the one to give the May basket; the next move was up to him.

"Sixish?" she suggested now, her spirits definitely flattened.

"Six it is." He tossed up his room key, caught it, winked at her, and said, "Pick you up at your place." Then he was gone, closing the door behind him.

Chapter 11

ALLISON COULDN'T SLEEP. If the exhilaration of the day's work-shops hadn't kept her awake, the butterflies in her stomach would have. She turned on the television and tried a cable station, but a horror movie was playing—hardly uplifting or relaxing. She flicked the TV off, flounced onto the bed, crossed her hands behind her head, and lay there like a ramrod.

Was he actually asleep over there while she lay here so keyed up over . . . over *everything* that it felt like she'd put a dime in the vibrator bed when she hadn't? How could he! The unsettled situation between them was as effective as any bottled stimulant on the druggist's shelves and getting more potent as the time for their "date" neared.

How should she act? As if she'd never shared a night of intimacy with Rick Lang that ended in near disaster? As if she had invited him to Madison, Wisconsin, solely to pose for her? As if she wasn't dying inside as each passing hour made her doubt she had the wherewithal to attract him as she once had?

By five o'clock her nerves were strung out like taut twine, and she ran a tub full of water—something she never did at home, it seemed sinful.

Sinking into bubbles up to her neck, she eased back, closing her eyes, willing herself to relax, be natural, just be her old full-of-piss-and-vinegar self. That was the girl he'd liked once. Crack a joke. Wear a smile. Banter. Tease.

But she felt like doing none of these. She felt like telling Rick Lang she loved him more than any man on the face of the earth, and if he didn't do something about it soon, she'd be a basket case.

She emerged from the bath wrinkled like a prune, having discovered that she had actually managed to fall asleep when she hadn't meant to. It was twenty minutes to six!

Forsaking shampoo, she settled for a quick recurling job with the hot iron, her usual light makeup, slightly heavier on the mascara for evening wear and a deeper shade of lipstick, almost umber, which shone like quicksilver when she checked her reflection in the mirror.

Cologne! She checked her watch—four minutes left. Rummaging through her bag, she came up with her favorite perfume and spared no immodesty, lavishing it on every intimate part of her body.

A knock on the door!

Oh Lord! He was two minutes early and she didn't have her dress on yet!

She flew to the coat rack, tore the yellow two-piece suit off the hanger, and clambered into the skirt, snatching a white eyelet blouse, trying to button up both at once.

He knocked again and called through the door, "Allison, are you awake?"

Her fingers seemed to be made of Silly Putty as she buttoned the minuscule pearl buttons of the blouse, which were round and insisted on slipping out of the holes nearly as fast as they went in.

"Allison?"

She yanked open the door, stopping his knuckles in midair as he raised them to rap again. For the second time that day his appearance brought her to a dead halt. This time he was dressed in an extremely formal vested suit of cocoa brown with an off-white shirt and Windsor-knotted tie in complementary stripes. The sight of Rick Lang in such clothing took Allison's breath away.

Her cheeks were as pink as crabapple blossoms, her hair lying in soft feathery ruff about her shoulders. His eyes traveled downward. Her hands were behind her back, closing the button on her skirt, and the strain at the front of the blouse

552

made the top button pop open. His eyes moved lower to her feet, in nylons but no shoes. He cocked an eyebrow.

"Everything went wrong . . . I'm sorry," she wailed.

Dark, smiling eyes moved back to hers. "There's not a thing wrong with what I can see."

"I tried to sleep, but I couldn't. So I decided to take a bath, then fell asleep in the tub, of all things. And when I woke up it was nearly twenty to six already!" She turned away to rummage through her suitcase, coming up with high spike heels, all black patent-leather straps. He watched, fascinated, as she leaned to brace a hand on the bed, her back to him while she slipped the sling-back pumps on one shapely heel, then the other. It was the first time he'd ever seen her in a skirt. Her legs were thin but curved, and from behind, in the flattering shoes, they totally captivated Rick's eyes, which traveled up their shapely length to the enticing curve of her derrière as she leaned over, working on the second shoe.

He saw her check her bodice, then rebutton the top button of her blouse, her back still toward him. Leaning over her suitcase, she took out something from a tiny white box, raised her elbows, and fastened it about her neck. The scent she'd put on was everywhere in the room, and as she lifted her graceful elbows, it filled his nostrils, mesmerizing him, just as he was mesmerized by the sight of her adding these last feminine touches.

She turned. A tiny gold heart hung from a delicate chain in the hollow of her throat. The vanity mirror was just beside the door where Rick stood. She moved toward it while his eyes followed. Her bewildering, powdery scent became headier as she neared him, leaned over the vanity toward the mirror, and put tiny gold hoop earrings into her pierced ears. His eyes traveled down to where she bent at the hip. When he looked up he found Allison watching him while she put the back on the second earring. Once more the top button of her blouse had come undone. He followed her fingers in the mirror as they closed it yet again.

From the coat rack she took a yellow long-sleeved jacket that matched her skirt. He crossed the short expanse to her side, and when she turned, Allison found him at her shoulder.

"I'll trade you," he said, producing from behind his back a

single long-stemmed red rose that suddenly seemed to be reflected in her cheeks as her startled eyes caressed it.

It occurred to Allison that while she was deriding him for calmly napping, he'd been out buying the flower. Wordlessly she took it, relinquishing the jacket to his waiting hands, closing her eyes, and breathing deeply of the flower's fragrance while her back was turned, and he assisted her into the jacket.

When she faced him again, she held the stem of the rose in both hands, looking down at it, then up into his eyes. "Rick, I don't deserve this." Tears suddenly burned her eyes. "Oh God, Rick, I'm so sorry."

His face was somber. He did not touch her. "I'm sorry, too."

"You have nothing to apologize for. I . . . I hurt you so badly. I was so unfair . . . I know that now."

"Allison, you weren't ready. You tried to tell me that, but I wouldn't listen."

"No, Rick, I was such a damn fool. But I had some growing up to do, some sorting out. I was mixed up and angry and unsure."

"And how are you now?"

She didn't know what to say, was afraid to admit how totally committed she'd become to making up everything to him, to letting their relationship thrive. If only he'd touch her, give her some clue to his feelings.

"I'm . . . I'm sorted out, and no longer angry, and sure." Touch me, hold me, tell me I'm forgiven, her heart cried.

But his touch was only a brief pat on her elbow. "Let's talk about it after dinner." He took her elbow and guided her out the door, down the hall and into the brisk May evening.

He drove to a restaurant called the Speakeasy where the waiters wore striped shirts and arm bands and parted their hair down the middle. But neither Allison nor Rick really noticed.

The menus were the size of billboards. Still Rick managed to study her over his. She looked up. The candle put lights into his eyes, color in his cheeks, and shadows about his lips, which still did not smile. Studying his somber face, Allison wondered again what he would say if she simply told him the truth that ached to be spoken.

I love you, Rick Lang. I want you in my bed. I want you in my life.

The waiter approached, tugging her back to earth.

While they waited for swordfish and well-done filet mignon, the wine steward brought wine, flamboyantly exercising his skill in removing cork, testing the bouquet, pouring, and offering a sample for Rick's approval.

Rick tasted, nodded. The steward filled two glasses and faded away.

"How did I do? Was I convincing?" Rick asked.

"Very." She brightened falsely. "I'd have sworn you were a connoisseur of . . ." She checked the label on the bottle, but could not pronounce it.

"Moonshine '82," Rick filled in, and they laughed at their ignorance. But the gay mood was forced.

"And I've never known anyone who ate filet well-done. Did you see the scowl the waiter gave you?"

She shrugged. "I feel rare enough tonight without rare steak, too."

He leaned forward, bracing tailored sleeves on the edge of the table, blue eyes moving over hers. "Do you? Do you really?"

"Yes, I do . . . really."

He lifted his glass in a toast. "Then here's to a rare night."

They drank, less of the wine than of each other across the tops of their glasses. Resting his footed goblet upon the linen cloth, Rick made small circles with it, studying it momentarily before his hand fell still and he watched her face as flickering candlelight changed its dancing shadows. Silently he reached, laid his hand, palm up, on the tabletop.

Her eyes flickered to it, then back to his, cautiously.

"Allison, if I don't touch you soon, I'm going to go crazy," he said quietly, only the hand reaching, the rest of him leaning back with casual grace, ankle crossed over knee as if he'd only said, "Allison, the temperature outside is seventy-two degrees," while every atom in her body went into motion until she felt explosive.

"Oh God, me too." She slid her palm over his and he slowly closed his fingers until they were squeezing hers so

555

tightly she thought her bones would break. He began moving his thumb, brushing it lightly across the backs of her knuckles as she sat stricken speechless, overwhelmed by the sensations that just his thumb could create within her body. She stared at their joined hands, wondering if he could feel the throbbing of her heart in her fingertips as she could.

"Do you dance?" he inquired quietly.

"Not very well."

"Me either, but I will if you will."

As they got to their feet the waiter brought Caesar salad. They turned toward the stamp-sized dance floor instead, where a man with an amiable smile played *Misty* on the piano.

Allison turned into Rick's arms, the two of them the only ones on the floor, neither even aware of it as his arm circled her waist and she moved near, resting her temple lightly against his jaw, her palm on his shoulder. Their movements were more of a gentle, unconscious sway than a dance, for they had not come here to dance, but to touch.

His after shave was faint, spicy, the shoulder of his suit coat firm and cool. The piano player began singing softly in a soulful voice, "Look at me, I'm as helpless as a kitten up a tree . . ." He smiled as he watched the handsome blond man wrap both arms around the tall, striking woman, and hers move up to circle his neck.

Rick rested his joined hands lightly on the hollow of Allison's spine, while his head dropped down and hers lifted. The words of the haunting old Erroll Garner song drifted about Allison, and she did feel helpless, clinging to a cloud, misty. Her hips rested lightly against Rick's, and the touch of his hands on the hollow of her spine sent shivers coursing upward. They moved in indolent swaying steps that took them nowhere but heaven as their thighs brushed and he leaned his forehead down to rest it on hers.

"I love you, Allison Scott, you know that, don't you?" he whispered.

She pulled back only far enough to see his face, while the beginning words of the song reverberated through her body, ringing now with triumph—*Look at me! Look at me! Look at me! Rick Lang just said he loves me!*

Her voice trembled and her eyes sparkled as she admitted,

"Yes . . . I know." She lay her fingertips on the back of his neck, above his collar—she suddenly had to touch his bare skin. "I love you, too, Rick Lang, you know that, don't you?"

"I've had my suspicions, but you put me through hell making me believe it."

"But you do?"

"I want to."

"Then do, because it's true."

He reached behind his neck to capture her right hand and reverted to the traditional waltz position. Her temple was again beside his ear. "Will you do something for me?" he asked.

"Anything."

"Maybe you shouldn't be so quick to answer 'anything.' This may be tough."

"Anything."

Again he stepped back and looked into her eyes. "Tell me about Jason."

Her steps faltered, a brief glint of uncertainty flickered in her eyes, but just then the music ended. He took her elbow and led her away from the floor. She watched the tips of her toes as they made their way back to the table. As Rick pulled her chair out, she felt a momentary sense of panic, then he was across from her, reaching for her hand again.

"Alllson, you've just told me you love me. Will you trust me enough to tell me about Jason—everything, so his ghost will be exorcised? And this time without anger. If you can talk about him without anger, I'll know you're free of him at last, and ready for what you and I . . . well, just ready."

Wide brown eyes flickered to Rick's, then to the flame of the candle.

"Tell me . . . all of it."

She began softly. "He was my favorite, wonderful, sensational model. But first and foremost, he was a hedonist, only I never realized it until he'd left me." Tears glimmered in her eyes. She swallowed, pulling her hand from Rick's to hide her face. "Oh God," she said to the tabletop, "I don't know how to tell it. I was such a fool."

"Give me your hand," he ordered gently, "and don't look away from me."

557

She drew a deep, shuddering sigh as she began again, her hand in Rick's. She told him everything, how she'd begun by taking Jason's photo, then accepted the idea of his moving in; how she'd paid all the bills; how he'd used his body to get her to close her eyes to his shortcomings and character faults; how they'd collected the portfolio of photos; how he'd stolen them; even about his signature on the easel picture. She laughed sadly, softly, looking up into Rick's eyes. "And you know what?" Strangely, it hurt hardly at all to admit, "It was the only time he ever mentioned the word love."

Allison glanced at the wine bottle. "Could I have a little more of that?"

Rick released her hand. "No. You don't need it. Eat your salad while you finish. It'll take away the hollow feeling until I can."

Again she met his eyes, which did not smile or make light of his words. Neither did they denigrate her for the past she'd just revealed so blatantly. She sighed deeply and ate her salad.

The night was damp and cool, but scented with golden mock orange and lilac in full bloom. They walked with measured steps, Allison matching hers to Rick's as they crossed the parking lot to the door of the motel. She was tucked securely against his hip, wishing he'd walk faster. But he sauntered with torturous slowness, lugging the heavy glass door open without relinquishing his hold on her, laughing with Allison as they struggled inside, two abreast, bruising their hips.

They took the stairs in unison, eagerness growing with each step. Halfway up he stopped.

"I can't wait any longer." His arm swept around her and forced her back against the handrail as he gave her a taste of what lay in store. The sweet intoxication of his lips made her head spin.

"You keep that up and I'll be lying bruised and broken at the bottom of these steps, Mr. Lang. Don't you know better than to make a lady dizzy halfway up a flight of stairs?"

"I beg your pardon, Miss Scott. Common sense seems to have fled."

She pulled his head down to hers and mumbled against his mouth, "Oh, goody."

In the hallway between their two doors he asked simply, "My room or yours?"

"Tell me, Mr. Lang," she asked piquantly, arms looped about his neck, head tilted to one side, "do you like the sun in the morning?"

"I love the sun in the morning."

"Then mine."

She produced her key, handed it to him, and when the door swung wide open they stood for a moment studying each other, the smiles gone from their faces.

"I feel it only fair to warn you," he said, "that I've never before told a woman I love her before I made love to her."

"And how about after?"

"No, Allison, not even after."

"Supposing you don't after . . . well, after this one." Her eyes skittered down to her nervous fingers, than back up to his. "Just forget what I said one time about forsaking all others, okay? I'm . . . heck, I'm fifty years behind the times."

"Allison, I—"

"Shh." She covered his lips with her fingertips. "Just kiss me, Rick, hold me, and let's start starting over."

His palms molded her face, lifting it to receive his kiss, which spoke of an ardency that drove all memory of the past from her mind. With their lips still joined, they moved inside her room. He caught the door with his heel, and when it slammed they fell against it, lost in each other's arms.

"Allison, I'll never hurt you, never knowingly," he promised in a gruff voice. "That other time when I thought I had . . ." He swallowed, pinning her tightly against the length of his body, clasping her head against his chest. "Please, darling, just be honest with me, always."

"I promise," she vowed as she kissed the side of his neck, then pressed her forehead against it, feeling the thrum of his heart there momentarily before backing out of his embrace and looking into his eyes while she slowly, methodically began removing her clothes.

As her jacket came off, his hands were still. As she

reached for the button at the back of her skirt, he slowly, slowly began tugging the knot from his tie. They watched each other remove article by article until she stood before him in half-slip, panties and bra. Then he ordered, "Stop . . . let me."

Her hands fell still as he reached for the clasp of her bra. He was barefooted, only trousers and shirt still on, the latter pulled out of his waistband, hanging open to reveal the bare skin of his chest underneath.

Her suitcase lay open on the bed. In one motion he closed it and swept it to the floor, then flipped the covers down over the foot of the mattress.

He tugged her to the bed, urging her down until they lay facing each other, his hand on the bare band of skin above her slip. As his face moved over hers, blocking out the light from the bedside lamp, her eyes closed. Soft, seeking kisses urged her trembling lips to open. Warm, gentle palms encouraged her back to relax. Hard, golden arms prompted her hips to move closer. And when they had, the rapture began. He mastered her hesitation by again moving with a slow hand, at first only the heel of it slipping to the side of her breast, brushing against the silky fabric that covered it, pressing, caressing, yet at a lazy pace that lulled and suggested and made her want more. He explored her back with a widespread hand, sliding down over the shallows of her spine, making the silken fabric of the half-slip seduce her skin before easing his fingers inside its elastic to let his flesh take its place. And so he pressed her womanly core hard against his swollen body, moving rhythmically against her until her hands began moving up and down his shirt, then inside, against the warm skin of his back.

"Oh, how I missed you, missed you," Allison whispered greedily.

"I missed you, too, every day, every minute."

His tongue danced desirously upon hers, and she slipped her hands over his arms, until he shrugged out of the shirt, and it lay forgotten beneath him. He cupped her breast fully, pushing it upward to forcibly change its shape as he lowered his head and ran his tongue just above the transparent lily-shaped lace that edged her bra, revealing the dark, dusky nipple behind it. She dropped back, soft sounds coming from her throat, her eyes drifting closed as he leaned across her body and continued kissing only the tops of her breasts. There was a sweet yearning pain in her tightly gathered nipples that only his mouth could calm.

She arched off the mattress in invitation, and his hands slipped behind to release the clasp of the bra. She opened her eyes to watch his blond head dip once again to her naked skin and shuddered when his wet tongue touched, tempted.

Her hands blindly sought his body, skimming from chest to hard belly, then lower, caressing, cupping, inciting his breath to beat rapidly against her skin.

She pushed him up and away, the better to reach, and he fell back, tense, waiting, his eyes closed and nostrils flaring while she sat beside him, leaning back on one palm as she watched her hand play over him. His chest rose and fell with a driving beat while he lay, wrists up, drifting in pleasure. She released the hidden hook on the waistband of his trousers, then unzipped them, feeling his hand brushing softly against her back, though he lay as before, eyes closed, only that hand in motion.

There was nothing to equal the sense of celebration she knew as she undressed him fully, brushing his clothing away until he lay naked, golden brown, flat bellied, aroused, silent, waiting. She touched him, and he jerked once as if a jolt of electricity had sizzled through him, lifting his back momentarily off the bed. Then he lay as before, his fingertips lightly grazing her back while she stroked his bare leg, from inner thigh to sharp-boned knee that bent over the edge of the mattress.

"I love you so much," she uttered. And without compunction she captured his heat in her hand, leaned over, and kissed it briefly. "You're so beautiful."

"Allison, darling, come here." He tugged at her elbow, and she fell back beside him. "It's inside that I want to be beautiful for you. It's an accident if what you see is beautiful. But for you I want to have a beautiful soul . . . like yours is to me." His eyes were eloquent as he spoke into hers.

"Rick, I love you . . . I love you . . . body, soul, inside, outside. How could I ever have thought you were like him?" She clung to his neck, kissing his jaw, cheek, the corner of his mouth, then opened her lips beneath his to let him delve into the wet silk of her mouth.

His body was quivering as he pulled away. "Hey, where did you learn what you did a minute ago?"

"I told you, Jason was a hedonist. He had no compunctions about making his wishes known. He reveled in it."

"And that's why the song triggered your panic that night we were making love?"

"Yes."

He kissed the hollow just beneath her lower lip, speaking against her skin, his words rough-edged with passion. "I only take as good as I give, Allison, and with me it's ladies first, okay?"

Her answer was one of silent language, spoken with lithe limb and straining muscle, with wet tongue and willing skin. He shimmered the remaining garments down her legs, leaving her clothed in nothing but a tiny gold heart in the hollow of her throat. From there his lips began their downward journey. They traveled her body at will, tasting desire in its every quiver and shiver. He kissed her stomach, the soft valleys beside hip, behind knees, her ankles, thighs, lost in the fragrance he'd once watched her apply to secret, hidden places.

"I love you, Allison... beautiful Allison," he murmured and lifted himself above her, poised on the brink of a beauty surpassing the visual. And a moment later their bodies became one.

During the minutes that followed, stroking her to climax, he gave her the sense of self each being must have before giving that self to another, unfettered. It had been taken from her by another, in an eon far removed from now, but was returned in all its glory by this man Allison Scott had finally come to trust.

When they lay exhausted, damp and disheveled in a faultless disarray, limbs languid and lifeless, apart from each other yet knowing they would never truly be apart, he ran a bare sole along her calf. "Now who turns you on more, me or my Hasselblad?"

Her voice came lazily from two feet away. "Right now, my

darling Richard, ain't no way you could turn me on. I done been turned till I can't turn no more."

A replete chuckle came from his side of the bed, then a lethargic hand flopped down wherever it happened to flop. It landed on her ribs, felt around, discovered its whereabouts and rectified the mistake.

"Oh yeah? Want me to prove differently?"

She swatted the hand away, but it returned promptly, along with another to gather her against his long, naked body before he yanked the blankets up to cover them.

"I was shivering, that's why they were puckered up."

"Oh, and here all this time I thought it was the mention of my Hasselblad that did it."

"Oh, that too."

"Anything else?"

They were snuggled so close a bedbug couldn't have crawled between them.

"Nothing comes to mind."

"Nothing?"

She reached beneath the covers while she teased, "Not one eentsy-weentsy little thing."

He yanked her hand up and pinned both wrists over her head, laying across her chest. "That, you little snot, was a low blow. Just for that I may not suggest what I was just on the verge of suggesting when your sharp little tongue did you out of something you'd sell your soul for."

She struggled to lift her head to rain kisses of apology and giggling persuasion on his chin, nose, and mouth, but he backed far enough away that she couldn't reach.

"I take it back," she promised. "Especially since I know it's only temporary."

"Hey, lady, you want my Hasselblad for life, or don't you?"

"Do you come along with it?"

The pressure on her wrists disappeared. His lips swept down toward hers, a suggestive glint in his eyes as he answered, "You're damn right."

"For life?" she inquired. "For honest-to-goodness life?"

"For life."

563

"Forsaking all others?"

"Forsaking all others."

And ten minutes later she sold her soul for the second time that night.

A Promise to Cherish

*With gratitude to my friends
in Independence and Kansas City –
Bea, who gave me the map
Barbra, who showed me the old orchard
and Vivien Lee, who took me to the "C C"*

Chapter 1

As THE FIRST suitcase came clunking down the luggage return of Stapleton International Airport in Denver, Lee Walker checked her watch impatiently, drummed four coral fingernails against her shoulder bag, and studied the conveyor belt with a frown. It moved like a sedated snail! She glanced at her watch a second time—only one hour and ten minutes before the bid letting! If the damn suitcase didn't roll out soon, she'd end up at City Hall in these faded blue jeans!

Lee glowered at the flapping porthole until at last her suitcase came through. She sighed deeply and strained to reach it.

She plucked it off the conveyor belt and flew—a tall, dark-skinned flash of loose black hair and aqua feathers, the worn patches on the backside of her tight jeans attracting the eyes of several men she adroitly sidestepped. The feathers in her hair lifted with each long-legged slap of her moccasins on the terminal floor until she came at last, panting and winded by the thin Denver air, to the Economy Rent-A-Car booth.

Twenty minutes later the same suitcase hit the bed in Room 110 of the Cherry Creek Motel. Lee reached to yank the shirttails free of her jeans at the same time that she released the catch on the suitcase and flipped it open. Her hand halted. Her jaw dropped open.

"Oh my God," she whispered. Lifeless fingers forgot about buttons. Stricken eyes stared at the strange contents of the suitcase while one hand covered her lips, the other clasped her suddenly queasy stomach. "Oh sh . . ." Her eyes took it in, but her mind balked. "No . . . it can't be!" But she was staring not at the mustard-colored envelope containing the bid for a sewage treatment plant she'd worked on for the last two weeks. Instead, a half-naked blonde tootsie lifted a pair of enormous breasts and smiled a come-hither message from the cover of a . . . a *Thrust* magazine.

For a moment Lee was struck motionless with disbelief. *Thrust?* She stood hunched over, horrified, her thoughts whirling. Then frantically she scrambled through the suitcase, throwing out item after item—a gray sweat suit, two pair of dress trousers, a man's shaving kit, two neatly folded shirts, royal blue jockey shorts—*royal blue?*—black socks, Rawhide deodorant, a pair of well-worn jogging shoes with filthy laces, a hair blower, and a brush with very dark brown hair caught in its white bristles.

She ran a thumb over them, then dropped it distastefully and quit scrambling through the contents to grab the identification tag dangling from the suitcase handle.

> Sam Brown
> 8990 Ward Parkway
> Kansas City, Missouri 64110

With a groan Lee sank to the bed, leaned forward, and clutched her forehead in both hands. *Oh, damn my hide, I've really done it now. Old Thorpe will gloat over this for months!* At the thought of Thorpe and his small, racist mind, panic swept Lee, tightening the skin across her temples, making the blood sing and swirl crazily as she burst to her feet. She checked her watch. Frantic thoughts tumbled about in her head, leaving her to stand in indecision, glancing from phone to suitcase to the car keys on the bed.

Countless dire possibilities insinuated themselves into Lee's thoughts while she wondered who to call first. Could she possibly retrieve her own suitcase and make it to the bid letting before two o'clock?

She wasted five minutes telephoning the airline's passenger information, who told her to call lost and found, who informed her they'd get back to her in half an hour. Frustrated and angry at both herself and the airline, which hadn't had an attendant checking baggage-claim stubs, Lee finally returned to the airport. When a search of the baggage department proved futile, there seemed little to do except call the home office in Kansas City and admit her blunder.

Lee's stomach churned as she dialed. She pictured the fat belly and seedy little eyes of Floyd Thorpe, the company president and owner, who never lost an opportunity to remind Lee exactly why he'd hired her. Oh, he'd been waiting for this. Like the self-righteous bigot he was, how he'd been waiting. She knew full well Thorpe gritted his teeth every time they passed each other in the office. He probably visited his psychotherapist every payday after signing her check.

Well, you wanted to compete in a man's world and earn a man's salary, and you are!

But never in her three years in the construction industry had Lee earned it so dearly.

Floyd Thorpe's voice fairly shook with rage. He let out a blue streak of cuss words, ending with an order for Lee to "get your liberated female ass to that bid letting and find out who the hell was low bidder, and when you have, get on the next plane home because I'm not—by God—paying for any goddam *woman* to stay in a Colorado motel and eat on my company expense account when she doesn't know her ass from a catch basin, and any government bureaucrat who think it's easy to find *minority* employees who are worth diddly can shove his Minority Business Enterprise Goals—"

That's where Lee hung up.

Sexist, bigoted bastard! she raged silently, feeling again the ineffable futility of trying to change the jaundiced views of men like Floyd A. Thorpe.

Lee had no delusions about why she'd been hired. Not only was she a woman, she was also one-quarter American Indian, and either fact qualified her employer as a minority contractor in the eyes of the federal government as long as she was a corporation officer or owner. Furthermore, the federal government had proclaimed that ten percent of all federal monies allocated for public improvements were to be paid to minority contractors.

Considering the marked advantage of those contractors in

today's business world, Floyd A. Thorpe would have given the diamonds out of the opera windows of his Diamond Jubilee Lincoln Continental Mark V to be an Indian woman himself—if he could possibly manage it without being red and female! But Floyd Thorpe was not only male, he was also as Caucasian as the president himself, and he never let Lee forget it. Whenever she was around, he spit juice from the ever-present poke of tobacco that bulged his cheek. He hoisted up his pot belly with strutting tugs on his overstrained belt. He told dirty jokes and talked like the sewer rat he was. It got worse and worse as Lee continued to refuse his invitations to become a vice-president of Thorpe Construction. And if Lee Walker didn't like it, Thorpe's overbearing attitude clearly stated, she could go home and chew hides, plant maize, and raise a few papooses.

As Lee now spun from the telephone and crossed the airport terminal, she too gritted her teeth. Yes, she wanted equal pay, so once again she had to lick his boots and go out there and earn it!

She arrived at the bid letting five minutes late. As usual, she was the only woman in the room. Up front the city engineer was opening a sealed envelope as Lee slipped into a folding chair at the back of the room. From her purse she took a tablet and pen, then glanced surreptitiously at the lap of the man next to her as he entered the amount of the bid being read.

She wrote it quickly on her own paper, then leaned over to ask, "How many have been opened?"

He counted with the tip of a mechanical pencil. "Only six so far."

"Do you mind if I copy them?"

"Not at all."

He angled the pad her way, and Lee took down the six names and amounts. Glancing around the room, she found an unusually large number of contractors represented. The nation's slumping economy, coupled with relatively little new-home construction, had contractors traveling farther and bidding tougher in order to get work.

The Denver suburb of Aurora had attracted much attention, for it was one of the fastest growing mid-size cities in the nation. Aurora had solved its most serious problem—a shortage of water—by obtaining its own water supply and bringing it down from Leadville, a hundred miles away. But that water needed filtering and chemical treatment before use, adequate sewage treatment and removal after use. Every contractor in the room understood the value of getting in on the ground floor of the city's growth. To win this bid would be like plucking the first ripe plum in a highly productive orchard.

Suddenly Lee's back stiffened as the voice of the city engineer rang across the room, reading the name on the front of the next envelope.

"Thorpe Construction Company of Kansas City."

Lee stiffened and her heart did a double-whammy. There must be some mistake! She searched the room for anyone else from Thorpe, but she was the only one present. How could the envelope have gotten there? She scarcely had time to wonder before a brass letter opener sliced through the thick envelope with a raspy sound of authority, and while Lee still floundered in stunned surprise, her bid was read aloud:

"Four million two hundred forty-nine thousand."

Her heart thudded like a bass drum and she pressed a palm against it. *My God! I'm the low bidder so far!* Across the room faces fell as those who'd been beaten out sighed with disappointment.

Lee knew nothing to equal the exhilaration of moments like this. The sweet taste of revenge was already making her mouth water as she thought of returning to Kansas City and flinging the news in the beady little mustard seed eyes of one Floyd A. Thorpe, alias F.A.T., as Lee often thought of him.

Another bid was read: four million six. Hers was still low!

It took every effort to sit calmly in her chair and wait. How often she'd sat in sessions like this and known this giddy elation until someone else bested her at the last moment. There could be only one winner, and the larger the number of submissions, the greater the glory; the larger the job, the greater the possible profits. And this one was big . . .

Lee chewed her lower lip, trying to contain her growing

excitement as three more bids were opened and read, none of them lower than hers.

Finally the city engineer grinned and announced the last bid. "Brown and Brown, Inc., Kansas City, Missouri," he said as he lifted the bulky envelope and slit it. The room was as silent as outer space. Even before he read the amount aloud, the city engineer's smile broadened, and Lee experienced a premonition of doom.

"Four million two hundred forty-five thousand!"

The blood seemed to drop to Lee's feet. She wilted against the back of her chair and strove not to let her disappointment show. She swallowed, closed her eyes momentarily, and breathed deeply while the scuffle of shoes and the metallic clank of chairs filled the room. Her body felt like lead, but she forced herself to her feet. To lose was tough. To be second was harder. But to be second by only four thousand dollars on a job worth over four million was agony.

Four thousand dollars—Lee restrained an ironic grunt. It might as well have been four cents!

Could there by anything harder than congratulating the winner at a time like this? The man beside Lee moved toward the cluster of people who'd converged, Lee presumed, around the winning estimator. She caught a glimpse of a dark head, wide shoulders . . . and immediately squared her own.

Protocol, she thought dismally, wishing she could forgo congratulations.

The man was accepting them with obvious relish. His wide smile was turned upon a competitor who railed good-naturedly, "You did it again, Sam, damn ya! Why don't you leave some for the rest of us?"

The smile became a laugh as his darkly tanned hand pumped the much lighter colored one. "Next time, Marv, okay? My luck can't hold forever." Others shook his hand, and exchanged brief business comments while Lee waited her chance to approach him. His wide hand was enclosed around another when his eyes swung to find her in front of him. Those eyes were deep brown in a tan face. Pale crinkles at the corners of his eyes suggested he had squinted many hours into the sun. His nose was narrow, Nordic; the lips widely smiling, pleased at the moment. His neck was thick and his posture more erect than any other man's in the room. Lee had a brief glimpse of a silver and turquoise cross resting in the cleft of his open collar as his shoulders swung her way. His palm slid free of the man still addressing him, as if the brown-eyed winner had forgotten him in the middle of a sentence.

"Congratulations . . . Sam, is it?" Lee extended her hand. His grip was like that of a front-end loader.

"That's right. Sam Brown. And thank you. This one was too close for comfort."

Lee's lips parted and her eyes widened. *Sam Brown?* The coincidence was too great to be believed! *Sam Brown?* The same Sam Brown who read girlie magazines? He certainly didn't look like the type who'd need to.

Lee quelled the inane urge to ask him if he used Rawhide deodorant and instead lifted her eyes to his hair for verification—it was indeed dark brown, straight, and appeared to be blow-combed into the stylish, unparted sweep that touched both ear and forehead and the very tip of his collar. In a crazy-clear recollection, royal blue jockey shorts flashed across Lee's mind, and she felt a flush begin to creep up from her navel.

"You don't have to tell me it was too close for comfort," Lee replied. "I'm the one who just came in second." Sam Brown's palm was hard and warm and captured hers too long. "I'm Lee Walker, Thorpe Construction."

His black brows lifted in surprise, and she freed her hand at last.

"Lee Walker?"

"Yes."

"Of Kansas City?"

"Yes."

The beginning of a grin appeared on his wide lips, and his dark eyes drifted down over her wrinkled plaid shirt, faded jeans, and scuffed moccasins. On their way back up, they took on a distinct glint of humor.

"I think I have something of yours," he said, leaning a little closer, his voice low and confidential.

Across her mind's eye paraded a file of personal items from her suitcase—bras, pants, tampons, her daily journal. His insinuating perusal made her uncomfortably aware that

575

she was dressed like a teenage runaway while attending a business function requiring professionalism in both comportment and dress. At the same time he—though missing his suitcase, too—was dressed in shiny brown loafers, neat cocoa brown trousers, an open throated peach-colored shirt, and a summer-weight oatmeal-colored sport coat.

The difference made Lee feel at a distinct disadvantage. She felt the heat reach her face and with it a wave of suspicion and anger. Yes he certainly *did* have something of hers—a job worth over four million dollars! But this was no place to accuse him. Other people stood within earshot, thus she was forced to reply with only half the rancor she felt.

"Then it *was* you who turned in my bid."

"It was."

"And I suppose you think I should thank you for it?"

His smile only deepened the indentations on either side of his lips. "Didn't anyone ever tell you always to carry anything of immediate importance on the plane with you?"

Stung by the fact that he was undeniably right, she could only glare and splutter, "Perhaps you should consider teaching a workshop on the *dos* and *don'ts* of preparing bids for a public bid letting. I'm sure the class could learn innumerable new techniques from you."

He had the grace to back off and decrease the wattage of his grin.

"How dare you turn in someone else's bid!" she challenged.

"Under the circumstances, I felt it the only honorable thing to do."

"Honorable!" she nearly yelped, then forcibly lowered her voice. "You honorably looked it over first, though, didn't you!"

His half grin changed to a scowl. "*You're* the one who got the wrong suitcase. I picked—"

"I don't care to discuss it here, if you don't mind," she hissed in a stage whisper, glancing in a semicircle to find too many curious ears nearby. "But I *do* want to discuss it!" Her eyes blazed, but she forced restraint into her tones, though she wanted to let him have it with both barrels. "Where is it?"

Contrarily he slipped a lazy hand into his trouser pocket

and slung his weight on one hip. "Where is what?"

"My suitcase," she ground out with deliberate diction as if explaining to a dimwit.

"Oh, that." He looked away disinterestedly. "It's in my car."

She waited with long-suffering patience but he refrained from offering to get it for her.

"Shall we trade?" she suggested with saccharine sweetness.

"Trade?" Again his dark gaze turned to her.

"I believe I have something of yours, too."

Now she had his full attention. He leaned closer. "You have *my* suitcase?"

"Not exactly, but I know where it is."

"Where?"

"I returned it to the airport."

His brows curled, and he checked his watch hurriedly. But at that moment an enormous red-faced man clapped a big paw on Sam Brown's shoulder and turned him around. "Sam, if we're going to talk about that subcontract, we'd better get going. I have"—he, too, bared a wrist to check the time—"at the outside, an hour and a half."

Brown nodded. "I'll be right with you, John. Give me a minute." He turned hastily back to Lee. "I'm sorry I have to run. Where are you staying? I'll bring your suitcase no later than six o'clock." He was already easing toward the door.

"Hey, wait a minute, I—"

"Sorry, but I have a previous commitment. What motel?" John was in the doorway, waiting impatiently.

"I have to catch a plane! Don't you dare leave!"

Sam Brown had reached the door. "What motel?" he insisted.

"Damn!" she muttered as her hands gripped her hips, and she all but stamped a foot in frustration. "Cherry Creek Motel, but I can't wait—"

"Cherry Creek Motel," he repeated, and raised an index finger. "I'll deliver it." Then he was gone.

For the next three hours Lee sat like a caged rabbit in Room 110 of the Cherry Creek Motel while her irritation grew with each passing minute. By six o'clock she felt like a time bomb. She was hot and dirty. Denver in July was like an inferno, and Lee wanted nothing so much as a cool, refreshing bath. But she couldn't take one without her suitcase. Old Thorpe was going to be hotter than a cannibal's stewpot when he found out she hadn't returned to Kansas City as ordered. A check on late-leaving flights confirmed that Lee had already missed the suppertime flight, and the next one didn't leave till 10:10 P.M. She was damned if she'd stay up half the night just to get into the office bright and early for Thorpe's self-righteous tirade. After all, it wasn't her fault. And she'd had a harrowing day and still had a bone to pick with the "honorable" Sam Brown.

Every time she thought of him, her temperature rose a notch. To leave her high and dry and sashay off without returning her property was bad enough, but worse was the dirty, underhanded trick he'd pulled with her bid. She couldn't wait to tear into him and tell him exactly what a sneaky, low, lying dog he was!

At 6:15 she stormed to the TV and slammed a palm against the off button. She didn't give two hoots what tomorrow's weather would be like in Denver. All she wanted was to get out of this miserable city!

When a knock finally sounded, Lee's head snapped up and she stopped pacing momentarily, then stormed across and flung the door open.

Sam Brown stood on the sidewalk with two identical suitcases in his hands.

"You're late!" she snapped, glaring up at him with black, angry eyes.

"Sorry I had to run off like that. I got here as soon as I could."

"Well, it's not soon enough. I've already missed my flight, and my boss is going to be livid!"

"I said I was sorry, but you're the one who caused all this by grabbing the wrong luggage at the airport."

"Me! How about you! How dare you run off with my suitcase!"

"As I said before, you ran off with mine."

She gritted her teeth, knowing a frustration so overwhelming it turned her vision blazing red. "I'm not talking about at the airport. I'm talking about after the bid letting. You left me here to sit and stew and not even a brush to brush my hair with or clean clothes so I could take a bath or . . . or . . ." Disgusted, she yanked a suitcase from his hand and flung it onto the bed. Again she spun on him and ordered, "You've got some explaining to do. I'd suggest you begin."

He stepped inside obligingly, closed the door, set the other suitcase down, glanced around, and asked, "May I?" Then, as unruffled as you please, he carefully tugged at the crease in his impeccable pants before easing down in one of the two chairs beside the small round table.

With her hands on her hips, Lee spat out, "No . . . you . . . may . . . not!"

But instead of getting up, he spread his knees, leaned both elbows on them, and let his hands dangle limply between them. "Listen, Miss Walker, it's been a helluva—"

"*Ms.* Walker," she interrupted.

He raised one brow, paused a moment, then repeated patiently, *"Ms.* Walker." He flexed his shoulder muscles, kneaded the back of his neck, and continued, "It's been a long day and I'd like to get out of these clothes."

"You opened my suitcase," she stated unsympathetically, scarcely able to keep her temper under control.

"I what?"

She leaned forward and riveted him with snapping, black eyes. "You opened my suitcase!"

"Why, hell yes, I opened it. I thought it was mine."

"But you did more than just open it! You looked through it!"

"Oh did I, now?"

"Are you denying it?"

"Well, what about you? Are you saying you didn't open mine?"

"Don't change the subject!"

"The subject, I believe, is suitcases, and women who are sore losers."

"Sore losers . . . *sore losers!*" She stepped closer, towering over him. "Why, you lying, cheating . . . crook!" she shouted.

"What the hell are you driving at, *Ms.* Walker?"

"You opened my suitcase, found my unsealed bid, saw that it already had all the necessary signatures, looked it over, and undercut me by a stinking four thousand dollars, then played the benevolent Good Samaritan by turning in my envelope at the bid letting . . ."

In one swift motion Sam Brown came up out of his chair, swung her around, and stabbed two blunt fingers in the middle of her chest. The poke sent her reeling backward till she landed with an undignified bounce on the bed.

"That's a mighty serious allegation, lady!"

"That's a might narrow margin . . . *man!*" she sneered, leaning back on her hands as he stood above her, one of his knees pressing hard against hers. His face wore a thunderous look, made all the more formidable by the swarthiness of his skin and brows. Suddenly, though, he backed off, hands on hips as he cast a deprecating glance along her length.

"Oh, one of those," he intoned knowingly.

She rebounded off the bed, planted a palm on his chest, shoved him back two feet, stepped around him, then faced him squarely.

"Yes, one of those. I'm sick and tired of men who think a woman can't compete in this all-male sewer and water industry of theirs!"

"That's not what I meant when I called you lady, so don't put ulterior meanings on it."

"Oh, isn't it? Then why did you make the distinction? Isn't it because once you realized that suitcase belonged to a woman, you also realized the bid must have been prepared by a woman and you couldn't face getting stung at a public bid letting by losing to her?"

He pointed a long brown finger at her nose and leaned at a dangerous angle from the hip.

"Lady . . ." he began, but cut the word in half and tried again. "Ms. Walker, you're an opinionated, egotistical . . . suffragette! What makes you think nobody else in the world can bid a job better than you?" He began pacing in the small space before the table and chairs. "My God, take a look at the economy, at the number of contractors who are folding every month. Count the number who showed up at that bid letting today. That job will keep crews working for an entire season! Everybody wanted it. The margin was bound to be narrow!"

"Four thousand on four million is too narrow to be accidental, especially from a man who had possession of my suitcase during the earlier part of the day."

A look of pure disgust turned his features to granite. He stood before her, stalk still, jaw clamped tight. Momentarily his expression altered to a heavy-lidded perusal. His lips softened. His eyes traveled slowly down the madras shirt, not quite reaching her hips before starting back up again. His voice fell to a distasteful purr as he backed a step away and mused with strained male tolerance. "From what I saw in your suitcase, it's to be expected you'd be testy at this time of the month, so I'll chalk this up to female taboos and won't take further issue over your ch—"

Crack!!

She smacked him across the side of the mouth with an open palm. It knocked him momentarily off balance, and he teetered back in stunned surprise.

"Why . . . you . . . degenerate," she grated. "I might have expected something like that out of a . . . pervert who carried porno magazines in his suitcase on a business trip!"

Four red stripes in the shape of her fingers appeared to the left of his lips. His fists clenched. The cords along his neck stood at attention. His eyes glowered like chips of resin, and his lips were a thin, tight line.

Fear coursed through Lee at her own temerity. What had she done? She was alone in a motel room with a total stranger who was dishonest enough to cheat her in business, and she'd just knocked him clear into next week. He might very well decide to knock her clear into the one after that!

Her own trembling hand covered her lips, but he only straightened his shoulders, muscle by muscle, his anger held fiercely in check as he relaxed slowly, slowly. Without a word he retrieved his suitcase, opened the door, and paused, his eyes never leaving Lee's face.

"Just *who* looked through *whose* suitcase," he drawled, then added sarcastically, ". . . *lady?*"

He paused long enough to cause a warm flush to darken her cheeks before disappearing from the door, taking a smug grin with him.

In his wake Lee slammed the door so hard the mirror on the wall threatened to come crashing to the floor.

Chapter 2

A MINUTE LATER Lee opened her suitcase only to stare, dismayed at its contents. *Oh no, not again*, she groaned. The distasteful magazine was still inside. It beckoned to Lee's seamier instincts. She began to close the suitcase, but a bit of royal blue peeked from beneath a folded dress shirt, making something forbidden and prurient tingle her insides. She crossed her arms nonchalantly over her waist, covertly glanced at the closed drapes, then slipped an innocent forefinger between the magazine pages, running it up and down thoughtfully several times before finally flipping the magazine open and crossing her arms tightly over her abdomen again.

She stared, mesmerized by the undeniably stunning body stretched backward over a wide boulder on a riverbank. The skin was oiled, shimmering beneath drops of river spray with limbs laid open, hiding nothing. The model's eyes were closed, the expression on her face a combination of lust and fulfillment. The sultry, open lips were parted, the tongue peeking out between perfect teeth. Her long, scarlet nails rested against the dark triangle of femininity.

Lee swallowed, blushed, but turned the page. There followed more of the same. Skin and sin, she thought—exactly what one might expect of a man like Sam Brown. Still, she turned one more page.

The blood surged to her face, to her toes, to the backs of her knees, as she stared at the pornographic film clip from a current movie. Her stomach went weightless. Her chest felt tight, and the short hairs of her arms and thighs stood at attention. The man and woman were intimately entwined, limbs and teeth bared...

Sam Brown, you are disgusting! Abruptly she slapped the magazine shut, slammed the suitcase closed, and drew her hand back as if it had been singed, just as a knock sounded at her door.

Her head snapped up. She swallowed and pressed cool palms against hot cheeks before crossing the room and opening the door with much more control than she felt.

It was Sam Brown again. But this time his sport coat was gone and only one button held his shirt together at the waist. The shirttails were matted into a network of wrinkles, and in the deep V collar she again caught sight of the small silver cross set in turquoise. She dropped her eyes quickly from that bare chest only to find his feet bare too.

"Seems we've done it again," he ventured.

"Seems," she said crisply, not smiling.

She found it impossible to confront his eyes right after having confronted his girlie magazine. *Don't be silly, Walker, he's not a mind reader.* But still she felt that if he got a closer look, he'd know what she'd been doing when he knocked.

"I was getting set to go for a run when..." He flipped a palm up. "Same song, second verse." He peered past her to his suitcase which she knew was lying on the bed with the top closed but unzipped. Still she stood like a palace guard, holding the edge of the door with one hand, blocking his entrance.

"Listen, what I said before was inexcusable. I'd like to apologize," Sam Brown offered.

"I should think you would," Lee returned tightly, the image from the magazine still vivid in her mind.

He handed her the correct suitcase. "Is that any way to reply when I'm trying to bury the hatchet? The least you can do is be civil."

"All right. I...I shouldn't have slapped you either. I'm sorry. There, will that do?" But her voice was hard and cynical.

"Not quite." He pointed to his belongings. "I'd like my stuff back, too. I want to take a run and work off all my recent anger and frustration, but my sweats are in there."

He tilted a peace-offering grin at her, and she stepped back stiffly and motioned for him to come in and take what was his. She watched the wrinkles on his shirttails as he lifted the cover of the suitcase to check cursorily inside. The magazine lay on top. He studied it a moment, then spun to face her, a dark glower lowering his eyebrows.

"Look, just because a man buys a skin magazine doesn't make him a pervert."

"To each his own," she granted, but her tone was undeniably judgmental.

"The rag's got damn good interviews and movie reviews and—" Suddenly he turned sour-faced, slammed the top down, and zipped it with three jerks of the wrist. "I don't know why the hell I should justify myself to you. And anyway, why do you think you have the right to convict a man according to what you find in his suitcase?"

She sighed with overstrained patience. "Listen, do you mind? I've been in these clothes all day, and I'd like a bath and some supper. It's been a rough day."

"Fine . . . fine." He yanked the suitcase off the bed. "I'm leaving!"

She was waiting to close the door on his heels, but before she could, he wheeled to face her. Almost angrily he stated, "I *am* sorry for what I said. It was totally out of line, but so are you for not gracefully accepting my apology and letting me off the hook. Those eyes of yours are gl—"

"I said, apology accepted."

"Then how about if I buy you dinner and we can talk about . . . whatever? Anything but suitcases."

"No thank you, Mr. Brown. Not interested. I work for one insufferable sexist and can't help being around him an unavoidable amount of time each week, but beyond him, I'm careful about who I spend my time with."

Deep wrinkles appeared in his forehead as he scowled down at her. He looked ominous and ready to blow his cork again, but Lee held her ground, facing him squarely, one hand on the edge of the door. She was conscious again of how erect his posture was—even more so as he held his anger tightly in check—shoulders squared back, the inverted triangle of bare skin on his chest as taut as the head of a drum. He wore a tight-lipped expression as his dark eyes seemed to penetrate her for a long, threatening moment. Then he turned on a bare heel and stalked away.

With a shaky sigh of relief, Lee closed the door, leaned her forehead against it for a moment, then slipped the dead bolt home.

The tension of the day had keyed her up until her neck and shoulders felt stiff with fatigue. She leaned far back from the waist, slipped a thin hand to the nape of her neck, and kneaded. Eyes closed, hair trailing free, she wondered what had prompted Sam Brown to invite her to dinner. Then, recalling his choice of reading material, she thought she knew the answer.

Lee flopped tiredly on the bed, crossed her arms behind her head, and tried to rid her thoughts of Sam Brown. But his face intruded, as she'd first seen it at the bid letting when he was accepting handshakes—smiling, laughing, pleased with himself. She remembered the tiny wrinkles at the corners of his eyes and wondered how old he was? Mid-thirties? When he scowled, he looked older—and he'd done plenty of scowling today! But his look of displeasure also made his undeniably handsome face even more good looking.

She tossed a limp forearm over her brow. Handsome is as handsome does, she thought tiredly. She'd chalk this day up to experience and forget she had ever laid eyes on the man.

The face of Floyd A. Fat Thorpe nudged Brown's aside, and Lee wondered which of the two was more disturbing. Thorpe was going to be more offensive than ever after this fiasco. Especially since she had deliberately disobeyed orders and stayed the night in Denver. There were times when competing in a man's world didn't seem worth it. But she had to prove to herself she could . . . hadn't she? Hadn't she had to prove it not only to herself but also to everyone else who had helped wreck her life?

She fell into a fitful sleep with the faces of Thorpe and Brown mingling in a collage of other disturbing faces from her past—Joel's, the judge's . . .

Awakening with a start, Lee jerked her wrist up—seven thirty!—slid off the bed, and began undressing all in one motion.

She ran a tubful of water, took a quick refreshing bath, and cursed the thin motel towels and cheap soap that scarcely lathered. Drying herself, she stepped to the vanity, then tossed the towel aside while she rummaged for her brush and began smoothing her hair. It reached just below her shoulder blades —a coarse, black mane thicker than wild prairie grass, so thick she leaned sideways at the waist as if its weight made her list. She leaned in the other direction, then stood straight, watching her breast rise and fall rhythmically with each brush stroke.

Her hand stopped in midair, the brush momentarily forgotten as she somberly assessed her naked reflection. Unbidden came the seductive pictures of the magazine and with them the vision of Sam Brown's face, his bare chest, his bare feet. She stared into her own dark eyes until her eyelids trembled, and she lowered her eyes. Her gaze moved down the long, lean neck to medium, pear-shaped breasts with dark nipples.

Hesitantly she brought the brush forward and ran the back of it around the outer edge of her right breast. The cool, yellow plastic was strangely smooth and welcome against her skin. She drifted it along the hollow beneath the breast, then up to the nipple. Tingles of remembrance came fluttering.

It had been a long time.

There were things a woman's body needed.

She closed her eyes as she turned the brush over, thinking of the whiskers on a firm jaw as she felt the light scrape of bristles along the side of her full breast, down her ribs, across her abdomen to the hollow of her hip.

A deep loneliness aroused memories of a past when her youthful dreams had consisted of rosy pictures of how life would turn out. Marriage, children, happy ever after. What had happened to all that? Why was she standing alone in a motel room in Denver, Colorado, remembering Joel Walker? He was married to someone else now, and, truth to tell, Lee no longer loved him. What she loved was the memory of those dreams she'd had when they'd first met, the wild want of each other's bodies that they'd thought was enough upon which to build a marriage. She ached for the time before all the mistakes had been made, before Jed and Matthew had been born.

Lee opened her eyes to find an empty, sad woman before her. A woman with pale stretch marks snaking from hip to abdomen as the only reminder of two pregnancies. She spread her fingers upon them and slumped against the vanity. Then she pushed herself erect and lifted her eyes. *Damn you, Lee, you promised yourself not to get bogged down in recriminations over what can't be changed!*

She took a firmer grip on the brush and began styling her hair, angrily brushing so hard her scalp hurt, dragging the heavy black mass around the back of her head and securing it just above and behind an ear in a heavy, smooth knot. Her skin was naturally bronze and needed neither foundation nor blush, but she accented her eyelids with silver shadow, curled her lashes, and applied eyeliner and mascara. Her lipstick was two-toned, a rich claret accented by white lipliner. She dashed a touch of perfume behind each ear and turned to get dressed.

She donned a pair of baggy white pants that tapered at the ankle above high-heeled wedgies of canvas and rope, then a cavalry-style shirt of pale blue stripes that buttoned off center and had short puffed sleeves ending in ruffles at the elbow. A generous ruffled collar stood up around Lee's jaws, which she knew emphasized her long, graceful neck. Stepping to the mirror, again she added the ever-present feathers—this time hanging them in her ears, light blue wisps that dangled when she turned to retrieve her purse and head down to dinner.

The dining room was almost empty. Night had nearly fallen and the lights of Denver were glimmering on one by one beyond the windows. Lee paused in the doorway, peering into the dimness where unobtrusive music played quietly. In a far corner a gray-haired couple was sipping coffee. The only other occupied table in the room was taken by Sam Brown. He glanced up from a newspaper as Lee paused in the doorway. Their eyes met briefly before he turned expressionlessly back to his reading, angling the paper to catch the last fading light from the window beside him. Lee waited, feeling awkward and conspicuous as she studied the back of the cash register. At last a waitress led her to a seat.

Unfortunately it was in the middle of the floor and faced Sam Brown. Again he lifted his eyes. Again they returned laconically to his newspaper, and Lee felt more than ever like the lead act in a one-ring circus.

The waitress handed Lee a menu. "Kind of slow tonight," the woman commented, her voice ringing like a clarion in the empty room.

"So I see."

"Can I get you anything from the bar?"

"Yes, a Smith and Kurn." Lee was conscious of Sam Brown's eyes directed her way again. "I know it's an after-dinner drink, but somehow I'm always too full then." She laughed nervously, damning herself for explaining, knowing she'd done it not for the waitress's benefit but for Sam Brown's. What did she care what he thought?

The waitress crossed to his table. She handed him a menu, and their voices also resounded clearly through the room.

"Something from the bar, sir?"

"An extra dry martini with pickled mushrooms, if you've got 'em."

My, aren't we fussy, Lee thought testily. Pickled mush-rooms!

"We sure do," the waitress replied, and moved away to leave the room with nothing but that dim music which could scarcely fill the uncomfortable tension spinning between their two tables.

Lee searched her menu, immediately spotted what she wanted, but taking refuge behind the wide folder for a full five minutes until the waitress finally arrived with her drink, giving Lee someplace else to focus her attention.

The chocolate-flavored drink was refreshing. Lee sipped and followed the waitress with her eyes as the uniformed back hid Sam Brown momentarily from view.

"We gave you a couple extra mushrooms. How's that?" came the pleasant question.

"Great, thank you." His deep voice reverberated in Lee's ears.

When the woman stepped back, Sam's eyes caught Lee's.

Immediately she ducked to take a sip of her drink. The glass felt slippery in her hand. She dried her palm on her thigh, and applied herself to the menu again, ever so studiously, damning the waitress for walking off without asking if she was ready to order.

The woman returned at last with pencil and pad. So far Lee had managed to keep her eyes off the table by the window.

"Can I take your order now?"

Does a one-legged duck swim in a circle? Lee bit back the snippy retort and forcibly pasted a pleasant smile on her face. She attempted to speak softly, but the words came ringing off the walls like gunshots.

"I'll have ocean perch, no potato, and Thousand Island dressing on my salad."

"Would you like something in place of the potato?"

"Would I ever, but I'm being firm with myself tonight." There followed a false laugh which Lee hardly recognized as her own while Brown's eyes probed once again. She suddenly felt as if she'd told him something personal that he had no right to know and damned herself for making the innocent comment.

He ordered prime rib, medium rare, baked potato with both butter and sour cream, the house dressing—without being told what it was, which for some reason irritated Lee, who ate in restaurants seldom enough not to be adventurous—and a cup of coffee.

This time when the waitress moved away, the eyes of the two diners met and hesitated on each other for a longer moment, Sam Brown now leaned back in his chair with lazy nonchalance, one shoulder angling lower than the other as he rested a negligent elbow on the table and touched the rim of his glass with five fingertips.

Lee sipped her drink and looked pointedly away, but the distracting memory of his magazine pictures came niggling again. She felt his eyes on her and for a moment had the disquieting impression he was stacking her up against his naked tootsies, wondering how she'd compare. To Lee's dismay, the memory of her stretch marks emblazoned itself across her mind.

"Did you get your bath?"

At the sound of his lazy question her eyes flew up, and she colored as if he'd just spoken an obscenity, then glanced quickly at the old couple in the corner. They were sipping silently, paying no attention whatsoever.

"Yes. Did you have your run?"

He smiled crookedly. "I tried, but the damn air in this city is so thin I felt like I was having a heart attack."

"A pity you didn't." She quirked one eyebrow and made the ice cubes bob with a poke of her finger.

"Still don't believe me, huh?"

She lifted her glass, eyed him over its rim, took a long, sweet sip, then slowly shook her head from side to side. "Uh-uh."

He shrugged indifferently, took a pull on his cocktail, and studied the view outside the window. The way he had one shoulder back farther than the other made the yellow knit shirt hug his chest like a wet buckskin. The front zipper was lowered several inches and the silver cross winked at Lee while she tried to pretend he wasn't there. But it was impossible when, a moment later, the old couple arose, paid their bill, and went away, leaving Lee and Sam the only two in the room.

The waitress returned, deposited their first courses, and disappeared again.

Lee dove into her salad like a sinner into a confessional. But every clink of fork upon bowl seemed amplified and disturbing. The sound of her own chewing seemed explosive in the room. She scarcely kept from wriggling in her chair while feeling Sam Brown's steady gaze resting on her in an increasingly distracting manner.

His voice split the quiet again. "You know this is ridiculous, don't you?"

She looked up to find him with hands resting idly next to his salad bowl.

"What is?" she managed.

"Sitting here like a couple of little kids who just had a fight over who broke the mud pie."

She couldn't think of a single sane reply. With an engaging

grin he went on. "So, you're gonna stay in your yard and I'm gonna stay in mine, and we're going to glare at each other over the fence and be lonely and miserable while neither of us will make the first move."

She stared at him, gulped down what felt like an entire, unbroken head of lettuce, and said not a word.

"Can I bring my salad over there?" he asked finally, then added charmingly, "If I promise not to break your mud pie?"

The wisp of a smile threatened her lips and before she could control it she had chuckled, the sound bringing a wash of relief. "Yes, come ahead. It's awful sitting here trying not to look at you."

He and his salad and his pickled mushrooms were up and across the floor in three seconds. He settled himself at her table, gave her an audacious grin, and declared, "There, that's better," then dug into his lettuce with gusto.

She had called him a liar, a cheat, and a pervert. What possible course of conversation could successfully follow that? she wondered uneasily. To her relief, he came up with one.

"I have to admit, you're the first lady estimator I've ever seen."

"I'm the first lady estimator *I've* ever seen," she admitted.

The deep lines on either side of his mouth dented in. "How long have you been one?"

"I began in the business three years ago and have been an estimator for a little over a year."

"Why?"

Her eyebrows curled in puzzlement. "What do you mean, why?"

"Why choose a career in a tough business like this that's traditionally been dominated by men?"

"Because it pays well."

He accepted that with a nod of the head. "You work for old Floyd Thorpe, huh?"

"Yes, I'm sorry to say I do."

"He's a hell-raiser that one—a real shyster."

Startled, she looked into his dark eyes. "You know him?"

"He's been around Kansas City a long time. Everybody

there knows old Floyd. It's his kind that give construction companies a bad reputation. He's as crooked as a dog's hind leg."

"But he knows how to make money so he's excused, right?" she questioned sarcastically.

Refusing to rise to the bait, Sam asked, "If you dislike him so much, why work for him?"

"With the construction industry tied directly to new-home starts, need you ask?"

He wiped his mouth on a napkin. "No, I guess there aren't a lot of job openings right now, are there?"

She poked at the fleshy wedge of tomato in her bowl as if it were Thorpe's fat belly. "The only opening I've seen lately is the one between Floyd Thorpe's front teeth when he spits his slimy tobacco juice at my feet."

Brown laughed appreciatively, prompting Lee to look up with a devilish expression on her face. "Can I share a very private joke with you? One that's exceedingly irreverent?"

"I love irreverent jokes."

Lee sucked on her bottom lip, then confessed, "Privately, when I'm disgusted with my boss, which I usually am, I call him by his initials."

"Which are?"

"F.A.T." Brown rocked back in his chair and laughed while she continued, "He doesn't like it generally known what his middle initial is. Maybe that's why I take such pleasure in including it."

The fine white lines about Brown's eyes disappeared as he crinkled a smile and watched as she jabbed repeatedly at the tomato. His eyes passed over high, wide cheekbones, the proud, straight nose, the black straight hair caught behind her ear, in a plump, smooth bun, the copper skin and near-black eyes.

"You're Indian, right?"

Her eyes flashed up defiantly, and the feathers swung against her jaws. "One quarter Cherokee. He never lets me forget it."

Brown glanced at the feathers but withheld comment. "What you're saying is old Fat knows which side his bread is buttered on, huh?"

"Exactly. He's asked me no less than five times to accept the *honorary* title of vice-president."

"Let me guess." Brown leaned forward. "That would qualify him as a minority contractor, right?"

She grinned ruefully. "*And* make him eligible to bid any and all Minority Business Enterprise jobs the federal government lets, either as prime contractor or subcontractor. As you know, they seem to be the best bet going right now."

He studied her from beneath black brows shaped like boomerangs. "I take it you've declined the vice-presidency."

"With great relish."

Again Sam Brown leaned back in his chair and laughed richly. "There are a few contractors in the Kansas City area who'd grin from ear to ear to hear somebody put one over on F.A. after all the times he's pulled underhanded deals."

"I'd grin wider myself if it weren't for the increase in pay I'm turning down just to make Fat Thorpe eat crow."

"Or—more aptly—Cherokee?" Sam quipped, watching her closely.

She chuckled and her dark eyes sparkled momentarily before a pensive look overcame them. She nudged a few remaining pieces of lettuce around her salad bowl and folded her knuckles beneath her chin. She braced one elbow on the table, rested her other forearm against the edge of the table, and stroked the damp sides of her cold glass. "You know," she mused to the ice cubes in the empty tumbler, "there are some things my pride just won't let me do. Not even for money."

"But I thought you said money was why you took the job."

"It was. But I earn enough to support myself now. That's all I need."

She saw his eyes drop to the hand toying with the glass. It bore only a large oval turquoise in a sterling silver setting.

"You're not married?" he asked.

His eyes moved higher, met hers, and her fingers stopped stroking the damp glass.

"No," she answered tersely, realizing she should qualify the answer, then disregarded her conscience, thinking she owed this man nothing. They were simply sharing a table—two strangers in a lonely city away from home.

Their main course arrived, and Sam Brown changed the

subject. "I take it *the Fat* is going to hit the fan when he hears you lost the bid, huh?"

Lee looked up, chuckled appreciatively, and noted, "You *do* have an irreverent sense of humor, don't you? He's always hitting the fan over one thing or another. It's a way of life with him. If it's not over losing the bid, it'll be over me staying overnight on his precious company credit card, which he warned me not to do."

"But you're doing it anyway?" A frown tilted his brows.

"It was either that or get into Kansas City in the middle of the night after missing the six P.M. flight out of here. After the day I've put in, I wasn't about to spend half the night in a plane."

"All because I had your suitcase, right?"

She met his eyes, but only shrugged and returned to her dinner.

The waitress brought coffee, interrupting them momentarily. When they were alone again, Lee studied Sam thoughtfully and asked, "If you've been around the K.C. area long enough to know about the questionable business practices of my illustrious boss, why haven't we met before?"

"Probably because we've been primarily involved with plumbing contracting and only recently decided to expand into sewer and water work."

"We?" she asked curiously. "Who's the other Brown in Brown and Brown?"

"It was my dad. He was the one who knew every contractor's secrets around town. He was in the contracting business for years."

"Was?"

"He died four years ago," Sam stated unemotionally, cutting into his prime rib.

"I . . . I'm sorry."

He looked up brightly. "Oh, don't be. My father had a hell of a good life, did everything he ever wanted to do, died a happy man . . . on a golf course, no less, on the sixth tee." His brown eyes twinkled. "That sixth tee always did give him trouble."

Even though Sam Brown pronounced all this with no apparent sadness, Lee felt awkward sharing his private history this way when she scarcely knew him. But he went on. "He was a hard-drinking, hard-working Norwegian—"

"A Norwegian named *Brown?*"

"Comes from Brunvedt, somewhere back along the line."

"I'm sorry . . . I interrupted."

"Well as I said, he was a hard-headed Norwegian, and when I say he did everything he wanted, that included disobeying doctor's orders. He'd had a small stroke and was given orders to take it easy for a few months, but when a stubborn Norwegian takes it into his head he's going to go golfing, there's no stopping him."

Lee found she was enjoying Sam Brown's company immensely by now and surprised even herself by replying, "And when a stubborn Norwegian takes it into his head that he's going to go to dinner with a woman, there's no stopping him either, is there?"

Sam angled a smile at the knot of hair behind her ear, then at her eyes, and finally her lips. It occurred to Lee that he looked nothing whatever like any Norwegian she'd ever met. His hair was a rich chestnut color, his eyes and skin so dark they seemed to reflect her very face as he reached blindly for his coffee cup and—without taking his eyes from her— teased, "Well, it wasn't so painful after all, was it?"

She wished she could answer otherwise, but she found it impossible. "Admittedly, no it wasn't."

"Maybe we can do it again sometime in Kansas City."

For a moment she was tempted, but recalling the less estimable aspects of his personality, she warned, "Don't plan on it. Not unless *I've* won the bid."

"Mmm . . ." He lifted his coffee. Devilish eyes sparkled above the cup. "Might be worth fixing the bid in your favor next time."

"I have no doubt you'd do it." She studied him for some time, then admitted, "I have a habit of coining titles for people I meet. You know what I've dubbed you?"

"What?"

Their eyes tangled in a delightful duel of wits.

"The Honorable Sam Brown."

"Hey, I like that . . . that's clever."

"And pure, unvarnished sarcasm. Brown, you're a completely dishonorable scoundrel, and I don't know why I'm sitting at this table with you right now."

He tipped his chair back until it balanced on two legs. "Because you wanted to find out if I'm as perverted as my reading material led you to suspect. They say every woman is attracted to the wrong kind of man at least once in her life. Who knows? Maybe I'm it for you."

"Then again maybe you're not." She tipped her head and studied him closely. He was a highly delicious looking male specimen—she'd grant him that. And his nasty sense of humor didn't hurt a bit. But Lee reminded herself again that he wasn't the sort with whom she should be bantering about sexually provocative things. Conversations such as this provoked vibrations that said much more than the mere words, and she was by no means ready for such vibrations again. Her wounds hadn't healed from the last disastrous relationship. But even while she chided herself for indulging in such give-and-take, Sam's eyes were steady on her as his chair came down on all fours. He leaned crossed arms on the table edge, and pitched slightly toward her.

"Tell me," he said, his voice gone low and intimate. "What'd you think of the one stretched out on the rock beside the river?"

Damned if she was going to look like some nilly-witted teenager caught peeping at African breasts in *National Geographic!* Lee looked Brown smack in the eye and replied levelly, "The photographer must have missed oiling the inner side of her right calf. The water didn't bead up there."

Sam Brown rewarded her with a full-throated, appreciative peal of laughter while Lee scolded herself for her own precociousness. A moment later he had flung his soiled napkin on the table, picked up the check and was standing behind her chair, waiting to pull it back. But before he did, he leaned close and, just beside an aqua feather, said, "Chief Sitting Bull would have excommunicated you from the tribe if he'd ha . . . ha . . ." He turned away just in time. *"Aaa-chooo!"*

She glanced over her shoulder with a cheeky grin. "My goodness, Brown, it looks like you're allergic to me. Don't get so close next time."

He was rubbing his nose with a handkerchief. "It's that perfume you're wearing."

"My apologies." She grinned, not feeling the least bit of contrition.

It's just as well, she thought. She had no business being with him in the first place. But still she had to smile, for on the way back to their rooms he sneezed three more times, and by the time they reached her door he was giving her a good six-foot clearance.

Chapter 3

FLOYD A. THORPE kept his office like he kept his teeth—brown around the edges. Rolls of plans, soil samples, drill bits, cast-iron pipe fittings, test plugs, incoming mail, hydrant wrenches, and used coffee cups created a random scattering of litter that was rarely cleared or dusted, for F.A. raised particular hell if anyone monkeyed with his "filing system." The room had an unpleasant smell, a mixture of rancid chewing tobacco, dust, stale alcohol, tar, and dried clay, topped off with the peculiar smell of cast iron. When Lee had taken the job at Thorpe Construction, F.A. had been in the middle of one of his sporadic drying-out periods, during which he became less abusive and more reasonable. The office had been cleaner, and so had he.

But he'd been off the wagon for months now. His nose shone like a beacon, and his cheeks wore the mottled red puffiness of the serious drinker. It was all Lee could do to face him the following morning across the junk on his desk.

"He what!" bellowed F.A.

Lee took a step backward. Thorpe's breakfast Manhattan was offensive the second time around.

"He got my suitcase by mistake, found the bid inside, and turned it in along with his own."

"And took the goddam job away from you like candy from a baby!" F.A. fumed and paced, then picked up a coffee can and spit into it. Lee studied a piece of P.V.C. pipe on a littered file cabinet behind him rather than observe the distasteful sight of his brown spume. "By a measly four thousand dollars!" F.A. whammed his fist into the center of the desk, lifting dust and making the telephone dance. He dropped into his desk chair and glowered at Lee, then turned suddenly pensive. "That's old Wayne Brown's kid, isn't it? Mmm . . . appears the kid's got more brains than his old man." Thorpe's eyes narrowed shrewdly, and he chuckled deep in his throat. Then he turned his beady eyes on Lee again. "I hope you learned your lesson from this. Everybody's out to screw everybody else in this world, and Sam Brown proved it!" With a quick shift of weight, he leaned back in his chair. "You thought any more about that vice-presidency I offered you?"

"Sorry, I prefer estimating."

Again he banged his fist on the desk. "Damn it, Walker, I put up with a lot from you, carrying your bids in a suitcase like some green recruit, then picking up the wrong damn one at the other end of the line and losing me a job worth over four million bucks! How long do you think I'm going to put up with screw-ups like this! I want your name on them corporation papers. It's the least you can do after the mess you made out of this Denver bid."

"I'm sorry about losing the suitcase, but the rest of it wasn't my fault. If Sam Brown checked my bid against his, he wouldn't admit it."

"Why, hell no, who would?" F.A.'s pot belly was so hard it scarcely depressed when he crossed his hands on it. "Tell you what, girlie. I'll give you till Friday to think it over. Either you help me out with this here minority business thing and agree to become vice-president, or you can find yourself someplace else to work. You're costin' me money, and unless you help me make a little of it back, I got no use for you."

Back in her own neat office, Lee strode angrily to her chair, deposited herself in it with great vexation, cursed under her breath, and considered marching back in there and telling F.A.T. where to put his vice-presidency *and* his tobacco cud! There'd be nothing so sweet as to walk out there and show that fat, smelly boar she didn't need his precious job or his calculating little mind one moment longer.

But the bitter truth was, she did.

She had no husband across town bringing in a paycheck from another job to support her. She was self-reliant now and needed a weekly salary to survive. Sam Brown had been right when he'd summed up the estimator's job market right now— there was none! Two years ago, before the recession had gripped the country, Kansas City and its surrounding suburbs had had perhaps twenty more general contractors than it did now. Now the industry grapevine buzzed constantly with news of this one or that one on the verge of folding, and they all held their breaths, hoping the next one to go under wouldn't be themselves.

The phone interrupted Lee's reverie. She punched line one and answered, "Lee Walker."

"You made it back."

The voice surprised Lee.

"Brown, is that you?"

"That's right, the Honorable Sam Brown. I looked for you on my flight. Thought we might sit together and share my magazine."

She didn't feel in the least like smiling but couldn't help it. Damn the man, making her laugh when he'd been the initial cause of the altercation she'd just had with Thorpe!

"Oh, you did, huh? I took an earlier flight. I've been back since ten o'clock."

A brief pause, then, "How did Thorpe take the news?"

She laughed, a single mirthless huff. "Need you ask?"

"Well, you win a few and you lose a few. He should know that by now."

"That isn't even remotely funny, Brown. Not after what you did to me! He came down on me like a tent when the circus is over, and what really irritates me is that Fat Thorpe actually seems to admire you for your duplicity. His exact words were, 'The kid's got more brains than his old man.' It appears you're two peas in a pod, you and my boss."

His unconcerned laughter came over the wire. "We're both a couple of degenerates, is that it?"

"That's it," she agreed.

"Well, how would you like a chance to try your hand at reforming me . . . say over dinner Friday night?"

Lee came close to sputtering, the dressing down she'd just

taken from F.A. still burning beneath her collar. "Dinner! What, again? And ruin my reputation around this town by being seen with a known pervert? I told you, Brown, I don't know why I ate with you the first time!"

"I'll take you to the American Restaurant," he bribed.

The American! Lee was suddenly crestfallen and undeniably tempted. The American Restaurant at the Crown Center was the *crème de la crème* of eateries in the Kansas City area.

"Brown, that's a dirty, rotten low blow, and you know it."

"I know," he agreed mirthfully, a smile in his voice.

"I told you, not until *I'm* the low bidder, and right now I'm not, as you well know." *The American Restaurant*, she thought woefully, kissing the chance good-bye.

"Okay, Cherokee, but I'll hold you to it . . . when you're low bidder."

"Ch . . ." Now Lee did sputter! "Ch . . . Cherokee! Brown, don't you ever call me that ag . . . Brown?" She clicked the disconnect button. "Brown!"

But he'd hung up. Then she did too, slamming the receiver down so hard it jumped back off the cradle. "Cherokee!" she spit out crossing her arms and glaring at the instrument guilty of carrying his damn sexy, teasing voice to her when she was in no mood to be manipulated by a smooth talker like him.

How dare he call her Cherokee when . . . when . . .

But a moment later her lips betrayed her and she found herself grinning at the phone. It was the last time she grinned that day.

Things went from bad to worse. Fat Thorpe pounded in and out, cussing like a marine and demanding test borings on jobs Lee knew were too wet to even consider bidding; ordering installation of inferior quality pipe they'd had trouble with before; demanding last minute changes in a bid she'd all but finished. He became more overbearing and demanding as the day passed. Lee required all her teeth-gritting strength to maintain her composure.

By the time she left the office, her nerves were at the breaking point. She arrived at her townhouse tired, angry, and depressed. In the front foyer she stripped off her shoes and pantyhose and left them lying in a heap. There was something about bare feet that seemed to take the stress off her head.

In the rear-facing kitchen she reached unseeingly into the refrigerator for a peach, and sank her teeth into it while roaming over to the sliding glass door and staring at her tiny private patio, fantasizing about calling the Human Rights Commission to complain that she was being discriminated against. But what could the complaint be? That Old Fat wanted to make her vice-president and give her a raise but she was declining the offer? There was nothing illegal about Thorpe's ploy to make his firm eligible as a minority contractor. It was only unethical! And Lee adamantly refused to be his patsy in the scheme.

She prowled the living room, heaping curses on Old Fat's fat head! Spying the newspaper, she checked the *Kansas City Star*, but as she'd suspected, no one wanted estimators. *The Construction Bulletin* turned up nothing more, and Lee's depression grew.

Sitting on the floor, her back to the sofa, she crossed her arms over upraised knees and rested her forehead there. The peach pit grew warm and slippery in her hand. She raised her head wearily and propped her chin on an arm, studying the precision pleats of the off-white custom-made draperies she was still paying off in monthly installments.

She'd worked so hard to get this place. She brushed a hand over the thick nap of the rich, rust carpet. She'd bought the townhouse only six months ago, and though she had a long way to go before it was completely decorated, she loved the furniture she'd managed to buy so far. She had modest dreams of adding decorator items piece by piece, of completing the finishing touches as she could afford them.

She sighed, slunk low onto her tailbone, and caught the nape of her neck on the cushion of the tuxedo sofa, which was covered with an arresting Mayan design of rich, deep earth tones, its soft depths strewn with plump matching cushions. Lee's eyes moved to the spots where she wanted side chairs.

But the room made her suddenly feel lonelier than ever. She studied the plants in the baskets, willing them to grow faster and fill up the extra space. Her eyes moved next to the only other item the room possessed—a loosely strung God's-eye on the wall behind the sofa, its rust, brown and ecru yarns so inexpertly stretched around the crossed dowels, that there could be no question it had been done by a child's hand.

Yes, the room was decidedly bare and lonely, but it was a beginning, and if she lost her job, she would lose this too.

Dejected, she wandered back to the kitchen, threw out the peach pit, rinsed off her hands and opened the refrigerator again only to find herself, some two minutes later, still staring into its almost empty space, remembering a day when she had shuffled and rearranged, trying to make room for family leftovers.

She closed the door on her memories, wishing the judge could see now what she'd made of herself since she'd faced him in court. Carrying a quart of milk onto the patio, she sank into a webbed lounge chair and drank the remainder of her supper right out of the red and white carton, too dispirited to care if it was in a glass or not.

It was much later when she finally plodded upstairs. The second floor of the townhouse had two bedrooms and a bath. As she neared the door of the smaller room, she slowed. Stopping, she reached inside and switched on the light. A pair of twin beds with heavy pine headboards took up the far wall. Between them stood a matching chest of drawers whose rich, dark wood looked richer against the bright scarlet carpet, but whose tops were bare—nothing there but a lamp and an unopened box of paper tissues. Still, the room was completely decorated. The bedspreads and draperies were crisp and new, with an all-over design of NFL insignias in a blaze of basic colors. On the wall beside one bed hung two Kansas City Chiefs pennants.

Lee studied the room sullenly, biting back tears that stung her eyes, feeling again the frustrating sense of unfairness that she could never shake at the thought of the boys.

She counted the days.

A brown and white cat padded silently into the room and preened his fur against Lee's ankle.

"Oh, P. Ewing, you've been on the bed again, haven't you?"

Lee looked down, watched the cat move sinuously against her, then crossed to one of the beds to plump its pillow and smooth the spread. On her way out she scooped up the cat, buried her face in his fur, and reached for the light switch. But she paused in the doorway and turned, assessing the silent room once more. "Oh, P. Ewing, what if I lose my job?" she lamented. "I'll have to give up this place."

On Friday morning Lee was working on a bid for a simple sewer and water installation in Overland Park, which would service an area where a shopping mall was to be built. The bid letting was scheduled for two that afternoon. These last few hours were always the worst. The phone constantly jangled with calls from salesmen giving last minute quotes on materials, from reinforced concrete pipe to catch basin castings. She'd just received a price quote on sod replacement which was several cents under the previous low bidder and was recomputing the labor subcontract cost when the phone rang. Preoccupied, fingers still flying over the calculator buttons, Lee reached unconsciously for the receiver, cradling it between shoulder and ear as her eyes continued scanning a column of numbers.

A moment later she realized she'd picked up a call meant for F.A. A smooth, masculine voice was saying, ". . . can come to terms on that twelve-inch reinforced concrete pipe we've had laying around the yard. The flaws are in the reinforcing, not in the concrete itself, so it'd be mighty tough to detect."

F.A. chuckled, then returned in a silky tone, "And we'll split the difference right up the middle?"

Horrified, Lee jerked the receiver away from her ear, clutching it in white knuckles, realizing she should have hung up the moment she'd identified the call as someone else's. But it had happened so fast! She rested the receiver on her job sheets and stared at the lighted button on the face of the phone, waiting, digesting what she'd heard. With each passing second her disgust grew. She'd heard it said many times that F.A. knew every dishonest trick in the book and wasn't afraid to use them. But she'd never had proof before. Using substandard materials, price fixing, collusion, buying off the competition before bids—there were countless deceits it was possible to practice. Some were illegal, some merely dishonest. But either way, until now it had been no more than hearsay.

The light blinked off, and Lee slipped the receiver silently back in place.

She was still sitting there in a turmoil when F.A. rounded the doorway into her office. This morning the gnawed stub of an unlit cigar was clenched in his teeth.

"Whoever you got to supply the twelve-inch reinforced concrete pipe on that Overland Park job, we won't be goin' with them. Gonna get that pipe from Jacobi."

"Oh?" Lee retorted coldly.

"Yeah, you can figure it at twelve-fifty a foot, materials only."

"And what margin of profit are you working on at twelve dollars and fifty cents a foot?"

His beady little eyes narrowed on her like laser beams. The cigar stub shifted to the opposite corner of his mouth. "Never mind, just figure it at twelve-fifty a foot."

Lee erupted from her chair. "No, *you* figure it at twelve-fifty a foot!"

"Me! That bid's due at two o'clock this afternoon and—"

"And it won't be turned in by me, not with flawed pipe from Jacobi figured into it!"

His sausagelike fingers slowly extracted the wet cigar from his lips. "So, Little Miss Big Ears has been listening in on somebody else's phone conversations, huh?"

"Yes, I heard you and Jacobi on the phone just now, but it was entirely unintentional. As a matter of fact, I only heard about ten seconds worth of the conversation."

"But it was enough to give you a sudden case of *morality*, is that it?" He managed to make the word sound quite dirty.

Lee's insides quivered. She pressed a thigh against the edge of her desk to steady the nerves that wanted to fly in six directions. "It's dishonest!"

Thorpe shifted till his shoulder leaned toward her like a baseball pitcher studying signals from a catcher. He jabbed the cigar butt before her nose. "It's profit. And don't you forget it!"

"Profit earned at the expense of the taxpayer . . . *and* the environment, I might add!"

"Well, bye-dee-ho!" F.A. ran his eyes around the walls of her office as if searching for something. "Too bad we ain't got

605

a stake around here so you can tie yourself to it and strike a match," he sneered.

Lee was already jerking her desk drawers open, setting her briefcase on the chair, snapping it open, separating personal items from company items.

"I refuse to be a party to your . . . your flawed materials or your scheme to qualify as a minority contractor. Why, I wouldn't be an officer of this company if Geronimo himself were president!" She piled up address book, legal pads, and portfolios in the center of her desk, each sharp slap like an exclamation point in the room.

"Geronimo wouldn't have the smarts it takes to run a business like this and turn a profit during a year as tough as this's been! In one phone call I clear a smooth ten thousand. Now what the hell kind of fool would turn down money like that?"

Lee stopped packing, rested her knuckles on the desktop, and skewered him with a feral glare. "And nobody's the wiser when five years from now the pipe breaks and untreated sewage infiltrates somebody's water supply, or . . . or runs into the Missouri River or—"

"A regular Albert Schweitzer, ain't you? Well, supposing I was to cut you in on a share of my take on this little deal, and you make me a minority contractor after all. Would a few thousand ease your conscience any?"

His cocky, self-assured belief that anybody could be bought off only sickened Lee all the more. She was suddenly very, very sure she was doing what should have been done months ago. Suddenly her anger disappeared and a renewed sense of well-being swept over her. Her lips relaxed; her voice quieted.

"Suppose it would. And what would be the next unethical thing you'd ask me to do? And the next? And how long would it be before you asked me to make the transition from unethical to illegal? You know, F.A., it isn't just the money—it's something much deeper than that. It's something born in an Indian that can't be programmed out. Call it elemental respect for the earth . . . or whatever you like. It's part of the reason I do what I do. I can't stop development or urban sprawl. But I *can* do my part to see that it doesn't completely annihilate the environment. I agree with you, Geronimo probably wouldn't be a rich man if he ran this company or one like it, but he'd probably rather drink clean water than deposit ten thousand dollars in the bank." Lee scanned her cleared desktop, then chuckled and smiled at F.A. "Come to think of it, Indians never were famous for saving for a rainy day, were they?"

Lee's belongings were piled on the desk and the chair. She snapped the briefcase shut, picked up an armful of notebooks and folders, and turned toward the door.

"But what about that bid for this afternoon?" Thorpe squawked.

"Finish it yourself."

"Girlie, you walk out of here, you give up unemployment checks, cause I ain't claimin' I laid you off. And don't look for no recommendations from—"

The outside door cut off his spate. As if his recommendation was worth anything at all around this town, Lee thought, as she headed toward the parking lot.

Her red Ford Pinto was parked right beside Thorpe's long, sleek Diamond Jubilee Mark V. The navy blue sedan was covered with a fine layer of dust, as if he'd recently driven through a jobsite. Lee dumped her load on the back seat of the Pinto, then straightened and studied Floyd's dusty status symbol. Imbedded in the glass of the opera window—still intact —was the illustrious but now lusterless diamond.

With a sardonic smile Lee leaned over, breathed on it, lifted an elbow, and polished it carefully. She stepped back to survey it critically, nodded once, then clambered into her Pinto and drove away.

But her cocky attitude had totally disappeared when, three days later, she'd turned up absolutely nothing resembling a job opening. As she paced the floor, she told herself she'd done the only thing possible. She was reviewing the miles she'd put on both her car and her feet during the past three days when her phone rang. Picking it up from the kitchen counter, the Honorable Sam Brown's was the last voice on earth she expected at the other end of the line.

"Who the hell are you trying to hide from?" he said without preamble.

"What!"

"I've been trying to get your damn phone number for three days!"

"And just who might this be?" she queried with undisguised sugar in every syllable.

"This, my little Indian, is the Honorable Sam Brown speaking. Just why in hell aren't you listed in the phone book?"

"Because I'm divorced and I don't want any obscene phone calls. And why didn't you just call Thorpe Construction for my number?"

"I did, but it seems Fat Floyd developed a conscience—belatedly, I might add—and declined to give out confidential information."

"Why that fat rat!"

"My sentiments exactly."

"So how did you get it?"

"I spent sixty-five bucks taking out a dumb redhead and buying her dinner, then plying her with a German wine because she works for Ma Bell."

Lee was dumbfounded. "You *whaaaat!*"

"And all she was good for at the end of the evening was a chaste good night kiss." He chuckled wickedly.

"I told you, Brown, I don't accept obscene phone calls."

"Too bad, cause the redhead finally gave over—your phone number, of course."

"Brown, you scheming weasel, are you saying you bribed the girl to get my unlisted number?"

"Call it what you will . . . I got it, didn't I?"

"For what?"

"I heard Fat Floyd gave you the ax."

"Well, you heard wrong. I quit."

"Bully for you. Have you got another job yet?"

"Are you kidding? I've been beatin' feet from one end of this town to the other, but it's hopeless."

"Listen, I've got a proposition for you."

"I'll just bet you do, but I'm not that desperate yet. If it's the same one you offered the redhead on her doorstep, keep it."

"You're the most suspicious woman I ever paid sixty-five dollars for, you know that?"

"And I'll bet there've been plenty, right?"

"Quit your goading, Cherokee, this is legitimate business. I'd like to talk to you about coming to work for me."

"You wh—"

"But I won't discuss it on the phone. I never carry out an interview by phone, only face to face. Are you busy tomorrow night?"

"Brown, you're crazy!"

He went on as if she hadn't spoken. "I'm busy all day tomorrow, including lunch, or we could get together then. But I'll be free by—oh, say, four thirty. Why don't we meet someplace for cocktails and discuss it then?"

"Brown, I can't come to work for you. It'd be like jumping from the pot into the fire!"

"Listen, I'd like to stay and listen to all this sweet talk, but I'm on the run as it is. Meet me at fifty-three oh-one State Line Road and we'll discuss it sensibly. Fifty-three oh-one State Line . . . got that?"

"Sam Brown, I don't trust you. What makes you think—"

But he'd done it again.

"Brown? . . . Brown, come back here!"

He'd left her with a dead receiver, and before the address escaped Lee's head, she was scrambling for a pencil.

Chapter 4

FIVE-THREE-OH-ONE State Line Road turned out to be a place so grandiose that Lee drove right past it two times without even considering it might be the right spot. It was magnificent. Perched imposingly at the crest of a hill, it dominated the view with a white facade that reminded Lee of an antebellum mansion. Staring up at it, she fully expected Scarlett O'Hara to come flouncing through the door. The horseshoe-shaped drive rose toward the building, encircling a curve of lush green grass and an imposing flower bed that provided the only clue to the building's identity—a stunning "C C" formed by vibrant red and white geraniums.

It appeared to be a country club, backing up to Ward Parkway, perhaps the most prestigious street in town with its countless fountains and mansions built by the oldest, moneyed forefathers. Lee had no doubt whatever that the place had a private membership of the highest echelon.

And Sam Brown was a member of *this?*

Leaving the car, Lee critically swished a hand over her skirt—thank God she hadn't worn slacks! Even the dress seemed less than adequate, for it was only a casual two-piece cotton outfit of brown and white stripes, the top an athletic looking slipover with ribbed waist, cap sleeves, and boatneck styling.

The shrubbery around the entrance looked artificial, it was so perfectly manicured. Tubs of potted flowers blossomed in colorful profusion on either side of the steps. Halting just short of them, Lee pulled a wand of lipgloss from her purse, checked her face in a tiny mirror, and applied a gleaming line of amber to her lips. Clamping her clutch bag beneath an elbow, she entered the "C C"—whatever it was!

She found herself in a vast room with high, wide windows off to the left through which the afternoon sun lit a tasteful grouping of antique furniture. A fireplace flanked the conversation area while enormous bouquets of silk flowers made the elegant old furniture appear even more valuable.

A discreet voice made her jump. "Ms. Walker?"

Lee turned to find a faultlessly dressed woman smiling at her from behind rimless glasses with a chain dangling from their bows. The woman looked like she might very well own the place.

"Yes?" a puzzled Lee returned.

"Ah, I thought so by Mr. Brown's description of you. You'll find him downstairs in the lounge. Just follow that stairway around and it'll take you right to him." With a graceful wave of her hand, the woman withdrew.

Lee followed the stairs as directed to find herself in a low-ceilinged bar with reduced lighting. She scarcely had time to note that Sam Brown wasn't there before a smiling black man in formal waiter's attire approached to ask, much as the woman upstairs had, "Ms. Walker?"

"Yes."

"Mr. Brown is waiting for you in the lounge, if you'll follow me."

He led the way to another elegant room much like the one upstairs, only smaller and more intimate, with soft lighting from tasteful table lamps. Again there was a fireplace on the far wall and a scattering of plush furniture placed in cozy groupings. Sam Brown stretched his tall frame up from one of the antique wing chairs flanking the fireplace.

"Here she is, Mr. Brown," the waiter announced.

"Thank you, Walter." To Lee, Sam said, "I see you found the place all right."

"Not without some trouble," she admitted, taking in his dark gaze as it swept her hair and face.

"Will the lady be wanting a cocktail?" Walter inquired.

"Yes, a Smith and Kurn," Brown answered before the waiter left them discreetly alone. Then he turned to Lee, gesturing. "Sit down, Ms. Walker."

In spite of herself she was pleased that he'd remembered her drink preference, and it tempered her voice as she chided, "Don't you Ms. Walker me, Sam Brown. Why didn't you warn me what kind of place this was?"

She perched on a Chippendale love seat while Brown chose the spot beside her rather than the chair he'd been occupying earlier. He turned sideways, lifting a knee partially onto the cushioned seat and resting his arm along its back. He scrutinized her with a half smile.

"Why? You look great, Cherokee."

"And don't call me Cherokee." She looked around furtively to see if anyone had heard, but they were alone in the lounge.

"If Ms. Walker and Cherokee are both out, what should I call you?"

She didn't know. "Try Lee," she finally suggested.

"All right, Lee, you had some trouble finding the place?"

"Trouble! I drove right past it two times and never even gave it a glance. What is it, anyway?"

"It's the Carriage Club."

"And you're a member, I take it."

"Aha." He reached for his cocktail from an oval table in front of the sofa. The entire grouping, including the pair of wing chairs, faced the fireplace, ensconcing them in a private circle of their own.

She turned her eyes to the coffee table. In addition to a bouquet of freshly cut spider mums and carnations, it held a silver bowl of macadamia nuts. Her gaze moved over richly papered walls to the polished andirons and screen in the fireplace. Slowly Lee's eyes traveled back to Sam Brown to find him studying her.

"Is this supposed to change my opinion of . . . the decadent rich?" she asked.

He shrugged, but his grin remained.

Just then Walter returned with her Smith and Kurn, set it on the table, and inquired, "And will there be anything else for you, Mr. Brown?"

"Another of the same."

As soon as Walter had faded away, Lee couldn't resist querying, "What? Aren't you going to ask for pickled mushrooms?"

"The decadent rich don't need to ask. Walter knows exactly how I prefer my drinks."

"So . . . you're a member of good standing?"

His only answer was the continued amiable expression on his face, and against her will, Lee Walker *was* thoroughly impressed.

"I came here to talk business, Mr. Brown," she said.

"Of course." He leaned forward slightly. "Unlike most of the contracting firms in this city, mine has had a good year. The plumbing half of the firm has sustained the sewer and water half until it can get on its feet. All I need is one good estimator."

"And what makes you think I'm good?"

"You damn near beat me out of that Denver job, and you did beat out an impressive lineup of competition. I want anybody who can do that working for me, not against me."

"I did beat you out, and you know it," she accused in a soft voice.

"Are we going to beat that old dead horse again?"

"I couldn't resist."

His brown eyes crinkled. Distracted, she reached for some nuts.

"Are you interested in the job offer?"

She didn't want to be, but—damn his dark eyes!—she was. Walter intruded momentarily to lean low with a silver tray, and even over his back Lee could feel Sam Brown's eyes following her hand as she lifted the nuts to her mouth, then licked away the salt that caught on her glossy lipstick.

She raised her eyes to confront him head on. "I want you to know right off the bat—I don't do anybody's dirty work. I bid 'em straight and fair."

"I'll pay you forty thousand a year, plus a company car and all the usual fringe benefits—profit sharing, insurance, use of a company credit card."

While shock waves catapulted through Lee, she watched Sam lazily stir his drink, then lift a red plastic saber upon

613

which four pickled mushrooms were skewered. His sparkling teeth slipped the first mushroom into his mouth, and his jaws began moving while hers went slack.

"Forty thousand a year?" The words scarcely peeped from her throat.

"Mmm-hmm." His eyes lingered indolently on hers as he clamped those perfect teeth around the second mushroom. Mesmerized, still not quite able to absorb his offer, she watched as he ate all four mushrooms.

Forty thousand dollars!

"You must be joking."

"Not at all. You'll work damn hard for it. If I say travel, you'll travel. We're bidding jobs in about eight states right now. Sometimes there'll be late nights if we're up against a deadline. Other times there'll be night flights in order to get connections to the right city. I pay my estimators well, but they earn every cent of it."

She was still too stunned to take it all in. "I don't even know where your offices are."

"On the other side of the creek, near Rainbow and Johnson Drive. I'll take you over later to see them, if you like."

Again she was astonished. The area he'd named was well known as one of the most prestigious in the city. It was generally referred to as the Plaza Area, named after the lush Country Club Plaza Shopping Center nearby. She was still pondering this when Sam Brown pulled a tie from the pocket of his blue linen sport coat, though she was so lost in thought she scarcely realized what he was doing. Without the aid of a mirror, he raised his collar, lay the tie underneath, buttoned his collar button, and began applying a Windsor knot to the tie by feel. Though her eyes were fixed on his hands, she was thinking instead of the pair of widewale corduroy armchairs she wanted so badly, thinking of the drapes she could pay off in no time, thinking of not having to give up the townhouse.

The ever-attentive Walter appeared as if out of nowhere. "Will there be anything more, Mr. Brown?"

"Ms. Walker and I will go into dinner now, Walter. Thank you."

"Of course, sir. I'll bring your drinks for you."

Lee finally slipped out of her reverie to realize that Sam

Brown was slipping a hand under her elbow and urging her to her feet. They followed at Walter's heels. "House rules," Sam whispered conspiratorially. "Men have to wear ties in the dining room."

Lee made a feeble attempt to pull away from his commanding grasp. This is all too perfect. It's going too fast!

"I'm not dressed—"

"You're dressed just fine." His eyes swept her from hair to her waist, and up again.

She felt obligated to resist one more time. "But . . . but I haven't even said I'd work for you, much less won a bid yet. And you invited me for a drink, not dinner."

He only grinned down at her cheek, squeezed the soft, bare skin of her inner elbow, and teased, "Let a man try to impress a lady when he's trying his damndest, okay, Cherokee?"

That word, perhaps more than any other, brought her back down to earth. Cherokee. But it was too late now. They'd reached the dining room doorway, which opened off the lounge. She felt helpless as she was propelled along beside him. His thumb was rough on her bare skin as they paused just inside, and he was again greeted by name. "Evening, Mr. Brown . . . ma'am. Your table is all ready." The man escorted them to a linen-covered table in front of a wide window that curved in a semicircle around half of the dining room. Lee looked onto a view of the swimming pool, ice rink, and tennis courts below. In the distance a line of tall trees indicated the meandering route of Brush Creek as it flowed eastward. The sun was slanting across the green lawn, from which Lee had difficulty pulling her eyes.

A nudge on the back of her knees reminded her that Sam Brown was solicitously waiting to push in her chair.

"Oh . . . thank you." She settled herself, subjected to the tantalizing scent that wafted about him as he sat down across from her. He had no more than hit the chair when yet another solicitous employee of the Carriage Club was immediately at hand to state, "The evening special is shrimp marinated in wine sauce, seasoned with tarragon and served with herb butter. And how are you this evening, Mr. Brown?" Menus were opened crisply and placed first in Lee's hands, then Sam's.

He raised his dark brows, and a smile lifted his lips.

"Hungry as a bear, Edward, and how are you?"

Edward leaned back and laughed softly. "I'm fine, sir. Leaving on my vacation tomorrow morning for my son's house in Tucson. He's got a new baby, you know, and we've never seen her."

"I imagine it's a little hard to keep your mind on marinated shrimp then, isn't it?"

"For you, sir, not at all. Service is the same as always."

They laughed together in the way of men who go through this ritual often. Lee noted the same camaraderie between Brown and yet another man who brought them goblets of ice water.

When they were alone with their menus at last, Lee admitted, "I am impressed, Brown. How could I help but be?"

"Tell me that when you've seen me in action in the office and it'll mean something."

She looked for signs of teasing and saw none.

This man, this Sam Brown, what did she know of him? Was he honorable or a scoundrel? Was his poise in these elegant surroundings an intentional smoke screen to hide his seamier side? He could charm the gold out of a person's teeth—she had no doubt about that—but could he also be ruthless? He was handsome enough to turn any woman's head, and that fact made it more difficult to assess his hidden traits. After all, she was making a business decision, and what he looked like had absolutely no bearing upon his character or his motives. Studying him now, Lee entwined her fingers, pressed her arms along the table edge, and bent forward until her breasts touched her wrists.

"Level with me, Brown. Would you hire me with the ulterior motive of exploiting me, like Thorpe did?"

She watched his eyes carefully as they registered faint surprise at her direct question, then glinted with brief amusement before that too disappeared and he asked matter-of-factly, "Could it be, Ms. Walker, that you have a hang-up about being Indian?" Immediately she bristled, but before she could respond he went on. "I did a little checking on you. You're good, you're honest, you're young and ambitious. A man could do worse than hire a person like that as an estimator, especially when his corporation has all its officers intact.

Besides that, it wouldn't be far for you to drive. That's always to an employer's advantage."

His answer set her back in her chair. "How do you know where I live?"

Again a glint of amusement filled his eyes. "You forget. Your suitcase had a tag on its handle just like mine did."

Of course! How could she forget what had led her here in the first place? Yet it was disconcerting to think he'd been asking people about her.

"Tell me, Mr. Brown," she began, "is there anything you don't know about me?"

He looked up from his menu and she became uncomfortably aware that she was wearing a necklace shaped like an Indian arrowhead strung around her neck on a leather thong. But his eyes returned to his menu as he answered, "Yes, I don't know why you bother to order your meals without potatoes when you don't need to. The food here is tremendous. Don't stint yourself tonight."

His answer raised an instant prickle of female vanity, but she warned herself to accept the compliment with a grain of salt. Just then the waiter approached to take their order.

The meal was delicious, as promised. They ate it while discussing upcoming jobs Sam would want her to bid, projects she had worked on, nothing more personal until, over coffee, he sat back with one shoulder drooping lower than the other in a way with which she was already becoming familiar.

"Actually, there is a question about you that puzzles me," he said.

She looked up, waiting.

"Why don't you have records of employment before Thorpe Construction?"

"I do. They're in St. Louis."

"St. Louis?" Sam quirked an eyebrow.

"Yes, that's where I lived before."

"Before what?" Though his eyes rested lightly on her, she had the feeling he was drilling into her head.

"Before I moved here three years ago," she answered with deliberate evasion.

"Ah." He tilted his chin up, and for a moment she thought he might question her further, but just then the waiter arrived and laid a small tray at Sam Brown's elbow and handed him a silver pen.

"Excuse me, Mr. Brown, your tab." Sam scrawled a quick signature and rose to his feet.

"Come on, I'll show you the office."

Lee breathed a sigh of relief at the interruption, for the subject of St. Louis was not one she wanted to pursue.

As they moved past the tables toward the doorway, they were interrupted by an impeccably dressed man who leaned back in a chair, half turning to extend a hand. "How's it going, Sam?"

"Fine. Took a job in Denver last week." Brown released his hold on Lee's elbow to shake hands, then politely performed introductions.

"Cassie and Don Norris . . . Lee Walker, my newest estimator."

Lee considered spouting a denial aloud, but instead she politely shook hands with the Norrises.

"Well, congratulations, Lee. You've chosen a damn fine company there," Don Norris offered. She murmured some comment, surprised at his unsolicited praise and hoping it was true. A moment later Sam urged her toward the door again.

As they moved through the lounge, she couldn't resist glancing up at Sam. "Your new estimator? Aren't you being a little presumptuous?"

Sam smiled and shrugged. "It eliminated a lengthy explanation. I could have said you were the woman who stole my suitcase in the Denver airport. Would that have been better?"

Lee turned to hide her grin as they reached the main lobby, crossed to the door, and stepped outside.

"You can ride with me," he suggested. "It's not far, and I can bring you back to your car afterward."

He led her to a classy, off-white Toronado. Inside, the car smelled like him—the agreeably masculine and tangy scent of what she took to be Rawhide cosmetics. The front seat was luxurious, equipped with a stereo that filled the void while they drove in the waning summer evening.

It had been a long time since Lee had been in a car with an attractive man—and Sam Brown was certainly that! She watched the contour of his wrist draped over the steering wheel, the gleam of a gold watch peeking from beneath his sleeve, the relaxed fingers with dark skin and well-kept nails. She recalled the pleasant meal they'd just shared, his easygoing camaraderie with everyone at the club, the compliment Norris had dropped in passing, Brown's glib sense of humor. She ventured a brief study of his hair, an ear, the side of his neck, but then his face swung her way and she looked quickly out her side window.

No doubt about it—she was beginning to like Sam Brown.

The office complex was new, modern, and pleasing to the eye. The late sun, slanting across its cinnamon-colored brick walls and smoked-glass windows, created deep triangles of shadow, accentuating the beauty of the buildings' architectural design. In keeping with Kansas City's claim that it had more fountains than any other city in the world except Rome, the buildings had been designed around a charming esplanade whose main attraction was a fountain whose running water created a design reminiscent of a dandelion gone to seed.

Sam guided Lee along curved concrete walks past cherry trees, and yews and more, every shrub so well-kept it appeared they were tended by a beautician instead of a gardener. The sprinkler system had come on, and as they sauntered between the buildings Lee breathed in the pungent scent of wet cedar chips clustered at the base of the decorative plants. Redwood benches had been placed strategically along the walks, and even the trash depositories were built of redwood, blending pleasantly into the environment. Tall ash trees had been planted alongside each building.

Sam unlocked the lobby door and held it open while Lee entered a spacious foyer carpeted in burnt orange. The stairs were carpeted as well and seemed to drop out of nowhere into the center of the lobby. A rich walnut handrail was smooth beneath Lee's palm as she ran her hand along it appreciatively.

If she'd expected Brown to be a smalltime hood, his surroundings were suggesting otherwise.

At Suite 204 he fitted a key into the lock, pushed the walnut door inward, and held it also as she passed before him. Fluorescent lights came on, flooding the reception area.

Lee glanced around nervously. There was something so gloomy and deserted about the silent, empty office. The room was decorated in tones of blue, from royal to wedgwood, and the walls were hung with posters depicting various moments in the company's history. They were framed in aluminum, fronted with glass, and hung on rich vinyl wallcovering that matched upholstered chairs and smoked-glass tables, where various construction magazines and equipment brochures lay.

The chink of keys brought Lee's attention back to Sam.

"This is obviously the reception area," he said, motioning her ahead of him around a free-standing wall that formed the backdrop for the receptionist's desk.

The payroll office was the first cubicle behind the wall. Inside, a computer hummed softly and photographs of two toddlers stood on a desk.

"The computer runs day and night," Sam informed Lee. "All our payroll and parts inventory are stored in it."

There was a separate office for the bookkeeper and his assistant, followed by a large open area, also carpeted in deep blue, where slant-topped drafting tables were lined up. The arrangement preserved an overall feeling of space, for the smoky windows ran nearly ceiling to floor, and the sight of the ash trees outside helped bring the outdoors in. The suite was at the southeast corner of the building, thus the fading sun left this area dimly lit, for Sam hadn't turned on the overhead lights here.

"This is where our draftsmen work," he explained unnecessarily. Lee was ever conscious of him hovering a step behind her. Occasionally the soft clink of keys told her how near he was. She looked across the pleasant, orderly expanse. Wide racks of blueprints hung neatly, like sheets on a clothesline. There were no rolled, wrinkled, or torn plans in sight. There were no chunks of dried clay on the carpet, no coffee-can cuspidors. "That's the copy room." Sam pointed, and Lee turned her head in time to catch the vague movement of his arm before he moved through the drafting area into a separate corner office. In the doorway he turned again to her, his stance inviting her in.

"Yours?" she asked.

He nodded.

Just inside the door she stopped, tingles of appreciation

running along her arms. The room was neat and orderly, and Lee couldn't help comparing it to Floyd Thorpe's pigpen. A modest-sized executive desk stood to one side, a credenza under the window. There was a game table, surrounded by rich leather armchairs on ball castors, which was obviously used as a conference table. The floor was carpeted in rich chocolate, the windows treated with vertical blinds of a lighter shade. Here again, plans and blueprints hung on neat racks. A tall schefflera plant stood in the corner where east and south-facing windows met.

Lee crossed to the south window and looked out. A moment later her nostrils were again filled with Sam's scent as he stepped behind her and pointed past the treetops. "That's where we were." From here she could see only the tip of the Carriage Club's main building. "Most of the time I move in a rather confined area."

"But a very pleasant one," she noted, turning and laying her fingertips on the polished surface of his desk. Her eyes met his, but there was no hint of teasing in them this time. "I like it very much."

The expression on his face told Lee it was one thing he'd wanted to hear. His fingers relaxed and the keys clinked softly.

"Would you like to see the estimating area?"

"I thought you'd never ask."

A smile broke on his face like sun over the horizon, and he led the way to another wide expanse much like that where the drafting tables were. Here the tables were flat and of desk height. The southern exposure gave the estimating area the same view as that from Sam's office. Lee looked out, thinking again of the three years she'd worked in Floyd Thorpe's office, wondering if she could possibly be wrong about Sam Brown's character, knowing it was fast losing importance in light of his fantastic offer and this enticing office.

"You're the first full-time estimator I've hired for the new portion of the business, so there's no designated area for you," Sam explained. "You'll just work in here with the plumbing estimators, if that's all right with you."

"Oh . . ." She turned from the window. "That's more than

621

all right, as I'm sure you're well aware. I've never seen a contractor's office as plush as this. But I'm sure you're well aware of that, too."

"Just because you dig in dirt for a living doesn't mean you have to live in it."

"No, not at all. Somebody should tell that to Floyd Thorpe."

He turned and indicated a desk across the way. "That would be yours."

The desks were placed in herringbone relationship to one another, giving the room an even more spacious aspect. Beside the desk Sam was pointing to stood a potted orange tree, that seemed to be thriving.

Lee crossed to *her* desk, pulled out *her* chair, and touched *her* orange tree. The chair rolled silently on a large slab of clear vinyl that protected the blue carpet. She sat down, and placed her palms flat on the desk top as if to test its temperature. A feeling of imminent excitement tightened her chest. My God, it was like a dream come true. She looked up at Sam, standing some distance across the room, watching every move she made.

"I think it fits." Accepting his offer, she was filled with anticipation.

"Agreed." He raised a hand and beckoned her over to him. "Come on, I'll drive you back to your car. You'll be spending enough time in that chair without staying in it now."

She pushed the chair back beneath the desk and moved to him. This time he didn't touch her, but before they rounded the corner she turned back, taking one last look at her desk.

Back in his car she didn't hear the music, didn't feel the plush seat, didn't watch his wrist on the wheel. She was too excited.

"My God, Brown, did you do all that or did your father?"

"He made it possible for me to do it. We didn't have that office until after he died."

She paused. "I imagine he would have loved it as much as I do."

"He was content at the old location," Sam said. "My mother was the one who encouraged me to move into the new building and add a touch of class to the operation. It turned out we'd made too damn much profit one year. The overhead became a healthy tax write-off after we rented this new place. Meanwhile we enjoy the surroundings."

"You know what I want to do the first day of work?" Lee rested her head back against the luxurious seat and closed her eyes.

"What?"

She rolled her head toward Sam and opened her eyes to find him studying the curve of her arched throat. "I want to bring my sack lunch and sit by that fountain and eat at high noon."

He laughed pleasantly, and she watched his lips change with the sound. "Whatever turns you on. There are several good restaurants in the complex—"

"Restaurants! Where's your sense of . . . of nature!"

"I get all the nature I need during the day. I spend more than half my time at jobsites. My old man taught me that's the only way to run a business—by keeping your eye on what's happening instead of leaving it up to someone else. At noon I like to go where it's cool and not dusty and let somebody serve me a decent meal on a plate."

Lee couldn't help wondering if he went out on the job dressed like that. His brown shoes certainly didn't look like they'd scuffed any dust today.

Just then, the Toronado turned into the horseshoe driveway of the Carriage Club, and Lee straightened in her seat. Brown swung the car into a parking spot, and before she could protest he was out his side and heading around to open her door. She beat him to the punch and met him beside the car.

He turned and together they ambled across the lot. "When do you want to start?" he asked.

She stopped him with a hand on his sleeve. "Brown, there's just one thing I have to ask for even before I say I'll take the job."

"What's that?"

She swallowed, knowing that what she had to ask was presumptuous. "I . . . I have to have the last week of August off." This was the last week of July—she knew it was a lot to ask. Nobody in the construction industry took time off during the busy summer season. As she stood waiting for Sam's response, she feared, too, that he might demand the reason for her request and sought frantically for a white lie. But in the end she had no need to produce one.

"Shouldn't be any problem," Sam said, "but usually we take vacations during the cold months when there's not much going on." He began moving on, but Lee grabbed his arm.

"Oh, I didn't mean I expect it off with pay! It's just..." She grew self-conscious holding his arm and dropped her hand.

"It's okay. As far as I can remember, there won't be any important bids around that time, so you can plan on it as yours."

"Thank you. In that case, back to your original question." She braved a sheepish smile. "Would Monday be too soon to start?"

He chuckled, came back to where she trailed along behind him, and lightly pressed a palm against the small of her back. "Are you that eager to work for this ... reprobate?" he teased.

Moving toward her car, she admitted artlessly, "I need to make the house payment next week, just like you do." She was far too aware of the warmth of his palm through the thin knit of her top, but then it disappeared.

"I don't make house payments. I live in the old family rattrap with my mother."

This was the second time he'd mentioned his mother, and Lee couldn't help but wonder. Another case of apron strings? Though she'd never have thought it of Sam Brown, she'd learned her lesson once with Joel. Furthermore, Sam wasn't the only one who'd done some calculating after reading an address on a suitcase. The family "rattrap" of which he spoke was on exclusive Ward Parkway. She didn't have to see the house to imagine what it must be like.

"Speaking of rattraps"—they'd reached her Pinto—"this one is mine."

He gave it a cursory glance, then returned his attention to her. "Is there anything else you need to know about the job?"

"Nothing I can think of. Oh, what are office hours?"

"On a normal day I usually come in around seven and knock off at five."

There seemed little more to say, and while she studied Sam Brown's expression, it ceased to say "business" and took on the distinctly alarming look of "pleasure."

A slow hand reached for the silver arrowhead necklace that rested against her chest, still warm from her skin, and his eyes followed. His fingers closed around it, and she thought she felt the thong tighten at the back of her neck.

Panic clawed its way up to her throat. She wanted to say "Brown, don't!" for she thought he was going to kiss her and, since he was about to become her boss, she couldn't let him set such a dangerous precedent. She wanted his job, but no other complications. Besides, he lived on Ward Parkway in the family "rattrap" with his mother . . . and . . . and . . . oh God, Brown, you smell so good . . . let go . . .

But she was never to know Sam Brown's intentions, for a moment later he dropped the arrowhead against her chest and turned away before an enormous sneeze erupted from him.

Lee was laughing before the second sneeze clutched him. He tugged a hanky from his hip pocket, rubbed his nose, and stepped back three feet.

"You and your damn Renaldo la Pizzio!"

Even though she jammed her hands on her hips, Lee was still amused as she scolded, "Oh, you had yourself a regular heyday with my private belongings, didn't you?"

"I could order you to get rid of it before you show up at the office."

"You could, but you won't. After all, they write exposés in Washington about orders like that."

But even as she chuckled, her body felt weak with relief, for if he *had* tried to kiss her, she wasn't sure how long she'd have resisted.

Chapter 5

THE NIGHT BEFORE her first day of work, Lee slept in that tenuous half-conscious state she often experienced before a day promising something special—a thin, filmy kind of sleep during which the excitement somehow managed to keep her so nearly alert that the morning alarm was stifled before its bell gave out more than a ting. She lay staring at the ceiling, which was tinted pale pink by the rising sun, and said in amazement, "Forty thousand dollars a year, can you beat that?"

Then she was on her feet, eagerness in every step as she switched on the radio, showered, washed her hair, took a sinful amount of time styling it, then applied her makeup. Her head was tilted back, a mascara wand darkening her stubby lashes, when she suddenly straightened, stared at her reflection, smiled, and told the woman in the mirror, "An orange tree . . . You have an orange tree by your desk!" Then the woman in the mirror replied, "Damn fool, Walker, finish your primping or you'll be late on your first day."

Lee considered long and hard before deciding between a warm rose slack outfit and a white slim skirt with a matching peplumed jacket. She chose the skirt in deference to the classy office, the white in deference to her own deep coloring. It complemented her dark skin and black hair so strikingly that Lee felt thoroughly pleased with her appearance when she was all dressed. The straight skirt added to her height and the peplum added to her hips—an altogether flattering combo.

After adding a single white bangle bracelet that matched white hoops in her ears, she was satisfied.

But as she smoothed the skirt one last time over her hips, she confronted her reflection in the mirror again and a worried frown formed between her eyebrows. Had she dressed so carefully to please Sam Brown? The possibility was disturbing. She dropped her eyes to the photographs of Jed and Matthew in a hinged frame on her dresser top. The familiar stab of loss cut through her momentarily, then she was removing the black combs that held her hair behind each ear, replacing them defiantly with others that trailed small, bronze feathers to the backs of her jaws.

You are what you are, Lee Walker, and you'd be wise not to forget it!

In the office Sam Brown seemed to scarcely notice what she was wearing. The sleeves of his plaid shirt were already rolled up past the elbows, and he held a set of plans in his hand. Though he greeted Lee with a pleasant, "Good morning . . . all set to meet the gang?" it was all business with Sam Brown.

Three others were already there when Lee arrived. Sam immediately introduced her as "the first permanent employee of the sewer and water division." Rachael Robinson, the office's gal friday, was efficient and energetic. She wore a pale yellow dress that looked smashing against her black skin and conveyed a very *now* look.

Immediately Lee could tell Frank Schultz was Sam Brown's right-hand man. Schultz was the head estimator of plumbing and had been working with Sam on the few sewer and water jobs they'd bid so far. A bull-headed Irishman named Duke was head superintendent of the outside crews, and under him worked several foremen who remained voices on the radio much of the time. Ron Chen was head book-keeper, a small Chinese man with thick glasses and an ingratiating smile. His second in command was his own twenty-year-old daughter, Terri, who worked part time and attended the University of Missouri at Kansas City the rest of the week. The computer was manned by an older, portly woman named Nelda Huffman, who looked more like a cleaning lady than a payroll clerk. The pictures on Nelda's desk proved to be of her grandchildren.

By the time all the employees of Brown & Brown had begun their work day, Lee Walker felt as if she were in the amphitheater of the United Nations Building! She realized that nobody here would notice a feather in her hair, although Rachael did comment on how stylish it was.

Brown & Brown was a pleasant change from Thorpe Construction. Though Lee didn't have her own office as she'd had previously, she didn't mind a bit. Among the entire office crew there was a noticeable camaraderie that made up for the lack of privacy. And the atmosphere was so harmonious, the decor so tasteful, that Lee felt almost childishly eager to do well, learn fast, and prove her abilities so she could feel justified in taking over the desk and the orange tree.

At coffee break the copy room became a gathering spot. It contained not only copying and duplicator machines, but also a refrigerator, microwave oven, and coffee percolator that was kept constantly replenished by Rachael, who seemed to be the office staff's cheerful "ladybug." Everyone seemed to like her.

The day began with a short session at which Sam Brown, Frank Schultz, and Rachael discussed helping Lee learn her way around the place. After Lee had filled out the usual new-employee forms, Frank explained the general bidding procedure, psychology, and ratio of profit on which they worked.

Sam was gone at noon, and Lee ate her sack lunch by the fountain, feeling totally refreshed when she returned. She saw Sam again late in the afternoon when he came in briefly, dusty leather workboots and khaki-colored jeans attesting to his having been out in the field. When Frank Schultz began cleaning off his desk top at the end of the afternoon, Lee couldn't believe it was going on five o'clock already. The day had raced by so fast it seemed as if she'd just walked in the door!

The following morning she, Sam, and Frank worked together on a small bid. Immediately Lee saw that changes here were discussed sensibly before being made. No last minute surprises were sprung unless it was by mutual agreement. They talked together about upcoming jobs listed in *The Construction Bulletin* and decided which ones Lee should order plans for. Sam asked if Frank would have time the following day to take Lee out and show her around the jobs in progress so she could get a handle on the equipment the company owned, and also give her a complete inventory of it so she knew exactly what work capacity they could handle.

The third day, she and Frank drove in a company pickup, from jobsite to jobsite. At each, Lee was introduced to crew members and foremen alike.

Walking into the skeleton of a two-story steel-frame building, Lee was surprised to see Sam Brown, in hardhat and workboots, waving hello. He picked his way across pipes and fittings, removing a pair of soiled leather workgloves as he came.

"Got troubles, boss?" Frank inquired.

"Naw, nothing Duke can't handle." Sam smiled over his shoulder as Lee heard Duke in the background, his voice like the roar of a bull elephant, telling some laborer to jack that son of a bitch up and see she didn't bust again or his ass'd be higher than the goddam water table! Lee was laughing as Sam turned back to her. The rough language of construction superintendents was nothing new to her.

"Everything going okay so far, Lee?" Sam's question was simple and inconsequential, nothing at all to make her heart jump. Maybe it was the ordinary way he'd called her Lee, or the way he lifted his hardhat off the back of his head and mopped his forehead with a sleeve that sent her pulse racing.

"Not a single complaint," she answered. "We've been to all the jobsites but one. I'm getting a good idea of how much equipment the company has, but I can see there's not much in the way of heavy stuff."

"We've leased most of the heavy stuff up till now and we'll continue to do that until we're sure we want to stay in the sewer and water work," Sam explained.

"A couple of the jobs we discussed yesterday would require a nine-eighty front-end loader and I haven't seen one yet."

"I know. We don't own one. The biggest we've got is a nine-fifty. That's why I wanted you to make the rounds with Frank. I've got some decisions to make about buying new equipment, and I want you in on them." There was something

629

elemental about him standing in the hot sun with a dusty boot on a section of pipe, settling the hardhat back on his head, then tugging back on the filthy leather gloves. His rolled-up sleeves exposed arms tanned to a cinnamon hue with hair bleached almost red by the sun. A bead of sweat trickled from under the hardhat along his temple, and Lee looked away.

In the background a machine started up, and Sam shouted to be heard above the noise. "Frank, could you run out to the Independence City Hall and pick up a set of plans for that Little Blue River job?"

"Sure, Sam. We'll be over that direction anyway."

"Good. Lee and I will run out and take a look at it Friday morning." At the mention of her name, she turned back to the trickle of sweat, but it had become no less irresistible, collecting dust as it moved downward. It drew her eyes as if it were whitewater on the Colorado River rather than a single droplet flowing along a man's hairline.

She pulled her eyes away again, hoping Sam hadn't noticed the direction of her gaze. At first she thought he hadn't, but in the end she wasn't sure, for as Frank pulled the pickup away from the bumpy construction site, Lee looked back over her shoulder to discover Sam standing where they'd left him, his feet planted firmly apart, his eyes following them.

On Thursday, just before Lee left for the day, Sam stopped by her desk. "It's been a helluva busy week. Sorry I haven't been around much."

Lee's elbows were propped on the desk top as she leaned over a long jobsheet. Turning, she almost bumped against Sam's thigh, he'd been standing so close. She tipped her chair back to look up at him.

"Frank has taken good care of me. The week's been great."

Sam crossed his arms, leaned against the edge of her desk, and stretched his legs out in front of him. "Good, glad to hear it. Listen, would you mind wearing something . . ." For a moment his eyes fell to her bare knee where her skirt was hitched up slightly. "Well, put on some slacks tomorrow, okay? We'll probably be walking through some rough stuff when we go out to look at that job."

"Sure, whatever you say."

"Have you got any boots?" Now his eyes drifted down her calves to the sling-back high heels on her feet.

"Aha. Got just the thing."

"Good. Bring 'em along. We'll be going out first thing in the morning, and the dew can be heavy."

"Anything else?"

"Yeah." For the first time he glanced up to give a quick survey of the room, but several desks were already empty, and nobody who remained paid them any attention. His gaze returned to Lee. "Have you been bringing those sack lunches like you said?"

"Every day. The fountain is delightful with cheese on rye."

"Could you make enough for two tomorrow?" His eyes softened as he smiled down at her.

"Of course. What's the occasion?"

"No occasion. We might end up someplace out in the boonies at lunchtime, so if you'll bring the food, I'll bring us some cola in a cooler."

"Friday is bologna and pickle day."

"Sweet or dill?"

"Dill."

"Sold." He stood up. "See you here at eight."

The following morning dawned murky and muggy after a night of intermittent thundershowers. Low, gray clouds hid the sunrise, and the thick, sultry air seemed cloyingly sticky.

She dressed in blue jeans, tennis shoes, and a casual cotton knit pullover of navy and white stripes with a sailor collar and a ribbed waist, and took along a pair of rubber, lace-up duck hunting boots, a can of mosquito spray, and a brown paper bag containing three bologna sandwiches, potato chips, pickles, and some chocolate chip cookies.

She and Sam set out right after he returned from his morning rounds of all the jobs. He stopped at Rachael's desk to advise her where they'd be. "If you need us, give a call on the radio."

"Right, boss."

"We'll take my truck," Sam informed Lee as they crossed the parking lot toward a sleek pickup identifiable by its stan-

631

dard company color—a rich, metallic brown with the logo
B & B in white on its doors. Sam looked down at Lee's feet.

"Didn't you bring any boots?"

"They're in my car. Be right back." She was only too
happy to move away from Sam Brown, for her eyes, too, had
meandered down the length of his strong legs, and the sight of
them was altogether too compelling. What was it about him?
Whenever she was close to him her thoughts strayed to his
masculinity, ever since that first night in Denver when she'd
found his magazine.

He'd backed the pickup around and was waiting when she
turned from the Pinto with full hands. This time her eyes were
arrested by the sight of his long, bronzed arm in its white
rolled-up sleeve as he stretched across the truck seat to push
the door open for her. *Shape up, Lee Walker, and think business!* Dragging her thoughts back to safer footing, she clambered up onto the high seat beside him and dumped her
collection on the floor.

A roll of plans, his workgloves and hardhat lay between
them, and with a murmured apology, Sam scooped them
closer to his hip to make more room for her.

"It's okay," Lee assured him, flashing him a quick smile.

But it wasn't okay. There was something too close about
the relatively confining space of the single seat. And—dammit!—did Sam Brown's vehicles always have to smell like
him? It was his world, this masculine domain of hardhats,
laced-up leather boots, and pickups with column shifts.

"I'll drive, you navigate," Sam ordered as they started out.
Almost gratefully, Lee opened the wide set of plans and studied the map. But even so, she found herself too aware of the
tan arm with its relaxed wrist that shifted gears, the hand
vibrating on the stick. Covertly she watched the tightening of
muscles beneath the left leg of his blue jeans as he raised it to
press in the clutch. He was a runner, she remembered, and
supposed those muscles were hard and well toned. The denim
fit his leg like a rind fits an orange.

Suddenly she realized they were sitting still and raised her
eyes from Sam's leg to find he'd been watching her. For how
long? She felt herself turning as red as the light that had
stopped them as he smiled lazily.

"I see you brought the bologna sandwiches." His face was stunningly dark against the open collar of his white shirt, and it did foolish things to the pit of her stomach.

"As ordered. Where's the Coke?" she managed to ask in a surprisingly normal voice.

He gestured with a shoulder and a lift of his chin. "In the back." His lazy eyes made her feel light-headed, but just then the light changed and they rolled forward. Sam's gaze moved away from her, and she returned to navigating.

"Exit on Two ninety-one south," she ordered.

"Two ninety-one south," he repeated. Then there was only the high whine of the wheels on the blacktop and the shuddering jiggle rising up through the seat beneath Lee as they rode silently. She watched the riffling of his shirtsleeves in the wind from the opened window, then studied the view beyond her own, striving to feel at ease in his presence.

Suddenly Rachael's voice crackled across the radio. "Base to unit one. Come in, Sam."

From the corner of her eye, Lee watched him pluck the mike from the dash. His index finger curled around the call button and the mike almost touched his lips. "Unit one, Sam here. Go ahead, Rachael."

"I've got a long-distance call from Denver. It's Tom Weatherall returning your call, so I thought you'd want to know."

"It's nothing important, just an inquiry I made about an equipment auction that's coming up. Tell him I'll get back to him on Monday."

"Right, boss . . . base clear."

"Thanks, Rachael. Unit one clear."

The white shirtsleeve strained diagonally across Sam's upper arm as he replaced the mike, and Lee turned her eyes resolutely away, again resisting the urge to study him. But to her chagrin, she found she need not look to remember. He was dressed in blue jeans, white shirt, and leather boots—no different from what a thousand laboring men wore every day. Yet he looked better than a thousand men, the basic no-nonsense work clothes lending him a magnetic sex appeal totally different from the dress slacks and sport coat he'd worn the first few times she'd seen him.

Keep your mind on your map, Walker, he didn't even kiss you.

They turned off 291 at her directions and took increasingly smaller roads until they came to a gravel road that led out into the country. "I think this is it." Lee pointed to an abandoned farm off to their right.

The pickup swerved to the side of the road to idle again while Sam hooked his left elbow over the steering wheel, rested his right hand along the back of the seat, and peered out her window. She was served up a tantalizing whiff of his aftershave as his knuckles passed before her face and he pointed.

"Looks like it'll start just this side of those trees and move off across the edge of that field. We might as well get out and walk it."

Lee was only too glad to escape the close proximity to Sam Brown, and she jumped from the cab with a shaky, indrawn breath of relief. She sat down on the running board to untie her tennis shoes and replace them with the olive drab waterproof boots, conscious now that Sam was standing with his hands on his hips watching her. She tucked her pantlegs into the boot tops, but left the yellow strings dangling. Still he stood, his weight balanced evenly on both feet, making her skin prickle with awareness. It had been a long time since a man had watched her change her clothes, even any as impersonal as shoes, and this man seemed to be studying the process all too closely. She straightened, got to her feet, and gave her ribbed waistband a businesslike tug to pull it back into place. His face wore a disturbingly appre- ciative half grin, his gaze centered on the thin band of skin at her waist, which quickly disappeared as she adjusted her shirt.

"What are you staring at, Brown?" she demanded.

He seemed to shake himself back to the present. "Estimators look different than they used to," he teased.

Keep it light, her saner self warned as his comment aroused a small thrill. She displayed one foot, lifting it before her. "Same as you, jeans and boots."

But as his eyes traveled down to her boots, she realized that instead of minimizing her femininity, they accented it. To her relief, at that moment Sam's hand slapped at his neck, then he made a grab at the air, missing the mosquito that had just bitten him.

"Come here, I'll give you a spray." Lee picked up the can from the floor of the truck.

With a grin, he noted, "You come prepared, don't you?"

"In Missouri, in August, the morning after a healthy rain?" she asked pointedly. He came to stand before her while she shook the can and sprayed the front of him in long sweeps from neck to boots, noting even in that quick journey certain spots where his jeans were more worn. *Damn you, Walker, what's the matter with you?* "Turn around, I'll do your back." But his back presented as enticing a set of muscles as his front. His shoulders were wide and firm as she sprayed them, heading down toward where his shirt scarcely crinkled as it disappeared into the narrow waist of his jeans. His buns were so flat that they scarcely curved beneath the denim. Again she remembered that he was a runner. It seemed a long, long way down to his wide-spread boots.

He craned to look at her over his shoulder. "Hurry up. This stuff stinks."

As she stood up, she couldn't resist teasing. "Don't be such a baby, Brown. I don't think it smells so bad." And as if to prove the point, she gave him a shot inside the back of his collar, then pulled the can farther back and emitted a cloud at the back of his head. He doubled forward and let out an immense sneeze.

She burst out laughing as he moved out of range and whirled.

"Damn it all, if it isn't one thing it's another."

She puckered her face and feigned an apology. "Oh, I'm so-o-o sorry."

A wicked grin lifted his mouth as he returned wryly, "Yes, I can see just how sorry you are."

He took a menacing step toward her, and she backed away. "Now, Brown, it was an accident!" she warned, holding out a hand to fend him off. But he advanced a step farther.

"So will this be." He wrenched the can from her hand and shook it, a gleam of menace in his eye.

"Brown, I'm warning you!"

"You started it, now stand and take your medicine."

There was nothing she could do but turn her back on him, squeeze her eyes shut, and wait. He took his sweet time about it, while she grew increasingly uncomfortable. Finally she felt the spray at the back of her neck. Then it moved downward and stopped at her hips. "Put your arms up," he ordered. She gritted her teeth, did as ordered, but immediately realized her mistake, for when her arms went up, so did the shirt. A long moment passed in silence, and she felt herself beginning to blush. Then the hiss of the spray finished its trip down her backside, and he nudged her with the can, ordering, "Turn around." She spun about, chancing a quick peek at the top of his hair as he hunkered down before her, but quickly shutting her eyes as the cloud of spray moved upward. It stopped again, at her hips, and she suffered an agonizing moment, wondering what he was doing before a direct shot hit her in her bare navel.

She yelped and jumped backward. "Damn you, Brown!"

He chuckled devilishly. "I couldn't resist."

She glared at him as he knelt on one knee, his eyes nearly on a level with the ribbed waistband that she now hugged protectively in place. She was fighting a losing battle of trying to forget that Sam Brown was a man—and he wasn't helping one bit! The only resource she could draw upon was feigned indignation. She yanked the can from his hand, then stalked to the truck and flung it through the open window.

"We've got work to do, Brown. Enough of this fooling around!" And, thankfully, he followed her lead and got back down to business.

They set off through knee-high grass laden with dew and embroidered with spider webs to which droplets of moisture clung. They moved slowly, the only sounds those of their footsteps swishing through the grass, which occasionally squeaked as it brushed wetly against Lee's rubber boots. They stopped and stood shoulder to shoulder, each holding one side of the wide blueprints as they studied them.

There were a hundred considerations to be made when deciding whether or not to bid a job such as this one. The first and most obvious was the amount of dirt to be moved, where to, and with what. As they walked, they scanned the ups and downs, considering, discussing, doing mental calculations.

They left the fairly level edge of the cornfield and came to a section of uneven roughland—pasture for the most part—with gullies and swales, many filled with muddy potholes after last night's rains. The dampness of the soil was a second important consideration, so Sam and Lee often knelt, side by side, lifting handfuls of soil, noting where they wanted to do test borings.

Lee was conscious of the smell of mosquito spray and wet earth, and of Sam Brown's inviting masculine scent, as they squatted with their shoulders almost touching. They moved on again, following the route the pipe would take, crossing a thick stand of prairie thistle in full purple bloom, until they came to a marsh where red-winged blackbirds perched atop bobbing cattails. The birds' voices raised a cacophony while Sam and Lee stood unmoving for several minutes—just listening and enjoying. It was peaceful and private. Lee became aware that Sam's eyes were seeking her out as he stood behind her, his thumbs hooked on his hipbones. It took great effort to keep from looking back, but she resolutely refrained. Assuming a businesslike air, she noted, "Lots of birds out here."

Sam gave a cursory glance at the swamp and grunted in agreement, but immediately his eyes swung back to her.

"The Department of Natural Resources will require a permit before we mess around with their nesting area. I'll make a note of it." But when she jotted down the note, she braved a glance at him and caught him studying her in a disturbing way. Immediately she looked at the set of plans, but his next question made her forget the figures before her eyes.

"How long have you been divorced?"

The air was utterly still, everything washed clean by the night rains which still lingered on leaf and stem, turning into diamond beads when the sun occasionally broke through the patchy clouds overhead. Lee met Sam's eyes, realizing that if she answered it would be harder than ever to get back to business.

"Three years," she replied.

He seemed to consider before finally asking, "Does he live here?"

"No."

"In St. Louis?"

Though posed in a casual tone, his question brought her to her senses. "We're supposed to be looking for a corner lathe with a red flag on it," she reminded him.

"Oh." He shrugged, as if her deliberate evasion were of little importance. "Oh yeah . . . well, forget I asked."

She tried to do just that, but for the remainder of their walk the unanswered question hung between them.

Chapter 6

BY THE TIME they finished their survey the sun was high and hot. They had made nearly a complete circle, which brought them at last to the foot of a hill below what had once been a thriving orchard and busy farmhouse. Lee could see the peak of the roof above the apple trees, and a large, rustic barn loomed up at her right. As they walked beneath the laden trees toward the crest of the hill, the shade felt soothing after the heat of the sun. The orchard had a scent of its own, a fecund mixture of loam and ripening fruit. Lee felt the lingering loneliness of old places whose thriving days have passed.

The house came into view. Like the barn, it had a fieldstone foundation. To Lee it seemed at once beautiful and sad, for the dreams that might have nurtured the building of this place were long dead with their dreamers. The voices of its past were long gone. Its windows, vacant now, had once reflected a yard filled with seasonal activity—cattle coming home at the end of deep afternoon, children at play...

At the thought, a sharp pain of regret knifed through Lee, and she clutched her stomach.

"Is something wrong?"

"No . . . no!" She turned back to Sam with assumed brightness and made a pretense of rubbing her stomach. "I . . . I'm just hungry, that's all."

He glanced in the direction of the truck. "I can probably make it up that old driveway yet. Why don't you wait here while I get the truck?"

He strode off, and she watched until he disappeared, swallowed up by the trees. The abandoned house drew her irresistibly, and her feet moved almost against her will. She wandered around the foundation, peeking in windows at old linoleum, remnants of wallpaper, a sagging pantry door, a rusted iron pump, a hole in the wall where a chimney had once been. She kicked at a fruit jar that had been left lying in the deep weeds and fought an intense ache brought on by the old place, whose memorabilia brought back memories of her own past.

A gay profusion of tiger lilies nodded on long stems beside the back stoop, and Lee sat down in the sun, dropping her forehead on her crossed arms and raised knees. The truck started, way off in the distance, but she scarcely heard it. Memories came flooding back, memories she wanted to blot out but couldn't—wallpaper on other walls . . . another kitchen sink with a child's dirty feet being washed at bedtime . . . a table with two people, then two plus a baby in a high chair . . . the view from another kitchen window . . . a swing set where a child fell and called for Mommy . . . another back door with a mother swooping through on her way to soothe the child's cries . . . another backyard with day lilies blossoming in lemon brightness . . .

The truck came gunning up the steep, rutted incline, sending rocks rolling behind it, then coming to a stop under the apple trees.

"Lee?" Sam called as he stepped out of the cab. She raised her head slowly, pulling herself back to the present. "Come on down here. It's cooler in the shade." When she didn't move, his hand slipped from the door and his shoulders tensed. "Hey, are you okay?"

He started toward her, and immediately she pulled herself together and jumped off the step, brushing off her backside with a jauntiness she didn't feel.

"Yeah . . . yeah, sure." She would have strode right past him, but he reached out a hand, and before she could prevent it, he swung her around and tipped up her unsteady chin. He studied her closely and, after a long, uncomfortable scrutiny, stated, "You've been crying."

She squelched the sudden, overwhelming urge to throw herself into his arms.

"I have not," she declared stubbornly.

He dropped his eyes to her nostrils, and she made an effort to keep them from quivering. His gaze continued down to her lips, which felt puffy, then back up to her glistening eyes and damp lashes.

"Do you want to talk about it?" he invited very quietly.

No . . . yes . . . oh, please, let me go before I do . . . His eyes invited her confidence, and the corners of his lips turned down as she hovered on the brink of telling him everything, which would prove utterly disastrous, she was sure.

"No," she finally answered.

He seemed to consider for a moment, then his hand fell, and his voice came gay and bright. "All right. Then we'll just eat our lunch." He swung blithely toward the cab, reached inside, and came up with the sack lunch, then left the truck door open and the radio tuned to a country station as he turned to assess the area under the apple trees. "The ground's probably wet. Why don't we sit on the tailgate?"

"Fine," Lee answered, still thrown off guard by Sam's sudden levity when she had expected him to press her for answers. He lowered the tailgate, set the bag down, and turned to her with the same carefree air.

"Need a boost?" Before she could answer, Lee found herself deposited on the cool, brown metal. The truck bounced a little as Sam joined her then twisted to retrieve the cooler and pull out two icy cans of cola before popping their tops and handing her one. He tipped up his own and swilled nearly half its contents before licking his lips, running a hand across his mouth, and sighing with satisfaction.

He looked down pointedly at the sandwich bag between their hips, and Lee realized she'd been watching him with undivided interest, trying to figure him out.

"Oh! Help yourself," she offered.

"Thanks."

He took a sandwich, sank his teeth into it, and swung his feet in rhythm to the soft country songs coming from the cab behind them.

"Aren't you going to eat?" he asked.

Lee was brought back from her wool-gathering and, dutifully taking a bite of the sandwich, discovered she was hungrier than she'd thought. Soon they were sitting in companionable silence, munching and sipping, listening to the birds and the radio.

When Sam finished eating, he leaned back on one palm, hooked a boot heel over the edge of the tailgate, and draped his elbow indolently over an updrawn knee, swinging the cola can idly between his fingers. Lee grew increasingly aware of his scrutiny and of the privacy of the old orchard and abandoned farmyard.

"Are you still hung up on your husband?" Startled, Lee turned to find Sam's brown eyes steady on her face. They were undeniably stunning, their lashes longer than her own. His unsmiling lips had a symmetry and fullness that must have broken a heart or two in their time, she thought.

Unsettled by her observation, she looked at some distant point and answered, "No."

"That's not why you were crying, then?"

She gave up the senseless argument that she hadn't been crying. "I . . . no."

"Over somebody else, then?"

"No, there's nobody else."

A long silence followed, and she sensed him looking at her hair, then at her profile. "Well, then . . ." The ensuing pause was electric. She still felt his eyes on her face but was afraid to look at him. The hand with the can left his knee, then a single, cold index finger lifted her chin until she was forced to meet his eyes. She stared mutely into them—stunning, steady brown eyes—telling herself to turn away sensibly. Instead, she sat as if transfixed as his lips moved closer . . . and closer . . .

"Brown, don't," she said at the last moment, turning aside. Her voice was reedy and strained.

"Well, if it's not your ex-husband and it's not somebody else, there's no reason why I shouldn't kiss you, is there?"

There were a hundred reasons why not, but they all escaped Lee at that moment as he tipped her face up once more. The noon sun sent splinters of light through minute openings in the branches overhead into their private domain, like miniature green-gold starbursts. Somewhere in the distance a meadowlark warbled.

"Brown, you're my boss and I don't think—"

His kiss cut off her argument as he leaned over, pressing a palm against the floor behind her, and meeting her lips above the brown paper bag and the remains of their meal. His lips were cold from the drink, but soft and appealing as he tipped his head to the side and moved it in lazy, seductive motions back and forth. The coolness left the skin of his inner lips and was replaced by warmth from her own.

Oh, Brown, Brown, you're too damn good at this.

Lee found her common sense at last and pulled back, but Sam continued leaning toward her in that nonchalant pose. The wrist and can were on his knee again, but his eyes were on her mouth.

"I've been thinking about that since long before our walk today," he said.

"Don't say things like that." She frowned at his chin to convince him she was serious, though she suspected she was the one who needed convincing for it had suddenly become very hard to breathe.

"Why not?" he asked with a half smile.

"Because it could cause innumerable problems, and I'm not up to handling them."

He leaned even closer. "No problems—I promise." While she was still trying to sort out rationality from response, he kissed her again, sending tiny shudders up her arms and fluid fire through her veins. His warm tongue circled her lips, and even as she told herself this was dangerous, this man was too appealing and far, far too expert, her lips parted and answered his tongue with a first hesitant response. The kiss grew warmer and wider and better until Sam Brown's softly sucking mouth melted Lee's resistance, and she leaned toward him, realizing how much—how very much—she had missed this.

Oh, Brown, we never should have started this.

But even as she thought it, his mouth left hers and she watched, mesmerized, as he slipped the can from her fingers and placed it to one side with his own. He confiscated her sandwich, which now wore two flat-pressed fingerprints.

643

Methodically, he cleared away the rest of their lunch and placed the bag beside the soft drink cans on his far side. When he turned back to her, his intention was clear.

The pulse jumped in Lee's throat, and a band seemed to cinch about her chest, bringing with it a sweet expectation that rivaled the sweet scent of the orchard. Sam's right hand slipped to her ribs, his left to cup her hip and slide her over until she bumped firmly up against him. Then her head was tipping back and his warm lips opened over hers again.

A thousand forgotten feelings swept over Lee as Sam's hand slipped beneath the ribbing at her waist and her fingers found his collarbone. It had been so long . . . so long. Then, in one deft motion, he pulled her across his chest and took her backward with him, falling onto the bed of the pickup, little caring that it was hard and dirty and cold.

Her shirt slid up as his hand moved over her bare back and warm fingers slipped underneath the narrow band of elastic that crossed beneath her shoulder blades. His other hand slid down over her backside and expertly adjusted her length atop his own until she felt exactly how tough and hard all that running had made his thighs. And while he kissed and tempted her with a strong molding of tongue upon tongue, something more grew tough and hard beneath Lee's body. Her own body leaped to life.

And—oh, God—it felt so wonderful to be held again, caressed again. Sam's compelling lips shut out all thought of stopping the warm hand that curved around the side of her breast while his other arm pressed against her spine. He slipped his fingers inside the front of her bra, between lace and skin, the tips not quite reaching her nipple. A moment later he'd reached around her to release the clasp between her shoulder blades. His warm palms moved between their bodies, finding her freed breasts and caressing them slowly before rolling their tips between his fingers as if they were flowers he'd plucked on their stroll through the meadow.

He was ardent and persuasive and so undeniably tempting as she lay on him. She knew all the dangers of succumbing to his tantalizing sorcery, but she told herself not to think of them as her body responded fully.

But then Sam suddenly rolled her to her hip and reached

for the snap on her jeans, and she plummeted to earth again.

"Brown . . . this is crazy, stop it!" She caught his straying hand and dragged it to safer territory. Everything inside her had gone zinging-singing, turned-on crazy with incredible desire for him. His eyes glinted down into hers like dark, metallic sparks, and his fingers curled into the back of her hand until she whispered fiercely, "Don't!"

To Lee's immense surprise and relief, he rolled away and fell flat on his back, his hands coming to rest, knuckles down on the corrugated metal beneath him.

"Sorry, Cherokee."

That name again! It did the strangest things to her stomach. She sat up and drew a steadying breath, wondering what had ever possessed her to let things get so far out of hand. She was thoroughly embarrassed now, for even with her back to him she could feel his eyes on her. But she had little choice except to reach behind her for her bra.

Once again Sam Brown did the unpredictable. He sat up immediately and slipped his hands under her shirt. "Here, let me. I'm the one who messed it up." With a total lack of compunction he pushed her shirt up and found the trailing ends of the bra and hooked them together again. His putting it back on had an even greater sexual impact than when he'd released it. Goose bumps erupted over her skin and left her more tinglingly aware of him than ever. But he unselfconsciously pulled the shirt down to her waist, smoothed it into place, and dropped his hands from her. He seemed to dismiss the entire episode with an almost cheery note. "You're probably right. We should stop."

She was astonished by his mercurial change of mood. Somehow she'd expected him to be demanding or angry at her rebuff. But he sat beside her now as if they'd shared nothing more than a bag lunch. At least that was the impression he gave until his lopsided grin returned and he drawled devilishly, "But it *was* fun."

She bit back a smile and scolded, "Brown, have you no scruples whatsoever?"

"Well, I didn't see you exactly high-tailing it in the other direction."

"Oh no?" She boosted herself up and dropped off the tailgate, then turned to inform him from that safe distance, "I think it's time we headed back to town."

He only grinned, curled his hands over the edge of the tailgate, and swung his legs loosely from the knees.

"Whatcha doing this weekend, Cherokee?"

"Cut that out, Brown. I said I don't want problems."

"I've got another name besides Brown, you know."

"That's all we need—a little more familiarity between us, and everyone in the office will have their jaws wagging."

"What time do you get up on Saturdays?"

How was a woman supposed to fight an irresistible tease like him? It was all she could do to keep a straight face.

"None of your business. Are you coming or not?"

He leaped nimbly from the truck, revealing three dirty stripes down the back of his white shirt. As he slammed the tailgate shut he suggested, "How about we rent some roller skates and try the skate trails?"

"I said no!" She added in exasperation, "Oh, Lord, you're as striped as a polecat, Brown. Hold still while I get rid of the evidence."

She stepped quickly up behind him to whisk the dirt away, but as her hands brushed over his hard back, he grinned over his shoulder—a devastatingly charming grin. "You scared I might make a pass at you again and catch you in a weaker moment?" She felt a telltale blush creep across her cheeks and immediately stepped back and jammed her hands into her pockets.

"You know what your problem is? You read too many girlie magazines!"

Sam laughed and plucked an apple off a tree, then draped his elbows on top of the tailgate behind him as he took a lazy bite.

"Well, I just thought, since you'd changed your brand of perfume—"

"That wasn't perfume, that was mosquito spray!"

Again his rich peal of appreciation lifted through the orchard before his teeth snapped through the skin of the apple. He considered her unhurriedly. "What about tomorrow?"

The man was undauntable. If he kept it up, he'd break her down yet! She stamped her foot and declared, "No, no, a thousand times no!" then spun from him, strode to the pickup, and got in.

He flung the apple core beneath the trees and climbed in beside her as she wondered frantically how to break the sexual tension spinning between them. But as Sam started the engine, he managed to break it himself by glancing at her from the corner of his eye and teasing, "You know, you're cuter 'n hell when you're on the warpath, Cherokee."

She could resist no longer and burst out laughing. He was an outlandish tease and a tempting creature. But he was her boss and the last man in the world she should encourage— assuming she wanted to encourage any man, which she didn't. Yet even as she promised herself sternly to avoid being alone with Sam Brown, a glow of well-being spread from her smiling lips all the way down to her tingling toes.

Chapter 7

LEE SPENT THE following morning at her usual Saturday drudgery—cleaning house. She had changed the sheets, cleaned the upstairs, vacuumed the steps, and was shoving the vacuum cleaner along the living room carpet when she thought she'd heard the doorchime. She heard it again more clearly and, mumbling a curse, turned the machine off with a bare toe.

She opened her front door and stopped dead still. There, his hips against the wrought-iron handrail, sat Sam Brown, practically naked!

"Hi," he greeted, puffing hard. "This is an obscene house call."

Without warning, Lee burst out laughing. She covered her mouth with both hands and bent forward, overcome with mirth. "Oh, Brown, I believe you!"

There he sat, wearing nothing but his beat-up running shoes, a pair of white jogging shorts with a green stripe, and a red headband. Sweat ran down his heaving chest, making it shine in the sun. There was little hair on it, but what there was burned like red-gold sparks as trickles of perspiration ran down the center hollow toward his navel. His legs were crossed at the ankle, but his shoulders slumped forward as he panted laboriously.

"Don't tell me you ran all the way over here," Lee said.

He nodded, still trying to catch his breath.

"But it must be eight miles!"

"Eight mi . . . hiles is nothing. I'm in goo . . . hood shape."

"I can see that." And she could, in spite of his breathlessness. He looked like poured copper, wet and smooth and sleek and sculptured, the muscles of his legs as hard as an Olympian's, his shoulders glossy and well developed.

"Must've lost six pounds of sw . . . sweat on the way ov . . . over here though."

"I can see that, too."

He drew in a large gulp of air, his breathing growing even while he continued to slump against the rail. "You wouldn't turn a man away thirsty, would you?"

"And risk a darn good job?" Lee returned impertinently. "Come on."

Sam boosted himself away from the railing and followed Lee inside, making her uncomfortably conscious of her bare feet and legs and the strip of exposed skin between her skimpy bandeau top of white stretch terry and the faded denim cutoffs with strings dangling down her legs. She resisted an urge to run a hand over the single coarse braid that fell down her back and was as frayed around the edges as her cutoffs. She led Sam along the short hall to the rear of the house, where the kitchen's sliding glass door stood open to her small, shady patio. He stood before it, hands on hips, letting the draft cool his sweating body, as she opened the refrigerator.

"Here." She moved behind him with two clinking glasses.

"Thanks."

"Let's go out on the patio where it's more comfortable." She slid the screen open, and he followed. There was only a single webbed lounge chair, and before he could protest, Lee plopped down on the concrete, facing the lounge chair with her legs crossed Indian fashion. "Have a seat," she said.

"No, here, you take—"

"Don't be silly. You're the one who just ran eight miles, not me. Anyway, the concrete is cool."

He shrugged, dropped into the lounge chair, took a sip of tea, and glanced around at her pots of bright red geraniums, asparagus fern, and vinca vine. It was cool and restful in the shade, but Lee felt warm and uncomfortable as Sam's eyes returned to her. What should she say to this man who refused to accept her brush-off and appeared at her door the next day with incorrigible brashness . . . then made her laugh!

"Do you run every day?"

"I try to."

"I don't think I'd care to on a day like today. It's supposed to get up to ninety-five degrees."

"That's why I run in the morning."

"Mmm." She sipped her drink, aware of his eyes, which made a periodic sweep of the geraniums but always returned to her bare knees.

"Did I interrupt something important?" He glanced toward the house, where the vacuum cleaner was sprawled across the living room floor.

"Just the weekly house cleaning." Lee grimaced, then added, "Ugh!"

Sam laughed, then the corners of his lips remained in a teasing grin. "Heap big disgusting job, cleaning the teepee?"

She couldn't stop her smile. "Show some respect, would you, Brown?"

"Well, you should see yourself"—he gestured with his glass—"sitting there barefooted with your legs crossed and that braid dangling down your back and your skin the color of a too ripe peach. The name Cherokee fits better than ever." He polished off the rest of his tea in one gulp and set the glass down, still grinning.

"You know"—she tipped her head to one side—"it puzzles me why I let you get away with it. If anybody else said things like that to me, I'd give 'em a black eye."

"You tried that once on me too, remember?"

"You deserved it."

He threw his head back, closed his eyes, and crossed his hands over his naked belly. "Yeah, I did."

How was a woman supposed to deal with a man like him? There he sat, as composed as a potentate, looking for all the world like he was going to take a nap on her patio.

"If you just stopped by to catch forty winks, do you mind if I finish my cleaning?"

He opened one eye. "Not at all." The eye closed again, and a moment later Lee slid the screen door open. The vacuum cleaner wheezed on, and for some reason she found herself smiling. She heard nothing more from Sam Brown until about fifteen minutes later, when she was watering the living room plants. He stepped inside and stopped in the hall behind her. "Would you mind if I used your bathroom before I head back?"

She turned to see him filling the living room doorway with his bare shoulders and chest. "It's upstairs, to your right."

He sprinted up the steps as she turned back to watering the plants. But a moment later she remembered the open door to the extra bedroom and turned, ready to bolt up and close it before he emerged from the bathroom. But as she reached the bottom step, the door above clicked open and the muffled thud of his footsteps sounded across the hall, pausing momentarily while she backed up, listening, a hand pressed to her heart. Again his footseps neared, and she scurried out to the kitchen, where she was busily scouring the sink when he found her again.

"Thanks for the iced tea. I've got an eight-mile run yet, so I guess I'd better go."

She ran her hands under the water, grabbed a towel, and followed him idly toward the front door, conscious of a great reluctance to see him leave. They stepped out onto the sunny front stoop, and he moved down two steps, then turned as she leaned against the railing with the towel slung over her shoulder. "I'll see you Monday, Cherokee," he finally said. The sun lit his hair to russet and his skin to copper as he gazed up at her without making a move. In another minute he would turn and jog off across the city. And all of a sudden she couldn't let him go. "It's eighty-five degrees already. There's no need for you to run all the way home. I can give you a ride if you want."

"What about your house cleaning?"

"It's all done."

"In that case, I accept."

Her heart went light and happy. "Give me a minute to put on some decent clothes, okay?"

She'd already stepped through the front door when his question stopped her. "Do you have to?"

Over her shoulder she threw him a scolding expression, but he only raised his palms, shrugged, and grinned.

She returned shortly, dressed in white pedal pushers and a

red spaghetti-strap top that bloused at the waist and just above her breasts. As her bare feet slapped down the steps, a pair of red canvas sandals swung jauntily from two fingers, and white feathers bounced in her ears. Sam was leaning against the back fender of her dusty Pinto. He nudged himself upright and opened her door, waiting while she got in.

When he was seated beside her, she put the car into reverse. "If I remember right," she said, "you live on Ward Parkway . . . in the family rattrap." She gave him a sidelong grin.

"Everybody's got to live somewhere."

He settled back for the ride, and fifteen minutes later Lee was following Sam's finger as it pointed toward the cobbled drive of a majestic, well-preserved mansion.

Cradling the wheel in her arms, she stared in undisguised awe. Realizing Sam hadn't moved, she turned to give him a sheepish grin, then gazed up the ivy-covered chimney of the enormous stucco tudor home. "Nice little rattrap you live in," she said wryly.

"Would you like to see it?"

"Are you kidding?"

"Mother's not home. She's out golfing." The mention of his mother made Lee quail momentarily, though she wanted very badly to go inside his home and see where he lived, how he lived.

He seemed to sense her hesitation and turned, resting a knee on the seat between them, an arm along its back. "I'd like very much to spend the day with you, Cherokee. What do you say we do the town? Anything at all—think of the craziest, most illogical things you've ever thought of doing, and we'll try every one of 'em. And no more of what happened in the orchard yesterday. That's a promise."

It was a promise she would not have extracted had the choice been left up to her. "I *work* for you! Doesn't it sound just a little . . . well . . ."

"Hell, is that all? You think that if we end up more than friends you'll lose your job if and when the romance is over?"

"Something like that. Or at least it'll be a lot more strained when we bump into each other in the office every day."

Engaging creases crinkled the corners of his eyes. "Maybe

652

I should fire you here and now so the problem doesn't arise."

"Brown, you're impossible." But she couldn't help smiling as she shook her head at his foolish reasoning. Yes, he was impossible. Impossible to resist, with his dark good looks and his engaging sense of humor. She thrust her worries aside and promised herself a day of carefree fun. She would laugh and return his bantering and teasing and accept the fact that she enjoyed his company immensely.

"Say yes," he coaxed.

She gave him a wry corner-of-the-eye smirk. "You gonna fire me if I don't?"

"No."

"Then, yes, damn you."

The house was all cool class with an open stairway that dropped from the biggest fanlight window Lee had ever seen. Sam ran upstairs, leaving her to look around while he took a quick shower and changed. She wandered from room to room, hands clasped behind her back as if afraid to touch what she wasn't supposed to. The living room had two enormous sets of fanlight doors opening onto a glass-walled sunroom that overlooked the side yard, where the Kansas City traditions had been sustained—lush flower beds curving around ancient magnolia trees; a small fountain spouting water from a cupid's ewer; and wrought-iron benches enclosed on three sides by precision-trimmed boxwood hedges.

"Ready?"

Lee turned to find that Sam had come up silently behind her on the thick, white carpeting. He looked as inviting as his house and yard. She forced her eyes back to the luscious view outside. "I had no idea," she murmured.

"It gets kind of lonely sometimes," he replied.

Again she turned. He was standing nearer, smelling of fresh soap and that everlasting Rawhide scent. His car keys were in his hand.

"Let's go get crazy," she said, giving him a devilish look meant to suggest just that.

They took the city by storm, skittering across it like crazy bedbugs. Sam knew Kansas City well, both its fun spots and its history, and he introduced Lee to both. They rented roller skates and wheeled through Loose Park, where the famed artist Christo had once covered the sidewalks with shimmering gold cloth and entitled his work "Wrapped Walkways." They bought bandages at the drugstore and entitled their works "Wrapped Knees." They bought a rhinestone ring at the Country Club Plaza and put it on the finger of a fountain nymph in the Crown Center, declaring a bond forever between the two magnificent landmarks whose creators, Lee learned, had both had the initials J. C. They got separated in the midst of the colorful *Festa Italiana* in Crown Center Square and recovered each other from the arms of exuberant Italian dancers. They ate ice cream at Swenson's and drank piña coladas at Kelly's Saloon, then nearly lost both on the Zambezi Zinger at Worlds of Fun, and settled their stomachs by lying flat on their backs between rows of markers at Mount Washington Cemetery. They spit into the "Mighty Mo" off the middle of the Hannibal Bridge, with laughing apologies to Octave Chanute, who hadn't taken two and a half years creating it just to have two zanies use it for this! They slipped into the Truman Library and left a note commemorating the date in the *Encyclopedia Britannica*—in Volume 7, page 754—promising to come back a year from then and see if it was still there.

All day they walked along Kansas City streets named after the city's founders—Meyer, Swope, Armour. Sam showed Lee Kessler Boulevard, named after the landscape architect who'd mapped out the entire beautification system of boulevards, gardens, and fountains which made the city a splendid kaleidoscope of beauty. He told her the history of William Rockhill Nelson, the founder of the *Kansas City Star*, who had fought for the city's approval of the unique boulevard network for fourteen years, and of how Jesse Clyde Nichols's visionary planning had brought sculpture, fountains and art objects to the city's intersections. They scampered, carefree, through the sun-splashed Kansas City day, and when night fell and the lights of the fountains lit their lilting waters to ruby, emerald, and sapphire, Lee and Sam sat on the edge of one eating Moo Goo Gai Pan and fried rice from little white cardboard containers.

"How's your knee?" Sam asked.

Lee lifted it and checked the bandage and the dried blood

on her white pedal pushers. "Still intact. Next time I won't let you talk me into doing three hundred sixty degree turns when I haven't been on skates in years."

He chuckled, but his eyes rested on her with a warm, appreciative glow.

"You're a helluva good sport, you know that, Cherokee?"

"Thanks. You ain't so bad yourself, Your Honor."

"You ready to call it a day?"

"Am I ever." She patted her stomach, sighed, then stacked the white cartons one inside the other. They meandered away from the fountain toward Sam's car, dropping their trash on the way . . . and somehow when he returned to her side, his hand took hers . . . and somehow she didn't mind a bit. A few minutes later, as their wide-swinging steps moved more lazily, Sam Brown looped an arm around Lee's neck and drew her close to his side. It felt good to be there, so she lifted a hand and hung it from his wrist, watching their feet go slower and slower.

Sam drove leisurely through the Kansas City night, listening to the night sounds of crickets and frogs through the open windows. The fountains along Ward Parkway *shushed* past, and Lee rested her head against the seat, wishing the evening needn't end at all. Sam pulled up in his driveway and turned off the engine. Neither of them moved.

"Thanks for a really fun day," she said softly.

"The pleasure was mine."

Still neither of them moved.

"I see Mother's home. Would you like to meet her?"

"Not tonight. It's late . . . and I've got bloody knees and Moo Goo Gai Pan on my shirt." The very thought of meeting his mother threatened to flaw the perfect day.

Lee felt Sam studying her across the car seat, and a moment later his voice came quietly. "Cherokee?"

"Yes?"

He hesitated before saying, "There's no Moo Goo Gai Pan on your shirt." Immediately she reached for her door handle, but his hand came out to detain her. "I'd really like you to meet my mother. Why are you running away?"

She laughed nervously and said to her lap, "I'm really not very good with mothers." She turned an entreating glance up

655

at him and added softly, "I'd rather not."

His thumb moved softly, brushing the crook of her elbow. "Do you mind telling me why?"

She considered doing just that, then answered without rancor, "Yes, I do mind."

Disregarding her answer, he went on, "Let me guess. It's got something to do with your being part Indian."

She was stunned that he'd figured out that much of the truth and felt as if, for a moment, he'd looked into her very soul.

"H . . . how did you know?"

His eyes moved to the feathers at her ears and with a single finger he set one in motion, then explained, "You're very defensive about it, you know."

"Everybody wears Indian jewelry these days. It's very in."

"Don't get mad, Cherokee. It's been a great day, and I want to keep it that way. But I wish you'd level with me. So far you haven't told me much of anything about your past." A long pause followed before he encouraged softly, "Why don't you tell me now?"

She considered for a moment and realized she wanted very badly to tell him. But it was hard to explain. It had been so long.

"I . . . I don't know where to begin."

"Begin with your husband. Was he white?"

"Yes." She dropped her eyes.

"And?"

"And . . ."

When she didn't go on, he urged softly, "Look at me, Cherokee. And what?"

His eyes were pools of shadow as he leaned across the dark confines of the car, and at the concern in his voice she suddenly found herself wanting to tell him things she'd promised herself never to reveal. But she needed to put some distance between herself and Sam Brown while she told him, so she opened her door and got out, leaving him to follow. As they ambled slowly toward her car, she began haltingly.

"Joel married me in one of those . . . those idiotic rebounds from the woman he should have married in the first place. A very white woman of whom his mother heartily approved.

He'd . . . he'd had a fight with her, so when he met me it was . . ." She sighed and looked up at the stars. "Oh, I don't know what it was. A chemical mix-up, maybe. A stupid impulse. But we didn't think it out at all. We just did it. Too fast, too . . ." She shrugged and hugged her arms as they moved across damp grass. "Nothing about it was right, not from the very first, except maybe the sex. But that's not enough to sustain a marriage. After a while his mother's disapproval of me began to wear on Joel, and he began blaming me for alienating him from his family. Within a year after our divorce, he married the girl his mother had been telling him all along he should have married." They stopped at her car. "So now you know why I'm not too good with mothers."

The lights from the house spilled in long white splashes across the dark lawn behind them. Sam stood with a hand in his trouser pocket. Lee waited for his response. When it came, she was pleasantly surprised. The hand came out of his pocket and captured her elbow and he spoke in a soft, cajoling voice.

"Now that that's out of the way, come here." His gentle grip swung her around to face him, then he looped his arms around her waist till their hips rested lightly against each other. And suddenly she forgot about mothers and personal histories, for Sam Brown's face was smiling down at her through the warm, flower-scented night. It seemed as if the beguiling fountains of Kansas City itself danced within Lee's heart as she waited for one thing she needed to make this day end in total perfection. Then he lowered soft, warm open lips over hers, and she lifted her own, slightly parted, readily accepting the brush of his tongue upon hers . . . but softly, gently.

Ah, Brown, the things you do inside me.

He held her lightly, only the tips of her breasts brushing his shirt while she rested her hands on his biceps. Sam's tongue stroked and coaxed, and Lee's answered, her fingertips slipped up beneath the ribbing of his short knit sleeves in an unconscious invasion of his firm, hidden skin. The kiss was unhurried, almost lazy, a sweet lingual blandishment while they leaned a little apart and began to rock indolently from side to side. It was an aperitif of a kiss, designed to whet the appetite for more. But when it ended—slowly, lingeringly—

657

they refrained from partaking further.

Sam lifted his head to tease softly, "That's better than Swenson's ice cream."

Lee smiled and leaned back against the circle of his hands. "Mmm . . . and it won't give you a stomachache, either."

He smiled impishly and settled his hips more firmly against hers. "Oh no?"

But she knew it wasn't his stomach that ached. She could feel what ached, pressed hard and inviting against her pedal pushers.

So she was surprised when a moment later she found herself pushed gently away and turned toward her car by the Honorable Sam Brown, who was proving increasingly honorable indeed.

Chapter 8

EARLY MONDAY MORNING, plans got under way for bidding the Little Blue River job. Again Lee noted the difference between the way things were done at Brown & Brown and at Thorpe Construction. Not only was there an ongoing sense of cooperation where she worked now, but there was also a thoroughness that surprised her.

Accurate records of soil workability were kept for all major jobs. Lee met the drill truck on site Monday afternoon to take soil samples directly from the steel auger. These were weighed, dried, and run through a series of nested copper sieves. The amounts of material retained on each of the variously gauged screens were weighed carefully and recorded on a gradation chart. Lee and Sam worked side by side sieving and recording the data. They compared their findings with those of former jobs under similar soil conditions and used the results to estimate the cost of such variables as dewatering and sheeting to prevent cave-ins.

They sat in the coffee room, Frank perched on the edge of a counter, Sam seated with his legs crossed and heels propped up on an empty chair. The sense of belonging Lee felt in her new job encouraged her to take full part in the decision making. To her surprise her personal relationship with Sam hardly entered into their business dealings.

"Do you mind using Tri-State Drilling for dewatering?" Sam asked. His elbows were pointed at the ceiling and his fingers were clasped behind his neck as he leaned back comfortably.

"I was thinking of asking Griffin Wellpoint for a quote," Lee replied. "I've had good luck in dealing with them in the past." She held her breath. It was the first time she'd directly opposed the wishes of either Sam or Frank.

Sam only shrugged. "Great. We've had good luck with Tri-State, too, so either one is fine."

Lee ordered quotes from Griffin for dewatering, along with those from another subcontractor for installing pilings through the swampy area, which had proved to be mostly peat. She asked landscape contractors for quotes on sodding, seeding, mulching, and fertilizing. As the days passed and she waited for these quotes, the calculator on her desk whirred constantly.

She computed labor costs for pipe installation per foot, according to depth and soil conditions. Material costs were broken down into unit prices—and in the case of pipe—per-foot prices—and these extended out into lump sums.

As the week wore on and the day of the bid letting drew nearer, suppliers sent quotes on pipes, valves, manhole castings and hydrants. Throughout the week the tension seemed to grow as bid day—Friday—approached. As usual, quotes from subcontractors came in late, holding up progress to some degree and lending a sense of uncertainty to the work on the bid.

Late Thursday, Sam stopped by Lee's desk and asked, "Have all those quotes come in from the subs yet?"

"Still waiting on one from Greenway. You know how it is."

He chuckled, but the sound seemed tense for Sam, who was usually relaxed and easygoing. "Yeah, I know how it is."

"You want this job badly, don't you?"

His eyes met Lee's and for the first time that week seemed to convey thoughts beyond soil evaluations and price per linear foot. "I've got a rather personal stake in this one. Don't you?"

Thoughts of the orchard in all its seductive glory came back. "Yes, I do."

He gazed down at her for a moment longer, then seemed to drag himself from his reverie to scratch the side of his neck and glance at the pale green job sheets draped across her desk.

"Anyway, we could use this job since the Denver one doesn't get rolling till spring. There'd be time enough to get this one finished before winter."

Friday morning brought the usual eleventh-hour craziness Lee had come to expect in estimating. Somehow the spirit of competition never seemed to surface in suppliers until just before bid time. Within two hours of the deadline Lee received a call from the pipe supplier who was lowering his quote by twelve thousand dollars. Immediately subtotals and totals had to be changed on the official proposal form. Since the call came at 11:30 with bid time set for 2:00, Lee skipped lunch to change the figures, then run another calculator check of the math.

Sam came in at 12:45 to find her at her desk, her fingers flying over the machine, her bare feet curled up on the caster guards of her desk chair. "How's it going?" he asked.

She scarcely looked up. "What time is it?"

"Quarter to one."

"Will you double-check the addition on these sheets?"

"Sure." She extended the sheets without even turning her eyes his way. "Didn't you have lunch?"

She did glance up then, for about a half second. "No. American Pipe called and lowered their bid by twelve thousand dollars."

Sam sat down hastily at a nearby desk and his fingers, too, started flying over a calculator. "Why didn't you say something?"

She paused, looked up, and smiled at his dark head. "I'm too tense to eat anyway."

He pushed the total button, the machine clicked into silence, and Sam smiled across at Lee. "Relax, Cherokee, it's just a damn job."

But it wasn't, and they both knew it. It was *their* job. Their first joint effort, and something inside of Lee said they just had to win it! Still, she appreciated Sam's effort to put her at ease, and her smile said as much before they both set to work again.

Fifteen minutes later the changes were all entered in ink on the official bid proposal, and Sam leaned over Lee's desk to initial each one and put his signature beside the company seal impressed on the final sheet. His shoulder was almost touching her jaw as he bent to scratch his name on the paper. During the week, she'd had little trouble controlling personal feelings that intruded during business hours, but now, as he stood close and she watched his dark hands moving on the white paper, she was drawn to him by their singularity of purpose. He dropped the pen, straightened, and smiled down at her feet.

"You can put your shoes back on now. It's done."

She grinned sheepishly. "Takes the pressure off the head."

"Maybe off yours, but not off mine." He gave her feet an appreciative grin just as a group of draftsmen returned from lunch. "Well, I'm holding you up, huh?" It was one o'clock, and she still had to drive clear across the city to the Independence City Hall.

She drew in a deep breath, raked a hand through her hair, and gave Sam a shaky smile. "Well, here goes."

Brown & Brown's new estimator gathered up her papers, slipped the bid into a large gold envelope, licked it, pressed it shut, and lifted her eyes to find that her boss had been watching her every move.

"Good luck, Cherokee," he said softly.

"Thanks, Your Honor," she returned. Then she slipped on her shoes, picked up her purse, and left the office.

Brown & Brown took the Little Blue River job for $750,000, only $7,900 below the next highest bidder. When the last bid was read and the announcement made, Lee felt adrenaline swoop into her bloodstream in a giddy swoosh. She rose to her feet to accept handshakes, and her knees felt wobbly and weak. Her palms had been sweating throughout the opening of the envelopes, but now they itched to get to a telephone and call the office.

She suffered through what seemed like hours of felicitations before finally escaping to the pay phone in the hall.

Rachael's perky voice answered, "Brown & Brown."

"Rachael, we got it!" Lee announced without prelude.

"Lee! That's wonderful!"

"Isn't it, though?" Lee bubbled. "I'm ecstatic . . . and a little shaky."

Rachael laughed. "That part never changes, honey."

A little chuckle released the last of her nervousness, then Lee requested, "Put Sam on, will you, Rachael?"

She listened to the silence on the line for a brief moment, basking in a deep sense of satisfaction as she waited for his voice. When it came, it sounded full of smiles.

"Nice going, Cherokee."

"Hallelujah, we did it, Brown!"

He laughed. "Feels good, huh?"

"Does it ever."

"Just how good?"

Understanding his cryptic question, she replied, "Only seventy-nine hundred dollars good . . . that's how good."

"You mean that's all you left!"

"Yes!"

At his laugh of satisfaction, Lee pictured the smile carving grooves into his cheeks, and the pale laugh lines disappearing about his eyes.

"Who came in second?"

"Just a minute, I'll read you the list."

She relayed the remainder of the bids, then Sam asked, "You're coming back to the office, aren't you? We've got to celebrate your first victory."

"I'll be there in an hour or so."

"Good, see you then."

In the business of estimating, the days of defeat far outnumbered those of victory. On winning days, a special elation seeped into everyone, creating a spirit of camaraderie and good humor. Coming back into the office to find that everyone in the house had already heard the good news, Lee stopped to accept congratulations and share lighthearted jokes with her coworkers. But one was foremost in her mind.

Sam was beaming as he strode across the blue carpet dressed in casual gray slacks and a pale blue dress shirt with the sleeves rolled up to the elbow. Lord, she'd never been as proud as she was then, facing Sam Brown. Her smile was infectious as he extended his wide hand and clasped hers, squeezing hard, shaking it just once and holding it only a fraction of a second longer than necessary.

"Congratulations, Lee."

"Thank you, Sam." She wished she could lay her other hand over his and tell him how much she'd appreciated his faith in her during the past week, and what a true pleasure it had been preparing the bid in the congenial atmosphere of his office, among his cooperative employees and—of course— with him. But his hand slipped away, and the group of men continued chattering. Rachael, Nelda, and Ron Chen joined the group, and to Lee it felt like Christmas Eve.

Some people were already clearing off their tables, others still standing around shooting the breeze, when Rachael pulled herself away from a drafting table and turned toward the front. "Well, hi, Mary, how are you?"

A darkly tanned woman of about sixty had entered the office and was moving familiarly toward the cluster of men and women. Most of them greeted her by name and exchanged anecdotal greetings. Obviously they all knew her. She was dressed in a classy looking summer suit with brown and white spectator pumps and a matching purse. She exuded an air of quiet confidence.

"I understand congratulations are in order around here," she commented as she approached.

To Lee's amazement, Sam broke away from the others and greeted the woman with a light kiss on the cheek.

"Hi, Mother. You out slumming?" he teased.

"I heard the news. Thought it was time I met your new estimator."

"She's right here." Sam looped an arm around his mother's shoulder and directed her toward Lee, who stood stock still with amazement.

"Mother, this is Lee Walker—Lee, my mother, Mary Brown." He had placed his hands on his mother's shoulders, and his dark, amused eyes twinkled down at Lee as color rose to her cheeks. Like a robot she extended her hand, which was clasped in very dark, coppery fingers with wide knuckles and several flashy diamonds.

"I'm happy to meet you, Mrs. Brown," Lee managed, unable to keep her eyes from fleeing back to Sam, who stood as before, with his hands on his mother's shoulders, an undisguised look of merriment crinkling the corners of his eyes.

"So you've won your first bid for Brown and Brown," the

woman noted in a friendly fashion as she studied Lee from a face with wide, high cheekbones and a blunt, broad nose. Her hair was graying now, but was unmistakably coal black underneath the lighter strands.

"I . . . uh . . . yes, but not alone. Frank and . . . and your son worked with me on it."

"Sam wanted it quite badly. He mentioned it several times this week. Well, congratulations." She smiled, then added, "And welcome to the company."

As Sam's hands fell from her shoulders, he grinned disarmingly at Lee, then turned to watch his mother visit with others before joining her. Just then the phone rang. One of the draftsmen picked it up.

"It's for you, Lee."

It was a salesman asking if she'd go out for a drink or dinner—standard procedure after winning a bid. The salesmen were always eager to write up orders. Lee was standing with her back to the room when she suddenly became aware that Sam had slipped quietly up behind her. She turned, glancing at him over her shoulder as she spoke into the receiver. "This afternoon?" She paused for the salesman's reply, then asked, "What time?" With the phone pressed to her ear, Lee watched Sam Brown reach for a pad and pencil and followed his movements as he wrote, "You owe me dinner . . ." He turned it her way and pierced her with a meaningful look as she tried valiantly to concentrate on what the voice on the phone was saying. Sam's hand moved again, adding, ". . . tonight." He punctuated the message with an exclamation point.

Lee turned her back on both Sam Brown and his message, stammering, "Ah . . . I'm sorry, Paul, what were you saying?" A quick glance over her shoulder told her that Sam had moved away again. "I'm sorry, Paul. Maybe we can make it Monday for lunch. I'm busy tonight."

They made arrangements to meet then, and by the time Lee hung up, the office was starting to empty. She looked around for Sam's mother, but found she had gone. Sam himself was coming toward Lee. She crossed her arms loosely over her chest and leaned against the desk as she watched him approach.

"Well, you've surprised me again, Your Honor." Lee smiled.

"Have I now?" His grin was utterly charming.

"You know perfectly well that you have. Your mother is more Indian than I am."

"Ah, you're very perceptive," he teased.

"Where is she?" Lee scanned the office again.

Sam shrugged, then smirked. "Probably gone home to clean the teepee."

A picture of his "teepee" flashed before Lee's mind, and she couldn't help laughing. "Sam Brown, you're impossible. Why didn't you tell me before this?"

"And let you stop thinking I hired you so I could become a minority contractor? I've had too much fun laughing about it to myself."

"At my expense?"

"It didn't cost you anything, did it?"

"Except my unflappable cool. I think you could've driven a front-end loader in my mouth when I got a look at her and realized she was your mother."

He smiled, but changed the subject abruptly. "What about that dinner?"

She cocked an eyebrow at him. "I take it you're holding me to my promise that I go out with you when I became low bidder."

"Exactly."

"And I *am* low bidder?"

"Yes you are."

"And I *do* keep my promises?"

His smile broadened. "I'll pick you up at your place at seven. Wear something dressy." He turned away, changed his mind, and returned momentarily to add, "And sexy." Then he left for good.

Lee chose white again—this time a sleek, lithe crepe de chine dress that slipped over her hips like water—not tight, not loose, but willowy. It was a simple cylinder, cinched by elastic above her breasts and at the waist, leaving her shoulders and upper chest bare, the perfect foil for a heavy turquoise and silver pendant shaped like a peyote bird that

666

dropped onto her chest from a silvery chain. She touched it and looked at her reflection in the mirror, remembering Sam Brown's mother. How like him not to tell her the truth, then let her find it out as she had. She smiled, then hurried to insert tiny droplets of dangling turquoise in her ears. On her feet went the briefest straps of white leather and high, high heels. She tricked her hair into a froth of sassy curls, their disheveled control confined only by a fine white headband that crossed her temples and disappeared amid the bouncy tangle on her head.

Just then the doorbell rang. Without thinking, Lee snatched the framed picture of her sons from the dresser top and stuffed it into a drawer. On her way out she took a moment to close the door to the second bedroom. Downstairs she paused and pressed a hand against her churning stomach, then took a deep breath and went to greet Sam Brown.

He was leaning against the railing again, but he seemed to unfold in slow motion, coming up off the wrought iron muscle by muscle. As his ankles uncrossed, as his hand came out of his trouser pocket, as he pulled himself to his feet, his eyes shimmered down the length of Lee, and a smile of undisguised appreciation lifted his sculptured lips. When his dark eyes met her even darker ones, he said flat out, "You look absolutely sensational, Cherokee."

His approval brought a sweet ripple of pride up her spine as she took in the crisp lapels of his navy blue suit.

"Thank you, Your Honor, so do you." Did he ever! His white shirt set off the rusty hue of his face like a well-chosen matting about a painting, and she wondered how she could have been so naive as to have missed the truth about his heritage all this time. Yet from the first, she'd realized he didn't look like any full-blooded Scandinavian she'd ever known. He'd had his fun with her . . . but now, studying him, she couldn't help rejoicing at the final outcome. Yes, he was stunning, his silk tie knotted so flawlessly that it stood away from his collar band as if aroused.

At the thought she dropped her eyes and turned to fetch a tiny beaded purse.

When he'd seen her solicitously to her side of the car and started the engine, he turned to study her again. She met his gaze levelly, unconcerned that he was undoubtedly reading the admiration in her perusal, just as she was in his.

"Tonight it's the American. I, too, keep my promises."

"But it was supposed to be my treat." She knew she couldn't afford the American Restaurant.

"Oh, you're wrong about that."

"But—"

"It's a company dinner, on the boss. I'll write it off as a business expense."

"Oh, in that case . . . the American it is." But Lee felt far removed from business concerns at the moment. And as the evening progressed, that distance widened.

They approached the Crown Center by way of its ten-acre square of terraced lawns and fountains, passing the massive tent pavilion and the thirty-foot-high umbrellas beneath whose yellow peaks they'd lost and found each other last Saturday. Alexander Calder's stabile "Shiva" loomed up before them, and minutes later they were entering the luxurious Westin Crown Center Hotel.

Its multilevel lobby was carved into a rocky hillside of natural limestone, creating a dramatic garden of tropical foliage and full grown trees through which tumbled a sixty-foot waterfall. The rushing water created a refreshing background music for hotel guests, shoppers from the adjacent Crown Center shops, and sightseers who sauntered along the elevated catwalks above the lobby.

Had Hans Christian Andersen been alive to dream up a fairy tale setting, he could not have invented any more compellingly romantic than that through which they passed, Lee thought. She found it difficult to keep her eyes from Sam, and when they found themselves the only two people on the elevator carrying them up to the restaurant, she gave in to the urge.

He was leaning against the left wall, she against the right. They studied each other wordlessly, caught up in a sense of impending intimacy. Horizons lay ahead for them—it seemed understood—which would change their relationship forever. The knowledge intensified the moment, though to all outward appearances they were as casual as before.

Lee's senses seemed honed to a fine edge. She was keenly

668

attuned to Sam's familiar scent, to his expression which grew more and more thoughtful and sexually aware as the night wore on. Seated in the restaurant's lofty expanse with chrome and mirrors at her elbow and Kansas City spread out before her, Lee watched cars follow the arteries leading northeast toward the heart of the city. Yet time and again her gaze was pulled back to Sam's. As if her consciousness had been fine tuned, she absorbed every detail around her with acute perception—the soft hiss of bubbles in her stemglass; the sleek texture of pickled mushrooms from the toothpick Sam teasingly held toward her; the brush of his pant leg against her bare ankle under the table; the bite of woven caning against her bare shoulders as she relaxed in her bentwood chair; the heat of the flame from their Steak Diane as the waiter performed his culinary act; the sharp, tangy taste of broccoli, suddenly delectable when she'd never liked it before; the scent of starch in linen as she wiped her lips, which grew impatient for what now seemed a certainty; the sluggardly passage of time as Sam drew out their anticipation by ordering Cherries Jubilee; the flash of fire as a match was struck to liqueur; Sam's lips, tipped up only slightly at the corner as he slipped a scarlet cherry from a spoon and gave her a glimpse of his tongue stroking the succulent sauce from it; the heat flooding her body at his wordless suggestion.

Lee lounged all willowy in her chair, but she noted how often Sam's glance fell to the ruched line where her dress met her chest, then lower to the discernible shadows hinting of dusky, bare nipples within her silken bodice. Each time it happened her stomach tingled. But she lounged on, playing his waiting game with a restraint that keyed their sensuality to a higher pitch.

From the restaurant, across the square, to the car, and all the way home . . . he never touched her. Not with his hands. But his eyes were as tactile as the brush of warm flesh as they lingered on her. The city was dark, alive, waiting . . . just like Lee.

At the curb in front of her house the engine stopped and his car door opened, then he opened her door and waited for her to step out. Again they moved up the sidewalk, up the steps to the door without a word, without a touch.

She had left the outside light off. The shrubbery and overhanging roof created deep shadows. Yet she turned to him, knowing his face without seeing it.

"Would you like to come in for a drink?" She remembered his preference for dry martinis with pickled mushrooms and added nervously, "I . . . I don't have any pickled mushrooms, but I do have olives."

A long, blank pause followed before he replied succinctly, "No, I wouldn't care for a drink or pickled mushrooms or olives."

Her stomach trembled, and she drew in a deep breath before asking softly, "What, then?"

She sensed him leaning toward her, just short of touching her as he answered in a husky voice, "I want you, Cherokee . . . you know that."

His answer sent her pulse pounding, and suddenly she didn't know what to say. She stood there in the dark, her nostrils filled with his scent, knowing the searching look in his eyes, though she could not see them. Then his voice came again, soft but intense. "Don't invite me in unless it's for that."

Still he didn't touch her, and though she wanted him to, she knew that once he did there'd be no turning back.

"You must know I still have reservations about it," she admitted shakily.

"Then why did you wear that dress tonight with nothing under it?"

He knew her better than she knew herself; it seemed foolish to deny it. She dropped her chin and admitted artlessly, "It was shameless of me, wasn't it?" She sensed him smiling in the dark doorway.

"Are you testing me, Cherokee, to see how far you can go before I make a move?"

"No . . . I . . ." Her hands fluttered and her voice grew unsteady. "I'm just nervous."

After a thoughtful silence, he mused, "You're an enigma, you know that? I've seen you in action at a bid letting where there's a good reason to be nervous, yet there you're as unruffled as can be. Out in the tough business world you scrap and fight with the best of 'em. But what happens to that confident woman when a man finds her attractive?" His voice went softer. "What do you have to be nervous about?"

Suddenly there were tens of answers Lee could have given, any one of which would have been enough to stop her. But she withheld them all, realizing it had been half her doing that they were here together on the brink of something that would be splendid, she was certain. She did want him, and complications always went along with that, thus she suppressed her doubts and asked in a wistful way he could not mistake, "Would you like to come in for nothing so simple as . . . as pickled mushrooms or olives?"

In answer he reached out and gave her bare shoulder a brief squeeze that sent goosebumps down her arm.

"Give me your key," he ordered quietly.

Her hand trembled as she forfeited it. It chinked into his hand and a moment later the door swung inward, then closed behind them, securing them in a blanket of blackness.

She came to a halt in the middle of the hall, her back to Sam as she clutched her tiny purse in both hands. Oh, it had been so different with that other man, the one whose name she could barely remember, who had come oh so briefly after Joel. But she hadn't forgotten the sudden chill that had overcome her body and turned it unwilling at the last minute. What if that happened now? And what if . . . what if . . .

She ran a frenzied mental assessment of her body and found only its shortcomings—not only the stretchmarks but also the loss of firmness, the unmistakable contour of hips that were wider now, the few extra pounds she perhaps should have lost . . . and there was a single vein on . . .

Sam's hands sought her waist in the dark, and his fingers spread wide on her ribs, pulling her against him as he pressed his mouth into the curve of her neck, riding it back along the warm silver chain, pushing her hair aside to kiss the nape of her neck.

"Cherokee," he murmured, "you're so tense. There's no need to be."

In the dark he found the purse she still clutched and pulled it from her fingers. She heard the soft thud as it landed on a carpeted step before he returned his attentions to her neck.

She released the breath she'd held captive for too long and

forced the muscles of her neck to relax one by one as he nuzzled the warm hollow behind her ear until her head dropped forward, then to the side.

"How long has it been?" he asked with gruff tenderness.

She knew a moment of trepidation before answering honestly, "Three years." Three long, empty years.

At her answer he circled her with both arms, just below her breasts, and she covered the sleeves of his suit jacket with her own arms and the backs of his hands with hers.

"You mean I'm the first since your husband?" he asked softly near her temple.

She swallowed thickly, then admitted, "Yes . . . no . . . well, almost."

She felt him move as if to look down at her questioningly, but his arms remained as before, warm and secure about her midriff.

"Almost?"

"There was one other man. I was lonely and . . ." Again she swallowed, thinking he'd pull away if she admitted what had happened. "Well, I thought I could, but . . . when I changed my mind things got ugly."

His arms tightened more firmly around her, and he rocked her soothingly a time or two. "Oh, Cherokee, can't you feel that's not going to happen to us?"

And suddenly she could. She relaxed against him as he wet the soft skin of her neck with the tip of his tongue and slipped a hand over her left breast, warm and resilient within the tissue-fine fabric of her dress. Shudders of pleasure made her skin prickle. Doubts fled magically. She no longer remembered that the skin he touched was not as firm as it had once been. She only reveled in how good it felt to be caressed again. She closed her eyes, and braved the question she, too, needed to have answered.

"How long has it been for you?"

His hand continued its gentle exploration even as he told her, "Three months."

"With who?"

The hand stilled on her breast. "Does it matter?"

"If she still means something to you, it does."

"She doesn't."

She relaxed even further, relieved more than she could say by his answer. The crepe dress seemed to have no more substance than a cobweb as he cupped his wide palms about the lower swell of both breasts and made the fabric slip seductively across her nipples, tempting them, making her insecurities retreat farther and farther, replacing them with the vast need to be touched again, fondled, loved.

"Oh, Cherokee, you feel so good," he murmured against her naked shoulder, dropping his head forward and crushing her back against him.

"So do you." She covered his hands and pressed them firmly against her breasts as if to absorb every nuance of tenderness. The wide palms moved beneath her hands, gentling and arousing at once, appeasing the need for quiet exploration. "Oh, Brown," she admitted breathily, "I've needed this for so long."

"I know," came his gruff voice beside her ear. "We all do." Then his fingertips familiarized themselves with the belled shapes of her nipples. He folded them between his thumbs and the edges of his hands, lifting her breasts at the same time, sending tiny tuggings of ache feathering along her nerves.

She hardly realized she'd sighed until his voice whispered in the hair above her ear, "That's better, Cherokee . . . relax."

And she was—oh, she was—for his hands seemed to stroke away her lingering misgivings, and the easy pace he'd set won her trust. His hands were very hard, both front and back, yet their touch was sensitive, and she made no effort to stop one from escaping her light hold. It slid over her stomach, where the fingers spread wide for a moment, then closed again before pressing into the hollow beside her hip. His touch became feather light as with a single fingertip he scribed a twining grapevine upon the mound of femininity within her silken skirt. He sent a perceptible shiver through her, for his movement over the crepe made it slip across equally silky undergarments until the sleek touch of her clothing sent ripples of sensuality up her spine. It made her powerfully aware of her own sexuality, this touch that was half caress, half tickle, and all arousal. She sensed him gauging her reaction, listening to the accelerated beat of her heart, feeling it beneath the palm that still pleasured her breast. At last he slipped his hand fully over the curve of her femininity, bringing her to know a wild rapture, a lush awakening.

He murmured her name—Lee, and sometimes Cherokee —kissing her ear, her jaw, her shoulder, as his hands rustled over her, learning her contours, then traveling once more up her stomach and sides until his thumbs hooked the elastic at the top of her dress, taking it down to her waist and freeing her breasts to his palms, which lingered only momentarily before one slipped low within her garments to touch her intimately for the first time. His voice was ragged as he uttered, "Oh, Cherokee, I've wanted this since the first night I saw you in that motel room."

She smiled in the dark thinking back to that night, realizing she'd been fighting a losing battle ever since. "I . . . I tried not to think of you, but it . . . it was impossible after that."

His touch drove the breath from her lungs and set her pulse thrumming, while behind her his body invited with its pressure, then with a faint side to side movement. But it was far easier to accept the first touch than bestow it. As if sensing her hesitancy, he rested his jaw against her temple and encouraged, "You know, you don't have to ask permission if there's anything you feel like doing."

Was he teasing? Only a little, and in an engaging way that sent a new awareness through her body. Yet girlish uncertainty mingled with womanly yearning. His midsection pressed firmly against her backside, verifying the message in his words while she hesitated yet a moment longer.

Then he begged softly, "Please, Cherokee . . ."

At last she drew her arm back, circling behind him to rest upon the tail of his suit jacket. His hand fell still upon her body, and his breath beat harshly against her ear as he waited . . . waited.

It had been so long . . . so long. But during these moments of sweet expectation she realized this intimacy had almost been predestined, for she and Sam had felt that spark from the first, and since then they had revealed bits and pieces of each other in the hope that each would find something more substantial to bring to his act. And now it was here, and her turn had come.

Her hand moved tentatively between them, and Sam

backed away, giving her space and the right to know him. Her heart was like a wild thing in her breast as she touched him for the first time, a tentative caress that brought a strange, thick sound from his throat. She explored him through tailored gabardine until he lost the power to remain still beneath her fingers and ordered gruffly, "Turn around, Cherokee." Suddenly she was spun about by her shoulders, and her arms were lifting while their open mouths met like a crashing of worlds. She pressed her willing body against his, circling his neck, losing her fingers in thick hair at the back of his head, and exploring the contour of his skull before she felt herself being lifted off her feet.

"Your shoes . . ." he ordered against her lips.

Her toes worked the straps off her heels, as first one clunk sounded behind her, then another. A moment later her bare feet rested again on the cool tile floor, and his palms slid within the elastic at her waist, passing along her lower back. Down went the skirt, and with it pantyhose and silky briefs, to form a pool of fabric at her feet. He encircled her with powerful arms, lifted her off the floor for a second time, and kicked the garments aside. Another drugging kiss stretched into an abandoned celebration of discovery while hands, mouths, and hips paid homage. When he lifted his head a long time later, he asked hoarsely, "How do you feel about undressing a man?"

Perhaps it was then that she realized she could easily fall in love with Sam Brown, with this sensitive man who made it all so easy and kissed away the last remaining doubt.

She smiled and replied throatily, "Turn me loose and I'll show you."

The pressure fell away, and she slipped her hands under his jacket. Before it hit the floor she was working the knot of his tie from side to side. It joined the jacket. As he unbuttoned his cuffs, his forearms softly brushed her breasts, and his voice came low and husky and certain. "We're going to be good together, Cherokee. I just know it."

At that moment she knew it too, and she reached for his shirttails and pulled them free of his trousers.

She did it all, all that he wanted of her, removing each article of clothing with a newfound sense of freedom. And when he too was naked and reaching, her hips were taken firmly against his once more. Her fingertips found his bare chest, and she raised up on tiptoe to settle her bare breasts securely against it, and he ran his palms over her back.

He asked only a single word. "Where?"

"In the living room," she murmured against his mouth before she was turned around and pulled back against his naked thighs while his legs nudged hers and they made their way onto soft, plush carpeting. She felt the pressure of his lips against her shoulder and answered their tacit command by bending with him. As they knelt, with one of his knees between hers, he aroused her with a magical touch until she lost all sense of time and drifted into a sensual paradise where a three-year void was eradicated by his knowing hands. The heat came slowly, starting in her toes, up her legs, along her flanks until her head pressed back against his shoulder and waves of pleasure broke across her skin.

She groaned, a strangled sound of abandon, and he clamped a steadying arm just below her breasts, holding her tightly against him while bringing her again the sense of self she'd lost somewhere along the years.

Behind her he was tense and rigid as his fingers curled into her shoulders, and a moment later she was turned and lowered quickly to her back and spread-eagled against the soft living room carpet.

It was a wild, primitive act they shared this first time, as if neither could control the tempo or the pressure. Celibacy had given Lee a need to match Sam's, so neither was concerned about the way they displayed their wantonness. It happened, as it was meant to happen, in an elemental and satisfying way neither had planned or anticipated. And when it was over and he fell heavily across her, they knew they'd shared something exceptional, even rare.

"Cherokee . . ." was all he could find the breath to say, but the single word was an accolade.

"Your Honor . . ." In other times, other contexts, the title had taken on a note of teasing, but now it was a sigh.

"You're wonderful," he praised.

"So are you . . . and . . . different than I expected."

He braced up, though his weight still pinned her lower

half. "And what did you expect?"

"I . . . I don't know." With both hands she soothed the damp hair from his temples. Though it was still dark, her eyes had adjusted to the dimness, and she could discern the outlines of his features. "All I know is I was very unsure, and . . . and feeling rather inadequate, and you made me forget all that."

He ran an index finger along the rim of her nose. "Inadequate? Why?"

How foolish it seemed now, yet minutes ago she had felt uncertain. "The second time a woman loses the confidence that comes so easily with the first time."

He kissed the tip of her nose with exquisite tenderness. "You're anything but inadequate, Cherokee. But in case you still have doubts, I'm volunteering to do my best to soothe them—indefinitely."

She tried to chuckle, but it was hard with his weight pressing the air from her lungs. She settled comfortably at his side and lay with her head on his arm while his hand rested on her hip.

She had forgotten the deep lethargy and satisfying afterglow of love. She basked in it now, resting in the curve of his arm, cherishing this lazy time which was the antithesis of what had just passed, but equally as necessary.

She curled up even more securely against his side, listening to the thud of his heart against her ear and running a finger from the corner of his lips to the soft center. His kissed her finger, which slipped into the moist, lush interior of his mouth before he bit it very gently, then continued holding it between his teeth.

Ruminating on the minutes just past, she murmured, "That was terrible, wasn't it?"

"What was so terrible about it?"

"Uninhibited," she mumbled, slightly chagrined at the memory.

"Are you saying you want to take it a little slower next time?"

"Next time?" She reached up and playfully yanked a handful of his hair. "You certainly take a lot for granted."

"Oh, do I now?" He rolled her on top of him and settled her along his length, then ran his hands down her spine until

677

his fingertips touched a part of her that disproved her words. And when they'd shared another ripple of mirth, he wrapped his arms around her securely and kissed her cheek.

"Cherokee, you're all woman, and you're more than enough to suit me. Mind if I hang around for a while?"

"Mmm . . . how long did you have in mind?"

"Oh . . . till morning, anyway." She heard the grin in his words, which brought a corresponding smile to her own lips.

But though she smiled and teased, "That long, huh?" the thought of morning was something to be reckoned with. Morning, with its bright revealing sun. She nudged the thought away, nestling against him, wanting him beside her throughout the night.

Morning would take care of itself.

Chapter 9

Lee watched dawn creep into the bedroom, all coral and cozy, illuminating their two bodies beneath strewn sheets, she on her belly, Sam on his back. Her eyes followed the brown and white cat that padded into the room, stopped beside the window where it lifted its nose to sniff the cool morning air, puffing the draperies gently from the sill, tapping the plastic bell on the end of the pull. Nose to the air, the cat stood for long minutes, then bounded onto the bed, landing in a most unfortunate spot.

Sam came up like a jack-in-the-box, uttering a sharp cry of surprise followed by an expletive. The cat went flying through the air like a missile as Lee braced up on both palms to observe Sam tenderly massaging his abused parts through the sheets.

She fell onto her belly again, chuckling into the pillow. "What's the matter? Was I too hard on you last night?"

"What the hell was that!"

"That was my cat, P. Ewing."

"Ohhh," he groaned. "I thought the bed was booby-trapped."

She laughed silently, hugged the pillow beneath one cheek, and peered up at him. "Can I help?"

He turned his head, all tousled and dark, and amusement curved his lips. "Your damn cat just . . . just pickled my mushrooms, woman, and you lie there making jokes?" It appeared he'd forgotten his discomforts now. He folded his arms behind his head and closed his eyes. "Don't talk to me, I'm pouting." But the corners of his lips twitched.

Lee studied him at leisure, noting that his beard had grown overnight, that his chest was wide and dark, that his nipples were the color of rosebuds. Pleasure came wafting over her at waking to the sight of such a man in her bed. He was as handsome as he was entertaining, and she let her eyes linger on his lips, brows, and eyelashes. She reached out and ran the tip of a fingernail just inside the rim of his nostril.

"Oh, Bro-o-w-wn?" she sing-songed seductively, going up and down the scale.

His nose twitched, but his eyes remained closed.

"Oh, Brow-w-wn . . ." she crooned again, tickling the edge of his other nostril. He wriggled his nose, then rubbed it distractedly before crossing his arms behind his head as before, with eyes still closed. She shimmied over beside him, propped her bare breasts coquettishly on his chest, and rested her chin on crossed wrists.

"Hey, Brown, you were right, this bed is booby-trapped. Wanna see?"

His chest shook silently, but he lay as before.

"Hmm?" she teased.

"Naw."

She snickered, unable to keep a straight face any longer. He opened one eye and looked down his nose at her.

"But I've got something here you might be interested in witnessing," he said.

"What's that?"

"A genuine Indian uprising."

They were dissolved by paroxysms of laughter then, even as his powerful arms closed around her and flipped her over. They shared a first good morning kiss, but before it ended the laughter had faded away. Lee held his face in both hands and said in a husky tone, "Oh, Brown, you're so good for me."

His ebony eyes ran over her face, touching her lips, nose, and tousled hair before meeting her own eyes.

"Lee," he requested in a strangely quiet way, "I'd like to hear you call me by my first name . . . just once."

She placed her palms in a light caress along his cheeks, then studied his face, feature by feature. It was a strong, compelling face, holding the color of the sun and his heritage in its copper tone. Her fingertips rested just beside his black-lashed eyes, which were as splendid in this new seriousness as ever they were when laughing. His cheekbones were high, his nose straight. She rested her thumbs on his full lips and brushed the soft skin lightly.

In the gentlest of voices she said his name. "Sam . . . Sam . . . Sam . . . I want you inside me again, Sam. You feel so good there." She drew his face down to hers, her mouth opening to receive his kiss as he moved over her, fitting his hips to hers, his firmness to her pliancy. Her eyes closed as his flesh stroked within hers—long, ardent strokes that took her back to that plane of rapture they'd shared more than once the night before.

"Open your eyes, Lee."

She opened them, losing herself in his brown, probing gaze that hovered just above her as their bodies blended rhythmically together. They watched each other's faces mirror what was happening inside as they moved closer to glory, reveling in not only what they took but also in what they gave.

As Lee witnessed a parade of feelings cross Sam's face, she found new meaning in the act, and realized with utter certainty that it was not one into which he had entered lightly.

When it was over and her hands had brushed away the sheen of moisture from Sam's back, she gathered him close, wondering if he would understand that what she'd just experienced seemed a blending of spirits as well as of bodies. Holding him tightly, she whispered against his neck, "Oh, we are good together, aren't we, Sam?"

"Yes we are, Cherokee. I told you that last night." He braced his elbows on either side of her, and his thumbs smoothed her hairline, and once again they assessed each other, but looking deeper now.

"I'm glad it wasn't just me," she began. "I mean . . . I needed this very badly and I thought maybe that's why it was . . . exceptional."

He smiled and kissed the side of her nose. "No, it wasn't

just you. It was exceptional for me too."

Her heart seemed to soar. "Was it really? You're not just saying that to be gallant?"

"Shall I stick around and convince you of that too?"

"Oh yes, Your Honor, please do."

And he did. They spent the weekend together, laughing and loving and learning about each other. And she came to know Sam Brown as a man of many facets.

That morning he insisted that she join him on an early run and produced from the trunk of his car a tote bag containing the same jogging clothes she'd seen once before. When she argued that it was Saturday, she had to clean the house, he said he'd help her when they got back. When she argued that she was out of shape, he said running would get her in shape —though he wasn't complaining. When she argued that it was hot, he said he'd cool her off.

They put on their sweatbands and headed out.

After a quarter of a mile Lee was lagging and panting. After half a mile her muscles burned. After that she tried to put her misery out of her mind, realizing what self-discipline it took to exercise like this every day. Her head hung. Her legs felt like deflated inner tubes. She followed Sam blindly, trailing doggedly at his heels and watching the slap of her feet . . .

He led her smack through the lawn sprinklers of Turner Golf Course!

She shrieked and threw her arms up over her head as the icy water brought her to a halt. "Brown, you're crazy!"

Still jogging, he turned to look at her over his shoulder. "I told you I'd cool you off," he called, then continued unceremoniously through the line of sprinklers. What could she do but laugh and follow?

When they returned home, he was the essence of solicitousness, laying her out on her stomach on the living room floor, then massaging her weary muscles with expert hands and soothing care. With her eyes closed and her cheek pressed against her crossed hands, she moaned, "Oh, Brown, how could you put me through that?"

"It'll keep you from getting fat and decadent," he replied cheerily, then completed her rubdown but refused to let her bask on the floor any longer. With a sharp slap on the rump, he ordered, "You have to keep moving or those muscles will tighten up."

With a groan she dragged herself up off the floor only to be hauled toward the shower. Without a flicker of embarrassment he joined her, and though it started out with Lee insisting she couldn't stand up for another minute, it ended with her soap-slicked body pressed flat against the cold ceramic tile and one knee hooked over Sam Brown's arm.

Afterward he made her breakfast, an ungodly concoction he called a Chinese omelette, declaring he had a passion for bean sprouts and water chestnuts. It was delicious after all, and the first meal a man had ever prepared for Lee. While they lounged at the table over cups of tea, Sam tipped his chair back on two legs, stretched a long arm toward the telephone on the counter behind him, called his mother, keeping his eyes on Lee all the time.

"Thought you might be worried," was the gist of his message.

When he'd hung up, he explained without compunction, "We don't interfere in each other's lives, but we share the same house. She'd do the same for me if she planned to be gone for an entire weekend."

And again, Lee looked at Sam in a new light.

There followed yet another surprise, for he was as good as his word and helped her with the house cleaning, showing an amazing lack of macho ego as he pushed the vacuum cleaner and emptied garbage cans. Joel had considered it "woman's work" and had never helped her with domestic tasks. Yet watching Sam Brown performing them now seemed to add to his masculinity rather than detract from it. She promised him a reward for his help and fulfilled that promise on the long sofa in the newly cleaned living room.

In the afternoon she remembered she'd made an appointment at the garage to have the oil changed in the Pinto. "Why not do it in the company shop and save yourself some money?" Sam suggested.

"Who, me?" she asked, surprised.

"Why not? The shop's got a hoist and any tools you need. Most of the guys who work for me take advantage of it. I don't mind."

"But . . ."

He leaned against the counter, crossed his arms, and cocked a dark eyebrow. "Don't tell me you're going to say, 'But I'm a woman.' Not after I just finished your vacuuming."

He had her there. She bit her tongue.

"I'll show you how, if you want me to. It's not hard," he offered.

And so Lee found herself doing the last thing in the world she'd ever have thought she'd do with Sam Brown—learning to buy the right size oil filter, the right weight oil; removing a drain plug, applying an oil-filter wrench, replacing the filter, then the plug, and finally the oil, and saving herself a considerable amount of money. And all at the suggestion of a man she'd once called rich and decadent.

But best of all, she'd earned Sam's respect, for as they headed back to her house, she knew he was pleased at the pluckiness she'd shown in her first attempt at auto maintenance.

They were scrubbing their hands at the bathroom sink when she looked up to find his approving eyes on her in the mirror. This time it was *he* who promised *her* a reward for her bravery, though he added with a charming grin that it would be the first time he'd ever made love to a mechanic.

While he went out to pick up a pizza, the "mechanic" prepared a homecoming.

Sam returned to a sight that stopped him dead in his tracks just inside the door. Lee posed at the far end of the hall haloed by the golden sunset coming through the patio door behind her. Her feet were bare. Her hair was loose. There were feathers in her ears and a white band around her forehead. Her palms rested on the walls above and beside her head while she slung her weight on one hip and the opposite thigh jutted forward. She wore nothing but a supple suede vest made up chiefly of swinging fringe. Several strands rode between her legs at the dark triangle of hair.

"Cherokee . . ." Sam breathed.

"Just so you don't get too used to me in a grease pit with a wrench in my hand."

"Come here, Cherokee," he said huskily.

They ate cold pizza.

At three o'clock in the morning Lee awakened with a charley horse in her leg and sprang up in pain. Sam was immediately at the foot of the bed, taking her calf in his hands and working the heel to ease the cramping muscles until the spasms passed.

"Better now, sweetheart?"

She sighed and relaxed. "Mmm-humm." His hands were like magic, soothing away the hurt. He'd called her sweetheart. She lay back, relaxed, letting him massage and manipulate the cramp away, thinking of what a study in contrasts Sam Brown had turned out to be. As if to bear out the point, a few minutes later he eased himself beside her again and pulled her into the curve of his body until they rested like two spoons in a drawer. As if to himself he mused, "Well, well . . . what's this now? I think I've discovered an Indian mound."

Lee burst out laughing and swatted him. "Sam Brown, you're awful!"

"Mmm . . . maybe I'll explore it."

"This one's been explored several times today."

"What? No more treasures left in it?"

Already he was searching for anything he might have missed. She knew that when he found it delight would surely follow, so she teased in return. "Well, there might be an old arrowhead left lying around."

Within minutes she had completely forgotten the lingering discomfort in her leg.

They ran again the next morning, then Lee cooked Sam breakfast while he did the Sunday crossword puzzle. Afterward she was sitting on the patio brushing her hair when he surprised her yet again by kneeling behind her, taking the brush from her hand, and pulling it gently through the tangled locks. As he braided the dark strands, they talked about their families and their pasts.

But there was one topic Lee never discussed—her children. She kept the door closed on the extra bedroom, hoping Sam wouldn't ask questions. And he didn't . . . until late Sunday afternoon, when they were once again lying naked on the living room floor.

She had fallen asleep and awoke to find Sam stretched out on his side, watching her, his jaw braced on a palm.

"Hi," he greeted softly.

"Hi." She smiled. "What are you doing?"

"Waiting."

"Have you been waiting long?"

"Not long. It's been an enjoyable wait."

She wondered how long he'd been studying her and resisted the urge to hide her stomach behind an arm. Even before he moved, she sensed what he was wondering.

Still lounging on his side, he dropped his eyes and slowly lifted his dark hand from his hip. It moved toward her stomach, then a single fingertip traced the faded line there, following it downward from her navel.

"What's this?" he asked in the quietest of voices, lifting his eyes to hers.

She swallowed and felt a flash of dread, wanting to be honest with him yet searching for an adequate lie. Finding none, she could only answer, "It's a stretch mark."

"And what's it from?" His unsmiling eyes remained locked with hers.

The words stuck in her throat, though she realized he deserved an answer—an honest answer. He had seen the marks many times during the past two days but had refrained from asking questions until it became apparent she was not going to offer an explanation without being prompted. She swallowed dryly, her throat tight with apprehension.

"It's . . . it's from a baby I once had."

A long moment passed, rife with unspoken questions. Then, without another word, he bent to her, resting his lips against the telltale line. Lee's heart threatened to burst beyond the bonds of her body as his warm mouth lingered. Tears suddenly filled her eyes at the sight of him twisted from the hip, his shoulder blade outlined sharply while he breathed softly against her skin.

When he raised his head at last, it was to study her eyes deeply as he asked, "When?"

"A long time ago."

He touched his thumb to the wet track from a tear. "Tears again, Cherokee, just like that day in the orchard?"

His compassion never failed to throw her off guard, for it was so unlike what she'd first expected from him. She turned her head sharply aside and stared out the window, unable to meet the concern in his gaze any longer. But he stretched out beside her again, wrapped her in his strong arms, and forced her to face him.

"Did it die, Cherokee?"

The natural assumption. She knew she should disabuse him of it here and now, but it was so hard . . . so hard. She closed her eyes, trapping more tears that wanted to escape, cutting off the sight of a tender, concerned Sam Brown, whom she knew she was deceiving by letting the misinterpretation go uncorrected.

"I can't talk about it. I . . . I just can't, Sam."

To Lee's surprise, he acquiesced. "Okay, we won't talk about it now." He brushed the hair back from her temple with his wide palm, then kissed the top of her head. "Anyway, I think it's time I was going."

They were silent as they went upstairs and found his clothes—the same he'd worn there Friday night—and a robe for her. She walked him to the door, but the gaiety they'd shared all weekend was gone. They stood without speaking for a long moment, Lee staring at his feet, and Sam at the keys in his palm. Finally he sighed and took her into his arms.

"Listen, I have to fly to Chicago tomorrow. I'll be gone for a few days."

She was taken by surprise at how abandoned his announcement made her feel. They had spent two days together—nothing more. How could she feel this bereft after only two days?

Her arms circled his shoulders, suddenly strong and clinging as she raised up on tiptoe, but after a brief return of the pressure, he backed away and grinned down at her.

"Promise me you'll run every day without me?"

She dredged up a bright smile. "Promise."

He kissed her lightly. "I'll be back on Thursday or so." Again they fell silent. He drew in a deep breath and looked as if he were coming to a decision he didn't like. "It'll probably be good for us to be apart for a while, huh?"

"Sure," she agreed with that same false brightness, while

her heart seemed to crack around the edges.

He gave her a last smile. "Get some sleep. You look exhausted."

Then he turned toward the door, and she found herself gripping its edge with both hands while calling after him, "Call me when you get back?"

"Of course."

But during the days that followed she wondered if he really would call. Why had that last conversation come up? *Why?* Each time she thought of it she felt like a fist was gripping her heart. He had guessed the truth, she was sure. He had guessed and wanted her to admit it, but when she'd backed away he'd decided it was time to take a second look at things. That's what he was doing on this trip to Chicago—evaluating her from a distance.

She lived with the fear that he would return having decided he didn't want to invest any more time in a woman who couldn't be totally honest with him, and she promised herself that if he called when he got back, she'd tell him the truth immediately.

In that brief time he had made himself an integral part of her life. He lingered in almost every corner of it—in the office, where she often glanced toward his open door, wondering how his business was going in Chicago, who he was with, if he missed her too; in her townhouse, where they had laughed and slept and made love and left memories in nearly every room; in her car, which reminded her of what fun it had been learning from him. Even running through the warm August evenings reminded her that he had already encouraged this change in her lifestyle, for she kept her promise and jogged after work each day, improving her wind control by breathing in long draughts as he'd taught her instead of in rhythm with her footsteps.

Sometimes she asked herself if this sudden obsession with Sam Brown was only sexual. Was she nothing more than a desperate divorcee who'd tumbled for the first man who gave her a second look? The idea frightened her, for ever since her divorce she'd feared doing that. Was she that kind of woman? Admittedly, it had been a long dry spell for her, which she'd certainly made up for with Sam Brown. Yet, what they had experienced that weekend had taken her feelings for him far beyond the sexual.

He had revealed himself to be a caring person, self-disciplined, amusing, devoted, compassionate, honest. What a surprise to discover such a myriad of admirable qualities hidden beneath the surface person she'd so mistrusted at first.

Recalling his attributes, she grew to miss him in a sometimes terrifying way and wished he'd call. But he didn't, though he checked in with Rachael every day. In a way Lee was hurt that he didn't ask to speak to her, but he'd said it would be good for them to be apart, and apparently he was giving the test a full chance.

Lee found him on her mind far, far too often and realized things had happened very fast between them. Too fast—like the first time with Joel when neither of them had stopped to think past the here and now. Hadn't she learned her lesson then? Yet here she was, plunged into loneliness over Sam after only a two-day relationship.

Relationship. She considered the word. Yes, she admitted, she and Sam Brown had related to one another in many ways. That was why their last conversation had come to bear such great significance and why his parting mood had left her utterly despondent. Once again she promised herself that the minute he called she'd tell him the truth.

Every time the phone rang in the office on Thursday, Lee's eyes went to the lighted button, wondering if it was him. Every time somebody's shadow crossed the doorway, she looked up with her heart in her throat. But he hadn't returned by five o'clock, and she drove home trying to decide whether or not she should run. What if he called while she was gone? In the end she kept her promise and went for the longest run she'd taken yet, pushing herself until her hip sockets ached and her thigh muscles quivered. Back home, she showered and put on faded blue jeans and a T-shirt with an advertisement for Water Products Company on its front. If he didn't call, if he didn't come, at least she wouldn't find herself at the end of the evening removing clothing that indicated she'd fussed and waited for him. But she polished her nails and braided her hair and put on a new brand of perfume she'd chosen for its light, uncloying scent. She opened the refrigerator perhaps a dozen times, but nothing appealed to her. She rehearsed exactly how she'd tell him, but each time she said the words her palms grew damp.

When the phone rang at 7:45, her heart seemed to skitter to her throat and her stomach went fluttery. It rang again. She lurched and grabbed it.

"Hello?"

Sam's baritone voice held an unexpected teasing note as he announced, "This is a collect obscene phone call from the Honorable Sam Brown to Cherokee Walker. Will she accept the charges?"

Joy sluiced through Lee, bringing a faint weakness to her knees. She beamed at the ceiling and answered, "Yes, she will."

"And is this Cherokee Walker?"

"It is."

"The one with the Indian braid on cleaning day and the mole way low on the left side of her rump?"

"Yes." A gurgle of laughter escaped her lips.

"And the one with the neat, sexy breasts just about the size of the palm of my hand?"

"The same." This was obviously no time for serious matters.

"The one who makes love on the living room floor and against the bathroom wall?"

"Sam, where are you?"

"I'm home, but I'll be at your house in exactly"—A pause followed as if he were checking his watch—"thirteen and a half minutes."

Her heart was hammering against her ribs, and she was smiling fit to kill. She was so relieved she forgot to say anything.

"Cherokee, are you still there?"

"Yes . . . yes, I'm still here."

Silence hummed for a moment before his voice came low and husky. "I missed you to beat hell, babe."

A great outthrusting pressure formed across her chest as she held the receiver in both hands and returned in a half whisper, "I missed you too. Hurry, Sam."

When had she last felt this giddy, this impatient? She was fifteen years old again, waiting for that special boy to walk into English class. She was sixteen, planning an appealing pose that a certain boy couldn't help but notice. She was seventeen and trying to appear casual while every nerve and muscle in her body was taut with anticipation. She conjured up the image of Sam Brown, and it was flawless and godlike, and she told herself it was only her breathless eagerness that made him perfect in her memory. Yet when reality stepped through her door, the memory paled in comparison.

He came in without knocking. She was standing at the kitchen end of the hall, where she waited for his knock after hearing the car door shut. At his unannounced entry, she drew in a quick breath, then stood unmoving, staring at Sam as he hesitated with his hand on the door—copper skin, chestnut hair, trousers of cinnamon brown, an open-throated ivory dress shirt, and a look in his dark eyes that said the past four days had been as long for him as they'd been for her.

"Cherokee . . ."

"Sam . . ."

She felt a moment of intense elation, took a hesitant step, and then they were flying toward each other and his arms were around her and hers were about his neck as he lifted her from the floor and turned in a joyous circle, holding her crushed high against his chest with her nose pressed against his crisp collar, where the scent of him was just as she remembered. She closed her eyes, the better to absorb the almost dizzying satisfaction at having him back again. Sam . . . Sam. . . . He let her slip down, and even before her toes touched the floor, they were kissing, with pounding hearts pressed together so tightly they seemed to beat within a single body. Their tongues conveyed not only impatience, not only eagerness, but also that far more poignant message—you're as good as I remembered . . . even better. She held the back of his head in two greedy palms, felt it move as his mouth worked compellingly upon hers and his strong arms circled so far around her ribs that his fingertips touched the soft swells at the sides of her breasts. Then his palms ran the length of her back, caressing it through the T-shirt from neck to waist in a touch that was curiously unsexual, but a comfirmation of her presence in his arms once again, a celebration at having her back where she belonged.

In much the same way she slipped her fingers inside the back of his collar, seeking warm skin, kneading the hard knots of his neck as if to reaffirm his presence.

When the first wild rush of greeting had finally passed, he lifted his head and his voice shook. "God, I missed you."

His words sent shudders of relief down her spine. His hands slipped under her shirt, and he folded his elbows along the center of her back till his wide palms came up through the neck of her T-shirt to cradle her head. She lay back against them, looking up at him, taking her fill of him.

"I missed you too . . . incredibly." Words seemed inadequate to describe how all-consuming her thoughts of him had been. She touched him in an effort to tell him in another way what her days had been like without him. She caressed his cheeks, his eyebrows, his lips . . . and as she did, his fingers massaged her head on either side of the thick braid. He closed his eyes and turned his parted lips against her fingertips as they brushed past.

"Chicago was almost a lost cause. I couldn't keep my mind on business," he confessed, still with his eyes closed, still with his lips turned against her fingers.

"The office wasn't the same without you."

He opened his eyes again. They held the look of a man who had truly come home.

"Wasn't it?"

She shook her head no. "I almost hated being there."

He smiled. "I'm glad. Misery loves company."

"Every time I knew Rachael had talked to you, I *was* miserable."

"Good, because I was too." His eyes wandered up to her hairline then, and his hands slipped from under her shirt to bracket her hips and settle them comfortably against his own.

"Did you run, like you promised?"

She laced her fingers around the back of his neck, leaning at the waist. "I ran like a dervish, trying to get you off my mind."

"Did it work?" The well-remembered grin was back.

"No." She squeezed his neck briefly. "It only made matters

worse. But you'd be proud of me. I must have gone three miles today."

"Three miles! Hey, that's good." At his approval she was suddenly very, very glad she'd persevered with the running and felt a great rush of pride.

"Oh, and I went shopping, too, and got some decent running shoes."

He backed away and looked down at her feet. "Let's see—oh, very nice. No more charley horses?" He settled her back where she'd been and ran his hands idly over the curve of her spine.

"Nope. I'm getting tougher all the time." Again she thrilled at his grin of approval. Then he observed, "You shopped for something else while I was gone too, didn't you?"

"What?"

His head dipped briefly to her neck while his hands moved unhurriedly over her buttocks. "Some new perfume, I think."

"Do you like it?"

"Aha." His lips confirmed the answer with a soft nip at the skin beneath one ear.

"And it doesn't make you sneeze?"

"Un-uh."

She rocked lazily against him, smiling to herself while her fingers remained locked at the back of his neck.

"Good, because after the shoes I can't afford to try another kind."

He laughed, lifting his head, white teeth flashing, then asked, "Have you eaten yet?"

"No, and I'm ravenous now that you're back."

"So am I. Let's go get something, and you can fill me in on everything that went on around the office while I was gone."

"I'm not exactly dressed . . ." She backed away, tugging at the hem of the baggy sweatshirt and looking down at it critically.

"You look sensational to me." Sam turned her toward the door, looped an arm over her shoulders, and gave her a nudge. "Now, let's get this damn eating over with so I can bring you back home and tell you again how much I missed you."

It wasn't until later that Lee realized the subtle change that had come over their relationship with Sam's homecoming. When it struck her, the significance was overwhelming. They had taken the time to catch up on each other's lives, talk business, eat supper together—all before they'd made love. And each moment had been equally satisfying.

Chapter 10

As AUGUST LENGTHENED, Lee and Sam grew used to seeing each other every day at the office and every evening, in private, but in spite of Lee's silent promises, she never brought up the subject of her children. Somehow the proper moment didn't present itself that first night, and as the days slipped by it became easier and easier to put it off.

Yet she saw more and more of Sam. She learned his favorite foods, favorite colors, favorite movie stars. They attended an outdoor concert at the Starlight Theater, and he helped her pick out chairs for her living room. They went to a preseason game of the Kansas City Chiefs at plush Arrowhead Stadium and ran together almost daily.

On the surface everything was calm, and their relationship thrived. But as the last week of August neared, an undeniable tension grew between them. Sam had never asked why she needed the week off, but she knew he wondered.

There were countless times when she could have told him, such as when he'd scooped up P. Ewing, looked the cat in the eye, and said, "Cat, I like your name. Where'd you get it?"

It was the perfect lead-in, so why didn't she take the opportunity to explain that it had come from Jed, who'd inadvertently stumbled upon it by exclaiming the kitten was "pew-ing" the first time it used the sandbox?

It would have been so much simpler had she listened to her conscience and told him in the beginning. But the longer she held the secret inside, the bigger it grew, until it lay like a malignancy she knew must be removed before it eventually killed her. But by now she'd put off telling him for so long that she'd become paranoid about it.

There were times when she looked up to find Sam's eyes studying her pensively, and she knew he was biting his tongue to keep from asking the question which by now he had every right to ask. Yet, honorably, he didn't. And the tension built . . . and built.

Until the night he took her to his home to have dinner with his mother. The evening was an unqualified success, and Lee realized it represented another step in their deepening relationship. But she knew too that Sam had not chosen this last evening before her week off without due consideration. He'd done it as if to say—there, another obstacle overcome; now it's your turn.

All the way home in the car tension grew between them. Outside, a storm raged with great slashes of lightning zagging over the plains followed by awesome thunderclaps. Rain pelted down. The windshield wipers beat out a rhythm and the tires hissed through the rainy streets while inside the car Sam refrained from taking Lee's hand, which he usually did when he drove.

At the townhouse he killed the engine and the lights, then laced his fingers on the steering wheel and stared straight ahead, as if waiting for an explanation.

"Lee—" he began at last.

But before he could get any farther, she interrupted, "There's no sense in two of us getting soaked. You stay here."

His silence seemed to say, "On our last night together?" Yet he continued brooding while the tension mounted still higher between them. Finally, unable to think of a graceful exit line, Lee leaned over and kissed his cheek. He sat as stiff as a ramrod, but as she reached for the door handle, his hand lashed out in the dark and grabbed her so roughly that she gasped. Immediately he loosened his grip, and his voice became contrite.

"Lee, I'm going to miss you."

"I . . . I'm going to miss you too." She waited breathlessly, but still he didn't ask the question, and still she didn't offer an explanation. She wanted so badly to be honest with him, but she was so afraid of looking inadequate in his eyes. The silence lengthened, and the tension in the car seemed ready to explode. Then, just when she thought she couldn't bear it another instant, Sam released her hand, sighed tiredly, and sank down against the seat. She searched his face in the shadows, and for a blinding second the car interior was lit by lightning. His eyes were closed, and he'd rolled his face away from her while he pinched the bridge of his nose.

"Lee, I'm not sure . . . no, let me start again." His hand fell away from his nose, but his voice was strained and held an undeniable note of weariness. "I think I love you, Lee."

It was the last thing she'd expected him to say. Tears sprang to her eyes, and her heart pounded. She reached for his hand on the seat between them, took it in both of hers, and lifted it to her mouth. It was more than a kiss she placed on the back of it. It was a taking in of the texture, warmth and security of it. And it was an apology.

She straightened the long, lax fingers and pressed her cheek and eyebrow against his knuckles.

"Oh, Sam," she breathed sadly against his hand, then carried it to the side of her neck and pressed it beneath her jaw where the pulse raced. "I think I love you too."

Everything inside Lee's body felt as temptestuous as the storm outside. She ran her fingertips down his inner wrist and felt his wild pulse, but he sat as before, wedged low in the seat.

"What should we do about it?" he asked, and she knew it was as close as he would come to forcing her to tell him why she was about to drop mysteriously out of his life for a week.

"Wait and see. We both said we 'think.'"

But even to Lee, her answer sounded inadequate, and she sensed his frustration mounting. "Wait?" he snapped, anger boiling to the surface again as he demanded in a hard tone, "How long?" His fingers closed tightly around hers.

"Sam, let me go in."

He seemed to consider a moment, as if calculating the effect of his question before asking, "Can I come in with you?"

Immediately she let go of his hand. "No, Sam, not tonight."

"Why?" He sat up straighter and seemed to strain toward her.

"I . . ." But she couldn't explain it. She only knew it had something to do with the boys coming tomorrow and a feeling of her own unworthiness. But before she could conjure up an answer, his voice cut coldly through the tense space between them.

"All right then, come here." And before she could guess his intentions, he reached for her in an insolent way he'd never before used with her and pulled her roughly across the seat until she fell against his chest. He began kissing her with a bruising lack of sensitivity.

"S . . . Sam, don't!" She struggled up, recoiling instinctively against him. But he grabbed her by both wrists, and he was frighteningly powerful in his anger as they poised, faced off in a half-prone position across the car seat. His fingers bit into the tender skin where her pulse raced. Tears trembled on her eyelids, and fear swelled up in her throat.

"Why do you pull away? I'm wishing the lady good-bye, that's all."

"Sam . . ." But before more words escaped her stiff lips, she was flung backward against his hard chest with her right hand wrenched between their bodies, rendering it useless. And all the while his voice grated near her ear. "I've just said I think I love you, and you told me the same thing. Considering that, I think you deserve a proper good-bye." She fought him with her single free hand, but he controlled it with amazingly little difficulty as he roughly opened the front fastening of her slacks and plunged his hand inside.

"Sam . . . why . . . why are you doing . . . this?" she sobbed.

But he was relentless. "Why?" His hand invaded the part of her body he had never touched with anything but utmost tenderness, but his voice made a mockery of the act. "This is what you keep me around for, isn't it? This is what you want me for, isn't it?"

He plundered her with consummate skill while an unspeakable sense of loss washed over Lee. She was sobbing quietly now, and somewhere in the back of her mind she knew she'd brought on this anger herself, for his confession of love had been an invitation for her to confide in him, yet she'd refused once again. Tears ran down her face as she finally gave up struggling and lay passively on his hard, aroused body, letting him do with her what he would.

But just as swiftly as it had come, the fight went out of him. His hand fell still while his chest still heaved with emotion. His heartbeat reverberated through the thin fabric of Lee's blouse, and he swallowed convulsively. At the sound, she too choked back the thick tears that clotted her throat. Slowly his fingertips withdrew to rest on the soft, warm skin of her stomach. Neither of them spoke.

In those moments, as she lay upon him, feeling him breathe torturously against the back of her neck, she saw the death of a love that might have been. She held back the sobs she wanted to release for the annihilation of something they'd built slowly and carefully, something that had shown such bright promise only a short time ago.

And—oh God, oh God—it hurt.

He had seized upon one of her greatest vulnerabilities and used it against her, knowing full well that his accusation would debase her. She wished she could go back ten minutes and live them again. But she could only fling the back of a wrist over her eyes while her throat muscles worked spasmodically. All the while she lay on top of him like a plucked flower, wilted by the very sun that had once given it life.

She opened her eyes and stared unseeingly at the rivulets of rain oozing down the windshield, turning an unearthly green in the intermittent flashes of lightning. For a minute she felt disoriented and removed from herself.

Then she summoned up the will to move and pulled herself up, slowly, slowly, sitting on his sprawled thighs and running shaky fingers through her tousled hair, unable yet to find the strength to remove herself from him completely.

"Cherokee—"

"Don't!" His rasping utterance was cut in half by the stiffening of her shoulders and the harsh word. She had thrown up a hand in warning but still sat on him, still with her back to him. There followed a deadly silence, broken only by the ongoing thrum of rain on the roof and low growls of thunder.

Then, muscle by muscle, she dragged her weary body to the far side of the seat and untangled her legs from his. In the same deliberate fashion he righted himself behind the wheel, then hung his hands on it, staring straight ahead for several seconds before slowly lowering his forehead onto his knuckles.

She tucked in her blouse, zipped and buttoned her slacks, and reached to slip her shoes from her feet, all with the stilted motions of an automaton. But when she reached for her purse and then for the door handle, Sam lifted his head and placed a detaining hand on her arm.

"Cherokee, I'm sorry. Let's talk about this."

"Don't touch me," she said lifelessly. "And don't call me Cherokee."

His hand fell away, but his voice held a note of entreaty. "This happened because you won't confide in me. If you go in now and stubbornly refuse to—"

The car door cut off his appeal as she stepped out into the torrents of rain and slammed it shut. A river of water rushed along the curb, but she scarcely felt it as her nylon-clad foot splashed through it. Then she was fleeing blindly toward the door. Behind her the engine started up, and the car tore away at breakneck speed, the tail lights fishtailing down the street on the slick pavement. At the stop sign up the block he only slowed, then tore off again with a second screech of tires and swerving of tail lights that bled off into the distance.

The night that followed was one of the worst in Lee's life. She was left utterly decimated by the rift between her and Sam while at the same time she realized she must buck up her spirits to face her sons. She damned Sam Brown for bringing this emotional turmoil into her life at a time that was already rife with it. Facing the boys brought again that sick-sweet lifting of the heart that was half joy, half pain, and as she knelt to greet them, it was with a foreknowledge that this visit was somehow doomed from the start.

Jed and Matthew had grown so much since she'd seen them. At six and eight, they now resisted her hello hugs. Telling herself not to feel slighted, she backed off, realizing she seemed strange to them and that it would take them a while to warm up. They loved her new townhouse, though, and claimed their new beds with exuberance and a few surprised "wows." They fell upon P. Ewing, seeming to have missed him more than their mother, and she looked on with heartsick emptiness, remembering how she and Joel had decided to get the cat because they'd been fighting more and more and thought the pet would be good for the boys.

Daddy, they said, was fine, and they liked his new wife, Tisha, real good. Tisha made the best lasagna in the world. No, Lee answered her younger son when he asked, she wasn't too handy at lasagna. How about spaghetti? But it seemed Matthew had lost the fetish for spaghetti she remembered.

They squealed with glee at her suggestion that she take them to a pro football game the second day they were there. But they didn't know the Kansas City players' names and before long squirmed in their seats and became occasionally disruptive, teasing each other and punching playfully, their bouncing and boisterousness drawing unfavorable glances from people in nearby seats. They left the game after the third quarter. On the way home Lee learned that soccer was their favorite game now. Daddy was coaching their team, and Tisha came to every game.

On Monday Lee won their hearts by taking them on an all-day outing to Worlds of Fun amusement park. They rode the Zulu, Orient Express, and Screamroller until Lee's feet hurt from standing around waiting. But after each ride she shared their renewed delight and robbed her pitifully poor pocketbook again and again for the junkfood they wanted. She forgot to bring suntan lotion, so by the end of the day the boys were both burned, thus irritable and uncomfortable in bed that night.

In her own bed, she thought about Sam and the day they'd ridden the Zambezi Zinger, but the day that had been so happy then only brought a bittersweet pang now and made her cry miserably. She missed him terribly, even while she hated him for the hurt he'd caused her. She considered calling him, but her emotional equilibrium was already strained to its limits by being with the boys again.

The boys. They hardly seemed like her sons anymore, and she felt increasingly inadequate. Nothing she did seemed right for their needs while everything Tisha did must be perfect. Tomorrow, she vowed, she'd make no mistakes.

That day she took them to the sixty acre Swope Park Zoo with its six hundred animals. But they'd been to Florida's Busch Gardens last year and had ridden down the African Safari Ride, where elephants spray you while you go past. The Swope trip seemed a definite second best to her sons.

Each night when they were asleep in their twin beds, Lee stepped to the doorway of their room and studied the dark heads on the pale pillow cases, and tears clogged her throat. At those moments, the disastrous days paled and were forgotten. She was desperately happy to have them here. The two sleeping children were hers again, flesh of her flesh, beings of her making. She loved them in a terrifying way, yet knew with a keen, piercing certainty that their stepmother's love was far more influential than her own. Soon she would become a shadow figure to them. Perhaps she already was.

Matthew had a bad dream the next night and awakened in tears. She sat on the edge of the bed while the backs of his sunburned hands smeared tears across his cheeks and he cried, "Where's Mommy?"

"I'm here, darling," she answered soothingly.

But, disoriented and accustomed to the securities of his life in another home, he cried, "No-o-o, I want Mommy."

By Friday both Jed and Matthew were discussing their friends at home and making plans for what they were going to play when they got back.

On Saturday they produced money "Mommy" had given them to buy a gift for Daddy. Lee took them to the store of stores—Halls, in the Crown Center—where there were items like nowhere else in the world. They bought Daddy a bar of soap shaped like a microphone so that he could sing in the shower.

On Sunday Lee dressed them each in a brand new outfit she'd bought and waited anxiously for their father to come and pick them up. She wondered what her reaction to Joel would be and felt a quailing in her stomach as the doorbell rang. The boys catapulted to answer it. But with him they babbled mostly about all the exciting things they'd done during the week. It was to Tisha, waiting in the car, to whom they ran with arms extended.

Joel looked healthy and happy, watching the boys gallop

across the lawn before he turned to her. She surveyed him with immense relief and realized he no longer posed a threat to her emotions. At some point she had stopped loving him, and she could face him now, comfortable with the fact.

"How are you, Lee?"

"Oh, I'm fine. Things are going well with my new job, and I've got the house now, and . . ." Her eyes wandered down the sidewalk to the boys, then back to Joel's face. "You and Tisha are doing a wonderful job with them, Joel."

"Thanks." He stood relaxed before her. "We're expecting another one in February."

"Well, congratulations!" She smiled. "I . . . well, please tell Tisha the same."

"I will." He made a move to leave and for the first time seemed slightly uncomfortable. "Well, I guess the guys will see you again at Christmas."

"Yes." The word sounded forlorn.

"Boys," Joel called, "come and kiss your mother good-bye."

They returned on the run, gave Lee the required kiss, then forgot everything except getting back into the car as fast as they could.

When they were gone, Lee wandered about the house like a lost soul, hugging her arms. The kitchen smelled like cherry popsicles and she found one melting down the sink, dropped there hastily when she'd said their daddy had arrived. She picked up the stick and threw it away, then rinsed the red liquid down the drain. But the pink stain remained. She stared at it for a long, long time until it grew wavery. A tear dripped down and landed beside it on the almond-colored porcelain, and a moment later she leaned an elbow on the sink edge and sobbed wretchedly. The sound of her crying made her weep all the harder, echoing as it did into the empty room. *My babies.* She clutched her stomach and let misery overwhelm her, leaning her face against her forearm until it grew slick. Her sobbing became so choppy and prolonged that it robbed Lee of breath, and she felt her knees buckle. She moved to the kitchen table and fell into a chair, dropping her head forward on her arms, crying until she thought there could be no more moisture in her body. *Where's Mommy?* P. Ewing came and rubbed up against her leg and purred, bringing a renewed freshet of misery. She needed a tissue, but had none in the kitchen, so she stumbled upstairs and blew her nose and dried her eyes. Clutching a handful of soggy tissues against her nose and mouth, she leaned against the bedroom doorway and felt her grief renewed at the sight of the twin beds and the pennants on the wall above them. Her head fell tiredly against the doorframe, and she cried until her throat and chest ached. *I love you, Jed. I love you, Matthew.* Her misery seemed to have eternal life. The convulsive sobs continued until her head was bursting, and she dragged herself to the bathroom for two aspirins. But at the sight of her ravaged face in the mirror, more tears burned her swollen eyelids and she thought that if she didn't hear the sound of another human voice soon, she would most certainly die.

She stumbled down to the kitchen and dialed, seeking help from the only person who could solace her. When she heard his voice, she tried to calm her own, but she lost control and sucked in unexpected gulps of air in the middle of words.

"Ss . . . S . . . ham?"

A moment of silence, then his concerned voice, "Lee, is that you?"

"S . . . Sam . . ." She couldn't get anything else out.

"Lee, what's the matter?" He sounded panicked.

"Oh, S . . . Sam, I n . . . need you so b . . . bad." A huge sob broke from her as she clutched the receiver with both hands.

"Lee, are you hurt?"

"No . . . No, n . . . not hurt . . . j . . . just hurting. Please . . . c . . . come . . ."

"Where are you?"

"At h . . . home," she choked.

"I'm coming."

When the line clicked, her arm wilted toward the floor with the phone dangling from her lifeless fingers and she begged him, "Pl . . . please hurry."

She was sitting slumped over the kitchen table ten minutes later when Sam Brown ran up the walk and burst through the front door. He skidded to a halt in the middle of the hall, chest heaving. "Lee?" He caught sight of her as she flew out of her chair. They met in the middle of the hall. She flung herself against him, sobbing abjectly and clinging to his comforting body as she burrowed into him.

"S . . . Sam, oh, Sam . . . h . . . hold me."

He crushed her to him protectively. "Lee, what is it? Are you all right?"

Her body was heaving so much no answer was possible just then. He closed his eyes and pressed a cheek against her disheveled hair as hot tears melded his shirt and his collarbone. Her tormented body was wracked by shudders so he wound his arms around her tightly, waiting for her to calm down.

"Sam . . . Sam . . ." she sobbed wretchedly, over and over.

Never had a body felt so good. His hard chest and arms were a haven of familiarity. His scent and texture comforted immeasurably while he stood like a rock, his feet widespread, his long length shielding her. Forgotten were the hurts they'd caused each other. All forgotten was the pain of separation. Barriers fell as she sought his strength, and he gave it willingly.

"I'm here," he assured her, spanning the back of her head with a wide hand and pressing her securely to him. "Tell me."

"My b . . . boys, m . . . my babies," she choked, the simple words becoming an outpouring of her soul while he remained unflinching, the solid foundation of her life.

"They were here?"

She could only nod against his neck.

"And now they're gone?"

Again she nodded and felt him stroke her hair. She pulled back. "How l . . . long have you known?"

His hands spanned almost the entire circumference of her head while his thumbs stroked the tears that were her healing. "Almost since the beginning."

She looked up through a bleary haze while her heart swelled with love for him. "Oh, Sam, I was s . . . so afraid to t . . . tell you." She buried herself against him.

"Why?" His voice was thick, and she heard in it vestiges of the hurt she'd caused and promised herself she would make it up to him. "Couldn't you trust me?"

Fresh tears spouted again while she clung to him. "I was so af . . . afraid of what you'd th . . . think of me." Her shoulders shook even as relief overwhelmed her because he knew at last.

"Shh, don't cry. Come here." He pushed her back gently and slipped an arm around her shoulders, urging her toward the stairs. He sat down on the third step and tugged her down between his knees on the step below, then pulled her back against him. His broad forearm crossed her chest and hugged her tightly while he squeezed her upper arm and rested his chin against the top of her hair. "Now tell me everything."

"I wanted to tell you the l . . . last time we were together. I wanted to so badly, b . . . but I didn't know what you'd think about a . . . a mother who had her kids taken away from her in a divorce court."

His lips pressed the top of her head. "Darling, I saw their beds the first day I came here. I've been waiting since then for you to tell me about it."

"You've known all that time. Oh, Sam, why didn't you ask?"

"I did once, but you let me believe they had died, and I realized then that *you* had to tell me. And that last night we were together, I . . . oh God, Cherokee, I'm so sorry for what I did. But it damn near killed me that you couldn't trust me enough to tell me then. I've had a miserable week, thinking of how I've hurt you and wondering if my suspicions about your kids were right. At times I even found myself wondering if you were with your ex-husband, and I told myself if you were, it was no more than I deserved." His arm tightened perceptibly across her chest.

"No, not that. He's married again and they're expecting another baby."

"You saw him this week, too?"

"Yes, he came to pick up the boys just before I called you."

"They live with him, then?" His quiet questions encouraged her to talk about them, and she marveled at having a man who understood her needs so well. His warm palm caressed her bare arm, and his voice was very soft and compelling.

"What are their names?"

She brushed his forearm and felt his breath warm on the top of her head. "Jed and Matthew." Just pronouncing their names brought a sharp sense of renewed heartache. She sat quietly for a long moment, thinking of their empty beds upstairs. But she rested her head against Sam's chest and drew strength from him as she continued. "Oh, Sam, I don't know if I'll ever get over 1 . . . losing them. That day in the courtroom was like . . . like judgment day, and I've been in hell ever since. It was totally unexpected. My lawyer was just as dumbfounded as I was when the judge declared that he was giving custody of the boys to Joel. But Joel had a high-powered attorney, one he could afford, and I had a less experienced one that I couldn't afford. I just never dreamed I'd lose. My attorney kept telling me there was something called the 'tender years concept,' meaning basically that little kids need their mother. The boys were only three and five then. But the judge said the court found it would be in the best interest of the children to have a strong male role model." Lee pulled away from Sam's body, crossed her arms on her knees, and rested her head on them. "Male role model, for God's sake. I didn't even know what it meant."

Sam studied her back, reached to cup a hand over her shoulders, and pulled her securely between his legs again.

"Go on," he ordered quietly, slipping his arm across her collarbone.

She closed her eyes and swallowed, then continued in a strained voice. "His lawyer brought up the subject of economics, and mine argued, but it seems economics enter into the . . . the emotional well-being of children. I had no means of support, no career, no prospects. I'd been a wife raising babies, how could I have?" A shudder went through her. She swallowed and opened her eyes. Tears slipped down her cheeks, and a lump lodged in her throat.

"Oh, Sam . . . have you any idea wh . . . what it's like to have your children t . . . taken away? What a failure you f . . . feel like?"

A hot tear dropped on his arm. He squeezed her shoulders and chest in a bone-crushing gesture of comfort, resting his cheek against her hair. "You're not a failure," he whispered thickly. "Not to me . . . because I love you."

How many times this week had she longed for those words? Yet at the moment they tore at her soul, for it was because she loved him too that she wanted to be perfect in his eyes. But she wasn't—oh, she wasn't—so, she went on purging herself. "This week I realized I'm totally inadequate as a mother. The courts were probably right to take them away from me. She's done a better job than I ever could. I d . . . did everything wrong. I l . . . let them get s . . . sunburned and I—"

"Lee, stop it."

"I didn't know how to c . . . comfort Matthew when he had a b . . . bad dream and—"

"Lee!"

"And I . . . I . . ." The tears broke free again, and she struggled on in self-recrimination. "I c . . . can't m . . . make—" He grabbed her roughly and swung her around until her face was pressed against his chest where the last word came out a muffled sob—"lasagna."

"Oh God, Cherokee, don't do this to yourself."

"I d . . . did everything wrong." She clung to the back of his shirt, wailing out her pitiful litany.

"Shh . . ." He patted her hair and held her head tightly with both hands.

"They ran to h . . . her and f . . . forgot all about m . . . me when she . . ."

His mouth stopped her words. He had jerked her roughly up to him and held her now in an awkward embrace, twisted as she was at the waist while they perched on their two different steps. He kissed her savagely, then lifted his head and held her jaw as he studied her face.

"They've been away from you for a long time, and they're used to her now. That doesn't mean you're a failure. Don't blame yourself. It breaks my heart to see you like this."

And from the depths of her misery she realized what she had in Sam Brown. Strength, understanding, compassion. Her hurt was his hurt for he absorbed it and his eyes became a reflection of the pain he saw in hers. She trembled on the brink of understanding the true depth of love. And, not wanting to put him through more agony, she finally made a shaky effort to control her tears. When they eventually lessened, he pushed her gently away from him, but only far enough to raise one hip and pull a handkerchief from his back pocket. When she'd dried her eyes and blown her nose, she felt better. Heaving a giant sigh, she sat down beside him on the same step. Bracing both elbows on her knees, Lee gingerly covered her burning eyelids with her fingertips and declared unsteadily, "My eyes hurt. I haven't cried this much since the divorce."

"Then you needed it."

She lowered her hands and looked at his understanding face.

"I'm sorry I unloaded on you. But thank you for . . . for being here. I needed you so much, Sam."

He studied her swollen eyes with their red rims, the fingers behind which she hid her cheeks. He reached and took one of her hands and interlaced his fingers with hers. "That's what love is all about, being there when you need each other, isn't it?"

She touched his cheek with her free hand. "Sam . . ." she said, quiet now, overwhelmed by love for him, certain that what he said was true.

Their eyes held, then he turned a kiss into her palm. "Have you decided yet whether you love me or not?"

"I think I decided on the day you came over here in your jogging shorts."

A brief smile lifted his lips, then they fell serious again. He said quietly, "I'd like to hear you say it once, Lee."

They were sitting side by side in a curiously childish position, holding hands with only the sides of their knees touching as she said into his eyes, "I love you, Sam Brown."

"Then let's get married."

Her startled eyes opened wide. She stared at him for a full ten seconds, then stammered, "G . . . get married!"

He gave her a lopsided grin. "Well, don't look so surprised, Cherokee. Not after the last wild and wonderful month we've spent together."

"B . . . but . . ."

"But what? I love you. You love me. We even *like* each other! We're both in the same line of work, have terrific senses of humor, and we're even the same breed. What could make more sense?"

"But I'm not ready to get married again. I . . ." She looked away. "I tried it once and look what it's put me through."

"Cherokee, you're not going to go through this again, not if you marry me."

"Sam, please . . ."

"Please?" His voice took on an edge. "Please what?"

"Please don't ask. Let's just keep things as they are."

"As they are? You mean sex every night at your house and nothing more than a polite hello at the office? I said I love you, Lee. I've never said it to another woman. I want to live with you and hang our clothes in the same closet and have a family to—"

"A family!" She jumped off the step and stood at his feet facing him. "Haven't you heard a thing I've said? I had that once, and it was the worst tragedy of my life! I lost my sons —the only ones I ever plan to have—in a divorce court. I'm not equipped to be a mother. I told you that!"

"That's all in your head, Lee. You'll be as good a mother as—"

"It's not in my head!" She swung away toward the living room. "I . . . I'm insecure and hurt, and I've failed once at being both a wife and a mother. I don't think I'd be very good at either one again."

He stood behind her in the middle of the living room.

"That's your answer, then? You won't marry me because you're afraid?"

She swallowed and felt the damnable tears spring to her eyes again. "Yes, Sam, that's my answer."

"Lee." He placed a hand on her shoulder, but she shrugged it away. "Lee, I won't accept it, not if you really love me. The only way to get over being afraid of something is to try it again. You're . . . we're not going to fail. We've got too damn much going for us. I just know it."

"It's out of the question, Sam. I just don't understand how you . . ." She turned to face him. "Sam, you can't know how a thing like losing your children can undermine your self-confidence. I swore when it happened that I'd never go through such a thing again. I'd prove to the world that the judge was wrong. I wasn't just a . . . a stupid *squaw* with . . . with no career and no visible earning power. I had things to prove, and I'm not done proving them yet."

"Squaw?" he retorted angrily. "Is that what this is all about?"

"It's part of it. Nobody will ever convince me that judge wasn't influenced against me because I was Indian and Joel wasn't. It has as much to do with the decision as the fact that I couldn't support the kids. Well, I couldn't do anything about my heritage, but I certainly could about my financial status. I set out to earn as much money as any man, in a job only men have traditionally done, but I have a long way to go before I reach my goals."

Sam's face was grim. "Lee, you've got a red chip on your shoulder about the size of the original Indian nations! You carry it there, daring anybody to knock it off—that's why most people try. When are you going to learn you're melted into the pot here, and stop flaunting your heritage?"

Fresh anger flared through Lee. "You don't understand a thing I've said here today! Not a thing!"

"I understand it all, Lee. I'm just not willing to buy some of it. I love you and I accept you exactly as you are, without any question that we could make a successful marriage—babies and all. You're the one who doesn't understand that if you really love somebody past histories should be forgotten and you should put your entire trust in the strength of that love."

She reached out to touch him, her face tight with pain. "I *do* love you, Sam, I do. But do I have to prove it by marrying you?" He removed her hand from his chest and held it in his own.

"That's the usual way, Lee." He looked up, and his dark eyes held a glint of hurt before he added softly, "The honorable way."

What could she say? After the way they'd parted last time, the hurts they both carried since then, how could she argue with him? She saw a grave weariness settle over his features as he stood holding her palm with the tips of his fingers, brushing his thumb across her knuckles.

She stared at him, already stricken with loss. "Sam, don't go."

Again she saw his weariness and the burden of sadness that her refusal had so suddenly brought upon him. He looked into her eyes, and his own were heavy with regret.

"I have to, Cherokee. This time I have to."

"Sam, I . . . I need you."

He stepped close again, drew up her face, and placed a

good-bye kiss on her lips, which were swollen yet from crying.

"Yes, I believe you do," came his tender reply.

He studied her black pupils, touched a thumb to the purple skin of one lower eyelid, then turned, and a moment later the door closed behind him.

Chapter 11

IF SHE WERE asked to define exactly who brought about the changes between them, Lee could not truthfully have named either Sam or herself. She only knew they'd reached an impasse that hurt deeply during the weeks that followed. Facing him each day at the office was sheer hell. He no longer passed her desk in the late afternoon to ask what time she'd be leaving for home. She no longer asked if he was coming over. Lee knew either of them could have broken down the invisible barrier that had sprung up between them. It would have taken no more than a single word, yet neither spoke it.

On the surface everything was the same. They consulted each other on bid work, bumped into each other in the copy room, pored over plans together. But through it all Sam maintained an incredibly unfluctuating air of normalcy, while Lee gave him neither pointed indifference nor veiled languishments. Instead they treated each other with neutral geniality, which made her wince inwardly. He opened doors for her if they were heading out together, and they chatted about jobs with a heartiness that distressed Lee's lovelorn soul.

One day in mid-September Sam passed her as she sat near the fountain eating lunch. He waved a roll of plans in greeting, never breaking stride as he called, "Hi, Lee. Enjoying the beautiful weather?" An acute sense of loss pierced her as she watched him stride purposefully into the building.

In late September six members of the office staff treated

Rachael to a birthday lunch at Leona's Restaurant in the Fairway Shops. They all piled into Sam's car for the short ride. Lee ended up in the back seat. Being there brought back memories of the days of intimacy with distressing clarity as she studied the back of Sam's head.

At Leona's, Lee found herself seated at a right angle to him. As they pulled their chairs in, their knees collided under the table. "Oh, excuse me!" Sam apologized. "It's these damn long legs of mine." His alacrity was as impersonal as if he had bumped Frank's knee, and again Lee felt raw inside. Yet she heard herself laugh and copy his nonchalance.

But for Lee being with him became a refined form of torture. At times she studied him across a room, wondering if he had intentionally plotted this insipid neutrality to punish her. Was he aware of it? Did he maintain this jovial air knowing that every day now put her over the rack? Or had he simply chalked up their affair to experience and moved on to greener pastures? If he loved her, as he claimed he did, how could he be so . . . so damn mundane! When he caught her looking at him, he smiled and turned back to whatever he was doing without the slightest sign of constraint and certainly without flashing any intimate messages with his eyes. But then, did she herself flash any?

September crept to a close, and the first hint of fall tinged the air. Sam called Lee into his office one day, but again he was his ineffable genial self, announcing that she'd been there two months and he was giving her a raise because he was very pleased with her work. Though it was a small boost in pay he said, he meant it as a vote of confidence and ushered her to the open door, where they stood for a minute in full view of the draftsmen. He smelled so familiar that saliva pooled beneath Lee's tongue. The sight of his shirtsleeves rolled up to the elbow, exposing summer-bronzed forearms, and the familiar way he slipped a hand into his trouser pocket as they talked, raised goosebumps of awareness across the low reaches of Lee's stomach.

Sam leaned against the door jamb and crossed his arms over his chest, discussing some aspect of the Little Blue River job, which was in full swing by this time. The apples in the orchard would be ripe now, the mosquitoes gone, the red-winged blackbirds and goldfinches flown south. *Oh, Sam, Sam, I haven't stopped loving you.* He continued to discuss business as if nothing had ever happened between them. *Sam . . . Your Honor . . . I want to reach for you, burrow against you, and be part of your life again.* It was time to make some major decisions about equipment, he was saying, while from Lee's body came both a physical and emotional outpouring of need for him. *How can you act as if it never happened when every nerve in my body feels touched by you?* ". . . so Rachael will make the plane reservations. Plan to be gone overnight," Sam was saying.

"I . . . what?" Lee stammered.

"Plan to be gone overnight," he repeated. "I just don't see how we can fly to Denver, attend the equipment auction, and get back here in one day, especially if we end up buying something. There'll be financial arrangements to make, and we'll have to find a yard to rent."

His words hit her like a blow in the stomach. He'd been standing there making plans for the two of them to attend the heavy-equipment auction in Denver with no more compunction than he'd announce the same to Frank or Ron or any of the other guys. Lord o' mercy, did he expect her to go off on an overnight jaunt with him and keep it totally platonic? What did he think she was made of . . . PVC, like the pipes they laid in the ground? His lack of sensitivity infuriated her . . . and the prospect of being alone with him left her weak and trembling.

They flew out of Kansas City on a golden mid-October day, and as the plane looped westward, leaving the cloverleaf design of K.C. International Airport behind them, Lee had a feeling of *déjà vu*, because they were going back to the same place where they'd met.

Before they crossed over mid-Kansas, Sam had slumped back and fallen asleep beside her. He woke up long enough to decline breakfast, leaving Lee to eat alone, ever aware of his slow, slumberous breathing at her shoulder, remembering mornings when she'd awakened to that sound on the other side of her bed. He was still sleeping peacefully when the seatbelt sign flashed on in preparation for landing. She studied his shuttered eyes, the long, dark lashes fanning his cheeks, his lips and limbs in repose, and a renewed sense of longing sprang up inside her. Hesitantly she touched his arm, which lay lax over the armrest between them.

"Sam?"

His eyes opened abruptly and looked directly into hers. There was a moment of disorientation, a sweet, compelling return to the days when they'd awakened together, a sensual smile of hello beginning to tip up his unwary mouth before he seemed to realize where he was and curbed the warm response.

"We'll be landing in a minute," Lee said, casting her eyes away when he clasped his hands, stiffened his elbows, and stretched, uncoiling and shivering in the old, familiar way.

"God, I slept like the dead," he said, reaching for his seat-belt.

You always did, she wanted to say. Their elbows bumped when they were latching their buckles, and Lee wondered how she would survive this torture for two days.

Inside Stapleton International Airport they stood side by side, watching the luggage bump toward them, both reaching for the first familiar suitcase when it arrived. Lee backed off, letting Sam retrieve it and check its I.D. tag. "This one's yours," he stated, setting it at her ankle with no further comment or clue to what he was thinking. His suitcase arrived, and they set off to rent a car.

Sam stowed their identical suitcases in the trunk, unlocked the passenger door, and waited while Lee got in. How many times had he done this for her when they were lovers? Yet now there was only the impersonal politeness he'd show to any woman as a matter of course. When he was behind the wheel Lee was assaulted by the familiarity of his movements, his scent, his hands on the steering wheel.

The auction was to be held at the Adams County Fairgrounds in Henderson. By the time they arrived, Lee was only too happy to escape the confines of the car with its taunting reminders and inescapable memories. But the day proved as distressing as the ride, for it was a remarkably mellow one, the kind in which lovers revel. The Colorado sky was a cloudless cerulean blue, none of Denver's usual brown haze blocking out its deep color. The state's famed aspens were at their peak of brightness too, shimmering like golden coins beneath a butterscotch sun. Accompanying Sam, inspecting machinery, discussing the needs of the company for the upcoming spring job here where their relationship had begun, Lee had difficulty concentrating on business. Time and again she drifted into thoughts of the man at her elbow—the texture of his skin beneath the golden mountain sun; the shadows of his shoulder blades under the knit shirt that delineated the well-remembered shape of his chest and arms; the sheen of his dark hair, which she had first touched in a brush in a motel room not far from where they now stood; the outline of his thigh muscles within his trousers, those muscles she'd first seen on her doorstep on a summer's morning that changed her life forever; his voice which had spoken countless intimacies into her ear and soothed her shattered soul with reassurances when she'd most needed them.

Being alone with him this way yet not alone at all only tightened the string of emotional tension to a higher pitch, until Lee felt as if one more inadvertent nudge of his arm against hers would snap that tensile thread.

He bid on several pieces of machinery, bought two, and made arrangements for payment and pickup with the auction-eering company's financier.

By the time they made their way back toward the rented car, it was late afternoon and the Denver freeways were packed. Lee had no idea where they were staying, but feared Rachael might have made reservations at the Cherry Creek again. To her relief, Sam drove to a different hotel—an airport high-rise. They checked in side by side, but took two separate rooms. Sam extended his company credit card without the slightest hint of uneasiness. He handed Lee one of the keys, and they rode up to the ninth floor together. The hall was carpeted and silent as they moved toward adjacent doors.

Lee thought Sam might suggest meeting for dinner, but instead he unlocked his door, glanced inside, and remarked casually, "Mmm . . . looks like a nice room." Then he picked up his suitcase, turned and answered the question that had been burning within her all day: "See you in the morning, Lee."

It would have been graceless and ill-advised to declare that she was lonely and missed his company and wanted terribly to spend the night with him. Instead she stepped into her own lonely cell and leaned weakly against the closed door to stare at the avocado green carpeting and matching bedspread without seeing either. What she saw was the face and hands and body of the man she loved, the man separated from her by a plaster wall and the equally as palpable barrier of their self-imposed strictures. To know he was there, so close, yet untouchable, was torture. While she stared at the lonely room, tears threatened. A tight constriction squeezed her chest. She crossed to the window and took in the view of the Denver skyline—the Great West Towers, Denver Square, and Anaconda Towers off in the distance. The sun was setting behind the Rockies, which appeared in the foreground like a triple-tiered Mexican skirt, fading from dark purple to light lavender in three distinct layers, from the earth skyward.

She turned away from the stunning view and fell across the bed, battling tears. *You know I love you, Sam. Why are you doing this to me?* When she cried, she felt better and got up to wash her face, refresh her makeup, and go down to dinner, since it was obvious Sam had no intention of asking her to join him for the meal.

As she ate in solitude, anger began to replace her hurt. Her ego smarted. *Damn you, Sam Brown, damn you! Damn you! Damn you!*

Back in her room, she flung her key down on the dresser and glared at the wall. A minute later she pressed her ear to it. She thought she could make out the sound of his T.V. but wasn't certain. She turned on her own, but it had no appeal whatsoever. She flounced onto her bed, plumping the pillows behind her back, but the short-lived anger had dissipated now, leaving her with despair and a crushing yearning that blotted out common sense.

At five minutes after nine o'clock she picked up the telephone and dialed Room 914.

"Yes?" he answered.

She closed her eyes and rested her hand against the headboard. Her heart beat like a tom-tom, and her tongue felt dry and swollen.

"Th . . . this is an obscene phone call from Room 912. W

. . . will you pl . . . please come and . . . and . . ." But her voice faltered as she clutched the phone and swallowed.

"And what?"

Oh God, he wasn't going to help her at all. He was going to keep up this sham. She swallowed her pride, closed her eyes, and admitted, "I was going to say and make love to me, but I need you for so many more reasons than that. I miss you so much that nothing is good in my life anymore."

She thought she heard him sigh tiredly and pictured him, perhaps leaning his back against the wall only inches behind her. The earth seemed to turn one complete revolution before he finally asked, "Are you sure now, Lee?"

Tears seeped from the corners of her eyes. "Oh, Sam, what have you been trying to do to me these past weeks?"

"Give you a chance to heal."

Through her misery she felt a first glimmer of hope. She let her eyes drift closed, realizing it was what she too had been doing.

"Sam, please . . . please come over here."

"Okay," he agreed softly, and hung up.

An instant later a soft tap sounded on her door.

When she'd opened it, she stepped far back, interlacing her fingers and pressing them against her stomach. They stared at each other for an interminable moment as he leaned a shoulder against the doorframe. He was dressed in black socks, gray trousers, and a pale blue dress shirt held together by a single button at the waist. The shirttails hung out of his pants and it looked disheveled, as did his hair.

"Were you asleep already?" Lee asked guiltily.

He shook his head tiredly, no. "I don't think I've slept for the last six weeks—except on that plane today." How had she failed to notice the pinched lines at the corners of his eyes and the tired droop of his mouth?

"Because of me?" she asked hopefully.

He pulled himself away from the doorframe and, with his head drooping forward, turned and slowly closed the door. His shoulders rose in a great sigh, and at last he faced her again. "What do you think?" he asked quietly.

She stared back at him, blinded by pain and tears that threatened to spill from her lashes. "I haven't known what to

think since you walked out of my house that night. I . . . you
. . . it's been . . ." Her palms flew to cover her face and sharp
sobs jerked her shoulders. "I . . . I . . . love you so," she
choked out against her hands.

He moved to stand before her, and his warm hands encircled her wrists, forcing them away from her face. He placed a
gentle kiss on the heel of each, where salty tears had left them
wet.

"I love you too," he said, his voice softened by pain.

With a small, throaty cry she flung herself against him,
arms looping up to circle his neck and cling. His arms, too,
clasped her tenaciously while he pressed his face against her
warm neck. He rocked her back and forth, back and forth,
standing with feet spread while holding her body firmly
molded to his, neither of them speaking, drawing comfort
from their nearness.

Her breasts, belly, and thighs flattened to his rigid body,
Lee's mind seemed filled with his name—Sam, Sam, Sam—
and the sweet realization that he was what she needed to complete not only her body but also her life, her *self*.

At last he raised his head and she hers. Their eyes delved,
dark into darker, speaking of the ache each had borne during
their separation, speaking of anguish about to end in triumph.

Their mouths met wordlessly and drank and sought to
make up for the emptiness of six weeks alone. Silky, wet
tongues twisted together, speaking of a want grown one hun-
dredfold since last they'd touched. The kiss lasted for endless,
reckless minutes—glorious! greedy!—until their hearts cla-
mored and their blood pounded. Sam bit Lee lightly, and her
tongue slid back to feel the texture of his teeth scraping atop
and below it. Her fingers found the warm hollow behind his
ear, and she made a throaty sound that sought to tell him
everything she felt for him.

His palms slid to her hips, moving them securely against
his own complementary curves. He pressed his face into the
scented side of her neck and as she tipped her head aslant, he
whispered roughly, "What are you doing with all these clothes
on?"

Her heart seemed to trip over itself as she raised her lips to

720

his ear and answered in a tremulous voice, "Waiting for you to ask me again to marry you."

His head lifted in surprise, and a smile tugged at the corners of his mouth. "Bring it up later, when we have nothing better to talk about."

Then he sobered again, running his eyes over her hair, face, and breasts in a sweeping glance that brought them back once more to the black, searching Cherokee eyes that were alight with love and longing.

He lifted her chin, and his face lowered, while with infinite tenderness he circled her lips with the tip of his tongue. Then they were kissing again, open-mouthed and seeking, while she felt the flutter of his fingers at the valley between her breasts.

He lifted his head, and their eyes met again, then dropped together to his bronze fingers that slipped buttons through holes, then tugged the blouse from the waistband of her slacks. Wordlessly he slid it from her shoulders. Wordlessly, too, he reached behind her and when he backed away again the white brassiere was draped over his dark hands. He tossed it behind her and looked down at her stomach. A moment later he had freed the button at her waist and lowered the zipper beneath it, revealing a wedge of skin above low-slung briefs. He dropped to one knee, pressing his face within the open garment, kissing her stomach where weeks ago he'd traced the line she was so afraid to explain. He traced it again, this time with the feather-light tip of his tongue.

"There's nothing I don't love about you . . . nothing," he vowed as his strong arms cinched her hips and his eyes slid closed. He turned the side of his face against her flesh while his voice grew gruff with emotion. "You never have to be afraid to tell me anything. Always remember that."

Tears trembled close to the surface as she twined her fingers in the hair at the back of his head and pressed him nearer. She closed her eyes against the sweet swelling sensations his words brought to her chest, welcoming the faintly abrasive scratch of his whiskers. The top of his hair brushed the undersides of her breasts, and she leaned low over his head, cradling it in both arms.

"Oh, Sam, I was so afraid to have you see those marks the

721

first time. Afraid of your disapproval, and . . . and wanting to be perfect when I couldn't be. But that's what love does to you, makes you want to be flawless for the one you love."

He pulled back to look up at her. "Cherokee . . ." His dark eyes were eloquent with approval even before he spoke the words. "I wouldn't change a single thing about you, don't you know that?" He reached one dark hand up to cup a breast, lifting it slightly as he brushed its crest with his thumb, yet looking beyond it to her eyes.

And suddenly she did know it, just as she knew she loved this warm, complex man. She threaded the fingers of both hands back through the hair of his temples, then held the sides of his head while savoring the moment and him.

"I know," she finally breathed softly. Then she leaned to kiss his lips, lightly at first, but with growing ardor, until she felt his hands moving over her skin to the loosened waistband that was soon being eased over the backs of her thighs. When it threatened to trip her, he stood, his hands sliding up her ribs to her armpits until she felt herself being lifted into space. He held her effortlessly, his mouth teasing her jaw while she pressed her hands to his hard shoulders and kicked herself free of impediments. But when the clothes dropped to the floor, he still held her aloft.

"Sam, Sam, let me go," she said, feeling helpless and impatient, wriggled provocatively against him.

"Never." He smiled back, then she was sliding down his body, freeing the single button that held his shirt together at the waist. While he shrugged it off hastily, she loosened his belt buckle.

Suddenly she realized he was standing motionless, and her fingers fell still. She looked up to find him watching her with the faint hint of a smile on his lips. How incredible that after all they'd been through she could feel this abrupt shyness, as if it were her first time. His hands hung loosely at his sides, and the expression on his face was a mixture of enjoyment and anticipation.

"Be my guest," he said softly.

Her lips fell open. A thrill spiraled through her while the breath seemed caught in her throat. Then she accepted his invitation, pulling the last garments from between them.

When they were naked, it took no more than a step and he was against her, forcing her back until her calves struck the bed and she toppled backward, pulling him with her. Their bodies were all grace and harmony while their mouths spoke wordless intimate messages and their hands roamed over each other, familiarizing themselves once again. "Oh, Sam, how I missed you." His shoulders were sleek and firm, his hair the texture of mink, the tendons of his neck resilient as she ran her hands over them. He leaned above her, kissing her temple, her eyelids, catching her lip between his teeth while her eyes drifted closed and she took pleasure in his adulation.

He moved down, turning them onto their sides while trailing kisses from the underside of her chin along her throat and down the hollow between her breasts, detouring to bestow a lingering kiss on each before moving on. His elbow hooked the curve of her waist, and his forearm pressed silkily against her back while he dipped a pleasurably wet tribute into her navel. He pressed her back, easing lower to trace once more those pale lines she no longer thought of hiding, learning their texture with the tip of his tongue.

"Cherokee . . ." His voice was rough, his lips soft while he nuzzled lower . . . and lower. "Cherokee . . ."

Then all was sensation—rough to smooth, ebb to flow, texture to sleekness, man to woman. She made some inarticulate sound deep in her throat, raising her body while drifting in an ethereal realm of sensuality.

He took her just short of fulfillment, then came to her, lifting himself over her once again to join the force of his love with hers in movements that were as much a part of love's expression as its innermost urge to give and to share.

Lee's head was thrown back, her eyes closed as she reached above her for something to hold on to, finding nothing but a pillow into which her fingers curled while he watched the pleasure in her trembling eyelids.

His name ripped from her throat as they shared again that shattering force of feeling they'd known before, followed by the dissolving sigh of satisfaction. A kiss on her forehead, the weight shifting away, taking her with it to her side, a heavy hand threaded through her hair, then a blissful lassitude as they lay in each other's arms.

"Cherokee?" he murmured after a long, long time.

"Hmm?"

His chest was warm and damp where her forehead rested against it.

"Can we talk now?"

"The answer is yes," she said, smiling at the ebullient feeling it gave her to say the word at last.

"The . . . what?" He jerked back in surprise.

"The answer is yes." She looked up innocently into his eyes. "Yes, I'll marry you. Yes, yes, yes!" She kissed his chest with a quick, light smack.

And naturally he had to tease, "I didn't ask you yet."

"You were gonna."

"Oh, was I now?"

She snuggled up against him, wrapping her arms around him and nestling comfortably with her head tucked under his chin.

He lifted a knee, rested it on her hip, and pressed the sole of his foot in the warm hollow at the back of her leg. "You know what I kept thinking the last six weeks?" His tone was reflective. "Of what a damn fool I was the night I asked you to marry me. My timing stank. I know that now. You were in an emotional mess that night, and I had no business bringing up the subject just then. I thought . . ." He sifted his fingers through her hair as if it were sand. "I thought I'd give you some time to gain your equilibrium after seeing your kids and your ex-husband again."

"You had me so scared, Sam." She squeezed her eyes shut, then hugged him close with fierce possessiveness. "I've never suffered as badly as I have during the last six weeks. You were so . . . so . . . unaffected by it all."

"Unaffected!" he exclaimed, pushing her back to see her face. "Woman, I was dying a little bit each day, waiting for you to come to me and say you'd changed your mind."

"You were?" She widened her eyes in surprise. "You didn't act like you were dying. You acted as if I was just one of the boys."

"Just one of the boys?" The grin was back as he ran his eyes then his hand over one naked breast. "Oh, Cherokee, hardly. It's not one of the boys I want to share my house

724

with ... and my life with ... to say nothing of my bed."

She smiled and felt a ripple of feminine vanity at his approval.

Then she fell serious, gazing up at him with concern. "Sam, have you really no fears at all?"

He pressed a kiss to her forehead. "None. Not since that first incredible weekend with you when we found out how much we can share."

"But ..." She searched his eyes deeply, hoping he wouldn't misconstrue what she was about to say. "I do have fears, Sam. Please understand."

"I know, Cherokee, I know now."

"At least give me some time before we start a family, okay?"

His head snapped back and he braced up on one palm, a dark hand grasping her shoulder and rolling her onto her back. "You mean it, Cherokee? You've been thinking about ... about kids?"

"Yes, Your Honor, I have to confess I have." She affected a scolding pout. "Not right away, mind you. After I have a little time to get used to the idea."

His smile was radiant, then to her amazement he gave a regular Indian war whoop and fell on his back beside her, rubbing his chest with an air of great satisfaction and smiling up at the ceiling.

She lay beside him, grinning at how happy she'd made him, wondering what one of their half-Indian babies would look like. It would have hair darker than his, beautiful eyes, with his long lashes instead of her short, stubby ones, and the prettiest lips this side of the Great Divide ...

Her reverie was interrupted by the growing awareness that Sam was no longer looking at the ceiling but at her naked breasts. The message in his eyes was clear even before a dark finger came teasing.

"Hey, Cherokee, what do you say we jump in the shower together and start all over and celebrate? I've got some time to make up for."

She burst out laughing and shoved his finger aside. "What have you been doing over there in your room all by yourself? Reading your porn magazines again?"

"How did you guess?"

She pretended to consider a minute. "On second thought, I'm not sure if I should hitch up for life with a man who reads porn magazines when he's got a perfectly capable wife." She sat up saucily and was heading for the edge of the bed when her progress was checked abruptly. A second later she squealed, "Brown! Let me go, Brown! I gotta go to the bathroom!"

"Not alone, Cherokee! You're going with me, straight to the shower!" In a flash she was slung ignominiously over his shoulder, her black hair dangling down past his posterior while one dark forearm clamped behind her knees and his other hand rested on her upturned derrière.

"Brown, put me down!"

"Like hell." He chuckled and stalked off toward the bathroom.

"Pervert!" she squawked.

"You damn betcha," he agreed, then turned to bite her enticing backside playfully as it bounced along on his shoulder.

She could hardly breathe by the time they reached the bathroom and he let her slip to her feet. She landed in the cold, hard bathtub, and a minute later the colder spray hit her full in the face. Before it warmed, they were kissing and slipping against each other and groping for the tiny bar of soap.

While Sam unwrapped it, she pushed her sodden hair out of her eyes.

"Hey, Brown, I've got just one more question, and I think I deserve an answer."

Disgruntled by the interruption, he curled his brows. "Okay, what—but hurry up and get it over with so we can get on with the important stuff."

"Did you read the amount of my bid that day we first met?"

A slow, sly grin climbed his cheek. He shut his eyes, leaned his head back till the shower spray hit him full in the face, then brought it forward, shook his head like a dog, and opened his spiky-lashed eyes again. "I'll tell you what." He pulled her up close, settled his hips against hers, and taunted with a grin, "You do *ev-v-v*erything I say and I'll think about answering that."

726

"Brown—" she started to scold playfully, but the word was cut in half by his wet lips, and a moment later the answer ceased to matter.

LAVYRLE SPENCER

Family Blessings

LaVyrle Spencer's latest novel is published in paperback
by HarperCollins in August 1995.
An extract from it appears in the following pages.

Chapter 1

For Christopher Lallek life couldn't have been better. It was payday, his day off, all the junk was scraped out of his old beat-up Chevy Nova, and his brand new Ford Explorer had come into Fahrendorff Ford. It was an Eddie Bauer model, top of the line, with a four litre V-6 engine, four-wheel-drive, air conditioning, tilt wheel, compact digital disc player and leather seats. The paint colour was called wild-strawberry, and it was wild, all right, wilder than anything he'd ever owned. Within an hour the papers would all be signed and he'd be slipping behind the wheel of his first new vehicle ever. All he needed was his paycheque.

He swung into the parking lot of the Anoka Police Station, cranked his old beater into a U-turn and, out of long practice, backed the car against the kerb beside two black-and-white squads parked the same way near the door.

He sprang out whistling 'I've Got Friends in Low Places' and took a happy leap onto the sidewalk, scanning the sky from behind a pair of mirrored sunglasses strung with hot-pink Croakies. Perfect day. Sunny. Couple of big white fluffy clouds in the east. Eighty degrees now shortly before noon, and by the time all the guys met at the lake it would be pushing ninety and the water would feel great. Greg was going to stop and price oversized inner tubes, Tom was bringing his Jet-Ski, and Jason had the use of his folks' speed boat for the day. Some of the guys would bring beer. Chris would pick up a couple of six-packs of soda and some salami and cheese, maybe a pint of that herring in cream sauce that he and Greg loved so much, and drive out there in his shiny new truck playing his new Vince Gill CD – hey, hell of a deal.

He unlocked the plate-glass door and walked into the squad room, still whistling. Nokes and Ostrinski, both in uniform, were standing beside the computer table, looking sober, talking.

'Hey, what's new, guys?'

They looked up and fell silent, watching him poke a hand into his mail cubicle, come up with an envelope and rip it open. 'Payday at last – hot damn!' He swung around, scanning the cheque, then slapped it against his palm. 'Eat your heart out, boys, my new Explorer came in at last and it's all dealer prepped and ready for pickup! If you want to go outside and administer last rites to my old Nova – '

It struck him suddenly that neither Nokes nor Ostrinski had moved. Or smiled. Nor had they said a word since he'd come in. From the patrol room two more uniformed officers came silently through the doorway, looking equally as solemn as the two already there.

'Murph, Anderson . . .' Christopher greeted, wary now. He'd been a police officer for nine years: he recognized this silence, this sombreness, this stillness too well.

'What's wrong?' His eyes darted from man to man.

His captain, Toby Anderson, spoke. 'It's bad news, Chris.'

Christopher's stomach seemed to drop two inches. Anderson's grave tone could mean only one thing.

'An officer went down.'

'Afraid so.'

'Who?'

Nobody spoke for ten seconds.

'Who!' Chris shouted, his dread mounting.

Anderson replied in a low, hoarse voice. 'Greg.'

'Greg!' Christopher's features registered bald-faced surprise, followed by disbelief. 'Wait a minute. Somebody's got their wires crossed here.'

Anderson only shook his head sadly. His gaze remained steadily on Christopher while the others studied their shoes.

'But you're wrong. He's not on-duty today. He left the apartment no more than an hour ago to come over here and get his cheque, then he was going to the bank. Then he had to stop by his mother's house, and as soon as I'd picked up my Explorer we were going to buy a water tube and go out to Lake George.'

'He wasn't on-duty, Chris. It happened on his way here.'

Christopher felt the truth shoot through his nerves to his extremities and turn them prickly. He felt his head go light.

'Oh, shit,' he whispered.

Anderson spoke again. 'A pickup ran a red light and hit him broadside.'

Shock created havoc inside Christopher and hammered his features into hard, unaccepting lines. He dealt with tragedies daily, but never before with the death of one of the force. Certainly not with the death of a best friend. He stood in the grip of conflicting reactions, his human side sending heat and weakness streaming through his insides, while the trained lawman maintained an analytical exterior. When he spoke his voice came out patchy and gruff. 'He was on his motorcycle.'

'Yes . . . he was.'

Anderson's pause, his throaty voice, precluded the need for details. Christopher's throat closed, his chest constricted and his knees began trembling, but he stood his ground and asked the questions he'd ask if Greg were some stranger, little realizing that shock had him operating as if by remote control.

'Who responded to the call?'

'Ostrinski.'

Christopher's eyes found the young police officer who appeared pale and shaken. 'Ostrinski?'

Ostrinski said nothing. He looked as though he'd been crying. His lips were puffy and his face pink.

'Well, go on . . . tell me,' Christopher insisted.

'I'm sorry, Chris, he was dead by the time I got there.'

Out of nowhere came a hot smack of anger. It sent Christopher whirling in a half-circle, flinging a chair out of his way. 'God *damn* it!' he shouted. 'Why Greg?' Beset by passion, he lashed out with the most simplistic blame. 'Why didn't he ride with me! I *told* him I didn't mind taking him by his mother's house! Why did he have to take his motorcycle?'

Anderson and Ostrinski reached out as if to comfort Christopher, but he recoiled. 'Don't! Just . . . just let me . . . I need . . . give me a minute here . . .' He spun away from them, marched two steps to an abrupt halt and exclaimed again, 'Shit!' Fear roiled within him, spawned by a shot of adrenalin that turned him hot, cold, trembly, made him feel as if his entire body could no longer fit inside his skin. Working as a cop, he'd seen reactions like this dozens of times and had never understood them. He'd often thought people hard when their response to the news of death took the form of anger. Suddenly it was happening to him, the quick flare of absolute rage that made him storm about like a warrior rather than cry like a bereaved friend.

As swiftly as the anger struck, it fled, leaving him shaken and nauseated. Tears came – hot, stinging tears – and a hurt in his throat.

'Aw, Greg,' he uttered in a strange cracked voice. 'Greg . . .'

His fellow officers came up behind him and offered support. This time he accepted the touch of their arms and hands on his shoulders. They murmured condolences, their voices, too, strangled by emotions. He turned, and suddenly Captain Anderson's arms were around him, big burly arms trained in the martial arts, clasping him hard while both men strained to withhold sobs.

'Why Greg?' Chris managed. 'It's just so damned unfair. Why not some . . . some dealer selling coke to school kids or some parent who's beating on his k . . . kids twice a week? Hell, we got a hundred of 'em in our files.'

'I know, I know . . . it's not fair.'

Christopher's tears streamed. He stood in his captain's grip, his chin pressed to Anderson's crisp collar with its fifteen-year chevrons, listening to the bigger man swallow repeatedly against his ear, feeling the captain's handcuff case pressing his belly while the other officers stood nearby feeling useless and vulnerable.

Anderson said, 'He was a good man . . . a good officer.'

'Twenty-five years old. Hell, he'd hardly even lived.'

Anderson gave him a bluff thump on the shoulder and released him. Christopher lowered himself to a chair and doubled forward, covering his face with both hands. Visions of

Greg flashed through his mind: earlier this morning in the apartment they shared, shuffling out of his bedroom with his brown hair standing on end, scratching his chest and offering the usual bachelor good morning: 'I gotta pee like a race horse. Outta my way!' Then plodding from the bathroom to the kitchen, where he stood holding the refrigerator door open for a good minute and a half, staring inside, asking, 'So what time're you going to get the new Explorer?' Reaching inside for a quart of orange juice and drinking half of it from the carton, belching, and finally letting the door close.

He couldn't be dead! It wasn't possible!

Only an hour ago he was standing by the kitchen cupboard eating a piece of toast, dressed in bathing trunks and a wrinkled teeshirt that said *Moustache Rides Free*! 'I gotta stop by my mom's,' he'd said, 'the end busted off one of her garden hoses and she asked me to put a new one on.'

Greg was always so good to his mother.

Greg's mother . . . aw, Jesus, Greg's poor mother. The thought of her brought a fresh shot of dread and grief. The woman had been through enough without this – she didn't need some strange police chaplain coming to her door to break the news.

*　　*　　*

Lee Reston looked up through her tears. She squeezed the back of his hand. 'What a horrible shock that must have been for you. And then you had to . . . to come over here and tell me.' He looked down at her hand covering his and relived the shock, but found some control deep down within that kept his hand steady and his eyes dry. He turned his hand over, linked his fingers with hers and whispered hoarsely, 'He loved you so damned much.'

She let her eyes close, battling for control; opened them to reveal large, rust-coloured irises brimming with tears. 'Thank you,' she whispered, squeezing his hand tenaciously.

In that moment while they sat connected by grief and sympathy for each other some ineffable bond was forged.

He had given her what she needed to make it through the next hour.

She had recognized that he'd had the toughest job of all, coming here to break the news to her.

'I'll be here for you . . . whatever you need,' he promised, and the promise went as deep as his love and grief for her son.

'Thank you, Christopher,' she said, squeezing his hand even harder, appreciating him fully for the first time, admitting how comforting a man's presence was, and that she'd undoubtedly call on him again and again throughout the terrible days ahead.

LaVyrle Spencer

LaVyrle Spencer's heartwarming novels are loved by thousands of readers across the world. Four-times winner of the Gold Medallion for Best Historical Romance, she 'tells a superb story capturing many human complexities and emotions that transcend age barriers' (*Los Angeles Daily News*). Her stories of contemporary love and family relationships have gained her the reputation of 'putting new life into the genre' (*New York Daily News*).

Titles available from HarperCollins include:

Bygones
LaVyrle Spencer

Bess Curran is a lively and successful interior designer, happy with her role as mother of two, content to be divorced from her ex-husband Michael. It's when her daughter, Lisa, asks her to an intimate dinner, that she senses something is up. Lisa is about to drop a bombshell: she wants to marry, she's having a baby, and she wants both her parents at the wedding.

Both for Bess, and for her teenage son, Randy, it's a terrible blow. They adore Lisa, they can't abide Michael, yet protocol demands that the family presents a united front.

Ever the professional, Bess decides to bless her daughter's day with love. That means meetings with her ex-husband: the man whose perfect teeth she could rearrange with a chisel; whose looks and wit make her spit and catch her breath all at once. For Michael is the man who has wounded her son yet loves him dearly; who irritates Bess but still causes a stir. Michael: once a husband, always a lover . . .

ISBN 0 586 21848 3

November of the Heart
LaVyrle Spencer

A commodore's daughter must be careful who she loves.

It is a warm summer's evening in 1895 at Rose Point Cottage on White Bear Lake. But Commodore Gideon Barnett's planned victory dinner has been spoilt – his team lost the boat race, and he just can't figure out why. Against his principles, he agrees to let his kitchen hand try to solve the problem.

Jens Harken is no ordinary odd-jobs man. Working 'below stairs' to pay his way in the New World, he happens to be a master boat builder. Soon he is designing a boat bound to win – the *Lorna D*. But he's not bargained for the enthusiasms of Barnett's daughter, the real Lorna.

Lorna, beautiful and determined, with lush auburn hair and a heart-shaped face, can't help falling for the charms of the blue-eyed, open-hearted Norwegian. Their love sets their world spinning. But it can only bring sorrow and shame to the family that holds Lorna so dear . . .

'This is a novel to cherish!'

Affaire de Coeur

ISBN 0 00 647608 2

Forgiving
LaVyrle Spencer

A magical new novel in the glorious Spencer tradition.

It is 1876 and young Sarah Merritt is a woman with a mission: to set up the only newspaper in the dusty gold-rush town of Deadwood, Dakota. But determined Sarah hasn't reckoned on the rawness of the town, or of its people, and she soon finds herself at loggerheads with the headstrong and arrogant local sheriff, Noah Campbell.

Enemies can be friends in the face of adversity, and when Noah discovers Sarah is also in Deadwood to find her sister Adelaide, he vows to help her. For Addie is working as an 'upstairs girl' in the bordello of Mrs Hossiter . . .

ISBN 0 586 21324 4

Memory and Desire
Lisa Appignanesi

Paris, Autumn 1934. Dr Jacob Jardine glimpses a figure from his deepest imaginings: Sylvie Kowalska, half temptress, half innocent child. Despite himself, he is drawn into a troubled, erotic world in which the past haunts the present. A world which casts Sylvie first as the darling of bohemian Paris and, when war erupts, as a fearless member of the Resistance.

New York, 1980. Katherine Jardine has cast off her European heritage, but is now forced to face a past – and a mother – she would rather forget. It appears she holds the key to a thirty-five-year-old mystery. But at its centre is Sylvie's enigmatic light, still burning bright. Her chaotic, ensnaring web of memory and desire still has the power to entangle lives across two continents and two generations . . .

'A superbly plotted saga of passion and heartbreak. Appignanesi will keep you guessing until the last full stop.'
Kate Saunders, *Cosmopolitan*

'A darkly erotic novel, *Memory and Desire* lays bare the many faces of a modern Eve.'   Sally Beauman

ISBN 0 00 617982 7

The Other Woman
Eileen Townsend

An unforgettable evocation of love and betrayal stretching from the 1880s to the First World War.

With *Of Woman Born*, *In Love and War* and *The Love Child*, Eileen Townsend has carved a place for herself as a remarkable dramatic novelist. Now with *The Other Woman* she evokes her most vivid and memorable world yet.

The Other Woman is the story of the orphan Mhairi McLeod, born on the mystical Isle of Skye, and of her quest for fortune and her heritage over forty turbulent years. An extraordinary heroine of her time, her happiness will be overshadowed by her illegitimacy, and by the rivalry of a woman whose blood ties bring both pain and pleasure.

ISBN 0 586 21277 9

Trespassing Hearts
Julie Ellis

Betsy Bernstein is a young Jewish graduate living in New York. An aspiring interior designer, she meets wealthy Gentile Paul Forrest and falls in love. But Paul's mother, a grasping socialite, will never accept her beloved son's choice of a Jewish girl. Nevertheless, when Betsy becomes pregnant, she and Paul throw caution to the winds and marry – but in secret.

With a young son, and Paul away, Betsy is determined to make a success of her interior design business. What she hasn't counted on is the astonishing wilfulness of her mother-in-law, or the prejudices of New York society – or the horrors of the Second World War.

From the bestselling author of *The Only Sin*, *Loyalties* and *No Greater Love* comes this stirring saga of courage, character and love.

ISBN 0 586 21854 8

Ellie
Frankie McGowan

She's smart, she's sexy, she's going places

Eleanor Carter is a top magazine journalist with her own column. It's a glamorous, easy life, for Ellie is politically correct, sexually adjusted and socially skilled. But her past is about to catch up with her, in the shape of property tycoon, Theo Stirling.

Suddenly, without reason, Ellie is fired. Her diary is empty, lunches are cancelled, doors are closed. But Ellie is that glorious mix of an alluring lady with the heart of a street-fighter. Having started at the bottom and climbed to the top, she's not going to fall down again . . .

'Recommended, it's a good read!'   *Essentials*

'A sure winner'   *Company*

ISBN 0 00 647312 1

Fortune's Child
William Gill

She had everything. She wanted more . . .

Marcus Ackerman is a gold-digger. Fabulously rich and powerful from prospecting in the mines of Chile, he cannot control the one love of his life – his daughter, Leonora. Creative, insecure, and all passion, Leonora adores her father. But nothing, not even his threats, can get in the way of her need to paint.

At art college in London, Leonora meets three men: David, Oliver and Nick. As diverse in character as in their skills, they are bonded by two desires: to succeed as world-class architects, and to win Leonora. For all three it is a question of balancing ambition with love – a combination only one can achieve . . .

'Intelligent, pacy and well written' *Sunday Times*

'A brilliant storyteller' Rosie Thomas

ISBN 0 586 21531 X

Favourite Titles from LaVyrle Spencer

☐ BYGONES £2.99   ☐ THE FULFILMENT £4.99
☐ FORGIVING £3.99   ☐ HUMMINGBIRD £4.99
☐ MORNING GLORY £4.99   ☐ BITTER SWEET £4.99
       ☐ NOVEMBER OF THE HEART £3.99

All these books are available from your local bookseller or can be ordered direct from the publishers.

To order direct just tick the titles you want and fill in the form below:

Name: _____

Address: _____

_____

Postcode: _____

Send to: HarperCollins Mail Order, Dept 8, HarperCollins *Publishers*, Westerhill Road, Bishopbriggs, Glasgow G64 2QT.
Please enclose a cheque or postal order or your authority to debit your Visa/Access account –

Credit card no: _____

Expiry date: _____

Signature: _____

– to the value of the cover price plus:

UK & BFPO: Add £1.00 for the first and 25p for each additional book ordered.

Overseas orders including Eire, please add £2.95 service charge.

Books will be sent by surface mail but quotes for airmail despatches will be given on request.

24 HOUR TELEPHONE ORDERING SERVICE FOR ACCESS/VISA CARDHOLDERS –
TEL: GLASGOW 041-772 2281 or LONDON 081-307 4052